Cities of the Interior

ANAÏS NIN

CITIES OF THE

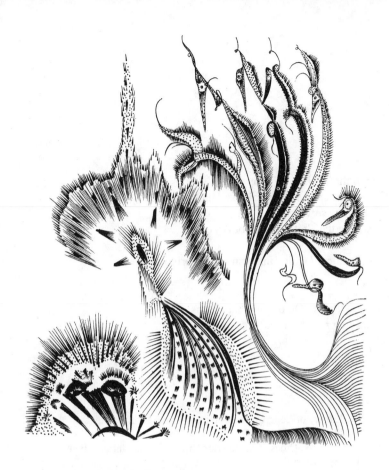

INTERIOR

Introduction by Sharon Spencer

Swallow Press   Ohio University Press   Athens

First Swallow / Ohio University Press printing 1980
02 01   7 6

Swallow Press / Ohio University Press
books are printed on acid-free paper ∞

Library of Congress Cataloging-in-Publication Data
Nin, Anais, 1903-1977.
        Cities of the Interior / by Anais Nin ; introduction
by Sharon Spencer.
            p.   cm.
            ISBN 0-8040-0665-2 (pbk.)
Contents: Ladders to Fire—Children of the Albatross—
The four-chambered heart—A spy in the house of love—
Seduction of the minotaur.
        I. Title.
        PS3527. I865C57   1991
        813' .52 – dc 20   91–14523
                                            CIP

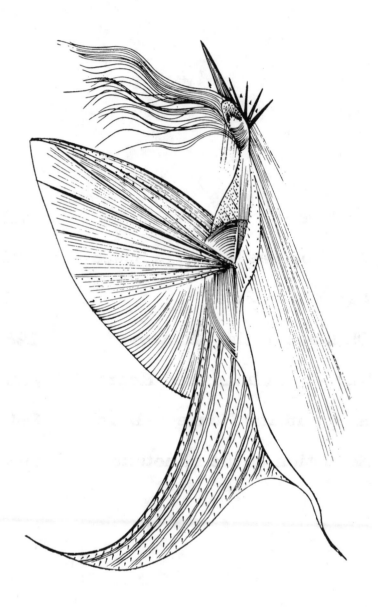

Preface

Until 1966, when Anais Nin, at the age of sixty-three, began to release portions of her much-rumored-about, lifelong diary, she was known to a small audience mainly as an "underground" writer of exquisite if somewhat "esoteric" fictions. The ongoing publication of her diary, which today is hailed by critics around the globe as the triumphant centerpiece of her artistic creation, and the attendant international recognition accorded her as a major writer have drawn renewed attention to Anais Nin's fictions, all of which were written and almost all of them published before the first appearance of the diary. When Anais Nin died in January 1977, she apparently did not leave behind any newly conceived, unpublished stories or novels. It seems that her need to express herself in fictional form subsided at the very moment she was finally able, after countless years of abortive attempts, to reveal the hitherto secreted, intimate, highly articulate record of a unique as well as exemplary life.

It has been suggested, in fact, that most of Anais Nin's fictions (excepting the erotica written "on order" in the early 1940s), from *The House of Incest* published in 1936 to *Collages* in 1964, were inspired by two motivating forces: a strong emotional need to "go public" with some of the experiences and conflicts first recorded and analyzed in the secret pages of her diary that for many complex reasons could be exposed at the time only in the guise of fiction, and her basic conviction that only the "truth" of lived experience, rather than invention, could provide the raw material for her fictions. Anais Nin herself encouraged such speculation from the very first when she stated in *The House of Incest* (originally subtitled "A

Fantasia of Neurosis") that her specific "truth," *i.e.* the secrets of her life she had confided only to her diary, would be "death-dealing" and could be given to the world only in the guise of "fairy-tales."

The five titles gathered in this volume, so aptly entitled *Cities of the Interior,* represent the central body of Anais Nin's fictions, those "outcroppings" from the diary which by now have assumed their rightful place as independent, if deeply connected, artistic creations. They were written in the United States over a span of almost twenty years during the 1940s and 1950s. Like her books published in Paris in the 1930s—the "prose poem" *The House of Incest,* which mistakenly earned her the tag of being a "surrealist," and the eventually revised *The Winter of Artifice*—these five "novels" also had a checkered and difficult publishing history. Stripped of the familiar ingredients of conventional storytelling (what Anais Nin in defending her fictional strategies often dismissed as mere "upholstery"), open-ended, and by dint of her "diary habit" focusing on psychological states and inner conflicts, these books often baffled readers brought up on American literary realism and gave unsympathetic critics reasons to dismiss them as mere psychoanalytical case histories, or to deplore their lack of social significance.

In 1974, when the second, revised version of the present volume was in preparation, Anais Nin, already gravely ill, recalled some of these difficulties in a preface and touched upon some of her artistic strategies, though she refrained then from drawing any connection between her diary and her fiction.

"The story of *Cities of the Interior* has never been told," Anais Nin wrote, "and it is time to clear up misunderstandings. I have never planned my novels ahead. I have always improvised on a theme. My only preconception was that it was to be a study of women. The first book turned out to be *Ladders to Fire*. All of the women I was to write about appeared in it, including Stella, whom I later dropped because she seemed so complete in herself rather than related to the other women."

When, after years of printing and publishing her own books Anais Nin found her first commercial publisher in New York, E. P. Dutton, she explained that *Ladders to Fire* "was part of a larger design, and that other novels would follow and round out the characters. The editors were aghast. They said the American public would never read a novel which threatened to continue, a *'roman fleuve'* as it is called in France."

So the book was published in 1946 as an independent novel "and nothing was said about development and continuity. For that reason, I did not develop a method of linking the various narratives.

"I began the next novel, *Children of the Albatross,* as if it were a new story. Though the same characters appeared, the theme was altogether different. Dutton's nervousness was dissipated." The book appeared in 1947, again as a separate work, and the link, Anais Nin wrote, "had to be made by the reader (or the critics) and naturally it was not."

Her third novel, *The Four-Chambered Heart,* after many delays and a change of publishers, came out in 1950, and again Anais Nin felt "much was lost by never stressing the continuity and interrelatedness of the novels." By 1954, when *A Spy in the House of Love* finally saw print, "the continuity was totally erased."

By that time Anais Nin's connections with commercial publishers in New York had been disrupted and her next work of fiction, *Solar Barque,* appeared in 1958 in a small, elegant, privately printed edition, with a series of black-and-white illustrations by eleven-year-old Peter Loomer. The thin book contained an end note: "This is volume five of a novel which will be published in one volume in 1959." The announced edition, of course, was Anais Nin's private effort to revive the four earlier, commercially published books which by then had gone out of print. She called the volume *Cities of the Interior*. "For the first time," she wrote in her preface, "the continuity was established."

Solar Barque, Anais Nin recalled, "focused on an episode of Lillian's life. At the time I thought it contained all I wished to say, but like a piece of music which continues to haunt one, the theme continued to develop in my head; and I took it up again and carried it to completion." Thus, *Solar Barque* became the opening section of *Seduction of the Minotaur,* published in 1961 by her new, loyal publisher, Alan Swallow, which now concludes the present edition of *Cities of the Interior*.

Today, with thirteen volumes drawn from the original diaries already in print, and the need for concealment finally removed, the attentive reader can trace the myriad interweavings between diary and fiction. It becomes clear that Anais Nin's "study of women"—"all the women I was to write about"— emerged from the ongoing investigation of her own conflicted and fragmented self, and that the settings and circumstances of her "fairy-tales" reflect the actual experiences and encounters of her own life.

Reading *Cities of the Interior* today, of course, also makes clear that as an artist, whether writing for the outside world or inside the labyrinth of her diary, Anais Nin was capable of giving universal significance and validity to what at first glance might have seemed mere personal experience.

Gunther Stuhlmann
Becket, Massachusetts, Winter 1992/1993

The Novel as Mobile in Space

T HE FIVE NOVELS OF *Cities of the Interior* were published individually during the 1940s and 1950s, a period that was unreceptive to introspective, lyrical prose. They met with critical misunderstanding and a hostility that has gradually mellowed into a grudging recognition by the U.S. literary establishment of Anaïs Nin's achievement in fiction. This has come about partly because of the publication beginning in 1966 of the volumes of Nin's great *Diary,* whose impact on the public has made people more aware of her other books at the same time that it has obscured them with its own fascinations.

But *Cities of the Interior* is itself a masterpiece. Like other arresting and original syntheses of life in art, this work, a set of five interconnected novels, presents difficulties to the general reader. The assumptions about reality that underlie its conception and the vision for a model of its composition are not those of the main influences on North American culture and, in fact, have been and are still current only among a small but growing group: people who believe that consciousness extends deeper than the data of the senses and far beyond the outlines of things and people.

The beliefs to which I refer go back in recent times to the Symbolist movement of the late nineteenth century, of which so great a poet as W. B. Yeats was a part, and in a much longer expanse of time to eras occurring before the Renaissance and stretching back into centuries and cultures in which the magical, the irrational, that special blend of chemistry and mysticism called alchemy, and the infinite life of the spirit were simply taken for granted. Certainly, as envisioned by men such as Rimbaud, Apollinaire, the German Expressionist painters and poets, Kandinsky, Breton, Aragon, Artaud, and Kurt Seligman (author of the *The Mirror of Magic*), modernism was "new" in its enthusiastic acceptance of the discoveries of modern science, but old—ancient, in fact—in its insistence on the indivisibility of matter and spirit and the power of the unconscious to animate and rejuvenate a life that had become, under the dominance of analytical, empirical science, as mechanical as a clock, its substance as dry as the metal pieces that interlock behind the time-keeper's face.

Cities of the Interior is a modernist work, but it has had the misfortune to be published after the first exciting decades of the movement had passed, repressed in some countries, in others suppressed because of urgent social problems: economic depression, war, and the reaction of the "cold war" period. The individual novels as well as the one-volume edition of *Cities* that was published in 1959 appeared a few years before the rediscovery and return in the 1960s to many of the political and aesthetic beliefs and ideals that characterized modernism. Finally, even though Nin's novel-cycle is a Symbolist and modernist work (not a Surrealist one, as has often been said, or charged), it is a timeless creation. *Cities of the Interior* is the achievement in fiction of the alchemical transformation of ordinary life into art. This is what Nin has always been striving for in writing.

Transformation and animation are ideals that Nin has formulated and expressed in her *Diary* and has struggled to fulfill since she began writing at the age of eleven. In 1952 while admiring a collage that was the gift of Jean (Janko) Varda, whom Nin called a "Merlin," she was transported from depression to ecstasy. She wrote, "It was as if I had stepped out of my life into a region of sand composed of crystals, of transparent women dancing, airy dresses, figures which no obstacle could stop, who could pass through walls being themselves constructed of apertures which allowed the breeze through, the feeling that through these floating figures with openings like windows, life could flow." Sadly, she concluded that Varda succeeded in expressing what she could not express because "his image being visible to the human eye was stronger than the moments I describe and enclose in a book."

Nin's sense of the relative impotence of words (she is a pianist's daughter) explains both why she has developed a poet's style in prose and why her writing has been so strongly influenced by the nonverbal arts. Motion, which she associates with freedom, has always been her great concern. Nin's writing is filled with images of ships, rivers, elevators, geological expeditions, voyages, excavations, labyrinths, tangled streets, prisons, cages, pools, dancing. "There is a way of living," she wrote, "which makes for greater airiness, space, ease, freedom. It is like an airplane's rise above the storms." For Nin the magic process through which psychic liberty is achieved is alchemy (art), the transformation of the ordinary or the base into the substance of highest value: gold. Except for the "charcoal burners," who wanted only money, serious alchemists envisioned the gold itself as symbolic. Their efforts were focused on a four-fold process to attain the gold, which the ancient alchemists regarded as the symbol of illumination and of salvation. For Nin, as for all of us who no longer believe in the power of churches to bestow illumination and salvation, the artist becomes a *voyant,* as Rimbaud said, or a wizard. Ingmar Bergman and Thomas Mann are among the many creators who have explored the theme of the artist as magician, a figure endowed with marvelous power.

With this aspiration and the ambition to explore the psyche of woman more deeply and more honestly than it had ever before been probed in fiction, Nin began in the late 1930s to write *Ladders to Fire,* the first published volume of the five novels. The fifth book is *Seduction of the Minotaur,* published in 1961, a portion of which is included in the one-volume edition of 1959, *Cities of the Interior: A Continuous Novel.* The timeless scope of this work is suggested in an obvious way by the metaphor "cities," which are, of course, ancient as well as modern. Nin set out to excavate the buried cities or psychic worlds of her three main characters: Lillian, Djuna, and Sabina. But the idea of continuity is much more complex. It suggests that the work is "open," like certain modern sculptures, that its creator intends it to extend into the surrounding space or context of life. At the same time that this book is not set off from life or carved out of it, bounded by the conventions of classically written symmetrical fiction with resolved conclusions, *Cities of the Interior* is always "open" to the addition of new parts. The five individual books are entirely self-contained. A reader can enjoy any one of them without moving to the other novels. A volume could be removed or a new one inserted into the cycle without in any way disturbing the overall composition. As Nin uses the word, "continuous" does not at all mean "to be continued." *Cities of the Interior* is not "continuous" in the sense of linear, progressive, or cumulative. There is no fixed starting point or concluding point. The books have been bound—because books, seemingly, *must* be bound —in the order in which they were written.

A reader can begin with any of the five volumes and move to the other four in any order. He will lose no essential connections. He can read one or two if he wishes, or even take up the novels in the reverse order of printing. In short, the five novels of *Cities of the Interior* are interchangeable in position in the total composition, which can be envisioned as a type of movable—truly mobile—modern sculpture, intersecting and interacting as it moves, not only among its own discrete parts, but also with the surrounding context of life. Nin's idea of continuity is circularity or total immersion in the movement of time. There are no beginnings and, as one of Nin's characters in *Collages* remarks, quoting the Koran, "Nothing is ever finished." In *Creative Evolution*, Bergson writes, "If matter appeared to us as a perpetual flowering, we should assign no termination to any of our actions."

To Nin life does, indeed, appear as a "perpetual flowering." In her novel cycle she has selected and expressed significant relationships and states of feeling and soul from the ever-changing, continuous process of the psychic lives of her three women figures. An alchemical motto reads: "Make a circle out of a man and a woman, out of this a square, out of this a triangle, make a circle and you will have the Philosopher's Stone." This geometric figure exactly illustrates the composition of *Cities of the Interior*. Imagine the outer circle as the total work, the five individual books as points on the circumference. Next, visualize inside this circle a triangle whose three points represent the women, each of whom suggests an element: Djuna, air; Sabina, fire; Lillian, earth. The square located within the triangle suggests the four novels which echo the symbolism of elements. In *Ladders* the earth-bound Lillian yearns to ascend to fire—passion—but must first descend the ladder to the fire—hell—of her own being. The design of *Children of the Albatross* is animated by the phosphorescent, airy, "transparent" children. At the end, Djuna's lover sails away to India. In *The Four Chambered Heart,* Djuna's own water voyage is a melancholy one as the houseboat she shares with Rango plies up and down the Seine, moving but not progressing. Finally, there is release, a baptism, as Djuna attempts to sink the boat. *A Spy in the House of Love* presents Sabina in images of fire and motion. At first she is represented as the firebird, but at the novel's close she is grounded, drooping, exhausted by her flight from one man to another. The center both of the inner and of the outer circles, as in the alchemical motto, is woman and man, their relationship in all its many forms. In *Seduction of the Minotaur* earth, air, fire, and water are united as Nin traces Lillian's course through the labyrinth of self.

Seduction of the Minotaur is central not only to an understanding of Nin's aspirations in fiction but also to the cycle of *Cities* and its basis, no doubt unconscious on the author's part, in the process of alchemy. The book is set in Golconda, a place which inspires a passage of lyric improvisation. (When Nin took LSD she envisioned herself as liquid gold.) Lillian works at a club called the Black Pearl (black is connected with one of the four alchemical processes). Her journey to Mexico in time present brings Lillian a series of experiences which are superimposed on selected painful experiences of her childhood. The superimpositions are fused in images, all of which are symbolic: the labyrinth, a prison, a doctor and the process of healing, diving and swimming, excavations, dancing. Polarities are resolved; there are both solar and lunar barques to carry the bodies of the physically dead to realms beyond this terrestrial one; inner and outer merge in Lillian's battle with her own minotaur, the masked woman who is her false self or persona; time present, in which she has no deep relationship with a man but many friendships, restores to her a past love for her estranged husband, Larry.

Mythology suggests that one way of escaping from a labyrinth is by air (today there are remains of five labyrinths in Europe and Egypt). In alchemical emblems the release from suffering and dedication to spiritual striving (symbolized by the condition of gold) is often portrayed by a creature without wings being borne aloft by a winged creature. *Seduction* closes as Lillian leaves Mexico in an airplane; she meditates upon her new understanding of her self and of her past; her meditation promises the rejuvenation of love. In Nin's writing the "dream" is always the miracle of love fulfilled.

Archeologists and anthropologists speculate that terrestrial labyrinths, besides being replicas of the heavenly constellations, were used for rituals to prepare initiates for the experience of death. *Seduction of the Minotaur* includes the only death in Nin's fiction (before *Collages* of 1964). It is that of Dr. Hernandez, the most complex male character in *Cities of the Interior*; he is the healer who plays an important part in Lillian's cure. The murder of Dr. Hernandez brings sorrow to the novel's conclusion, but it is a natural sorrow, an acceptable grief because it is a part of life as essential as self-confrontation, joy, or love.

My own visually symbolic vision of *Cities of the Interior* is a very personal one, and it is intended merely as suggestive. Symbolism, distinct from allegory, is always fluid, particularly now that we have come to recognize the universe itself as open and the nature of reality as a constantly evolving process, an activity so rapid and so complex that we cannot apprehend it except by lifting from it certain still moments, composing these into images and forms which we can contemplate long enough to orient ourselves in the continuous process of time and change. Such instants of arrest or stasis are what artists give us in their compositions. Perhaps this has always been so, but modern artists, certainly Joyce, Proust, Woolf, and Faulkner, to name only a few, were fully aware that this was what they were doing when they composed novels, not representing a copy of reality but making a composition of significant moments selected from an endless process of such moments. Bergson designated these frozen instants as "snapshots."

Nin's writing is not, however, primarily visual. Her style and her structures are intimately related to the nonverbal arts of painting, dance, and music, not only in the obvious sense that she writes about artists, but more deeply, because she has so brilliantly adapted techniques of the other arts to prose. The visual arts appeal to her because of their power to bring images to life, to give them color; her characters often discover truths about themselves when they look at paintings. But Nin's writing is essentially musical, "symphonic," as she herself has said. Its beauty and its evocative power lie in the equally strong development of three modes of symbolism: words, characterizations, and structures. These are individually perfected, then fused by force of imagination into a synthesis that renders psychic states in images that are more rhythmic and auditory than visual. Painting brings to her writing color and solidity of forms outlined; through the music of her prose Nin places her characters within the flow of time, while dance suggests the constant interplay between the human being in motion, interacting as he moves with the space around him. If they are truly to live, Nin's characters are obliged to remain in motion. Although she recognizes that there is meaningless motion, like Sabina's flights from man to man, Nin insists upon ceaseless change as essential to psychic life.

This raises the question of Nin's concept of the self, a concept without which the construct of *Cities of the Interior* would not have been possible. Here an exchange of ideas with the analyst and brilliant thinker Otto Rank is important. His books *Art and Artist* and *Will Therapy and Truth and Reality* are essential to a reader with an interest in the creative personality. For Rank and for Nin, once his patient, the self is not an entity but a process. The self is never fixed, though it is the center of being; it is always forming and re-forming itself through relationships of identification, friendship, or love, and the endless absorption and interpretation of sensations, ideas, and experiences. The self is itself a mobile, a process, as Bergson argued, of constant becoming. At the same time, it is a tool, an instrument which serves to connect dimensions of consciousness and of reality. Nin wrote, "My self is like the self of Proust. It is an instrument to connect life and the myth." She has made many statements about the nature of the self, not so much in essence, as in its relationships with other people. Unequivocally, she wrote, "The quest of the self through the intricate maze of modern confusion is the central theme of my work." "We know," she has observed, "that *we are composites in reality,* collages of our fathers and mothers, of what we read, of television influences and films, of friends and associates. . . ." The self, then, is condemned to submit to constant motion, to change; if it is to grow, it is committed to a life of constant transition between its own boundaries, which are never fixed, and the equally fluid territories of other people's psyches. It is precisely through this constant process of change, adjustment, and readjustment that the self discovers and rediscovers itself or, in short, lives. Through knowing others we form ourselves and perceive the world. Nin writes, "I could identify with characters unlike myself, enter their visions of the universe, and *in essence* achieve the truest objectivity of all, *which is to be able to see what the other sees, to feel what the other feels."*

This act of fusion or of merging with another, however, poses the threat of loss of self. This is both a danger and a challenge. Nin has made this challenge the subject of her fiction. Again and again she probes relationships of fusion. Usually they involve a man and a woman, but sometimes, as in *Ladders to Fire,* she explores the way in which members of the same sex seek to strengthen their sense of self by intense identification with another. In every intense and intimate relationship there is the peril that the self of the weaker may be submerged in that of the stronger, but if it is not, if both persons maintain their authenticity, act and are acted upon, then both will have evolved.

Imagine the self as Jung does, as the center of being, including all dimensions, conscious and unconscious. Then imagine that this center possesses the power of motion. The very center, the self, changes and moves, thus moving the entire circle of the self and affecting each ray that extends toward the circumference. We return to the image of the circle. It is only apparently fixed and immobile. When the center moves, so does the entire form, turning endlessly when growth is constant, holding into meaningful form an ever-evolving pattern of energy. Nin as the author is at the center of *Cities of the Interior.* At different times and under the pressure of various influence, Nin herself evolves into the personages of her characters. Of course, they are, as many have observed, aspects of her self. So are the characters of all novelists. As the author evolves, so do her characters, engaging in relationships with one another and with the secondary characters (often comic glosses on the main figures). The concept of the novel as a continuous creation, a mobile turning in space, is made possible by the concept of the self as a mobile turning in space, the space of experiences and of other people.

I return to the figure of the dance. Partly, it was the power of dance that attracted Nin to the women in Varda's collage. Djuna, the character who most resembles Nin, her persona at any rate, is a dancer, as Nin herself once was. Now we can see fused the ideas of art as alchemy, the perception of continuity as circular, and the meditative, worshipful interpretation of dance as observed in Eastern religions. In their book *Mandala*, José and Miriam Argüelles write: "The amazingly fluid capacity for transformation also describes the law upon which Shiva's dance is based—the dance of the continual turning of the four-spoked cosmic wheel whose hub is eternity, and which transforms everything as it gradually rolls along its course." The most beautiful and the most revealing image in all of Anaïs Nin's writing is the figure of the dancer with which *House of Incest* closes:

> And she danced; she danced with the music and with the rhythm of earth's circles; she turned with the earth turning, like a disk, turning all faces to light and to darkness evenly, dancing towards daylight.

The key to Anaïs Nin's "continuous" creation lies in this image. To enter it means that the reader too must learn to move to a new rhythm and into a deeper way of experiencing a novel.

SHARON SPENCER
New York City, 1974

Ladders to Fire

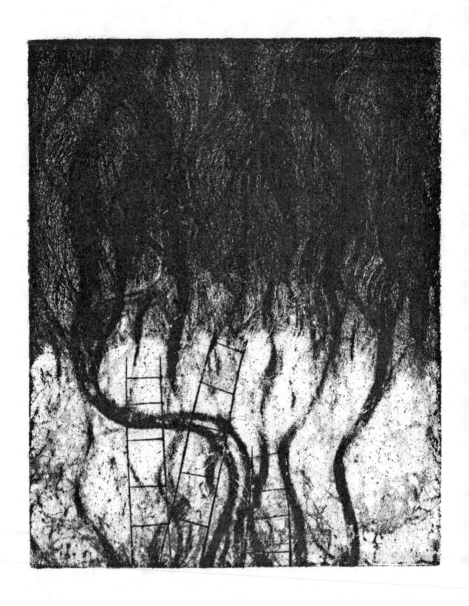

This Hunger

LILLIAN WAS ALWAYS in a state of fermentation. Her eyes rent the air and left phosphorescent streaks. Her large teeth were lustful. One thought of a negress who had found a secret potion to turn her skin white and her hair red.

As soon as she came into a room she kicked off her shoes. Necklaces and buttons choked her and she loosened them, scarves strangled her and she slackened them. Her hand bag was always bursting full and often spilled over.

She was always in full movement, in the center of a whirlpool of people, letters, and telephones. She was always poised on the pinnacle of a drama, a problem, a conflict. She seemed to trapeze from one climax to another, from one paroxysm of anxiety to another, skipping always the peaceful region in between, the deserts and the pauses. One marvelled that she slept, for this was a suspension of activity. One felt sure that in her sleep she twitched and rolled, and even fell off the bed, or that she slept half sitting up as if caught while still talking. And one felt certain that a great combat had taken place during the night, displacing the covers and pillows.

When she cooked, the entire kitchen was galvanized by the strength she put into it; the dishes, pans, knives, everything bore the brunt of her strength, everything was violently marshalled, challenged, forced to bloom, to cook, to boil. The vegetables were peeled as if the skins were torn from their resisting flesh, as if they were the fur of animals being peeled by the hunters. The fruit was stabbed, assassinated, the lettuce was murdered with a machete. The flavoring was poured like hot lava and one expected the salad to wither, shrivel instantly. The bread was sliced with a vigor which recalled heads falling from the guillotine. The bottles and glasses were knocked hard against each other as in bowling games, so that the wine, beer and water were conquered before they reached the table.

What was concocted in this cuisine reminded one of the sword swallowers at the fair, the fire-eaters and the glass-eaters of the Hindu magic sects. The same chemicals were used in the cooking as were used in the composition of her own being: only those which caused the most violent reaction, contradiction, and teasing, the refusal to answer questions but the love of putting them, and all the strong spices of human relationship which bore a relation to black pepper, paprika, soybean sauce, ketchup and red peppers. In a laboratory she would have caused explosions. In life she caused them and was afterwards aghast at the damage. Then she would hurriedly set about to atone for the havoc, for the miscarried phrase, the fatal honesty, the reckless act, the disrupting scene, the explosive

4

and catastrophic attack. Everywhere, after the storms of her appearance, there was emotional devastation. Contacts were broken, faiths withered, fatal revelations made. Harmony, illusion, equilibrium were annihilated. The next day she herself was amazed to see friendships all askew, like pictures after an earthquake.

The storms of doubt, the quick cloudings of hypersensitivity, the bursts of laughter, the wet furred voice charged with electrical vibrations, the resonant quality of her movements, left many echoes and vibrations in the air. The curtains continued to move after she left. The furniture was warm, the air was whirling, the mirrors were scarred from the exigent way she extracted from them an ever unsatisfactory image of herself.

Her red hair was as unruly as her whole self; no comb could dress it. No dress would cling and mould her, but every inch of it would stand out like ruffled feathers. Tumult in orange, red and yellow and green quarreling with each other. The rose devoured the orange, the green and blue overwhelmed the purple. The sport jacket was irritated to be in company with the silk dress, the tailored coat at war with the embroidery, the everyday shoes at variance with the turquoise bracelet. And if at times she chose a majestic hat, it sailed precariously like a sailboat on a choppy sea.

Did she dream of being the appropriate mate for the Centaur, for the Viking, for the Pioneer, for Attila or Genghis Khan, of being magnificently mated with Conquerors, the Inquisitioners or Emperors?

On the contrary. In the center of this turmoil, she gave birth to the dream of a ghostly lover, a pale, passive, romatic, anaemic figure garbed in grey and timidity. Out of the very volcano of her strength she gave birth to the most evanescent, delicate and unreachable image.

She saw him first of all in a dream, and the second time while under the effects of ether. His pale face appeared, smiled, vanished. He haunted her sleep and her unconscious self.

The third time he appeared in person in the street. Friends

introduced them. She felt the shock of familiarity known to lovers.

He stood exactly as in the dream, smiling, passive, static. He had a way of greeting that seemed more like a farewell, an air of being on his way.

She fell in love with an extinct volcano.

Her strength and fire were aroused. Her strength flowed around his stillness, encircled his silence, encompassed his quietness.

She invited him. He consented. Her whirlpool nature eddied around him, agitating the fixed, saturnian orbit.

"Do you want to come . . . do you?"

"I never know what I want," he smiled because of her emphasis on the "want," "I do not go out very much." From the first, into this void created by his not wanting, she was to throw her own desires, but not meet an answer, merely a pliability which was to leave her in doubt forever as to whether she had substituted her desire for his. From the first she was to play the lover alone, giving the questions and the answers too.

When man imposes his will on woman, she knows how to give him the pleasure of assuming his power is greater and his will becomes her pleasure; but when the woman accomplishes this, the man never gives her a feeling of any pleasure, only of guilt for having spoken first and reversed the roles. Very often she was to ask: "Do you want to do this?" And he did not know. She would fill the void, for the sake of filling it, for the sake of advancing, moving, feeling, and then he implied: "You are pushing me."

When he came to see her he was enigmatic. But he was there.

As she felt the obstacle, she also felt the force of her love, its impetus striking the obstacle, the impact of the resistance. This collision seemed to her the reality of passion.

He had been there a few moments and was already preparing for flight, looking at the geography of the room, marking the exits "in case of fire," when the telephone rang.

"It's Serge asking me to go to a concert," said Lillian with the proper feminine inflection of: "I shall do your will, not mine." And this time Gerard, although he was not openly and violently in favor of Lillian, was openly against Serge, whoever he was. He showed hostility. And Lillian interpreted this favorably. She refused the invitation and felt as if Gerard had declared his passion. She laid down the telephone as if marking a drama and sat nearer to the Gerard who had manifested his jealousy.

The moment she sat near him he recaptured his quality of a mirage: paleness, otherworldliness, obliqueness. He appropriated woman's armor and defenses, and she took the man's. Lillian was the lover seduced by obstacle and the dream. Gerard watched her fire with a feminine delectation of all fires caused by seduction.

When they kissed she was struck with ecstasy and he with fear.

Gerard was fascinated and afraid. He was in danger of being possessed. Why in danger? Because he was already possessed by his mother and two possessions meant annihilation.

Lillian could not understand. They were two different loves, and could not interfere with each other.

She saw, however, that Gerard was paralyzed, that the very thought of the two loves confronting each other meant death.

He retreated. The next day he was ill, ill with terror. He sought to explain. "I have to take care of my mother."

"Well," said Lillian, "I will help you."

This did not reassure him. At night he had nightmares. There was a resemblance between the two natures, and to possess Lillian was like possessing the mother, which was taboo. Besides, in the nightmare, there was a battle between the two possessions in which he won nothing but a change of masters. Because both his mother and Lillian (in the nightmare they were confused and indistinguishable), instead of living out their own thoughts, occupying their own hands, playing their own instruments, put all their strength, wishes, desires, their wills on him. He felt that in the nightmare they carved him out like a statue, they talked for him, they acted for him, they fought for him, they never let him alone. He was merely the possessed. He was not free.

Lillian, like his mother, was too strong for him. The battle between the two women would be too strong for him. He could not separate them, free himself and make his choice. He was at a disadvantage. So he feared: he feared his mother and the outcries, the scenes, dramas, and he feared Lillian for the same reason since they were of the same elements: fire and water and aggression. So he feared the new invasion which endangered the pale little flame of his life. In the center of his being there was no strength to answer the double challenge. The only alternative was retreat.

When he was six years old he had asked his mother for the secret of how children were born. His mother answered: "I made you."

"You made me?" Gerard repeated in utter wonder. Then he had stood before a mirror and marvelled: "You made this hair? You made this skin?"

"Yes," said his mother. "I made them."

"How difficult it must have been, and my nose! And my teeth! And you made me walk, too." He was lost in admiration of his mother. He believed her. But after a moment of gazing at the mirror he said: "There is one thing I can't believe. I can't believe that you made my eyes!"

His eyes. Even today when his mother was still making him, directing him, when she cut his hair, fashioned him, carved him, washed his clothes, what was left free in this encirclement of his being were his eyes. He could not act, but he could see.

But his retreat was inarticulate, negative, baffling to Lillian. When she was hurt, baffled, lost, she in turn retreated, then he renewed his pursuit of her. For he loved her strength and would have liked it for himself. When this strength did not threaten him, when the danger was removed, then he gave way to his attraction for this strength. Then he pursued it. He invited and lured it back, he would not surrender it (to Serge or anyone

8

else). And Lillian who suffered from his retreat suffered even more from his mysterious returns, and his pursuits which ceased as soon as she responded to them.

He was playing with his fascination and his fear.

When she turned her back on him, he renewed his charms, enchanted her and won her back. Feminine wiles used against woman's strength like women's ambivalent evasions and returns. Wiles of which Lillian, with her straightforward manly soul, knew nothing.

The obstacle only aroused Lillian's strength (as it aroused the knights of old) but the obstacle discouraged Gerard and killed his desire. The obstacle became his alibi for weakness. The obstacle for Gerard was insurmountable. As soon as Lillian overcame one, Gerard erected another. By all these diversions and perversions of the truth he preserved from her and from himself the secret of his weakness. The secret was kept. The web of delusion grew around their love. To preserve this fatal secret: you, Lillian, are too strong; you, Gerard, are not strong enough (which would destroy them), Gerard (like a woman) wove false pretexts. The false pretexts did not deceive Lillian. She knew there was a deeper truth but she did not know what it was.

Weary of fighting the false pretexts she turned upon herself, and her own weakness, her self-doubts, suddenly betrayed her. Gerard had awakened the dormant demon doubt. To defend his weakness he had unknowingly struck at her. So Lillian began to think: "I did not arouse his love. I was not beautiful enough." And she began to make a long list of self-accusations. Then the harm was done. She had been the aggressor so she was the more seriously wounded. Self-doubt asserted itself. The seed of doubt was implanted in Lillian to work its havoc with time. The real Gerard receded, faded, vanished, and was reinstated as a dream image. Other Gerards will appear, until . . .

After the disappearance of Gerard, Lillian resumed her defensive attitude towards man, and became again the warrior. It became absolutely essential to her to triumph in the smallest issue of an argument. Because she felt so insecure about her own value it became of vital importance to convince and win over everyone to her assertions. So she could not bear to yield, to be convinced, defeated, persuaded, swerved in the little things.

She was now afraid to yield to passion, and because she could not yield to the larger impulses it became essential also to not yield to the small ones, even if her adversary were in the right. She was living on a plane of war. The bigger resistance to the flow of life became one with the smaller resistance to the will of others, and the smallest issue became equal to the ultimate one. The pleasure of yielding on a level of passion being unknown to her, the pleasure of yielding on other levels became equally impossible. She denied herself all the sources of feminine pleasure: of being invaded, of being conquered. In war, conquest was imperative. No approach from the enemy could be interpreted as anything but a threat. She could not see that the real issue of the war was a defense of her being against the invasion of passion. Her enemy was the lover who might possess her. All her intensity was poured into the small battles; to win in the choice of a restaurant, of a movie, of visitors, in opinions, in analysis of people, to win in all the small rivalries through an evening.

At the same time as this urge to triumph continuously, she felt no appeasement or pleasure from her victories. What she won was not what she really wanted. Deep down, what her nature wanted was to be made to yield.

The more she won (and she won often for no man withstood this guerrilla warfare with any honors—he could not see the great importance that a picture hung to the left rather than to the right might have) the more unhappy and empty she felt.

No great catastrophe threatened her. She was not tragically struck down as others were by the death of a loved one at war.

10

There was no visible enemy, no real tragedy, no hospital, no cemetery, no mortuary, no morgue, no criminal court, no crime, no horror. There was nothing.

She was traversing a street. The automobile did not strike her down. It was not she who was inside of the ambulance being delivered to St. Vincent's Hospital. It was not she whose mother died. It was not she whose brother was killed in the war.

In all the registers of catastrophe her name did not appear. She was not attacked, raped, or mutilated. She was not kidnapped for white slavery.

But as she crossed the street and the wind lifted the dust, just before it touched her face, she felt as if all these horrors had happened to her, she felt the nameless anguish, the shrinking of the heart, the asphyxiation of pain, the horror of torture whose cries no one hears.

Every other sorrow, illness, or pain is understood, pitied, shared with all human beings. Not this one which was mysterious and solitary.

It was ineffectual, inarticulate, unmoving to others as the attempted crying out of the mute.

Everybody understands hunger, illness, poverty, slavery and torture. No one understood that at this moment at which she crossed the street with every privilege granted her, of not being hungry, of not being imprisoned or tortured, all these privileges were a subtler form of torture. They were given to her, the house, the complete family, the food, the loves, like a mirage. Given and denied. They were present to the eyes of others who said: "You are fortunate," and invisible to her. Because the anguish, the mysterious poison, corroded all of them, distorted the relationships, blighted the food, haunted the house, installed war where there was no apparent war, torture where there was no sign of instruments, and enemies where there were no enemies to capture and defeat.

Anguish was a voiceless woman screaming in a nightmare.

She stood waiting for Lillian at the door. And what struck Lillian instantly was the aliveness of Djuna: if only Gerard had been like her! Their meeting was like a joyous encounter of equal forces.

Djuna responded instantly to the quick rhythm, to the intensity. It was a meeting of equal speed, equal fervor, equal strength. It was as if they had been two champion skiers making simultaneous jumps and landing together at the same spot. It was like a meeting of two chemicals exactly balanced, fusing and foaming with the pleasure of achieved proportions.

Lillian knew that Djuna would not sit peacefully or passively in her room awaiting the knock on her door, perhaps not hearing it the first time, or hearing it and walking casually towards it. She knew Djuna would have her door open and would be there when the elevator deposited her. And Djuna knew by the swift approach of Lillian that Lillian would have the answer to her alert curiosity, to her impatience; that she would hasten the elevator trip, quicken the journey, slide over the heavy carpet in time to meet this wave of impatience and enthusiasm.

Just as there are elements which are sensitive to change and climate and rise fast to higher temperatures, there were in Lillian and Djuna rhythms which left them both suspended in utter solitude. It was not in body alone that they arrived on time for their meetings, but they arrived primed for high living, primed for flight, for explosion, for ecstasy, for feeling, for all experience. The slowness of others in starting, their slowness in answering, caused them often to soar alone.

To Djuna Lillian answered almost before she spoke, answered with her bristling hair and fluttering hands, and the tinkle of her jewelry.

"Gerard lost everything when he lost you," said Djuna before Lillian had taken off her coat. "He lost life."

Lillian was trying to recapture an impression she had before seeing Djuna. "Why, Djuna, when I heard your voice over the telephone I thought you were delicate and fragile. And you

12

look fragile but somehow not weak. I came to ... well, to protect you. I don't know what from."

Djuna laughed. She had enormous fairytale eyes, like two aquamarine lights illumining darkness, eyes of such depth that at first one felt one might fall into them as into a sea, a sea of feeling. And then they ceased to be the pulling, drawing, absorbing sea and they became beacons, with extraordinary intensity of vision, of awareness, of perception. Then one felt one's chaos illumined, transfigured. Where the blue, liquid balls alighted every object acquired significance.

At the same time their vulnerability and sentience made them tremble like delicate candlelight or like the eye of the finest camera lens which at too intense daylight will suddenly shut black. One caught the inner chamber like the photograper's dark room, in which sensitivity to daylight, to crudity and grossness would cause instantaneous annihilation of the image.

They gave the impression of a larger vision of the world. If sensitivity made them retract, contract swiftly, it was not in any self-protective blindness but to turn again to that inner chamber where the metamorphosis took place and in which the pain became not personal, but the pain of the whole world, in which ugliness became not a personal experience of ugliness but the world's experience with all ugliness. By enlarging and situating it in the totality of the dream, the unbearable event became a large, airy understanding of life which gave to her eyes an ultimately triumphant power which people mistook for strength, but which was in reality courage. For the eyes, wounded on the exterior, turned inward, but did not stay there, and returned with the renewed vision. After each encounter with naked unbearable truths, naked unbearable pain, the eyes returned to the mirrors in the inner chambers, to the transformation by understanding and reflection, so that they could emerge and face the naked truth again.

In the inner chambers there was a treasure room. In it dwelt her racial wealth of Byzantine imagery, a treasure room of hierarchic figures, religious symbols. Old men of religion, who had assisted at her birth and blessed her with their wisdom. They appeared in the colors of death, because they had at first endangered her advance into life. Their robes, their caps, were made of the heavily embroidered materials of rituals illumined with the light of eternity. They had willed her their wisdom of life and death, of past and future, and therefore excluded the present. Wisdom was a swifter way of reaching death. Death was postponed by living, by suffering, by risking, by losing, by error. These men of religion had at first endangered her life, for their wisdom had incited her in the past to forego the human test of experience, to forego the error and the confusion which was living. By knowing she would reach all, not by touching, not by way of the body. There had lurked in these secret chambers of her ancestry a subtle threat such as lurked in all the temples, synagogues, churches—the incense of denial, the perfume of the body burnt to sacrificial ashes by religious alchemy, transmuted into guilt and atonement.

In the inner chamber there were also other figures. The mother madonna holding the child and nourishing it. The haunting mother image forever holding a small child.

Then there was the child itself, the child inhabiting a world of peaceful, laughing animals, rich trees, in valleys of festive color. The child in her eyes appeared with its eyes closed. It was dreaming the fertile valleys, the small warm house, the Byzantine flowers, the tender animals and the abundance. It was dreaming and afraid to awaken. It was dreaming the lightness of the sky, the warmth of the earth, the fecundity of the colors.

It was afraid to awaken.

Lillian's vivid presence filled the hotel room. She was so entirely palpable, visible, present. She was not parcelled into a woman who was partly in the past and partly in the future, or one whose spirit was partly at home with her children, and partly elsewhere. She was here, all of her, eyes and ears, and hands and warmth and interest and alertness, with a sympathy which surrounded Djuna—questioned, investigated, absorbed, saw, heard. . . .

"You give me something wonderful, Lillian. A feeling that I have a friend. Let's have dinner here. Let's celebrate."

Voices charged with emotion. Fullness. To be able to talk as one feels. To be able to say all.

"I lost Gerard because I leaped. I expressed my feelings. He was afraid. Why do I love men who are afraid? He was afraid and I had to court him. Djuna, did you ever think how men who court a woman and do not win her are not hurt? And woman gets hurt. If woman plays the Don Juan and does the courting and the man retreats she is mutilated in some way."

"Yes, I have noticed that. I suppose it's a kind of guilt. For a man it is natural to be the aggressor and he takes defeat well. For woman it is a transgression, and she assumes the defeat is caused by the aggression. How long will woman be ashamed of her strength?"

"Djuna, take this."

She handed her a silver medallion she was wearing.

"Well, you didn't win Gerard but you shook him out of his death."

"Why," said Lillian, "aren't men as you are?"

"I was thinking the same thing," said Djuna.

"Perhaps when they are we don't like them or fear them. Perhaps we like the ones who are not strong. . . ."

Lillian found this relation to Djuna palpable and joyous. There was in them a way of asserting its reality, by constant signs, gifts, expressiveness, words, letters, telephones, an exchange of visible affection, palpable responses. They exchanged jewels, clothes, books, they protected each other, they expressed concern, jealousy, possessiveness. They talked. The relationship was the central, essential personage of this dream without pain. This relationship had the aspect of a primitive figure to which both enjoyed presenting proofs of worship and devotion. It was an active, continuous ceremony in which there entered no moments of indifference, fatigue, or misunderstandings or separations, no eclipses, no doubts.

"I wish you were a man," Lillian often said.

"I wish you were."

Outwardly it was Lillian who seemed more capable of this metamorphosis. She had the physical strength, the physical dynamism, the physical appearance of strength. She carried tailored clothes well; her gestures were direct and violent. Masculinity seemed more possible to her, outwardly. Yet inwardly she was in a state of chaos and confusion. Inwardly she was like nature, chaotic and irrational. She had no vision into this chaos: it ruled her and swamped her. It sucked her into miasmas, into hurricanes, into caverns of blind suffering.

Outwardly Djuna was the essence of femininity . . . a curled frilled flower which might have been a starched undulating petticoat or a ruffled ballet skirt moulded into a sea shell. But inwardly the nature was clarified, ordered, understood, dominated. As a child Djuna had looked upon the storms of her own nature—jealousy, anger, resentment—always with the knowledge that they could be dominated, that she refused to be devastated by them, or to destroy others with them. As a child, alone, of her own free will, she had taken on an oriental attitude of dominating her nature by wisdom and understanding. Finally, with the use of every known instrument—art, aesthetic forms, philosophy, psychology—it had been tamed.

But each time she saw it in Lillian, flaring, uncontrolled, wild, blind, destroying itself and others, her compassion and love were aroused. "That will be my gift to her," she thought with warmth, with pity. "I will guide her."

Meanwhile Lillian was exploring this aesthetic, this form,

16

this mystery that was Djuna. She was taking up Djuna's clothes one by one, amazed at their complication, their sheer femininity. "Do you wear this?" she asked, looking at the black lace nightgown. "I thought only prostitutes wore this!"

She investigated the perfumes, the cosmetics, the refined coquetries, the veils, the muffs, the scarves. She was almost like a sincere and simple person before a world of artifice. She was afraid of being deceived by all this artfulness. She could not see it as aesthetic, but as the puritans see it: as deception, as immorality, as belonging with seduction and eroticism.

She insisted on seeing Djuna without make-up, and was then satisfied that make-up was purely an enhancement of the features, not treachery.

Lillian's house was beautiful, lacquered, grown among the trees, and bore the mark of her handiwork all through, yet it did not seem to belong to her. She had painted, decorated, carved, arranged, selected, and most of it was made by her own hands, or refashioned, always touched or handled or improved by her, out of her very own activity and craftsmanship. Yet it did not become her house, and it did not have her face, her atmosphere. She always looked like a stranger in it. With all her handiwork and taste, she had not been able to give it her own character.

It was a home; it suited her husband, Larry, and her children. It was built for peace. The rooms were spacious, clear, brightly windowed. It was warm, glowing, clean, harmonious. It was like other houses.

As soon as Djuna entered it, she felt this. The strength, the fervor, the care Lillian spent in the house, on her husband and children came from some part of her being that was not the deepest Lillian. It was as if every element but her own nature had contributed to create this life. Who had made the marriage? Who had desired the children? She could not remember the first impetus, the first choice, the first desire for these, nor how they came to be. It was as if it had happened in her sleep. Lillian, guided by her background, her mother, her sisters, her habits, her home as a child, her blindness in regard to her own desires, had made all this and then lived in it, but it had not been made out of the deeper elements of her nature, and she was a stranger in it.

Once made—this life, these occupations, the care, the devotion, the family—it never occurred to her that she could rebel against them. There was no provocation for rebellion. Her husband was kind, her children were lovable, her house was harmonious; and Nanny, the old nurse who took care of them all with inexhaustible maternal warmth, was their guardian angel, the guardian angel of the home.

Nanny's devotion to the home was so strong, so predominant, and so constantly manifested that the home and family seemed to belong to her more than to Lillian. The home had a reality for Nanny. Her whole existence was centered on it. She defended its interests, she hovered, reigned, watched, guarded tirelessly. She passed judgments on the visitors. Those who were dangerous to the peace of the home, she served with unappetizing meals, and from one end of the meal to the other, showed her disapproval. The welcome ones were those her instinct told her were good for the family, the home, for their unity. Then she surpassed herself in cooking and service. The unity of the family was her passionate concern: that the children should understand each other and love each other; that the children should love the father, the mother; that the mother and father should be close. For this she was willing to be the receiver of confidences, to be the peacemaker, to reestablish order.

She was willing to show an interest in any of Lillian's activities as long as these ultimately flowed back to the house. She could be interested in concerts if she brought the overflow of the music home to enhance it. She could be interested in painting while the results showed visibly in the house.

When the conversation lagged at the table she supplied diversion. If the children quarrelled she upheld the rights of each one in soothing, wise explanations.

She refused one proposal of marriage.

When Lillian came into the house, and felt lost in it, unable to really enter into, to feel it, to participate, to care, as if it were all not present and warm but actually a family album, as if her son Paul did not come in and really take off his snow-covered boots, but it was a snapshot of Paul taking off his boots, as if her husband's face were a photograph too, and Adele was actually the painting of her above the piano ... then Lillian rushed to the kitchen, unconsciously seeking Nanny's worries, Nanny's anxieties (Paul is too thin, and Adele lost her best friend in school) to convince herself of the poignant reality of this house and its occupants (her husband had forgotten his rubbers).

If the children had not been growing up (again according to Nanny's tabulations and calculations) Lillian would have thought herself back ten years. Her husband did not change.

Nanny was the only one who had felt the shock the day that Lillian decided to have her own room. And Lillian might not have changed the rooms over if it had not been for a cricket.

Lillian's husband had gone away on a trip. It was summer. Lillian felt deeply alone, and filled with anxiety. She could not understand the anxiety. Her first thought always was: Larry is happy. He is well. He looked very happy when he left. The children are well. Then what can be the matter with me? How can anything be the matter with me if they are well?

There were guests at the house. Among them was one who vaguely resembled Gerard, and the young man in her dreams, and the young man who appeared to her under anaesthetic. Always of the same family. But he was bold as a lover. He courted her swiftly, impetuously.

A cricket had lodged itself in one of the beams of her room.

19

Perfectly silent until the young man came to visit her, until he caressed her. Then it burst into frenzied cricket song.

They laughed.

He came again the next night, and at the same moment the cricket sang again.

Always at the moment a cricket should sing.

The young man went away. Larry returned. Larry was happy to be with his wife.

But the cricket did not sing. Lillian wept. Lillian moved into a room of her own. Nanny was depressed and cross for a week.

When they sat together, alone, in the evenings, Larry did not appear to see her. When he talked about her he always talked about the Lillian of ten years ago; how she looked then, how she was, what she said. He delighted in reviving scenes out of the past, her behaviour, her high temper and the troubles she got herself into. He often repeated these stories. And Lillian felt that she had known only one Larry, a Larry who had courted her and then remained as she had first known him. When she heard about the Lillian of ten years ago she felt no connection with her. But Larry was living with her, delighting in her presence. He reconstructed her out of his memory and sat her there every evening they had together.

One night they heard a commotion in the otherwise peaceful village. The police car passed and then the ambulance. Then the family doctor stopped his car before the gate. He asked for a drink. "My job is over," he said, "and I need a drink badly." Lillian gave him one, but at first he would not talk.

Later he explained: The man who rented the house next door was a young doctor, not a practicing one. His behavior and way of living had perplexed the neighbors. He received no one, allowed no one into the house. He was somber in mood, and attitude, and he was left alone. But people complained persistently of an unbearable odor. There were investigations. Finally it was discovered that his wife had died six months earlier, in California. He had brought her body back and he was living with it stretched on his bed. The doctor had seen her.

Lillian left the room. The odor of death, the image of death . . . everywhere.

No investigation would be made in her house. No change. Nanny was there.

But Lillian felt trapped without knowing what had trapped her.

Then she found Djuna. With Djuna she was alive. With Djuna her entire being burst into living, flowering cells. She could feel her own existence, the Lillian of today.

She spent much time with Djuna.

Paul felt his mother removed in some way. He noticed that she and his father had little to say to each other. He was anxious. Adele had nightmares that her mother was dying. Larry was concerned. Perhaps Lillian was not well. She ate little. He sent for the doctor. She objected to him violently. Nanny hovered, guarded, as if she scented danger. But nothing changed. Lillian waited. She always went first to the kitchen when she came home, as if it were the hearth itself, to warm herself. And then to each child's room, and then to Larry.

She could do nothing. Djuna's words illuminated her chaos, but changed nothing. What was it Djuna said: that life tended to crystallize into patterns which became traps and webs. That people tended to see each other in their first "state" or "form" and to adopt a rhythm in consequence. That they had greatest difficulty in seeing the transformations of the loved one, in seeing the becoming. If they did finally perceive the new self, they had the greatest difficulty nevertheless in changing the rhythm. The strong one was condemned to perpetual strength, the weak to perpetual weakness. The one who loved you best

21

condemned you to a static role because he had adapted his being to the past self. If you attempted to change, warned Djuna, you would find a subtle, perverse opposition, and perhaps sabotage! Inwardly and outwardly, a pattern was a form which became a prison. And then we had to smash it. Mutation was difficult. Attempts at evasion were frequent, blind evasions, evasions from dead relationships, false relationships, false roles, and sometimes from the deeper self too, because of the great obstacle one encountered in affirming it. All our emotional history was that of the spider and the fly, with the added tragedy that the fly here collaborated in the weaving of the web. Crimes were frequent. People in desperation turned about and destroyed each other. No one could detect the cause or catch the criminal. There was no visible victim. It always had the appearance of suicide.

Lillian sensed the walls and locks. She did not even know she wanted to escape. She did not even know she was in rebellion. She did it with her body. Her body became ill from the friction, lacerations and daily duels with her beloved jailers. Her body became ill from the poisons of internal rebellion, the monotony of her prison, the greyness of its days, the poverty of the nourishment. She was in a fixed relationship and could not move forward.

Anxiety settled upon the house. Paul clung to his mother longer when they separated for short periods. Adele was less gay.

Larry was more silent.

Nanny began to weep noiselessly. Then she had a visitor. The same one she had sent away ten years earlier. The man was growing old. He wanted a home. He wanted Nanny. Nanny was growing old. He talked to her all evening, in the kitchen. Then one day Nanny cried without control. Lillian questioned her. She wanted to get married. But she hated to leave the family. The family! The sacred, united, complete family. In this big house, with so much work. And no one else to be had. And she wanted Lillian to protest, to cling to her—as the children did before, as Larry had done a few years back, each time the suitor had come again for his answer. But Lillian said quietly, "Nanny, it is time that you thought of yourself. You have lived for others all your life. Get married. I believe you should get married. He loves you. He waited for you such a long time. You deserve a home and life and protection and a rest. Get married."

And then Lillian walked into the dining room where the family was eating and she said: "Nanny is going to get married and leave us."

Paul then cried out: "This is the beginning of the end!"

Larry looked up from his meal, for the first time struck with a clearer glimpse of what had been haunting the house.

Through the high building, the wind complained, playing a frenzied flute up and down the elevator shafts.

Lillian and Djuna opened the window and looked at the city covered with a mist. One could see only the lighted eyes of the buildings. One could hear only muffled sounds, the ducks from Central Park lake nagging loudly, the fog horns from the river which sounded at times like the mournful complaints of imprisoned ships not allowed to sail, at others like gay departures.

Lillian was sitting in the dark, speaking of her life, her voice charged with both laughter and tears.

In the dark a new being appears. A new being who has not the courage to face daylight. In the dark people dare to dream everything. And they dare to tell everything. In the dark there appeared a new Lillian.

There was just enough light from the city to show their faces chalk white, with shadows in the place of eyes and mouth, and an occasional gleam of white teeth. At first it was like two

23

children sitting on a see-saw, because Lillian would talk about her life and her marriage and the disintegration of her home, and then Djuna would lean over to embrace her, overflowing with pity. Then Djuna would speak and Lillian would lean over and want to gather her in her arms with maternal compassion.

"I feel," said Lillian, "that I do everything wrong. I feel I do everything to bring about just what I fear. You will turn away from me too."

Lillian's unsatisfied hunger for life had evoked in Djuna another hunger. This hunger still hovered at times over the bright film of her eyes, shading them not with the violet shadows of either illness or sensual excess, of experience or fever, but with the pearl-grey shadow of denial, and Djuna said:

"I was born in the most utter poverty. My mother lying in bed with consumption, four brothers and sisters loudly claiming food and care, and I having to be the mother and nurse of them all. We were so hungry that we ate all the samples of food or medicines which were left at the house. I remember once we ate a whole box of chocolate-coated constipation pills. Father was a taxi driver but he spent the greatest part of what he made on drink along the way. As we lived among people who were all living as we were, without sufficient clothing, or heat or food, we knew no contrast and believed this was natural and general. But with me it was different. I suffered from other kinds of pangs. I was prone to the most excessive dreaming, of such intensity and realism that when I awakened I felt I lost an entire universe of legends, myths, figures and cities of such color that they made our room seem a thousand times more bare, the poverty of the table more acute. The disproportion was immense. And I'm not speaking merely of the banquets which were so obviously compensatory! Nor of the obvious way by which I filled my poor wardrobe. It was more than that. I saw in my dreams houses, forests, entire cities, and such a variety of personages that even today I wonder how a child, who had not even seen pictures, could invent such designs in textures, such colonnades, friezes, fabulous animals, statues, colors, as I did. And the activity! My dreams were so full of activity that at times I felt it was the dreams which exhausted me rather than all the washing, ironing, shopping, mending, sweeping, tending, nursing, dusting that I did. I remember I had to break soap boxes to burn in the fireplace. I used to scratch my hands and bruise my toes. Yet when my mother caressed me and said, you look tired, Djuna, I almost felt like confessing to her that what had tired me was my constant dreaming of a ship which insisted on sailing through a city, or my voyage in a chaise through the snow-covered steppes of Russia. And by the way, there was a lot of confusion of places and methods of travel in my dreams, as there must be in the dreams of the blind. Do you know what I think now? I think what tired me was the intensity of the pleasures I had together with the perfect awareness that such pleasure could not last and would be immediately followed by its opposite. Once out of my dreams, the only certitude I retained from these nocturnal expeditions was that pleasure could not possibly last. This conviction was strengthened by the fact that no matter how small a pleasure I wanted to take during the day it was followed by catastrophe. If I relaxed for one instant the watch over my sick mother to eat an orange all by myself in some abandoned lot, she would have a turn for the worse. Or if I spent some time looking at the pictures outside of the movie house one of my brothers or sisters would cut himself or burn his finger or get into a fight with another child. So I felt then that liberty must be paid for heavily. I learned a most severe accounting which was to consider pleasure as the jewel, a kind of stolen jewel for which one must be willing to pay vast sums in suffering and guilt. Even today, Lillian, when something very marvelous happens to me, when I attain love or ecstasy or a perfect moment, I expect it to be followed by pain."

Then Lillian leaned over and kissed Djuna warmly: "I want to protect you."

"We give each other courage."

The mist came into the room. Djuna thought: She's such a hurt woman. She is one who does not know what she suffers from, or why, or how to overcome it. She is all unconscious, motion, music. She is afraid to see, to analyze her nature. She thinks that nature just is and that nothing can be done about it. She would never have invented ships to conquer the sea, machines to create light where there was darkness. She would never have harnessed water power, electric power. She is like the primitive. She thinks it is all beyond her power. She accepts chaos. She suffers mutely. . . .

"Djuna, tell me all that happened to you. I keep thinking about your hunger. I feel the pangs of it in my own stomach."

"My mother died," continued Djuna. "One of my brothers was hurt in an accident while playing in the street and crippled. Another was taken to the insane asylum. He harmed nobody. When the war started he began to eat flowers stolen from the florists. When he was arrested he said that he was eating flowers to bring peace to the world. That if everybody ate flowers peace would come to the world. My sister and I were put in an orphan asylum. I remember the day we were taken there. The night before I had a dream about a Chinese pagoda all in gold, filled with a marvelous odor. At the tip of the pagoda there was a mechanical bird who sang one little song repeatedly. I kept hearing this song and smelling the odor all the time and that seemed more real to me than the callous hands of the orphan asylum women when they changed me into a uniform. Oh, the greyness of those dresses! And if only the windows had been normal. But they were long and narrow, Lillian. Everything is changed when you look at it through long and narrow windows. It's as if the sky itself were compressed, limited. To me they were like the windows of a prison. The food was dark, and tasteless, like slime. The children were cruel to each other. No one visited us. And then there was the old watchman who made the rounds at night. He often lifted the corners of our bedcovers, and let his eyes rove and sometimes more than his eyes. ... He became the demon of the night for us little girls."

There was a silence, during which both Lillian and Djuna became children, listening to the watchman of the night become the demon of the night, the tutor of the forbidden, the initiator breaking the sheltered core of the child, breaking the innocence and staining the beds of adolescence.

"The satyr of the asylum," said Djuna, "who became also our jailer because when we grew older and wanted to slip out at night to go out with the boys, it was he who rattled the keys and prevented us. But for him we might have been free at times, but he watched us, and the women looked up to him for his fanaticism in keeping us from the street. The orphan asylum had a system which permitted families to adopt the orphans. But as it was known that the asylum supplied the sum of thirty-five dollars a month towards the feeding of the child, those who responded were most often those in need of the thirty-five dollars. Poor families, already burdened with many children, came forward to 'adopt' new ones. The orphans were allowed to enter these homes in which they found themselves doubly cheated. For at least in the asylum we had no illusion, no hope of love. But we did have illusions about the adoptions. We thought we would find a family. In most cases we did not even imagine that these families had children of their own. We expected to be a much wanted and only child! I was placed in one of them. The first thing that happened was that the other children were jealous of the intruder. And the spectacle of the love lavished on the legitimate children was terribly painful. It made me feel more abandoned, more hungry, more orphaned than ever. Every time a parent embraced his child I suffered so much that finally I ran away back to the asylum. And I was not the only one. And besides this emotional starvation we got even less to eat—the allowance being spent on the whole family. And now I lost my last treasure: the dreaming. For nothing in the dreams took the place of the human warmth I had witnessed. Now I felt utterly poor, because I could not create a human companion."

This hunger which had inhabited her entire being, which had thinned her blood, transpired through her bones, attacked the roots of her hair, given a fragility to her skin which was never to disappear entirely, had been so enormous that it had marked her whole being and her eyes with an indelible mark. Although her life changed and every want was filled later, this appearance of hunger remained. As if nothing could ever quite fill it. Her being had received no sun, no food, no air, no warmth, no love. It retained open pores of yearning and longing, mysterious spongy cells of absorption. The space between actuality, absolute deprivation, and the sumptuosity of her imagination could never be entirely covered. What she had created in the void, in the emptiness, in the bareness continued to shame all that was offered her, and her large, infinitely blue eyes continued to assert the immensity of her hunger.

This hunger of the eyes, skin, of the whole body and spirit, which made others criminals, robbers, rapers, barbarians, which caused wars, invasions, plundering and murder, in Djuna at the age of puberty alchemized into love.

Whatever was missing she became: she became mother, father, cousin, brother, friend, confidant, guide, companion to all.

This power of absorption, this sponge of receptivity which might have fed itself forever to fill the early want, she used to receive all communication of the need of others. The need and hunger became nourishment. Her breasts, which no poverty had been able to wither, were heavy with the milk of lucidity, the milk of devotion.

This hunger . . . became love.

While wearing the costume of utter femininity, the veils and the combs, the gloves and the perfumes, the muffs and the heels of femininity, she nevertheless disguised in herself an active lover of the world, the one who was actively roused by the object of his love, the one who was made strong as man is made strong in the center of his being by the softness of his love.

Loving in men and women not their strength but their softness, not their fullness but their hunger, not their plenitude but their needs.

They had made contact then with the deepest aspect of themselves—Djuna with Lillian's emotional violence and her compassion for this force which destroyed her and hurled her against all obstacles, Lillian with Djuna's power of clarification. They needed each other. Djuna experienced deep in herself a pleasure each time Lillian exploded, for she herself kept her gestures, her feeling within an outer form, like an Oriental. When Lillian exploded it seemed to Djuna as if some of her violent feeling, so long contained within the forms, were released. Some of her own lightning, some of her own rebellions, some of her own angers. Djuna contained in herself a Lillian too, to whom she had never given a moment's freedom, and it made her strangely free when Lillian gave vent to her anger or rebellions. But after the havoc, when Lillian had bruised herself, or more seriously mutilated herself (war and explosion had their consequences) then Lillian needed Djuna. For the bitterness, the despair, the chaos submerged Lillian, drowned her. The hurt Lillian wanted to strike back and did so blindly, hurting herself all the more. And then Djuna was there, to remove the arrows implanted in Lillian, to cleanse them of their poison, to open the prison door, to open the trap door, to protect, to give transfusion of blood, and peace to the wounded.

But it was Lillian who was drowning, and it was Djuna who was able always at the last moment to save her, and in her moments of danger, Lillian knew only one thing: that she must possess Djuna.

It was as if someone had proclaimed: I need oxygen, and therefore I will lock some oxygen in my room and live on it.

29

So Lillian began her courtship.

She brought gifts. She pulled out perfume, and jewelry and clothes. She almost covered the bed with gifts. She wanted Djuna to put all the jewelry on, to smell all the perfumes at once, to wear all her clothes. Djuna was showered with gifts as in a fairytale, but she could not find in them the fairytale pleasure. She felt that to each gift was tied a little invisible cord or demand, of exactingness, of debt, of domination. She felt she could not wear all these things and walk away, freely. She felt that with the gifts, a golden spider wove a golden web of possession. Lillian was not only giving away objects, but golden threads woven out of her very own substance to fix and to hold. They were not the fairytale gifts which Djuna had dreamed of receiving. (She had many dreams of receiving perfume, or receiving fur, or being given blue bottles, lamés, etc.) In the fairytale the giver laid out the presents and then became invisible. In the fairytales and in the dreams there was no debt, and there was no giver.

Lillian did not become invisible. Lillian became more and more present. Lillian became the mother who wanted to dress her child out of her own substance, Lillian became the lover who wanted to slip the shoes and slippers on the beloved's feet so he could contain these feet. The dresses were not chosen as Djuna's dresses, but as Lillian's choice and taste to cover Djuna.

The night of gifts, begun in gaiety and magnificence, began to thicken. Lillian had put too much of herself into the gifts. It was a lovely night, with the gifts scattered through the room like fragments of Miro's circus paintings, flickering and leaping, but not free. Djuna wanted to enjoy and she could not. She loved Lillian's generosity, Lillian's largeness, Lillian's opulence and magnificence, but she felt anxiety. She remembered as a child receiving gifts for Christmas, and among them a closed mysterious box gaily festooned with multicolored ribbons. She remembered that the mystery of this box affected her more than the open, exposed, familiar gifts of tea cups, dolls, etc. She opened the box and out of it jumped a grotesque devil who, propelled by taut springs, almost hit her face.

In these gifts, there is a demon somewhere; a demon who is hurting Lillian, and will hurt me, and I don't know where he is hiding. I haven't seen him yet, but he is here.

She thought of the old legends, of the knights who had to kill monsters before they could enjoy their love.

No demon here, thought Djuna, nothing but a woman drowning, who is clutching at me . . . I love her.

When Lillian dressed up in the evening in vivid colors with her ever tinkling jewelry, her face wildly alive, Djuna said to her, "You're made for a passionate life of some kind."

She looked like a white negress, a body made for rolling in natural undulations of pleasure and desire. Her vivid face, her avid mouth, her provocative, teasing glances proclaimed sensuality. She had rings under her eyes. She looked often as if she had just come from the arms of a lover. An energy smoked from her whole body.

But sensuality was paralyzed in her. When Djuna sought to show Lillian her face in the mirror, she found Lillian paralyzed with fear. She was impaled on a rigid pole of puritanism. One felt it, like a heavy silver chastity belt, around her soft, rounded body.

She bought a black lace gown like Djuna's. Then she wanted to own all the objects which carried Djuna's personality or spirit. She wanted to be clasped at the wrists by Djuna's bracelet watch, dressed in Djuna's kind of clothes.

(Djuna thought of the primitives eating the liver of the strong man of the tribe to acquire his strength, wearing the teeth of the elephant to acquire his durability, donning the lion's head and mane to appropriate his courage, gluing feathers on themselves to become as free as the bird.)

Lillian knew no mystery. Everything was open with her. Even the most ordinary mysteries of women she did not guard. She was open like a man, frank, direct. Her eyes shed lightning but no shadows.

One night Djuna and Lillian went to a night club together to watch the cancan. At such a moment Djuna forgot that she was a woman and looked at the women dancing with the eyes of an artist and the eyes of a man. She admired them, revelled in their beauty, in their seductions, in the interplay of black garters and black stockings and the snow-white frills of petticoats.

Lillian's face clouded. The storm gathered in her eyes. The lightning struck. She lashed out in anger: "If I were a man I would murder you."

Djuna was bewildered. Then Lillian's anger dissolved in lamentations: "Oh, the poor people, the poor people who love you. You love these women!"

She began to weep. Djuna put her arms around her and consoled her. The people around them looked baffled, as passers-by look up suddenly at an unexpected, freakish windstorm. Here it was, chaotically upsetting the universe, coming from right and left, great fury and velocity—and why?

Two women were looking at beautiful women dancing. One enjoyed it, and the other made a scene.

Lillian went home and wrote stuttering phrases on the back of a box of writing paper: Djuna, don't abandon me; if you abandon me, I am lost.

When Djuna came the next day, still angry from the inexplicable storm of the night before, she wanted to say: are you the woman I chose for a friend? Are you the egotistical, devouring child, all caprice and confusion who is always crossing my path? She could not say it, not before this chaotic helpless writing on the back of the box, a writing which could not stand alone, but wavered from left to right, from right to left, inclining, falling, spilling, retreating, ascending on the line as if for flight off the edge of the paper as if it were an airfield, or plummeting on the paper like a falling elevator.

If they met a couple along the street who were kissing, Lillian became equally unhinged.

If they talked about her children and Djuna said: I never

liked real children, only the child in the grown-up, Lillian answered: you should have had children.

"But I lack the maternal feeling for children, Lillian, though I haven't lacked the maternal experience. There are plenty of children, abandoned children right in the so-called grown-ups. While you, well you are a real mother, you have a real maternal capacity. You are the mother type. I am not. I only like being the mistress. I don't even like being a wife."

Then Lillian's entire universe turned a somersault again, crashed, and Djuna was amazed to see the devastating results of an innocent phrase: "I am not a maternal woman," she said, as if it were an accusation. (Everything was an accusation.)

Then Djuna kissed her and said playfully: "Well, then, you're a *femme fatale!*"

But this was like fanning an already enormous flame. This aroused Lillian to despair: "No, no, I never destroyed or hurt anybody," she protested.

"You know, Lillian, someday I will sit down and write a little dictionary for you, a little Chinese dictionary. In it I will put down all the interpretations of what is said to you, the right interpretation, that is: the one that is not meant to injure, not meant to humiliate or accuse or doubt. And whenever something is said to you, you will look in my little dictionary to make sure, before you get desperate, that you have understood what is said to you."

The idea of the little Chinese dictionary made Lillian laugh. The storm passed.

But if they walked the streets together her obsession was to see who was looking at them or following them. In the shops she was obsessed about her plumpness and considered it not an attribute but a defect. In the movies it was emotionalism and tears. If they sat in a restaurant by a large window and saw the people passing it was denigration and dissection. The universe hinged and turned on her defeated self.

She was aggressive with people who waited on her, and then was hurt by their defensive abandon of her. When they did not wait on her she was personally injured, but could not see the injury she had inflicted by her demanding ways. Her commands bristled everyone's hair, raised obstacles and retaliations. As soon as she appeared she brought dissonance.

But she blamed the others, the world.

She could not bear to see lovers together, absorbed in each other.

She harassed the quiet men and lured them to an argument and she hated the aggressive men who held their own against her.

Her shame. She could not carry off gallantly a run in her stocking. She was overwhelmed by a lost button.

When Djuna was too swamped by other occupations or other people to pay attention to her, Lillian became ill. But she would not be ill at home surrounded by her family. She was ill alone, in a hotel room, so that Djuna ran in and out with medicines, with chicken soup, stayed with her day and night chained to her antics, and then Lillian clapped her hands and confessed: "I'm so happy! Now I've got you all to myself!"

The summer nights were passing outside like gay whores, with tinkles of cheap jewelry, opened and emollient like a vast bed. The summer nights were passing but not Lillian's tension with the world.

She read erotic memoirs avidly, she was obsessed with the lives and loves of others. But she herself could not yield, she was ashamed, she throttled her own nature, and all this desire, lust, became twisted inside of her and churned a poison of envy and jealousy. Whenever sensuality showed its flower head, Lillian would have liked to decapitate it, so it would cease troubling and haunting her.

At the same time she wanted to seduce the world, Djuna, everybody. She would want to be kissed on the lips and more warmly and then violently block herself. She thrived on this hysterical undercurrent without culmination. This throbbing sensual obsession and the blocking of it; this rapacious love without polarity, like a blind womb appetite; delighting in making the temperature rise and then clamping down the lid.

In her drowning she was like one constantly choking those around her, bringing them down with her into darkness.

Djuna felt caught in a sirocco.

She had lived once on a Spanish island and experienced exactly this impression.

The island had been calm, silvery and dormant until one morning when a strange wind began to blow from Africa, blowing in circles. It swept over the island charged with torpid warmth, charged with flower smells, with sandalwood and patchouli and incense, and turning in whirlpools, gathered up the nerves and swinging with them into whirlpools of dry enervating warmth and smells, reached no climax, no explosion. Blowing persistently, continuously, hour after hour, gathering every nerve in every human being, the nerves alone, and tangling them in this fatal waltz; drugging them and pulling them, and whirlpooling them, until the body shook with restlessness—all polarity and sense of gravity lost. Because of this insane waltz of the wind, its emollient warmth, its perfumes, the being lost its guidance, its clarity, its integrity. Hour after hour, all day and all night, the body was subjected to this insidious whirling rhythm, in which polarity was lost, and only the nerves and desires throbbed, tense and weary of movement—all in a void, with no respite, no climax, no great loosening as in other storms. A tension that gathered force but had no release. It abated not once in forty-eight hours, promising, arousing, caressing, destroying sleep, rest, repose, and then vanished without releasing, without culmination. . . .

This violence which Djuna had loved so much! It had become a mere sirocco wind, burning and shrivelling. This violence which Djuna had applauded, enjoyed, because she could not possess it in herself. It was now burning her, and their friendship. Because it was not attached to anything, it was not creating anything, it was a trap of negation.

"You will save me," said Lillian always, clinging.

Lillian was the large foundering ship, yes, and Djuna the

36

small lifeboat. But now the big ship had been moored to the small lifeboat and was pitching too fast and furiously and the lifeboat was being swamped.

(She wants something of me that only a man can give her. But first of all she wants to become me, so that she can communicate with man. She has lost her ways of communicating with man. She is doing it through me!)

When they walked together, Lillian sometimes asked Djuna: "Walk in front of me, so I can see how you walk. You have such a sway of the hips!"

In front of Lillian walked Lillian's lost femininity, imprisoned in the male Lillian. Lillian's femininity imprisoned in the deepest wells of her being, loving Djuna, and knowing it must reach her own femininity at the bottom of the well by way of Djuna. By wearing Djuna's feminine exterior, swaying her hips, becoming Djuna.

As Djuna enjoyed Lillian's violence, Lillian enjoyed Djuna's feminine capitulations. The pleasure Djuna took in her capitulations to love, to desire. Lillian breathed out through Djuna. What took place in Djuna's being which Lillian could not reach, she at least reached by way of Djuna.

"The first time a boy hurt me," said Lillian to Djuna, "it was in school. I don't remember what he did. But I wept. And he laughed at me. Do you know what I did? I went home and dressed in my brother's suit. I tried to feel as the boy felt. Naturally as I put on the suit I felt I was putting on a costume of strength. It made me feel sure, as the boy was, confident, impudent. The mere fact of putting my hands in the pockets made me feel arrogant. I thought then that to be a boy meant one did not suffer. That it was being a girl that was responsible for the suffering. Later I felt the same way. I thought man had found a way out of suffering by objectivity. What the man called being reasonable. When my husband said: Lillian, let's be reasonable, it meant he had none of the feeling I had, that he could be objective. What a power! Then there was another thing. When I felt his great choking anguish I discovered one

37

relief, and that was action. I felt like the women who had to sit and wait at home while there was a war going on. I felt if only I could join the war, participate, I wouldn't feel the anguish and the fear. All through the last war as a child I felt: if only they would let me be Joan of Arc. Joan of Arc wore a suit of armor, she sat on a horse, she fought side by side with the men. She must have gained their strength. Then it was the same way about men. At a dance, as a girl, the moment of waiting before they asked me seemed intolerable, the suspense, and the insecurity; perhaps they were not going to ask me! So I rushed forward, to cut the suspense. I rushed. All my nature became rushed, propelled by the anxiety, merely to cut through all the moment of anxious uncertainty."

Djuna looked tenderly at her, not the strong Lillian, the overwhelming Lillian, the aggressive Lillian, but the hidden, secret, frightened Lillian who had created such a hard armor and disguise around her weakness.

Djuna saw the Lillian hidden in her coat of armor, and all of Lillian's armor lay broken around her, like cruel pieces of mail which had wounded her more than they had protected her from the enemy. The mail had melted, and revealed the bruised feminine flesh. At the first knowledge of the weakness Lillian had picked up the mail, wrapped herself in it and had taken up a lance. The lance! The man's lance. Uncertainty resolved, relieved by the activity of attack!

The body of Lillian changed as she talked, the fast coming words accelerating the dismantling. She was taking off the shell, the covering, the defenses, the coat of mail, the activity.

Suddenly Lillian laughed. In the middle of tears, she laughed: "I'm remembering a very comical incident. I was about sixteen. There was a boy in love with me. Shyly, quietly in love. We were in the same school but he lived quite far away. We all used bicycles. One day we were going to be separated for a week by the holidays. He suggested we both bicycle together towards a meeting place between the two towns. The week of separation seemed too unbearable. So it was agreed: at a certain hour we would leave the house together and meet half way."

Lillian started off. At first at a normal pace. She knew the rhythm of the boy. A rather easy, relaxed rhythm. Never rushed. Never precipitate. She at first adopted his rhythm. Dreaming of him, of his slow smile, of his shy worship, of his expression of this worship, which consisted mainly in waiting for her here, there. Waiting. Not advancing, inviting, but waiting. Watching her pass by.

She pedaled slowly, dreamily. Then slowly her pleasure and tranquillity turned to anguish: suppose he did not come? Suppose she arrived before him? Could she bear the sight of the desolate place of their meeting, the failed meeting? The exaltation that had been increasing in her, like some powerful motor, what could she do with this exaltation if she arrived alone, and the meeting failed? The fear affected her in two directions. She could stop right there, and turn back, and not face the possibility of disappointment, or she could rush forward and accelerate the moment of painful suspense, and she chose the second. Her lack of confidence in life, in realization, in the fulfillment of her desires, in the outcome of a dream, in the possibility of reality corresponding to her fantasy, speeded her bicycle with the incredible speed of anxiety, a speed beyond the human body, beyond human endurance.

She arrived before him. Her fear was justified! She could not measure what the anxiety had done to her speed, the acceleration which had broken the equality of rhythm. She arrived as she had feared, at a desolate spot on the road, and the boy had become this invisible image which taunts the dreamer, a mirage that could not be made real. It had become reality eluding the dreamer, the wish unfulfilled.

The boy may have arrived later. He may have fallen asleep and not come at all. He may have had a tire puncture. Nothing mattered. Nothing could prevent her from feeling that she was not Juliet waiting on the balcony, but Romeo who had to leap across space to join her. She had leaped, she had acted Romeo, and when woman leaped she leaped into a void.

Later it was not the drama of two bicycles, of a road, of two separated towns; later it was a darkened room, and a man and woman pursuing pleasure and fusion.

At first she lay passive dreaming of the pleasure that would come out of the darkness, to dissolve and invade her. But it was not pleasure which came out of the darkness to clasp her. It was anxiety. Anxiety made confused gestures in the dark, crosscurrents of forces, short circuits, and no pleasure. A depression, a broken rhythm, a feeling such as men must have after they have taken a whore.

Out of the prone figure of the woman, apparently passive, apparently receptive, there rose a taut and anxious shadow, the shadow of the woman bicycling too fast; who, to relieve her insecurity, plunges forward as the desperado does and is defeated because this aggressiveness cannot meet its mate and unite with it. A part of the woman has not participated in this marriage, has not been taken. But was it a part of the woman, or the shadow of anxiety, which dressed itself in man's clothes and assumed man's active role to quiet its anguish? Wasn't it the woman who dressed as a man and pedalled too fast?

Jay. The table at which he sat was stained with wine. His blue eyes were inscrutable like those of a Chinese sage. He ended all his phrases in a kind of hum, as if he put his foot on the pedal of his voice and created an echo. In this way none of his phrases ended abruptly.

Sitting at the bar he immediately created a climate, a tropical day. In spite of the tension in her, Lillian felt it. Sitting at a bar with his voice rolling over, he dissolved and liquefied the hard click of silver on plates, the icy dissonances of glasses, the brittle sound of money thrown on the counter.

He was tall but he carried his tallness slackly and easily, as easily as his coat and hat, as if all of it could be discarded and sloughed off at any moment when he needed lightness or nimbleness. His body large, shaggy, as if never definitely chiselled, never quite ultimately finished, was as casually his as his passing moods and varying fancies and fortunes.

He opened his soft animal mouth a little, as if in expectancy of a drink. But instead, he said (as if he had absorbed Lillian's face and voice in place of the drink), "I'm happy. I'm too happy." Then he began to laugh, to laugh, to laugh, with his head shaking like a bear, shaking from right to left as if it were too heavy a head. "I can't help it. I can't help laughing. I'm too happy. Last night I spent the night here. It was Christmas and I didn't have the money for a hotel room. And the night before I slept at a movie house. They overlooked me, didn't sweep where I lay. In the morning I played the movie piano. In walked the furious manager, then he listened, then he gave me a contract starting this evening. Christ, Lillian, I never thought Christmas would bring me anything, yet it brought you."

How gently he had walked into her life, how quietly he seemed to be living, while all the time he was drawing bitter caricatures on the bar table, on the backs of envelopes. Drawing bums, drunks, derelicts.

"So you're a pianist . . . that's what I should have been. I'm not bad, but I would never work hard enough. I wanted also to be a painter. I might have been a writer too, if I had worked enough. I did a bit of acting too, at one time. As it is, I guess I'm the last man on earth. Why did you single me out?"

This man who would not be distinguished in a crowd, who could pass through it like an ordinary man, so quiet, so absorbed, with his hat on one side, his steps dragging a little, like a lazy devil enjoying everything, why did she see him hungry, thirsty, abandoned?

Behind this Jay, with his southern roguishness, perpetually calling for drinks, why did she see a lost man?

41

He sat like a workman before his drinks, he talked like a cart driver to the whores at the bar; they were all at ease with him. His presence took all the straining and willing out of Lillian. He was like the south wind: blowing when he came, melting and softening, bearing joy and abundance.

When they met, and she saw him walking towards her, she felt he would never stop walking towards her and into her very being: he would walk right into her being with his soft lazy walk and purring voice and his mouth slightly open.

She could not hear his voice. His voice rumbled over the surface of her skin, like another caress. She had no power against his voice. It came straight from him into her. She could stuff her ears and still it would find its way into her blood and make it rise.

All things were born anew when her dress fell on the floor of his room.

He said: "I feel humble, Lillian, but it is all so good, so good." He gave to the word good a mellowness which made the whole room glow, which gave a warmer color to the bare window, to the woolen shirt hung on a peg, to the single glass out of which they drank together.

Behind the yellow curtain the sun seeped in: everything was the color of a tropical afternoon.

The small room was like a deep-set alcove. Warm mist and warm blood; the high drunkenness which made Jay flushed and heavy blooded. His sensual features expanded.

"As soon as you come, I'm jubilant." And he did somersaults on the bed, two or three of them.

"This is fine wine, Lillian. Let's drink to my failure. There's no doubt about it, no doubt whatever that I'm a failure."

"I won't let you be a failure," said Lillian.

"You say: I want, as if that made things happen."

"It does."

"I don't know what I expect of you. I expect miracles." He looked up at her slyly, then mockingly, then gravely again. "I have no illusions," he said.

Then he sat down with his heavy shoulders bowed, and his head bowed, but Lillian caught that swift, passing flash, a moment's hope, the lightning passage of a spark of faith left in his indifference to his fate. She clung to this.

Jay—gnome and sprite and faun, and playboy of the mother-bound world. Brightly gifted, he painted while he enjoyed the painting; the accidental marvels of colors, the pleasant shock of apparitions made in a game with paint. He stopped painting where the effort began, the need for discipline or travail. He danced while he was allowed to improvise, to surprise himself and others, to stretch, laugh, and court and be courted; but stopped if there were studying, developing or disciplining or effort or repetition involved. He acted, he acted loosely, flowingly, emotionally, while nothing more difficult was demanded of him, but he evaded rehearsals, fatigue, strain, effort. He pur ued no friend, he took what came.

He gave himself to the present moment. To be with the friend, to drink with the friend, to talk with the friend, he forgot what was due the next day, and if it were something which demanded time, or energy, he could not meet it. He had not provided for it. He was asleep when he should have been awake, and tired when his energy was required, and absent when his presence was summoned. The merest expectation from a friend, the most trivial obligation, sent him running in the opposite direction. He came to the friend while there was pleasure to be had. He left as soon as the pleasure vanished and reality began. An accident, an illness, poverty, a quarrel—he was never there for them.

It was as if he smelled the climate: was it good? Was there the odor of pleasure, the colors of pleasure? Expansion, forgetfulness, abandon, enjoyment? Then he stayed. Difficulties? Then he vanished.

Lillian and Jay.

It was a merciless winter day. The wind persecuted them around the corners of the street. The snow slid into their collars. They could not talk to each other. They took a taxi.

The windows of the taxi had frosted, so they seemed completely shut off from the rest of the world. It was small and dark and warm. Jay buried his face in her fur. He made himself small. He had a way of becoming so passive and soft that he seemed to lose his height and weight. He did this now, his face in her fur, and she felt as if she were the darkness, the smallness of the taxi, and were hiding him, protecting him from the elements. Here the cold could not reach him, the snow, the wind, the daylight. He sheltered himself, she carried his head on her breast, she carried his body become limp, his hands nestling in her pocket. She was the fur, the pocket, the warmth that sheltered him. She felt immense, and strong, and illimitable, the boundless mother opening her arms and her wings, flying to carry him somewhere; she his shelter and refuge, his secret hiding place, his tent, his sky, his blanket.

The soundproof mother, the shockproof mother of man!

This passion warmer, stronger than the other passion, annihilating desire and becoming the desire, a boundless passion to surround, envelop, sustain, strengthen, uphold, to answer all needs. He closed his eyes. He almost slept in her warmth and furriness. He caressed the fur, he feared no claws, he abandoned himself, and the waves of passion inspired by his abandon intoxicated her.

44

He usually wore colored shirts to suit his fancy. Once he wore a white one, because it had been given to him. It did not suit him. Whiteness and blackness did not suit him. Only the intermediate colors.

Lillian was standing near him and they had just been discussing their life together. Jay had admitted that he would not work. He could not bear repetition, he could not bear a "boss," he could not bear regular hours. He could not bear the seriousness.

"Then you will have to be a hobo."

"I'll be a hobo, then."

"A hobo has no wife," said Lillian.

"No," he said. And added nothing. If she became part of the effort, he would not cling to her either.

"I will have to work, then," she said. "One of us has to work."

He said nothing.

Lillian was doubly disturbed by the unfamiliarity of the scene, the portentousness of it, and by the familiarity of the white shirt. The white shirt disturbed her more than his words. And then she knew. The white shirt reminded her of her husband. Just before he put on his coat she had always seen him and obscurely felt: how straight and rigid he stands in his white shirt. Black and white. Definite and starched, and always the same. But there it was. She was not sure she had liked the white shirt. From it came authority, a firm guidance, a firm construction. And now she was again facing a white shirt but with a strange feeling that there was nothing in it: no rigidity, no straight shoulders, no man. If she approached she would feel something fragile, soft and wavering: the shirt was not upheld by the body of the man. If she broke suddenly at the idea of assuming the responsibility, if she broke against this shirt it would collapse, turn to sand, trickle sand and soft laughter and elusive flickering love.

Against this white shirt of the husband she had lain her head once and heard a strong heart beat evenly, and now it was as

45

if it were empty, and she were in a dream of falling down soft sand dunes to softer and more sliding shifty sand dunes. . . . Her head turned.

She kept herself on this new equilibrium by a great effort, fearing to touch the white shirt of weakness and to feel the yielding, the softness and the sand.

When she sewed on buttons for him she was sewing not only buttons but also sewing together the sparse, disconnected fragments of his ideas, of his inventions, of his unfinished dreams. She was weaving and sewing and mending because he carried in himself no thread of connection, no knowledge of mending, no thread of continuity or repair. If he allowed a word to pass that was poisoned like a primitive arrow, he never sought the counter-poison, he never measured its fatal consequences. She was sewing on a button and the broken pieces of his waywardness; sewing a button and his words too loosely strung; sewing their days together to make a tapestry; their words together, their moods together, which he dispersed and tore. As he tore his clothes with his precipitations towards his wishes, his wanderings, his rambles, his peripheral journeys. She was sewing together the little proofs of his devotion out of which to make a garment for her tattered love and faith. He cut into the faith with negligent scissors, and she mended and sewed and rewove and patched. He wasted, and threw away, and could not evaluate or preserve, or contain, or keep his treasures. Like his ever torn pockets, everything slipped through and was lost, as he lost gifts, mementos—all the objects from the past. She sewed his pockets that he might keep some of their days together, hold together the key to the house, to their room, to their bed. She sewed the sleeve so he could reach out his arm and hold her, when loneliness dissolved her. She sewed the lining so that the warmth would not seep out of their days together, the soft inner skin of their relationship.

He always admitted and conceded to his own wishes first, before she admitted hers. Because he was sleepy, she had to become the panoply on which he rested. Her love must fan him if he were warm and be the fire if he were cold. In illness he required day and night nursing, one for the illness, the other for the pleasure he took in her attentiveness.

His helplessness made him the *"homme fatal"* for such a woman. He reached without sureness or nimbleness for the cup, for the food, Her hand flew to finish off the uncertain gesture, to supply the missing object. His hunger for anything metamorphosed her into an Aladdin's lamp: even his dreams must be fulfilled.

Towards the greater obstacles he assumed a definitely non-combatant attitude. Rather than claim his due, or face an angry landlord, or obtain a rightful privilege, his first impulse was to surrender. Move out of the house that could not be repaired, move out of the country if his papers were not in order, move out of a woman's way if another man stalked too near. Retreat, surrender.

At times Lillian remembered her husband, and now that he was no longer the husband she could see that he had been, as much as the other men she liked; handsome and desirable, and she could not understand why he had never been able to enter her being and her feelings as a lover. She had truly liked every aspect of him except the aspect of lover. When she saw him, with the clarity of distance and separation, she saw him quite outside of herself. He stood erect, and self-sufficient, and manly. He always retained his normal male largeness and upstanding protectiveness.

But Jay . . . came towards her almost as a man who limps and whom one instinctively wishes to sustain. He came as the man who did not see very well, slightly awkward, slightly stumbling. In this helplessness, in spite of his actual stature (he was the same height as her husband) he gave the air of being smaller, more fragile, more vulnerable. It was this fear in the man, who seemed inadequate in regard to life, trapped in it, the victim of it, which somehow affected her. In a smaller, weaker dimension he seemed to reach the right proportion for his being to enter into hers. He entered by the route of her compassion. She opened as the refuge opens; not conscious that it was a man who entered (man of whom she had a certain suspicion) but a child in need. Because he knocked as a beggar begging for a retreat, as a victim seeking solace, as a weakling seeking sustenance, she opened the door without suspicion.

It was in her frenzy to shelter, cover, defend him that she laid her strength over his head like an enormous starry roof, and the stretching immensity of the boundless mother was substituted for the normal image of the man covering the woman.

Jay came and he had a cold. And though he at first pretended it was of no importance, he slowly melted entirely into her, became soft and tender, waiting to be pampered, exaggerating his cough. And they wandered through the city like two lazy southerners, he said, like two convalescents. And she pampered him laughingly, ignoring time, eating when they were hungry, and seeing a radium sunlight lighting up the rain, seeing only the shimmer of the wet streets and not the greyness. He confessed that he craved a phonograph, and they shopped together and brought it back in a taxi. They slept soundly inside the warmth of this closeness, in the luxury of their contentment. It was Jay who touched everything with the magic of his contentment. It was Jay who said: isn't this ham good, isn't this salad good, isn't this wine good. Everything was good and savory, palatable and expansive.

He gave her the savor of the present, and let her care for the morrow.

This moment of utter and absolute tasting of food, of color, this moment of human breathing. No fragment detached, errant, disconnected or lost. Because as Jay gathered the food on the table, the phonograph to his room, he gathered her into the present moment.

His taking her was not to take her or master her. He was the lover inside of the woman, as the child is inside of the woman. His caresses were as if he yearned and craved to be taken in not only as a lover; not merely to satisfy his desire but to remain within her. And her yearning answered this, by her desire to be filled. She never felt him outside of herself. Her husband had stood outside of her, and had come to visit her as a man, sensually. But he had not lodged himself as Jay had done, by reposing in her, by losing himself in her, by melting within her, with such feeling of physical intermingling as she had had with her child. Her husband had come to be renewed, to emerge again, to leave her and go to his male activities, to his struggles with the world.

The maternal and the feminine cravings were all confused in her, and all she felt was that it was through this softening and through this maternal yieldingness that Jay had penetrated where she had not allowed her husband's manliness to enter, only to visit her.

He liked prostitutes. "Because one does not have to make love to them, one does not have to write them beautiful letters." He liked them, and he liked to tell Lillian how much he liked them. He had to share all this with Lillian. He could not conceal any part of it from her, even if it hurt her. He could retain and hold nothing back from her. She was his confessor and his companion, his collaborator and his guardian angel. He

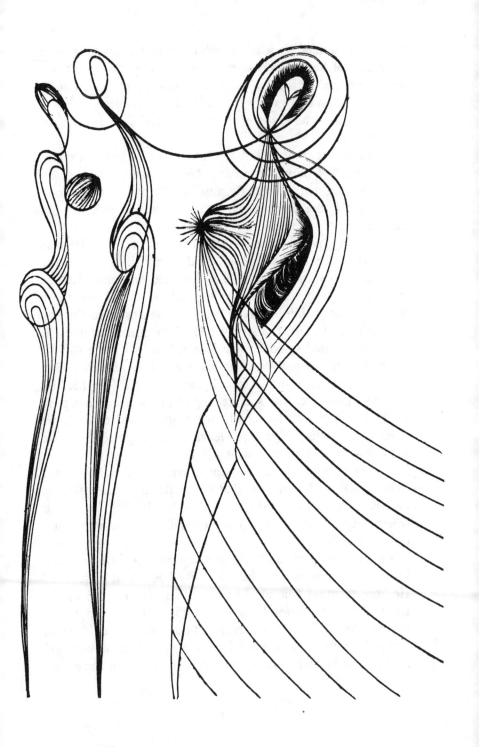

did not see her weep when he launched into descriptions. At this moment he treated her as if she were a man (or the mother). As if the spectacle of his life could amuse her. "I even think if you had seen me that time, you could have enjoyed it."

He liked her to assume the burden of their life together, its material basis. Yet when she came to him, she must be all ready to discard this mantle of responsibilities, and become a child with him. His sense of humor took wayward forms.

His favorite prank: something that could be thrown away, which others valued; something that could be broken which others preserved. Traditions, habits, possessions. His greatest enjoyment was in demolition.

One of his most joyous experiences had been when a neighbor pianist who lived on the same quiet little street with him many years ago had been obliged to visit his mother at the hospital on the same day as the piano house had promised him an exchange of pianos. The man had been looking forward to this for many months. He begged Jay to attend to this. It was a complicated affair, getting the old piano out and the new one in. It was to be done by two different houses. One, a moving man, was to take the old piano out, then the piano house was to deliver the new. Jay had laughed it all off, and walked out unconcernedly, never remembering the promise he made. When he came home he found the two pianos in the street, before the entrance of the house, and the rain pouring down on them. The sight of the two pianos in the rain sent him into an absolute state of gaiety. "It was the most surrealistic sight I have ever seen." His laughter was so contagious that Lillian laughed with him, at the same time as she felt, somehow, a kind of pain at the image of pianos drenched in rain, and a pain even for the unknown pianist's feeling on his return home.

He seized only upon the comedy of the events.

At times Lillian asked herself: what will he make of me some day, when will he hurt me? And what if he does: I will try to love him gaily, more easily and loosely. To endure space and distance and betrayals. My courage is born today. Here lies Jay, breathing into my hair, over my neck. No hurt will come from me. No judgment. No woman ever judged the life stirring within her womb. I am too close to you. I will laugh with you even if it is against me.

Against me. Now the pain about the pianos left out in the rain suddently touched her personally, and she understood why she had not been able to laugh freely. Those pianos were not only those of Jay's friend in the past, but her own too, since she had given up playing in order to work for Jay's support. She had surrendered any hope of becoming a concert pianist to attend better to their immediate needs. Jay's mockery wounded her, for it exposed his insensitiveness to anyone's loss, and to her loss too, his incapacity to feel for others, to understand that with the loss of her pianist self she had lost a very large part of herself, annihilated an entire portion of her personality, sacrificed it to him.

It was her piano Jay had left out in the rain, to be ruined. . . .

He was wearing bedroom slippers and he was painting, with a bottle of red wine beside him. Circles of red wine on the floor. Stains. The edge of the table was burnt by cigarette stubs.

He didn't care. He said that what he had painted today was not as good as yesterday, but he didn't care. He was enjoying it just the same. He wasn't worrying about art. Everything was good, hang perfection, and he was out of cigarettes and if she would give him one he might finish that watercolor. She had come to interrupt him, that was good too, that was life; life was more important than any painting, let the interruptions come, specially in the form of a woman; let people walk in, it was good, to paint was good, not to paint was just as good, and eating and love making were even better, and now he was finished and he was hungry, and he wished they might go to the movies, good or bad. . . .

The room was black. Jay was asleep in her arms, now, heavily asleep. She heard the organ grinder grinding his music. It was Saturday night. Always a holiday with him, always Saturday night with the crowds laughing and shouting and the organ grinder playing.

"According to the Chinese," said Jay, awakening, "there was a realm between heaven and earth . . . this must be it."

Tornadoes of desire and exquisite calms. She felt heavy and burnt.

"I want to keep you under lock and key, Lillian."

Suddenly he leaped up with a whiplike alacrity and exuberance and began to talk about his childhood, about his life in the streets, about the women he had loved and ditched, and the women who had ditched and bitched him, as he put it. He seemed to remember everything at once, as though it was a ball inside of him which unravelled of itself, and as it unravelled made new balls which he would unravel again another day. Had he actually done all these things he was relating to Lillian with such kaleidoscopic fury and passion? Had he really killed a boy in school with a snow ball? Had he really struck his first wife down when she was with child? Had he really butted his head against a wall in sudden anger because the woman he loved had rejected him? Had he really taken abortions and thrown them off the ferry boat in order to pick up a little extra change? Had he really stolen silver from a blind news vendor?

All the layers of his past he unravelled and laid before her, his masks, his buffooneries, and she saw him pretending, driven by obscure revenges, by fears, by weaknesses.

She saw him in the past and in the world, another man from the one she knew. And like all women in love she discarded this man of the past, holding others responsible for his behavior; and thinking· before me he sheds all his poses and

53

defenses. The legend of hardness and callousness she did not believe. She saw him innocent, as we always see the loved one, innocent and even a victim.

She felt that she knew which was the rind and which the core of the man. "You always know," he said, "what is to be laughed away."

Then he rolled over and fell asleep. No noise, no care, no work undone, no imperfection unmastered, no love scene unresumed, no problem unsolved, ever kept him awake. He could roll over and forget. He could roll over with such grand indifference and let everything wait. When he rolled over the day ended. Nothing could be carried over into the next day. The next day would be absolutely new and clean. He just rolled over and extinguished everything. Just rolling over.

Djuna and Jay. For Djuna Jay does not look nonchalant but rather intent and listening, as if in quest of some revelation, as if he were questioning for the first time.

"I've lived so blindly. . . . No time to think much. Tons and tons of experience. Lillian always creating trouble, misery, changes, flights, dramas. No time to digest anything. And then she says I die when she leaves, that pain and war are good for me."

Djuna notices that although he is only forty years old, his hair is greying at the temple.

"Your eyes are full of wonder," he said, "as if you expected a miracle every day. I can't let you go now. I want to go places with you, obscure little places, just to be able to say: here I came with Djuna. I'm insatiable, you know. I'll ask you for the impossible. What it is, I don't know. You'll tell me, probably. You're quicker than I am. And you're the first woman with whom I feel I can be absolutely sincere. You make me happy because I can talk with you. I feel at ease with you. This is a little drunken, but you know what I mean. You always seem to know what I mean."

"You change from a wise old man to a savage. You're both timid and cruel too, aren't you?"

"There is something here it is impossible for Lillian to understand, or to break either. I feel we are friends. Don't you see? Friends. Christ, have a man and woman ever been friends, beyond love and beyond desire, and beyond everything, friends? Well, this is what I feel with you."

She hated the gaiety with which she received these words, for that condemnation of her body to be the pale watcher, the understanding one upon whom others laid their burdens, laying their heads on her lap to sleep, to be lulled from others' wounds. And even as she hated her own goodness, she heard herself say quietly, out of the very core of this sense of justice: "The destroyers do not always destroy, Jay."

"You see more, you just see more, and what you see is there all right. You get at the core of everything."

And now she was caught between them, to be the witch of words, a silent swift shadow darkened by uncanny knowledge, forgetting herself, her human needs, in the unfolding of this choking blind relationship: Lillian and Jay lacerating each other because of their different needs.

Pale beauty of the watcher shining in the dark.

Both of them now, Jay and Lillian, entered Djuna's life by gusts, and left by gusts, as they lived.

She sat for hours afterwards sailing her lingering mind like a slow river boat down the feelings they had dispersed with prodigality.

"In my case," said Jay, alone with her, "what's difficult is to keep any image of myself clear. I have never thought about myself much. The first time I saw myself full length, as it were, was in you. I have grown used to considering your image of me as the correct one. Probably because it makes me feel good. I was like a wheel without a hub."

"And I'm the hub, now," said Djuna, laughing.

Jay was lying on the couch in the parlor, and she had left him to dress for an evening party. When she was dressed she opened the door and then stood before her long mirror perfuming herself.

The window was open on the garden and he said: "This is like a setting for Pelleas and Melisande. It is all a dream."

The perfume made a silky sound as she squirted it with the atomizer, touching her ear lobes, her neck. "Your dress is green like a princess," he said, "I could swear it is a green I have never seen before and will never see again. I could swear the garden is made of cardboard, that the trembling of the light behind you comes from the footlights, that the sounds are music. You are almost transparent there, like the mist of perfume you are throwing on yourself. Throw more perfume on yourself, like a fixative on a water color. Let me have the atomizer. Let me put perfume all over you so that you won't disappear and fade like a water color."

She moved towards him and sat on the edge of the couch: "You don't quite believe in me as a woman," she said, with an immense distress quite out of proportion to his fancy.

"This is a setting for Pelleas and Melisande," he said, "and I know that when you leave me for that dinner I will never see you again. Those incidents last at the most three hours, and the echoes of the music maybe a day. No more."

The color of the day, the color of Byzantine paintings, that gold which did not have the firm surface of lacquer, that gold made of a fine powder easily decomposed by time, a soft powdery gold which seemed on the verge of decomposing, as if each grain of dust, held together only by atoms, was ever ready to fall apart like a mist of perfume; that gold so thin in substance that it allowed one to divine the canvas behind it, the space in the painting, the presence of reality behind its thinness, the fibrous space lying behind the illusion, the absence of color and depth, the condition of emptiness and blackness underneath the gold powder. This gold powder which had fallen now on the garden, on each leaf of the trees, which was flowering inside the room, on her black hair, on the skin of his wrists, on his frayed suit sleeve, on the green carpet, on her green dress, on the bottle of perfume, on his voice, on her anxiety—the very breath of living, the very breath he and she took in to live and breathed out to live—that very breath could mow and blow it all down.

The essence, the human essence always evaporating where the dream installs itself.

The air of that summer day, when the wind itself had suspended its breathing, hung between the window and garden; the air itself could displace a leaf, could displace a word, and a displaced leaf or word might change the whole aspect of the day.

The essence, the human essence always evaporating where the dream installed itself and presided.

Every time he said he had been out the night before with friends and that he had met a woman, there was a suspense in Lillian's being, a moment of fear that he might add: I met the woman who will replace you. This moment was repeated for many years with the same suspense, the same sense of the fragility of love, without bringing any change in his love. A kind of superstition haunted her, running crosscurrent to the strength of the ties binding them, a sense of menace. At first because the love was all expansion and did not show its roots; and later, when the roots were apparent, because she expected a natural fading and death.

This fear appeared at the peak of their deepest moments, a precipice all around their ascensions. This fear appeared through the days of their tranquillity, as a sign of death rather than a sign of natural repose. It marked every moment of silence with the seal of a fatal secret. The greater the circle spanned by the attachment, the larger she saw the fissure through which human beings fall again into solitude.

The woman who personified this danger never appeared. His description gave no clues. Jay made swift portraits which he seemed to forget the next day. He was a man of many friends. His very ebullience created a warm passage but an onward flowing one, forming no grooves, fixing no image permanently. His enthusiasms were quickly burned out, sometimes in one evening. She never sought out these passing images.

Now and then he said with great simplicity: "You are the only one. You are the only one."

And then one day he said: "The other day I met a woman you would like. I was sorry you were not there. She is coming with friends this evening. Do you want to stay? You will see. She has the most extraordinary eyes."

"She has extraordinary eyes? I'll stay. I want to know her." (Perhaps if I run fast enough ahead of the present I will outdistance the shock. What is the difference between fear and intuition? How clearly I have seen what I imagine, as clearly as a vision. What is it I feel now, fear or premonition?)

Helen's knock on the door was vigorous, like an attack. She was very big and wore a severely tailored suit. She looked like a statue, but a statue with haunted eyes, inhuman eyes not made for weeping, full of animal glow. And the rest of her body a statue pinned down to its base, immobilized by a fear. She had the immobility of a Medusa waiting to transfix others into stone: hypnotic and cold, attracting others to her mineral glow.

She had two voices, one which fell deep like the voice of a man, and another light and innocent. Two women disputing inside of her.

She aroused a feeling in Lillian which was not human. She felt she was looking at a painting in which there was an infinity of violent blue. A white statue with lascivious Medusa hair. Not a woman but a legend with enormous space around her.

Her eyes were begging for an answer to an enigma. The pupils seemed to want to separate from the whites of the eyes.

Lillian felt no longer any jealousy, but a curiosity as in a dream. She did not feel any danger or fear in the meeting, only an enormous blue space in which a woman stood waiting. This space and grandeur around Helen drew Lillian to her.

Helen was describing a dream she often had of being carried away by a Centaur, and Lillian could see the Centaur holding Helen's head, the head of a woman in a myth. People in myths were larger than human beings.

Helen's dreams took place in an enormous desert where she was lost among the prisons. She was tearing her hands to get free. The columns of these prisons were human beings all bound in bandages. Her own draperies were of sackcloth, the woolen robes of punishment.

And then came her questions to Lillian: "Why am I not free? I ran away from my husband and my two little girls many years ago. I did not know it then, but I didn't want to be a mother, the mother of children. I wanted to be the mother of creations and dreams, the mother of artists, the muse and the mistress. In my marriage I was buried alive. My husband was a man without courage for life. We lived as if he were a cripple, and I a nurse. His presence killed the life in me so completely that I could hardly feel the birth of my children. I became afraid of nature, of being swallowed by the mountains, stifled by the forest, absorbed by the sea. I rebelled so violently against my married life that in one day I destroyed everything and ran away, abandoning my children, my home and my native country. But I never attained the life I had struggled to reach. My escape brought me no liberation. Every night I dream the same dream of prisons and struggles to escape. It is as if only my body escaped, and not my feelings. My feelings were left over there like roots dangling when you tear a plant too violently. Violence means nothing. And it does not free one. Part of my being remained with my children, imprisoned in the past. Now I have to liberate myself wholly, body and soul, and I don't know how. The violent gestures I make only tighten the knot of resistance around me. How can one liquidate the past? Guilt and regrets can't be shed like an old coat."

Then she saw that Lillian was affected by her story and she added: "I am grateful to Jay for having met you."

Only then Lillian remembered her painful secret. For a moment she wanted to lay her head on Helen's shoulder and confess to her: "I only came because I was afraid of you. I came because I thought you were going to take Jay away from me." But now that Helen had revealed her innermost dreams and pains, Lillian felt: perhaps she needs me more than she needs Jay. For he cannot console. He can only make her laugh.

At the same time she thought that this was equally effective. And she remembered how much Jay liked audacity in women, how some feminine part of him liked to yield, liked to be chosen, courted. Deep down he was timid, and he liked audacity in women. Helen could be given the key to his being, if Lillian told her this. If Lillian advised her to take the first step, because he was a being perpetually waiting to be ignited, never set off by himself, always seeking in women the explosion which swept him along.

All around her there were signs, signs of danger and loss.

Without knowing consciously what she was doing, Lillian began to assume the role she feared Jay might assume. She became like a lover. She was full of attentiveness and thoughtfulness. She divined Helen's needs uncannily. She telephoned her at the moment Helen felt the deepest loneliness. She said the gallant words Helen wanted to hear. She gave Helen such faith as lovers give. She gave to the friendship an atmosphere of courtship which accomplished the same miracles as love. Helen began to feel enthusiasm and hunger again. She forgot her illness to take up painting, her singing, and writing. She recreated, redecorated the place she was living in. She displayed art in her dressing, care and fantasy. She ceased to feel alone.

On a magnificent day of sun and warmth Lillian said to her: "If I were a man, I would make love to you."

Whether she said this to help Helen bloom like a flower in warmth and fervor, or to take the place of Jay and enact the courtship she had imagined, which she felt she had perhaps deprived Helen of, she did not know.

But Helen felt as rich as a woman with a new love.

At times when Lillian rang Helen's bell, she imagined Jay ringing it. And she tried to divine what Jay might feel at the sight of Helen's face. Every time she fully conceded that Helen was beautiful. She asked herself whether she was enhancing Helen's beauty with her own capacity for admiration. But then Jay too had this capacity for exalting all that he admired.

Lillian imagined him coming and looking at the paintings. He would like the blue walls. It was true he would not like her obsessions with disease, her fear of cancer. But then he would laugh at them, and his laughter might dispel her fears.

In Helen's bathroom, where she went to powder and comb her hair, she felt a greater anguish, because there she was nearer to the intimacy of Helen's life. Lillian looked at her kimono, her bedroom slippers, her creams and medicines as if trying to divine with what feelings Jay might look at them. She remembered how much he liked to go behind the scenes of people's lives. He liked to rummage among intimate belongings and dispel illusions. It was his passion. He would come out triumphantly with a jar: and this, what is this for? as if women were always seeking to delude him. He doubted the most simple things. He had often pulled at her eyelashes to make certain they were not artificial.

What would he feel in Helen's bathroom? Would he feel tenderness for her bedroom slippers? Why were there objects which inspired tenderness and others none? Helen's slippers did not inspire tenderness. Nothing about her inspired tenderness. But it might inspire desire, passion, anything else—even if she remained outside of one, like a sculpture, a painting, a form, not something which penetrated and enveloped one. But inhuman figures could inspire passion. Even if she were the statue in a Chirico painting, unable to mingle with human beings, even if she could not be impregnated by others or live inside of another all tangled in threads of blood and emotion.

When they went out together Lillian always expected the coincidence which would bring the three of them together to the same concert, the same exhibit, the same play. But if it never happened. They always missed each other. All winter long the coincidences of city life did not bring the three of them together. Lillian began to think that this meeting was not destined, that it was not she who was keeping them apart.

Helen's eyes grew greener and sank more and more into the myth. She could not feel. And Lillian felt as if she were keeping from her the man who might bring her back to life. Felt almost as if she were burying her alive by not giving her Jay.

Perhaps Lillian was imagining too much.

Meanwhile Helen's need of Lillian grew immense. She was not contented with Lillian's occasional visits. She wanted to fill the entire void of her life with Lillian. She wanted Lillian to stay over night when she was lonely. The burden grew heavier and heavier.

Lillian became frightened. In wanting to amuse and draw Helen away from her first interest in Jay, she had surpassed herself and become this interest.

Helen dramatized the smallest incident, suffered from insomnia, said her bedroom was haunted at night, sent for Lillian on every possible occasion.

Lillian was punished for playing the lover. Now she must be the husband, too. Helen had forgotten Jay but the exchange had left Lillian as a hostage.

Not knowing how to lighten the burden she said one day: "You ought to travel again. This city cannot be good for you. A place where you have been lonely and unhappy for so long must be the wrong place."

That very night there was a fire in Helen's house, in the apartment next to hers. She interpreted this as a sign that Lillian's intuitions for her were wise. She decided to travel again.

They parted at the corner of a street, gaily, as if for a short separation. Gaily, with green eyes flashing at one another.

63

They lost each other's address. It all dissolved very quickly, like a dream.

And then Lillian felt free again. Once again she had worn the warrior armor to protect a core of love. Once again she had worn the man's costume.

Jay had not made her woman, but the husband and mother of his weakness.

Lillian confessed to Jay that she was pregnant. He said: "We must find the money for an abortion." He looked irritated. She waited. She thought he might slowly evince interest in the possibility of a child. He revealed only an increased irritation. It disturbed his plans, his enjoyment. The mere idea of a child was an intrusion. He let her go alone to the doctor. He expressed resentment. And then she understood.

She sat alone one day in their darkened room.

She talked to the child inside of her.

"My little one not born yet, I feel your small feet kicking against my womb. My little one not born yet, it is very dark in the room you and I are sitting in, just as dark as it must be for you inside of me, but it must be sweeter for you to be lying in the warmth than it is for me to be seeking in this dark room the joy of not knowing, not feeling, not seeing; the joy of lying still in utter warmth and this darkness. All of us forever seeking this warmth and this darkness, this being alive without pain, this being alive without anxiety, fear or loneliness. You are impatient to live, you kick with your small feet, but you ought to die. You ought to die in warmth and darkness because you are a child without a father. You will not find on earth this father as large as the sky, big enough to hold your whole being and your fears, larger than house or church. You will not find a father who will lull you and cover you with his greatness and his warmth. It would be better if you died inside of me, quietly, in the warmth and in the darkness."

Did the child hear her? At six months she had a miscarriage and lost it.

Lillian was giving a concert in a private home which was like a temple of treasures. Paintings and people had been collected with expert and exquisite taste. There was a concentration of beautiful women so that one was reminded of a hothouse exhibit.

The floor was so highly polished there were two Lillians, two white pianos, two audiences.

The piano under her strong hands became small like a child's piano. She overwhelmed it, she tormented it, crushed it. She played with all her intensity, as if the piano must be possessed or possess her.

The women in the audience shivered before this *corps à corps*.

Lillian was pushing her vigor into the piano. Her face was full of vehemence and possessiveness. She turned her face upwards as if to direct the music upwards, but the music would not rise, volatilize itself. It was too heavily charged with passion.

She was not playing to throw music into the blue space, but to reach some climax, some impossible union with the piano, to reach that which men and women could reach together. A moment of pleasure, a moment of fusion. The passion and the blood in her rushed against the ivory notes and overloaded them. She pounded the coffer of the piano as she wanted her own body pounded and shattered. And the pain on her face was that of one who reached neither sainthood nor pleasure. No music rose and passed out of the window, but a sensual

65

cry, heavy with unspent forces. . . .

Lillian storming against her piano, using the music to tell all how she wanted to be stormed with equal strength and fervor.

This tidal power was still in her when the women moved towards her to tell her it was wonderful. She rose from the piano as if she would engulf them, the smaller women; she embraced them with all the fervor of unspent intensity that had not reached a climax—which the music, like too delicate a vessel, the piano with too delicate a frame, had not been able to contain.

It was while Lillian was struggling to tear from the piano what the piano could not possibly give her that Djuna's attention was wafted towards the window.

In the golden salon, with the crystal lamps, the tapestries and the paintings there were immense bay windows, and Djuna's chair had been placed in one of the recesses, so that she sat on the borderline between the perfumed crowd and the silent, static garden.

It was late in the afternoon, the music had fallen back upon the people like a heavy storm cloud which could not be dispersed to lighten and lift them, the air was growing heavy, when her eyes caught the garden as if in a secret exposure. As everyone was looking at Lillian, Djuna's sudden glance seemed to have caught the garden unaware, in a dissolution of peace and greens. A light rain had washed the faces of the leaves, the knots in the tree trunks stared with aged eyes, the grass was drinking, there was a sensual humidity as if leaves, trees, grass and wind were all in a state of caress.

The garden had an air of nudity.

Djuna let her eyes melt into the garden. The garden had an air of nudity, of efflorescence, of abundance, of plenitude.

The salon was gilded, the people were costumed for false roles, the lights and the faces were attenuated, the gestures were starched—all but Lillian whose nature had not been stylized, compressed or gilded, and whose nature was warring with a piano.

Music did not open doors.

Nature flowered, caressed, spilled, relaxed, slept.

In the gilded frames, the ancestors were mummified forever, and descendants took the same poses. The women were candied in perfume, conserved in cosmetics, the men preserved in their elegance. All the violence of naked truths had evaporated, volatilized within gold frames.

And then, as Djuna's eyes followed the path carpeted with detached leaves, her eyes encountered for the first time three full-length mirrors placed among the bushes and flowers as casually as in a boudoir. Three mirrors.

The eyes of the people inside could not bear the nudity of the garden, its exposure. The eyes of the people had needed the mirrors, delighted in the fragility of reflections. All the truth of the garden, the moisture, and the worms, the insects and the roots, the running sap and the rotting bark, had all to be reflected in the mirrors.

Lillian was playing among vast mirrors. Lillian's violence was attenuated by her reflection in the mirrors.

The garden in the mirror was polished with the mist of perfection. Art and artifice had breathed upon the garden and the garden had breathed upon the mirror, and all the danger of truth and revelation had been exorcised.

Under the house and under the garden there were subterranean passages and if no one heard the premonitory rumblings before the explosion, it would all erupt in the form of war and revolution.

The humiliated, the defeated, the oppressed, the enslaved. Woman's misused and twisted strength. . . .

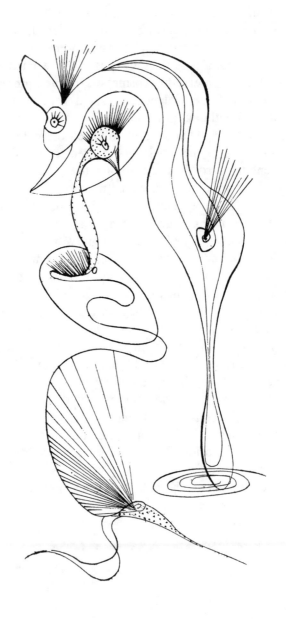

Bread and the Wafer

WHEN JAY WAS NOT TALKING or painting he sang. He sang under his breath or loudly according to his occupation. He dressed and ate to a rhythm, as if he were executing a primitive ritual with his big body that had not been quite chiselled off with the finish of a classical sculptor but whose outline had remained rugged as if it were not yet entirely separated from the wood or stone out of which it had been carved. One expected to feel the roughness of it as when one touched a clay figure before it had been thrust into the potter's oven.

He had retained so much of the animal, a graceful awkward-

ness in his walk, strong rhythmic gestures in full accord with
the pull of the muscles, an animal love of stretching, yawning,
relaxing, of sleeping anywhere, of obeying every impulse of
his body. A body without nerves or tensions.

When he stood upon his well-planted, well-separated feet it
was as if like a tree he would immediately take root there. As
he had taken roots lustily in Paris now, in the café, in his
studio, in his life with Lillian.

Wherever he found himself he was well, as if the living roots
of his body could sprout in any ground, at any time, under any
sky. His preference went, however, to artificial lights, crowds,
and he grew, talked, and laughed best in the center of a stream
of people.

If he were waiting he would fill the waiting with explosions
of song, or fall into enthusiastic observations. The spectacle of
the street was enough for him; whatever was there was enough
for him, for his boundless satisfaction.

Placed before a simple meal he would begin his prestidigita-
tions: this steak is wonderful . . . how *good* it is. How awfully
good! And the onions. . . . He made sounds of delight. He
poured his enthusiasm over the meal like a new condiment.
The steak began to glow, to expand, to multiply under the
warmth of his fervor. Every dish was wrapped in amorous
appreciation, as if it had been brought to the table with a fire
burning under it and was flaming in rum like a Christmas
pudding.

"Good, good, good," said his palate, said his roseate cheeks,
said his bowed assenting head, said his voice, all expanding
in prodigious additions, as if he were pushing multiple buttons
of delight, and colors burst from the vegetables, meat, salad,
cheese and wine. Even the parsley assumed a festive air like
a birthday candle on a cake. "Ah, ah, ah, the salad!" he said,
pouring over it a voice like an unguent along with the olive oil.

His pleasure donned the white cap of the proud chef playing
gay scales of flavors, festooning the bread and wine with the
high taste of banquets.

70

The talk, too, burst its boundaries. He started a discussion, let it take fire and spread, but the moment it took too rigid a form he began to laugh, spraying it, liquefying it in a current of gaiety.

To laugh. To laugh. "I'm not laughing at you. I'm not laughing at anyone, at anybody. I just can't help myself. I don't care a bit, not a bit, who's right."

"But you must care," said Faustin, speaking through a rigid mask of sadness which made his face completely static, and one was surprised that the words could come through the closed mouth. "You must care, you must hold on to something."

"I never hold on," said Jay. "Why hold on? Whatever you hold on to dies. There comes Colette. Sit here, Colette. How was the trade today? Colette, these people are talking about holding on. You must hold on, you must care, they say. Do you hold on, Colette? They pass like a stream, don't they, and you'd be surprised if the same ones bobbed up continuously, surprised and maybe bored. It's a good stream, isn't it, just a stream that does not nestle into you to become an ulcer, a good washing stream that cleanses as it flows, and flows clean through."

With this he drank fully from his Pernod, drank indeed as if the stream of absinthe, of ideas, feelings, talk, should pass and change every day guided only by thirst.

"You're drunk," said Colette. "You don't make sense."

"Only the drunks and the insane make sense, Colette, that's where you're wrong. Only the drunks and the insane have discarded the unessential for chaos, and only in chaos there is richness."

"If you go on this way," said Faustin, his finger pointing upward like a teacher of Sanskrit, "someone will have to take care of you while you spill in all directions recklessly. You'll need taking care of, for yours is no real freedom but an illusion of freedom, or perhaps just rebellion. Chaos always turns out to be the greatest trap of all in which you'll find yourself more securely imprisoned than anyone."

At the words "taking care" Jay had turned automatically towards Lillian and read in her eyes that fixed, immutable love which was his compass.

When Faustin was there at the café conversation would always start at the top of a pyramid without any gradual ascension. It would start with the problems of form, being and becoming, physiognomics, destiny versus incident, the coming of the fungoid era, the middle brain and the tertiary moon!

Faustin talked to build. He insisted that each talk should be a complete brick to add to a careful construction. He always started to draw on the marble-top table or on the tablecloth: this is our first premise, this is our second premise, and now we will reach the third. No sooner had he made on the table the semblance of a construction than there would come into Jay's eyes an absinthe glint which was not really the drink but some layer of his being which the drink had peeled away, which was hard, cruel, mischievous. His phrases would begin to break and scatter, to run wild like a machine without springs, gushing forth from the contradictory core of him which refused all crystallizations.

It happened every time the talk approached a definite conclusion, every time some meaning was about to be extracted from confusion. It was as if he felt that any attempt at understanding were a threat to the flow of life, to his enjoyment. As if understanding would threaten the tumultuous current or arrest it.

They were eating in a small café opposite the Gare St. Lazare, a restaurant wide open on the street. They were eating on the street and it was as if the street were full of people who were eating and drinking with them.

With each mouthful Lillian swallowed, she devoured the noises of the street, the voices and the echoes they dropped, the swift glances which fell on her like pieces of lighted wick from guttering candles. She was only the finger of a whole bigger body, a body hungry, thirsty, avid.

The wine running down her throat was passing through the throat of the world. The warmth of the day was like a man's hand on her breast, the smell of the street like a man's breath on her neck. Wide open to the street like a field washed by a river.

Shouts and laughter exploded near them from the art students on their way to the *Quatz' Arts* Ball. Egyptians and Africans in feather and jewelry, with the sweat shining on their brown painted bodies. They ran to catch the bus and it was like a heaving sea of glistening flesh shining between colored feathers and barbaric jewelry, with the muscles swelling when they laughed.

A few of them entered the restaurant, shouting and laughing. They circled around their table, like savages dancing around a stake.

The street organ was unwinding *Carmen* from its roll of tinfoil voices.

The same restaurant, another summer evening; but Jay is not there. The wine has ceased passing down Lillian's throat. It has no taste. The food does not seem rich. The street is separated from the restaurant by little green bushes she had not noticed before; the noises seem far from her, and the faces remote. Everything now happens outside, and not within her own body. Everything is distant and separated. It does not flow inside of her and carry her away.

Because Jay is not there? Does it mean it was not she who had drunk the wine, eaten the food, but that she had eaten and drunk through the pores of his pleasure and his appetite? Did she receive her pleasure, her appetite, through his gusto, his lust, his throat?

That night she had a dream: Jay had become her iron lung.

She was lying inside of him and breathing through him. She felt a great anxiety, and thought: if he leaves me then I will die. When Jay laughed she laughed; when he enjoyed she enjoyed. But all the time there was this fear that if he left her she would no longer eat, laugh or breathe.

When he welcomed friends, was at ease in groups, accepted and included all of life, she experienced this openness, this total absence of retraction through him. When alone, she still carried some constriction which interfered with deep intakes of life and people. She had thought that by yielding to him they would be removed.

She felt at times that she had fallen in love with Jay's freedom, that she had dreamed he would set her free, but that somehow or other he had been unable to accomplish this.

At night she had the feeling that she was being possessed by a cannibal.

His appetite. The gifts she made him of her feelings. How he devoured the response of her flesh, her thoughts about him, her awareness of him. As he devoured new places, new people, new impressions. His gigantic devouring spirit in quest of substance.

Her fullness constantly absorbed by him, all the changes in her, her dissolutions and rebirths, all this could be thrown into the current of his life, his work, and be absorbed like twigs by a river.

He had the appetite of the age of giants.

He could read the fattest books, tackle the most immense paintings, cover the vastest territories in his wanderings, attack the most solemn system of ideas, produce the greatest quantity of work. He excluded nothing: everything was food. He could eat the trivial and the puerile, the ephemeral and the gross, the scratchings on a wall, the phrase of a passerby, the defect on a face, the pale sonata streaming from a window, the snoring of a beggar on a bench, flowers on the wallpaper of a hotel room, the odor of cabbage on a stairway, the haunches of a bareback rider in the circus. His eyes devoured details, his hands leaped to grasp.

His whole body was like a sensitive sponge, drinking, eating, absorbing with a million cells of curiosity.

She felt caught in the immense jaws of his desire, felt herself dissolving, ripping open to his descent. She felt herself yielding up to his dark hunger, her feelings smouldering, rising from her like smoke from a black mass.

Take me, take me, take my gifts and my moods and my body and my cries and my joys and my submissions and my yielding and my terror and my abandon, take all you want.

He ate her as if she were something he wanted to possess inside of his body like a fuel. He ate her as if she were a food he needed for daily sustenance.

She threw everything into the jaws of his desire and hunger. Threw all she had known, experienced and given before. She gathered all to feed his ravenousness; she went into the past and brought back her past selves, she took the present self and the future self and threw them into the jaws of his curiosity, flung them before the greed of his questions.

The red lights from a hotel sign shone into the studio. A red well. A charging, a hoofing, a clanging, a rushing through the body. Thumping. The torrent pressure of a machine, panting, sliding back and forth, back and forth.

Swing. Swing. The bed-like stillness and downiness of summer foliage. Roll. Roll. Clutch and fold. Steam. Steam. The machine on giant oiled gongs yielding honey, rivers of honey on a bed of summer foliage. The boat slicing open the lake waters, ripples extending to the tips of the hair and the roots of the toes.

No stronger sea than this sea of feelings she swam into with him, was rolled by, no waves like the waves of desire, no foam like the foam of pleasure. No sand warmer than skin, the sand and quicksands of caresses. No sun more powerful than the sun of desire, no snow like the snow of her resistance melting in blue joys, no earth anywhere as rich as flesh.

She slept, she fell into trances, she was lost, she was renewed, she was blessed, pierced by joy, lulled, burned, consumed, purified, born and reborn within the whale belly of the night.

At the beginning of their life together he had constantly reverted to his childhood as if to deposit in her hands all the mementoes of his early voyages.

In all love's beginnings this journey backwards takes place: the desire of every lover to give his loved one all of his different selves, from the beginning.

What was most vivid in Jay's memory was the treachery of his parents.

"I was about six years old when a brand-new battleship docked at the Brooklyn Navy yard. All the boys in the neighborhood had been taken to see it but me. They kept describing it in every detail until I could dream of it as if I had seen it myself. I wanted desperately for my father to take me to it. He kept postponing the visit. Then one day he told me to wash my hands and ears carefully, to put on my best suit and said he was taking me to see the battleship. I washed myself as never before. I walked beside my father neat, and proud and drunk with gaiety. I kept telling him the number of guns we would see, the number of portholes. My father listened with apparent interest. He walked me into a doctor's office instead, where I had my tonsils taken out. The pain was a million times multiplied by the shock of disillusion, of betrayal, by the violent contrast between my dream, my expectations, and the brutal reality of the operation."

As he told this story it was clear to Lillian that he still felt the shock of the deception and had never forgiven his father. The intensity of the wish had been made even greater by the poverty of his childhood which made the visit to the battleship a unique pleasure discussed by his playmates for a whole year and not easily forgotten.

"One very cold, snowy night my mother and I were walking towards the river. I was very small, five years old maybe. My mother was walking too fast for me, and I felt terribly cold, especially my hands. My mother carried a muff. Every now and then she took her right hand out of the muff to grab mine when we crossed the streets. The warmth of her hand warmed me all through. Then she would drop my hand again and nestle hers back in her muff. I began to weep: I wanted to put my hand inside of her muff but she wouldn't let me. I wept and raged as if it were a matter of life and death—probably was, for me. I wanted the warmth and her naked hands. The more I wept and pulled at the muff the harsher my mother got. Finally she slapped my hand so I would let the muff go."

As he told this his blue eyes became the eyes of an irrevocably angry child. Lillian could see clear through his open eyes as through the wrong end of a telescope, a diminutive Jay raging, cold and thwarted, with his blue frozen hands reaching for his mother's muff.

This image was not being transmitted to Lillian the woman, but to the responsive child in herself understanding and sharing his anger and disillusion. It was the child in herself who received it as it sank through and beyond the outer layer of the woman who sat there listening with a woman's full body, a woman's face. But of this response there was no outer sign showing for Jay to see: the child in her lay so deeply locked within her, so deeply buried, that no sign of its existence or of its response was apparent. It did not beckon through her eyes which showed only a woman's compassion, nor alter her gestures nor the pose of her body which was the pose of a woman listening to a child and looking at his smallness without herself changing stature. At this moment, like Jay, she could have slipped out of her maturity, of her woman's body, and exposed her child's face, eyes, movements, and then Jay would have seen it, known that he had communicated with it, touched it by way of his own childhood, and the child might have met the child and become aware of its similar needs.

By her attitude she did not become one with him in this return to his past self. What she overtly extended to him was one who seemed done with her child self and who would replace the harsh mother, extend the muff and the warm naked hands.

She became, at that instant, indelibly fixed in his eyes not as another child with possibly equal needs, but as the stronger one in possession of the power to dispense to all *his* needs.

From now on was established an inequality in power: he was the cold and hungry one, she the muff and the warm naked hands.

From now on her needs, concealed and buried as mere interferences with the accomplishment of this role, were condemned to permanent muteness. Strong direction was given to her activity as the muff, as the provider of innumerable battleships in compensation for the one he had been cheated of. Giving to him on all levels, from book to blanket to phonograph to fountain pen to food, was always and forever the battleship he had dreamed and not seen. It was the paying off of a debt to the cheated child.

Lillian did not know then that the one who believes he can pay this early debt meets a bottomless well. Because the first denial has set off a fatality of revenge which no amount of giving can placate. Present in every child and criminal is this conviction that no retribution will repair the injury done. The man who was once starved may revenge himself upon the world not by stealing just once, or by stealing only what he needs, but by taking from the world an endless toll in payment of something irreplaceable, which is the lost faith.

This diminutive Jay who appeared in the darkness when he evoked his childhood was also a personage who could come nearer to her own frightened self without hurting her than the assertive, rather ruthless Jay who appeared in the daytime when he resumed his man's life. When he described his smallness and how he could enter saloons to call for his father without having to swing the doors open, it seemed to Lillian that she could encompass this small figure better in the range of her vision than the reckless, amorphous, protean Jay whose personality flowed into so many channels like swift mercury.

When Jay described the vehemence, the wildness, the hunger with which he went out into the streets to play, it seemed to her that he was simultaneously describing and explaining the vehemence, the hunger, the wildness with which he went out at night now and left her alone, so that the present became strangely innocent in her mind.

When he talked about his impulses towards other women he took on the expression not of a man who had enjoyed another woman sensually, but of a gay, irrepressible child whose acts were absolutely uncontrollable; it became no longer infidelity but a childish, desperate eagerness to "go to the street and play."

She saw him in the present as the same child needing to boast of his conquests out of a feeling of helplessness, needing to be admired, to win many friends, and thus she attenuated in herself the anxiety she experienced at his many far-flung departures from her.

When she rebelled at times he looked completely baffled by her rebellions, as if there were nothing in his acts which could harm her. She always ended by feeling guilty: he had given her his entire self to love, including the child, and now, out of noblesse oblige, she could not possibly act . . . like his harsh mother!

He looked at the sulphur-colored Pernod and drank it.

He was in the mood to paint his self-portrait for anyone who wanted to listen: this always happened after someone had attacked his painting, or claimed some overdue debt.

So Jay drank Pernod and explained: "I'm like Buddha who chose to live in poverty. I abandoned my first wife and child for a religious life. I now depend on the bowl of rice given to me by my followers."

"What do you teach?" asked a young man who was not susceptible to the contagion of Jay's gaiety.

"A life from which all suffering is absent."

But to the onlooker who saw them together, Lillian, ever alert to deflect the blows which might strike at him, it seemed much more as if Jay had merely unburdened all sadnesses upon her rather than as if he had found a secret for eliminating them altogether. His disciples inevitably discovered they, too, must find themselves a Lillian to achieve his way of life.

"I'm no teacher," said Jay. "I'm just a happy man. I can't explain how I arrived at such a state." He pounded his chest with delight. "Give me a bowl of rice and I will make you as joyous as I am."

This always brought an invitation to dinner.

"Nothing to worry about," he always said to Lillian. "Someone will always invite me to dinner."

In return for the dinner Jay took them on a guided tour of his way of life. Whoever did not catch his mood could go overboard. He was no initiator. Let others learn by osmosis!

But this was only one of his self-portraits. There were other days when he did not like to present himself as a laughing man who communicated irresponsibility and guiltlessness, but as the great barbarian. In this mood he exulted the warrior, the invaders, the pillagers, the rapers. He believed in violence. He saw himself as Attila avenging the impurities of the world by bloodshed. He saw his paintings then as a kind of bomb.

As he talked he became irritated with the young man who had asked him what he taught, for Jay noticed that he walked back and forth constantly but not the whole length of the studio. He would take five long steps, stop mechanically, and turn back like an automaton. The nervous compulsion disturbed Jay and he stopped him: "I wish you'd sit down."

"Excuse me, I'm really sorry," he said, stopping dead. A look of anxiety came to his face. "You see, I've just come out of jail. In jail I could only walk five steps, no more. Now when I'm in a large room, it disturbs me. I want to explore it, familiarize myself with it, at the same time I feel compelled to walk no further."

"You make me think of a friend I had," said Jay, "who was very poor and a damned good painter and of the way he escaped from his narrow life. He was living at the Impasse Rouet, and as you know probably, that's the last step before you land at the Hospital, the Insane Asylum or the Cemetery. He lived in one of those houses set far back into a courtyard, full of studios as bare as cells. There was no heat in the house and most of the windows were cracked and let the wind blow through. Those who owned stoves, for the most part, didn't own any coal. Peter's studio had an additional anomaly: it had no windows, only a transom. The door opened directly on the courtyard. He had no stove, a cot whose springs showed through the gored mattress. No sheets, and only one old blanket. No doorbell, of course. No electricity, as he couldn't pay the bill. He used candles, and when he had no money for candles he got fat from the butcher and burnt it. The concierge was like an old octopus, reaching everywhere at once with her man's voice and inquisitive whiskers. Peter was threatened with eviction when he hit upon an idea. Every year, as you know, foreign governments issued prizes for the best painting, the best sculpture. Peter got one of the descriptive pamphlets from the Dutch embassy where he had a friend. He brought it to the concierge and read it to her, then explained: Fact one: he was the only Dutch painter in Paris. Fact two: a prize would be given to the best painting produced by a Dutchman, amounting to half a million francs. The concierge was smart enough to see the point. She agreed to let the rent slide for a month, to lend him money for paints and a little extra change for cigarettes while he painted something as big as the wall of his cell. In return, with the prize money, he promised to buy her a little house in the country for her old age—with garden. Now he could paint all day. It was spring; he left his door open and the concierge settled in the courtyard with her heavy red hands at rest on her lap and thought that each brush stroke added to her house and garden. After two months she got impatient. He was still painting, but he was also eating, smoking cigarettes, drinking aperitifs and even sleeping at times more than eight hours. Peter rushed to the embassy and asked his friend to pay him an official call. The friend managed to borrow the official car with the Dutch coat of arms and paid the painter a respectful visit. This reassured her for another month. Every evening they read the booklet together: "the prize will be handed over in cash one week after the jury decides upon its value. . . ." The concierge's beatitude was contagious. The entire house benefited from her mellowness. Until one morning when the newspapers published the name and photograph of the genuine Dutch painter who had actually won the prize and then without warning she turned into a cyclone. Peter's door was locked. She climbed on a chair to look through the transom to make sure he was not asleep or drunk. To her great horror she saw a body hanging from the ceiling. He had hanged himself! She called for help. The police forced the door open. What they cut down was a mannequin of wax and old rags, carefully painted by Peter.

"The funny thing," added Jay after a pause, "is that after this his luck turned. When he hanged his effigy he seemed to have killed the self who had been a failure."

The visitors left.

Then all the laughter in him subsided into a pool of serenity. His voice became soft. Just as he loved the falsities of his roles, he loved also to rest from these pranks and attitudes and crystallize in the white heat of Lillian's faith.

And when all the gestures and talk seemed lulled, suddenly he sprang up again with a new mood, a fanatic philosopher who walked up and down the studio punctuating the torrent of his ideas with fist blows on the tables. A nervous lithe walk, while he churned ideas like leaves on a pyre which never turned to ash.

Then all the words, the ideas, the memories, were drawn together like the cords of a hundred kites and he said:

82

"I'd like to work now."

Lillian watched the transformation in him. She watched the half open mouth close musingly, the scattered talk crystallizing. This man so easily swayed, caught, moved, now collecting his strength again. At that moment she saw the big man in him, the man who appeared to be merely enjoying recklessly, idling, roaming, but deep down set upon a terribly earnest goal: to hand back to life all the wealth of material he had collected, intent on making restitution to the world for what he had absorbed with his enormous creator's appetite.

There remained in the air only the echoes of his resonant voice, the hot breath of his words, the vibration of his pounding gestures.

She rose to lock the door of the studio upon the world. She drew in long invisible bolts. She pulled in rustless shutters. Silence. She imprisoned within herself that mood and texture of Jay which would never go into his work, or be given or exposed to the world, that which she alone could see and know.

While Lillian slept Jay reassembled his dispersed selves.

At this moment the flow in him became purposeful.

In his very manner of pressing the paint tube there was intensity; often it spurted like a geyser, was wasted, stained his clothes and the floor. The paint, having appeared in a minor explosion, proceeded to cause a major one on the canvas.

The explosion caused not a whole world to appear, but a shattered world of fragments. Bodies, objects, cities, trees, animals were all splintered, pierced, impaled.

It was actually a spectacle of carnage.

The bodies were dismembered and every part of them misplaced. In the vast dislocation eyes were placed where they had never visited a body, the hands and feet were substituted for the face, the faces bore four simultaneous facets with one empty void between. Gravity was lost, all relation between the figures were like those of acrobats. Flesh became rubber, trees flesh, bones became plumage, and all the life of the interior, cells, nerves, sinew lay exposed as by a merely curious surgeon not concerned with closing the incisions. All his painter's thrusts opening, exposing, dismembering in the violent colors of reality.

The vitality with which he exploded, painted dissolution and disintegration, with which his energy broke familiar objects into unfamiliar components, was such that people who walked into a room full of his painting were struck only with the power and force of these brilliant fragments as by an act of birth. That they were struck only by broken pieces of an exploded world, they did not see. The force of the explosion, the weight, density and brilliance was compelling.

To each lost, straying piece of body or animal was often added the growth and excrescences of illness, choking moss on southern trees, cocoons of the unborn, barnacles and parasites.

It was Jay's own particular jungle in which the blind warfare of insects and animals was carried on by human beings. The violence of the conflicts distorted the human body. Fear became muscular twistings like the tangled roots of trees, dualities sundered them in two separate pieces seeking separate lives. The entire drama took place at times in stagnant marshes, in petrified forests where every human being was a threat to the other.

The substance that could weld them together again was absent. Through the bodies irretrievable holes had been drilled and in place of a heart there was a rubber pump or a watch.

The mild, smiling Jay who stepped out of these infernos always experienced a slight tremor of uneasiness when he passed from the world of his painting to Lillian's room. If she was awake she would want to see what he had been doing. And she was always inevitably shocked. To see the image of her ınner nightmares exposed affected her as the sight of a mirror affects a cat or a child. There was always a moment of strained silence.

This underground of hostility she carried in her being, of which her body felt only the blind impacts, the shocks, was now clearly projected.

Jay was always surprised at her recoil, for he could see how Lillian was a prolongation of this warfare on canvas, how at the point where he left violence and became a simple, anonymous, mild-mannered man, it was she who took up the thread and enacted the violence directly upon people.

But Lillian had never seen herself doing it.

Jay would say: "I wish you wouldn't quarrel with everyone, Lillian."

"I wish you wouldn't paint such horrors. Why did you paint Faustin without a head? That's what he's proudest of—his head."

"Because that's what he should lose, to come alive. You hate him too. Why did you hand him his coat the other night in such a way that he was forced to leave?"

In the daylight they repudiated each other. At night their bodies recognized a familiar substance: gunpowder, and they made their peace together.

In the morning it was he who went out for bread, butter and milk for breakfast, while she made the coffee.

When she locked the studio for the night, she locked out anxiety. But when Jay got into his slack morning working clothes and stepped out jauntily, whistling, he had a habit of locking the door again—and in between, anxiety slipped in again.

He locks the door, he has forgotten that I am here.

Thus she interpreted it, because of her feeling that once he had taken her, he deserted her each time anew. No contact was ever continuous with him. So he locked the door, forgot she was there, deserted her.

When she confessed this to Djuna, Djuna who had continued to write for Lillian the Chinese dictionary of counter-interpretations, she laughed: "Lillian, have you ever thought that he might be locking you in to keep you for himself?"

Lillian was accurate in her feeling that when Jay left the studio he was disassociated from her, and not from her alone, but from himself.

He walked out in the street and became one with the street. His mood became the mood of the street. He dissolved and became eye, ear, smile.

There are days when the city exposes only its cripples, days when the bus must stop close to the curb to permit a one-legged man to board it, days when a man without legs rests his torso on a rolling stand and propels himself with his hands, days when a head is held up by a pink metal truss, days when blind men ask to be guided, and Jay knew as he looked, absorbing every detail, that he would paint them, even though had he been consulted all the cripples of the world would be destroyed excepting the smiling old men who sat on benches beatifically drunk, because they were his father. He had so many fathers, for he was one to see the many. *I believe we have a hundred fathers and mothers and lovers all interchangeable, and that's the flaw in Lillian, for her there is only one mother, one father, one husband, one lover, one son, one daughter, irreplaceable, unique—her world is too small. The young girl who just passed me with lightning in her eyes is my daughter. I could take her home as my daughter in place of the one I lost. The world is full of fathers, whenever I need one I only need to stop and talk to one . . . this one sitting there with a white beard and a captain's cap . . .*

"Do you want a cigarette, Captain?"

"I'm no captain, Monsieur, I was a Legionnaire, as you can

see by my beard. Are you sure you haven't a butt or two? I'd rather have a butt. I like my independence, you know, I collect butts. A cigarette is charity. I'm a hobo, you know, not a beggar."

His legs were wrapped in newspapers. "Because of the varicose veins. They sort of bother me in the winter. I could stay with the nuns, they would take care of me. But imagine having to get up every morning at six at the sound of a bell, of having to eat exactly at noon, and then at seven and having to sleep at nine. I'm better here. I like my independence." He was filling his pipe with butts.

Jay sat beside him.

"The nuns are not bad to me. I collect crusts of old bread from the garbage cans and I sell them to the hospital for the soup they serve to pregnant women."

"Why did you leave the Legion?"

"During my campaigns I received letters from an unknown godmother. You can't imagine what those letters were, Monsieur, I haven't got them because I wore them out reading them there, in the deserts. They were so warm I could have heated my hands over them if I had been fighting in a cold country. Those letters made me so happy that on my first furlough I looked her up. That was quite a task, believe me, she had no address! She sold bananas from a little cart, and she slept under the bridges. I spent my furlough sitting with her like this with a bottle of red wine. It was a good life; I deserted the Legion."

He again refused a cigarette and Jay walked on.

The name of a street upon an iron plate, Rue Dolent, Rue Dolent decomposed for him into dolorous, doliente, douleur. The plate is nailed to the prison wall, the wall of China, of our chaos and our mysteries, the wall of Jericho, of our religions and our guilts, the wall of lamentation, the wall of the prison of Paris. Wall of soot, encrusted dust. No prison breaker ever crumbled this wall, the darkest and longest of all leaning heavily upon the little Rue Dolent Doliente Douleur which, although on the free side of the wall, is the saddest street of all Paris. On one side are men whose crimes were accomplished in a moment of rage, rebellion, violence. On the other, grey figures too afraid to hate, to rebel, to kill openly. On the free side of the wall they walk with iron bars in their hearts and stones on their feet carrying the balls and chains of their obsessions. Prisoners of their weakness, of their self-inflicted illnesses and slaveries. No need of guards and keys! They will never escape from themselves, and they only kill others with the invisible death rays of their impotence.

He did not know any longer where he was walking. The personages of the street and the personages of his paintings extended into each other, issued from one to fall into the other, fell into the work, or out of it, stood now with, now without, frames. The man on the sliding board, had he not seen him before in Coney Island when he was a very young man and walking with a woman he loved? This half-man had followed them persistently along the boardwalk, on a summer night made for caresses, until the woman had recoiled from his pursuit and left both the half-man and Jay. Again the man on wheels had appeared in his dream, but this time it was his mother in a black dress with black jet beads on it as he had seen her once about to attend a funeral. Why he should deprive his mother of the lower half of her body, he didn't know. No fear of incest had ever barred his way to women, and he had always been able to want them all, and the more they looked like his mother the better.

He saw the seven hard benches of the pawnshop where he had spent so many hours of his life in Paris waiting to borrow a little cash on his paintings, and felt the bitterness he had tasted when they underestimated his work! The man behind the counter had eyes dilated from appraising objects. Jay laughed out loud at the memory of the man who had pawned his books and continued to read them avidly until the last minute like one condemned to future starvation. He had painted them all pawning their arms and legs, after seeing them pawn the stove that would keep them warm, the coat that would save them from pneumonia, the dress that would attract customers. A grotesque world, hissed the Dean of Critics. A distorted world. *Well and good. Let them sit for three hours on one of the seven benches of the Paris pawnshop. Let them walk through the Rue Dolent. Perhaps I should not be allowed to go free, perhaps I should be jailed with the criminals. I feel in sympathy with them. My murders are committed with paint. Every act of murder might awaken people to the state of things that produced it, but soon they fall asleep again, and when the artist awakens them they are quick to take revenge. Very good that they refuse me money and honors, for thus they keep me in these streets and exposing what they do not wish me to expose. My jungle is not the innocent one of Rousseau. In my jungle everyone meets his enemy. In the underworld of nature debts must be paid in the same specie: no false money accepted. Hunger with hunger, pain with pain, destruction with destruction.*

The artist is there to keep accounts.

From his explorations of the Dome, the Select, the Rotonde, Jay once brought back Sabina, though with these two people it would be difficult to say which one guided the other home or along the street, since both of them had this aspect of overflowing rivers rushing headlong to cover the city, making houses, cafés, streets and people seem small and fragile, easily swept along. The uprooting power of Jay's impulses added to Sabina's mobility reversed the whole order of the city.

Sabina brought in her wake the sound and imagery of fire engines as they tore through the streets of New York alarming the heart with the violent gong of catastrophe.

All dressed in red and silver, the tearing red and silver siren

89

cutting a pathway through the flesh. The first time one looked at Sabina one felt: everything will burn!

Out of the red and silver and the long cry of alarm, to the poet who survives in a human being as the child survives in him, to this poet Sabina threw an unexpected ladder in the middle of the city and ordained: climb!

As she appeared, the orderly alignment of the city gave way before this ladder one was invited to climb, standing straight in space like the ladder of Baron Münchhausen which led to the sky.

Only Sabina's ladder led to fire.

As she walked heavily towards Lillian from the darkness of the hallway into the light of the door Lillian saw for the first time the woman she had always wanted to know. She saw Sabina's eyes burning, heard her voice so rusty and immediately felt drowned in her beauty. She wanted to say: I recognize you. I have often imagined a woman like you.

Sabina could not sit still. She talked profusely and continuously with feverish breathlessness, like one in fear of silence. She sat as if she could not bear to sit for long, and when she walked she was eager to sit down again. Impatient, alert, watchful, as if in dread of being attacked; restless and keen, making jerking gestures with her hands, drinking hurriedly, speaking rapidly, smiling swiftly and listening to only half of what was said to her.

Exactly as in a fever dream, there was in her no premeditation, no continuity, no connection. It was all chaos—her erratic gestures, her unfinished sentences, her sulky silences, her sudden walks through the room, her apologizing for futile reasons (I'm sorry, I lost my gloves), her apparent desire to be elsewhere.

She carried herself like one totally unfettered who was rushing and plunging on some fiery course. She could not stop to reflect.

She unrolled the film of her life stories swiftly, like the accelerated scenes of a broken machine, her adventures, her escapes from drug addicts, her encounters with the police, parties at which indistinct incidents took place, hazy scenes of flagellations in which no one could tell whether she had been the flagellator or the victim, or whether or not it had happened at all.

A broken dream, with spaces, reversals, contradictions, galloping fantasies and sudden retractions. She would say: "he lifted my skirt," or "we had to take care of the wounds," or "the policeman was waiting for me and I had to swallow the drug to save my friends," and then as if she had written this on a blackboard she took a huge sponge and effaced it all by a phrase which was meant to convey that perhaps this story had happened to someone else, or she may have read it, or heard it at a bar, and as soon as this was erased she began another story of a beautiful girl who was employed in a night club and whom Sabina had insulted, but if Jay asked why she shifted the scene, she at once effaced it, cancelled it, to tell about something else she had heard and not seen at the night club at which she worked.

The faces and the figures of her personages appeared only half drawn, and when one just began to perceive them another face and figure were interposed, as in a dream, and when one thought one was looking at a woman it was a man, an old man, and when one approached the old man who used to take care of her, it turned out to be the girl she lived with who looked like a younger man she had first loved and this one was metamorphosed into a whole group of people who had cruelly humiliated her one evening. Somewhere in the middle of the scene Sabina appeared as the woman with gold hair, and then later as a woman with black hair, and it was equally impossible to keep a consistent image of whom she had loved, betrayed, escaped from, lived with, married, lied to, forgotten, deserted.

She was impelled by a great confessional fever which forced her to lift a corner of the veil, but became frightened if anyone listened or peered at the exposed scene, and then she took a giant sponge and rubbed it all out, to begin somewhere else, thinking that in confusion there was protection. So Sabina beckoned and lured one into her world, and then blurred the passageways, confused the images and ran away in fear of detection.

From the very first Jay hated her, hated her as Don Juan hates Doña Juana, as the free man hates the free woman, as man hates in woman this freedom in passion which he grants solely to himself. Hated her because he knew instinctively that she regarded him as he regarded woman: as a possible or impossible lover.

He was not for her a man endowed with particular gifts, standing apart from other men, irreplaceable as Lillian saw him, unique as his friends saw him. Sabina's glance measured him as he measured women: endowed or not endowed as lovers.

She knew as he did, that none of the decorations or dignities conferred upon a man or woman could alter the basic talent or lack of talent as a lover. No title of architect emeritus will confer upon them the magic knowledge of the body's structure. No prestidigitation with words will replace the knowledge of the secret places of responsiveness. No medals for courage will confer the graceful audacities, the conquering abductions, the exact knowledge of the battle of love, when the moment for seduction, when for consolation, when for capitulation.

The trade, art and craft that cannot be learned, which requires a divination of the fingertips, the accurate reading of signals from the fluttering of an eyelid, an eye like a microscope to catch the approval of an eyelash, a seismograph to catch the vibrations of the little blue nerves under the skin, the capacity to prognosticate from the direction of the down as from the inclination of the leaves some can predict rain, tell where storms are brooding, where floods are threatening, tell which regions to leave alone, which to invade, which to lull and which to take by force.

No decorations, no diplomas for the lover, no school and no traveller's experience will help a man who does not hear the beat, tempo and rhythms of the body, catch the ballet leaps of desire at their highest peak, perform the acrobatics of tenderness and lust, and know all the endless virtuosities of silence.

Sabina was studying his potentialities with such insolence, weighing the accuracy of his glance. For there is a black lover's glance well known to women versed in this lore, which can strike at the very center of woman's body, which plants its claim as in a perfect target.

Jay saw in her immediately the woman without fidelity, capable of all desecrations. That a woman should do this, wear no wedding ring, love according to her caprice and not be in bondage to the one. (A week before he was angry with Lillian for considering him as the unique and irreplaceable one, because it conferred on him a responsibility he did not wish to assume, and he was wishing she might consider an understudy who would occasionally relieve him of his duties!)

For one sparkling moment Jay and Sabina faced each other in the center of the studio, noting each other's defiance, absorbing this great mistrustfulness which instantly assails the man and women who recognize in each other the law-breaking lovers; erecting on this basic mutual mistrust the future violent attempts to establish certitude.

Sabina's dress at first like fire now appeared, in the more tangible light of Lillian's presence, as made of black satin, the texture most similar to skin. Then Lillian noticed a hole in Sabina's sleeve, and suddenly she felt ashamed not to have a hole in her sleeve too, for somehow, Sabina's poverty, Sabina's worn sandals, seemed like the most courageous defiance of all, the choice of a being who had no need of flawless sleeves or new sandals to feel complete.

Lillian's glance which usually remained fixed upon Jay, grazing lightly over others, for the first time absorbed another human being as intently.

Jay looked uneasily at them. This fixed attention of Lillian revolving around him had demanded of him, the mutable one, something he could not return, thus making him feel like a man accumulating a vast debt in terms he could never meet.

In Sabina's fluctuating fervors he met a challenge: she gave him a feeling of equality. She was well able to take care of herself and to answer treachery with treachery.

Lillian waited at the corner of the Rue Auber. She would see Sabina in full daylight advancing out of a crowd. She would make certain that such an image could materialize, that Sabina was not a mirage which would melt in the daylight.

She was secretly afraid that she might stand there at the corner of the Rue Auber exactly as she had stood in other places watching the crowd, knowing no figure would come out of it which would resemble the figures in her dreams. Waiting for Sabina she experienced the most painful expectancy: she could not believe Sabina would arrive by these streets, cross such a boulevard, emerge from a mass of faceless people. What a profound joy to see her striding forward, wearing her shabby sandals and her shabby black dress with royal indifference.

"I hate daylight," said Sabina, and her eyes darkened with anger. The dark blue rings under her eyes were so deep they marked her flesh. It was as if the flesh around her eyes had been burned away by the white heat and fever of her glance.

They found the place she wanted, a place below the level of the street.

Her talk like a turbulent river, like a broken necklace spilled around Lillian.

"It's a good thing I'm going away. You would soon unmask me."

At this Lillian looked at Sabina and her eyes said so clearly: "I want to become blind with you," that Sabina was moved and turned her face away, ashamed of her doubts.

"There are so many things I would love to do with you, Lillian. With you I would take drugs. I would not be afraid."

"You afraid?" said Lillian, incredulously. But one word rose persistently to the surface of her being, one word which was like a rhythm more than a word, which beat its tempo as soon as Sabina appeared. Each step she took with Sabina was marked as by a drum beat with the word: danger danger danger danger.

"I have a feeling that I want to be you, Sabina. I never wanted to be anyone but myself before."

"How can you live with Jay, Lillian? I hate Jay. I feel he is like a spy. He enters your life only to turn around afterwards and caricature. He exposes only the ugly."

"Only when something hurts him. It's when he gets hurt that he destroys. Has he caricatured you?"

"He painted me as a whore. And you know that isn't me. He has such an interest in evil that I told him stories. . . . I hate him."

"I thought you loved him," said Lillian simply.

All Sabina's being sought to escape Lillian's directness in a panic. Behind the mask a thousand smiles appeared, behind the eyelids ageless deceptions.

This was the moment. If only Sabina could bring herself to say what she felt: Lillian, do not trust me. I want Jay. Do not love me, Lillian, for I am like him. I take what I want no matter who is hurt.

"You want to unmask me, Lillian."

"If I were to unmask you, Sabina, I would only be revealing myself: you act as I would act if I had the courage. I see you exactly as you are, and I love you. You should not fear exposure, not from me."

This was the moment to turn away from Jay who was bringing her not love, but another false role of play, to turn towards Lillian with the truth, that a real love might take place.

Sabina's face appeared to Lillian as that of a child drowning behind a window. She saw Sabina as a child struggling with her terror of the truth, considering before answering what might come closest to the best image of herself she might give Lillian. Sabina would not say the truth but whatever conformed to what she imagined Lillian expected of her, which was in reality not at all what Lillian wanted of her, but what she, Sabina, thought necessary to her idealized image of herself. What Sabina was feverishly creating always was the reverse of what she acted out: a woman of loyalty and faithfulness. To maintain this image at all costs she ceased responding to Lillian's soft appeal to the child in need of a rest from pretenses.

"I don't deny Jay is a caricaturist, but only out of revengefulness. What have you done to deserve his revenge?"

Again Sabina turned her face away.

"I know you're not a *femme fatale,* Sabina. But didn't you want him to think you were?"

With this peculiar flair she had for listening to the buried child in human beings, Lillian could hear the child within Sabina whining, tired of its inventions grown too cumbersome, weary of its adornments, of its disguises. Too many costumes, valances, gold, brocade, veils, to cover Sabina's direct thrusts towards what she wanted, and meanwhile it was this audacity, this directness, this unfaltering knowledge of her wants which Lillian loved in her, wanted to learn from her.

But a smile of immeasurable distress appeared in Sabina, and then was instantly effaced by another smile: the smile of seduction. When Lillian was about to seize upon the distress, to enter the tender, vulnerable regions of her being, then Sabina concealed herself again behind the smile of a woman of seduction.

Pity, protection, solace, they all fell away from Lillian like gifts of trivial import, because with the smile of seduction Sabina assumed simultaneously the smile of an all-powerful enchantress.

Lillian forgot the face of the child in distress, hungrily demanding a truthful love, and yet, in terror that this very truth might destroy the love. The child face faded before this potent smile to which Lillian succumbed.

She no longer sought the meaning of Sabina's words. She looked at Sabina's blonde hair tumbling down, at her eyebrows peaked upward, at her smile slanting perfidiously, a gem-like smile which made a whirlpool of her feelings.

A man passed by and laughed at their absorption.

"Don't mind, don't mind," said Sabina, as if she were familiar with this situation. "I won't do you any harm."

"You can't do me any harm."

Sabina smiled. "I destroy people without meaning to. Everywhere I go things become confused and terrifying. For you I would like to begin all over again, to go to New York and become a great actress, to become beautiful again. I won't appear any more with clothes that are held together with safety pins! I've been living stupidly, blindly, doing nothing but drinking, smoking, talking. I'm afraid of disillusioning you, Lillian."

They walked down the streets aimlessly, unconscious of their surroundings, arm in arm with a joy that was rising every moment, and with every word they uttered. A swelling joy that mounted with each step they took together and with the occasional brushing of their hips as they walked.

The traffic eddied around them but everything else, houses and trees were lost in a fog. Only their voices distinct, carrying such phrases as they could utter out of their female labyrinth of oblique perceptions.

Sabina said: "I wanted to telephone you last night. I wanted to tell you how sorry I was to have talked so much. I knew all the time I couldn't say what I wanted to say."

"You too have fears, although you seem so strong," said Lillian.

"I do everything wrong. It's good that you don't ever ask questions about facts. Facts don't matter. It's the essence that matters. You never ask the kind of question I hate: what city? what man? what year? what time? Facts. I despise them."

Bodies close, arm in arm, hands locked together over her

breast. She had taken Lillian's hand and held it over her breast as if to warm it.

The city had fallen away. They were walking into a world of their own for which neither could find a name.

They entered a softly lighted place, mauve and diffuse, which enveloped them in velvet closeness.

Sabina took off her silver bracelet and put it around Lillian's wrist.

"It's like having your warm hand around my wrist. It's still warm, like your own hand. I'm your prisoner, Sabina."

Lillian looked at Sabina's face, the fevered profile taut, so taut that she shivered a little, knowing that when Sabina's face turned towards her she could no longer see the details of it for its blazing quality. Sabina's mouth always a little open, pouring forth that eddying voice which gave one vertigo.

Lillian caught an expression on her face of such knowingness that she was startled. Sabina's whole body seemed suddenly charged with experience, as if discolored from it, filled with violet shadows, bowed down by weary eyelids. In one instant she looked marked by long fevers, by an unconquerable fatigue. Lillian could see all the charred traces of the fires she had traversed. She expected her eyes and hair to turn ashen.

But the next moment her eyes and hair gleamed more brilliantly than ever, her face became uncannily clear, completely innocent, an innocence which radiated like a gem. She could shed her whole life in one moment of forgetfulness, stand absolutely washed of it, as if she were standing at the very beginning of it.

So many questions rushed to Lillian's mind, but now she knew Sabina hated questions. Sabina's essence slipped out between the facts. So Lillian smiled and was silent, listening merely to Sabina's voice, the way its hoarseness changed from rustiness to a whisper, a faint gasp, so that the hotness of her breath touched her face.

She watched her smoke hungrily, as if smoking, talking and moving were all desperately necessary to her, like breathing, and she did them all with such reckless intensity.

When Lillian and Sabina met one night under the red light of the café they recognized in each other similar moods: they would laugh at him, the man.

"He's working so hard, so hard he's in a daze," said Lillian. "He talks about nothing but painting."

She was lonely, deep down, to think that Jay had been at his work for two weeks without noticing either of them. And her loneliness drew her close to Sabina.

"He was glad we were going out together, he said it would give him a chance to work. He hasn't any idea of time—he doesn't even know what day of the week it is. He doesn't give a damn about anybody or anything."

A feeling of immense loneliness invaded them both.

They walked as if they wanted to walk away from their mood, as if they wanted to walk into another world. They walked up the hill of Montmartre with little houses lying on the hillside like heather. They heard music, music so off tune that they did not recognize it as music they heard every day. They slid into a shaft of light from where this music came—into a room which seemed built of granified smoke and crystallized human breath. A room with a painted star on the ceiling, and a wooden, pock-marked Christ nailed to the wall. Gusts of weary, petrified songs, so dusty with use. Faces like empty glasses. The musicians made of rubber like the elastic rubber-soled night.

We hate Jay tonight. We hate man.

The craving for caresses. Wanting and fighting the want. Both frightened by the vagueness of their desire, the indefiniteness of their craving.

A rosary of question marks in their eyes.

Sabina whispered: "Let's take drugs tonight."

She pressed her strong knee against Lillian, she inundated her with the brilliance of her eyes, the paleness of her face.

Lillian shook her head, but she drank, she drank. No drink equal to the state of war and hatred. No drink like bitterness.

Lillian looked at Sabina's fortuneteller's eyes, and at the taut profile.

"It takes all the pain away; it wipes out reality."

She leaned over the table until their breaths mingled.

"You don't know what a relief it is. The smoke of opium like fog. It brings marvelous dreams and gaiety. Such gaiety, Lillian. And you feel so powerful, so powerful and content. You don't feel any more frustration, you feel that you are lording it over the whole world with marvelous strength. No one can hurt you then, humiliate you, confuse you. You feel you're soaring over the world. Everything becomes soft, large, easy. Such joys, Lillian, as you have never imagined. The touch of a hand is enough . . . the touch of a hand is like going the whole way. . . . And time . . . how time flies. The days pass like an hour. No more straining, just dreaming and floating. Take drugs with me, Lillian."

Lillian consented with her eyes. Then she saw that Sabina was looking at the Arab merchant who stood by the door with his red Fez, his kimono, his slippers, his arms loaded with Arabian rugs and pearl necklaces. Under the rugs protruded a wooden leg with which he was beating time to the jazz.

Sabina laughed, shaking her whole body with drunken laughter. "You don't know, Lillian . . . this man . . . with his wooden leg . . . you never can tell . . . he may have some. There was a man once, with a wooden leg like that. He was arrested and they found that his wooden leg was packed with snow. I'll go and ask him."

And she got up with her heavy, animal walk, and talked to the rug merchant, looking up at him alluringly, begging, smiling up at him in the same secret way she had of smiling at Lillian. A burning pain invaded Lillian to see Sabina begging. But the merchant shook his head, smiled innocently, shook his head firmly, smiled again, offered his rugs and the necklaces.

When she saw Sabina returning empty handed, Lillian drank again, and it was like drinking fog, long draughts of fog.

They danced together, the floor turning under them like a

100

phonograph record. Sabina dark and potent, leading Lillian.

A gust of jeers seemed to blow through the place. A gust of jeers. But they danced, cheeks touching, their cheeks chalice white. They danced and the jeers cut into the haze of their dizziness like a whip. The eyes of the men were insulting them. The eyes of men called them by the name the world had for them. Eyes. Green, jealous. Eyes of the world. Eyes sick with hatred and contempt. Caressing eyes, participating. Eyes ransacking their conscience. Stricken yellow eyes of envy caught in the flare of a match. Heavy torpid eyes without courage, without dreams. Mockery, frozen mockery from the frozen glass eyes of the loveless.

Lillian and Sabina wanted to strike those eyes, break them, break the bars of green wounded eyes, condemning them. They wanted to break the walls confining them, suffocating them. They wanted to break out from the prison of their own fears, break every obstacle. But all they found to break were glasses. They took their glasses and broke them over their shoulders and made no wish, but looked at the fragments of the glasses on the floor wonderingly as if their mood of rebellion might be lying there also, in broken pieces.

Now they danced mockingly, defiantly, as if they were sliding beyond the reach of man's hands, running like sand between their insults. They scoffed at those eyes which brimmed with knowledge for they knew the ecstasy of mystery and fog, fire and orange fumes of a world they had seen through a slit in the dream. Spinning and reeling and falling, spinning and turning and rolling down the brume and smoke of a world seen through a slit in the dream.

The waiter put his ham-colored hand on Sabina's bare arm: "You've got to get out of here, you two!"

They were alone.

They were alone without daylight, without past, without any thought of the resemblance between their togetherness and the union of other women. The whole world was being pushed to one side by their faith in their own uniqueness. All comparisons proudly discarded.

Sabina and Lillian alone, innocent of knowledge, and innocent of other experiences. They remembered nothing before this hour: they were innocent of associations. They forgot what they had read in books, what they had seen in cafés, the laughter of men and the mocking participation of other women. Their individuality washed down and effaced the world: they stood at the beginning of everything, naked and innocent of the past.

They stood before the night which belonged to them as two women emerging out of sleep. They stood on the first steps of their timidity, of their faith, before the long night which belonged to them. Blameless of original sin, of literary sins, of the sin of premeditation.

Two women. Strangeness. All the webs of ideas blown away. New bodies, new souls, new minds, new words. They would create it all out of themselves, fashion their own reality. Innocence. No roots dangling into other days, other nights, other men or women. The potency of a new stare into the face of their desire and their fears.

Sabina's sudden timidity and Lillian's sudden awkwardness. Their fears. A great terror slashing through the room, cutting icily through them like a fallen sword. A new voice. Sabina's breathless and seeking to be lighter so as to touch the lightness of Lillian's voice like a breath now, an exhalation, almost a voicelessness because they were so frightened.

Sabina sat heavily on the edge of the bed, her earthly weight like roots sinking into the earth. Under the weight of her stare Lillian trembled.

Their bracelets tinkled.

The bracelets had given the signal. A signal like the first

tinkle of beads on a savage neck when they enter a dance. They took their bracelets off and put them on the table, side by side.

The light. Why was the light so still, like the suspense of their blood? Still with fear. Like their eyes. Shadeless eyes that dared neither open, nor close, nor melt.

The dresses. Sabina's dress rolled around her like long sea weed. She wanted to turn and drop it on the floor but her hands lifted it like a Bayadere lifting her skirt to dance and she lifted it over her head.

Sabina's eyes were like a forest; the darkness of a forest, a watchfulness behind ambushes. Fear. Lillian journeyed into the darkness of them, carrying her blue eyes into the red-brown ones. She walked from the place where her dress had fallen holding her breasts as if she expected to be mortally thrust.

Sabina loosened her hair and said: "You're so extraordinarily white." With a strange sadness, like a weight, she spoke, as if it were not the white substance of Lillian but the whiteness of her newness to life which Sabina seemed to sigh for. "You're so white, so white and smooth." And there were deep shadows in her eyes, shadows of one old with living: shadows in the neck, in her arms, on her knees, violet shadows.

Lillian wanted to reach out to her, into these violet shadows. She saw that Sabina wanted to be she as much as she wanted to be Sabina. They both wanted to exchange bodies, exchange faces. There was in both of them the dark strain of wanting to become the other, to deny what they were, to transcend their actual selves. Sabina desiring Lillian's newness, and Lillian desiring Sabina's deeply marked body.

Lillian drank the violet shadows, drank the imprint of others, the accumulation of other hours, other rooms, other odors, other caresses. How all the other loves clung to Sabina's body, even though her face denied this and her eyes repeated: I have forgotten all. How they made her heavy with the loss of herself, lost in the maze of her gifts. How the lies, the loves, the dreams, the obscenities, the fevers weighed down her body, and how Lillian wanted to become leadened with her, poisoned with her.

Sabina looked at the whiteness of Lillian's body as into a mirror and saw herself as a girl, standing at the beginning of her life unblurred, unmarked. She wanted to return to this early self. And Lillian wanted to enter the labyrinth of knowledge, to the very bottom of the violet wells.

Through the acrid forest of her being there was a vulnerable opening. Lillian trod into it lightly. Caresses of down, moth invasions, myrrh between the breasts, incense in their mouths. Tendrils of hair raising their heads to the wind in the finger tips, kisses curling within the conch-shell necks. Tendrils of hair bristling and between their closed lips a sigh.

"How soft you are, how soft you are," said Sabina.

They separated and saw it was not this they wanted, sought, dreamed. Not this the possession they imagined. No bodies touching would answer this mysterious craving in them to become each other. Not to possess each other but to become each other. Not to take, but to imbibe, absorb, change themselves. Sabina carried a part of Lillian's being, Lillian a part of Sabina, but they could not be exchanged through an embrace. It was not that.

Their bodies touched and then fell away, as if both of them had touched a mirror, their own image upon a mirror. They had felt the cold wall, they had felt the mirror that never appeared when they were taken by man. Sabina had merely touched her own youth, and Lillian her free passions.

As they lay there the dawn entered the room, a grey dawn which showed the dirt on the window panes, the crack in the table, the stains on the walls. Lillian and Sabina sat up as if the dawn had opened their eyes. Slowly they descended from dangerous heights, with the appearance of daylight and the weight of their fatigue.

With the dawn it was as if Jay had entered the room and were now lying between them. Every cell of their dream seemed to burst at once, with the doubt which had entered Lillian's mind.

If she had wanted so much to be Sabina so that Jay might love in her what he admired in Sabina, could it be that Sabina wanted of Lillian this that made Jay love her?

"I feel Jay in you," she said.

The taste of sacrilege came to both their mouths. The mouths he kissed. The women whose flavor he knew. The one man within two women. Jealousy, dormant all night; now lying at their side, between their caresses, slipping in between them like an enemy.

(Lillian, Lillian, if you arouse hatred between us, you break a magic alliance! He is not as aware of us as we are of each other. We have loved in each other all he has failed to love and see. Must we awake to the great destructiveness of rivalry, of war, when this night contained all that slipped between his fingers!)

But jealousy had stirred in Lillian's flesh. Doubt was hardening and crystallizing in Lillian, crystallizing her features, her eyes, tightening her mouth, stiffening her body. She shivered with cold, with the icy incision of this new day which was laying everything bare.

Bare eyes looking at each other with naked, knife-pointed questions.

To stare at each other they had to disentangle their hair, Sabina's long hair having curled around Lillian's neck.

Lillian left the bed. She took the bracelets and flung them out of the window.

"I know, I know," she said violently, "you wanted to blind me. If you won't confess, he will. It's Jay you love, not me. Get up. I don't want him to find us here together. And he thought we loved each other!"

"I do love you, Lillian."

"Don't you dare say it," shouted Lillian violently, all her being now craving wildly for complete devastation.

They both began to tremble.

Lillian was like a foaming sea, churning up wreckage, the debris of all her doubts and fears.

Their room was in darkness. Then came Jay's laughter, creamy and mould-breaking. In spite of the darkness Lillian could feel all the cells of his body alive in the night, vibrating with abundance. Every cell with a million eyes seeing in the dark.

"A fine dark night in which an artist might well be born," he said. "He must be born at night, you know, so that no one will notice that his parents gave him only seven months of human substance. No artist has the patience to remain nine months in the womb. He must run away from home. He is born with a mania to complete himself, to create himself. He is so multiple and amorphous that his central self is constantly falling apart and is only recomposed by his work. With his imagination he can flow into all the moulds, multiply and divide himself, and yet whatever he does, he will always be two."

"And require two wives?" asked Lillian.

"I need you terribly," he said.

Would the body of Sabina triumph over her greater love?

"There are many Sabinas in the world, but only one like you," said Jay.

How could he lie so close and know only what she chose to tell him, knowing nothing of her, of her secret terrors and fear of loss.

He was only for the joyous days, the days of courage, when she could share with him all the good things he brought with his passion for novelty and change.

But he knew nothing of her; he was no companion to her sadness. He could never imagine anyone else's mood, only his own. His own were so immense and loud, they filled his world and deafened him to all others. He was not concerned to know whether she could live or breathe within the dark caverns of his whale-like being, within the whale belly of his ego.

Somehow he had convinced her that this expansiveness was a sign of bigness. A big man could not belong to one person. He had merely overflowed into Sabina, out of over-richness.

106

And they would quarrel some day. Already he was saying: "I suspect that when Sabina gives one so many lies it is because she has nothing else to give but mystery, but fiction. Perhaps behind her mysteries there is nothing."

But how blinded he was by false mysteries! Because Sabina made such complicated tangles of everything—mixing personalities, identities, missing engagements, being always elsewhere than where she was expected to be, chaotic in her hours, elusive about her occupations, implying mystery and suspense even when she said goodbye . . . calling at dawn when everyone was asleep, and asleep when everyone else was awake. Jay with his indefatigable curiosity was easily engaged in unravelling the tangle, as if every tangle had a meaning, a mystery.

But Lillian knew, too, how quickly he could turn about and ridicule if he were cheated, as he often was, by his blind enthusiasms. How revengeful he became when the mysteries were false.

"If only Sabina would die," thought Lillian, "if she would only die. She does not love him as I do."

Anxiety oppressed her. Would he push everything into movement again, disperse her anxieties with his gaiety, carry her along in his reckless course?

Lillian's secret he did not detect: that of her fear. Once her secret had almost pierced through, once when Jay had stayed out all night. From her room she could see the large lights of the Boulevard Montparnasse blinking maliciously, Montparnasse which he loved and those lights, and the places where he so easily abandoned himself as he gave himself to everything that glittered,—rococo women, spluttering men in bars, anyone who smiled, beckoned, had a story to tell.

She had waited with the feeling that where her heart had been there was now a large hole; no heart or blood beating anymore but a drafty hole made by a precise and rather large bullet.

Merely because Jay was walking up and down Montparnasse

in one of his high drunken moods which had nothing to do with drink but with his insatiable thirst for new people, new smiles, new words, new stories.

Each time the white lights blinked she saw his merry smile in his full mouth, each time the red lights blinked she saw his cold blue eyes detached and mocking, annihilating the mouth in a daze of blue, iced gaiety. The eyes always cold, the mouth warm, the eyes mocking and the mouth always repairing the damage done. His eyes that would never turn inward and look into the regions of deep events, the regions of personal explorations: his eyes intent on not seeing discords or dissolutions, not seeing the missing words, the lost treasures, the wasted hours, the shreds of the dispersed self, the blind mobilities.

Not to see the dark night of the self his eyes rose frenziedly to the surface seeking in fast-moving panoramas merely the semblance of riches. . . .

"Instead of love there is appetite," thought Lillian. "He does not say: 'I love you,' but 'I need you.' Our life is crowded like a railroad station, like a circus. He does not feel things where I feel them: the heart is definitely absent. That's why mine is dying, it has ceased to pound tonight, it is being slowly killed by his hardness."

Away from him she could always say: he does not feel. But as soon as he appeared she was baffled. His presence carried such a physical glow that it passed for warmth. His voice was warm like the voice of feeling. His gestures were warm, his hands liked touch. He laid his hands often on human beings, and one might think it was love. But it was just a physical warmth, like the summer. It gave off heat like a chemical, but no more.

"He will die of hardness, and I from feeling too much. Even when people knock on the door I have a feeling they are not knocking on wood but on my heart. All the blows fall directly on my heart."

Even pleasure had its little stabs upon the heart. The perpetual heart-murmur of the sensibilities.

"I wish I could learn his secret. I would love to be able to go out for a whole night without feeling all the threads that bind me to him, feeling my love for him all around me like a chastity belt."

And now he was lying still on the breast of her immutable love and she had no immutable love upon which to lay her head, no one to return to at dawn.

He sat up lightly saying: "Oh, Sabina has no roots!"

"And I'm strangling in my roots," thought Lillian.

He had turned on the light to read now, and she saw his coat hugging the back of the chair, revealing in the shape of its shoulders the roguish spirit that had played in it. If she could only take the joys he gave her, his soft swagger, the rough touch of his coat, the effervescence of his voice when he said: that's good. Even his coat seemed to be stirring with his easy flowing life, even to his clothes he gave the imprint of his liveliness.

To stem his outflowing would be like stemming a river of life. She would not be the one to do it. When a man had decided within himself to live out every whim, every fancy, every impulse, it was a flood for which no Noah's Ark had ever been provided.

Lillian and Djuna were walking together over dead autumn leaves that crackled like paper. Lillian was weeping and Djuna was weeping with her and for her.

They were walking through the city as it sank into twilight and it was as if they were both going blind together with the bitterness of their tears. Through this blurred city they walked hazily and half lost, the light of a street lamp striking them now and then like a spotlight throwing into relief Lillian's

109

distorted mouth and the broken line of her neck where her head fell forward heavily.

The buses came upon them out of the dark, violently, with a deafening clatter, and they had to leap out of their way, only to continue stumbling through dark streets, crossing bridges, passing under heavy arcades, their feet unsteady on the uneven cobblestones as if they had both lost their sense of gravity.

Lillian's voice was plaintive and monotonous, like a lamentation. Her blue eyes wavered but always fixed on the ground as if the whole structure of her life lay there and she were watching its consummation.

Djuna was looking straight before her, through and beyond the dark, the lights, the traffic, beyond all the buildings. Eyes fixed, immobile like glass eyes, as if the curtain of tears had opened a new realm.

Lillian's phrases surged and heaved like a turgid sea. Unformed, unfinished, dense, heavy with repetitions, with recapitulations, with a baffled, confused bitterness and anger.

Djuna found nothing to answer, because Lillian was talking about God, the God she had sought in Jay.

"Because he had the genius," she said, "I wanted to serve him, I wanted to make him great. But he is treacherous, Djuna. I am more confused and lost now than before I knew him. It isn't only his betrayals with women, Djuna, it's that he sees no one as they are. He only adds to everyone's confusions. I put myself wholly in his hands. I wanted to serve someone who would create something wonderful, and I also thought he would help me to create myself. But he is destructive, and he is destroying me."

This seeking of man the guide in a dark city, this aimless wandering through the streets touching men and seeking the guide—this was a fear all women had known . . . seeking the guide in men, not in the past, or in mythology, but a guide with a living breath who might create one, help one to be born as a woman, a guide they wished to possess for themselves alone, in their own isolated woman's soul. The guide for

110

woman was still inextricably woven with man and with man's creation.

Lillian had thought that Jay would create her because he was the artist, that he would be able to see her as clearly as she had seen in him the great painter, but Jay's inconsistencies bewildered her. She had placed her own image in his hands for him to fashion: make of me a big woman, someone of value.

His own chaos had made this impossible.

"Lillian, no one should be entrusted with one's image to fashion, with one's self-creation. Women are moving from one circle to another, rising towards independence and self-creation. What you're really suffering from is from the pain of parting with your faith, with your old love when you wish to renew this faith and preserve the passion. You're being thrust out of one circle into another and it is this which causes you so much fear. You know you cannot lean on Jay, but you don't know what awaits you, and you don't trust your own awareness."

Lillian thought that she was weeping because Jay had said: Leave me alone, or let me work, or let me sleep.

"Oh, Lillian, it's such a struggle to emerge from the past clean of regrets and memories and of the desire to regress. No one can accept failure."

She wanted to take Lillian's hand and make her raise her head and lead her into a new circle, raise her above the pain and confusion, above the darkness of the present.

These sudden shafts of light upon them could not illumine where the circle of pain closed and ended and woman was raised into another circle. She could not help Lillian emerge out of the immediacy of her pain, leap beyond the stranglehold of the present.

And so they continued to walk unsteadily over what Lillian saw merely as the dead leaves of his indifference.

Jay and Lillian lived in the top floor studio of a house on the Rue Montsouris, on the edge of Montparnasse—a small street without issue lined with white cubistic villas.

When they gave a party the entire house opened its doors from the ground floor to the roof, since all the artists knew each other. The party would branch off into all the little street with its quiet gardens watched by flowered balconies.

The guests could also walk down the street to the Park Montsouris lake, climb on a boat and fancy themselves attending a Venetian feast.

First came the Chess Player, as lean, brown, polished, and wooden in his gestures as a chess piece; his features sharply carved and his mind set upon a perpetual game.

For him the floors of the rooms were large squares in which the problem was to move the people about by the right word. To control the temptation to point such a person to another he kept his hands in his pockets and used merely his eyes. If he were talking to someone his eyes would design a path in the air which his listener could not help but follow. His glance having caught the person he had selected made the invisible alliance in space and soon the three would find themselves on the one square until he chose to move away and leave them together.

What his game was no one knew, for he was content with the displacements and did not share in the developments. He would then stand in the corner of the room again and survey the movements with a semitone smile.

No one ever thought of displacing him, of introducing him to strangers.

But he thought it imperative to bring about an encounter between the bearded Irish architect and Djuna, because he had conceived a house for many moods, a house whose sliding panels made it one day very large for grandiose states of being, one day very small for intimate relationships. He had topped it with a removable ceiling which allowed the sky to play roof, and designed both a small spiral staircase for secret escapades

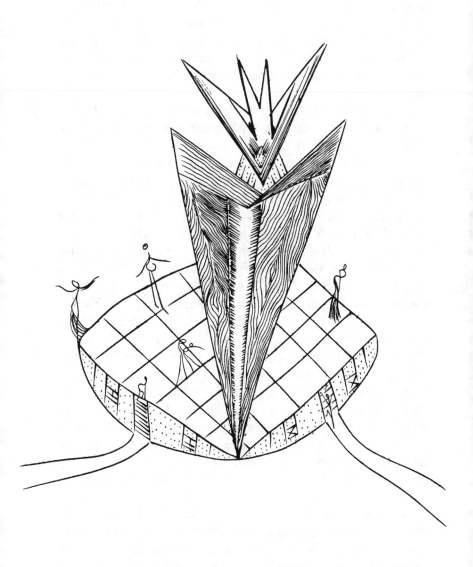

and a vast one for exhibitionism. Besides, it turned on a pivot to follow the changing whims of the sun, and who but Djuna should know this house which corresponded to her many moods, to her smiling masks and refusal to show her night face, her shadows and her darkness, she who turned on artificial pivots always towards the light, who was adept at sliding panels to make womb enclosures suitable to intimate confessions, and equally capable of opening them all at once to admit the entire world.

Djuna smiled at the Chess Player's accuracy, and he left them standing on the square while the Irish architect began with silken mouthfuls of words to design this house around Djuna as if he were spewing a cocoon and she would leave the party like a snail with a house built around her to the image of her needs. On her black dress he was drawing a blue print.

On this square something was being constructed and so the Chess Player moved on, his eyes made of the glass one could look through without being seen and now he seized upon Faustin, the Zombie, the one who had died under the first blow struck at him by experience. Most of those who die like this in the middle of their life await a resuscitation, but Faustin awaited nothing: every line of his body sagged with acceptance, the growing weight of his flesh cushioned inertia, submission. The blood no longer circulated and one could see the crystal formations of fear and stagnation as in those species of fish living in the deepest waters without eyes, ears, fins, motion, shaped like loaves of bread, nourishing themselves through static cells of the skin. His one obsession was not to free himself of his death but to stand like a black sentinel at the gate and prevent others escaping from their traps. He lived among the artists, the rebels, never acquiescing in their rebellions, but waiting for the moment of Jay's fullest sunburst of enthusiasm to puncture it with irony, waiting for Lillian's wildest explosions to shame her as an exhibitionist, watching for Djuna's blurred absences from reality to point out her delinquencies from the present. His very expression set the stage for the murder; he had a way of bearing himself which was like the summation of all the prohibitions: do not trespass, do not smoke, do not spit, do not lean out of the window, no thoroughfare, do not speed.

With his black eyes and pale face set for homicide he waited in a corner. Wherever he was, a black moth would enter the room and begin its flights of mourning, black-gloved, black-creped, black-soled, inseminating the white walls with future sadnesses. The silence which followed his words clearly marked the withering effect of them and the time it took for the soil to bloom again. Always at midnight he left, following a rigid compulsion, and the Chess Player knew he must act hastily if he were going to exploit the Zombie's death rays and test their effect upon the living.

He walked the Zombie towards the fullest bloom of all, towards the camellia face of Sabina which opened at a party like the crowned prize-winner of the flower shows and gave every man the sensation he held the tip of a breast in his teeth. Would Sabina's face close when the shadow of Faustin fell across it, when the black moth words and the monotonous voice fell upon her ears curtained intricately by her anarchic hair?

She merely turned her face away: she was too richly nourished with pollen, seeds and sap to wither before any man, even a dead one. Too much love and desire had flown through the curves of her body, too many sighs, whispers, lay folded in the cells of her skin. Through the many rivers of her veins too much pleasure had coursed; she was immune.

Faustin the Zombie felt bitterly defeated, for he loved to walk in the traces of Jay's large patterns and collect his discarded mistresses. He loved to live Jay's discarded lives, like a man accepting a second-hand coat. There was always a little warmth left in them.

From the moment of his defeat, he ceased to attend the Party, even in his role of zombie, and the Chess Player whose role it was to see that the Party was attended at all cost, even at the cost of pretending, was disturbed to see this shadowy figure walking now always between the squares, carefully setting his foot on that rim of Saturn, the rim of nowhere which surrounds all definite places. One fallen piece.

The Chess Player's eyes fell on Djuna but she had escaped all seizure by dissolving into the music. This was a game he could not play: giving yourself. Djuna gave herself in the most unexpected ways. She lived in the cities of the interior, she had no permanent abode. She was always arriving and leaving undetected, as through a series of trap doors. The life she led there no one knew anything about. It never reached the ears of reporters. The statisticians of facts could never interview her. Then unexpectedly, in a public place, in a concert hall, a dance hall, at a lecture, at a party, she gave the immodest spectacle of her abandon to Stravinsky, her body's tense identification with the dancer, or revealed a passionate interest in the study of phosphenes.

And now she sat very neatly shaped in the very outline of the guitar played by Rango, her body tuned by the keys of her fingers as if Rango were playing on the strands of her hair, of her nerves, and the black notes were issuing from the black pupils of her eyes.

At least she could be considered as attending the party: her eyes were not closed, as they had been a half hour earlier when she was telling the Chess Player about phosphenes: phosphenes are the luminous impressions and circles seen with the eyelids closed, after the sudden compression of the eyeball. "Try it!"

The guitar distilled its music. Rango played it with the warm sienna color of his skin, with the charcoal pupil of his eyes, with the underbrush thickness of his black eyebrows, pouring into the honey-colored box the flavors of the open road on which he lived his gypsy life: thyme, rosemary, oregano, marjoram and sage. Pouring into the resonant sound-box the sensual swing of his hammock hung across the gypsy-cart and the dreams born on his mattress of black horsehair.

Idol of the night clubs, where men and women barred the doors and windows, lit candles, drank alcohol, and drank from his voice and his guitar the potions and herbs of the open road, the charivaris of freedom, the drugs of leisure and laziness, the maypole dance of the fireflies, the horse's neighing fanfaronade, the fandangoes and ridottos of sudden lusts.

Shrunken breasts, vacillating eyes, hibernating virilities, all drank out of Rango's guitar and sienna voice. At dawn, not content with the life transfusion through cat guts, filled with the sap of his voice which had passed into their veins, at dawn the women laid hands upon his body like a tree. But at dawn Rango swung his guitar over his shoulder and walked away.

Will you be here tomorrow, Rango?

Tomorrow he might be playing and singing to his black horse's philosophically swaying tail on the road to the south of France.

Now arrived a very drunken Jay with his shoal of friends: five pairs of eyes wide open and vacant, five men wagging their heads with felicity because they are five. One a Chinese poet, tributary of Lao Tze; one Viennese poet, echo of Rilke; Hans the painter derived from Paul Klee; an Irish writer feebly stemming from Joyce. What they will become in the future does not concern them: at the present moment they are five praising each other and they feel strong and they are tottering with felicity.

They had had dinner at the Chinese restaurant, a rice without salt and meat with tough veins, but because of the shoal beatitude Jay proclaimed he had never eaten such rice, and five minutes later forgetting himself he said: "Rice is for the dogs!" The Chinese poet was hurt, his eyelids dropped humbly.

Now as they walked up the stairs he explained in neat phrases the faithfulness of the Chinese wife and Jay foamed with amazement: oh, such beautiful faithfulness!—he would marry a Chinese woman. Then the Chinese poet added: In China all tables are square. Jay almost wept with delight at this, it was the sign of a great civilization. He leaned over perilously and said with intimate secretiveness: In New Jersey when I was a boy tables were always round; I always hated round tables.

117

Their feet were not constructed for ascensions at the present moment; they might as well remain midway and call at Soutine's studio.

On the round stairway they collided with Stella susurrating in a tafetta skirt and eating fried potatoes out of a paper bag. Her long hair swayed as if she sat on a child's swing.

Her engaging gestures had lassoed an artist known for his compulsion to exhibit himself unreservedly, but he was not yet drunk enough and was for the moment content with strumming on his belt. Stella, not knowing what spectacle was reserved for her in his imagination, took the offering pose of women in Florentine paintings, extending the right hip like a holy water stand, both hands open as if inviting pigeons to eat from her palms, stylized, liturgical, arousing in Manuel the same impulse which had once made him set fire to a ballet skirt with a cigarette.

But Manuel was displaced by a figure who moved with stately politeness, his long hair patined with brilliantine, his face set in large and noble features by the men who carved the marble faces in the hall of fame.

He bowed graciously over women's hands with the ritualistic deliberateness of a Pope. His decrees, issued with handkissing, with soothing opening and closing of doors, extending of chairs, were nevertheless fatal: he held full power of decision over the delicate verdict: is it tomorrow's art?

No one could advance without his visa. He gave the passports to the future. Advance . . . or else: My dear man, you are a mere echo of the past.

Stella felt his handkissing charged with irony, felt herself installed in a museum *not* of modern art—blushed. To look at her in this ironic manner while scrupulously adhering to medieval salutations this man must know that she was one to keep faded flowers.

For he passed on with royal detachment and gazed seriously for relief at the steel and wood mobiles turning gently in the breeze of the future, like small structures of nerves vibrating in the air without their covering of flesh, the new cages of our future sorrows, so abstract they could not even contain a sob.

Jay was swimming against the compact stream of visitors looking for re-enforcement to pull out the Chinese poet who had stumbled into a very large garbage can in the front yard, and who was neatly folded in two, severely injured in his dignity. But he was arrested on his errand by the sight of Sabina and he thought why are there women in whom the sediment of experience settles and creates such a high flavor that when he had taken her he had also possessed all the unexplored regions of the world he had wanted to know, the men and women he would never have dared to encounter. Women whose bodies were a labyrinth so that when he was lying beside her he had felt he was taking a journey through the ancient gorge where Paracelsus dipped his sick people in fishing nets into lukewarm water, like a journey back into the womb, and he had seen several hundred feet above his head the little opening in the cathedral archway of the rocks through which the sun gleamed like a knife of gold.

But too late now to dwell on the panoramic, great voyage flavors of Sabina's body: the Chinese poet must be saved.

At this moment Sabina intercepted a look of tenderness between Jay and Lillian, a tenderness he had never shown her. The glance with which Lillian answered him was thrown around him very much like a safety net for a trapezist, and Sabina saw how Jay, in his wildest leaps, never leaped out of range of the net of protectiveness extended by Lillian.

The Chess Player noted with a frown that Sabina picked up her cape and made her way to the imitation Italian balcony. She was making a gradual escape; from the balcony to balcony, she would break the friendly efforts made to detain her, and reach the exit. He could not allow this to go on, at a Party everyone should pursue nothing but his individual drama. Because Lillian and Jay had stood for a moment on the same square and Sabina had caught Jay leaping spuriously into the safety net of Lillian's protectiveness, now Sabina acted like one pierced by a knife and left the game for a balcony.

Where she stood now the noises of the Party could not reach her. She heard the wind and rain rushing through the trees like the lamentation of reeds in shallow tropical waters.

Sabina was lost.

The broken compass which inhabited her and whose wild fluctuations she had always obeyed, making for tumult and motion in place of direction, was suddenly fractured so that she no longer knew the relief of tides, ebbs and flows and dispersions.

She felt lost.

The dispersion had become too vast, too extended. For the first time a shaft of pain appeared cutting through the nebulous pattern. Pain lies only in reflection, in awareness. Sabina had moved so fast that all pain had passed swiftly as through a sieve, leaving a sorrow like children's sorrows, soon forgotten, soon replaced by a new interest. She had never known a pause.

And suddenly in this balcony, she felt alone.

Her cape, which was more than a cape, which was a sail, which was the feelings she threw to the four winds to be swelled and swept by the wind in motion, lay becalmed.

Her dress was becalmed.

It was as if now she wore nothing that the wind could catch, swell and propel.

For Sabina, to be becalmed meant to die.

Jealousy had entered her body and refused to run through it like sand through an hourglass. The silvery holes of her sieve against sorrow granted her at birth through which everything passed through and out painlessly, had clogged. Now the pain had lodged itself inside of her.

She had lost herself somewhere along the frontier between her inventions, her stories, her fantasies, and her true self. The boundaries had become effaced, the tracks lost, she had walked into pure chaos, and not a chaos which carried her like the wild gallopings of romantic riders in operas and legends, but a cavalcade which suddenly revealed the stage prop: a papier-mâché horse.

120

She had lost her boat, her sails, her cape, her horse, her seven-league boots, and all of them at once, leaving her stranded on a balcony, among dwarfed trees, diminished clouds, a miserly rainfall.

In the semi-darkness of that winter evening, her eyes were blurred. And then as if all the energy and warmth had been drawn inward for the first time, killing the senses, the ears, the touch, the palate, all movements of the body, all its external ways of communicating with the exterior, she suddenly felt a little deaf, a little blind, a little paralyzed; as if life, in coiling upon itself into a smaller, slower inward rhythm, were thinning her blood.

She shivered, with the same tremor as the leaves, feeling for the first time some small withered leaves of her being detaching themselves.

The Chess Player placed two people on a square.

As they danced a magnet pulled her hair and his together, and when they pulled their heads away, the magnet pulled their mouths together and when they separated the mouths, the magnet clasped their hands together and when they unclasped the hands their hips were soldered. There was no escape. When they stood completely apart then her voice spiralled around his, and his eyes were caught in the net grillage which barred her breasts.

They danced off the square and walked into a balcony.

Mouth meeting mouth, and pleasure striking like a gong, once, twice, thrice, like the beating wings of large birds. The bodies traversed by a rainbow of pleasure.

By the mouth they flowed into each other, and the little grey street ceased to be an impasse in Montparnasse. The balcony was now suspended over the Mediterranean, the Aegean sea, the Italian lakes, and through the mouth they flowed and coursed through the world.

While on the wall of the studio there continued to hang a large painting of a desert in smoke colors, a desert which parched the throat. Imbedded in the sand many little bleached bones of lovelessness.

"The encounter of two is pure, in two there is some hope of truth," said the Chess Player catching the long floating hair of Stella as she passed and confronting her with a potential lover.

Behind Stella hangs a painting of a woman with a white halo around her head. Anxiety had carved diamond holes through her body and her airiness came from this punctured faith through which serenity had flown out.

What Stella gave now was only little pieces of herself, pieces carefully painted in the form of black circles of wit, squares of yellow politeness, triangles of blue friendliness, or the mock orange of love: desire. Only little pieces from her external armor. What she gave now was a self which a man could only carry across the threshold of an abstract house with only one window on the street and this street a desert- with little white bones bleaching in the sun.

Deserts of mistrust.

The houses are no longer hearths, they hang like mobiles turning to the changing breeze while they love each other like ice skaters on the top layers of their invented selves, blinded with the dust of attic memories, within the windowless houses of their fears.

The guests hang their coats upon a fragile structure like the bar upon which ballet dancers test their limb's wit.

The Party spreads like an uneasy octopus that can no longer draw in his tentacles to seize and strangle the core of its destructiveness.

In each studio there is a human being dressed in the full regalia of his myth fearing to expose a vulnerable opening, spreading not his charms but his defences, plotting to disrobe, somewhere along the night—his body without the aperture of the heart or his heart with a door closed to his body. Thus keeping one compartment for refuge, one uninvaded cell.

And if you feel a little compressed, a little cramped in your daily world, you can take a walk through a Chirico painting. The houses have only facades, so escape is assured; the colonnades, the volutes, valances extend into the future and you can walk into space.

The painters peopled the world with a new variety of fruit and tree to surprise you with the bitterness of what was known for its sweetness and the sweetness of what was known for its bitterness, for they all deny the world as it is and take you back to the settings and scenes of your dreams. You slip out of a Party into the past or the future.

This meandering led the Chess Player to stray from his geometrical duties, and he was not able to prevent a suicide. It was Lillian who stood alone on a square; Lillian who had begun the evening like an African dancer donning not only all of her Mexican silver jewelry but a dress of emerald green of a starched material which had a bristling quality like her mood.

She had moved from one to another with gestures of her hands inciting others to foam, to dance. She teased them out of their nonchalance or detachment. People would awaken from their lethargies as in a thunderstorm; stand, move, ignite, catching her motions, her hands beating a meringue of voices, a soufflé of excitement. When they were ready to follow her into some kind of tribal dance, she left them, to fall again into limpness or to walk behind her enslaved, seeking another electrical charge.

She could not even wait for the end of the Party to commit her daily act of destruction. So she stood alone in her square defended by her own bristles and began: "No one is paying any attention to me. I should not have worn this green dress: it's too loud. I've just said the wrong thing to Brancusi. All these people have accomplished something and I have not. They put me in a panic. They are all so strong and so sure of themselves. I feel exactly as I did in my dream last night: I had been asked to play at a concert. There were so many people. When I went to play, the piano had no notes, it was a lake, and I tried to play on the water and no sound came. I felt defeated and humiliated. I hate the way my hair gets wild. Look at Stella's hair so smooth and clinging to her face. Why did I tease her? She looked so tremulous, so frightened, as if pleading not to be hurt. Why do I rush and speak before thinking? My dress is too short."

In this invisible hara-kiri she tore off her dress, her jewels, tore off every word she had uttered, every smile, every act of the evening. She was ashamed of her talk, of her silences, of what she had given, and of what she had not given, to have confided and not to have confided.

And now it was done. A complete house-wrecking service. Every word, smile, act, silver jewel, lying on the floor, with the emerald green dress, and even Djuna's image of Lillian to which she had often turned for comfort, that too lay shattered on the ground. Nothing to salvage. A mere pile of flaws. A little pile of ashes from a bonfire of self-criticism.

The Chess Player saw a woman crumpling down on a couch as if her inner frame had collapsed, smiled at her drunkenness and took no note of the internal suicide.

Came the grey-haired man who makes bottles, Lawrence Vail, saying: "I still occasionally and quite frequently and very perpetually empty a bottle. This is apt to give one a guilty feeling. Is it not possible I moaned and mooned that I have neglected the exterior (of the bottle) for the interior (of the bottle)? Why cast away empty bottles? The spirits in the bottle are not necessarily the spirit of the bottle. The spirit of the spirits of the bottle are potent, potential substances that should not be discarded, eliminated in spleen, plumbing and hangover. Why not exteriorize these spirits on the body of the bottle. . . ."

The Chess Player saw it was going to happen.

He saw Djuna slipping off one of the squares and said: "Come here! Hold hands with Jay's warm winey white-trash friends. It is too early in the evening for you to be slipping off."

Djuna gave him a glance of despair, as one does before falling.

She knew it was now going to happen.

This dreaded mood which came, warning her by dimming the lights, muffling the sounds, effacing the faces as in great

124

snowstorms.

She would be inside of the Party as inside a colored ball, being swung by red ribbons, swayed by indigo music. All the objects of the Fair around her—the red wheels, the swift chariots, the dancing animals, the puppet shows, the swinging trapezes, words and faces swinging, red suns bursting, birds singing, ribbons of laughter floating and catching her, teasing hands rustling in her hair, the movements of the dance like all the motions of love: taking, bending, yielding, welding and unwelding, all the pleasures of collisions, every human being opening the cells of his gaiety.

And then wires would be cut, lights grow dim, sounds muffled, colors paled.

At this moment, like the last message received through her inner wireless from the earth, she always remembered this scene: she was sixteen years old. She stood in a dark room brushing her hair. It was a summer night. She was wearing her nightgown. She leaned out of the window to watch a party taking place across the way.

The men and women were dressed in rutilant festive colors she had never seen before, or was she dressing them with the intense light of her own dreaming, for she saw their gaiety, their relation to each other as something unparallelled in splendor. That night she yearned so deeply for this unattainable party, fearing she would never attend it, or else that if she did she would not be dressed in those heightened colors, she would not be so shining, so free. She saw herself attending but invisible, made invisible by timidity.

Now when she had reached this Party, where she had been visible and desired, a new danger threatened her: a mood which came and carried her off like an abductor, back into darkness.

This mood was always provoked by a phrase out of a dream: "This is not the place."

(What place? Was it the first party she wanted and none other, the one painted out of the darkness of her solitude?)

The second phrase would follow: "He is not the one."

Fatal phrase, like a black magic potion which annihilated the present. Instantly she was outside, locked out, thrust out by no one but herself, by a mood which cut her off from fraternity.

Merely by wishing to be elsewhere, where it might be more marvelous, made the near, the palpable seem then like an obstruction, a delay to the more marvelous place awaiting her, the more wonderful personage kept waiting. The present was murdered by this insistent, whispering, interfering dream, this invisible map constantly pointing to unexplored countries, a compass pointing to mirage.

But as quickly as she was deprived of ears, eyes, touch and placed adrift in space, as quickly as warm contact broke, she was granted another kind of ear, eye, touch, and contact.

She no longer saw the Chess Player as made of wood directed by a delicate geometric inner apparatus, as everyone saw him. She saw him before his crystallization, saw the incident which alchemized him into wood, into a chess player of geometric patterns. There, where a blighted love had made its first incision and the blood had turned to tree sap to become wood and move with geometric carefulness, there she placed her words calling to his warmth before it had congealed.

But the Chess Player was irritated. He addressed a man he did not recognize.

From the glass bastions of her city of the interior she could see all the excrescences, deformities, disguises, but as she moved among their hidden selves she incurred great angers.

"You demand we shed our greatest protections!"

"I demand nothing. I wanted to attend a Party. But the Party had dissolved in this strange acid of awareness which only dissolves the callouses, and I see the beginning."

"Stand on your square," said the Chess Player. "I shall bring you someone who will make you dance."

"Bring me one who will rescue me! Am I dreaming or dying? Bring me one who knows that between the dream and death there is only one frail step, one who senses that between this murder of the present by a dream, and death, there is only one shallow breath. Bring me one who knows that the dream with-out exit, without explosion, without awakening, is the passage-way to the world of the dead! I want my dress torn and stained!"

A drunken man came up to her with a chair. Of all the chairs in the entire house he had selected a gold one with a red brocade top.

Why couldn't he bring me an ordinary chair?

To single her out for this hierarchic offering was to con-demn her.

Now it was going to happen, inevitably.

The night and the Party had barely begun and she was being whisked away on a gold chair with a red brocade top by an abductor who would carry her back to the dark room of her adolescence, to the long white nightgown and hair brush, and to dream of a Party that she could never attend.

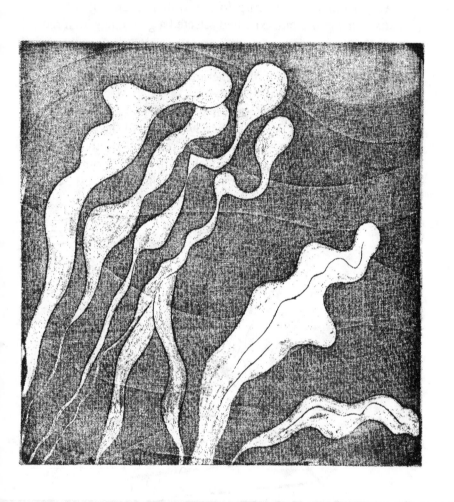

Children
of the Albatross

The Sealed Room

STEPPING OFF THE BUS at Montmartre Djuna arrived in the center of the ambulant Fair and precisely at the moment when she set her right foot down on the cobblestones the music of the merry-go-round was unleashed from its mechanical box and she felt the whole scene, her mood, her body, transformed by its gaiety exactly as in her childhood her life in the orphan asylum had been suddenly transformed from a heavy nightmare to freedom by her winning of a dance scholarship.

As if, because of so many obstacles her childhood and adolescence had been painful, heavy walking on crutches and had suddenly changed overnight into a dance in which she discovered the air, space and the lightness of her own nature.

Her life was thus divided into two parts: the bare, the pedestrian one of her childhood, with poverty weighing her feet, and then the day when her interior monologue set to music led her feet into the dance.

Pointing her toe towards the floor she would always think: I danced my way out of the asylum, out of poverty, out of my past.

She remembered her feet on the bare floor of their first apartment. She remembered her feet on the linoleum of the orphan asylum. She remembered her feet going up and down the stairs of the home where she had been "adopted" and had suffered her jealousy of the affection bestowed on the legitimate children. She remembered her feet running away from that house.

She remembered her square-toed lusterless shoes, her mended stockings, and her hunger for new and shining shoes in shop windows.

She remembered the calluses on her feet from house work, from posing for painters, from working as a mannequin, from cold, from clumsy mendings and from ill-fitting shoes.

She remembered the day that her dreaming broke into singing, and became a monologue set to music, the day when the dreams became a miniature opera shutting out the harsh or dissonant sounds of the world.

She remembered the day when her feet became restless in their prison of lusterless leather and they began to vibrate in obedience to inner harmonizations, when she kicked off her shoes and as she moved her worn dress cracked under her arms and her skirt slit at the knees.

The flow of images set to music had descended from her head to her feet and she ceased to feel as one who had been split into two pieces by some great invisible saber cut.

In the external world she was the woman who had submitted to mysterious outer fatalities beyond her power to alter, and in her interior world she was a woman who had built many tunnels deeper down where no one could reach her, in which she deposited her treasures safe from destruction and in which she built a world exactly the opposite of the one she knew.

But at the moment of dancing a fusion took place, a welding, a wholeness. The cut in the middle of her body healed, and she was all one woman moving.

Lifted and impelled by an inner rhythm, with a music box playing inside her head, her foot lifted from drabness and immobility, from the swamps and miasmas of poverty, carried her across continents and oceans, depositing her on the cobblestones of a Paris square on the day of the Fair, among shimmering colored tents, the flags of pleasure at full mast, the merry-go-rounds turning like dervish dancers.

She walked to a side street, knocked on a dark doorway opened by a disheveled concierge and ran down the stairway to a vast underground room.

As she came down the stairway she could already hear the piano, feet stamping, and the ballet master's voice. When the piano stopped there was always his voice scolding, and the whispering of smaller voices.

Sometimes as she entered the class was dissolving, and a flurry of little girls brushed by her in their moth ballet costumes, the little girls from the Opera, laughing and whispering, fluttering like moths on their dusty ballet slippers, flurries of snow in the darkness of the vast room, with drops of dew from exertion.

Djuna went down with them along the corridors to the dressing rooms which at first looked like a garden, with the puffed white giant daisies of ballet skirts, the nasturtiums and poppies of Spanish skirts, the roses of cotton, the sunflowers, the spider webs of hair nets.

The small dressing room overflowed with the smell of cold cream, face powder, and cheap cologne, with the wild confusion of laughter, confessions from the girls, with old dancing slippers, faded flowers and withering tulle.

132

As soon as Djuna cast off her city clothes it was the trepidating moment of metamorphosis.

The piano slightly out of tune, the floor's vibrations, the odor of perspiration swelled the mood of excitement born in this garden of costumes to the accompaniment of whisperings and laughter.

When she extended her leg at the bar, the ballet master placed his hand on it as if to guide the accuracy of her pointed toe.

He was a slender, erect, stylized man of forty, not handsome in face; only in attitudes and gestures. His face was undefined, his features blurred. It was as if the dance were a sculptor who had taken hold of him and had carved style, form, elegance out of all his movements, but left the face unimportant.

She always felt his hand exceptionally warm whenever he placed it on her to guide, to correct, improve or change a gesture.

When he placed his hand on her ankle she became intensely aware of her ankle, as if he were the magician who caused the blood to flow through it; when he placed his hand on her waist she became intensely aware of her waist as if he were the sculptor who indented it.

When his hand gave the signal to dance then it was not only as if he had carved the form of her body and released the course of her blood but as if his hand had made the co-ordination between blood and gestures and form, and the *leçon de danse* became a lesson in living.

So she obeyed, she danced, she was flexible and yielding in his hands, plying her body, disciplining it, awakening it.

It became gradually apparent that she was the favorite. She was the only one at whom he did not shout while she was dressing. He was more elated at her progress, and less harsh about her faults.

She obeyed his hands, but he found it more imperative than with other pupils to guide her by touch or by tender inflections of his voice.

He gave of his own movements as if he knew her movements would be better if he made them with her.

The dance gained in perfection, a perfection born of an accord between their gestures; born of her submission and his domination.

When he was tired she danced less well. When his attention was fixed on her she danced magnificently.

The little girls of the ballet troupe, mature in this experience, whispered and giggled: you are the favorite!

Yet not for a moment did he become for her a man. He was the ballet master. If he ruled her body with this magnetic rulership, a physical prestige, it was as a master of her dancing for the purpose of the dance.

But one day after the lessons, when the little girls from the Opera had left and there still hung in the air only an echo of the silk, flurry, snow and patter of activities, he followed her into the dressing room.

She had not yet taken off the voluminous skirt of the dance, the full-blown petticoat, the tight-fitting panties, so that when he entered the dressing room it seemed like a continuation of the dance. A continuation of the dance when he approached her and bent one knee in gallant salutation, and put his arms around her skirt that swelled like a huge flower. She laid her hand on his head like a queen acknowledging his worship. He remained on one knee while the skirt like a full-blown flower opened to allow a kiss to be placed at the core.

A kiss enclosed in the corolla of the skirt and hidden away, then he returned to the studio to speak with the pianist, to tell her at what time to come the next day, and to pay her, while Djuna dressed, covering warmth, covering her tremor, covering her fears.

He was waiting for her at the door, neat and trim.

He said: "Why don't you come and sit at the café with me?"

She followed him. Not far from there was the Place Clichy, always animated but more so now as the site of the Fair.

The merry-go-rounds were turning swiftly. The gypsies were

reading fortunes in little booths hung with Arabian rugs.

Workmen were shooting clay pigeons and winning cut-glass dishes for their wives.

The prostitutes were enjoying their watchful promenades, and the men their loitering.

The ballet master was talking to her: "Djuna (and suddenly as he said her name, she felt again where he had deposited his tribute), I am a simple man. My parents were shoemakers in a little village down south. I was put to work as a boy in an iron factory where I handled heavy things and was on the way to becoming deformed by big muscles. But during my lunch hour I danced. I wanted to be a ballet dancer, and I practiced at one of the iron bars in front of a big furnace. And today— look!" He handed her a cigarette case all engraved with names of famous ballet dancers. "Today," he said proudly, "I have been the partner of all these women. If you would come with me, we could be happy. I am a simple man, but we could dance in all the cities of Europe. I am no longer young but I have a lot of dancing in me still. We could be happy. . . ."

The merry-go-round turned and her feelings with it, riding again the wooden horses of her childhood in the park, which was so much like flying, riding around from city to city reaching eagerly for the prizes, for bouquets, for clippings, for fame, flinging all of one's secret desires for pleasure on the outside like a red shawl, with this joyous music at the center always, the body recovered, the body dancing. (Hadn't she been the woman in quest of her body once lost by a shattering blow— submerged, and now floating again on the surface where un- crippled human beings lived in a world of pleasure like the Fair?)

How to explain to this simple man, how to explain? *There is something broken inside of me.* I cannot dance, live, love as easily as others. Surely enough, if we traveled around the world, I would break my leg somewhere. Because this inner break is invisible and unconvincing to others, I would not rest until I had broken something for everyone to see, to understand. How to explain to this simple man, I could dance continuously with success, without breaking. *I am the dancer who falls,* always, into traps of depression, breaking my heart and my body almost at every turn, losing my tempo and my lightness, falling out of groups, out of grace, out of perfection. There is too often something wrong. Something you cannot help me with. . . . Supposing we found ourselves in a strange country, in a strange hotel. You are alone in a hotel room. Well, what of that? You can talk to the bar man, or you can sit before your glass of beer and read the papers. Everything is simple. But when I am alone in a hotel room something happens to me at times which must be what happens to children when the lights are turned out. Animals and children. But the animals howl their solitude, and children can call for their parents and for lights. But I. . . .

"What a long time it takes you to answer me," said the ballet master.

"I'm not strong enough," said Djuna.

"That's what I thought when I first saw you. I thought you couldn't take the discipline of a dancer's life. But it isn't so. You look fragile and all that, but you're healthy. I can tell healthy women by their skin. Yours is shining and clear. No, I don't think you have the strength of a horse, you're what we call *'une petite nature.'* But you have energy and guts. And we'll take it easy on the road."

In the middle of a piece of music the merry-go-round suddenly stopped. Something had gone wrong with the motor! The horses slowed down their pace. The children lost their hilarity. The boss looked troubled, and the mechanic was called and like a doctor came with his bag.

The Fair lost its spinning frenzy.

When the music stopped, one could hear the dry shots of the amateur hunters and the clay pigeons falling behind the cardboard walls.

136

The dreams which Djuna had started to weave in the asylum as if they were the one net in which she could exist, leaping thus always out of reach of unbearable happenings and creating her own events parallel to the ones her feelings could not accept, the dreams which gave birth to worlds within worlds, which, begun at night when she was asleep, continued during the day as an accompaniment to acts which she now discovered were rendered ineffectual by this defensive activity, with time became more and more violent.

For at first the personages of the dream, the cities which sprang up, were distinct and bore no resemblance to reality. They were images which filled her head with the vapors of fever, a drug-like panorama of incidents which rendered her insensible to cold, hunger and fatigue.

The day her mother was taken to the hospital to die, the day her brother was injured while playing in the street and developed a gentle insanity, the day at the asylum when she fell under the tyranny of the only man in the place, were days when she noted an intensification of her other world.

She could still weep at these happenings, but as people might lament just before they go under an anesthetic. "It still hurts," says the voice as the anesthetic begins to take effect and the pain growing duller, the body complaining more out of a mere remembrance of pain, automatically, just before sinking into a void.

She even found a way to master her weeping.

No mirrors were allowed in the orphan asylum, but girls had made one by placing black paper behind one of the small windows. Once a week they set it up and took turns looking at their faces.

Djuna's first glimpse of her adolescent face was in this black mirror, where the clear coloring of her skin was as if touched with mourning, as if reflected at the bottom of a well.

Even long afterwards it was difficult for her to overcome this first impression of her face painted upon black still waters.

But she discovered that if she was weeping, and she looked

at the weeping in a mirror, the weeping stopped. It ceased to be her own. It belonged to another.

Henceforth she possessed this power: whatever emotion would ravish or torment her, she could bring it before a mirror, look at it, and separate herself from it. And she thought she had found a way to master sorrow.

There was a boy of her age who passed under her window and who had the power to move her. He had a lean, eager face, eyes which seemed liquid with tenderness, and his gestures were full of gentleness.

His passage had the power to make her happy or unhappy, warm or cold, rich or poor. Whether he walked abstractedly on the other side of the street or on her side, whether he looked up at her window or forgot to look up, determined the mood of her day.

Because of his manner, she felt she trusted him entirely, that if he should come to the door and ask her to follow him she would do so without hesitation.

In her dreams at night she dissolved in his presence, lost herself in him. Her feelings for him were the opposite of an almost continuous and painful tension whose origin she did not know.

In contrast to this total submission to the unknown boy's gentleness, her first encounter with man was marked with defiance, fear, hostility.

The man, called the Watchman by the girls, was about forty years old when Djuna was sixteen. He was possessed of unlimited power because he was the lover of the Directress. His main attribute was power. He was the only man in the asylum, and he could deal privileges, gifts, and give permissions to go out at night.

This unique role gave him a high prestige. He was polite, carried himself with confidence, and was handsome in a neutral way which adapted him easily to any kind of image the orphans wished to fashion of him.

He could pass for the tall man, the brown-haired man, the

138

blond man; given a little leeway, he answered all the descriptions of gypsy card readers.

An added piquancy was attained by the common knowledge that he was the favorite of the Directress, who was very much hated. In winning his favor, one struck indirect blows at her authority, and achieved a subtle revenge for her severity.

The girls thought of him as possessing an even greater power than hers, for she who submitted to no one, had often been seen bowing her head before his reproaches.

The one he chose felt endowed immediately with greater beauty, greater charm and power than the other girls. He was appointed the arbiter, the connoisseur, the bestower of decorations.

To be chosen by the Watchman was to enter the realm of protection. No girl could resist this.

Djuna could distinguish his steps at a great distance. It seemed to her that he walked more evenly than anyone she knew, evenly and without stops or change of rhythm. He advanced through the hallways inexorably. Other people could be stopped, or eluded. But his steps were those of absolute authority.

He knew at what time Djuna would be passing through this particular hallway alone. He always came up to her, not a yard away, but exactly beside her.

His glance was always leveled at her breasts, and two things would happen simultaneously: he would offer her a present without looking at her face, as if he were offering it to her breasts, and then he would whisper: "Tonight I will let you out if you are good to me."

And Djuna would think of the boy who passed by under her window, and feel a wild beating of her heart at the possibility of meeting him outside, of talking to him, and her longing for the boy, for the warm liquid tenderness of his eyes was so violent that no sacrifice seemed too great—her longing and her feeling that if he knew of this scene, he would rescue her, but that there was no other way to reach him, no other way to defeat authority to reach him than by this concession to authority.

In this barter there was no question of rebellion. The way the Watchman stood, demanded, gestured, was all part of a will she did not even question, a continuation of the will of the father. There was the man who demanded, and outside was the gentle boy who demanded nothing, and to whom she wanted to give everything, whose silence even, she trusted, whose way of walking she trusted with her entire heart, while this man she did not trust.

It was the *droit du seigneur*.

She slipped the Watchman's bracelet around the lusterless cotton of her dress, while he said: "The poorer the dress the more wonderful your skin looks, Djuna."

Years later when Djuna thought the figure of the Watchman was long since lost she would hear echoes of his heavy step and she would find herself in the same mood she had experienced so many times in his presence.

No longer a child, and yet many times she still had the feeling that she might be overpowered by a will stronger than her own, might be trapped, might be somehow unable to free herself, unable to escape the demands of man upon her.

Her first defeat at the hands of man the father had caused her such a conviction of helplessness before tyranny that although she realized that she was now in reality no longer helpless, the echo of this helplessness was so strong that she still dreaded the possessiveness and willfulness of older men. They benefited from this regression into her past, and could override her strength merely because of this conviction of unequal power.

It was as if maturity did not develop altogether and completely, but by little compartments like the airtight sections of a ship. A part of her being would mature, such as her insight, or interpretative faculties, but another could retain a childhood conviction that events, man and authority together were stronger than one's capacity for mastering them, and that one was doomed to become a victim of one's pattern.

It was only much later that Djuna discovered that this belief in the great power of others became the fate itself and caused the defeats.

But for years, she felt harmed and defeated at the hands of men of power, and she expected the boy, the gentle one, the trusted one, to come and deliver her from tyranny.

Ever since the day of Lillian's concert when she had seen the garden out of the window, Djuna had wanted a garden like it.

And now she possessed a garden and a very old house on the very edge of Paris, between the city and the Park.

But it was not enough to possess it, to walk through it, sit in it. One still had to be able to live in it.

And she found she could not live in it.

The inner fever, the restlessness within her corroded her life in the garden.

When she was sitting in a long easy chair she was not at ease.

The grass seemed too much like a rug awaiting footsteps, to be trampled with hasty incidents. The rhythm of growth too slow, the falling of the leaves too tranquil.

Happiness was an absence of fever. The garden was feverless and without tension to match her tensions. She could not unite or commune with the plants, the languor, the peace. It was all contrary to her inward pulse. Not one pulsation of the garden corresponded to her inner pulsation which was more like a drum beating feverish time.

Within her the leaves did not wait for autumn, but were torn off prematurely by unexpected sorrows. Within her, leaves did not wait for spring to sprout but bloomed in sudden hothouse exaggerations. Within her there were storms contrary to the lazy moods of the garden, devastations for which nature had no equivalent.

Peace, said the garden, peace.

The day began always with the sound of gravel crushed by automobiles.

141

The shutters were pushed open by the French servant, and the day admitted.

With the first crushing of the gravel under wheels came the barking of the police dog and the carillon of the church bells.

Cars entered through an enormous green iron gate, which had to be opened ceremoniously by the servant.

Everyone else walked through the small green gate that seemed like the child of the other, half covered with ivy. The ivy did not climb over the father gate.

When Djuna looked at the large gate through her window it took on the air of a prison gate. An unjust feeling, since she knew she could leave the place whenever she wanted, and since she knew more than anyone that human beings placed upon an object, or a person this responsibility of being the obstacle, when the obstacle lay within one's self.

In spite of this knowledge, she would often stand at the window staring at the large closed iron gate as if hoping to obtain from this contemplation a reflection of her inner obstacles to a full open life.

She mocked its importance; the big gate had a presumptuous creak! Its rusty voice was full of dissonant affectations. No amount of oil could subdue its rheumatism, for it took a historical pride in its own rust: it was a hundred years old.

But the little gate, with its overhanging ivy like disordered hair over a running child's forehead, had a sleepy and sly air, an air of always being half open, never entirely locked.

Djuna had chosen the house for many reasons, because it seemed to have sprouted out of the earth like a tree, so deeply grooved it was within the old garden. It had no cellar and the rooms rested right on the ground. Below the rugs, she felt, was the earth. One could take root here, feel as one with the house and garden, take nourishment from them like the plants.

She had chosen it too because its symmetrical façade covered by a trellis overrun by ivy showed twelve window faces. But one shutter was closed and corresponded to no room. During some transformation of the house it had been walled up.

142

Djuna had taken the house because of this window which led to no room, because of this impenetrable room, thinking that someday she would discover an entrance to it.

In front of the house there was a basin which had been filled, and a well which had been sealed up. Djuna set about restoring the basin, excavated an old fountain and unsealed the well.

Then it seemed to her that the house came alive, the flow was re-established.

The fountain was gay and sprightly, the well deep.

The front half of the garden was trim and stylized like most French gardens, but the back of it some past owner had allowed to grow wild and become a miniature jungle. The stream was almost hidden by overgrown plants, and the small bridge seemed like a Japanese bridge in a glass-bowl garden.

There was a huge tree of which she did not know the name, but which she named the Ink Tree for its black and poisonous berries.

One summer night she stood in the courtyard. All the windows of the house were lighted.

Then the image of the house with all its windows lighted— all but one—she saw as the image of the self, of the being divided into many cells. Action taking place in one room, now in another, was the replica of experience taking place in one part of the being, now in another.

The room of the heart in Chinese lacquer red, the room of the mind in pale green or the brown of philosophy, the room of the body in shell rose, the attic of memory with closets full of the musk of the past.

She saw the whole house on fire in the summer night and it was like those moments of great passion and deep experience when every cell of the self lighted simultaneously, a dream of fullness, and she hungered for this that would set aflame every room of the house and of herself at once!

In herself there was one shuttered window.

She did not sleep soundly in the old and beautiful house.

She was disturbed.

She could hear voices in the dark, for it is true that on days of clear audibility there are voices which come from within and speak in multiple tongues contradicting each other. They speak out of the past, out of the present, the voices of awareness—in dialogues with the self which mark each step of living.

There was the voice of the child in herself, unburied, who had long ago insisted: I want only the marvelous.

There was the low-toned and simple voice of the human being Djuna saying: I want love.

There was the voice of the artist in Djuna saying: I will create the marvelous.

Why should such wishes conflict with each other, or annihilate each other?

In the morning the human being Djuna sat on the carpet before the fireplace and mended and folded her stockings into little partitioned boxes, keeping the one perfect unmended pair for a day of high living, partitioning at the same time events into little separate boxes in her head, dividing (that was one of the great secrets against shattering sorrows), allotting and rearranging under the heading of one word a constantly fluid, mobile and protean universe whose multiple aspects were like quicksands.

This exaggerated sense, for instance, of a preparation for the love to come, like the extension of canopies, the unrolling of ceremonial carpets, the belief in the state of grace, of a perfection necessary to the advent of love.

As if she must first of all create a marvelous world in which to house it, thinking it befell her adequately to receive this guest of honor.

Wasn't it too oriental, said a voice protesting with mockery —such elaborate receptions, such costuming, as if love were such an exigent guest?

She was like a perpetual bride preparing a trousseau. As other women sew and embroider, or curl their hair, she embellished her cities of the interior, painted, decorated, prepared a great *mise en scène* for a great love.

144

It was in this mood of preparation that she passed through her kingdom the house, painting here a wall through which the stains of dampness showed, hanging a lamp where it would throw Balinese theater shadows, draping a bed, placing logs in the fireplaces, wiping the dull-surfaced furniture that it might shine. Every room in a different tone like the varied pipes of an organ, to emit a wide range of moods—lacquer red for vehemence, gray for confidences, a whole house of moods with many doors, passageways, and changes of level.

She was not satisfied until it emitted a glow which was not only that of the Dutch interiors in Dutch paintings, a glow of immaculateness, but an effulgence which had caused Jay to discourse on the gold dust of Florentine paintings.

Djuna would stand very still and mute and feel: my house will speak for me. My house will tell them I am warm and rich. The house will tell them inside of me there are these rooms of flesh and Chinese lacquer, sea greens to walk through, inside of me there are lighted candles, live fires, shadows, spaces, open doors, shelters and air currents. Inside of me there is color and warmth.

The house will speak for me.

People came and submitted to her spell, but like all spells it was wonderful and remote. Not warm and near. No human being, they thought, made this house, no human being lived here. It was too fragile and too unfamiliar. There was no dust on her hands, no broken nails, no sign of wear and tear.

It was the house of the myth.

It was the ritual they sensed, tasted, smelled. Too different from the taste and smell of their own houses. It took them out of the present. They took on an air of temporary guests. No familiar landscape, no signpost to say: this is your home as well.

All of them felt they were passing, could not remain. They were tourists visiting foreign lands. It was a voyage and not a port.

Even in the bathroom there were no medicine bottles on

the shelves proclaiming: soda, castor oil, cold cream. She had transferred all of them to alchemist bottles, and the homeliest drug assumed an air of philter.

This was a dream and she was merely a guide.

None came near enough.

There were houses, dresses, which created one's isolation as surely as those tunnels created by ferrets to elude pursuit by the male.

There were rooms and costumes which appeared to be made to lure but which were actually effective means to create distance.

Djuna had not yet decided what her true wishes were, or how near she wanted them to come. She was apparently calling to them but at the same time, by a great ambivalence and fear of their coming too near, of invading her, of dominating or possessing her, she was charming them in such a manner that the human being in her, the warm and simple human being, remained secure from invasion. She constructed a subtle obstacle to invasion at the same time as she constructed an appealing scene.

None came near enough. After they left she sat alone, and deserted, as lonely as if they had not come.

She was alone as everyone is every morning after a dream.

What was this that was weeping inside of her costume and house, something smaller and simpler than the edifice of spells?

She did not know why she was left hungry.

The dream took place. Everything had contributed to its perfection, even her silence, for she would not speak when she had nothing meaningful to say (like the silence in dreams between fateful events and fateful phrases, never a trivial word spoken in dreams!).

The next day, unknowing, she began anew.

She poured medicines from ugly bottles into alchemist bottles, creating minor mysteries, minor transmutations.

Insomnia. The nights were long.

Who would come and say: that is *my* dream, and take up

146

the thread and make all the answers?

Or are all dreams made alone?

Lying in the fevered sheets of insomnia, there was a human being cheated by the dream.

Insomnia came when one must be on the watch, when one awaited an important visitor.

Everyone, Djuna felt, saw the dancer on light feet but no one seized the moment when she vacillated, fell. No one perceived or shared her difficulties, the mere technical difficulties of loving, dancing, believing.

When she fell, she fell alone, as she had in adolescence.

She remembered feeling this mood as a girl, that all her adolescence had proceeded by oscillations between weakness and strength. She remembered, too, that whenever she became entangled in too great a difficulty she had these swift regressions into her adolescent state. Almost as if in the large world of maturity, when the obstacle loomed too large, she shrank again into the body of a young girl for whom the world had first appeared as a violent and dangerous place, forcing her to retreat, and when she retreated she fell back into smallness.

She returned to the adolescent deserts of mistrust of love.

Walking through snow, carrying her muff like an obsolete wand no longer possessed of the power to create the personage she needed, she felt herself walking through a desert of snow.

Her body muffled in furs, her heart muffled like her steps, and the pain of living muffled as by the deepest rich carpets, while the thread of Ariadne which led everywhere, right and left, like scattered footsteps in the snow, tugged and pulled within her memory and she began to pull upon this thread (silk for the days of marvel and cotton for the bread of everyday living which was always a little stale) as one pulls upon a spool, and she heard the empty wooden spool knock against the floor of different houses.

Holding the silk or cotton began to cut her fingers which bled from so much unwinding, or was it that the thread of Ariadne had led into a wound?

The thread slipped through her fingers now, with blood on it, and the snow was no longer white.

Too much snow on the spool she was unwinding from the tightly wound memories. Unwinding snow as it lay thick and hard around the edges of her adolescence because the desire of men did not find a magical way to open her being.

The only words which opened her being were the muffled words of poets so rarely uttered by human beings. They alone penetrated her without awakening the bristling guards on watch at the gateways, costumed like silver porcupines armed with mistrust, barring the way to the secret recesses of her thoughts and feelings.

Before most people, most places, most situations, most words, Djuna's being, at sixteen, closed hermetically into muteness. The sentinels bristled: someone is approaching! And all the passages to her inner self would close.

Today as a mature woman she could see how these sentinels had not been content with defending her, but they had constructed a veritable fort under this mask of gentle shyness, forts with masked holes concealing weapons built by fear.

The snow accumulated every night all around the rim of her young body.

Blue and crackling snowbound adolescence.

The young men who sought to approach her then, drawn by her warm eyes, were startled to meet with such harsh resistance.

This was no mere flight of coquetry inviting pursuit. It was a fort of snow (for the snowbound, dream-swallower of the frozen fairs). An unmeltable fort of timidity.

Yet each time she walked, muffled, protected, she was aware of two young women walking: one intent on creating trap doors of evasion, the other wishing someone might find the entrance that she might not be so alone.

With Michael it was as if she had not heard him coming, so gentle were his steps, his words. Not the walk or words of the hunter, of the man of war, the determined entrance of older men, not the dominant walk of the father, the familiar walk of the brother, not like any other man she knew.

Only a year older than herself, he walked into her blue and white climate with so light a tread that the guards did not hear him!

He came into the room with a walk of vulnerability, treading softly as upon a carpet of delicacies. He would not crush the moss, no gravel would complain under his feet, no plant would bow its head or break.

It was a walk like a dance in which the gentleness of the steps carried him through air, space and silence in a sentient minuet in accord with his partner's mood, his leaf-green eyes obeying every rhythm, attentive to harmony, fearful of discord, with an excessive care for the other's intent.

The path his steps took, his velvet words, miraculously slipped between the bristles of her mistrust, and before she had been fully aware of his coming, by his softness he had entered fully into the blue and white climate.

The mists of adolescence were not torn open, not even disturbed by his entrance.

He came with poems, with worship, with flowers not ordered from the florist but picked in the forest near his school.

He came not to plunder, to possess, to overpower. With great gentleness he moved towards the hospitable regions of her being, towards the peaceful fields of her interior landscape, where white flowers placed themselves against green backgrounds as in Botticelli paintings of spring.

At his entrance her head remained slightly inclined towards the right, as it was when she was alone, slightly weighed down by pensiveness, whereas on other occasions, at the least approach of a stranger, her head would raise itself tautly in preparation for danger.

And so he entered into the flowered regions behind the forts, having easily crossed all the moats of politeness.

His blond hair gave him the befitting golden tones attributed to most legendary figures.

Djuna never knew whether this light of sun he emitted came out of his own being or was thrown upon him by her dream of him, as later she had observed the withdrawal of this light from those she had ceased to love. She never knew whether two people woven together by feelings answering each other as echoes threw off a phosphorescence, the chemical sparks of marriage, or whether each one threw upon the other the spot-light of his inner dream.

Transient or everlasting, inner or outer, personal or magical, there was now this lighting falling upon both of them and they could only see each other in its spanning circle which dazzled them and separated them from the rest of the world.

Through the cocoon of her shyness her voice had been hardly audible, but he heard every shading of it, could follow its nuances even when it retreated into the furthest impasse of the ear's labyrinth.

Secretive and silent in relation to the world, she became exalted and intense once placed inside of this inner circle of light.

This light which enclosed two was familiar and natural to her.

Because of their youth, and their moving still outside of the center of their own desires blindly, what they danced together was not a dance in which either took possession of the other, but a kind of minuet, where the aim consisted in *not* appropriating, *not* grasping, *not* touching, but allowing the maximum space and distance to flow between the two figures. To move in accord without collisions, without merging. To encircle, to bow in worship, to laugh at the same absurdities, to mock their own movements, to throw upon the walls twin shadows which will never become one. To dance around this danger: the danger of becoming one! To dance keeping each to his own path. To allow parallelism, but no loss of the self into the other. To play at marriage, step by step, to read the same book together, to dance a dance of elusiveness on the rim of desire, to remain within circles of heightened lighting without touching the core that would set the circle on fire.

A deft dance of unpossession.

They met once at a party, imprinted on each other forever the first physical image: she saw him tall, with an easy bearing, an easily flowing laughter. She saw all: the ivory color of the skin, the gold metal sheen of the hair, the lean body carved with meticulous economy as for racing, running, leaping; tender fingers touching objects as if all the world were fragile; tender inflections of the voice without malice or mockery; eyelashes always ready to fall over the eyes when people spoke harshly around him.

He absorbed her dark, long, swinging hair, the blue eyes never at rest, a little slanted, quick to close their curtains too, quick to laugh, but more often thirsty, absorbing like a mirror. She allowed the pupil to receive these images of others but one felt they did not vanish altogether as they would on a mirror: one felt a thirsty being absorbing reflections and drinking words and faces into herself for a deep communion with them.

She never took up the art of words, the art of talk. She remained always as Michael had first seen her: a woman who talked with her Naiad hair, her winged eyelashes, her tilted head, her fluent waist and rhetorical feet.

She never said: I have a pain. But laid her two arms over the painful area as if to quiet a rebellious child, rocking and cradling this angry nerve. She never said: I am afraid. But entered the room on tiptoes, her eyes watching for ambushes.

She was already the dancer she was to become, eloquent

with her body.

They met once and then Michael began to write her letters as soon as he returned to college.

In these letters he appointed her Isis and Arethusa, Iseult and the Seven Muses.

Djuna became the woman with the face of all women.

With strange omissions: he was neither Osiris nor Tristram, nor any of the mates or pursuers.

He became uneasy when she tried to clothe *him* in the costume of myth figures.

When he came to see her during vacations they never touched humanly, not even by a handclasp. It was as if they had found the most intricate way of communicating with each other by way of historical personages, literary passions, and that any direct touch even of finger tips would explode this world.

With each substitution they increased the distance between their human selves.

Djuna was not alarmed. She regarded this with feminine eyes: in creating this world Michael was merely constructing a huge, superior, magnificent nest in some mythological tree, and one day he would ask her to step into it with him, carrying her over the threshold all costumed in the trappings of his fantasy, and he would say: this is our home!

All this to Djuna was an infinitely superior way of wooing her, and she never doubted its ultimate purpose, or climax, for in this the most subtle women are basically simple and do not consider mythology or symbolism as a substitute for the climaxes of nature, merely as adornments!

The mist of adolescence, prolonging and expanding the wooing, was merely an elaboration of the courtship. His imagination continued to create endless detours as if they had to live first of all through all the loves of history and fiction before they could focus on their own.

But the peace in his moss-green eyes disturbed her, for in her eyes there now glowed a fever. Her breasts hurt her at night, as if from overfullness.

His eyes continued to focus on the most distant points of all, but hers began to focus on the near, the present. She would dwell on a detail of his face. On his ears for instance. On the movements of his lips when he talked. She failed to hear some of his words because she was following with her eyes and her feelings the contours of his lips moving as if they were moving on the surface of her skin.

She began to understand for the first time the carnation in Carmen's mouth. Carmen was eating the mock orange of love: the white blossoms which she bit were like skin. Her lips had pressed around the mock-orange petals of desire.

In Djuna all the moats were annihilated: she stood perilously near to Michael glowing with her own natural warmth. Days of clear visibility which Michael did not share. His compass still pointed to the remote, the unknown.

Djuna was a woman being dreamed.

But Djuna had ceased to dream: she had tasted the mock orange of desire.

More baffling still to Djuna grown warm and near, with her aching breasts, was that the moss-green serenity of Michael's eyes was going to dissolve into jealousy without pausing at desire.

He took her to a dance. His friends eagerly appropriated her. From across the room full of dancers, for the first time he saw not her eyes but her mouth, as vividly as she had seen him. Very clear and very near, and he felt the taste of it upon his lips.

For the first time, as she danced away from him, encircled by young men's arms, he measured the great space they had been swimming through, measured it exactly as others measure the distance between planets.

The mileage of space he had put between himself and Djuna. The lighthouse of the eyes alone could traverse such immensity!

And now, after such elaborations in space, so many figures interposed between them, the white face of Iseult, the burning

153

face of Catherine, all of which he had interpreted as mere elaborations of his enjoyment of her, now suddenly appeared not as ornaments but as obstructions to his possession of her.

She was lost to him now. She was carried away by other young men, turning with them. They had taken her waist as he never had, they bent her, plied her to the movements of the dance, and she answered and responded: they were mated by the dance.

As she passed him he called out her name severely, reproachfully, and Djuna saw the green of his eyes turned to violet with jealousy.

"Djuna! I'm taking you home."

For the first time he was willful, and she liked it.

"Djuna!" He called again, angrily, his eyes darkening with anger.

She had to stop dancing. She came gently towards him, thinking: "He wants me all to himself," and she was happy to yield to him.

He was only a little taller than she was, but he held himself very erect and commanding.

On the way home he was silent.

The design of her mouth had vanished again, his journey towards her mouth had ceased the moment it came so near in reality to his own. It was as if he dared to experience a possibility of communion only while the obstacle to it was insurmountable, but as the obstacle was removed and she walked clinging to his arm, then he could only commune with her eyes, and the distance was again reinstated.

He left her at her door without a sign of tenderness, with only the last violet shadows of jealousy lurking reproachfully in his eyes. That was all.

Djuna sobbed all night before the mystery of his jealousy, his anger, his remoteness.

She would not question him. He confided nothing. They barred all means of communication with each other. He would not tell her that at this very dance he had discovered an intermediate world from which all the figures of women were absent. A world of boys like himself in flight away from woman, mother, sister, wife or mistress.

In her ignorance and innocence then, she could not have pierced with the greatest divination where Michael, in his flight from her, gave his desire.

In their youthful blindness they wounded each other. He excused his coldness towards her: "You're too slender. I like plump women." Or again: "You're too intelligent. I feel better with stupid women." Or another time he said: "You're too impulsive, and that frightens me."

Being innocent, she readily accepted the blame.

Strange scenes took place between them. She subdued her intelligence and became passive to please him. But it was a game, and they both knew it. Her ebullience broke through all her pretenses at quietism.

She swallowed countless fattening pills, but could only gain a pound or two. When she proudly asked him to note the improvements, his eyes turned away.

One day he said: "I feel your clever head watching me, and you would look down on me if I failed."

Failed?

She could not understand.

With time, her marriage to another, her dancing which took her to many countries, the image of Michael was effaced.

But she continued to relate to other Michaels in the world. Some part of her being continued to recognize the same gentleness, the same elusiveness, the same mystery.

Michael reappeared under different bodies, guises, and each time she responded to him, discovering each time a little more until she pierced the entire mystery open.

But the same little dance took place each time, a little dance of insolence, a dance which said to the woman: "I dance alone, I will not be possessed by a woman."

The kind of dance tradition had taught woman as a ritual to provoke aggression! But this dance made by young men before the women left them at a loss for it was not intended to be answered.

Years later she sat at a café table in Paris between Michael and Donald.

Why should she be sitting between Michael and Donald?

Why were not all cords cut between herself and Michael when she married and when he gave himself to a succession of Donalds?

When they met in Paris again, he had this need to invent a trinity: to establish a connecting link between Djuna and all the changing, fluctuating Donalds.

As if some element were lacking in his relation to Donald.

Donald had a slender body, like an Egyptian boy. Dark hair wild like that of a child who had been running. At moments the extreme softness of his gestures made him appear small, at others when he stood stylized and pure in line, erect, he seemed tall and firm.

His eyes were large and entranced, and he talked flowingly like a medium. His eyelids fell heavily over his eyes like a woman's, with a sweep of the eyelashes. He had a small straight nose, small ears, and strong boyish hands.

When Michael left for cigarettes they looked at each other, and immediately Donald ceased to be a woman. He straightened his body and looked at Djuna unflinchingly.

With her he asserted his strength. Was it her being a woman which challenged his strength? He was now like a grave child in the stage of becoming a man.

With the smile of a conspirator he said: "Michael treats me as if I were a woman or a child. He wants me not to work and to depend on him. He wants to go and live down south in a kind of paradise."

156

"And what do you want?"

"I am not sure I love Michael. . . ."

That was exactly what she expected to hear. Always this admission of incompleteness. Always one in flight or the three sitting together, always one complaining or one loving less than the other.

All this accompanied by the most complicated harmonization of expressions Djuna had ever seen. The eyes and mouth of Donald suggesting an excitement familiar to drug addicts, only in Donald it did not derive from any artificial drugs but from the strange flavor he extracted from difficulties, from the maze and detours and unfulfillments of his loves.

In Donald's eyes shone the fever of futile watches in the night, intrigue, pursuits of the forbidden, all the rhythms and moods unknown to ordinary living. There was a quest for the forbidden and it was this flavor he sought, as well as the strange lighting which fell on all the unknown, the unfamiliar, the tabooed, all that could remind him of those secret moments of childhood when he sought the very experiences most forbidden by the parents.

But when it came to the selection of one, to giving one's self to one, to an open simplicity and an effort at completeness, some mysterious impulse always intervened and destroyed the relationship. A hatred of permanency, of anything resembling marriage.

Donald was talking against Michael's paradise as it would destroy the bitter-sweet, intense flavor he sought.

He bent closer to Djuna, whispering now like a conspirator. It was his conspiracy against simplicity, against Michael's desire for a peaceful life together.

"If you only knew, Djuna, the first time it happened! I expected the whole world to change its face, be utterly transformed, turned upside down. I expected the room to become inclined, as after an earthquake, to find that the door no longer led to a stairway but into space, and the windows overlooked the sea. Such excitement, such anxiety, and such a fear of not achieving fulfillment. At other times I have the feeling that I am escaping a prison, I have a fear of being caught again and punished. When I signal to another like myself in a café I have the feeling that we are two prisoners who have found a laborious way to communicate by a secret code. All our messages are colored with the violent colors of danger. What I find in this devious way has a taste like no other object overtly obtained. Like the taste of those dim and secret afternoons of our childhood when we performed forbidden acts with great anxiety and terror of punishment. The exaltation of danger, I'm used to it now, the fever of remorse. This society which condemns me . . . do you know how I am revenging myself? I am seducing each one of its members slowly, one by one. . . ."

He talked softly and exultantly, choosing the silkiest words, not disguising his dream of triumphing over all those who had dared to forbid certain acts, and certain forms of love.

At the same time when he talked about Michael there came to his face the same expression women have when they have seduced a man, an expression of vain glee, a triumphant, uncontrollable celebration of her power. And so Donald was celebrating the feminine wiles and ruses and charms by which he had made Michael fall so deeply in love with him.

In his flight from woman, it seemed to Djuna, Michael had merely fled to one containing all the minor flaws of women.

Donald stopped talking and there remained in the air the feminine intonations of his voice, chanting and never falling into deeper tones.

Michael was back and sat between them offering cigarettes.

As soon as Michael returned Djuna saw Donald change, become woman again, tantalizing and provocative. She saw Donald's body dilating into feminine undulations, his face open in all nakedness. His face expressed a dissolution like that of a woman being taken. Everything revealed, glee, the malice, the vanity, the childishness. His gestures like those of a second-rate actress receiving flowers with a batting of the eyelashes, with an oblique glance like the upturned cover of a bedspread, the edge of a petticoat.

He had the stage bird's turns of the head, the little dance of alertness, the petulance of the mouth pursed for small kisses that do not shatter the being, the flutter and perk of prize birds, all adornment and change, a mockery of the evanescent darts of invitation, the small gestures of alarm and promise made by minor women.

Michael said: "You two resemble each other. I am sure Donald's suits would fit you, Djuna."

"But Donald is more truthful," said Djuna, thinking how openly Donald betrayed that he did not love Michael, whereas she might have sought a hundred oblique routes to soften this truth.

"Donald is more truthful because he loves less," said Michael.

Warmth in the air. The spring foliage shivering out of pure coquetry, not out of discomfort. Love flowing now between the three, shared, transmitted, contagious, as if Michael were at last free to love Djuna in the form of a boy, through the body of Donald to reach Djuna whom he could never touch directly, and Djuna through the body of Donald reached Michael—and the missing dimension of their love accomplished in space like an algebra of imperfection, an abstract drama of incompleteness at last resolved for one moment by this trinity of woman sitting between two incomplete men.

She could look with Michael's eyes at Donald's finely designed body, the narrow waist, the square shoulders, the stylized gestures and dilated expression.

She could see that Donald did not give his true self to Michael. He acted for him a caricature of woman's minor petulances and caprices. He ordered a drink and then changed his mind, and when the drink came he did not want it at all.

Djuna thought: "He is like a woman without the womb in which such great mysteries take place. He is a travesty of a marriage that will never take place."

Donald rose, performed a little dance of salutation and

flight before them, eluding Michael's pleading eyes, bowed, made some whimsical gesture of apology and flight, and left them.

This little dance reminded her of Michael's farewells on her doorsteps when she was sixteen.

And suddenly she saw all their movements, hers with Michael, and Michael's with Donald, as a ballet of unreality and unpossession.

"Their greatest form of activity is flight!" she said to Michael.

To the tune of Debussy's *"Ile Joyeuse,"* they gracefully made all the steps which lead to no possession.

(When will I stop loving these airy young men who move in a realm like the realm of the birds, always a little quicker than most human beings, always a little above, or beyond humanity, always in flight, out of some great fear of human beings, always seeking the open space, wary of enclosures, anxious for their freedom, vibrating with a multitude of alarms, always sensing danger all around them. . . .)

"Birds," said a research scientist, "live their lives with an intensity as extreme as their brilliant colors and their vivid songs. Their body temperatures are regularly as high as 105 to 110 degrees, and anyone who has watched a bird at close range must have seen how its whole body vibrates with the furious pounding of its pulse. Such engines must operate at forced draft: and that is exactly what a bird does. The bird's indrawn breath not only fills its lungs, but also passes on through myriads of tiny tubules into air sacs that fill every space in the bird's body not occupied by vital organs. Furthermore the air sacs connect with many of the bird's bones, which are not filled with marrow as animals' bones are, but are hollow. These reserve air tanks provide fuel for the bird's intensive life, and at the same time add to its buoyancy in flight."

Paul arrived as the dawn arrives, mist-laden, uncertain of his gestures. The sun was hidden until he smiled. Then the blue of his eyes, the shadows under his eyes, the sleepy eyelids, were all illuminated by the wide, brilliant smile. Mist, dew, the uncertain hoverings of his gestures were dispelled by the full, firm mouth, the strong even teeth.

Then the smile vanished again, as quickly as it had come. When he entered her room he brought with him this climate of adolescence which is neither sun nor full moon but the intermediate regions.

Again she noticed the shadows under his eyes, which made a soft violet-tinted halo around the intense blue of the pupils.

He was mantled in shyness, and his eyelids were heavy as if from too much dreaming. His dreaming lay like the edges of a deep slumber on the rim of his eyelids. One expected them to close in a hypnosis of interior fantasy as mysterious as a drugged state.

This constant passing from cloudedness to brilliance took place within a few instants. His body would sit absolutely still, and then would suddenly leap into gaiety and lightness. Then once again his face would close hermetically.

He passed in the same quick way between phrases uttered with profound maturity to sudden innocent inaccuracies.

It was difficult to remember he was seventeen.

He seemed more preoccupied with uncertainty as to how to carry himself through this unfamiliar experience than with absorbing or enjoying it.

Uncertainty spoiled his pleasure in the present, but Djuna felt he was one to carry away his treasures into secret chambers of remembrance and there he would lay them all out like the contents of an opium pipe being prepared, these treasures no longer endangered by uneasiness in living, the treasures becoming the past, and there he would touch and caress every word, every image, and make them his own.

In solitude and remembrance his real ·life would begin. Everything that was happening now was merely the preparation of the opium pipe that would later send volutes into space to enchant his solitude, when he would be lying down away from danger and unfamiliarity, lying down to taste of an experience washed of the dross of anxiety.

He would lie down and nothing more would be demanded of the dreamer, no longer expected to participate, to speak, to act, to decide. He would lie down and the images would rise in chimerical visitations and from a tale more marvelous in every detail than the one taking place at this moment marred by apprehension.

Having created a dream beforehand which he sought to preserve from destruction by reality, every movement in life became more difficult for the dreamer, for Paul, his fear of errors being like the opium dreamer's fear of noise or daylight.

And not only his dream of Djuna was he seeking to preserve like some fragile essence easily dispelled but even more dangerous, his own image of what was expected of him by Djuna, what he imagined Djuna expected of him—a heavy demand upon a youthful Paul, his own ideal exigencies which he did not know to be invented by himself creating a difficulty in every act or word in which he was merely re-enacting scenes rehearsed in childhood in which the child's naturalness was always defeated by the severity of the parents giving him the perpetual feeling that no word and no act came up to this impossible standard set for him. A more terrible compression than when the Chinese bound the feet of their infants, bound them with yards of cloth to stunt the natural growth. Such tyrannical cloth worn too long, unbroken, uncut, would in the end turn one into a mummy. . . .

Djuna could see the image of the mother binding Paul in the story he told her: He had a pet guinea pig, once, which he loved. And his mother had forced him to kill it.

She could see all the bindings when he added: "I destroyed a diary I kept in school."

"Why?"

"Now that I was home for a month, my parents might have

162

read it."

Were the punishments so great that he was willing rather to annihilate living parts of himself, a loved pet, a diary reflecting his inner self?

"There are many sides of yourself you cannot show your parents."

"Yes," An expression of anxiety came to his face. The effect of their severity was apparent in the way he sat, stood— even in the tone of resignation in which he said: "I have to leave soon."

Djuna looked at him and saw him as the prisoner he was— a prisoner of school, of parents.

"But you have a whole month of freedom now."

"Yes," said Paul, but the word freedom had no echo in his being.

"What will you do with it?"

He smiled then. "I can't do much with it. My parents don't want me to visit dancers."

"Did you tell them you were coming to visit me?"

"Yes."

"Do they know you want to be a dancer yourself?"

"Oh, no." He smiled again, a distressed smile, and then his eyes lost their direct, open frankness. They wavered, as if he had suddenly lost his way.

This was his most familiar expression: a nebulous glance, sliding off people and objects.

He had the fears of a child in the external world, yet he gave at the same time the impression of living in a larger world. This boy, thought Djuna tenderly, is lost. But he is lost in a large world. His dreams are vague, infinite, formless. He loses himself in them. No one knows what he is imagining and thinking. He does not know, he cannot say, but it is not a simple world. It expands beyond his grasp, he senses more than he knows, a bigger world which frightens him. He cannot confide or give himself. He must have been too often harshly condemned.

Waves of tenderness flowed out to him from her eyes as they sat without talking. The cloud vanished from his face. It was as if he sensed what she was thinking.

Just as he was leaving Lawrence arrived breathlessly, embraced Djuna effusively, pranced into the studio and turned on the radio.

He was Paul's age, but unlike Paul he did not appear to carry a little snail house around his personality, a place into which to retreat and vanish. He came out openly, eyes aware, smiling, expectant, in readiness for anything that might happen. He moved propelled by sheer impulse, and was never still.

He was carrying a cage which he laid in the middle of the room. He lifted its covering shaped like a miniature striped awning.

Djuna knelt on the rug to examine the contents of the cage and laughed to see a blue mouse nibbling at a cracker.

"Where did you find a turquoise mouse?" asked Djuna.

"I bathed her in dye," said Lawrence. "Only she licks it all away in a few days and turns white again, so I had to bring her this time right after her bath."

The blue mouse was nibbling eagerly. The music was playing. They were sitting on the rug. The room began to glitter and sparkle.

Paul looked on with amazement.

(This pet, his eyes said, need not be killed. Nothing is forbidden here.)

Lawrence was painting the cage with phosphorescent paint so that it would shine in the dark.

"That way she won't be afraid when I leave her alone at night!"

While the paint dried Lawrence began to dance.

Djuna was laughing behind her veil of long hair.

Paul looked at them yearningly and then said in a toneless voice: "I have to leave now." And he left precipitately.

"Who is the beautiful boy?" asked Lawrence.

"The son of tyrannical parents who are very worried he

should visit a dancer."

"Will he come again?"

"He made no promise. Only if he can get away."

"We'll go and visit him."

Djuna smiled. She could imagine Lawrence arriving at Paul's formal home with a cage with a blue mouse in it and Paul's mother saying: "You get rid of that pet!"

Or Lawrence taking a ballet leap to touch the tip of a chandelier, or singing some delicate obscenity.

"C'est une jeune fille en fleur," he said now, clairvoyantly divining Djuna's fear of never escaping from the echoes and descendants of Michael.

Lawrence shrugged his shoulders. Then he looked at her with his red-gold eyes, under his red-gold hair. Whenever he looked at her it was contagious: that eager, ardent glance falling amorously on everyone and everything, dissolving the darkest moods.

No sadness could resist this frenzied carnival of affection he dispensed every day, beginning with his enthusiasm for his first cup of coffee, joy at the day's beginning, an immediate fancy for the first person he saw, a passion at the least provocation for man, woman, child or animal. A warmth even in his collisions with misfortunes, troubles and difficulties.

He received them smiling. Without money in his pocket he rushed to help. With generous excess he rushed to love, to desire, to possess, to lose, to suffer, to die the multiple little deaths everyone dies each day. He would even die and weep and suffer and lose with enthusiasm, with ardor. He was prodigal in poverty, rich and abundant in some invisible chemical equivalent to gold and sun.

Any event would send him leaping and prancing with gusto: a concert, a play, a ballet, a person. Yes, yes, yes, cried his young firm body every morning. No retractions, no hesitations, no fears, no caution, no economy. He accepted every invitation.

His joy was in movement, in assenting, in consenting, in expansion.

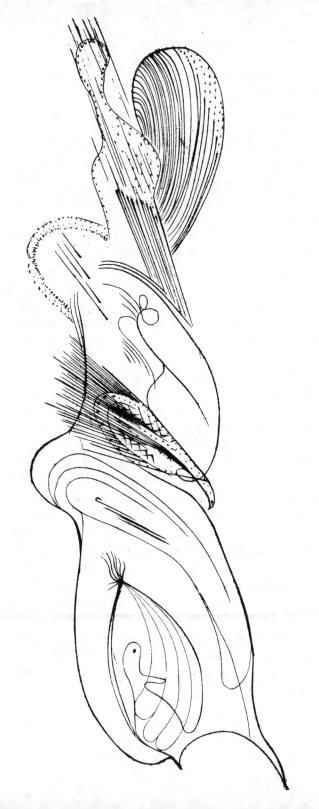

Whenever he came he lured Djuna into a swirl. Even in sadness they smiled at each other, expanding in sadness with dilated eyes and dilated hearts.

"Drop every sorrow and dance!"

Thus they healed each other by dancing, perfectly mated in enthusiasm and fire.

The waves which carried him forward never dropped him on the rocks. He would always come back smiling: "Oh, Djuna, you remember Hilda? I was so crazy about her. Do you know what she did? She tried to palm off some false money on me. Yes, with all her lovely eyes, manners, sensitiveness, she came to me and said so tenderly: let me have change for this ten-dollar bill. And it was a bad one. And then she tried to hide some drugs in my room, and to say I was the culprit. I nearly went to jail. She pawned my typewriter, my box of paints. She finally took over my room and I had to sleep for the night on a park bench."

But the next morning he was again full of faith, love, trust, impulses.

Dancing and believing.

In his presence she was again ready to believe.

To believe in Paul's eyes, the mystery and the depth in them, the sense of some vast dream lying coiled there, undeciphered.

Lawrence had finished the phosphorescent painting. He closed the curtains and the cage shone in the dark. Now he decided to paint with phosphorescence everything paintable in the room.

The next day Lawrence appeared with a large pot of paint and he was stirring it with a stick when Paul telephoned: "I can get away for a while. May I come?"

"Oh, come, come," said Djuna.

"I can't stay very late. . . ." His voice was muffled, like that of a sick person. There was a plaintiveness in it so plainly audible to Djuna's heart.

"The prisoner is allowed an hour's freedom," she said.

When Paul came Lawrence handed him a paintbrush and

in silence the two of them worked at touching up everything paintable in the room. They turned off the lights. A new room appeared.

Luminous faces appeared on the walls, new flowers, new jewels, new castles, new jungles, new animals, all in filaments of light.

Mysterious translucence like their unmeasured words, their impulsive acts, wishes, enthusiasms. Darkness was excluded from their world, the darkness of loss of faith. It was now the room with a perpetual sparkle, even in darkness.

(They are making a new world for me, felt Djuna, a world of greater lightness. It is perhaps a dream and I may not be allowed to stay. They treat me as one of their own, because I believe what they believe, I feel as they do. I hate the father, authority, men of power, men of wealth, all tyranny, all authority, all crystallizations. I feel as Lawrence and Paul: outside there lies a bigger world full of cruelties, dangers and corruptions, where one sells out one's charms, one's playfulness, and enters a rigid world of discipline, duty, contracts, accountings. A thick opaque world without phosphorescence. I want to stay in this room forever not with man the father but with man the son, carving, painting, dancing, dreaming, and always beginning, born anew every day, never aging, full of faith and impulse, turning and changing to every wind like the mobiles. I do not love those who have ceased to flow, to believe, to feel. Those who can no longer melt, exult, who cannot let themselves be cheated, laugh at loss, those who are bound and frozen.)

She laid her head on Lawrence's shoulder with a kind of gratitude.

(Nowhere else as here with Lawrence and with Paul was there such an iridescence in the air; nowhere else so far from the threat of hardening and crystallizing. Everything flowing. . . .)

Djuna was brushing her hair with her fingers, in long pensive strokes, and Lawrence was talking about the recurrent big problem of a job. He had tried so many. How to work without losing one's color, one's ardor, personal possessions and freedom. He was very much like a delicate Egyptian scarab who dreaded to lose his iridescence in routine, in duty, in monotony. The job could kill one, or maim one, make one a robot, an opaque personage, a future undertaker, a man of power with gouty limbs and a hardening of the arteries of faith!

Lawrence was now working in a place which made decorations for shop windows. He liked to work at night, to go on strange expeditions in the company of mannequins, papiermâché horses, to live on miniature stages building jungles, sea landscapes, fabulous animals. To flirt with naked mannequins whose arms came off as easily as other women's gloves, who deposited their heads on the floor and took off their wigs when they took off their hats. He became an expert at dismantling women!

Lawrence lived and breathed color and there was no danger of his dying of drabness, for even accidents took on a most vivid shade and a spilled pot of *gouache* was still a delight to the eyes.

He brought Djuna gifts of chokers, headdresses, earrings made of painted clay which crumbled quickly like the trappings for a costume play.

She had always liked objects without solidity. The solid ones bound her to permanency. She had never wanted a solid house, enduring furniture. All these were traps. Then you belonged to them forever. She preferred stage trappings which she could move into and out of easily, without regret. Soon after they fell apart and nothing was lost. The vividness alone survived.

She remembered once hearing a woman complain that armchairs no longer lasted twenty years, and Djuna answered: "But I couldn't love an armchair for twenty years!"

And so change, mutations like the rainbow, and she preferred Lawrence's gifts from which the colored powder and crystals fell like the colors on the wings of butterflies after yielding their maximum of charm.

Paul was carving a piece of copper, making such fine incisions with the scissors that the bird which finally appeared between his slender fingers bristled with filament feathers.

He stood on the table and hung it by a thread to the ceiling. The slightest breath caused it to turn slowly.

Paul had the skin of a child that had never been touched by anything of this earth: no soap, no washrag, no brush, no human kiss could have touched his skin! Never scrubbed, rubbed, scratched, or wrinkled by a pillow. The transparency of the child skin, of the adolescent later to turn opaque. What do children nourish themselves with that their skin has this transparency, and what do they eat of later which brings on opaqueness?

The mothers who kiss them are eating light.

There is a phosphorescence which comes from the magic world of childhood.

Where does this illumination go later? Is it the substance of faith which shines from their bodies like phosphorescence from the albatross, and what kills it?

Now Lawrence had discovered a coiled measuring tape of steel in Djuna's closet while delving for objects useful for charades.

When entirely pulled out of its snail covering it stretched like a long snake of steel which under certain manipulations could stand rigid like a sword or undulate like silver-tipped waves, or flash like lightning.

Lawrence and Paul stood like expert swordsmen facing each other for a duel of light and steel.

The steel band flexed, then hardened between them like a bridge, and at each forward movement by one it seemed as if the sword had pierced the body of the other.

At other moments it wilted, wavered like a frightened snake, and then it looked bedraggled and absurd and they both laughed.

But soon they learned never to let it break or waver and it became like a thunderbolt in their hands. Paul attacked with audacity and Lawrence parried with swiftness.

At midnight Paul began to look anxious. His luminosity clouded, he resumed his hesitant manner. He ceased to occupy the center of the room and moved out of the focus of light and laughter. Like a sleepwalker, he moved away from gaiety.

Djuna walked with him towards the door. They were alone and then he said: "My parents have forbidden me to come here."

"But you were happy here, weren't you?"

"Yes, I was happy."

"This is where you belong."

"Why do you think I belong here?"

"You're gifted for dancing, for painting, for writing. And this is your month of freedom."

"Yes, I know. I wish . . . I wish I were free. . . ."

"If you wish it deeply enough you will find a way."

"I would like to run away, but I have no money."

"If you run away we'll all take care of you."

"Why?"

"Because we believe in you, because you're worth helping."

"I have nowhere to go."

"We'll find you a room somewhere, and we will adopt you. And you will have your month of life."

"Of life!" he repeated with docility.

"But I don't want you to do it unless you feel ready, unless you want it so much that you're willing to sacrifice everything else. I only want you to know you can count on us, but it must be your decision, or it will not mean anything."

"Thank you." This time he did not clasp her hand, he laid his hand within hers as if nestling it there, folded, ivory smooth and gentle, at rest, in an act of trustingness.

Then before leaving the place he looked once more at the room as if to retain its enfolding warmth. At one moment he had laughed so much that he had slid from his chair. Djuna had made him laugh. At that moment many of his chains must have broken, for nothing breaks chains like laughter, and

Djuna could not remember in all her life a greater joy than this spectacle of Paul laughing like a released prisoner.

Two days later Paul appeared at her door with his valise.

Djuna received him gaily as if this were the beginning of a holiday, asked him to tie the velvet bows at her wrist, drove him to where Lawrence lived with his parents and where there was an extra room.

She would have liked to shelter him in her own house, but she knew his parents would come there and find him.

He wrote a letter to his parents. He reminded them that he had only a month of freedom for himself before leaving for India on the official post his father had arranged for him, that during this month he felt he had a right to be with whatever friends he felt a kinship with. He had found people with whom he had a great deal to share and since his parents had been so extreme in their demands, forbidding him to see his friends at all, he was being equally extreme in his assertion of his freedom. Not to be concerned about him, that at the end of the month he would comply with his father's plans for him.

He did not stay in his room. It had been arranged that he would have his meals at Djuna's house. An hour after he had laid down his valise in Lawrence's room he was at her house.

In his presence she did not feel herself a mature woman, but again a girl of seventeen at the beginning of her own life. As if the girl of seventeen had remained undestroyed by experience—like some deeper layer in a geological structure which had been pressed but not obliterated by the new layers.

(He seems hungry and thirsty for warmth, and yet so fearful. We are arrested by each other's elusiveness. Who will take flight first? If we move too hastily fear will spring up and separate us. I am fearful of his innocence, and he of what he believes to be my knowingness. But neither one of us knows what the other wants, we are both arrested and ready to vanish, with such a fear of being hurt. His oscillations are like mine, his muteness like mine at his age, his fears like my fears.)

She felt that as she came nearer there was a vibration through his body. Through all the mists as her body approached to greet him there was an echo of her movements within him.

With his hand within hers, at rest, he said: "Everyone is doing so much for me. Do you think that when I grow up I will be able to do the same for someone else?"

"Of course you will." And because he had said so gently "when I grow up" she saw him suddenly as a boy, and her hand went out swiftly towards the strand of boyish hair which fell over his eyes and pulled it.

That she had done this with a half-frightened laugh as if she expected retaliation made him feel at ease with her.

He did retaliate by trying jiujitsu on her arm until she said: "You hurt me." Then he stopped, but the discovery that her bones were not as strong as the boys' on whom he had tested his knowledge made him feel powerful. He had more strength than he needed to handle her. He could hurt her so easily, and now he was no longer afraid when her face came near his and her eyes grew larger and more brilliant, or when she danced and her hair accidentally swung across her face like a silk whip, or when she sat like an Arab holding conversation over the telephone in answer to invitations which might deprive him of her presence. No matter who called, she always refused, and stayed at home to talk with him.

The light in the room became intensely bright and they were bathed in it, bright with the disappearance of his fear.

He felt as ease to sit and draw, to read, to paint, and to be silent. The light around them grew warm and dim and intimate.

By shedding in his presence the ten years of life which created distance between them, she felt herself re-entering a smaller house of innocence and faith, and that what she shed was merely a role: she played a role of woman, and this had been the torment, she had been pretending to be a woman, and now she knew she had not been at ease in this role, and now with Paul she felt she was being transformed into a stature and substance nearer to her true state.

With Paul she was passing from an insincere pretense at maturity into a more vulnerable world, escaping from the more difficult role of tormented woman to a smaller room of warmth.

For one moment, sitting there with Paul, listening to the Symphony in D Minor of César Franck, through his eyes she was allowed behind the mirror into a smaller silk-lined house of faith.

In art, in history, man fights his fears, he wants to live forever, he is afraid of death, he wants to work with other men, he wants to live forever. He is like a child afraid of death. The child is afraid of death, of darkness, of solitude. Such simple fears behind all the elaborate constructions. Such simple fears as hunger for light, warmth, love. Such simple fears behind the elaborate constructions of art. Examine them all gently and quietly through the eyes of a boy. There is always a human being lonely, a human being afraid, a human being lost, a human being confused. Concealing and disguising his dependence, his needs, ashamed to say: I am a simple human being in too vast and too complex a world. Because of all we have discovered about a leaf . . . it is still a leaf. Can we relate to a leaf, on a tree, in a park, a simple leaf: green, glistening, sun-bathed or wet, or turning white because the storm is coming. Like the savage, let us look at the leaf wet or shining with sun, or white with fear of the storm, or silvery in the fog, or listless in too great heat, or falling in the autumn, drying, reborn each year anew. Learn from the leaf: simplicity. In spite of all we know about the leaf: its nerve structure phyllome cellular papilla parenchyma stomata venation. Keep a human relation—leaf, man, woman, child. In tenderness. No matter how immense the world, how elaborate, how contradictory, there is always man, woman, child, and the leaf. Humanity makes everything warm and simple. Humanity. Let the waters of humanity flow through the abstract city, through abstract art, weeping like rivulets, cracking rocky mountains, melting icebergs. The frozen worlds in empty cages of mobiles where hearts lie exposed like wires in an electric bulb. Let them burst at the tender touch of a leaf.

The next morning Djuna was having breakfast in bed when Lawrence appeared.

"I'm broke and I'd like to have breakfast with you."

He had begun to eat his toast when the maid came and said: "There's a gentleman at the door who won't give his name."

"Find out what he wants. I don't want to dress yet."

But the visitor had followed the servant to the door and stood now in the bedroom.

Before anyone could utter a protest he said in the most classically villainous tone: "Ha, ha, having breakfast, eh?"

"Who are you? What right have you to come in here," said Djuna.

"I have every right: I'm a detective."

"A detective!"

Lawrence's eyes began to sparkle with amusement.

The detective said to him: "And what are you doing here, young man?"

"I'm having breakfast." He said this in the most cheerful and natural manner, continuing to drink his coffee and buttering a piece of toast which he offered Djuna.

"Wonderful!" said the detective. "So I've caught you. Having breakfast, eh? While your parents are breaking their hearts over your disappearance. Having breakfast, eh? When you're not eighteen yet and they can force you to return home and never let you out again." And turning to Djuna he added: "And what may your interest in this young man be?"

Then Djuna and Lawrence broke into irrepressible laughter.

"I'm not the only one," said Lawrence.

At this the detective looked like a man who had not expected his task to be so easy, almost grateful for the collaboration.

"So you're not the only one!"

Djuna stopped laughing. "He means anyone who is broke can have breakfast here."

"Will you have a cup of coffee?" said Lawrence with an impudent smile.

"That's enough talk from you," said the detective. "You'd better come along with me, Paul."

"But I'm not Paul."

"Who are you?"

"My name is Lawrence."

"Do you know Paul—? Have you seen him recently?"

"He was here last night for a party."

"A party? And where did he go after that?"

"I don't know," said Lawrence. "I thought he was staying with his parents."

"What kind of a party was this?" asked the detective.

But now Djuna had stopped laughing and was becoming angry. "Leave this place immediately," she said.

The detective took a photograph out of his pocket, compared it with Lawrence's face, saw there was no resemblance, looked once more at Djuna's face, read the anger in it, and left.

As soon as he left her anger vanished and they laughed again. Suddenly Djuna's playfulness turned into anxiety. "But this may become serious, Lawrence. Paul won't be able to come to my house any more. And suppose it had been Paul who had come for breakfast!"

And then another aspect of the situation struck her and her face became sorrowful. "What kind of parents has Paul that they can consider using force to bring him home."

She took up the telephone and called Paul. Paul said in a shocked voice: "They can't take me home by force!"

"I don't know about the law, Paul. You'd better stay away from my house. I will meet you somewhere—say at the ballet theater—until we find out."

For a few days they met at concerts, galleries, ballets. But no one seemed to follow them.

Djuna lived in constant fear that he would be whisked away and that she might never see him again. Their meetings took on the anxiety of repeated farewells. They always looked at each other as if it were for the last time.

Through this fear of loss she took longer glances at his face, and every facet of it, every gesture, every inflection of his voice thus sank deeper into her, to be stored away against future loss—deeper and deeper it penetrated, impregnated her more as she fought against its vanishing.

She felt that she not only saw Paul vividly in the present but Paul in the future. Every expression she could read as an indication of future power, future discernment, future completion. Her vision of the future Paul illumined the present. Others could see a young man experiencing his first drunkenness, taking his first steps in the world, oscillating or contradicting himself. But she felt herself living with a Paul no one had seen yet, the man of the future, willful, and with a power in him which appeared intermittently.

When the clouds and mists of adolescence would vanish, what a complete and rich man he would become, with this mixture of sensibility and intelligence motivating his choices, discarding shallowness, never taking a step into mediocrity, with an unerring instinct for the extraordinary.

To send a detective to bring him home by force, how little his parents must know this Paul of the future, possessed of that deep-seated mine of tenderness hidden below access but visible to her.

She was living with a Paul no one knew as yet, in a secret relationship far from the reach of the subtlest detectives, beyond the reach of the entire world.

Under the veiled voice she felt the hidden warmth, under the hesitancies a hidden strength, under the fears a vaster dream more difficult to seize and to fulfill.

Alone, after an afternoon with him, she lay on her bed and while the bird he had carved gyrated lightly in the center of the room, tears came to her eyes so slowly she did not feel them at first until they slid down her cheeks.

Tears from this unbearable melting of her heart and body —a complete melting before the face of Paul, and the muted way his body spoke, the gentle way he was hungering, reaching, groping, like a prisoner escaping slowly and gradually, door by door, room by room, hallway by hallway, towards the light. The prison that had been built around him had been of darkness: darkness about himself, about his needs, about his true nature.

The solitary cell created by the parents.

He knew nothing, nothing about his true self. And such blindness was as good as binding him with chains. His parents and his teachers had merely imposed upon him a false self that seemed right to them.

This boy they did not know.

But this melting, it must not be. She turned her face away, to the right now, as if to turn away from the vision of his face, and murmured: "I must not love him, I must not love him."

The bell rang. Before she could sit up Paul had come in.

"Oh, Paul, this is dangerous for you!"

"I had to come."

As he stopped in his walking towards her his body sought to convey a message. What was his body saying? What were his eyes saying?

He was too near, she felt his eyes possessing her and she rushed away to make tea, to place a tray and food between them, like some very fragile wall made of sand, in games of childhood, which the sea could so easily wash away!

She talked, but he was not listening, nor was she listening

to her own words, for his smile penetrated her, and she wanted to run away from him.

"I would like to know . . ." he said, and the words remained suspended.

He sat too near. She felt the unbearable melting, the loss of herself, and she struggled to close some door against him. "I must not love him, I must not love him!"

She moved slightly away, but his hair was so near her hand that her fingers were drawn magnetically to touch it lightly, playfully.

"What do you want to know?"

Had he noticed her own trembling? He did not answer her. He leaned over swiftly and took her whole mouth in his, the whole man in him coming out in a direct thrust, firm, willful, hungry. With one kiss he appropriated her, asserted his possessiveness.

When he had taken her mouth and kissed her until they were both breathless they lay side by side and she felt his body strong and warm against hers, his passion inflexible.

He laid his hand over her with hesitations. Everything was new to him, a woman's neck, a shoulder, a woman's hooks and buttons.

Between the journeys of discovery he had flickering instants of uncertainties until the sparks of pleasure guided his hand.

Where he passed his hand no one else had ever passed his hand. New cells awakened under his delicate fingers never wakened before to say: this is yours.

A breast touched for the first time is a breast never touched before.

He looked at her with his long blue eyes which had never wept and her eyes were washed luminous and clear, her eyes forgot they had wept.

He touched her eyelashes with his eyelashes of which not one had fallen out and those of hers which had been washed away by tears were replaced.

His hair which had never been crushed between feverish

179

pillows, knotted by nightmares, mingled with hers and untangled it.

Where sadness had carved rich caverns he sank his youthful
thrusts grasping endless sources of warmth.

Only before the last mystery of the body did he pause. He
had thrust and entered and now he paused.

Did one lie still and at peace in the secret place of woman?
In utter silence they lay.

Fever mounting in him, the sap rising, the bodies taut with
a need of violence.

She made one undulatory movement, and this unlocked in
him a whirlpool of desire, a dervish dance of all the silver
knives of pleasure.

When they awakened from their trance, they smiled at each
other, but he did not move. They lay merged, slimness to
slimness, legs like twin legs, hip to hip.

The cotton of silence lay all around them, covering their
bodies in quilted softness.

The big wave of fire which rolled them washed them ashore
tenderly into small circles of foam.

On the table there was a huge vase filled with tulips. She
moved towards them, seeking something to touch, to pour
her joy into, out of the exaltation she felt.

Every part of her body that had been opened by his hands
yearned to open the whole world in harmony with her mood.

She looked at the tulips so hermetically closed, like secret
poems, like the secrets of the flesh. Her hands took each tulip,
the ordinary tulip of everyday living and she slowly opened
them, petal by petal, opened them tenderly.

They were changed from plain to exotic flowers, from closed
secrets to open flowering.

Then she heard Paul say: "Don't do that!"

There was a great anxiety in his voice. He repeated: "Don't. do that!"

She felt a great stab of anxiety. Why was he so disturbed?

She looked at the flowers. She looked at Paul's face lying on the pillow, clouded with anxiety, and she was struck with fear. Too soon. She had opened him to love too soon. He was not ready.

Even with tenderness, even with delicate fingers, even with the greatest love, it had been too soon! She had forced time, as she had forced the flowers to change from the ordinary to the extraordinary. He was not ready!

Now she understood her own hesitations, her impulse to run away from him. Even though he had made the first gesture, she, knowing, should have saved him from anxiety.

(Paul was looking at the opened tulips and seeing in them something else, not himself but Djuna, the opening body of Djuna. Don't let her open the flowers as he had opened her. In the enormous wave of silence, the hypnosis of hands, skin, delight, he had heard a small moan, yet in her face he had seen joy. Could the thrust into her have hurt her? It was like stabbing someone, this desire.)

"I'm going to dress, now," she said lightly. She could not close the tulips again, but she could dress. She could close herself again and allow him to close again.

Watching her he felt a violent surge of strength again, stronger than his fears. "Don't dress yet."

Again he saw on her face a smile he had never seen there in her gayest moments, and then he accepted the mystery and abandoned himself to his own joy.

His heart beat wildly at her side, wildly in panic and joy together at the moment before taking her. This wildly beating heart at her side, beating against hers, and then the cadenced, undulating, blinding merging together, and no break between their bodies afterwards.

After the storm he lay absolutely still over her body, dreaming, quiet, as if this were the place of haven. He lay given, lost, entranced. She bore his weight with joy, though after a while it numbed and hurt her. She made a slight movement, and then he asked her: "Am I crushing you?"

"You're flattening me into a thin wafer," she said, smiling, and he smiled back, then laughed.

"The better to eat you, my dear."

He kissed her again as if he would eat her with delight.

Then he got up and made a somersault on the carpet, with light exultant gestures.

She lay back watching the copper bird gyrating in the center of the room.

His gaiety suddenly overflowed, and taking a joyous leap in the air, he came back to her and said:

"I will call up my father!"

She could not understand. He leaned over her body and keeping his hand over her breast he dialed his father's telephone number.

Then she could see on his face what he wanted to tell his father: call his father, tell him what could not be told, but which his entire new body wanted to tell him: I have taken a woman! I have a woman of my own. I am your equal, Father! I am a man!

When his father answered Paul could only say the ordinary words a son can say to his father, but he uttered these ordinary words with exultant arrogance, as if his father could see him with his hand on Djuna's body: "Father, I am here."

"Where are you?" answered the father severely. "We're expecting you home. You can continue to see your friends but you must come home to please your mother. Your mother has dinner all ready for you!"

Paul laughed, laughed as he had never laughed as a boy, with his hand over the mouth of the telephone.

On such a day they are expecting him for dinner!

They were blind to the miracle. Over the telephone his father should hear and see that he had a woman of his own:

she was lying there smiling.

How dare the father command now! Doesn't he hear the new voice of the new man in his son?

He hung up.

His hair was falling over his eager eyes. Djuna pulled at it. He stopped her. "You can't do that any more, oh no." And he sank his teeth into the softest part of her neck.

"You're sharpening your teeth to become a great lover," she said.

When desire overtook him he always had a moment of wildly beating heart, almost of distress, before the invading tide. Before closing his eyes to kiss her, before abandoning himself, he always carefully closed the shutters, windows and doors.

This was the secret act, and he feared the eyes of the world upon him. The world was full of eyes upon his acts, eyes watching with disapproval.

That was the secret fear left from his childhood: dreams, wishes, acts, pleasures which aroused condemnation in the parents' eyes. He could not remember one glance of approval, of love, of admiration, of consent. From far back he remembered being driven into secrecy because whatever he revealed seemed to arouse disapproval or punishment.

He had read the *Arabian Nights* in secret, he had smoked in secret, he had dreamed in secret.

His parents had questioned him only to accuse him later.

And so he closed the shutters, curtains, windows, and then went to her and both of them closed their eyes upon their caresses.

There was a knitted blanket over the couch which he particularly liked. He would sit under it as if it were a tent. Through the interstices of the knitting he could see her and the room as through an oriental trellis. With one hand out of the blanket he would seek her little finger with his little finger and hold it.

As in an opium dream, this touching and interlacing of two little fingers became an immense gesture, the very fragile bridge of their relationship. By this little finger so gently and so lightly pulling hers he took her whole self as no one else had.

He drew her under the blanket thus, in a dreamlike way, by a small gesture containing the greatest power, a greater power than violence.

Once there they both felt secure from all the world, and from all threats, from the father and the detective, and all the taboos erected to separate lovers all over the world.

Lawrence rushed over to warn them that Paul's father had been seen driving through the neighborhood.

Paul and Djuna were having dinner together and were going to the ballet.

Paul had painted a feather bird for Djuna's hair and she was pinning it on when Lawrence came with the warning.

Paul became a little pale, then smiled and said: "Wafer, in case my father comes, could you make yourself less pretty?"

Djuna went and washed her face of all make-up, and then she unpinned the airy feather bird from her hair, and they sat down together to wait for the father.

Djuna said: "I'm going to tell you the story of Caspar Hauser, which is said to have happened many years ago in Austria. Caspar Hauser was about seventeen years old when he appeared in the city, a wanderer, lost and bewildered. He had been imprisoned in a dark room since childhood. His real origin was unknown, and the cause for the imprisonment. It was believed to be a court intrigue, that he might have been put away to substitute another ruler, or that he might have been an illegitimate son of the Queen. His jailer died and the boy found himself free. In solitude he had grown into manhood with the spirit of a child. He had only one dream in his possession, which he looked upon as a memory. He had once lived in a castle. He had been led to a room to see his mother. His mother stood behind a door. But he had never reached her. Was it a dream or a memory? He wanted to find this castle again, and his mother. The people of the city adopted him as a curiosity. His honesty, his immediate, childlike instinct about people, both infuriated and interested them. They tampered with him. They wanted to impose their beliefs on him, teach him, possess him. But the boy could sense their falsities, their treacheries, their self-interest. He belonged to his dream. He gave his whole faith only to the man who promised to take him back to his home and to his mother. And this man betrayed him, delivered him to his enemies. Just before his death he had met a woman, who had not dared to love him because he was so young, who had stifled her feeling. If she had dared he might have escaped his fate."

"Why didn't she dare?" asked Paul.

"She saw only the obstacle," said Djuna. "Most people see only the obstacle, and are stopped by it."

(No harm can befall you now, Paul, no harm can befall you. You have been set free. You made a good beginning. You were loved by the first object of your desire. Your first desire was answered. I made such a bad beginning! I began with a closed door. This harmed me, but you at least began with fulfillment. You were not hurt. You were not denied. I am the only one in danger. For that is all I am allowed to give you, a good beginning, and then I must surrender you.)

They sat and waited for the father.

Lawrence left them. The suspense made him uneasy.

Paul was teaching Djuna how to eat rice with chopsticks. Then he carefully cleaned them and was holding them now as they talked as if they were puppets representing a Balinese shadow theater of the thoughts neither one dared to formulate.

They sat and waited for the father.

Paul was holding the chopsticks like impudent puppets, gesticulating, then he playfully unfastened the first button of her blouse with them, deftly, and they laughed together.

"It's time for the ballet," said Djuna. "Your father is evidently not coming, or he would be here already."

She saw the illumination of desire light his face.

"Wait, Djuna." He unfastened the second button, and the third.

Then he laid his head on her breast and said: "Let's not go anywhere tonight. Let's stay here."

Paul despised small and shallow waves. He was drawn to a vastness which corresponded to his boundless dreams. He must possess the world in some big way, rule a large kingdom, expand in some absolute leadership.

He felt himself king as a child feels king, over kingdoms uncharted by ordinary men. He would not have the ordinary, the known. Only the vast, the unknown could satisfy him.

Djuna was a woman with echoes plunging into an endless past he could never explore completely. When he tasted her he tasted a suffering which had borne a fragrance, a fragrance which made deeper grooves. It was enough that he sensed the dark forests of experience, the unnamed rivers, the enigmatic mountains, the rich mines under the ground, the overflowing caves of secret knowledges. A vast ground for an intrepid adventurer.

Above all she was his "ocean," as he wrote her. "When a man takes a woman to himself he possesses the sea."

The waves, the enormous waves of a woman's love!

She was a sea whose passions could rise sometimes into

186

larger waves than he felt capable of facing!

Much as he loved danger, the unknown, the vast, he felt too the need of taking flight, to put distance and space between himself and the ocean for fear of being submerged!

Flight: into silence, into a kind of invisibility by which he could be sitting there on the floor while yet creating an impression of absence, able to disappear into a book, a drawing, into the music he listened to.

She was gazing at his little finger and the extreme fragility and sensitiveness of it astonished her.

(He is the transparent child.)

Before this transparent finger so artfully carved, sensitively wrought, boned, which alighted on objects with a touch of air and magic, at the marvel of it, the ephemeral quality of it, a wave of passion would mount within her and exactly like the wave of the ocean intending merely to roll over, cover the swimmer with an explosion of foam, in a rhythm of encompassing, and withdrawing, without intent to drag him to the bottom.

But Paul, with the instinct of the new swimmer, felt that there were times when he could securely hurl himself into the concave heart of the wave and be lifted into ecstasy and be delivered back again on the shore safe and whole; but that there were other times when this great inward curve disguised an undertow, times when he measured his strength and found it insufficient to return to shore.

Then he took up again the lighter games of his recently surrendered childhood.

Djuna found him gravely bending over a drawing and it was not what he did which conveyed his remoteness, but his way of sitting hermetically closed like some secret Chinese box whose surface showed no possibility of opening.

He sat then as children do, immured in his particular lonely world then, having built a magnetic wall of detachment.

It was then that he practiced as deftly as older men the great objectivity, the long-range view by which men eluded all personal difficulties: he removed himself from the present and the personal by entering into the most abstruse intricacies of a chess game, by explaining to her what Darwin had written when comparing the eye to a microscope, by dissertating on the pleuronectidae or flat fish, so remarkable for their asymmetrical bodies.

And Djuna followed this safari into the worlds of science, chemistry, geology with an awkwardness which was not due to any laziness of mind, but to the fact that the large wave of passion which had been roused in her at the prolonged sight of Paul's little finger was so difficult to dam, because the feeling of wonder before this spectacle was to her as great as that of the explorers before a new mountain peak, of the scientists before a new discovery.

She knew what excitement enfevered men at such moments of their lives, but she did not see any difference between the beauty of a high flight above the clouds and the subtly colored and changing landscape of adolescence she traversed through the contemplation of Paul's little finger.

A study of anthropological excavations made in Peru was no more wonderful to her than the half-formed dreams unearthed with patience from Paul's vague words, dreams of which they were only catching the prologue; and no forest of precious woods could be more varied than the oscillations of his extreme vulnerability which forced him to take cover, to disguise his feelings, to swing so movingly between great courage and a secret fear of pain.

The birth of his awareness was to her no lesser miracle than the discoveries of chemistry, the variations in his temperature, the mysterious angers, the sudden serenities, no less valuable than the studies of remote climates.

But when in the face of too large a wave, whose dome seemed more than a mere ecstasy of foam raining over the marvelous shape of his hands, a wave whose concaveness seemed more than a temporary womb in which he could lie for the fraction of an instant, the duration of an orgasm, he sat like a Chinese secret box with a surface revealing no possible opening to the infiltrations of tenderness or the flood of passion, then her larger impulse fractured with a strange pain into a multitude of little waves capped with frivolous sunspangles, secretly ashamed of its wild disproportion to the young man who sat there offering whatever he possessed— his intermittent manliness, his vastest dreams and his fear of his own expansions, his maturity as well as his fear of this maturity which was leading him out of the gardens of childhood.

And when the larger wave had dispersed into smaller ones, and when Paul felt free of any danger of being dragged to the bottom, free of that fear of possession which is the secret of all adolescence, when he had gained strength within his retreat, then he returned to tease and stir her warmth into activity again, when he felt equal to plunging into it, to lose himself in it, feeling the intoxication of the man who had conquered the sea. . . .

Then he would write to her exultantly: you are the sea. . . .

But she could see the little waves in himself gathering power for the future, preparing for the moment when he would be the engulfing one.

Then he seemed no longer the slender adolescent with dreamy gestures but a passionate young man rehearsing his future scenes of domination.

He wore a white scarf through the gray streets of the city, a white scarf of immunity. His head resting on the folds was the head of the dreamer walking through the city selecting by a white magic to see and hear and gather only according to his inner needs, slowly and gradually building as each one does ultimately, his own world out of the material at hand

189

from which he was allowed at least a freedom of selection.

The white scarf asserted the innumerable things which did not touch him: choked trees, broken windows, cripples, obscenities penciled on the walls, the lascivious speeches of the drunks, the miasmas and corrosions of the city.

He did not see or hear them.

After traversing deserted streets, immured in his inner dream, he would suddenly open his eyes upon an organ grinder and his monkey.

What he brought home again was always some object by which men sought to overcome mediocrity: a book, a painting, a piece of music to transform his vision of the world, to expand and deepen it.

The white scarf did not lie.

It was the appropriate flag of his voyages.

His head resting fittingly on its white folds was immune to stains. He could traverse sewers, hospitals, prisons, and none left their odor upon him. His coat, his breath, his hair, when he returned, still exhaled the odor of his dream.

This was the only virgin forest known to man: this purity of selection.

When Paul returned with his white scarf gleaming it was all that he rejected which shone in its folds.

He was always a little surprised at older people's interest in him.

He did not know himself to be the possessor of anything they might want, not knowing that in his presence they were violently carried back to their first dream.

Because he stood at the beginning of the labyrinth and not in the heart of it, he made everyone aware of the turn where they had lost themselves. With Paul standing at the entrance of the maze, they recaptured the beginning of their voyage, they remembered their first intent, their first image, their first desires.

They would don his white scarf and begin anew.

And yet today she felt there was another purity, a greater

purity which lay in the giving of one's self. She felt pure when she gave herself, and Paul felt pure when he withdrew himself.

The tears of his mother, the more restrained severity of his father, brought him home again.

His eighteenth birthday came and this was the one they could not spend together, this being his birthday in reality, the one visible to his parents. Whereas with Djuna he had spent so many birthdays which his parents could not have observed, with their limited knowledge of him.

They had not attended the birthday of his manhood, the birthday of his roguish humorous self, of his first drunkenness, his first success at a party; or the birthday of his eloquent self on the theme of poetry, painting or music. Or the birthday of his imagination, his fantasy, of his new knowledge of people, of his new assertions and his discoveries of unknown powers in himself.

This succession of birthdays that had taken place since he left home was the highest fiesta ever attended by Djuna, the spectacle of unpredictable blooms, of the shells breaking around his personality, the emergence of the man.

But his real birthday they could not spend together.

His mother made dinner for him, and he played chess with his father—they who loved him less and who had bound and stifled him with prohibitions, who had delayed his manhood.

His mother made a birthday cake iced and sprinkled with warnings against expansion, cautions against new friends, designed a border like those of formal gardens as if to outline all the proprieties with which to defeat adventure.

His father played chess with him silently, indicating in the carefully measured moves a judgment upon all the wayward dances of the heart, the caprices of the body, above all a judg-

191

ment upon such impulses as had contributed to Paul's very presence there, the act of conjunction from which had been formed the luminous boy eating at their table.

The cake they fed him was the cake of caution: to fear all human beings and doubt the motivations of all men and women not listed in the Social Directory.

The candles were not lit to celebrate his future freedom, but to say: only within the radius lighted by these birthday candles, only within the radius of father and mother are you truly safe.

A small circle. And outside of this circle, evil.

And so he ate of this birthday cake baked by his mother, containing all the philters against love, expansion and freedom known to white voodoo.

A cake to prevent and preserve the child from becoming man!

No more nights together, when to meet the dawn together was the only marriage ceremony accorded to lovers.

But he returned to her one day carrying the valise with his laundry. On his return home he had packed his laundry to have it washed at home. And his mother had said: "Take it back. I won't take care of laundry you soiled while living with strangers."

So quietly he brought it back to Djuna, to the greater love that would gladly take care of his belongings as long as they were the clothes he soiled in his experience with freedom.

The smallness of his shirts hurt her, like a sign of dangers for him which she could not avert. He was still slender enough, young enough to be subjected to tyranny.

They were both listening to César Franck's Symphony in D Minor.

And then the conflicting selves in Djuna fused into one mood as they do at such musical crossroads.

The theme of the symphony was gentleness.

She had first heard it at the age of sixteen one rainy afternoon and associated it with her first experience of love, of a love without climax which she had known with Michael. She had interwoven this music with her first concept of the nature of love as one of ultimate, infinite gentleness.

In César Franck's symphony there was immediate exaltation, dissolution in feeling and the evasion of violence. Over and over again in this musical ascension of emotion, the stairway of fever was climbed and deserted before one reached explosion.

An obsessional return to minor themes, creating an endless tranquillity, and at sixteen she had believed that the experience of love was utterly contained in this gently flowing drug, in the delicate spirals, cadences, and undulations of this music.

César Franck came bringing messages of softness and trust, accompanying Paul's gestures and attitudes, and for this she trusted him, a passion without the storms of destruction.

She had wanted such nebulous landscapes, such vertiginous spirals without explosions: the drug.

Listening to the symphony flowing and yet not flowing (for there was a static groove in which it remained imprisoned, so similar to the walled-in room of her house, containing a mystery of stillness), Djuna saw the Obelisk in the Place de la Concorde, the arrow of stone placed at the center of a gracefully turbulent square, summating gardens, fountains and rivers of automobiles. One pointed dart of stone to pierce the night, the fog, the rain, the sun, aiming faultlessly into the clouds.

And there was the small, crazy woman Matilda, whom everyone knew, who came every morning and sat on one of the benches near the river, and stayed there all day, watching the passers-by, eating sparingly and lightly of some mysterious food in crumbs out of a paper bag, like the pigeons. So familiar

193

to the policeman, to the tourists, and to the permanent in-habitants of the Place de la Concorde, that not to see her there would have been as noticeable, as disturbing, as to find the Obelisk gone, and the square left without its searchlight into the sky.

Matilda was known for her obstinacy in sitting there through winter and summer, her indifference to climate, her vague answers to those who sought her reasons for being there, her tireless watchfulness, as if she were keeping a rendezvous with eternity.

Only at sundown did she leave, sometimes gently incited by the policeman.

Since there was not total deterioration in her clothes, or in her health, everyone surmised she must have a home and no one was ever concerned about her.

Djuna had once sat beside her and Matilda at first would not speak, but addressed herself to the pigeons and to the falling autumn leaves, murmuring, whispering, muttering by turns. Then suddenly she said to Djuna very simply and clearly: "My lover left me sitting here and said he would come back."

(The policeman had said: I have seen her sitting there for twenty years.)

"How long have you been sitting here and waiting?" Djuna asked.

"I don't know."

She ate of the same bread she was feeding the pigeons. Her face was wrinkled but not aged, through the wrinkles shone an expression which was not of age, which was the expression of alert waiting, watchfulness, expectation of the young.

"He will come back," she said, for the first time a look of defiance washing her face of its spectator's pallor, the pallor of the recluse who lives without intimate relationship to stir the rhythms of the blood, this glazed expression of those who watch the crowd passing by and never recognize a face.

"Of course he will," said Djuna, unable to bear even the shadow of anxiety on the woman's face.

Matilda's face recovered its placidity, its patience.

"He told me to sit here and wait."

A mortal blow had stopped the current of her life, but had not shattered her. It had merely paralyzed her sense of time, she would sit and wait for the lost lover and the years were obliterated by the anesthesia of the deadened cell of time: five minutes stretched to infinity and kept her alive, alive and ghostly, with the cell of time, the little clock of reality inside the brain forever damaged. A faceless clock pointing to anguish. And with time was linked pain, lodged in the same cell (neighbors and twins), time and pain in more or less intimate relationship.

And what was left was this shell of a woman immune to cold and heat, anesthetized by a great loss into immobility and timelessness.

Sitting there beside Matilda Djuna heard the echoes of the broken cell within the little psychic stage of her own heart, so well enacted, so neat, so clear, and wondered whether when her father left the house for good in one of his moods of violence as much damage had been done to her, and whether some part of her being had not been atrophied, preventing complete openness and complete development in living.

By his act of desertion he had destroyed a cell in Djuna's being, an act of treachery from a cruel world setting her against all fathers, while retaining the perilous hope of a father returning under the guise of the men who resembled him, to re-enact again the act of violence.

It was enough for a man to possess certain attributes of the father—any man possessed of power—and then her being came alive with fear as if the entire situation would be re-enacted inevitably: possession, love and desertion, replacing her on a bench like Matilda, awaiting a denouement.

Looking back, there had been a momentous break in the flow, a change of activity.

Every authoritarian step announced the return of the father and danger. For the father's last words had been: "I will come back."

Matilda had been more seriously injured: the life flow had stopped. She had retained the first image, the consciousness that she must wait, and the last words spoken by the lover had been a command for eternity: wait until I come back.

As if these words had been uttered by a proficient hypnotist who had then cut off all her communications with the living, so that she was not permitted even this consolation allowed to other deserted human beings: the capacity to transfer this love to another, to cheat the order given, to resume life with others, to forget the first one.

Matilda had been mercifully arrested and suspended in time, and rendered unconscious of pain.

But not Djuna.

In Djuna the wound had remained alive, and whenever life touched upon this wound she mistook the pain she felt for being alive, and her pain warning her and guiding her to deflect from man the father to man the son.

She could see clearly all the cells of her being, like the rooms of her house which had blossomed, enriched, developed and stretched far and beyond all experiences, but she could see also the cell of her being like the walled-in room of her house in which was lodged violence as having been shut and condemned within her out of fear of disaster.

There was a little cell of her being in which she still existed as a child, which only activated with a subtle anger in the presence of the father, for in relation to him she lost her acquired power, her assurance, she was rendered small again and returned to her former state of helplessness and dependence.

And knowing the tragic outcome of this dependence she felt hostility and her route towards the man of power bristled with this hostility—an immediate need to shut out violence.

Paul and Djuna sat listening to César Franck's Symphony in D Minor, in this little room of gentleness and trust, barring violence from the world of love, seeking an opiate against

196

destruction and treachery.

So she had allied herself with the son against the father. He had been there to forbid and thus to strengthen the desire. He had been there, large and severe, to threaten the delicate, precarious bond, and thus to render it desperate and make each encounter a reprieve from death and loss.

The movements of the symphony and her movements had been always like Paul's, a ballet of oscillations, peripheral entrances and exits, figures designed to become invisible in moments of danger, pirouetting with all the winged knowledge of birds to avoid collision with violence and severity.

Together they had taken leaps into the air to avoid obstacles.

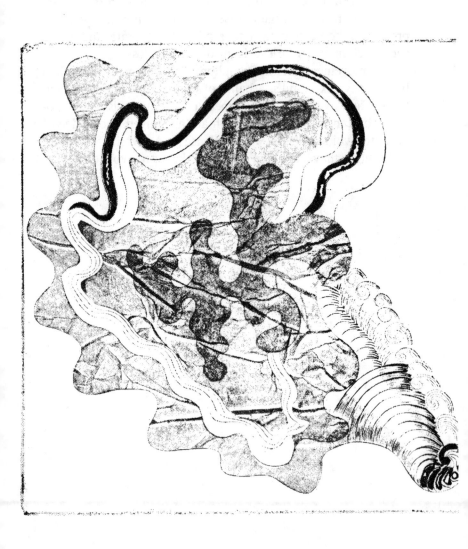

The Café

THE CAFÉS WERE THE WELLS of treasures, the caves of Ali
Baba.

The cafés were richer even than the oriental cities where
all living was plied openly under your eyes so that you were
offered all the activities of the world to touch and smell. You
saw your shoes being made from the skinning of the animal
to the polishing of the leather. You saw the weaving of cloth
and the dyeing in pails of multicolored liquids. You saw the
scribes writing letters for the illiterate, the philosopher meditating, the religious man chanting as he squatted and the lepers

199

disintegrating under your eyes, within the touch of your hand.

And so in the café, with one franc for a glass of wine and even less for coffee, you could hear stories from the Pampas, share in African voodoo secrets, read the pages of a book being written, listen to a poem, to the death rattles of an aristocrat, the life story of a revolutionary. You could hear the hummed theme of a symphony, watch the fingers of a jazz drummer drumming on the table, accept an invitation from a painter who would take you to the Zoo to watch the serpents eat their daily ration of white mice, consult a secretive Hindu on his explorations of occult streets, or meet an explorer who would take you on his sailboat around the world.

The chill of autumn was tempered by little coal stoves and glass partitions.

A soft rain covered the city with a muted lid, making it intimate like a room, shutting out sky and sun as if drawing curtains, lighting lamps early, kindling fires in the fireplaces, pushing human beings gently to live under the surface, inciting them to sprout words, sparkling colors out of their own flesh, to become light, fire, flowers and tropical fiestas.

The café was the hothouse, densely perfumed with all the banned oils, the censured musks, the richest blooms accelerated by enclosure, warmth, and crossgraftings from all races.

No sunsets, no dawns, but exhibits of paintings rivaling all in luxuriance. Rivers of words, forests of sculptures, huge pyramids of personalities. No need of gardens.

City and cafés became intimate like a room that was carpeted, quilted for the easy intermingling of man's inner landscapes, his multiple secret wishes vibrating from table to table as elbows and the _garçon_ not only carried brimming glasses but endless messages and signals as the servants did in the old Arabian tales.

Day and night were colliding gently at twilight, throwing off erotic sparks.

Day and night met on the boulevards.

Sabina was always breaking the molds which life formed around her.

She was always trespassing boundaries, erasing identifications.

She could not bear to have a permanent address or to give her telephone number.

Her greatest pleasure consisted in being where no one knew she was, in an out-of-the-way café, a little-known hotel, if possible a room from which the number had been scratched off.

She changed her name as criminals efface their tracks.

She herself did not know what she was preserving from detection, what mystery she was defending.

She hated factual questions as to her activities. Above all she hated to be registered in any of the official books. She hated to give her birth hour, her genealogy, and all her dealings with passport authorities were blurred and complicated.

She lived entirely by a kind of opportunism, all her acts dictated by the demands of the present situation. She eluded tabulations only to place herself more completely at the disposal of anyone's fantasy about her.

She kept herself free of all identifications the better to obey some stranger's invention about her.

As soon as a man appeared the game began.

She must keep silent. She must let him look at her face and let his dream take form. She must allow time and silence for his invention to develop.

She let him build an image. She saw the image take form in his eyes. If she said what she wanted to say he might think her an ordinary woman!

This image of herself as a *not* ordinary woman, an image which was trembling now in his eyes, might suddenly disappear. Nothing more difficult to live up to than men's dreams. Nothing more tenuous, elusive to fulfill than men's dreams.

She might say the wrong phrase, make the wrong gesture, smile the wrong smile, and then see his eyes waver vulnerably for one instant before turning to the glassy brilliance of disillusion.

She wanted desperately to answer man's most impossible wishes. If the man said: you seem perverse to me, then she would set about gathering together all her knowledge of perversity to become what he had called her.

It made life difficult. She lived the tense, strained life of an international spy. She moved among enemies set on exposing her pretenses. People felt the falseness at times and sought to uncover her.

She had such a fear of being discovered!

She could not bear the light of common, everyday simplicities! As other women blink at the sunlight, she blinked at the light of common everyday simplicities.

And so this race which must never stop. To run from the slanting eyes of one to the caressing hands of another to the sadness of the third.

As she collided with people they lost their identities also: they became objects of desire, objects to be consumed, fuel for the bonfire. Their quality was summarized as either inflammable or noninflammable. That was all that counted. She never distinguished age, nationality, class, fortune, status, occupation or vocation.

Her desire rushed instantaneously, without past or future. A point of fire in the present to which she attached no contracts, no continuity.

Her breasts were always heavy and full. She was like a messenger carrying off all she received from one to carry it to the other, carrying in her breasts the words said to her, the book given her, the land visited, the experience acquired, in the form of stories to be spun continuously.

Everything lived one hour before was a story to tell the following hour to the second companion. From room to room what was perpetuated was her pollen-carrying body.

When someone asked her: where are you going now? whom are you going to meet? she lied. She lied because this current sweeping her onward seemed to cause others pain.

Crossing the street she nourished herself upon the gallant smile of the policeman who stopped the traffic for her. She culled the desire of the man who pushed the revolving door for her. She gathered the flash of adoration from the drugstore clerk: are you an actress? She picked the bouquet of the shoe salesman trying on her shoes: are you a dancer? As she sat in the bus she received the shafts of the sun as a personal intimate visit. She felt a humorous connivance with the truck driver who had to pull the brakes violently before her impulsive passages and who did so smiling.

Every moment this current established itself, this state of flow, of communication by seduction.

She always returned with her arms full of adventures, as other women return with packages. Her whole body rich with this which nourished her and from which she nourished others. The day finished always too early and she was not empty of restlessness.

Leaning out of the window at dawn, pressing her breasts upon the window sill, she still looked out of the window hoping to see what she had failed to grasp, to possess. She looked at the ending night and the passersby with the keen alertness of the voyager who can never reach terminations as ordinary people reach peaceful terminals at the end of each day, accepting pauses, deserts, rests, havens, as she could not accept them.

She believed only in fire. She wanted to be at every explosion of fire, every convergence of danger. She lived like a fireman, tense for all the emergencies of conflagrations. She was a menace to peaceful homes, tranquil streets.

She was the firebug who was never detected.

Because she believed that fire ladders led to love. This was the motive for her incendiary habits. But Sabina, with all her fire ladders, could not find love.

At dawn she would find herself among ashes again.

And so she could not rest or sleep.

As soon as the day dawned peaceful, uneventful, Sabina

slipped into her black satin dress, lacquered her nails the color of her mood, pulled her black cape around her and set out for the cafés.

At dawn Jay turned towards Lillian lying beside him and his first kiss reached her through the net of her hair.

Her eyes were closed, her nerves asleep, but under his hand her body slipped down a dune into warm waves lapping over each other, rippling her skin.

Jay's sensual thrusts wakened the dormant walls of flesh, and tongues of fire flicked towards his hard lashings piercing the kernel of mercury, disrupting a current of fire through the veins. The burning fluid of ecstacy eddying madly and breaking, loosening a river of pulsations.

The core of ecstacy bursting to the rhythmic pounding, until his hard thrusts spurted burning fluid against the walls of flesh, impulsion within the womb like a thunderbolt.

Lillian's panting decreased, and her body reverberated in the silence, filled with echoes . . . antennae which had drunk like the stems of plants.

He awakened free, and she did not.

His desire had reached a finality, like a clean saber cut which dealt pleasure, not death.

She felt impregnated.

She had greater difficulty in shifting, in separating, in turning away.

Her body was filled with retentions, residues, sediments.

He awakened and passed into other realms. The longer his stay in the enfolding whirls, the greater his energy to enter activity again. He awakened and he talked of painting, he awakened laughing, eyes closed with laughter, laughing on the edge of his cheeks, laughter in the corner of his mouth, the laughter of great separateness.

She awakened unfree, as if laden with the seeds of his being, wondering at what moment he would pull his whole self away as one tears a plant out by the roots, leaving a crevice in the earth. Dreading the break because she felt him a master of this act, free to enter and free to emerge, whereas she felt dispossessed of her identity and freedom because Jay upon awakening did not turn about and contemplate her even for a moment as Lillian, a particular woman, but that when he took her, or looked at her he did so gaily, anonymously, as if any woman lying there would have been equally pleasant, natural, and not Lillian among all women.

He was already chuckling at some idea for a painting, already hungry for breakfast, ready to open his mail and embark on multiple relationships, curious about the day's climate, the changes in the street, the detailed news of the brawl of the night before which had taken place under their window.

Fast fast fast moving away, his mind already pursuing the wise sayings of Lao-tse, the theories of Picasso, already like a vast wheel at the fair starting on a wide circle which at no point whatever seemed to include her, because she was there like bread for him, a nonidentifiable bread which he ate of as he would eat any bread, not even troubling with the ordinary differentiations: today my bread is fresh and warm, and today it is a little dry, today it lacks salt, today it is lifeless, today it is golden and crisp.

She did not reach out to possess Jay, as he believed, but she reached out because so much of Jay had been deposited, sown, planted within her that she felt possessed, as if she were no longer able to move, breathe, live independently of him. She felt her dependence, lost to herself, given, invaded, and at his mercy, and the anxiety of this, the defenselessness caused a clinging which was the clinging of the drowning. . . .

As if she were bread, she would have liked Jay at least to notice all variations in moods and flavors. She would have liked Jay to say: you are my bread, a very unique and marvelous bread, like none other. If you were not here I would die of instantaneous starvation.

Not at all. If he painted well, it was the spring day. If he were gay, it was the Pernod. If he were wise, it was the little book of Lao-tse's sayings. If he were elated, it was due to a worshipful letter in the mail.

And me, and me, said a small, anxious voice in Lillian's being, where am I?

She was not even the woman in his paintings.

He was painting Sabina. He painted her as a mandrake with fleshy roots, bearing a solitary purple flower in a purple bell-shaped corolla of narcotic flesh. He painted her born with red-gold eyes always burning as from caverns, from holes in the earth, from behind trees. Painted her as one of the luxuriant women, a tropical growth, excommunicated from the bread line as too rich a substance for everyday living, placing her there merely as a denizen of the world of fire, and was content with her intermittent, parabolic appearances.

So, if she was not in his paintings, Lillian thought, where was she? When he finished painting he drank. When he drank he exulted in his powers and palmed it all on the holy ghost inside of him, each time calling the spirit animating him by a different name that was not Lillian. Today it was the holy ghost, and the spring light and a dash of Pernod.

He did not say what Lillian wanted to hear: "You are the holy ghost inside of me. You make my spring."

She was not even sure of that—of being his holy ghost. At times it seemed to her that he was painting with Djuna's eyes. When Djuna was there he painted better. He did not paint her. He only felt strong and capable when he tackled huge masses, strong features, heavy bodies. Djuna's image was too tenuous for him.

But when she was there he painted better.

Silently she seemed to be participating, silently she seemed to be transmitting forces.

Where did her force come from? No one knew.

She merely sat there and the colors began to organize themselves, to deepen, as if he took the violet from her eyes when she was angry, the blue when she was at peace, the gray when she was detached, the gold when she was melted and warm, and painted with them. Using her eyes as a color chart.

In this way he passed from the eyes of Lillian which said: "I am here to warm you." Eyes of devotion.

To the eyes of Sabina which said: "I am here to consume you."

To the eyes of Djuna which said: "I am here to reflect your painter's dream, like a crystal ball."

Bread and fire and light, he needed them all. He could be nourished on Lillian's faith but it did not illumine his work. There were places into which Lillian could not follow him. When he was tormented by a half-formed image he went to Djuna, just as once walking through the streets with her he had seen a child bring her a tangled skein of string to unravel.

He would have liked the three women to love each other. It seemed to him that then he would be at peace. When they pulled against each other for supremacy it was as if different parts of his own body pulled against each other.

On days when Lillian accepted understanding through the eyes of Djuna, when each one was connected with her role and did not seek to usurp the other's place he was at peace and slept profoundly.

(If only, thought Lillian, lying in the disordered bed, when he moved away I could be quiet and complete and free. He seems bound to me and then so completely unbound. He changes. One day I look at him and there is warmth in him, and the next a kind of ruthlessness. There are times when he kisses me and I feel he is not kissing me but any woman, or all the women he has known. There are times when he seems made of wax, and I can see on him the imprint of all those he has seen during the day. I can hear their words. Last night he even fraternized with the man who was courting me. What does this mean? Even with Edgar who was trying to take me away from him. He was in one of his moods of effusive display, when he loved everybody. He is promiscuous. I can't bear how near they come, they talk in his face, they breathe his breath. Anyone at all has this privilege. Anyone can talk to him, share his house, and even me. He gives away everything. Djuna says I lack faith. . . . Is that what it is? But how can I heal myself? I thought one could get healed by just living and loving.)

Lying in bed and listening to Jay whistling while he shaved in the bathroom, Lillian wondered why she felt simultaneously in bondage and yet unmarried, unappeased, and all her conversations with Djuna with whom she was able to talk even better than to monologue with herself once more recurred to her before she allowed herself to face the dominant impulse ruling her: to run away from Jay.

Passion gathered its momentum, its frenzy, from the effort to possess what was unpossessable in reality, because it sprang from an illusion, because it gained impetus from a secret knowledge of its unfulfillable quality, because it attacked romantic organisms, and incited to fever in place of a natural union by feelings. Passion between two people came from a feverish desire to fuse elements which were unfusable. The extreme heat to which human beings subjected themselves in this experiment, as if by intensity the unfusable elements could be melted into one—water with fire, fire with earth, rock and water. An effort doomed to defeat.

Lillian could not see all this, but felt it happening, and knew that this was why she had wept so bitterly at their first quarrel: not weeping over a trivial difference but because her instinct warned her senses that this small difference indicated a wider one, a difference of elements, by which the relationship would ultimately be destroyed.

In one of his cheerful, human moods Jay had said: "If my friends bother you so much, we shall put them all against a wall and shoot them."

But Lillian knew that if today Jay surrendered today's set

of friends, he would renew the same kind of relationships with a new set, for they reflected the part of him she did not feel close to, the part in fact she was at war with.

Lillian's disproportionate weeping had seemed childish to Jay who saw only the immediate difference, but Lillian was weeping blindly with a fear of death of the relationship, with her loss of faith sensing the first fissure as the first symbol of future dissolution, and knowing from that moment on that the passion between them would no longer be an affirmation of marriage but a struggle against death and separation.

(Djuna said: You can't bear to let this relationship die. But why must it die, Djuna? Do you believe all passion must die? Is there nothing I can do to avoid failure? Passion doesn't die of natural death. Everyone says passion dies, love dies, but it's we who kill it. Djuna believes this. Djuna said: You can fight all the symptoms of divorce when they first appear, you can be on your guard against distortions, against the way people wound each other and instill doubt, you can fight for the life and continuity of this passion, there *is* a knowledge which postpones the death of a relationship, death is not natural, but, Lillian, you cannot do it alone, there are seeds of death in his character. One cannot fight alone for a living relationship. It takes the effort of two. Effort, effort. The word most foreign to Jay. Jay would never make an effort. Djuna, Djuna, couldn't you talk to him? Djuna, will you talk to him? No, it's useless, he does not want anything that is difficult to reach. He does not like effort or struggles. He wants only his pleasure. It isn't possessiveness, Djuna, but I want to feel at the center so that I can allow him the maximum freedom without feeling each time that he betrays everything, destroys everything.)

She would run away.

When Jay saw her dressing, powdering her face, pulling up her stockings, combing her hair, he noticed no change in her gestures to alarm him, for did she not always comb her hair and powder and dress with the flurry of a runaway. Wasn't she always so uneasy and overquick, as if she had been frightened?

He went to his studio and Lillian locked the door of the bedroom and sat at her piano, to seek in music that wholeness which she could not find in love. . . .

Just as the sea often carries bodies, wrecks, shells, lost objects carved by the sea itself in its own private studio of sculpture to unexpected places, led by irrational currents, just so did the current of music eject fragments of the self believed drowned and deposited them on the shore altered, recarved, rendered anonymous in shape. Each backwash, each cross-current, throwing up new material formed out of the old, from the ocean of memories.

Driftwood figures that had been patiently recarved by the sea with rhythms broken by anger, patiently remolding forms to the contours of knotted nightmares, woods stunted and distorted by torments of doubts.

She played until this flood of debris rose from the music to choke her, closed the piano with anger, and rose to plan her escape.

Escape. Escape.

Her first instinctive, blind gesture of escape was to don the black cape copied from Sabina's at the time of their relationship.

She wrapped Sabina's cape around her, and put two heavy bracelets around her wrist (one for each wrist, not wanting any more to be in bondage to one, never to one; she would split the desire in two, to rescue one half of herself from destruction).

And for the first time since her marriage to Jay, she climbed the worn stairs of a very old hotel in Montparnasse, experiencing the exaltation familiar to runaways.

The more she could see of the worn carpet and its bare skeleton, the more acrid the smell of poverty, the more bare the room, this which might have lowered the diapason of another's mood only increased the elation of hers, becoming transfigured by her conviction that she was making a voyage which would forever take her away from the prison of anxiety, the pain of dependence on a human being she could not trust. Her mood of liberation spangled and dappled shabbiness with light like an impressionist painting.

Her sense of familiarity with this scene did not touch her at first: a lover was waiting for her in one of the rooms of this hotel.

Could anyone help her to forget Jay for a moment? Could Edgar help her, Edgar with his astonished eyes saying to her: You are wonderful, you are wonderful! Drunkenly repeating you are wonderful! as they danced under Jay's very eyes not seeing, not seeing her dancing with Edgar in the luminous spotlight of a night club, but when her dress opened a little at the throat she could smell the mixed odor of herself and Jay.

She was taking revenge now for his effusive confessions as to the pleasures he had taken with other women.

She had been made woman by Jay, he alone held in his hands all the roots of her being, and when he had pulled them, in his own limitless motions outward and far, he had inflicted such torture that he had destroyed the roots all at once and sent her into space, sent her listening to Edgar's words gratefully, grateful for Edgar's hands on her pulling her away from Jay, grateful for his foolish gift of flowers in silver paper (because Jay gave her no gifts at all), and she would imagine Jay watching this scene, watching her go up the stairs to Edgar's room, wearing flowers in a silver paper, and she enjoyed imagining his pain, as he witnessed the shedding of her clothes, witnessed her lying down beside Edgar. (You are the man of the crowd, Jay, and so I lie here beside a stranger. What makes me lonely, Jay, are the cheap and gaudy people you are friendly with, and I lie here with a stranger who is only caressing you inside of me. He is complaining like a woman: you are not thinking of me, you are not filled with me.)

But no sooner had she shed her cape copied from Sabina's than she recognized the room, the man, the scene, and the feelings as not belonging to her, not having been selected by her, but as having been borrowed from Sabina's repertoire of stories of adventures.

Lillian was not free of Jay since she had invited him to witness the scene enacted solely to punish his unfaithfulness. She was not free, she was being Sabina, with the kind of man Sabina would have chosen. All the words and gestures prescribed by Sabina in her feverish descriptions, for thus was much experience transmitted by contagion, and Lillian, not yet free, had been more than others predisposed to the contagion by lowered resistance!

She was ashamed, not of the sensual meeting, but for having acted in disguise, and eluded responsibility.

When the stranger asked her for her name she did not say Lillian, but Sabina.

She returned home to shed her cape and her acts, pretending not to know this woman who had spent hours with a stranger.

To put the responsibility on Sabina.

Escape escape escape—into what? Into borrowing the self of Sabina for an hour. She had donned the recklessness of Sabina, borrowed her cape for a shy masquerade, pretending freedom.

The clothes had not fitted very well.

But after a while, would this cease to be a role and did the borrowing reveal Lillian's true desires?

The possibility of being this that she borrowed.

Blindly ashamed of what she termed unfaithfulness (when actually she was still so tied to Jay it was merely within the precincts of their relationship that she could act, with his presence, and therefore unsevered from him), she discarded all the elements of this charade, cape, bracelets, then bathed and dressed in her own Lillian costume and went to the café where she sat beside Sabina who had already accumulated several plates by which the waiter was able to add the number of drinks.

212

When Jay felt exhausted after hours of painting he went to see Djuna.

He always softened as he thought of Djuna. She was to him more than a woman. It had been difficult at first to see her simply as a woman. His first impression had been an association with Florentine painting, his feeling that no matter what her origin, her experiences, her resemblances to other women, she was for him like a canvas which had been covered first of all with a coating of gold paint, so that whatever one painted over it, this gold on which he had dissertated during one of his early visits to her, was present as it remained present in the Florentine paintings.

But even though his obsession for dispelling illusions, which made him pull at her eyelashes to see if they were real, which made him open jars and bottles in the bathroom to see what they contained, even though he always had the feeling that women resorted to tricks and contrived spells which man must watch out for, he still felt that she was more than a woman, and that given the right moment, she was willing to shed the veils, the elusiveness, and to be completely honest.

It was not her clarity either, which he called honesty. Her clarity he distrusted. She always made wonderful patterns— he admitted that. There was a kind of Grecian symmetry to her movements, her life, and her words. They looked convincingly harmonious, clear—too clear. And in the meanwhile where was she? Not on the clear orderly surface of her ideas any longer, but submerged, sunk in some obscure realm like a submarine. She had only appeared to give you all her thoughts. She had only seemed to empty herself in this clarity. She gave you a neat pattern and then slipped out of it herself and laughed at you. Or else she gave you a neat pattern and then slipped out of it herself and then the utterly tragic expression of her face testified to some other realm she had entered and not allowed one to follow her into, a realm of despair even, a realm of anguish, which was only betrayed by her eyes.

What was the mystery of woman? Only this obstinacy in concealing themselves—merely this persistence in creating mysteries, as if the exposure of her thoughts and feelings were gifts reserved for love and intimacy.

He suspected that some day an honest woman would clear all this away. He never suspected for a moment that this mystery was a part of themselves they did not know, could not see.

Djuna, he ruminated, was a more ornamented woman, but an honest one.

He had long ago found a way to neutralize the potencies of woman by a simplification all his own, which was to consider all women as sharing but one kind of hunger, a hunger situated between the two pale columns of the legs. Even the angels, said Jay, even the angels, and the mothers, and the sisters, were all made the same way, and he retained this focus upon them from the time when he was a very little boy playing on the floor of his mother's kitchen and an enormous German woman had come straight to them from the immigration landing, still wearing her voluminous peasant skirts, her native costume, and she had stood in the kitchen asking his mother to help her find work, using some broken jargon impossible to understand—everyone in the house dismayed by her foreignness, her braids, her speech. As if to prove her capabilities through some universal gesture, she had started to knead the dough expertly, kneading with fervor, while Jay's mother watched her with increasing interest.

Jay was playing on the floor with matches, unnoticed, and he found himself covered as by a huge and colorful tent by the perfoliate skirt of the German woman, his glance lost where two pale columns converged in a revelation which had given him forever this perspective of woman's being, this vantage point of insight, this observatory and infallible focus, which prevented him from losing his orientation in the vastest maze of costumes, classes, races, nationalities—no external variations able to deprive him of this intimate knowledge of woman's most secret architecture. . . .

Chuckling, he thought of Djuna's expression whenever she opened the door to receive him.

The dreamer wears fur and velvet blinkers.

Chuckling, Jay thought of himself entering the house, and of her face shining between these blinkers of her vision of him as a great painter, shutting out with royal indifference all other elements which might disturb this vision.

He could see on her face this little shrine built by the dreamer in which she placed him as a great painted. Won by her fervor, he would enter with her into her dream of him, and begin to listen raptly to her way of transmuting into gold everything he told her!

If he had stolen from the Zombie's pocketbook she said it was because the Zombie was provocatively miserly. If he complained that he was oversleeping when he should be working Djuna translated it that he was catching up on sleep lost during the period when he had only a moving-picture hall to sleep in.

She only heard and saw what she wanted to hear and see. (Damn women!) Her expression of expectancy, of faith, her perpetual absolution of his acts disconcerted him at times.

The more intently he believed all she believed while he was with her, the more precipitately he fell out of grace when he left her, because he felt she was the depository of his own dream, and that she would keep it while he turned his back on it.

One of the few women, chuckled Jay, who understood the artificial paradise of art, the language of man.

As he walked, the city took on the languid beauty of a woman, which was the beauty of Paris, especially at five o'clock, at twilight, when the fountains, the parks, the soft lighting, the humid streets like blue mirrors, all dissolved into a haze of pearl, extending their fripperies and coquetries.

At the same hour New York took on its masculine and aggressive beauty, with its brash lighting, its steel arrows and giant obelisks piercing the sky, an electric erectness, a rigid city pitiless to lovers, sending detectives to hotel rooms to track them down, at the same hour that the French waiter said to the couples: do you wish a *cabinet particulier*—at the same hour that in New York all the energies were poured into steel structures, digging oil wells, harnessing electricity, for power.

Jay walked leisurely, like a ragpicker of good moments, walked through streets of joy, throwing off whatever disturbed him, gathering only what pleased him, noticing with delight that the washed and faded blue of the café awning matched the washed faded blue face of the clock in the church spire.

Then he saw the café table where Lillian sat talking with Sabina, and knowing his dream of becoming a great painter securely stored in the eyes of Djuna (damn women!) he decided to sin against it by sinking into the more shallow fantasies born of absinthe.

Djuna awakened from so deep a dream that opening her eyes was like pushing aside a heavy shroud of veils, a thousand layers of veils, and with a sensation similar to that of the trapezist who has been swinging in vast spaces, and suddenly feels again in his two hands the coarse touch of the swing cord.

She awakened fully to the painful knowledge that this was a day when she would be possessed by a mood which cut her off from fraternity.

It was also at those moments that she would have the clearest intuitions, sudden contacts with the deepest selves of others, divine the most hidden sorrow.

But if she spoke from this source, others would feel uneasy, not recognizing the truth of what she said. They always felt exposed and were quick to revenge themselves. They rushed to defend this exposure of the self they did not know, they were not familiar with, or did not like. They blamed her for excess of imagination, for exaggeration.

They persisted in living on familiar terms only with the surface of their personalities, and what she reached lay deeper where they could not see it. They felt at ease among their falsities, and the nakedness of her insight seemed like forcing open underworlds whose entrance was tacitly barred in everyday intercourse.

They would accuse her of living in a world of illusion while they lived in reality.

Their falsities had such an air of solidity, entirely supported by the palpable.

But she felt that on the contrary, she had contact with their secret desires, secret fears, secret intents. And she had faith in what she saw.

She attributed all her difficulties merely to the overquickness of her rhythm. Proofs would always follow later, too late to to be of value to her human life, but not too late to be added to this city of the interior she was constructing, to which none had access.

Yet she was never surprised when people betrayed the self she saw, which was the maximum rendition of themselves. This maximum she knew to be a torment, this knowledge of all one might achieve, become, was a threat to human joy and life. She felt in sympathy with those who turned their back on it. Yet she also knew that if they did, another torment awaited them: that of having fallen short of their own dream.

She would have liked to escape from her own demands upon herself.

But even if at times she was taken with a desire to become blind, to drift, to abandon her dreams, to slip into negation, destruction, she carried in herself something which altered the atmosphere she sought and which proved stronger than the place or people she had permitted to infect her with their disintegration, their betrayal of their original dream of themselves.

Even when she let herself be poisoned with all that was

human, defeat, jealousy, sickness, surrender, blindness, she carried an essence which was like a counter-poison and which reversed despair into hope, bitterness into faith, abortions into births, weight into lightness.

Everything in her hands changed substance, quality, form, intent.

Djuna could see it happen against her will, and did not know why it happened.

Was it because she began every day anew as children do, without memory of defeat, rancor, without memory of disaster? No matter what happened the day before, she always awakened with an expectation of a miracle. Her hands always appeared first from out of the sheets, hands without memories, wounds, weights, and these hands danced.

That was her awakening. A new day was a new life. Every morning was a beginning.

No sediments of pain, sadness yes, but no stagnating pools of accumulated bitterness.

Djuna believed one could begin anew as often as one dared.

The only acid she contained was one which dissolved the calluses formed by life around the sensibilities.

Every day she looked at people with the eyes of faith. Placing an unlimited supply of faith at their disposal. Since she did not accept the actual self as final, seeing only the possibilities of expansion, she established a climate of infinite possibilities.

She did not mind that by this expectation of a miracle, she exposed herself to immense disappointments. What she suffered as a human being when others betrayed themselves and her she counted as nothing—like the pains of childbirth.

She believed that the dream which human beings carry in themselves was man's greatest hunger. If statistics were taken there would be found more deaths by aborted dreams than from physical calamities, more deaths by dream abortions than child abortions, more deaths by infection from despair than from physical illness.

Carrying this ultimate knowledge she was often the victim

of strange revenges: people's revenge against the image of their unfulfilled dream. If they could annihilate her they might annihilate this haunting image of their completed selves and be done with it!

She only knew one person who might rescue her from this world, from this city of the interior lying below the level of identity.

She might learn from Jay to walk into a well-peopled world and abandon the intense selectivity of the dream (*this* personage fits into my dream and this one does not).

The dreamer rejects the ordinary.

Jay invited the ordinary. He was content with unformed fragments of people, incomplete ones: a minor doctor, a feeble painter, a mediocre writer, an average of any kind.

For Djuna it must always be: an extraordinary doctor, a unique writer, a summation of some kind, which could become a symbol by its completeness, by its greatness in its own realm.

Jay was the living proof that it was in this acceptance of the ordinary that pleasure lay. She would learn from him. She would learn to like daily bread. He gave her everything in its untransformed state: food, houses, streets, cafés, people. A way back to the simplicities.

Somewhere, in the labyrinth of her life, bread had been transformed on her tongue into a wafer, with the imponderability of symbols. Communion had been the actual way she experienced life—as communion, not as bread and wine. In place of bread, the wafer, in place of blood, the wine.

Jay would give her back a crowded world untransmuted. He had mocked her once saying he had found her portrait in one page of the dictionary under *Trans:* transmutations, transformation, transmitting, etc.

In the world of the dreamer there was solitude: all the exaltations and joys came in the moment of preparation for living. They took place in solitude. But with action came anxiety, and the sense of insuperable effort made to match the dream, and with it came weariness, discouragement, and the flight into solitude again. And then in solitude, in the opium den of remembrance, the possibility of pleasure again.

What was she seeking to salvage from the daily current of living, what sudden revulsions drove her back into the solitary cell of the dream?

Let Jay lead her out of the cities of the interior.

She would work as usual, hours of dancing, then she would take her shoes to be repaired, then she would go to the café.

The shoemaker was working with his window open on the street. As often as Djuna passed there he would be sitting in his low chair, his head bowed over his work, a nail between his lips, a hammer in his hand.

She took all her shoes to him for repairing, because he had as great a love of unique shoes as she did. She brought him slippers from Montenegro whose tips were raised like the prows of galleys, slippers from Morocco embroidered in gold thread, sandals from Tibet.

His eyes traveled up from his work towards the package she carried as if she were bringing him a gift.

He took the fur boots from Lapland he had not seen before, and was moved by the simplicity of their sewing, the reindeer guts sewn by hand. He asked for their history.

Djuna did not have to explain to him that as she could not travel enough to satisfy the restlessness of her feet, she could at least wear shoes which came from the place she might never visit. She did not have to explain to him that when she looked at her feet in Lapland boots she felt herself walking through deserts of snow.

The shoes carried her everywhere, tireless shoes walking forever all over the world.

This shoemaker repaired them with all the curiosity of a great traveler. He respected the signs of wear and tear as if she were returning from all the voyages she had wanted to make. It was not alone the dust or mud of Paris he brushed off but of Egypt, Greece, India. Every shoe she brought him was his voyage too. He respected wear as a sign of distance, broken straps as an indication of discoveries, torn heels as an accident happening only to explorers.

He was always sitting down. From his cellar room he looked up at the window where he could see only the feet of the passers-by.

"I love a foot that has elegance," he said. "Sometimes for days I see only ugly feet. And then perhaps one pair of beautiful feet. And that makes me happy."

As Djuna was leaving, for the first time he left his low working chair and moved forward to open the door for her, limping.

He had a club foot.

Once she had been found in the corner of a room by her very angry parents, all covered by a shawl. Their anxiety in not finding her for a long time turned to great anger.

"What are you doing there hiding, covered by a shawl?"

She answered: "Traveling. I am traveling."

The Rue de la Sante, the Rue Dolent, the Rue des Saint Pères became Bombay, Ladoma, Budapest, Lavinia.

The cities of the interior were like the city of Fez, intricate, endless, secret and unchartable.

Then she saw Jay sitting at the café table with Lillian, Donald, Michael, Sabina and Rango, and she joined them.

Faustin the Zombie, as everyone called him, awakened in a room he thought he had selected blindly but which gave the outward image of his inner self as accurately as if he had turned every element of himself into a carpet or a piece of furniture.

First of all it was not accessible to the door when it opened, but had to be reached by a dark and twisted corridor. Then he had contrived to cover the windows in such a manner with a glazed material that the objects, books and furniture appeared to be conserved in a storage room, to be at once dormant and veiled. The odor they emitted was the odor of hibernation.

One expected vast hoods to fall over the chairs and couch. Certain chairs were dismally isolated and had to be forcibly dragged to enter into relation with other chairs. There was an inertia in the pillows, an indifference in the wilted texture of the couch cover. The table in the center of the room blocked all passageways, the lamp shed a tired light. The walls absorbed the light without throwing it back.

His detachment affected the whole room. Objects need human warmth like human beings to bloom. A lamp sheds a meager or a prodigal light according to one's interior lighting. Even specks of dust are inhabited by the spirit of the master. There are rooms in which the dust is brilliant. There are rooms in which even carelessness is alive, as the disorder of someone rushing to more important matters. But here in Faustin's room there was not even the disorder caused by emotional draughts!

The walls of the rooming house were very thin, and he could hear all that took place in the other rooms.

This morning he awakened to a clear duet between a man and a woman.

Man: It's unbelievable, we've been together six years now, and I still have an illusion about you! I've never had this as long with any woman.
Woman: Six years!
Man: I'd like to know how often you have been unfaithful.
Woman: Well, I don't want to know how many times you were.
Man: Oh, me, only a few times. Whenever you went away and I'd get lonely and angry that you had left me. One summer at the beach ... do you remember the model Colette?
Woman: I didn't ask you. I don't want to know.
Man: But I do. I know you went off with that singer. Why did you? A singer. I couldn't make love to a singer!
Woman: But you made love to a model.
Man: That's different. You know it's not important. You know you're the only one.

Woman: You'd think it was important if I had.

Man: It's different for a woman. Why? Why did you, what made you go with that singer, why, when I love you so much and desire you so often?

Silence.

Woman: I don't believe we should talk about this. I don't want to know about you. (Crying.) I never wanted to think about it and now you made me.

Man: You're crying! But it's nothing. I forgot it immediately. And in six years only a few times. Whereas you, I'm sure it was many times.

Woman: (still crying) I didn't ask you. Why did you have to tell me?

Man: I'm just more sincere than you are.

Woman: It isn't sincerity, it's revenge. You told me just to hurt me.

Man: I told you because I thought it would drive you into being honest with me.

Silence.

Man: How obstinate you are. Why are you crying?

Woman: Not over your unfaithfulness!

Man: Over your own then?

Woman: I'm crying over unfaithfulness in general—how people hurt each other.

Man: Unfaithfulness in general! What a fine way to evade the particular.

Silence.

Man: I'd like to know how you learned all you know about love-making. Who did you learn from? You know what very few women do.

Woman: I learned . . . from talking with other women. I also have a natural gift.

Man: I suppose it was Maurice who taught you the most. It enrages me to see how much you know.

Woman: I never asked you where you learned. Besides, it's always personal. Each couple invents their own way.

Man: Yes, that's true. Sometimes I made you cry with joy, didn't I?

Woman: (crying) Why do you use the past tense?

Man: Why did you go off with that singer?

Woman: If you insist so much I will tell you something.

Man: (in a very tense voice) About the singer?

Woman: No, someone else. Once I tried to be unfaithful. You were neglecting me. I took rather a fancy to someone. And all might have gone well except that he had the same habit you have of starting with: you have the softest skin in the world. And when he said this, just as you do, I remembered your saying that, and I left the man, I ran away. Nothing happened.

Man: But just the same he had time to note the quality of your skin.

Woman: I'm telling you the truth.

Man: You have nothing to cry about now. You have taken your revenge.

223

Woman: I'm crying about unfaithfulness in general, all the betrayals.
Man: I will never forgive you.
Woman: Once in six years!
Man: I'm sure it was that singer.

Faustin, lying down, smoking as he listened, felt the urgent need to comment. He knocked angrily on the wall. The man and the woman were silent.

"Listen," he said, in his loudest voice, "I heard your entire conversation. I would say in this case the man is very unjust and the woman right. She was more faithful than the man. She was faithful to a personal emotion, to a personal rite."

"Who are you?" said the man in the other room, angrily.

"No one in particular, just a neighbor."

There was a long silence. Then the sound of a door being closed violently. Faustin heard one person moving about with soft rustles. Judging from the steps, it was the man who had gone out.

Faustin lay down again, meditating on his own anxiety.

He felt at this moment like a puppet, but he became aware that all this had happened many times before to him, but never as clearly.

All living had taken place for him in the other room, and he had always been the witness. He had always been the commentator.

He felt a guilt for having listened, which was like the guilt he felt at other times for never being the one in action. He was always accompanying someone to a marriage, not his own, to a hospital, to a burial, to a celebration in which he played no part but that of the accompanist.

He was allowing them all to live for him, and then articulating a judgment. He was allowing Jay to paint for him, and then he was the one to write ironic articles on his exhibits. He was allowing Sabina to devastate others with her passion, and smiling at those who were consumed or rejected. Now at this moment he was ashamed not to be the one consumed or rejected. He allowed Djuna to speak, Michael to face the tragic consequences of his deviations in love. He was allowing others to cry, to complain, to die.

And all he did was to speak across a protective wall, to knock with anger and say: you are right, and you are wrong.

Rendered uneasy by these meditations, he dressed himself and decided to go to the café.

He was called Uncle Philip by everyone, even by those who were not related to him.

He had the solicitous walk of an undertaker, the unctuous voice of a floorwalker.

His hands were always gloved, his heels properly resoled, his umbrella sheathed.

It was impossible to imagine him having been a child, or even an adolescent. It was admitted he possessed no photographs of that period, and that he had the taste never to talk about this obviously nonexistent facet of his personality. He had been born gray-haired, slender and genteel.

Attired in the most neutral suit, with the manners of someone about to announce a bereavement, Uncle Philip nevertheless did not fulfill such threats and was merely content to register and report minutely on the activity of the large, colorful, international family to which he was related.

No one could mention a country where Uncle Philip did not have a relative who . . .

No one could mention any world, social, political, artistic, financial, political, in which Uncle Philip did not possess a relative who . . .

No one ever thought of inquiring into his own vocation. One accepted him as a witness.

By an act of polite prestidigitation and punctuality, Uncle Philip managed to attend a ceremony in India where one of the members of the family was decorated for high bravery. He could give all the details of the function with a precision of colors resembling scenes from the *National Geographic Magazine*.

And a few days later he was equally present at the wedding of another member in Belgium, from which he brought back observations on the tenacious smell of Catholic incense.

A few days later he was present as godfather of a newborn child in Hungary and then proceeded to attend in Paris the first concert of importance given by still another relative.

Amiable and courteous as he shared in the backstage celebrations, he remained immune to the contagion of colors, gaiety and fame. His grayness took no glow from the success, flowers, and handshakes. His pride in the event was historical, and shed no light on his private life.

He was the witness.

He felt neither honored nor disgraced (he also attended death by electric chair of a lesser member).

He appeared almost out of nowhere, as a family spirit must, and immediately after the ceremony, after he partook of the wine, food, rice, sermon or verdict, he vanished as he had come and no one remembered him.

He who had traveled a thousand miles to sustain this family tree, to solder the spreading and dissipated family unity, was instantly forgotten.

Of course it was simple enough to follow the careers of the more official members of the family, those who practiced orthodox marriages and divorces, or such classical habits as first nights, presentations at the Court of England, decorations from the Academie Francaise. All this was announced in the papers and all Uncle Philip had to do was to read the columns carefully every morning.

But his devotion to the family did not limit itself to obvious attendance upon the obvious incidents of the family tree. He was not content with appearing at cemeteries, churches, private homes, sanatoriums, hospitals.

He pursued with equal flair and accuracy the more mysterious developments. When one relative entered upon an irregular union Uncle Philip was the first to call, assuming that all was perfectly in order and insisting on all the amenities.

The true mystery lay in the contradiction that the brilliance of these happenings (for even the performance at the electric chair was not without its uniqueness, the electric power failing to achieve its duty) never imparted any radiation to Uncle Philip; that while he moved in a profusion of family-tree blossoms, yet each year he became a little more faded, a little more automatic, a little more starched—like a wooden figure representing irreparable ennui.

His face remained unvaryingly gray, his suits frayed evenly, his soles thinned smoothly, his gloves wore out not finger by finger but all at once, as they should.

He remained alert to his duties, however. His genius for detecting step by step the most wayward activities led him to his most brilliant feat of all.

One relative having wanted to travel across the Atlantic with a companion who was not her husband, deceived all her friends as to the date of her sailing and boarded a ship leaving a day earlier.

As she walked up and down the deck with her compromising escort, thinking regretfully of the flowers, fruit and books which would be delivered elsewhere and lost to her, she encountered Uncle Philip holding a small bouquet and saying in an appropriate voice: *"Bon voyage!* Give my regards to the family when you get to America!"

The only surprising fact was that Uncle Philip failed to greet them at their arrival on the other side.

"Am I aging?" asked Uncle Philip of himself as he awakened, picked up the newspaper at his door, the breakfast tray, and went back to his bed.

He was losing his interest in genealogical trees.

He thought of the café and of all the people he had seen there, watched, listened to. From their talk they seemed to have been born without parents, without relatives. They had all run away, forgotten, or separated from the past. None of them acknowledged parents, or even nationalities.

When he questioned them they were irritated with him, or fled from him.

He thought they were rootless, and yet he felt they were bound to each other, and related to each other as if they had founded new ties, a new kind of family, a new country.

He was the lonely one, he the *esprit de famille*.

The sap that ran through the family tree had not bloomed in him as the sap that ran through these people as they sat together.

He wanted to get up and dress and sit with them. He remembered a painting he had seen in a book of mythology. All in coral and gold, a vast tree, and sitting at each tip of a branch, a mythological personage, man, woman, child, priest or poet, scribe, lyre player, dancer, goddess, god, all sitting in the same tree with a mysterious complacency of unity.

When Donald had been ejected from his apartment because he had not been able to pay his rent, all of them had come in the night and formed a chain and helped him to move his belongings out of the window, and the only danger had been one of discovery due to their irrepressible laughter.

When Jay sold a painting he came to the café to celebrate and that night everyone ate abundantly.

When Lillian gave a concert they all went together forming a compact block of sympathy with effusive applause.

When Stella was invited by some titled person or other to stay at a mansion in the south of France, she invited them all.

When the ballet master fell ill with asthma and could no longer teach dancing, he was fed by all of them.

There was another kind of family, and Uncle Philip wished he could discover the secret of their genealogy.

With this curiosity he dressed and went off to the café.

228

Michael liked to awaken first and look upon the face of Donald asleep on the pillows, as if he could extract from the reality of Donald's face asleep on a pillow within reach of his hand, a certitude which might quiet his anxiety, a certitude which, once awake, Donald would proceed to destroy gradually all through the day and evening.

At no time when he was awake could Donald dispense the word Michael needed, dispense the glance, the smallest act to prove his love.

Michael's feelings at that moment exactly resembled Lillian's feelings in regard to Jay.

Like Lillian he longed for some trivial gift that would prove Donald had wanted to make him a gift. Like Lillian he longed for a word he could enclose within his being that would place him at the center. Like Lillian he longed for some moment of passionate intensity that would be like those vast fires in the iron factory from which the iron emerged incandescent, welded, complete.

He had to be content with Donald asleep upon his pillow. With Donald's presence.

But no sooner would his eyes open than Donald would proceed to weave a world as inaccessible to Michael as the protean, fluid world of Jay became inaccessible to Lillian.

This weaving began always with Donald's little songs of nonsense with which he established the mood of the day on a pitch too light for Michael to seize, and which he sang not to please himself, but with a note of defiance, of provocation to Michael:

> Nothing is lost but it changes
> into the new string old string
> into the new bag old bag . . .

"Michael," said Donald, "today I would like to go to the zoo and see the new weasel who cried so desperately when she was left alone."

Michael thought: "How human of him to feel sympathy for the weasel crying in solitude in its cage." And Donald's sympathy for the weasel encouraged him to say tenderly: "Would you cry like that if you were left alone?"

"Not at all," said Donald, "I wouldn't mind at all. I like to be alone."

"You wouldn't mind if I left you?"

Donald shrugged his shoulders and sang:

> in the new pan old tin
> in the new shoe old leather
> in the new silk old hair
> in the new hat old straw . . .

"Anyhow," said Donald, "what I like best in the zoo is not the weasel, it's the rhinoceros with his wonderful tough hide."

Michael felt inexplicably angry that Donald should like the rhinoceros and not the weasel. That he should admire the toughness of the rhinoceros skin, as if he were betraying him, expressing the wish that Michael should be less vulnerable.

How how how could Michael achieve invulnerability when every gesture Donald made was in a different rhythm from his own, when he remained uncapturable even at the moments when he gave himself.

Donald was singing:

> in the new man the child
> and the new not new
> the new not new
> the new not new

Then he sat down to write a letter and the way he wrote his letter was so much in the manner of a schoolboy, with the attentiveness born of awkwardness, an unfamiliarity with concentration, an impatience to have the task over and done with that the little phrase in his song which Michael had not allowed to become audible to his heart now became louder and more ominous: in the new man the child.

As Donald sat biting the tip of his pen, Michael could see him preparing to trip, skip, prance, laugh, but always within a circle in which he admitted no partner.

To avoid the assertion of a difference which would be em-

230

phasized in a visit to the zoo, Michael tempted Donald with a visit to the Flea Market, knowing this to be one of Donald's favorite rambles.

There, exposed in the street, on the sidewalk, lay all the objects the imagination could produce and summon.

All the objects of the world with the added patina of having been possessed already, loved and hated, worn and discarded.

But there, as Michael moved and searched deliberately he discovered a rare book on astronomy, and Donald found the mechanism of a music box without the box, just a skeleton of fine wires that played delicately in the palm of his hand. Donald placed it to his ear to listen and then said: "Michael, buy me this music box. I love it."

In the open air it was scarcely audible, but Donald did not offer it to Michael's ear, as if he were listening to a music not made for him.

Michael bought it for him as one buys a toy for a child, a toy one is not expected to share. And for himself he bought the book on astronomy which Donald did not even glance at.

Donald walked with the music box playing inside of his pocket, and then he wanted reindeer horns, and he wanted a Louis Fifteenth costume, and he wanted an opium pipe.

Michael studied old prints, and all his gestures were slow and lagging with a kind of sadness which Donald refused to see, which was meant to say: "Take me by the hand and let me share your games."

Could he not see, in Michael's bearing, a child imprisoned wishing to keep pace with Donald, wishing to keep pace with his prancing, wishing to hear the music of the music box?

Finally they came upon the balloon woman, holding a floating bouquet of emerald-green balloons, and Donald wanted them all.

"All?" said Michael in dismay.

"Maybe they will carry me up in the air. I'm so much lighter than the old woman," said Donald.

But when he had taken the entire bunch from the woman,

and held them and was not lifted off the ground as he expected, he let them fly off and watched their ascension with delight, as if part of himself were attached to them and were now swinging in space.

Now it seemed to Michael that this divorce which happened every day would stretch intolerably during the rest of their time together, and he was wishing for the night, for darkness.

A blind couple passed them, leaning on each other. Michael envied them. (How I envy the blind who can love in the dark. Never to see the eye of the lover without reflection or remembrance. Black moment of desire knowing nothing of the being one is holding but the fiery point in darkness at which they could touch and spark. Blind lovers throwing themselves in the void of desire lying together for a night without dawn. Never to see the day upon the body that was taken. Could love go further in the darkness? Further and deeper without awakening to the sorrows of lucidity? Touch only warm flesh and listen only to the warmth of a voice!)

There was no darkness dark enough to prevent Michael from seeing the eyes of the lover turning away, empty of remembrance, never dark enough not to see the death of a love, the defect of a love, the end of the night of desire.

No love blind enough for him to escape the sorrows of lucidity.

"And now," said Donald, his arms full of presents, "let's go to the café."

Elbows touching, toes overlapping, breaths mingling, they sat in circles in the café while the passers-by flowed down the boulevard, the flower vendors plied their bouquets, the newsboys sang their street songs, and the evening achieved the marriage of day and night called twilight.

An organ grinder was playing at the corner like a fountain of mechanical birds singing wildly Carmen's provocations in this artificial paradise of etiolated trees, while the monkey rattled his chains and the pennies fell in the tin cup.

They sat rotating around each other like nearsighted planets, they sat mutating, exchanging personalities.

Jay seemed the one nearest to the earth, for there was the dew of pleasure upon his lips, there was this roseate bloom of content on his cheeks because he was nearest to the earth. He could possess the world physically whenever he wished, he could bite into it, eat it, digest it without difficulty. He had an ample appetite, he was not discriminating, he had a good digestion. So his face shone with the solid colors of Dutch paintings, with the blood tones of a well-nourished man, in a world never far from his teeth, never made invisible or insubstantial, for he carried no inner chamber in which the present scene must repeat itself for the commentator.

He carried no inner chamber in which this scene must be stored in order to be possessed. He carried no echo and no retentions. No snail roof around his body, no veils, no insulators.

His entrances and exits were as fluid, mobile, facile, as his drinking and its consequences. For him there was no sense of space between human beings, no distance to traverse, no obstacles to overcome to reach one another, no effort to make.

Because of his confidence in the natural movements of the planets, a pattern all arranged beforehand by some humorous astrologer, he always showed a smiling face in this lantern slide of life in Paris, and felt no strings of bondage, of restraint, and no tightrope walking as the others did.

From the first moment when he had cut utterly the umbilical cord between himself and his mother by running away from home at the age of fourteen and never once returning, he had known this absence of spools, lassos, webs, safety nets. He had eluded them all.

Thus in the sky of the café tables rotating, the others circled around him to drink of his gaiety, hoping to catch his secret formula.

Was it because he had accepted that such an indifference to effort led men to the edge of the river, to sleep under bridges, was it because he had decided that he did not mind sleeping under bridges, drinking from the fountain, smoking cigarette butts, eating soup from the soup line of the Hospital de la Santé?

Was this his secret? To relinquish, to dispossess one's self of all wishes, to renounce, to be attached to no one, to hold no dream, to live in a state of anarchy?

Actually he never reached the last stage. He always met someone who assumed the responsibility of his existence.

But he could sense whoever unwound from the center of a spool and rewound himself back into it again at night, or the one who sought to lasso the loved one into an indissoluble spiral, or the one who flung himself from heights intent on catching the swing midway and fearful of a fatal slip into abysms.

This always incited him to grasp giant scissors and cut through all the patterns.

He began to open people before the café table as he opened bottles, not delicately, not gradually, but uncorking them, hurling direct questions at them like javelins, assaulting them with naked curiosity.

A secret, an evasion, a shrinking, drove him to repeat his thrusts like one hard of hearing: what did you say?

No secrets! No mystifications allowed! Spill open! Give yourself publicly like those fanatics who confess to the community.

He hated withdrawals, shells, veils. They aroused the barbarian in him, the violator of cities, the sacker and invader.

Dive from any place whatever!

But dive!

With large savage scissors he cut off all the moorings. Cut off responsibilities, families, shelters. He sent every one of them towards the open sea, into chaos, into poverty, into solitude, into storms.

At first they bounced safely on the buoyant mattress of his enthusiasms. Jay became gayer and gayer as his timid passengers embarked on unfamiliar and tumultous seas.

Some felt relieved to have been violated. There was no other way to open their beings. They were glad to have been done violence to as secrets have a way of corroding their containers. Others felt ravaged like invaded countries, felt hopelessly exhibited and ashamed of this lesser aspect of themselves.

As soon as Jay had emptied the person, and the bottle, of all it contained, down to the sediments, he was satiated.

Come, said Jay, display the worst in yourself. To laugh it is necessary to present a charade of our diminished states. To face the natural man, and the charm of his defects. Come, said Jay, let us share our flaws together. I do not believe in heroes. I believe in the natural man.

(I now know the secret of Jay's well-being, thought Lillian. *He does not care.* That is his secret. He does not care! And I shall never learn this from him. I will never be able to feel as he does. I must run away from him. I will return to New York.)

And at this thought, the cord she had imagined tying her and Jay together for eternity, the cord of marriage, taut with incertitude, worn with anxiety, snapped, and she felt unmoored.

While he unmoored others, by cutting through the knots of responsibilities, he had inadvertently cut the binding, choking cord between them. From the moment she decided to sail away from him she felt elated.

All these tangled cords, from the first to the last, from the mother to the husband, to the children, and to Jay, all dissolved at once, and Jay was surprised to hear Lillian laugh in a different tone, for most times her laughter had a rusty quality which brought it closer to a sob, as if she had never determined which she intended to do.

At the same hour at the tip of the Observatory astronomers were tabulating mileage between planets, and just as Djuna had learned to measure such mileage by the oscillations of her heart (he is warm and near, he is remote and cool) from her first experience with Michael, past master in the art of creating distance between human beings, Michael himself arrived with Donald and she could see instantly that he was suffering from his full awareness of the impenetrable distance between himself and Donald, between himself and the world of adolescence he wanted to remain in forever and from which his lack of playfulness and recklessness barred him.

As soon as Michael saw Djuna's eyes he had the feeling of being restored to visibility, as if by gazing into the clear mirrors of her compassion he were reincarnated, for the relentless work accomplished by Donald's exclusion of him from his boyish world deprived him of his very existence.

Djuna needed only to say: Hello, Michael! for him to feel he was no longer a kindly protective ghost necessary to Donald's existence. For Djuna saw him handsome, gifted in astronomy and mathematics, rich with many knowledges, eloquent when properly warmed.

Hello, Michael! Djuna said, and the 100000000000000000000000000 miles between himself and human beings became like a small pencil addition on a note paper and not a state of being. They were laid aside like a student's abstractions, and now he was sitting in a café and Donald at his right was merely a very beautiful boy of which there were so many, cut out like a clay pigeon at the fair, with only a façade, and that is what Djuna had called him from the very beginning (the first time she had said it he had been angry and brooded on the insufferable jealousy of woman). Hello, Michael! How is your clay pigeon today?

Such fine threads passed between Michael and Djuna. He could always seize the intermediary color of her mood. That was his charm, his quality, this fine incision from his knowledge of woman, this capacity for dealing in essences.

This love without possibility of incarnation which took place between Djuna and all the descendants of Michael, the lineage

236

of these carriers of subtleties known only to men of his race.

They had found a territory which existed beyond sensual countries, and by a communion of swift words could charm each other actively in spite of the knowledge that this enchantment would have no ordinary culmination.

"Djuna," said Michael, "I see all your thoughts running in all directions, like minnows."

Then immediately he knew this in her was a symptom of anxiety, and he avoided the question which would have wounded her: "Has Paul's father sent him to India?"

For in the way she sat there he knew she was awaiting a mortal blow.

At this moment there appeared on the marble-topped tables the stains of drink, the sediments and dregs of false beatitudes.

At this moment the organ grinder changed his tune, and ceased to shower the profligacies of *Carmen*.

The laughter of Pagliacci bleached by city fumes, wailed like a loon out of the organ, so that the monkey cornered by a joviality which had neither a sound of man or monkey rattled his chains in greater desperation and saluted with his red Turkish hat every stranger who might deliver him from this loud-speaker tree to which he had been tied.

He danced a pleading dance to be delivered from this tree from which the twisting of a handle brought forth black birds of corrugated melodies.

But as the pennies fell he remembered his responsibilities, his prayer for silent trees vanished from his eyes as he attempted a gesture of gratitude with his red Turkish hat.

Djuna walked back again into her labyrinthian cities of the interior.

Where music bears no titles flowing like a subterranean

river carrying all the moods, sensations and impressions into dissolutions forming and reforming a world in terms of flow . . .

where houses wear but façades exposed to easy entrances and exits

where streets do not bear a name because they are the streets of secret sorrows

where the birds who sing are the birds of peace, the birds of paradise, the colored birds of desire which appear in our dreams

there are those who feared to be lost in this voyage without compass, barometers, steering wheel or encyclopedias

but Djuna knew that at this surrender of the self began a sinking into deeper layers of awareness deeper and deeper starting at the topsoil of gaiety and descending through the geological stairways carrying only the delicate weighing machine of the heart to weigh the imponderable

through these streets of secret sorrows in which the music was anonymous and people lost their identities to better be carried and swept back and forth through the years to find only the points of ecstasy . . .

registering only the dates and titles of emotion which alone enter the flesh and lodge themselves against the flux and loss of memory

that only the important dates of deep feeling may recur again and again each time anew through the wells, fountains and rivers of music. . . .

The Four-Chambered Heart

THE GUITAR DISTILLED ITS MUSIC.

Rango played it with the warm copper color of his skin, with the charcoal pupil of his eyes, with the underbrush thickness of his eyebrows, pouring into the honey-colored box the flavors of the open road on which he lived his gypsy life: thyme, rosemary, oregano, marjoram, and sage. Pouring into the resonant box the sensual swing of his hammock hung across the gypsy cart and the dreams born on his mattress of black horsehair.

Idol of the night clubs, where men and women barred doors

241

and windows, lit candles, drank alcohol, and drank from his voice and his guitar the potions and herbs of the open road, the charivaris of freedom, the drugs of leisure and laziness.

At dawn, not content with the life transfusion through catguts, filled with the sap of his voice which had passed into their veins, at dawn the women wanted to lay hands upon his body. But at dawn Rango swung his guitar over his shoulder and walked away.

Will you be here tomorrow, Rango?

Tomorrow he might be playing and singing to his black horse's philosophically swaying tail, on the road to the south of France.

Toward this ambulant Rango, Djuna leaned to catch all that his music contained, and her ear detected the presence of this unattainable island of joy which she pursued, which she had glimpsed at the party she had never attended but watched from her window as a girl. And like some lost voyager in a desert, she leaned more and more eagerly toward this musical mirage of a pleasure never known to her, the pleasure of freedom.

"Rango, would you play once for my dancing?" she asked softly and fervently, and Rango stopped on his way out to bow to her, a bow of consent which took centuries of stylization and nobility of bearing to create, a bow indicating the largesse of gesture of a man who had never been bound.

"Whenever you wish."

As they planned for the day and hour, and while she gave him her address, they walked instinctively toward the river.

Their shadows walking before them revealed the contrast between them. His body occupied twice the space of hers. She walked unswerving like an arrow, while he ambled. His hands trembled while lighting her cigarette, and hers were steady.

"I'm not drunk," he said, laughing, "but I've been drunk so often that my hands have remained unsteady for life, I guess."

"Where is your cart and horse, Rango?"

"I have no cart and horse. Not for a long time. Not since Zora fell ill, years ago."

"Zora?"

"My wife."

"Is your wife a gypsy, too?"

"Neither my wife nor I. I was born in Guatemala, at the top of the highest mountain. Are you disappointed? That legend was necessary to keep up, for the night club, to earn a living. It protects me, too. I have a family in Guatemala who would be ashamed of my present life. I ran away from home when I was seventeen. I was brought up on a ranch. Even today my friends say: 'Rango, where is your horse? You always look as if you had left your horse tied to the gate.' I lived with the gypsies in the south of France. They taught me to play. They taught me to live as they do. The men don't work; they play the guitar and sing. The women take care of them by stealing food and concealing it under their wide skirts. Zora never learned that! She got very ill. I had to give up roaming. We're home now. Do you want to come in?"

Djuna looked at the gray stone house.

She had not yet effaced from her eyes the image of Rango on the open road. The contrast was painful and she took a step backward, suddenly intimidated by a Rango without his horse, without his freedom.

The windows of the house were long and narrow. They seemed barred. She could not bear yet to see how he had been captured, tamed, caged, by what circumstances, by whom.

She shook his big hand, the big warm hand of a captive, and left him so swiftly he was dazed. He stood bewildered and swaying, awkwardly lighting another cigarette, wondering what had made her take flight.

He did not know that she had just lost sight of an island of joy. The image of an island of joy evoked by his guitar had vanished. In walking toward a mirage of freedom, she had entered a black forest, the black forest of his eyes darkening when he said: "Zora is very ill." The black forest of his wild hair as he bowed his head in contrition: "My family would be ashamed of the life I lead today." The black forest of his bewilderment as he stood about to enter a house too gray, too shabby, too cramped for his big, powerful body.

Their first kiss was witnessed by the Seine River carrying gondolas of street lamps' reflections in its spangled folds, carrying haloed street lamps flowering on bushes of black lacquered cobblestones, carrying silver filigree trees opened like fans beyond whose rim the river's eyes provoked them to hidden coquetries, carrying the humid scarfs of fog and the sharp incense of roasted chestnuts.

Everything fallen into the river and carried away except the balcony on which they stood.

Their kiss was accompanied by the street organ and it lasted the whole length of the musical score of Carmen, and when it ended it was too late; they had drunk the potion to its last drop.

The potion drunk by lovers is prepared by no one but themselves.

The potion is the sum of one's whole existence.

Every word spoken in the past accumulated forms and colors in the self. What flows through the veins besides blood is the distillation of every act committed, the sediment of all the visions, wishes, dreams, and experiences. All the past emotions converge to tint the skin and flavor the lips, to regulate the pulse and produce crystals in the eyes.

The fascination exerted by one human being over another is not what he emits of his personality at the present instant of encounter but a summation of his entire being which gives off this powerful drug capturing the fancy and attachment.

No moment of charm without long roots in the past, no

moment of charm is born on bare soil, a careless accident of beauty, but is the sum of great sorrows, growths, and efforts.

But love, the great narcotic, was the hothouse in which all the selves burst into their fullest bloom . . .

love the great narcotic was the revealer in the alchemist's bottle rendering visible the most untraceable substances

love the great narcotic was the *agent provocateur* exposing all the secret selves to daylight

love the great narcotic-lined fingertips with clairvoyance pumped iridescence into the lungs for transcendental x-rays printed new geographies in the lining of the eyes adorned words with sails, ears with velvet mutes

and soon the balcony tipped their shadows into the river, too, so that the kiss might be baptized in the holy waters of continuity.

Djuna walked along the Seine the next morning asking the fishermen and the barge sailors for a boat to rent in which she and Rango might live.

As she stood by the parapet wall, and then leaned over to watch the barges, a policeman watched her.

(Does he think I am going to commit suicide? Do I look like someone who would commit suicide? How blind he is! I never wanted less to die, on the very day I am beginning to live!)

He watched her as she ran down the stairs to talk to the owner of *Nanette*, a bright red barge. *Nanette* had little windows trimmed with beaded curtains just like the superintendent's windows in apartment houses.

(Why bring to a barge the same trimmings as those of a house? They are not made for the river, these people, not for voyages. They like familiarity, they like to continue their life on earth, while Rango and I want to run away from houses, cafés, streets, people. We want to find an island, a solitary cell, where we can dream in peace together. Why should the policeman think I may jump into the river at this moment when I never felt less like dying? Or does he stand there to reproach me for slipping out of my father's house last night after ten o'clock, with such infinite precautions, leaving the front door ajar so he would not hear me leave, deserting his house with a beating heart because now his hair is white and he no longer understands anyone's need to love, for he has lost everything, not to love, but to his games of love; and when you love as a game, you lose everything, as he lost his home and wife, and now he clings to me, afraid of loss, afraid of solitude.)

That morning at five-thirty she had awakened, gently untangled her body from Rango's arms and reached her room at six, and at six-thirty her father had knocked on the door because he was ill and wanted care.

(Ali Baba protects the lovers! Gives them the luck of bandits, and no guilt; for love fills certain people and expands them beyond all laws; there is no time, no place for regrets, hesitations, cowardices. Love runs free and reckless; and all the gentle trickeries perpetrated to protect others from its burns—those who are not the lovers but who might be the victims of this love's expansion—let them be gentle and gay about these trickeries, gentle and gay like Robin Hood, or other games of children; for Anahita, the moon goddess, will then judge and mete out punishment, Mr. Policeman. So wait for her orders, for I am sure you would not understand if I told you my father is delightfully clear and selfish, tender and lying, formal and incurable. He exhausts all the loves given to him. If I did not leave his house at night to warm myself in Rango's burning hands I would die at my task, arid and barren, sapless, while my father monologues about his past, and I yawn yawn yawn . . . It's like looking at family albums, at stamp collections! Understand me, Mr. Policeman, if you can: if that were all I had, I would indeed be in danger of jumping into the Seine, and you would have to take a chill rescuing me. See, I have money for a taxi, I sing a song of thanksgiving to the taxi which nourishes the dream and carries it unbreakable, fragile but unbreakable everywhere. The taxi is the nearest object to a seven-leagued boot, it perpetuates the reverie, my vice, my luxury. Oh, you can, if you wish, arrest me for reverie, vagabondage of the wildest sort, for it is the cell, the mysterious, the padded, the fecund cell in which everything is born; everything that man ever accomplished is born in this little cell . . .)

The policeman passed by and did not arrest her, so she confided in him and found him rich with knowledge. He knew of many barges here and there. He knew one where they served fried potatoes and red wine to fishermen, another where hobos could spend the night for five cents, one where a woman in trousers carved big statues, another one turned into a swimming pool for boys, another one called the barge of the red lights, for men, and beyond this one there was a barge that had been used by a troupe of actors to travel all through France, and there she might inquire as it was empty and had been deemed unsafe for long voyages . . .

It was anchored near the bridge, long and wide, with a strong prow from which hung the heavy anchor chain. It had no windows on the side, but a glass trap door on deck which an old watchman threw open for her. She descended a narrow and steep stairway to find herself in a broad room, with light falling from skylight windows, and then there were a smaller room, a hallway, and more small cabins on each side.

The large center room which had been used for the stage was still full of discarded sets and curtains and costumes. The

247

small cabins which branched off on both sides had once been dressing rooms for the ambulant actors. They were now filled with pots of paint, firewood, tools, old sacks, and newspapers. At the prow of the barge was a vast room papered with glossy tarpaper. The skylight windows showed only the sky, but two openings in the wall, working like drawbridges on a chain, were cut only a few inches above water level and focused on the shore.

The watchman occupied one of the small cabins. He wore a beret and dark blue denim blouse like the French peasants.

He explained: "I was the captain of a pleasure yacht once. The yacht blew up and I lost my leg. But I can fetch water for you, and coal and wood. I can pump the water every day. This barge has to be watched for leaks. It's pretty old, but the wood is strong."

The walls of the barge curved like the inside of a whale belly. The old beams were stained with marks of former cargoes: wood, sand, stone, and coal.

As Djuna left, the old watchman picked up a piece of wood which held a pail at each end, hanging on a cord. He balanced it on his shoulders like a Japanese water carrier, and began to jump on his one leg after her, keeping a miraculous balance on the large cobblestones.

The winter night came covering the city, dusting the street lamps with fog and smoke so that their light dissolved into an aureole of sainthood.

When Djuna and Rango met, he was sad that he had found nothing to shelter them. Djuna said: "I have something for you to see; if you like it, it might do for us."

As they walked along the quays, as they passed the station through a street being repaired, she picked up one of the red lanterns left by the repair men, and carried it, all lit, across the bridge. Halfway they met the same policeman who had helped her find the barge. Djuna thought: "He will arrest me for stealing a street lantern."

But the policeman did not stop her. He smiled, knowing where she was going, and merely appraised Rango's build as they passed.

The old watchman appeared suddenly at the trap door and shouted: "Hey, there! Who goes there? Oh, it's you, petite madame. Wait. I'll open for you." And he threw the trap door fully open.

They descended the turning stairway and Rango smelled the tar with delight. When he saw the room, the shadows, the beams, he exclaimed: "It's like *The Tales of Hoffmann*. It's a dream. It's a fairy tale."

Old grandfather of the river, ex-captain of a pleasure yacht, snorted insolently at this remark and went back to his cabin.

"This is what I wanted," said Rango.

He bent down to enter the very small room at the tip of the barge which was like a small pointed prison with barred windows. The enormous anchor chain hung before the iron bars. The floor had been worn away, rotted with dampness, and they could see through the holes the layer of water which lies at the bottom of every ship, like the possessive fingers of the sea and the river asserting its ownership of the boat.

Rango said: "If ever you're unfaithful to me, I will lock you up in this room."

With the tall shadows all around them, the medieval beams cracking above their heads, the lapping water, the mildew at the bottom, the anchor chain's rusty plaintiveness, Djuna believed his words.

"Djuna, you're taking me to the bottom of the sea to live, like a real mermaid."

"I must be a mermaid, Rango. I have no fear of depths and a great fear of shallow living. But you, poor Rango, you're from the mountain, water is not your element. You won't be happy."

"Men from the mountains always dream of the sea, and above all things I love to travel. Where are we sailing now?"

As he said this, another barge passed up the river close to theirs. The whole barge heaved; the large wooden frame cracked like a giant's bones.

Rango lay down and said: "We're navigating."

"We're out of the world. All the dangers are outside, out in the world." All the dangers . . . dangers to the love, they believed as all lovers believe, came from the outside, from the world, never suspecting the seed of death of love might lie within themselves.

"I want to keep you here, Djuna. I would like it if you never left the barge."

"I wouldn't mind staying here."

(If it were not for Zora, Zora awaiting food, awaiting medicines, awaiting Rango to light the fire.)

"Rango, when you kiss me the barge rocks."

The red lantern threw fitful shadows, feverish red lights, over their faces. He named it the aphrodisiac lamp.

He lighted a fire in the stove. He threw his cigarette into the water. He kissed her feet, untied her shoes, he unrolled her stockings.

They heard something fall into the water.

"It's a flying fish," said Djuna.

He laughed: "There are no flying fish in the river, except you. When you're in my arms, I know you're mine. But your feet are so swift, so swift, they carry you as lightly as wings, I never know where, too fast, too fast away from me."

He rubbed his face, not as everyone does, with the palm of the hand. He rubbed it with his fists closed as children do, as bears and cats do.

He caressed her with such fervor that the little red lantern fell on the floor, the red glass broke, the oil burst into many small wild flames. She watched it without fear. Fire delighted her, and she had always wanted to live near danger.

After the oil was absorbed by the thick dry wooden floor, the fire died out.

They fell asleep.

The drunken grandfather of the river, ex-captain of a pleasure yacht, had lived alone on the barge for a long time. He had been the sole guardian and owner of it. Rango's big body, his dark Indian skin, his wild black hair, his low and vehement voice frightened the old man.

When Rango lit the stove at night in their bedroom, the old man in his cabin would begin to curse him for the noise he made.

Also he resented that Rango did not let him wait on Djuna, and he would mutter against him when he was drunk, mutter threats in apache language.

One night Djuna arrived a little before midnight. A windy night with dead leaves blowing in circles. She was always afraid to walk alone down the stairs from the quays. There were no lights. She stumbled on hobos asleep, on whores plying their trade behind the trees. She tried to overcome her fear and would run down the steps along the edge of the river.

But finally they had agreed that she would throw a stone from the street to the roof of the barge to warn Rango of her arrival and that he would meet her at the top of the stairs.

This night she tried to laugh at her fears and to walk down alone. But when she reached the barge there was no light in the bedroom, and no Rango to meet her, but the old watchman popped out of the trap door, vacillating with drink, red-eyed and stuttering.

Djuna said: "Has Monsieur arrived?"

"Of course, he's in there. Why don't you come down? Come

down, come down."

But Djuna did not see any light in the room, and she knew that if Rango were there, he would hear her voice and come out to meet her.

The old watchman kept the trap door open, saying as he stamped his feet: "Why don't you come down? What's the matter with you?" with more and more irritability.

Djuna knew he was drunk. She feared him, and she started to leave. As his rage grew, she felt more and more certain she should leave.

The old watchman's imprecations followed her.

Alone at the top of the stairs, in the silence, in the dark, she was filled with fears. What was the old man doing there at the trap door? Had he hurt Rango? Was Rango in the room? The old watchman had been told he could no longer stay on the barge. Perhaps he had avenged himself. If Rango were hurt, she would die of sorrow.

Perhaps Rango had come by way of the other bridge.

It was one o'clock. She would throw another stone on the roof and see if he responded.

As she picked up the stone, Rango arrived.

Returning to the barge together, they found the old watchman still there, muttering to himself.

Rango was quick to anger and violence. He said: "You've been told to move out. You can leave immediately."

The old watchman locked himself in his cabin and continued to hurl insults.

"I won't leave for eight days," he shouted. "I was captain once, and I can be a captain any time I choose again. No black man is going to get me out of here. I have a right to be here."

Rango wanted to throw him out, but Djuna held him back. "He's drunk. He'll be quiet tomorrow."

All night the watchman danced, spat, snored, cursed, and threatened. He drummed on his tin plate.

Rango's anger grew, and Djuna remembered other people saying: "The old man is stronger than he looks. I've seen him knock down a man like nothing." She knew Rango was stronger, but she feared the old man's treachery. A stab in the back, an investigation, a scandal. Above all, Rango might be hurt.

"Leave the barge and let me attend to him," said Rango.

Djuna dissuaded him, calmed his anger, and they fell asleep at dawn.

When they came out at noon, the old watchman was already on the quays, drinking red wine with the hobos, spitting into the river as they passed, with ostentatious disdain.

The bed was low on the floor; the tarred beams creaked over their heads. The stove was snoring heat, the river water patted the barge's sides, and the street lamps from the bridge threw a faint yellow light into the room.

When Rango began to take Djuna's shoes off, to warm her feet in his hands, the old man of the river began to shout and sing, throwing his cooking pans against the wall:

> Nanette gives freely
> what others charge for.
> Nanette is generous,
> Nanette gives love
> Under a red lantern

Rango leaped up, furious, eyes and hair wild, big body tense, and rushed to the old man's cabin. He knocked on the door. The song stopped for an instant, and was resumed:

> Nanette wore a ribbon
> In her black hair.
> Nanette never counted
> All she gave. . . .

Then he drummed on his tin plate and was silent.

"Open the door!" shouted Rango.

253

Silence.

Then Rango hurled himself against the door, which gave way and tore into splinters.

The old watchman lay half naked on a pile of rags, with his beret on his head, soup stains on his beard, holding a stick which shook from terror.

Rango looked like Peter the Great, six feet tall, black hair flying, all set for battle.

"Get out of here!"

The old man was dazed with drunkenness, and he refused to move. His cabin smelled so badly that Djuna stepped back. There were pots and pans all over the floor, unwashed, and hundreds of old wine bottles exuding a rancid odor.

Rango forced Djuna back into the bedroom and went to fetch the police.

Djuna heard Rango return with the policeman, and heard his explanations. She heard the policeman say to the watchman: "Get dressed. The owner told you to leave. I have an injunction here. Get dressed."

The watchman lay there, fumbling for his clothes. He could not find the top of his pants. He kept looking down into one of the pant's legs as if surprised at its smallness. He mumbled. The policeman waited. They could not dress him because he would turn limp. He kept muttering: "Well, what do I care? I used to be captain of a yacht. Something white and smart, not one of these broken-down barges. I used to have a white suit, too. Suppose you do throw me into the river, it's all the same to me. I don't care if I die. I'm not a bad old man. I run errands for you, don't I? I fetch water, don't I? I bring coal. What if I do sing a bit at night?"

"You don't just sing a bit," said Rango. "You make a hell of a noise every time you come home. You bang your pails together, you raise hell, you bang on the walls, you're always drunk, you fall down the stairs."

"I was sound asleep, wasn't I? Sound asleep, I tell you. Who knocked the door down, tell me? Who broke into my cabin? I'll not get out. I can't find my pants. These aren't mine, they're too small."

Then he began to sing:

> Laissez moi tranquille,
> Je ferais le mort.
> Ma chandelle est morte
> Et ma femme aussi.

Then Rango, the policeman, and Djuna all began to laugh. No one could stop laughing. The old man looked so dazed and innocent.

"You can stay if you're quiet," said Rango.

"If you're not quiet," said the policeman, "I'll come back and fetch you and throw you in jail."

"*Je ferais le mort,*" said the old man. "You'll never know I'm here."

He was now thoroughly bewildered and docile. "But no one has a right to knock a door down. What manners, I tell you! I've knocked men down often enough, but never knocked a door down. No privacy left. No manners."

When Rango returned to the bedroom, he found Djuna still laughing. He opened his arms. She hid her face against his coat and said: "You know, I love the way you broke that door." She felt relieved of some secret accumulation of violence, as one does watching a storm of nature, thunder and lightning discharging anger for us.

"I loved your breaking down that door," repeated Djuna.

Through Rango she had breathed some other realm she had never attained before. She had touched through his act some climate of violence she had never known before.

The Seine River began to swell from the rains and to rise high above the watermark painted on the stones in the Middle

Ages. It covered the quays at first with a thin layer of water, and the hobos quartered under the bridge had to move to their country homes under the trees. Then it lapped the foot of the stairway, ascended one step, and then another, and at last settled at the eighth, deep enough to drown a man.

The barges stationed there rose with it; the barge dwellers had to lower their rowboats and row to shore, climb up a rope ladder to the wall, climb over the wall to the firm ground. Strollers loved to watch this ritual, like a gentle invasion of the city by the barges' population.

At night the ceremony was perilous, and rowing back and forth from the barges was not without difficulties. As the river swelled, the currents became violent. The smiling Seine showed a more ominous aspect of its character.

The rope ladder was ancient, and some of its solidity undermined by time.

Rango's chivalrous behavior was suited to the circumstances; he helped Djuna climb over the wall without showing too much of the scalloped sea-shell edge of her petticoat to the curious bystanders; he then carried her into the rowboat, and rowed with vigor. He stood up at first and with a pole pushed the boat away from the shore, as it had a tendency to be pushed by the current against the stairway, then another current would absorb it in the opposite direction, and he had to fight to avoid sailing down the Seine.

His pants rolled up, his strong dark legs bare, his hair wild in the wind, his muscular arms taut, he smiled with enjoyment of his power, and Djuna lay back and allowed herself to be rescued each time anew, or to be rowed like a great lady of Venice.

Rango would not let the watchman row them across. He wanted to be the one to row his lady to the barge. He wanted to master the tumultuous current for her, to land her safely in their home, to feel that he abducted her from the land, from the city of Paris, to shelter and conceal her in his own tower of love.

At the hour of midnight, when others are dreaming of fire-sides and bedroom slippers, of finding a taxi to reach home from the theatre, or pursuing false gaieties in the bars, Rango and Djuna lived an epic rescue, a battle with an angry river, a journey into difficulties, wet feet, wet clothes, an adventure in which the love, the test of the love, and the reward tele-scoped into one moment of wholeness. For Djuna felt that if Rango fell and were drowned she would die also, and Rango felt that if Djuna fell into the icy river he would die to save her. In this instant of danger they realized they were each other's reason for living, and into this instant they threw their whole beings.

Rango rowed as if they were lost at sea, not in the heart of a city; and Djuna sat and watched him with admiration, as if this were a medieval tournament and his mastering of the Seine a supreme votive offering to her feminine power.

Out of worship and out of love he would let no one light the stove for her either, as if he would be the warmth and the fire to dry and warm her feet. He carried her down the trap door into the freezing room damp with winter fog. She stood shivering while he made the fire with an intensity into which he poured his desire to warm her, so that it no longer seemed like an ordinary stove smoking and balking, or Rango an ordinary man lighting wood with damp newspapers, but like some Valkyrian hero lighting a fire in a Black Forest.

Thus love and desire restored to small actions their large dimensions, and renewed in one winter night in Paris the full stature of the myth.

She laughed as he won his first leaping flame and said: "You are the God of Fire."

He took her so deeply into his warmth, shutting the door of their love so intimately that no corroding external air might enter.

And now they were content, having attained all lovers' dream of a desert island, a cell, a cocoon, in which to create a world together from the beginning.

In the dark they gave each other their many selves, avoiding only the more recent ones, the story of the years before they met as a dangerous realm from which might spring dissensions, doubts, and jealousies. In the dark they sought rather to give each other their earlier, their innocent, unpossessed selves.

This was the paradise to which every lover liked to return with his beloved, recapturing a virgin self to give one another.

Washed of the past by their caresses, they returned to their adolescence together.

Djuna felt herself at this moment a very young girl, she felt again the physical imprint of the crucifix she had worn at her throat, the incense of mass in her nostrils. She remembered the little altar at her bedside, the smell of candles, the faded artificial flowers, the face of the virgin, and the sense of death and sin so inextricably entangled in her child's head. She felt her breasts small again in her modest dress, and her legs tightly pressed together. She was now the first girl he had loved, the one he had gone to visit on his horse, having traveled all night across the mountains to catch a glimpse of her. Her face was the face of this girl with whom he had talked only through an iron gate. Her face was the face of his dreams, a face with the wide space between the eyes of the madonnas of the sixteenth century. He would marry this girl and keep her jealously to himself like an Arab husband, and she would never be seen or known to the world.

In the depth of this love, under the vast tent of this love, as he talked of his childhood, he recovered his innocence too, an innocence much greater than the first, because it did not stem from ignorance, from fear, or from neutrality in experience. It was born like an ultimate pure gold out of many tests, selections, from voluntary rejection of dross. It was born of courage, after many desecrations, from much deeper layers of the being inaccessible to youth.

Rango talked in the night. "The mountain I was born on was an extinct volcano. It was nearer to the moon. The moon there was so immense it frightened man. It appeared at times with a red halo, occupying half of the sky, and everything was stained red. . . . There was a bird we hunted, whose life was so tough that after we shot him the Indians had to tear out two of his feathers and plunge them into the back of the bird's neck, otherwise it would not die. . . . We killed ducks in the marshes, and once I was caught in quicksands and saved myself by getting quickly out of my boots and leaping to safe ground. . . . There was a tame eagle who nestled on our roof. . . . At dawn my mother would gather the entire household together and recite the rosary. . . . On Sundays we gave formal dinners which lasted all afternoon. I still remember the taste of the chocolate, which was thick and sweet, Spanish fashion. . . . Prelates and cardinals came in their purple and gold finery. We led the life of sixteenth-century Spain. The immensity of nature around us caused a kind of trance. So immense it gave sadness and loneliness. Europe seemed so small, so shabby at first, after Guatemala. A toy moon, I said, a toy sea, such small houses and gardens. At home it took six hours by train and three weeks on horseback to reach the top of the mountain where we went hunting. We would stay there for months, sleeping on the ground. It had to be done slowly because of the strain on the heart. Beyond a certain height the horses and mules could not stand it; they would bleed through mouth and ears. When we reached the snow caps, the air was almost black with intensity. We would look down sharp cliffs, thousands of miles down, and we would see below, the small, intensely green, luxuriant tropical jungle. Sometimes for hours and hours my horse would travel alongside a waterfall, until the sound of the falling water would hypnotize me. And all this time, in snow and wildness, I dreamed of a pale slender woman. . . . When I was seventeen, I was in love with a small statue of a Spanish virgin, who had the wide space between the eyes which you have. I dreamed of this woman, who was you, and I dreamed of cities, of living in cities. . . . Up in the mountain where I was born one never walked on level ground, one walked always on stairways, an eternal stairway toward the sky, made of gigantic square stones. No one knows how the Indians were able to pile these stones one upon another; it seems humanly impossible. It seemed more like a stairway made by gods, because the steps were higher than a man's step could encompass. They were built for giant gods, for the Mayan giants carved in granite, those who drank the blood of sacrifices, those who laughed at the puny efforts of men who tired of taking such big steps up the flanks of mountains. Volcanoes often erupted and covered the Indians with fire and lava and ashes. Some were caught descending the rocks, shoulders bowed, and frozen in the lava, as if cursed by the earth, by maledictions from the bowels of the earth. We sometimes found traces of footsteps bigger than our own. Could they have been the white boots of the Mayans? Where I was born the world began. Where I was born lay cities buried under lava, children not yet born destroyed by volcanoes. There was no sea up there, but a lake capable of equally violent storms. The wind was so sharp at times it seemed as if it would behead one. The clouds were pierced by sandstorms, the lava froze in the shape of stars, the trees died of fevers and shed ashen leaves, the dew steamed where it fell, and clouds rose from the earth's parched cracked lips. . . . And there I was born. And the first memory I have is not like other children's; my first memory is of a python devouring a cow. . . . The poor Indians did not have the money to buy coffins for their dead. When bodies are not placed in coffins a combustion takes place, little explosions of blue flames, as the sulphur burns. These little blue flames seen at night are weird and frightening. . . . To reach our house we had to cross a river. Then came the

front patio which was as large as the Place Vendôme. . . .
Then came the chapel which belonged to our ranch. A priest
was sent for from town every Sunday to say mass. . . . The
house was large and rambling, with many inner patios. It was
built of pale coral stucco. There was one room entirely filled
with firearms, all hanging on the walls. Another room filled
with books. I still remember the cedar-wood smell of my
father's room. I loved his elegance, manliness, courage. . . .
One of my aunts was a musician; she married a very brutal
man who made her unhappy. She let herself die of hunger,
playing the piano all through the night. It was hearing her
play night after night, until she died, and finding her music
afterward, which drew me to the piano. Bach, Beethoven, the
best, which at that time were very little known in such far-off
ranches. The schools of music were only frequented by girls.
It was thought to be an effeminate art. I had to give up going
there and study alone, because the girls laughed at me. Although I was so big, and so rough in many ways, loved hunting, fighting, horseback riding, I loved the piano above everything else. . . . The mountain man's obsession is to get a
glimpse of the sea. I never forgot my first sight of the ocean.
The train arrived at four in the morning. I was dazzled, deeply
moved. Even today when I read the *Odyssey* it is with the
fascination of the mountain man for the sea, of the snow man
for warm climates, of the dark, intense Indian for the Greek
light and mellowness. And it is that which draws me to you,
too, for you are the tropics, you have the sun in you, and the
softness, and the clarity. . . ."

What had happened to this body made for the mountain,
for violence and war? A little blue flame of music, of art, from
the body of the aunt who had died playing Bach, a little blue
flame of restless sulphur had passed into this body made for
hunting, for war and the tournaments of love. It had lured him
away from his birthplace, to the cities, to the cafés, to the
artists.

But it had not made of him an artist.

It had been like a mirage, stealing him from other lives, depriving him of ranch, of luxury, of parents, of marriage and children, to make of him a nomad, a wanderer, a restless, homeless one who could never go home again: "Because I am ashamed, I have nothing to show, I would be coming back as a beggar."

The little blue flame of music and poetry shone only at night, during the long nights of love, that was all. In the daytime it was invisible. As soon as day came, his body rose with such strength that she thought: he will conquer the world.

His body—which had not been chiseled like a city man's, not with the precision and finesse of some highly finished statue, but modeled in a clay more massive, more formless too, cruder in outline, closer to primitive sculpture, as if it had kept a little of the heavier contours of the Indian, of animals, of rocks, earth, and plants.

His mother used to say: "You don't kiss me like a boy, but like a little animal."

He began his day slowly, like a cub, rubbing his eyes with closed fists, yawning with eyes closed, a humorous, a sly, upward wrinkle from mouth to high cheekbone, all his strength, as in the lion, hidden in a smooth form, no visible sign of effort.

He began his day slowly, as if man's consciousness were something he had thrown off during the night, and had to be recovered like some artificial covering for his body.

In the city, this body made for violent movements, to leap, to face a danger of some kind, to match the stride of a horse, was useless. It had to be laid aside like a superfluous mantle. Firm muscles, nerves, instincts, animal quickness were useless. It was the head which must awaken, not the muscles and sinews. What must awaken was awareness of a different kind of danger, a different kind of effort, all of it to be considered, matched, mastered in the head, by some abstract wit and wisdom.

The physical euphoria was destroyed by the city. The supply of air and space was small. The lungs shrank. The blood thinned. The appetite was jaded and corrupt.

The vision, the splendor, the rhythm of the body were instantly broken. Clock time, machines, auto horns, whistles, congestion, caught man in their cogs, deafened, stupefied him. The city's rhythm dictated to man; the imperious order to remain alive actually meant to become an abstraction.

Rango's protest was to set out to deny and destroy the enemy. He set out to deny clock time and he would miss, first of all, all that he reached for. He would make such detours to obey his own rhythm and not the city's that the simplest act of shaving and buying a steak would take hours, and the vitally important letter would never be written. If he passed a cigar store, his habit of counter-discipline would be stronger than his own needs and he would forget to buy the cigarettes he craved, but later when about to reach the house of a friend for lunch he would make a long detour for cigarettes and arrive too late for lunch, to find his angry friend gone, and thus once more the rhythm and pattern of the city were destroyed, the order broken, and Rango with it, Rango left without lunch.

He might try to reach the friend by going to the café, would find someone else and fall into talk about bookbinding and meanwhile another friend was waiting for Rango at the Guatemalan Embassy, waiting for his help, his introduction, and Rango never appeared, while Zora waited for him at the hospital, and Djuna waited for him in the barge, while the dinner she had made spoiled on the fire.

At this moment Rango was standing looking at a print on the bookstalls, or throwing dice over a café counter to gamble for a drink, and now that the city's pattern had been destroyed, lay in shambles, he returned and said to Djuna: "I am tired." And laid a despondent, a heavy head on her breasts, his heavy body on her bed, and all his unfulfilled desires, his aborted moments, lay down with him like stones in his pockets, weighing him down, so that the bed creaked with the inertia of his words: "I wanted to do this, I wanted to do that, I want to change the world, I want to go and fight, I want. . . ."

But it is night already, the day has fallen apart, disintegrated in his hands. Rango is tired, he will take another drink from the little barrel, eat a banana, and start to talk about his childhood, about the bread tree, the tree of the shadows that kill, the death of the little Negro boy his father had given him for his birthday, a little Negro boy who had been born the same day as Rango, but in the jungle, and who would be his companion on hunting trips, but who died almost immediately from the cold up in the mountains.

Thus at twilight when Rango had destroyed all order of the city because the city destroyed his body, and the day lay like a cemetery of negations, of rebellions and abortions, lay like a giant network in which he had tangled himself as a child tangles himself in an order he cannot understand, and is in danger of strangling himself . . . then Djuna, fearing he might suffocate, or be crushed, would tenderly seek to unwind him, just as she picked up the pieces of his broken glasses to have them made again. . . .

They had reached a perfect moment of human love. They had created a moment of perfect understanding and accord. This highest moment would now remain as a point of comparison to torment them later on when all natural imperfections would disintegrate it.

The dislocations were at first subtle and held no warning of future destruction. At first the vision was clear, like a perfect crystal. Each act, each word would be imprinted on it to shed light and warmth on the growing roots of love, or to distort it slowly and corrode its expansion.

Rango lighting the lantern for her arrival, for her to see the red light from afar, to be reassured, incited to walk faster, elated by this symbol of his presence and his fervor. His pre-

paring the fire to warm her. . . . These rituals Rango could
not sustain, for he could not maintain the effort to arrive on
time since his lifelong habit had created the opposite habit: to
elude, to avoid, to disappoint every expectation of others, every
commitment, every promise, every crystallization.

The magic beauty of simultaneity, to see the loved one
rushing toward you at the same moment you are rushing
toward him, the magic power of meeting exactly at midnight
to achieve union, the illusion of one common rhythm achieved
by overcoming obstacles, deserting friends, breaking other
bonds—all this was soon dissolved by his laziness, by his habit
of missing every moment, of never keeping his word, of living
perversely in a state of chaos, of swimming more naturally in
a sea of failed intentions, broken promises, and aborted wishes.

The importance of rhythm in Djuna was so strong that no
matter where she was, even without a watch, she sensed the
approach of midnight and would climb on a bus, so instinctively accurate that very often as she stepped off the bus the
twelve loud gongs of midnight would be striking at the large
station clock.

This obedience to timing was her awareness of the rarity of
unity between human beings. She was fully, painfully aware
that very rarely did midnight strike in two hearts at once, very
rarely did midnight arouse two equal desires, and that any dislocation in this, any indifference, was an indication of dis-
unity, of the difficulties, the impossibilities of fusion between
human beings.

Her own lightness, her freedom of movement, her habit of
sudden vanishings made her escapes more possible, whereas
Rango, on the contrary, had never been known to leave except when the bottles, the people, the night, the café, the streets
were utterly empty.

But for her, his inability to overcome the obstacles which
delayed him lessened the power of his love.

Little by little, she became aware that he had two fires to
light, one at home for Zora, and one on the barge. When he

arrived late and wet, she was moved by his tiredness and her awareness of his burdens at home, and she began to light the fire for him.

He loved to sleep late, while she would be awakened by the passing of coal barges, by foghorns, and by the heavy traffic over the bridge. So she would dress quietly and she would run to the café at the corner and return with coffee and buns to surprise him on awakening.

"How human you are, Djuna, how warm and human...."

"But what did you expect me to be?"

"Oh, you look as if the very day you were born you took one look at the world and decided to live in some region between heaven and earth which the Chinese called the Wise Place."

The immense clock on the Quai d'Orsay station which sent people traveling, showed such an enormous, reproachful face in the morning: it is time to take care of Zora, it is time to take care of your father, it is time to return to the world, time time time....

As she knew how much she had loved to see the red lantern gleaming behind the window of the barge as she walked toward it, when Rango fell back into his habit of lateness, it was she who lit the lantern for him, mastering her fear of the dark barge, the drunken watchman, the hobos asleep, the moving figures behind the trees.

When she discovered how strong was his need of wine, she never said: don't drink. She bought a small barrel at the flea market, had it filled with red wine, and placed it at the head of the bed within reach of his hand, having faith that their life together, their adventures together, and the stories they told each other to pass the time, would soon take the place of the wine. Having faith that their warmth together would take the place of the warmth of the wine, believing that all the natural intoxications of caresses would flow from her and not the barrel....

Then one day he arrived with a pair of scissors in his pocket.

Zora was in the hospital for a few days. It was she who always cut his hair. He hated barbers. Would Djuna like to cut his hair?

His heavy, his brilliant, his curling black hair, which neither water nor oil could tame. She cut it as he wished, and felt, for a moment, like his true wife.

Then Zora returned home, and resumed her care of Rango's hair.

And Djuna wept for the first time, and Rango did not understand why she wept.

"I would like to be the one to cut your hair."

Rango made a gesture of impatience. "I don't see why you should give that any importance. It doesn't mean anything. I don't understand you at all."

If it were not for music, one could forget one's life and be born anew, washed of memories. If it were not for music one could walk through the markets of Guatemala, through the snows of Tibet, up the steps of Hindu temples, one could change costumes, shed possessions, retain nothing of the past.

But music pursues one with some familiar air and no longer does the heart beat in an anonymous forest of heartbeats, no longer is it a temple, a market, a street like a stage set, but now it is the scene of a human crisis reenacted inexorably in all its details, as if the music had been the score of the drama itself and not its accompaniment.

The last scene between Rango and Djuna might have faded into sleep, and she might have forgotten his refusal to let her cut his hair once more, but now the organ grinder on the quay turned his handle mischievously, and aroused in her the evocation of another scene. She would not have been as disturbed by Rango's evasiveness, or his defense of Zora's rights to the cutting of his hair, if it had not added itself to other scenes which the organ grinder had attended with similar tunes, and which he was now recreating for her, other scenes where she had not obtained her desire, had not been answered.

The organ grinder playing Carmen took her back inexorably

268

like an evil magician to the day of her childhood when she had asked for an Easter egg as large as herself, and her father had said impatiently: "What a silly wish!" Or to another time when she had asked him to let her kiss his eyelids, and he had mocked her, or still another time when she had wept at his leaving on a trip and he had said: "I don't understand your giving this such importance."

Now Rango was saying the same thing: "I don't understand why you should be sad at not being able to cut my hair any longer."

Why could he not have opened his big arms to her, sheltered her for an instant and said: "It cannot be, that right belongs to Zora, but I do understand how you feel, I do understand you are frustrated in your wish to care for me as a wife. . . ."

She wanted to say: "Oh, Rango, beware. Love never dies of a natural death. It dies because we don't know how to replenish its source, it dies of blindness and errors and betrayals. It dies of illnesses and wounds, it dies of weariness, of witherings, of tarnishings, but never of natural death. Every lover could be brough to trial as the murderer of his own love. When something hurts you, saddens you, I rush to avoid it, to alter it, to feel as you do, but you turn away with a gesture of impatience and say: 'I don't understand.' "

It was never one scene which took place between human beings, but many scenes converging like great intersections of rivers. Rango believed this scene contained nothing but a whim of Djuna's to be denied.

He failed to see that it contained at once all of Djuna's wishes which had been denied, and these wishes had flown from all directions to meet at this intersection and to plead once more for understanding.

All the time that the organ grinder was unwinding the songs of *Carmen* in the orchestra pit of this scene, what was conjured was not this room in a barge, and these two people, but a series of rooms and a procession of people, accumulating to reach immense proportions, accumulating analogies and repetitions of small defeats until it contained them all, and the continuity of the organ grinder's accompaniment welded, compressed them all into a large injustice. Music expanding the compressed heart created a tidal wave of injustice for which no Noah's Ark had ever been provided.

The fire sparkled high; their eyes reflected all its dances joyously.

Djuna looked at Rango with a premonition of difficulties, for it so often happened that their gaiety wakened in him a sudden impulse to destroy their pleasure together. Their joys together never a luminous island in the present but stimulating his remembrance that she had been alive before, that her knowledge of caresses had been taught to her by others, that on other nights, in other rooms, she had smiled. At every peak of contentment she would tremble slightly and wonder when they would begin to slide into torment.

This evening the danger came unsuspected as they talked of painters they liked, and Rango said suddenly: "And to think that you believed Jay a great painter!"

When she defended a friend from Rango's irony and wit it always aroused his jealousy, but to defend an opinion of a painter, Djuna thought, could be achieved without danger.

"Of course, you'll defend Jay," said Rango, "he was a part of your former life, of your former values. I will never be able to alter that. I want you to think as I do."

"But Rango, you couldn't respect someone who surrendered an opinion merely to please you. It would be hypocrisy."

"You admire Jay as a painter merely because Paul admired him. He was Paul's great hero in painting."

"What can I say, Rango? What can I do to prove to you that I belong to you? Paul is not only far away but you know we

270

will never see each other again, that we were not good for each other. I have completely surrendered him, and I could forget him if you would let me. You are the one constantly reminding me of his existence."

At these moments Rango was no longer the fervent, the adoring, the warm, the big, the generous one. His face would darken with anger, and he made violent gestures. His talk became vague and formless, and she could barely catch the revealing phrase which might be the key to the storm and enable her to abate or deflect it.

A slow anger at the injustice of the scene overtook her. Why must Rango use the past to destroy the present? Why did he deliberately seek torment?

She left the table swiftly, and climbed to the deck. She sat near the anchor chain, in the dark. The rain fell on her and she did not feel it; she felt lost and bewildered.

Then she felt him beside her. "Djuna! Djuna!"

He kissed her, and the rain and the tears and his breath mingled. There was such a desperation in his kiss that she melted. It was as if the quarrel had peeled away a layer and left a core like some exposed nerve, so that the kiss was magnified, intensified, as if the pain had made a fine incision for the greater penetration of pleasure.

"What can I do?" she murmured. "What can I do?"

"I'm jealous because I love you."

"But Rango, you have no cause for jealousy."

It was as if they shared his illness of doubt and were seeking a remedy, together.

It seemed to her that if she said, "Jay was a bad painter," Rango could see the obviousness of such a recantation, its absurdity. Yet how could she restore his confidence? His entire body was pleading for reassurance, and if her whole love was not enough what else could she give him to cure his doubt?

When they returned to the room the fire was low.

Rango did not relax. He found some books piled next to the

wastebasket which she had intended to throw away. He picked them up and studied them, one by one, like a detective.

Then he left the ones she had discarded and walked to those aligned on the book shelf.

He picked one up at random and read on the fly leaf: "From Paul."

It was a book on Jay, with reproductions of his paintings.

Djuna said: "If it makes you happy, you can throw it away with the others."

"We'll burn them," he said.

"Burn them all," she said with bitterness.

To her this was not only an offering of peace to his tormenting jealousy, but a sudden anger at this pile of books whose contents had not prepared her for moments such as this one. All these novels so carefully concealing the truth about character, about the obscurities, the tangles, the mysteries. Words words words words and no revelation of the pitfalls, the abysms in which human beings found themselves.

Let him burn them all; they deserved their fate.

(Rango thinks he is burning moments of my life with Paul. He is only burning words, words which eluded all truths, eluded essentials, eluded the bare demon in human beings, and added to the blindness, added to the errors. Novels promising experience, and then remaining on the periphery, reporting only the semblance, the illusions, the costumes, and the falsities, opening no wells, preparing no one for the crises, the pitfalls, the wars, and the traps of human life. Teaching nothing, revealing nothing, cheating us of truth, of immediacy, of reality. Let him burn them, all the books of the world which have avoided the naked knowledge of the cruelties that take place between men and women in the pit of solitary nights. Their abstractions and evasions were no armor against moments of despair.)

She sat beside him by the fire, partaking of this primitive bonfire. A ritual to usher in a new life.

If he continued to destroy malevolently, they might reach

a kind of desert island, a final possession of each other. And at times this absolute which Rango demanded, this peeling away of all externals to carve a single figure of man and woman joined together, appeared to her as a desirable thing, perhaps as a final, irrevocable end to all the fevers and restlessness of love, as a finite union. Perhaps a perfect union existed for lovers willing to destroy the world around them. Rango believed the seed of destruction lay in the world around them, as for example in these books which revealed to Rango too blatantly the difference between their two minds.

To fuse then, it was, at least for Rango, necessary to destroy the differences.

Let them burn the past then, which he considered a threat to their union.

He was driving the image of Paul into another chamber of her heart, an isolated chamber without communicating passage into the one inhabited by Rango. A place in some obscure recess, where flows eternal love, in a realm so different from the one inhabited by Rango that they would never meet or collide, in these vast cities of the interior.

"The heart . . . is an organ . . . consisting of four chambers. . . . A wall separates the chambers on the left from those on the right and no direct communication is possible between them. . . ."

Paul's image was pursued and hid in the chamber of gentleness, as Rango drove it away, with his holocaust of the books they had read together.

(Paul, Paul, this is the claim you never made, the fervor you never showed. You were so cool and light, so elusive, and I never felt you encircling me and claiming possession. Rango is saying all the words I had wanted to hear you say. You never came close to me, even while taking me. You took me as men take foreign women in distant countries whose language they cannot speak. You took me in silence and strangeness. . . .)

When Rango fell asleep, when the aphrodisiac lantern had

burnt out its oil, Djuna still lay awake, shaken by the echoes of his violence, and by the discovery that Rango's confidence would have to be reconstructed each day anew, that none of these maladies of the soul were curable by love or devotion, that the evil lay at the roots, and that those who threw themselves into palliating the obvious symptoms assumed an endless task, a task without hope of cure.

The word most often on his lips was *trouble.*

He broke the glass, he spilled the wine, he burnt the table with cigarettes, he drank the wine which dissolved his will, he talked away his plans, he tore his pockets, he lost his buttons, he broke his combs.

He would say: "I'll paint the door. I will bring oil for the lantern. I will repair the leak on the roof." And months passed: the door remained unpainted, the leak unrepaired, the lantern without oil.

He would say: "I would give my life for a few months of fulfillment, of achievement, of something I could be proud of."

And then he would drink a little more red wine, light another cigarette. His arms would fall at his side; he would lie down beside her and make love to her.

When they entered a shop, she saw a padlock which they needed for the trap door and said: "Let's buy it."

"No," said Rango, "I have seen one cheaper elsewhere."

She desisted. And the next day she said: "I'm going near the place where you said they sold cheap padlocks. Tell me where it is and I'll get it."

"No," said Rango. "I'm going there today. I'll get it." Weeks passed, months passed, and their belongings kept disappearing because there was no padlock on the trap door.

No child was being created in the womb of their love, no

child, but so many broken promises, each day an aborted wish, a lost object, a misplaced unread book, cluttering the room like an attic with discarded possessions.

Rango only wanted to kiss her wildly, to talk vehemently, to drink abundantly, and to sleep late in the mornings.

His body was in a fever always, his eyes ablaze, as if at dawn he were going to don a heavy steel armor and go on a crusade like the lover of the myths.

The crusade was the café.

Djuna wanted to laugh, and forget his words, but he did not allow her to laugh or to forget. He insisted that she retain this image of himself created in his talks at night, the image of his intentions and aspirations. Every day he handed her anew a spider web of fantasies, and he wanted her to make a sail of it and sail their barge to a port of greatness.

She was not allowed to laugh. When at times she was tempted to surrender this fantasy, to accept the Rango who created nothing, and said playfully: "When I first met you, you wanted to be a hobo. Let me be a hobo's wife," then Rango would frown severely and remind her of a more austere destiny, reproaching her for surrendering and diminishing his aims. He was unyielding in his desire that she should remind him of his promises to himself and to her.

This insistence on his dream of another Rango touched her compassion. She was deceived by his words and his ideal of himself. He had appointed her not only guardian angel, but a reminder of his ideals.

She would have liked at times to descend with him into more humanly accessible regions, into a carefree world. She envied him his reckless hours at the café, his joyous friendships, his former life with the gypsies, his careless adventures. The night he and his bar companions stole a rowboat and rowed up the Seine singing, looking for suicides to rescue. His awakenings sometimes in far-off benches in unknown quarters of the city. His long conversations with strangers at dawn far from Paris, in some truck which had given him a ride. But she was not allowed into this world with him.

Her presence had awakened in him a man suddenly whipped by his earlier ideals, whose lost manhood wanted to assert itself in action. With his conquest of Djuna he felt he had recaptured his early self before his disintegration, since he had recaptured his first ideal of woman, the one he had not attained the first time, the one he had completely relinquished in his marriage to Zora—Zora, the very opposite of what he had first dreamed.

What a long detour he had taken by his choice of Zora, who had led him into nomadism, into chaos and destruction.

But in this new love lay the possibility of a new world, the world he had first intended to reach and had missed, had failed to reach with Zora.

Sometimes he would say: "Is it possible that a year ago I was just a bohemian?"

She had unwittingly touched the springs of his true nature: his pride, his need of leadership, his early ambition to play an important role in history.

There were times when Djuna felt, not that his past life had corrupted him—because in spite of his anarchy, his destructiveness, the core of him had remained human and pure—but that perhaps the springs in him had been broken by the tumultuous course of his life, the springs of his will.

How much could love accomplish: it might extract from his body the poisons of failure and bitterness, of betrayals and humiliations, but could it repair a broken spring, broken by years and years of dissolution and surrenders?

Love for the uncorrupted, the intact, the basic goodness of another, could give a softness to the air, a caressing sway to the trees, a joyousness to the fountains, could banish sadness, could produce all the symptoms of rebirth. . . .

He was like nature, good, wild, and sometimes cruel. He had all the moods of nature: beauty, timidity, violence, and tenderness.

Nature was chaos.

276

"Way up into the mountains," Rango would begin again, as if he were continuing to tell her stories of the past which he loved, never of the past of which he was ashamed, "on a mountain twice as high as Mont Blanc, there is a small lake inside of a bower of black volcanic rocks polished like black marble, in the middle of eternal snow peaks. The Indians went up to visit it, to see the mirages. What I saw in the lake was a tropical scene, richly tropical, palms and fruits and flowers. You are that to me, an oasis. You drug me and at the same time you give me strength."

(The drug of love was no escape, for in its coils lie latent dreams of greatness which awaken when men and women fecundate each other deeply. Something is always born of man and woman lying together and exchanging the essences of their lives. Some seed is always carried and opened in the soil of passion. The fumes of desire are the womb of man's birth and often in the drunkenness of caresses history is made, and science, and philosophy. For a woman, as she sews, cooks, embraces, covers, warms, also dreams that the man taking her will be more than a man, will be the mythological figure of her dreams, the hero, the discoverer, the builder. . . . Unless she is the anonymous whore, no man enters woman with impunity, for where the seed of man and woman mingle, within the drops of blood exchanged, the changes that take place are the same as those of great flowing rivers of inheritance, which carry traits of character from father to son to grandson, traits of character as well as physical traits. Memories of experience are transmitted by the same cells which repeated the design of a nose, a hand, the tone of a voice, the color of an eye. These great flowing rivers of inheritance transmitted traits and carried dreams from port to port until fulfillment, and gave birth to selves never born before. . . . No man or woman knows what will be born in the darkness of their intermingling; so much besides children, so many invisible births, exchanges of soul and character, blossoming of unknown selves, liberation of hidden treasures, buried fantasies. . . .)

There was this difference between them: that when these thoughts floated up to the surface of Djuna's consciousness, she could not communicate them to Rango. He laughed at her. "Mystic nonsense," he said.

As Rango chopped wood, lighted the fire, fetched water from the fountain one day with energy and ebullience, smiling a smile of absolute faith and pleasure, then Djuna felt: wonderful things will be born.

But the next day he sat in the café and laughed like a rogue, and when Djuna passed she was confronted with another Rango, a Rango who stood at the bar with the bravado of the drunk, laughing with his head thrown back and his eyes closed, forgetting her, forgetting Zora, forgetting politics and history, forgetting rent, marketing, obligations, appointments, friends, doctors, medicines, pleasures, the city, his past, his future, his present self, in a temporary amnesia, which left him the next day depressed, inert, poisoned with his own angers at himself, angry with the world, angry with the sky, the barge, the books, angry with everything.

And the third day another Rango, turbulent, erratic, dark, like Heathcliff, said Djuna, destroying everything. That was the day that followed the bouts of drinking: a quarrel with Zora, a fight with the watchman. Sometimes he came back with his face hurt by a brawl at the café. His hands shook. His eyes glazed, with a yellow tinge. Djuna would turn her face away from his breath, but his warm, his deep voice would bring her face back saying: "I'm in trouble, bad trouble. . . ."

On windy nights the shutters beat against the walls like the bony wings of a giant albatross.

The wall against which the bed lay was wildly licked by the small river waves and they could hear the lap lap lap against the mildewed flanks.

In the darkness of the barge, with the wood beams groaning, the rain falling in the room through the unrepaired roof, the steps sounded louder and more ominous. The river seemed reckless and angry.

Against the smoke and brume of their caresses, these brusque changes of mood, when the barge ceased to be the cell of a mysterious new life, an enchanted refuge; when it became the site of compressed angers, like a load of dynamite boxes awaiting explosion.

For Rango's angers and battles with the world turned to poison. The world was to blame for everything. The world was to blame for Zora having been born very poor, of an insane mother, of a father who ran away. The world was to blame for her undernourishment, her ill health, her precocious marriage, her troubles. The doctors were to blame for her not getting well. The public was to blame for not understanding her dances. The house owner should have let them off without paying rent. The grocer had no right to claim his due. They were poor and had a right to mercy.

The noise of the chain tying and untying the rowboat, the fury of the winter Seine, the suicides from the bridge, the old watchman banging his pails together as he leaped over the gangplank and down the stairs, the water seeping too fast into the hold of the barge not pumped, the dampness gathering and painting shoes and clothes with mildew. Holes in the floor, unrepaired, through which the water gleamed like the eyes of the river, and through which the legs of the chairs kept falling like an animal's leg caught in a trap.

Rango said: "My mother told me once: how can you hope to play the piano, you have the hands of a savage."

"No," said Djuna, "your hands are just like you. Three of the fingers are strong and savage, but these last two, the smallest, are sensitive and delicate. Your hand is just like you; the core is tender within a dark and violent nature. When you trust, you are tender and delicate, but when you doubt, you are dangerous and destructive."

"I always took the side of the rebel. Once I was appointed chief of police in my home town, and sent with a posse to capture a bandit who had been terrorizing the Indian villages. When I got there I made friends with the bandit and we played cards and drank all night."

"What killed your faith in love, Rango? You were never betrayed."

"I don't accept your having loved anyone before you knew me."

Djuna was silent, thinking that jealousy of the past was unfounded, thinking that the deepest possessions and caresses were stored away in the attics of the heart but had no power to revive and enter the present lighted rooms. They lay wrapped in twilight and dust, and if an old association caused an old sensation to revive it was but for an instant, like an echo, intermittent and transitory. Life carries away, dims, and mutes the most indelible experiences down the River Styx of vanished worlds. The body has its cores and its peripheries and such a mysterious way of maintaining intruders on the outer rim. A million cells protect the core of a deep love from ghostly invasions, from any recurrences of past loves.

An intense, a vivid present was the best exorcist of the past.

So that whenever Rango began his inquisitorial searchings into her memory, hoping to find an intruder, to battle Paul, Djuna laughed: "But your jealousy is necrophilic! You're opening tombs!"

"But what a love you have for the dead! I'm sure you visit them every day with flowers."

"Today I have not been to the cemetery, Rango!"

"When you are here I know you are mine. But when you go up those little stairs, out of the barge, walking in your quick quick way, you enter another world, and you are no longer mine."

"But you, too, Rango, when you climb those stairs, you enter another world, and you are no longer mine. You belong to

Zora then, to your friends, to the café, to politics."

(Why is he so quick to cry treachery? No two caresses ever resemble each other. Every lover holds a new body until he fills it with his essence, and no two essences are the same, and no flavor is ever repeated. . . .)

"I love your ears, Djuna. They are small and delicate. All my life I dreamed of ears like yours."

"And looking for ears you found me!"

He laughed with all of himself, his eyes closing like a cat's, both lids meeting. His laughter made his high cheekbone even fuller, and he looked at times like a very noble lion.

"I want to become someone in the world. We're living on top of a volcano. You may need my strength. I want to be able to take care of you."

"Rango, I understand your life. You have a great force in you, but there is something impeding you, blocking you. What is it? This great explosive force in you, it is all wasted. You pretend to be indifferent, nonchalant, reckless, but I feel you care deep down. Sometimes you look like Peter the Great, when he was building a city on a swamp, rescuing the weak, charging in battle. Why do you drown the dynamite in you in wine? Why are you so afraid to create? Why do you put so many obstacles in your own way? You drown your strength, you waste it. You should be constructing. . . ."

She kissed him, seeking and searching to understand him, to kiss the secret Rango so that it would rise to the surface, become visible and accessible.

And then he revealed the secret of his behavior to her in words which made her heart contract: "It's useless, Djuna. Zora and I are victims of fatality. Everything I've tried has failed. I have bad luck. Everyone has harmed me, from my family on, friends, everyone. Everything has become twisted, and useless."

"But Rango, I don't believe in fatality. There is an inner pattern of character which you can discover and you can alter. It's only the romantic who believes we are victims of a destiny. And you always talk against the romantic."

Rango shook his head vehemently, impatiently. "You can't tamper with nature. One just is. Nature cannot be controlled. One is born with a certain character and if that is one's fate, as you say, well, there is nothing to be done. Character cannot be changed."

He had those instinctive illuminations, flashes of intuition, but they were intermittent, like lightning in a stormy sky, and then in between he would go blind again.

The goodness which at times shone so brilliantly in him was a goodness without insight, too; he was not even aware of the changes from goodness to anger, and could not conjure any understanding against his violent outbursts.

Djuna feared those changes. His face at times beautiful, human, and near, at others twisted, cruel, and bitter. She wanted to know what caused the changes, to avert the havoc they caused, but he eluded all efforts at understanding.

She wished she had never told him anything about her past. She remembered what incited her to talk. It was during the early part of the relationship, when one night he had leaned over and whispered: "You are an angel. I can't believe you can be taken like a woman." And he had hesitated for an instant to embrace her.

She had rushed to disprove it, eagerly denying it. She had as great a fear of being told that she was an angel as other women had of their demon being exposed. She felt it was not true, that she had a demon in her as everyone had, but that she controlled it rigidly, never allowing it to cause harm.

She also had a fear that this image of the angel would eclipse the woman in her who wanted an earthy bond. An angel to her was the least desirable of bedfellows!

To talk about her past had been her way to say: "I am a woman, not an angel."

"A sensual angel," then he conceded. But what he registered was her obedience to her impulses, her capacity for love, her gift of herself, on which to base henceforth his doubts of her fidelity.

"And you're Vesuvius," she said laughing. "Whenever I talk about understanding, mastering, changing, you get as angry as an earthquake. You have no faith that destiny can be changed."

"The Mayan Indian is not a mystic, he is a pantheist. The earth is his mother. He has only one word for both mother and earth. When an Indian died they put real food in his tomb, and they kept feeding him."

"A symbolical food does not taste as good as real food!"

(It is because he is of the earth that he is jealous and possessive. His angers are of the earth. His massive body is of the earth. His knees are of iron, so strong from pressing against the flanks of wild horses. His body has all the flavors of the earth: spices, ginger, chutney, musk, pimiento, wine, opium. He has the smooth neck of a statue, a Spanish arrogance of the head, an Indian submission, too. He has the awkward grace of an animal. His hands and feet are more like paws. When he catches a fleeing cat he is swifter than the cat. He squats like an Indian and then leaps on powerful legs. I love the way his high cheekbones swell with laughter. Asleep he shows the luxuriant charcoal eyelashes of a woman. The nose so round and jovial; everything powerful and sensual except his mouth. His mouth is small and timid.)

What Djuna believed was that like a volcano his fire and strength would erupt and bring freedom, to him and to her. She believed the fire in him would burn all the chains which bound him. But fire too must have direction. His fire was blind. But she was not blind. She would help him.

In spite of his physical vitality, he was helpless, he was bound and tangled. He could set fire to a room and destroy, but he could not build as yet. He was bound and blind as nature is. His hands could break what he held out of strength, a strength he could not measure, but he could not build. His inner chaos was the chain around his body, his conviction that one was born a slave of one's nature, to be led inevitably to

283

destruction by one's blind impulses.

"What do you want your life to be?"

"A revolution every day."

"Why, Rango?"

"I love violence. I want to serve ideas with my body."

"Men die every day for ideas which betray them, for leaders who betray them, for false ideals."

"But love betrays, too," said Rango. "I have no faith."

(Oh, god, thought Djuna, will I have the strength to win this battle against destruction, this private battle for a human love?)

"I need independence," said Rango, "as a wild horse needs it. I can't harness myself to anything. I can't accept any discipline. Discipline discourages me."

Even asleep his body was restless, heavy, feverish. He threw off all the blankets, lay naked, and by morning the bed seemed like a battlefield. So many combats he had waged within his dreams; so tumultuous a life even in sleep.

Chaos all around him, his clothes always torn, his books soiled, his papers lost. His personal belongings, of which he remembered an object now and then which he missed, wanted to show Djuna, were scattered all over the world, in rooming-house cellars where they were kept as hostages for unpaid rent.

All the little flames burning in him at once, except the wise one of the holy ghost.

It saddened Djuna that Rango was so eager to go to war, to fight for his ideas, to die for them. It seemed to her that he was ready to live and die for emotional errors as women did, but that like most men he did not call them emotional errors; he called them history, philosophy, metaphysics, science. Her feminine self was sad and smiled, too, at this game of endowing personal and emotional beliefs with the dignity of impersonal names. She smiled at this as men smile at women's enlargement of personal tragedies to a status men do not believe applicable to personal lives.

While Rango took the side of wars and revolutions, she took the side of Rango, she took the side of love.

Parties changed every day, philosophies and science changed, but for Djuna human love alone continued. Great changes in the maps of the world, but none in this need of human love, this tragedy of human love swinging between illusion and human life, sometimes breaking at the dangerous passageway between illusion and human life, sometimes breaking altogether. But love itself as continuous as life.

She smiled at man's great need to build cities when it was so much harder to build relationships, his need to conquer countries when it was so much harder to conquer one heart, to satisfy a child, to create a perfect human life. Man's need to invent, to circumnavigate space when it is so much harder to overcome space between human beings, man's need to organize systems of philosophy when it was so much harder to understand one human being, and when the greatest depths of human character lay but half explored.

"I must go to war," he said. "I must act. I must serve a cause."

Rango gave her the feeling of one who reproduced in life gestures and scenes and atmosphere already imprinted on her memory. Where had she already seen Rango on horseback, wearing white fur boots, furs and corduroys, Rango with his burning eyes, somber face, and wild black hair?

Where had she already seen Rango's face in passion worshipful like a man receiving communion, the profane wafer on the tongue?

Seeing him lying at her side was like one of those memories which assail one while traveling through foreign lands to which one was not bound in any conscious way, and yet at each step recognizing its familiarity, with an exact prescience of the scene awaiting one around the corner of the street.

Memory, or race memories, or the influence of tales, fairy tales, legends, and ballads heard in childhood?

Rango came from sixteenth-century Spain, the Spain of the troubadours, with its severity, its rigid form, the domination of the church, the claustration of women, the splendor of Catholic ceremonies, and a vast, secret tumultuous river of sensuality running below the surface, uncontrollable, and detectable only through those persistent displays of guilt and atonement common to all races.

Rango recreated for Djuna a natural blood-and-flesh paradise so different from the artificial paradises created in art by city children. In her childhood spent in cities, and not in forests, she had created paradises of her own inventions, with a language of her own, outside and beyond life, as certain birds create a nest in some inaccessible branch of a tree, inaccessible to disaster but also difficult to preserve.

But Rango's paradise was an artless paradise of life in a forest, in mountains, lakes, mirages, with strange animals and strange flowers and trees, all of it warm and accessible.

Because she had been a child of the cities, the paradise of her childhood had been born of fairy tales, legends, and mythology, obscuring ugliness, cramped rooms, miserly backyards.

Rango had had no need to invent. He had possessed mountains of legendary magnificence, lakes of fantastic proportions, extraordinary animals, a house of great beauty. He had known fiestas which lasted for a week, carnivals, orgies. He had taken his ecstasies from the rarefied air of heights, his drugs from religious ceremonies, his physical pleasures from battles, his poetry from solitude, his music from Indian dances, and been nourished on tales told by his Indian nurse.

To visit the first girl he had loved he had had to travel all night on horseback, he had leaped walls, and risked her mother's fury and possible death at the hands of her father. It was all written in the *Romancero!*

The paradise of her childhood was under a library table covered to the ground by a red cloth with fringes, which was her house, in which she read forbidden books from her father's vast library. She had been given a little piece of oilcloth on which she wiped her feet ostentatiously before entering this tent, this Eskimo hut, this African mud house, this realm of the myth.

The paradise of her childhood had been in books.

The house in which she had lived as a child was the house of the spirit which does not live blindly but is ever, out of passionate experience, building and adorning its four-chambered heart—an extension and expansion of the body, with many delicate affinities establishing themselves between her and the doors and passageways, the lights and shadows of her outward abode, until she was incorporated into it in the entire expressiveness of what is outward as related to the inner significance, until there was no more distinction between outward and inward at all.

(I'm fighting a dark force in Rango, loving nature in him, through him, and yet fighting the destructions of nature. When my life culminates in a heaven of passion, it is most dangerously balanced over a precipice. The further I seek to soar into the dream, the essence, touching the vaults of the sky, the tighter does the cord of reality press my neck. Will I break seeking to rescue Rango? Fatigue of the heart and body. . . . Intermittently I see and feel the dampness, poverty, a sick Zora, food on the table with wine stains, cigarette ashes, and bread crumbs of past meals. Only now and then do I notice the rust in the stove, the leak in the roof, the rain on the rug, the fire that has gone out, the sour wine in a cup. And thus I descend through trap doors without falling into a trap but knowing there is another Rango I cannot see, the one who lives with Zora, who awaits to appear in the proper lighting. And I am afraid, afraid of pain. . . . Now I understand why I loved Paul . . . because he was afraid. When we lay down and caressed each other we caressed this self-same fear and understood it, under the blanket, fear of violence. We recognized it in the dark, with our hands and our mouths. We touched it and were moved by it, because it was our secret which we shared through the body. Everyone says: you must take sides, choose a political party, choose a philosophy, choose a dogma. . . . I chose the dream of human love. Whatever I ally myself to is to be close to my love. With it I hope to defeat tragedy, to defeat violence. I dance, I sew, I mend, I cook for the sake of this dream. In this dream nobody dies, nobody is sick, nobody separates. I love and dance with my dream unfurled, trusting darkness, trusting the labyrinth, into the furnaces of love. Some say: the dream is escape. Some say: the dream is madness. Some say: the dream is sickness. It will betray you. The Rango I see is not the one Zora sees, or the world sees. This is the witchcraft of love. You can take sides in religion, you can take sides in history, and there are others with you, you are not alone. But when you take the side of love, the opium of love, you are alone. For the doctors call the dream a symptom, the historians escape, the philosophers a drug, and even your lover will not make the perilous journey with you. . . . Hang your dream of love on the mast of this barge of caresses . . . a flag of fire. . . .)

The enemy was not outside as Rango believed.

What he most wanted to avoid, which was that Djuna should remember her days with Paul, or desire Paul's return, or yearn for his presence, was the very feeling he caused by his violence. Because his violence drove her away from him. The sense of devastation left by his angry words, or his distorted interpretations of her acts, his doubts, caused such an anxious climate that at times to escape from the tension, like a child seeking peace and gentleness, she did remember Paul. . . .

Then Rango committed a second error: he wanted Djuna and Zora to be friends.

Djuna never knew whether he believed this would achieve a unity in his torn and divided life, whether he was thinking only of himself, or of sharing his burden with Djuna, or whether he had such faith in Djuna's creation of human beings that he hoped she could heal Zora and perhaps win Zora's affection and put an end to the tension he felt whenever he returned home.

The obscurities and labyrinths of Rango's mind remained always mysterious to her. There were twists and deformities in his nature which she could not clarify. Not only because he never knew himself what took place within him, not only because he was full of contradictions and confusions, but because he resented and rebelled against any examination, probing, or questioning of his motives.

So came the day when he said: "I wish you would visit Zora. She is very ill and you might help her."

Until now there had been very little mention of Zora. Certain words of Rango's had accumulated in Djuna's mind: Rango had married Zora when he was seventeen. Six years before he met Djuna they had begun to live together without a physical bond, "as brother and sister." She was constantly ill and Rango had a great compassion for her helplessness. Djuna did not know whether more than compassion bound them together, more than the past.

She knew that this appeal was made to her good self, and that she must, to answer it, subdue her own wishes not to be entangled in Rango's life with Zora, and to avoid a relationship which could only cause her pain. She was being asked to bring a certain aspect of herself among her other aspects as others are asked to wear a certain costume out of their multiple wardrobe.

She was invited to bring her good self only, in which Rango believed utterly, and yet she felt a rebellion against this good self which was too often called upon, was too often invited, to

the detriment of other selves who were now like numerous wallflowers! The Djuna who wanted to laugh, to be carefree, to have a love all of her own, an integrated life, a rest from troubles.

Secretly she had often dreamed of her other selves, the wild, the free, the natural, the capricious, the whimsical, the mischievous ones. But the constant demand upon the good one was atrophying the others.

But there are invitations which are like commands.

There are heraldic worlds of spiritual and emotional aristocracy which have nothing to do with conventional morality, which give to certain acts a quality of noblesse oblige, a faithfulness to the highest capacities of a personality, a sort of life on the altitudes, a devotion to the idealized self. The artists who had overthrown conventions submitted to this code and knew the sadness and guilt which came from any failing in this voluntary standard. All of them suffered at times from a guilt resembling the guilt of the religious, the moralists, the bourgeois, while apparently living in opposition to them. It was the incurable guilt of the idealist seeking to reach an image of one's self one could be proud of.

They had merely created fraternities, duties, communal taboos of another sort, but to which they adhered at the cost of great personal sacrifices.

Djuna did not know how this good self had attained such prominence. She did not know how it had come to be born at all, for she considered it thrust upon her, not adopted by her. She felt much less good than she was expected to be. It gave her a feeling of treachery, of deception.

She did not have the courage to say: I would rather not see Zora, not know your other life. I would rather retain my illusion of a single love.

In childhood she remembered she played dangerous games. She sought adventures and difficulties. She fabricated paper wings and threw herself out of a second-story window, escaping injury by a miracle. She did not want to be the sweet and gentle

heroine in charades and games, but the dark queen of intrigue.
She preferred Catherine de' Medici to the flavorless and innocent princesses.

She was often tangled in her own high rebellions, in her
devastating bad tempers, and in lies.

But her parents repeated obsessionally: You must be good.
You must keep your dress clean. You must be kind, thank
the lady, hide your pain if you fall, do not reach for anything
you want, do not attract attention to yourself, do not be vain
about the ribbon in your hair, efface yourself, be silent and
modest, give up to your brothers the games they want, curb
your temper, do not talk too much, do not invent stories about
things which never happened, *be good or else you will not be
loved.* And when she was accused of any of these offenses,
both parents turned away from her and she was denied the
good-night or good-morning kiss which was essential to her
happiness. Her mother carried out her threats of loss into
games which seemed like tragedies to Djuna the child: once
swimming in a lake before Djuna's anxious eyes, she had pretended to disappear and be drowned. When she reappeared
on the surface Djuna was already hysterical. Another time,
in a vast railroad station, when Djuna was six years old, the
mother hid behind a column and Djuna found herself alone
in the crowd, lost, and again she wept hysterically.

The good self was formed by these threats: an artificial
bloom. In this incubator of fear, her goodness bloomed merely
as the only known way to hold and attract love.

There were other selves which interested her more but
which she learned to conceal or to stifle: her inventive, fantasy-
weaving self who loved tales, her high-tempered self who
flared like heat lightning, her stormy self, the lies which were
not lies but an improvement on reality.

She had loved strong language like ginger upon the lips.
But her parents had said: "From you we don't expect this, not
from you." And appointed her as a guard upon her brothers,
asking her to enforce their laws, just as Rango had appointed

her now a guard against his disintegrations.

So that she had learned the only reconciliation she could find: she learned to preserve the balance between crime and punishment. She took her place against the wall, face to the wall, and then muttered, "Damn damn damn damn," as many times as she pleased, since she was simultaneously punishing herself and felt absolved, with no time wasted on contrition.

And now this good self could no longer be discarded. It had a compulsive life, its legend, its devotees! Every time she yielded to its sway she increased her responsibilities, for new devotees appeared, demanding perpetual attendance.

If Rango asked her today to take care of Zora, it was because he had heard, and he knew, of many past instances when she had taken care of others.

This indestructible good self, this false and wearying good self who answered prayers: Djuna, I need you; Djuna, console me; Djuna, you carry palliatives (why had she studied the art of healing, all the philters against pain?); Djuna, bring your wand; Djuna, we'll take you to Rango, not the Rango of the joyous guitar and the warm songs, but Rango, the husband of a woman who is always ill. It will break your heart, Djuna of the fracturable heart, your heart will fracture with a sound of wind chimes and the pieces will be iridescent. Where they fall new plants will grow instantly, and it is to the advantage of a new crop of breakable hearts that yours should fracture often, for the artist is like the religious man, he believes that denial of worldly possessions and acceptance of pain and trouble will give birth to the marvelous—sainthood or art.

(This goodness is a role, too tight around me; it is a costume I can no longer wear. There are other selves trying to be born, demanding at least a hearing!)

Your past history influenced your choice, Djuna; you have shown capabilities to lessen pain and so you are not invited to the fiestas.

Irrevocable extension of past roles, and no reversal possible.

Too many witnesses to past compassions, past abdications,

and they will look scandalized by any alteration of your character and will reawaken your old guilts. Face to the wall! This time so that Rango may not see your rebellion in your face. Rango's wife is mortally ill and you are to bring your philters.

But she had made an important discovery.

This bond with Rango, this patience with his violent temper, this tacit fraternity of her gentleness and his roughness, this collaboration of light and shadow, this responsibility for Rango which she felt, her compulsion to rescue him from the consequences of his blind rages, were because Rango lived out for her this self she had buried in her childhood. All that she had denied and repressed: chaos, disorder, caprice, destruction.

The reason for her indulgence; everyone marveled (how could you bear his jealousy, his angers?) at the way he destroyed what she created so that each day she must begin anew: to understand, to order, to reconstruct, to mend; the reason for her acceptance of the troubles caused by his blindness was that Rango *was* nature, uncontrolled, and that the day she had buried her own laziness, her own jealousy, her own chaos, these atrophied selves awaited liberation and began to breathe through Rango's acts. For this complicity in the dark she must share the consequences with him.

The realm she had tried to skip: darkness, confusion, violence, destruction, erupted secretly through relationship with Rango. The burden was placed on his shoulders. She must therefore share the torments, too. She had not annihilated her natural self; it reasserted itself in Rango. And she was his accomplice.

The dark-faced Rango who opened the door of his studio below street level was not the joyous carefree guitarist Djuna had first seen at the party, nor was it the fervent Rango of the nights at the barge, nor was it the oscillating Rango of the café, the ironic raconteur, the reckless adventurer. It was another Rango she did not know.

In the dark hallway his body appeared silhouetted, his high forehead, the fall of his hair, his bow, full of nobility, grandeur. He bowed gravely in the narrow hallway as if this cavernous dwelling were his castle, he the seigneur and she a visitor of distinction. He emerged prouder, taller, more silent, too, out of poverty and barrenness, since they were of his own choice. If he had not been a rebel, he would be greeting her at the vast entrance of his ranch.

Down the stairs into darkness. Her hand touched the walls hesitantly to guide herself, but the walls had such a rough surface and seemed to be sticky to the touch so that she withdrew it and Rango explained: "We had a fire here once. I set fire to the apartment when I fell asleep while smoking. The landlord never repaired the damage as we haven't paid rent for six months."

A faint odor of dampness rose from the studio below, which was the familiar odor of poor studios in Paris. It was compounded of fog, of the ancient city breathing its fetid breath through cellar floors; it was the odor of stagnation, of clothes not often washed, of curtains gathering mildew.

She hesitated again until she saw the skylight windows above her head; but they were covered with soot and let in a dim northern light.

Rango then stood aside, and Djuna saw Zora lying in bed.

Her black hair was uncombed and straggled around her parchment-colored skin. She had no Indian blood, and her face was almost a direct contrast to Rango's. She had heavy, pronounced features, a wide full mouth, all cast in length, in sadness, a defeated pull downward which only changed when she raised her eyelids; then the eyes had in them an unexpected shrewdness which Rango did not have.

She was wearing one of Rango's shirts, and over that a

kimono which had been dyed black. The red and black squares of the shirt's colors showed at the neck and wrists. The stripes once yellow still showed through the black dye of the kimono.

On her feet she wore a pair of Rango's big socks filled with cotton wool at the toes, which seemed like disproportionate clown's feet on her small body.

Her shoulders were slightly hunched, and she smiled the smile of the hunchback, of a cripple. The arching of her shoulders gave her an air of having shrunk herself together to occupy a small space. It was the arch of fear.

Even before her illness, Djuna felt, she could never have been handsome but had a strength of character which must have been arresting. Yet her hands were childish and clasped things without firmness. And in the mouth there was the same lack of control. Her voice, too, was childish.

The studio was now half in darkness, and the oil lamp which Rango brought cast long shadows.

The mist of dampness in the room seemed like the breath of the buried, making the walls weep, detaching the wallpaper in long wilted strips. The sweat of centuries of melancholic living, the dampness of roots and cemeteries, the moisture of agony and death seeping through the walls seemed appropriate to Zora's skin from which all glow and life had withdrawn.

Djuna was moved by Zora's smile and plaintive voice. Zora was saying: "The other day I went to church and prayed desperately that someone should save us, and now you are here. Rango is always bewildered, and does nothing." Then she turned to Rango: "Bring me my sewing box."

Rango brought her a tin cracker box which contained needles, threads, and buttons in boxes labeled with medicine names: injections, drops, pills.

The material Zora took up to sew looked like a rag. Her small hands smoothed it down mechanically, yet the more she smoothed it down the more it wilted in her hands, as if her touch were too anxious, too compressing, as if she transmitted to objects some obnoxious withering breath from her sick flesh.

And when she began to sew she sewed with small stitches, closely overlapping, so closely that it was as if she were strangling the last breath of color and life in the rag, as if she were sewing it to the point of suffocation.

As they talked she completed the square she had already begun, and then Djuna watched her rip apart her labor and quietly begin again.

"Djuna, I don't know if Rango told you, but Rango and I are like brother and sister. Our physical life . . . was over years ago. It was never very important. I knew that sooner or later he would love another woman, and I am glad it's you because you're kind, and you will not take him away from me. I need him."

"I hope we can be . . . kind to each other, Zora. It's a difficult situation."

"Rango told me that you never tried, or even mentioned, his leaving me. How could I not like you? You saved my life. When you came I was about to die for lack of care and food. I don't love Rango as a man. To me he is a child. He has done me so much harm. He just likes to drink, and talk, and be with friends. If you love him, I am glad, because of the kind of woman you are, because you are full of quality."

"You're very generous, Zora."

Zora leaned over to whisper now: "Rango is mad, you know. He may not seem so to you because he is leaning on you. But if it were not for you I would be out in the street, homeless. We've often been homeless, and I'd be sitting on my valises, out on the sidewalk, and Rango just waving his arms and helpless, never knowing what to do. He lets everything terrible happen, and then he says: 'It's destiny.' With his cigarette he set fire to our apartment. He was nearly burnt to death."

There was a book lying at the foot of her bed, and Djuna opened it while Zora was carefully unstitching all she had sewed before.

"It's a book about illness," said Zora. "I love to read about

297

illness. I go to the library and look up descriptions of the symptoms I have. I've marked all the pages which apply to me. Just look at all these markings. Sometimes I think I have all the sicknesses one can have!" She laughed. Then looking at Djuna plaintively, almost pleadingly, she said: "All my hair is falling out."

When Djuna left that evening, Rango and she were no longer man and woman in a chamber of isolated love for each other. They were suddenly a trinity, with Zora's inexorable needs conducting all their movements, directing their time together, dictating the hours of separation.

Rango had placed Zora under Djuna's protection and her love for Rango had to extend in magnitude to include Zora.

Zora talked to Djuna. If it was Djuna who had planned to come to Zora and show the most exemplary devotion, she found herself merely passive before the friendliness of Zora.

It was Zora who talked, with her eyes upon her sewing and unsewing. "Rango is a changed man, and I'm so happy, Djuna. He is kinder to me. He was very unhappy before and he took it out on me. A man cannot live without love and Rango was not easy to satisfy. All the women wanted him, but he would see them once perhaps and come back dejected, and refuse to see them again. He always found something wrong with them. With you he is content. And I am happy because I knew this had to happen sometime, but I'm happy it's you because I trust you. I used to fear some woman coming and taking him where I would never see him again. And I know you wouldn't do that."

Djuna thought: "I love Rango so much that I want to share his burdens, love and serve what he loves and serves, share his conviction that Zora is an innocent victim of life, worthy of all sacrifices."

This was for both Rango and Djuna the atonement for the marvelous hours in the barge. All great flights away from life land one in such places of atonement as this room, with Zora sewing rags and talking about dandruff, about ovarian insufficiency, about gastritis, about thyroid and neuritis.

Djuna had brought her a colorful Indian-print dress and Zora had dyed it black. And now she was reshaping it and it looked worn and dismal already. She wore a shawl pinned with a brooch which had once held stones in its clasps and was now empty, thrusting bare silver branches out like the very symbol of denudation. She wore two overcoats sewn together, the inner one showing at the edges.

While they sat sewing together, Zora lamented over Rango: "Why must he always live with so many people around him?"

Knowing that Rango liked to spend hours and hours alone with her, Djuna feared to say: "Perhaps he is just seeking warmth and forgetfulness, running away from illness and darkness."

When Rango was with her he seemed dominating, full of dignity and pride. When he entered Zora's room he seemed to shrink. When he first entered there was a copper glow in his face; after a moment the glow vanished.

"Why do men live in shoals?" persisted Zora.

Djuna looked at Rango lighting the fire, warming water, starting to cook. There was something so discouraged in the pose of his body, expressing agreement with Zora's enumeration of his faults, so diminished, which Djuna could not bear to witness.

Zora was in the hospital.

Djuna was cooking for Rango now, and also a special soup

which Rango was to take to Zora at noon.

As Djuna passed through the various rooms to find Zora she saw a woman sitting up in bed combing her hair and tying a blue ribbon around it. Her face was utterly wasted, and yet she had powdered it, and rouged her lips, and there was on it not only the smile of a woman dying but also the smile of a woman who wanted to die with grace, deploying her last flare of feminine coquetry for her interview with death.

Djuna was moved by this courage, the courage to meet death with one's hair combed, and this gentle smile issuing from centuries of conviction that a woman must be pleasing to all eyes, even to the eyes of death.

When she reached Zora's bed she was faced with the very opposite, an utter absence of courage, although Zora was less ill than the other woman.

"The soup is not thin enough," said Zora. "It should have been strained longer." And she laid it aside and shook her head while Djuna and Rango pleaded that she should eat it anyway for the sake of gaining strength.

Her refusal to eat caused Rango anxiety, and Zora watched this anxiety on his face and savoured it.

He had brought her a special bread, but it was not the one she wanted.

Djuna had brought her some liver concentrate in glass containers. Zora looked at them and said: "They are not good. They're too dark. I'm sure they're not fresh and they will poison me."

"But Zora, the date is printed on the box, the drugstore can't sell them when they're old."

"They're very old, I can see it. Rango, I want you to get me some others at La Muette drugstore."

La Muette was one hour away. Rango left on his errand and Djuna took the medicine away.

When they met in the evening Rango said: "Give me the liver medicine. I'll take it back to the drugstore."

They walked to the drugstore together. The druggist was

incensed and pointed to the recent date on the box.

What amazed Djuna was not that Zora should give way to a sick woman's whims, but that Rango should be so utterly convinced of their rationality.

The druggist would not take it back.

Rango was angry and tumultuous, but Djuna was rebelling against Rango's blindness and when they returned to the house-boat she opened one of the containers and before Rango's eyes she swallowed it.

"What are you doing?" asked Rango with amazement.

"Showing you that the medicine is fresh."

"You believe the druggist and not Zora?" he said angrily.

"And you believe in a sick person's whim," she said.

Zora was always talking about her future death. She began all her conversations with: "When I die. . . ." Rango was mantained in a state of panic, fearing her death, and lived each day accordingly: "Zora is in grave danger of death," he would say, to excuse her demands upon his time.

At first Djuna was alarmed by Zora's behavior, and shared Rango's anxieties. Her gestures were so vehement, so mag-nified, that Djuna believed they might be those of a dying woman. But as these gestures repeated themselves day after day, week after week, month after month, year after year, Djuna lost her fear of Zora's death.

When Zora said: "I have a burning sensation in my stomach," she made the gestures of a person writhing in a brasier of flames.

At the hospital, where Djuna sometimes accompanied her, the nurses and doctors no longer listened to her. Djuna caught glances of irony in the doctor's eyes.

Zora's gestures to describe her troubles became for Djuna

a special theatre of exaggeration, which at first caused terror, and then numbed the senses.

It was like the Grand Guignol, where knowing every scene was overacted to create horror finally created detachment and laughter.

But what helped Djuna to overcome her terror was something else which happened that winter: there was an epidemic of throat infection which swept Paris and which Djuna caught.

It was painful but came without fever, and there was no need to stay in bed.

That same day Rango rushed to the barge, distressed and vehement. He could not stay with Djuna because Zora was terribly ill. "You might come back with me, if you wish. Zora has a heart attack, an inflamed throat, and she's suffocating."

When they arrived, the doctor was there examining Zora's throat. Zora lay back pale and rigid, as if her last hour had come. Her gestures, her hands upon her throat, her strained face were a representation of strangulation.

The doctor straightened up and said: "Just the same throat infection everybody has just now. You don't have to stay in bed. Just keep warm, and eat soups only."

And Djuna, with the same throat trouble, was out with Rango.

The first year Djuna had suffered from Rango's panic. The second year from pity; the third year detachment and wisdom came. But Rango's anxiety never diminished.

Djuna awakened one morning and asked herself: "Do I love this woman who magnifies her illness a thousand times, unconcerned with curing it, but savoring its effect on others? Why does Zora contort herself in a more than life-size pain for all the world to see and hear?"

Many times Djuna had been baffled by the fact that when someone said to Zora, "You look better, so much better," Zora was not pleased. A frown would come between her eyes, an expression of distress.

At the hospital one day, the doctor did not linger very long at Zora's bedside, and when he walked away Djuna laid her hand on his arm: "Please tell me what's the matter with my friend?"

"She's a pathological case," he said.

Djuna saw the second face of Zora.

It was an expression she had seen before and could not place. And then she remembered.

It was the expression upon the face of professional beggars.

Her enumeration of the troubles she had endured that day was like the plaintive incantation too perfectly molded by time and repetition.

Under the tone of sorrow there was a practice in the tone of sorrow.

Yet Djuna felt ashamed to doubt the sincerity of Zora's complaints, as one is ashamed to doubt a beggar's poverty. Yet she felt, as one does occasionally before a beggar, that a pain too often studied for public exposure had become a pain necessary to the beggar, his means of livelihood, his claim to existence, to protection. If he were deprived of it, he would be deprived of his right to compassion.

It was as if true compassion should be reserved for troubles not exploited, but of recent occurrence and deeply felt. The poverty of the professional lamenter was an asset rather than a tragedy.

Djuna wanted to forget her intuition, in favor of the tradition which dictated that a beggar's needs cannot be judged, because there is a noblesse oblige which dictates: his cup is empty and yours is full, therefore there is only one action possible; and even if an investigation revealed the beggar not to be blind and to have amassed a fortune under his pallet, even then, such hesitations before an empty cup are so distressing that the role of the believer is easier, easier to be deceived than to doubt. . . .

Djuna was sometimes disconcerted by the shrewd look in Zora's eyes while she detailed her day's hardships; as startled to catch this expression as to see a blind man who was crossing the street alone and walking into danger—causing you a sharp compassion—to see him suddenly turn upon you eyes fully aware of the impending danger.

But Djuna wanted to believe, because Rango believed. She discarded this first glimpse of Zora's second face as people often discard first intuitions until they reach the end of a friendship, the end of a love, and then this long-buried first impression reappears only to prove that the animal senses in human beings warning them clearly of dangers, of traps, may be accurate but are often discarded in favor of a blind compulsion in the opposite direction to that of self-preservation. Proving that human beings have a sense of danger but that some other desire, some other compulsion, lures and draws them precisely toward these traps, toward self-destruction.

Djuna felt now like a puppet. She felt the need to give Rango a perpetually healthy, perpetually spirited woman because at home he had a perpetually sick, depressed wife. Rango's needs set the tone, mood, and activities of her days. She obeyed the strings blindly. She allowed Rango's anxieties to infect her, merely so he would not be alone with his burden. The strings were in Zora's hands. The hierarchy was firmly established: if Zora had a cold, a headache, Rango must stay at home (even if this cold were caused by Zora washing her hair in the middle of a winter day and going out with her hair still wet). It was forbidden to rebel or question the origin of the trouble, or to suggest that Zora might consider others, consider preventing these troubles.

Zora could not cook, could not shop, could not clean, she could not be alone at night. If friends came to see her, Rango must be at home to save her pride.

When Djuna had first known Rango he spent most of his

nights out at the café. Often he did not come home till dawn, and oftener still he did not come home at all when he was spending a night with one of his mistresses.

At first Zora had said: "I'm so glad to know Rango is not drinking, that he is with you instead of at the café."

But after awhile she developed new fears. Rango said: "Poor Zora, she is so afraid at night. The other evening someone knocked at her door for a long time and just stood there waiting. She was so frightened that the man would come in and rape her that she piled all the furniture in front of the door and did not sleep all night."

Rango spent every other night at the barge, and then only twice a week as Zora's complaints increased, and then one night a week.

And on that one night Zora came and knocked on the door.

She was in pain, she said. Rango rushed out and took her home. She was convulsed with pains. The doctor was called, and could not find the cause. Only at dawn did she confess: she had heard that cleaning fluid was good for the stomach, so she had drunk a glass of it.

Rango left Djuna to watch over Zora while he went to buy the medicines which the doctor advised.

Djuna tended Zora, and Zora smiled at her innocently. Could Zora be so unaware of the consequences of her acts?

Whenever they were alone together they fell naturally into a sincere relationship. Djuna's compassion would once more be aroused and Zora would nestle into it securely. At these moments Djuna believed a relationship was being constructed to which Zora would be loyal, one of mutual giving. It was only later that Djuna would discover what Zora had achieved with her behavior, and that would always be, in the end, something to harm and stifle the relationship between Rango and Djuna.

But it was all so subtly done that Djuna could never detect it.

When Zora talked about Rango, it seemed at first a natural harmless sick woman's complaining; it seemed not as if she wanted to harm Rango in Djuna's eyes, but as if she wanted Djuna's sympathy for her difficult life with Rango. It was only later when alone that Djuna became aware of how much dissension and doubt Zora had managed to insert in her monotonous lamentations against Rango.

Djuna would prepare herself for these talks which hurt her by thinking: "She is talking about another Rango, not the one I know. The Rango I love is different. This is the Rango that was born of his life with Zora. She is responsible for what he was with her."

This night, calmed by Djuna's ministrations, Zora began to talk: "You love Rango in such a different way than I do. I never loved Rango physically. I never loved any man physically. I don't know what it is to respond to a man. . . . You know, sometimes when I get these crying spells, I think to myself: maybe it's because I can't melt physically. I don't feel anything, and so crying is a relief, I cry instead. . . ."

Djuna was moved by this, and then appalled. Rango did not know about Zora's coldness. Was this the secret of her destructiveness toward him?

She wished she did not have to become an intimate part of their lives together. She wished she could escape the clutch of Zora's dependence.

She was silent. Zora was beginning her usual long, monotonous recital of Rango's faults: It was Rango who had made her ill. It was Rango who had ruined her career. Rango was to blame for everything.

Zora blamed Rango, and Rango blamed the world. Both of them were equally blind in the knowledge of their own character and responsibilities. Djuna did not know yet, but sensed the cause of their downfall.

Djuna rebelled against Rango's blind subservience to Zora's helplessness, and yet she found herself in the same position: unable to avoid the slavery.

Zora never asked a favor. She demanded, and then proceeded to criticize how the orders were carried out, with a sense of her right to be served and no acknowledgment or lightest form of thankfulness.

Zora was now talking about her career as a dancer: "I was the first to present Guatemalan dances to Paris audiences. I was very successful, so much so that an agent came from New York and arranged a tour for me. I made money, I made many friends. But there was a woman in the show traveling with me who wanted to kill me."

"Oh, no, Zora."

"Yes, for no reason at all. She invited me to lunch with her every day and gave me tomatoes and eggs. They made me terribly ill. They were poisoned."

"Perhaps they weren't poisoned; perhaps eggs and tomatoes don't agree with you."

"She did it on purpose, I tell you. I was too much of a success."

(That's madness, thought Djuna. If only Rango would realize this, we could live in peace. If he would detach himself and admit: she is very ill, she is unbalanced. We could take care of her but not let her destroy our life together. But Rango sees everything as distortedly as she does. If only he would *see*. It would save us all.)

"Zora, what I can't understand was why, if you were so successful as a dancer, if you reached the heights there, and could travel, and do all you wanted . . . what happened? What caused the downfall in your life? Was it your health?"

Zora hesitated. Djuna was painfully tense, awaiting an answer to this question, feeling that if Zora answered it their three lives would be altered.

But Zora never answered direct questions.

Djuna regretted having used the word downfall. Downfall was the wrong word for Zora and Rango, since all their troubles were caused by an evil world, came from a hostile aggression from the world.

Zora sank into apathy. Would she deviate as Rango did, elude, answer so elliptically that the question would be lost in a maze of useless vagaries.

She reopened her eyes and began her recitation where she had left off: "In New York I stopped the show. The agent came to see me with a long contract. I could make as much money as I wanted to. I had fur coats and beautiful evening dresses, I could travel. . . ."

"And then?"

"Then I left everything and went home to Guatemala."

"Home to Guatemala?"

Zora laughed, irrepressibly, hysterically, for such a long time that Djuna was frightened. A spasm of cough stopped her. "You should have seen the face of the agent, when I didn't sign the contract. Everybody's face. I enjoyed that. I enjoyed their faces more than I enjoyed the money. I left them all just like that and went home. I wanted to see Guatemala again. I laughed all the way, thinking of their faces when I quit."

"Were you sick then?"

"I was always sick, from childhood. But it wasn't that. I'm independent."

Djuna remembered Rango telling her the story of a friend who had worked to obtain an engagement for Zora in Paris, a contract to dance at a private house. He had promised to meet this friend at the café. "I came five hours late, and she was in a state." Whenever he told this story he laughed. The idea of this friend waiting, foaming and furious, sitting at the café, aroused his humor.

"I stayed six months in Guatemala. When the money was gone I returned to New York. But nobody would sign me up. They told each other about the broken contract. . . ."

Rango arrived with the medicine. Zora refused to take it. Bismuth would calm her pain and the burn, but she refused to take it. She turned her face to the wall and fell asleep, holding Djuna and Rango's hand, both enchained to her caprices.

Djuna's head was bowed. Rango said: "You must be exhausted. You'd better go home. Sometimes I think. . . ." Djuna raised imploring eyes to his face, wildly hoping that they would be united by the common knowledge that Zora was a sick, unstable child who needed care but who could not be allowed to direct, to infect their lives with her destructiveness.

Rango looked at her, his eyes not seeing what she saw. "Sometimes I think you're right about Zora. She does foolish things. . . ." And that was all.

He walked to the door with her. . . . She looked into the bleak and empty street. It was just before dawn. She needed warmth, sleep. She needed to be as blind as Rango was, to continue living this way. The knowledge she had was useless. It only added to her burden, the knowing that so much effort, care, devotion were being utterly wasted, that Zora would never be well, that it was wrong to devote two lives to one twisted human being. . . . This knowledge estranged her from Rango, whose blind faith she could not share. It burdened her, isolated her. Tonight, through fatigue, she wanted so much to lay her head on Rango's shoulder, to fall asleep in his arms, but there was already another head on his shoulder, a heavy burden.

As if in fear that Djuna should ask him to come with her, he said: "She cannot be left alone."

Djuna was silent. She could not divulge what she knew.

When she did protest against the excessive demands and whims of Zora, even gently, Rango would say: "I am between two fires, so you must help me."

To help him meant to yield to Zora, knowing that she would in the end destroy their relationship.

Every day Djuna suppressed her knowledge, her lucidity; Rango would have considered them an attack upon a defenseless Zora.

Noblesse oblige enforced silence, and all her awareness of the destruction being wreaked upon their relationship—when Zora was the greatest beneficiary of this relationship—only served to increase her suffering.

Zora had mysteriously won all the battles; Rango and Djuna

could never spend a whole night together.

What corrodes a love are the secrets.

This doubt of Zora's sanity which she dared not word to Rango, which made every sacrifice futile, created a fissure in the closeness to Rango. A simple, detached understanding of this would have made Rango less enslaved, less anxious, and would have brought Djuna and Rango closer together, whereas his loyalty to all the irrational demands of Zora, her distorted interpretation of his acts as well as Djuna's, was a constant irritant to Djuna's intelligence and awareness.

The silence with which she accomplished her duties now became a gradual isolation in her emotions.

It was strange to be cooking, to be running errands, to be searching for new doctors, to be buying clothes, to be furnishing a new room for Zora, while knowing that Zora was working against them all and would never get well because her illness was her best treasure, was her weapon of power over them.

But Rango needed desperately to believe. He believed that every new medicine, every new doctor would restore her health.

Djuna felt now as she had as a child, when she had repudiated her religious dogmas but must continue to attend mass, rituals, kneel in prayer, to please her mother.

Any departure from what she believed he considered a betrayal of her love.

At every turn Zora defeated this battle for health. When she got a new room in the sun, she kept the blinds down and shut out air and light. When they went to the beach together up the river, her bathing suit, given to her by Djuna, was not ready. She had ripped it apart to improve its shape. When they went to the park she wore too light a dress and caught cold. When they went to a restaurant she ate the food she knew would harm her, and predicted that the next day she would be in bed all day.

She made pale attempts to take up her dancing again, but never when alone, only when Djuna and Rango were there to witness her pathetic attempts, and when the exertion would cause her heart to beat faster she would say to Rango: "Put your hand here. See how badly my heart goes when I try to work again."

At times Djuna's detachment, her self-protective numbness would be annihilated by Rango, as when he said once: "We are killing her."

"We are killing her?" echoed Djuna, bewildered and shocked.

"Yes, she said once that it was my unfaithfulness which made her ill."

"But unfaithful to what, Rango? She was not your wife, she was your sick child, long before I came. It was understood between you that your relationship was fraternal, that sooner or later you would need a woman's love. . . ."

"Zora didn't mind when I had just a desire for a woman, a passing desire. . . . But I gave you more than that. That's what Zora cannot accept."

"But Rango, she told me that she was happy and secure with our relationship, because she felt protected by both of us, she knew I would not take you away from her, she said she had gained two loves and lost nothing. . . ."

"One can say such things, and yet feel betrayed, feel hurt. . . ."

Rango convinced Djuna that their love must be atoned for. Even if Zora had always been ill, even as a child, even though their love protected her, yet they must atone . . . atone . . . atone. Never enough devotion could make up for what pain they caused her. . . . Not enough to rise early in the morning to market for tempting foods for Zora, never enough to dress her, to answer her every whim, to surrender Rango over and over again.

Djuna fell into an overwhelming, blind, stupefying devotion to Zora. She became the sleeping dreamer seeking nothing but one brief moment of fiery joy with Rango, and then atoning for it the rest of the time.

Rango would ring her bell and call her out during the night to watch Zora while he went for medicines.

The sleeping dreamer Djuna walked up a muddy hill on a rainy afternoon to the hospital bringing Zora her winter coat, so divested and stripped of her possessions that her father was beginning to notice it and demanded explanations: "Where is your coat? Why aren't you wearing stockings? You're beginning to dress like a tramp recently. Is this the influence of your new friends? Who are you associating with?"

Rango's grateful kisses over her eyelids were the blinding, drugging hypnosis, and she let her father believe that she was "fancying herself a bohemian now," that she was playing at being poor.

That afternoon at the hospital Rango left her alone with Zora. The moment he left the room Zora said: "Reach for that bottle on the shelf. It's a disinfectant. Pour some here in the bassinet. The nurse is stingy with it. She measures only a few drops. She doesn't want me to get well. She's saving the stuff. And I know more of it would cure me."

"But Zora, this stuff is strong. It will burn your skin. You can't use a lot of it. The nurse isn't trying to economize."

An expression of utter maliciousness came into Zora's eyes: "You want me to die, don't you? So you can live with Rango. That's why you won't give me the medicine."

Djuna gave her the bottle and watched Zora pouring the strong liquid in the bassinet. She would burn her skin, but she would at least believe that Djuna was on her side.

Rango's long oriental eyes which opened and closed like a cat's, his oblique dark eyes, would soon close hers upon reality, upon all reasoning.

He did not observe the coincidences as Djuna did unconsciously. Whenever Djuna went away for a few days Zora would be moderately ill. Whenever Djuna returned there would be an aggravation, and thus Djuna and Rango could not meet that evening.

Djuna instinctively knew this to be so accurate and inevitable that she would prepare herself for it. On her way back from a trip she would say to herself: "Don't get exalted at the idea of seeing Rango, for surely Zora will get very ill when you come back and Rango will not be free. . . ."

And then because Rango could not explode or revolt against an illness (which he thought genuine and inevitable), could not see how its developments obeyed Zora's destructive will, he revolted at other situations, unjustly, inaccurately. Djuna learned to detect the origin of the revolt, to know it was an aborted revolt at home which he diverted and brought to other scenes or circumstances. He exploded wildly over politics, he attacked the illnesses of other women, he incited other husbands to revolt and would seek them out and take them to the café almost by force, just as Djuna indulged now and then in a tirade against helpless or childish women in general because she did not dare to speak openly against Zora's childishness.

From so many scenes at home Rango escaped to Djuna as a refuge. He would place the whole weight of his head and arms on her knees, and if it happened that Djuna was tired, she did not reveal it for fear of overburdening a man too heavily burdened already. She disguised her own needs, her weaknesses, her handicaps, her own fears or troubles. She concealed them all from him. Thus grew in his mind an image of her infinite energy, infinite power to overcome obstacles. Any flaw in this irritated him like a failed promise. He needed her strength.

Because he seemed to love Zora for her weakness, to be so indulgent toward her inadequacies, her fumbling inability to open a door, incapacity to buy a stamp and mail a letter, to visit a friend alone, Djuna felt a deep unbalance, a deep injustice taking place. For the extreme childishness of Zora

313

robbed her relation to Rango of all its naturalness. It set the two women at opposite poles, not as rivals, but as opposites, destruction against construction, weakness against strength, taking against giving.

To break the hypnosis came certain shocks, which Djuna was losing her power to interpret.

When she had gradually passed to Zora most of her belongings, all of her jewelry—to such an extreme that she had to surrender going to certain places and seeing certain friends where she could not appear dressed as carelessly as she was— she arrived unexpectedly at Zora's and found her sitting among six opened trunks.

"I'm working on a costume for a new dance," said Zora.

The trunks overflowed with clothes. Not theatre costumes only, but coats, dresses, stockings, underwear, shoes.

Djuna looked bewildered and Zora began to show her all that the trunks contained, explaining: "I bought all this when things were going well for me in New York."

"But you could wear them now!"

"Yes, I could, but they look too nice. I just like to keep them and look at them now and then."

And all the time she had been wearing torn shoes, mended stockings, dresses too light for winter, when not wearing all that she had extracted from Djuna.

This discovery stunned Djuna. It proved what she had felt all the time obscurely, that Zora's dramatization of the poor, the cold, the scantily dressed, the pathetic woman, was a voluntary role which suited her deepest convenience. That this drabness, which constantly aroused Rango's pity, was deliberate, that, at any moment, she could have been better dressed than Djuna.

That night Djuna could not refrain from asking Rango: "Did you know when I gave up my fur coat for Zora to wear this winter that she had one in her trunk all the time?"

"Yes," said Rango. "Zora has a lot of the gypsy in her. Gypsies always keep their finery for certain occasions, and

315

like to look at it now and then, but seldom wear it."

"Am I going mad?" asked Djuna of herself. "Or is Rango as mad as Zora? He is not aware of the absurdity, the cruelty of this. He thinks it's natural that I should dispossess myself for a woman obsessed with the desire to arouse pity."

But as this incident threatened her faith in Rango, she soon closed her eyes again.

The actor does not suffer any cramps because he knows the role he plays he will be able to discard at some stated time, and walk free again to be himself.

But Djuna's role in life seemed inescapable. She was doomed to be devoted to a cause she did not believe in. Zora would never get well; Rango would never be free. She suffered from pains which were like cramps, because in all these unnatural positions she took, these contortions of giving, of surrender, there was a strain from the knowledge that she could never, as long as she loved Rango, ever be free and herself again.

Out of physical exhaustion she would occasionally run away.

This time to conceal her exhaustion from Rango she took the Dover-Calais boat intending to hide in London for a few days at the house of a friend.

Sitting on deck, on a foggy afternoon, she felt so utterly tired and discouraged that she fell asleep. Tired tired tired, her body sank into deep sleep on the deck chair. Sleep. A deep deep sleep . . . until she felt a hand on her shoulder as if calling. She would not open her eyes; she would not respond. She dreaded to awaken. She feigned a complete sleep and turned her head away from the hand that was beckoning . . .

But the voice persisted: "Mademoiselle, mademoiselle. . . ."

A voice pleading.

She felt the spray on her face, the swaying of the ship, and began to hear the voices around her.

She opened her eyes.

A man was leaning over her, his hand still on her shoulder.

"Mademoiselle, forgive me. I know I should have let you sleep. Forgive me."

316

"Why did you wake me? I was so tired, so tired." She was not fully awake yet, not awake enough to be angry, or even reproachful.

"Forgive me. I can explain, if you will let me. I am not trying to flirt, believe me. I'm a *grand blessé de guerre*. I can't tell you how seriously wounded, but it's left me so I can't bear fog, damp, rain, or the sea. Pains. Such pains all over the body. I have to make this trip often, for my work. It's torture, you know. Going back to England now. . . . When the pains start there is nothing I can do but to talk to someone. I had to talk to someone. I looked all around me. I looked into every face. I saw you asleep. I know it was inconsiderate, but I felt: that's the woman I can talk to. It will help me—do you mind?"

"I don't mind," said Djuna.

And they talked, all the way, on the train too, all the way to London. When she reached London she was near collapse. She took the first hotel room she could find and slept for twelve hours. Then she returned to Paris.

No more questioning, no more interpretations, no more examinations of her life. She was resigned to her destiny. It was her destiny. The *grand blessé de guerre* on the ship had made her feel it, had convinced her.

So she made a pirouette charged with sadness, on the revolving stages of awareness, and returned to this role she had been fashioned for, even down to the face, even when asleep.

But when people play a role motivated by false impulses, moved by compulsions formed by fear, by distortions, rather than by a deep need, the only symptom which reveals that it is a role and that acts do not correspond to the true nature, is the sense of unbearable tension.

The ways to measure one's insincerities are few, but Djuna knew that the most infallible one was joylessness. Any task accomplished without joy was a falsity to one's true nature. When Djuna indulged in an extravagant giving to Zora she felt no joy because it was misinterpreted by both Rango and Zora. If there was a natural goodness in Djuna it was not this magnified, this self-destructive annihilation of all of herself.

But this role could last a lifetime, since Rango denied the possibility of change by clairvoyance, the possibility of a lucid change of direction. They were rudderless and at the mercy of Zora's madness.

She did not even gain the prestige granted to the professional actor, for there is this about roles played in life, and that is that no one is deceived. The most obtuse, the most insensitive people feel a dissonance, sense an imposture, and, whereas the actor is respected for creating an illusion on the stage, no one is respected for seeking to create an illusion in life.

She planned another escape, this time with Rango and Zora. She felt that taking them to the sea, into nature, might heal them all, might strengthen Zora and bring them peace.

It was a most arduous undertaking to get Zora to pack and to free Rango from all his tangles. They missed not one but several trains. Zora had two trunks of belongings. Rango had debts and his debtors were reluctant to let him leave Paris. They overslept in the mornings.

Rango borrowed some money and bought Djuna a present, a slender white leather belt from Morocco. It was his first present and Djuna was overjoyed and wore it proudly. But when the three met at the station she found Zora wearing an identical belt, so her own lost its charm for her and she threw it away.

The fishing port they reached in the morning lay in the sun. The crescent-shaped harbor sheltered yachts and fishing boats from all over the world. The cafés were all gathered on the edge and as they sat having coffee they saw the boats come to life, the sailors and voyagers emerging from their cabins. They saw the small portholes open, the hatches lifted, and sails

318

spread. They saw the sailors starting to polish brass and wash decks.

Behind them rose the hills planted with white houses built during the Moor's invasion of the Mediterranean coast.

The place was animated, like a perpetual carnival. The fluttering, glitter, and mobility of the harbor and ships were reflected in the cafés and visitors. Women's scarves answered the coquetries of the sails. The eyes, skins, and smiles were as polished as the brass. Women's sea-shell necklaces reflected the sky and the sea.

Rango found a place for Zora and himself at the top of a hill within a forest. Djuna took a room in a hotel farther down the hill and nearer to the harbor.

When Rango came down the hill on his bicycle and met Djuna at one of the cafés on the port, the sun was setting.

The night and the sea were velvety and caressing, unfolding a core of softness. As the plants exhaled a more mysterious flowering, people, too, shed their brighter day selves and donned colors and perfumes more appropriate to secret blooms. They dilated with the leaves, the shadows, at the approach of night.

The automobiles which passed carried all the flags of pleasure unfurled in audacious smiles, insolent scarves.

All the voices were pitched to a tone of intimacy. Sea, earth, and bodies seeking alliances, wearing their plumage of adventure, coral and turquoise, indigo and orange. Human corollas opening in the night, inviting pursuit, seeking capture, in all the dilations which allow the sap to rise and flow.

Then Rango said: "I must leave. Zora is afraid of the dark."

To make it easier for Rango she bicycled back with him, but when she returned alone to her room all the exhalations of the sea tempted her out again, and she returned to the port and sat at the same table where she had sat with Rango and watched the gaiety of the port as she had watched that first party out of her window as a girl, feeling again that all pleasure was unattainable for her.

People were dancing in the square to an accordion played by the village postmaster. The letter carrier invited her to dance, but all the time she felt Rango's jealous and reproachful eyes on her. Every porthole, every light, seemed to be watching her dance with reproach.

So at ten o'clock she left the port and its festivities and bicycled back to her small hotel room.

As she climbed the last turn in the hill, pushing her bicycle before her, she saw a flashlight darting over her window which gave on the ground floor. She could not see who was wielding it, but she felt it was Rango and she called out to him joyously, thinking that perhaps Zora had fallen asleep and he was free and had come to be with her.

But Rango responded angrily to her greeting: "Where have you been?"

"Oh, Rango, you're too unjust. I couldn't stay in my room at eight o'clock. It's only ten now, and I'm back early, and alone. How can you be angry?"

But he was.

"You're too unjust," she said, and passing by him, almost running, she went into her room and locked the door.

The few times that she had held out against him, such as the time he had arrived at midnight instead of for dinner as he had promised, she had noticed that Rango's anger abated, and that his knock on the door had not been imperious, but gentle and timid.

That is what happened now. And his timidity disarmed her anger.

She opened the door. And Rango stayed with her and they sought closeness again, as if to resolder all that his violence broke.

"You're like Heathcliff, Rango, and one day everything will break."

He had an incurable jealousy of her friends, because to him friends were the accomplices in the life she led outside of his precincts. They were the possible rivals, the witnesses, and

320

perhaps the instigators to unfaithfulness. They were the ones secretly conniving to separate them.

But graver still was his jealousy of the friends who reflected an aspect of Djuna not included in her relationship to Rango, or which revealed aspects of Djuna not encompassed in the love, an unknown Djuna which she could not give to Rango. And this was a playful, a light, a peace-loving Djuna, the one who delighted in harmony, not in violence, the one who found outside of passion luminous moods and regions unknown to Rango. Or still the Djuna who believed understanding could be reached by effort, by an examination of one's behavior, and that destiny could be reshaped, one's twisted course redirected with lucidity.

She attracted those who knew how to escape the realm of sorrow by fantasy. Other extensions of Paul appeared, and one in particular of whom Rango was as jealous as if he had been a reincarnation of Paul. Though he knew it was an innocent friendship, still he stormed around it. He knew the boy could give Djuna a climate which his violence and intensity destroyed.

It was her old quest for a paradise again, a region outside of sorrow.

Lying on the sand with Paul the second (while Rango and Zora slept through half of the day) they built ninepins out of driftwood, they dug labyrinths into the sand, they swam underwater looking for sea plants, and drugged themselves with tales.

Their only expression of a bond was his reaching for her little finger with his, as Paul had once done, and this was like an echo of her relation to Paul, a fragile bond, a bond like a game, but life-giving through its very airiness and delicacy.

Iridescent, ephemeral hours of relief from darkness.

When Rango came, blurred, soiled by his stagnant life with Zora, from quarrels, she felt stronger to meet this undertow of bitterness.

She wore a dress of brilliant colors, indigo and saffron; she brushed her hair until it glistened, and proclaimed in all her gestures a joyousness which she hoped would infect Rango.

But as often happened, this very joyousness alarmed him; he suspected the cause of it, and he set about to reclaim her from a region she had not traversed with him, the region of peace, faith, and gentleness he could never give her.

True that Paul the second had only appropriated her little finger and laid no other claim on her, true that Rango's weight upon her body was like the earth, stronger and warmer, true that when his arms fell at her side with discouragement they were so heavy that she could not have lifted them, true that those made only of earth and fire were never illuminated, never lifted or borne above it, never free of it, but hopelessly entangled in its veins.

Her dream of freeing Rango disintegrated day by day. When she gave them the sun and the sea, they slept. Zora had ripped her bathing suit and was sewing it again. She would sew it for years.

It was clear to Djuna now that the four-chambered heart was no act of betrayal, but that there were regions necessary to life to which Rango had no access. It was not that Djuna wanted to house the image of Paul in one chamber and Rango in another, nor that to love Rango she must destroy the chamber inhabited by Paul—it was that in Djuna there was a hunger for a haven which Rango was utterly incapable of giving to her, or attaining with her.

If she sought in Paul's brother a moment of relief, a moment of forgetfulness, she also sought in the dark, at night, someone without flaw, who would protect her and forgive all things.

Whoever was without flaw, whoever understood, whoever contained an inexhaustible flow of love was god the father whom she had lost in her childhood.

Alone at night, after the torments of her life with Rango, after her revolts against this torment which she had vainly tried to master with understanding of Rango, defeated by Rango's own love of this inferno, because he said it was real, it was life, it was heightened life, and that happiness was a mediocre ideal, held in contempt by the poets, the romantics, the artists—alone at night when she acknowledged to herself that Rango was doomed and would never be whole again, that he was corrupted in his love of pain, in his belief that war and troubles heightened the flavor of life, that scenes were necessary to the climax of desire, like fire, suddenly in touching the bottom of the abysmal loneliness in which both relationships left her, she felt the presence of god again, as she had felt him as a child, or still at another time when she had been close to death.

She felt this god again, whoever he was, taking her tenderly, holding her, putting her to sleep. She felt protected, her nerves unknotted, she felt peace. She fell asleep, all her anxieties dissolved. How she needed him, whoever he was, how she needed sleep, she needed peace, she needed god the father.

In the orange light of the fishing port, the indigo spread of the sea, the high flavor of the morning rolls, the joyousness of early mornings on the wharf, the scenes with Rango became more and more like hallucinations.

Rango walking through the reeds seemed like a Balinese, with his dark skin and blazing eyes.

When they sat at the beach late at night around a fire and roasted meat, he seemed so in harmony with nature, crouching on his strong legs, nimble with his hands. When they returned from long bicycle rides, after hours of pedaling against a brisk wind, tired and thirsty but drugged with physical euphoria and content, then the returns to his obsessions seemed more like a sickness.

Djuna knew all the prefaces to trouble. If during the ride she had sung in rhythm with others, or laughed, or acquiesced, Rango would begin: "This morning I found your bicycle and the boy's against the wall of the café, so close together, as if you had spent the night together."

"But Rango, he arrived after me, he merely placed his bicycle next to mine. Everyone has breakfast at the same café. It doesn't mean anything."

At times Djuna felt that Rango had caught Zora's madness. Then she felt compassion for him, and would answer with patience, as you would a sick person.

She knew that we love in others some repressed self. In consoling Rango, reassuring him, was she consoling some secret Djuna who had once been jealous and not dared to reveal it?

(We love shadows of our hidden selves in others. Once I must have been as jealous as Rango, but I did not reveal it, even to myself. I must have experienced such jealousy in so hidden a realm of my own nature that I was not even aware of it. Or else I would not be so patient with Rango. I would not feel compassion. He is destroying us both by this jealousy. I want to protect him from the consequences ... He is driving me away from him. I should run away now, yet I feel responsible. When we see another daring to be what we did not dare, we feel responsible for him. ...)

But once she awakened so exhausted by Rango's demon that she decided to frighten him, to run away, hoping it might cure him.

She packed and went to the station. But there was no train until evening. She sat disconsolately to wait.

And Rango arrived. He looked distracted. "Djuna! Djuna, forgive me. I must have been mad. I didn't tell you the truth. A friend of mine has been making absinthe in his cellar and every day at noon we have been sampling it. I must have taken a good deal of it all these days."

She forgave him. She also thought, in an effort always to absolve him: "His slavery to Zora's needs is so tremendous and he does not dare to rebel. She has a gift for making him feel that he never does enough, and to burden him with guilt, and that may be why, when he comes to me, he has to rebel and be angry about something, he has to explode. I am his scapegoat."

And she was tied to Rango through this breathing tube, tied to his explosions. She might one day come to believe, as he did, that violence was necessary to dive to the depths of experience.

On these revolving stages of the unconscious, the last hidden jungles of our nature which we have controlled and harnessed almost to extermination, sealing all the wells, it is no wonder when we seek to open these sealed wells again to find a flow of life we find instead a flow of anger.

Thus in anger Rango threw like a geyser this nature's poison, and then refused to admit responsibility for the storms. His angers came like lightning, and each time Djuna was delivered of her own.

But the black sun of his jealousy eclipsed the Mediterranean sun, churned the sea's turquoise gentleness.

There were times when she lay alone on the sand and sought to remember what she had tried to reach through the body of Rango, what her first sight of him, playing on his guitar and evoking his gypsy life, had awakened in her.

Through him, to extend into pure nature.

There were times when she remembered his first smile, the ironic smile of the Indian which came from afar like the echo of an ancient Indian smile at the beginning of Mayan worlds; the earthy walk issued from bare footsteps treading paths into the highest mountains of the world, into the most immune lakes and impenetrable forests.

In her dream of him she returned to the origins of the world, hearing footsteps in Rango which were echoes of primeval footsteps hunting.

She remembered, above all, stories, the one Rango had told her about sitting on a rock on top of a glacier and asserting he had felt the spinning of the earth!

She had kissed eyes filled with remembrance of splendors, eyes which had seen the Mayans bury their gold treasures at the bottom of the lakes out of reach of the plundering Spaniards.

She had kissed the Indian princes of her childhood fairytales.

She had plunged with love and desire into the depths of ancient races, and sought heights and depths and magnificence.

And found . . . found deserts where vultures perpetuated their encirclement, no longer distinguishing between the living and the dead.

Found a muted city resting on ruined columns, cracked cupolas, tombs, with owls screaming like women in childbirth.

In the shadows of volcanoes there were fiestas, orgies, dances, and guitars.

But Rango had not taken her there.

To love he brought only his fierce anxieties; she had embraced, kissed, possessed a mirage. She had walked and walked, not into the fiestas and the music, not into laughter, but into the heart of an Indian volcano. . . .

THE TRAP WAS INVISIBLE BY DAY.

The trap was a web of senseless duties. No sooner were Djuna's eyes open than she saw Zora vividly, lying down, pale, with soft flabby hands touching everything with infantile awkwardness. Zora missing her aim, dropping what she held, fumbling with a door, and moving so abnormally slow and with such hazy, uncertain gestures that it took her two hours to get dressed.

Compassion was the cover with which Djuna disguised to

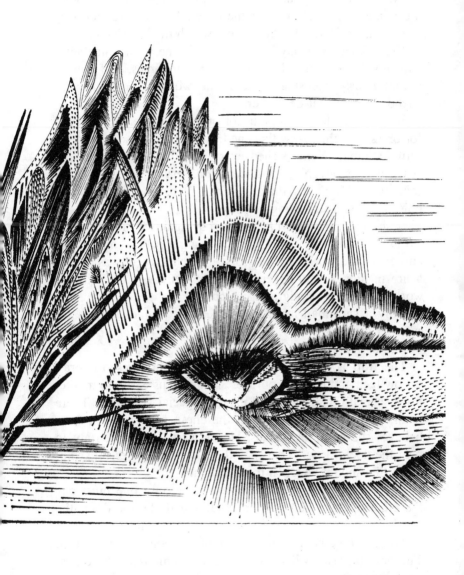

her own eyes her revulsion for Zora's whining voice, unkempt body, and shrewd glance, for her beggar's clothes which were a costume to attract pity, for the listless hair she was too lazy to brush, for the dead skin through which the blood stagnated.

If one knew what lay in Zora's mind, one would turn away with revulsion. Djuna had heard her sometimes, half asleep, monotonously accusing doctors, the world, Rango, herself, friends, for all that befell her.

Revulsion. There is a guilt not only for acts committed but for one's thoughts. Now that the trap had grown so grotesque, futile, stifling, Djuna wished every day that Zora might die. A useless life, grasping food, devotion, service, and giving absolutely nothing, less than nothing. A useless life, exuding poison, envy, a strangling tyranny.

If she died, Rango's life might soar again, a fire, his body strong and exuberant, his imagination propelling him to all corners of the world. At his worst moments, there was always a fire in him. In Zora there was coldness. Only the mind at work, deforming, denigrating, accusing.

Only a showman left in her. "See my wound, see what I suffer. Love me."

But love is not given for such reasons.

The trap is inescapable. Djuna has nightmares of Zora's yellow face and lack of courage. She awakens early, to market for a special bread, a special meat, a special vegetable. There is an appointment for x-rays of the chest, for this week Zora believes she has tuberculosis. Hours wasted on this, only to hear the doctor say: "There's nothing wrong. Hysterical symptoms. She should be taken to a psychiatrist."

There is a visit to the pawnbroker, because one must pay the other doctor, the one who made the futile, the dramatic, test for cancer. Djuna's allowance for the month is finished.

There is no escape. The day crumbles soon after it is born. The only tree she will see will be the anemic tree of the hospital garden.

A useless, abortive sacrifice gives sadness.

328

The day is the trap, but she does not dare revolt. If she wants her half-night with Rango, this is the only path to reach it. At the end of the day there will be his fervent kisses, his emotion, his desire, the bites of hunger on the shoulder, vibrations of pleasure shaking the body, the guttural moans of men and women returning to their primitive origin. . . .

Sometimes there is no time for undressing. At others, the climax is postponed teasingly, arousing frenzy. The dross of the day is burned away.

When Djuna thinks during the day, "I must run away. I must leave Rango to his chosen torment," it is the remembrance of this point of fire which binds her.

How can Rango admire Zora's rotting away—not even a noble suicide, but a fixed obsession to die slowly, dragging others along with her? A life ugly and monstrous. If she washes a dish, she complains. If she sews a button, she laments.

These are Djuna's thoughts, and she must atone for them too. Zora, take this bread I traveled an hour to find, it won't nourish you, you are too full of poison within your body. Your first words to me were hypocritical, your talk about praying to be helped, and being glad I was the one, yes, because I was one who could be easily caught through compassion. You knew I would act toward you as you would never have acted toward me. I have tried to imagine you in my place, and I couldn't. I know you would be utterly cruel.

On her way back to the barge she bought new candles, and a fur rug to lie on, because Rango believed it was too bourgeois to sleep on a bed like everybody else. They slept on the floor. Perhaps a fur, the bed of Eskimos, would be appropriate.

When Rango came, he looked at the candles and the fur like a lion looking at a lettuce leaf. But lying on it, his bronze desire is aroused and the primitive bed is baptized in memory of cavernous dwellings.

At this hour children are reading fairy tales from which Rango and Djuna were led to expect such marvels, the impossible. Rango had imagined a life without work, without responsibilities. Djuna had wanted a life of desire and freedom, not comfort but the smoothness of magical happenings, not luxury but beauty, not security but fulfillment, not perfection but a perfect moment like this one . . . but without Zora waiting to lie between them like an incubus. . . .

Djuna was unprepared for Rango's making the first leap out of the trap. It came unexpectedly at midnight as they were about to separate. Out of the fog of enswathing caresses came his voice: "We're leading a selfish life. There are many things happening in the world; we should be working for them. You are like all the artists, with your big floodlights fixed on the sky, and never on earth, where things are happening. There is a revolution going on, and I want to help."

Djuna did not think of the world or the revolution needing Rango, Rango and his bohemian indiscipline, his love of red wine, his laziness. She felt that Zora's persecutions were driving him away. He was caught between a woman who wanted to die, and one who wanted to live! He had hoped to amalgamate the women, so he would not feel the tension between his two selves. He had thought only of his own emotional comfort. He had overlooked Zora's egoistic ferocity, and Djuna's clairvoyance. The alliance was a failure.

Now he was driven to risk his life for some impersonal task.

She was silent. She looked at his face and saw that his mouth looked unhappy, wounded, and revealed his desperateness. He kept it tightly shut, as women do when they don't want to weep. His mouth which was not in keeping with his lion's head, which was the mouth of a child, small and vulnerable; the mouth which aroused her indulgence.

Parting at the corner of the street, they kissed desperately as if for a long voyage. A beggar started to play on his violin, then stopped, thinking they were lovers who would never see each other again.

The blood beat in her ears as she walked away, her body parting from Rango in anticipation, hair parting from hair, hands unlocking, lips closing against the last kiss, surrendering him to a more demanding mistress: the revolution.

The earth was turning fast. Women cannot walk out of the traps of love, but men can; they have wars and revolutions to attend to. What would happen now? She knew. One signed five sheets of paper and answered minute, excruciatingly exact questions. She had seen the questionnaire. One had to say whether one's wife or husband believed in the revolution; one had to tell everything. Rango would be filling these pages slowly, with his nervous, rolling, and swaying handwriting. Everything. He would probably say that his wife was a cripple, but the party would not condone a mistress.

Then suddenly the earth ceased turning and the blood no longer rang in her ear. Everything stood deathly still because she remembered the dangers. . . . She remembered Rango's friend who had been found with a bullet hole in his temple, near the café where they met. She remembered Rango's story about one of the men who worked for the revolution in Guatemala: the one who had been placed in a jail half full of water until his legs rotted away in strips of moldy flesh, until his eyes turned absolutely white.

The next evening Rango was late. Djuna forgot that he was always late. She thought: he has signed all the papers, and been told that a member of the party cannot have a mistress.

It was nine o'clock. She had not eaten. It was raining. Friends came into the café, talked a little, and left. The time seemed long because of the anxiety. This is the way it would be, the waiting, and never knowing if Rango were still alive. He would be so easily detected. A foreigner, dark skin, wild hair, his very appearance was the one policemen expected from a man working for the revolution.

What had happened to Rango? She picked up a newspaper. Once he had said: "I picked up a newspaper and saw on the front page the photograph of my best friend, murdered the night before."

That is the way it would happen. Rango would kiss her as he had kissed her the night before at the street corner, with the violin playing, then the violin would stop, and that very night. . . .

She questioned her instinct. No, Rango was not dead.

She would like to go to church, but that was forbidden, too. Despair was forbidden. This was the time for stoicism.

She was jealous of Rango's admiration for Gauguin's mother, a South American heroine, who had fought in revolutions and shot her own husband when he betrayed the party.

Djuna walked past the church and entered. She could not pray because she was seeking to transform herself into the proper mate for a revolutionist. But she always felt a humorous, a private, connivance with god. She felt he would always smile with irony upon her most wayward acts. He would see the contradictions, and be indulgent. There was a pact between them, even if she were considered guilty before most tribunals. It was like her friendliness with the policemen of Paris.

And now Rango walked toward her! (See what a pact she had with god that he granted her wishes no one else would have dared to expect him to grant!)

Rango had been ill. No, he had not signed the papers. He had overslept. Tomorrow. *Mañana*.

Djuna had forgotten this Latin deity: *Mañana*.

At the Café Martiniquaise, near the barge, Rango and Djuna sat drinking coffee.

The place was dense with smoke, voices, faces, heaving and swaying like a compact sonorous wave, washing over them at times and enswathing them, at others retreating as if subdued, only to return again louder and more suffocating to engulf their voices.

Djuna could never identify such a tide of faces dissolved by lights and shadows, slightly blurred in outlines from drink.

But Rango could say immediately: "There's a pimp, there's a prizefighter. There's a drug addict."

Two friends of Rango's walked in, with their hands in their pockets, greeted them obliquely, with heavy lids half dropped over glazed eyes. They had deep purple shadows under the eyes and Rango said: "It startles me to see my friends disintegrating so fast, even dying, from drugs. I'm no longer drawn to this kind of life."

"You were drawn toward destruction before, weren't you?"

"Yes," said Rango, "but not really. When I was a young man, at home, what I liked most was health, physical energy and well-being. It was only later, here in Paris the poets taught me not to value life, that it was more romantic to be desperate, more noble to rebel, and to die, than to accept what ordinary life had to offer. I'm not drawn to that any more. I want to live. That was not the real me. Zora says you changed me, yet I can't think of anything you said or did to accomplish it. But every time we are together I want to accomplish something, something big. I don't want any more of this literary credo, about the romantic beauty of living desperately, dangerously, destructively."

Djuna thought with irony that she had not meant to give birth to a rebel. She had changed, too, because of Rango. She had acquired some of his gypsy ways, some of his nonchalance, his bohemian indiscipline. She had swung with him into the disorders of strewn clothes, spilled cigarette ashes, slipping into bed all dressed, falling asleep thus, indolence, timelessness. . . . A region of chaos and moonlight. She liked it there. It was the atmosphere of earth's womb, where awareness could not reach and illumine all the tragic aspects of unfulfilled desires. In the darkness, chaos, warmth, one forgot. . . . And the silence. She liked the silence most of all. The silence in which the body, the senses, the instincts, are more alert, more powerful, more sensitized, live a more richly perfumed and intoxicating life, instead of transmuting into thoughts, words, into exquisite abstractions, mathematics of emotion in place of the violent impact, the volcanic eruptions of fever, lust, and delight.

Irony. Now Rango was projecting himself out of this realm, and wanted action. No more time for the guitar which had ensorcelled her, no more time to visit the gypsies as he had once promised, no more time to sleep in the morning as she had been learning, or to acquire by osmosis his art of throwing off responsibilities, his self-indulgence, his recklessness. . . .

As they sat in the café, he condemned his past life. He was full of contrition for the wasted hours, the wasted energy, the wasted years. He wanted a more austere life, action and fulfillment.

Suddenly Djuna looked down at her coffee and her eyes filled with stinging tears; the tears of irony burn the skin more fiercely. She wept because she had aroused in Rango the desire to serve a purpose which was not hers, to live now for others when already he lived for Zora, and had so little to give her of himself. She wept because they were so close in that earthy darkness, close in the magnetic pull between their skins, their hair, their bodies, and yet their dreams never touched at any point, their vision of life, their attitudes. She wept over the many dislocations of life, forbidding the absolute unity.

Rango did not understand.

In the realm of ideas he was always restless, impatient, and like some wild animal who feared to be corralled. He often described how the horses, the bulls, were corralled in his ranch. He delighted in the fierceness of the battle. For him to examine, to understand, to interpret was exactly like some corralling activity, of which he was suspicious.

But for the moment, she was breathing the odor of his hair. For the moment there was this current between their skin and flesh, these harmonizations of contrasting colors, weight, quality, odors. Everything about him was pungent and violent. They were as his friends said, like Othello and Désdemona.

Mañana he would be a party member.

334

When you lose your wings, thought Djuna, this is the way you live. You buy candles for the meeting of Rango's friends, but these candles do not give a light that will delight you, because you do not believe in what you are doing.

Sadness never added to her weight; it caught her in flight as she danced in spirals misplacing air pools like an arrow shot at a bird which did not bring it down but merely increased its flutterings.

She had every day a greater reluctance to descend into familiar daily life, because the hurt, the huntsman's bow, came from the earth, and therefore flight at a safe distance became more and more imperative.

Her mobility was now her only defense against new dangers. While you're in movement it is harder to be shot at, to be wounded even. She had adopted the basic structure of the nomads.

Rango had said: "Prepare the barge for a meeting tonight. It will be an ideal place. No superintendents to tell tales to the police. No neighbors."

He had signed all the papers. They must be more careful.

The barge was being put to a greater usefulness.

There are two realms to live in now. (Do I hold the secret drug which permits me to hold on to the ecstasies while entering the life of the world, activities in the world, contingencies? I feel it coming to me while I am walking. It is a strange sensation, like drunkenness. It catches me in the middle of the street like a tremendous wave, and a numbness passes through my veins which is the numbness of the marvelous. I know it by its power, by the way it lifts my body, the air which passes under my feet. The cold room I left in the morning, the drab bedcovers, the stove full of ashes, the sour wine at the bottom of the glass were all illuminated by the force of love for Rango. It was as if I had learned to fly over the street and were permitted to do so for an instant . . . making every color more intense, every caress more penetrating, every moment more magnificent. . . . But I knew by the anxiety that it might not last. It is a state of grace of love, which some achieve by wine and others by prayer and fasting. It is a state of grace but I cannot discover what makes one fall out of it. The danger lies in flying low, in awakening. She knew she was flying lower now that Rango was to act in the world. The air of politics was charged with dust. People aspired to reach the planets, but it was a superfluous voyage; there was a certain way of breathing, of walking, of seeing, which transported human beings into space, into transparency. The extraordinary brilliancy of the games people played beyond themselves, the games of their starry selves. . . .)

She bought wood for the fire. She swept the barge. She concealed the bed and the barrel of wine.

Rango would guide the newcomers to the barge, and remain on the bridge to direct them.

The Guatemalans arrived gradually. The darker Indian-blooded ones in Indian silence, the paler Spanish-blooded ones with Spanish volubility. But both were intimidated by the place, the creaking wood, the large room resembling the early meeting places of the revolutionaries, the extended shadows, the river noises, chains, oars, the disquieting lights from the bridge, the swaying when other barges passed. Too much the place for conspirators. At times life surpasses the novel, the drama. This was one of them. The setting was more dramatic than they wished. They stood awkwardly around.

Rango had not yet come. He was waiting for those who were late.

Djuna did not know what to do. This was a role for which she had no precedent. Politeness or marginal talk seemed out of place. She kept the stove filled with wood and watched the flames as if her guardianship would make them active.

When you lose your wings, and wear a dark suit bought in the cheapest store of Paris, to become anonymous, when you discard your earrings, and the polish on your nails, hoping to express an abdication of the self, a devotion to impersonal service, and still you do not feel sincere, you feel like an actress, because you expect conversion to come like a miracle, by the grace of love for one party member. . . .

They know I am pretending.

That is how she interpreted the silence.

In her own eyes, she stood judged and condemned. She was the only woman there, and they knew she was there only because she was a woman, tangled in her love, not in the revolution.

Then Rango came, breathless, and anxious: "There will be no meeting. You are ordered to disperse. No explanations."

They were relieved to go. They left in silence. They did not look at her.

Rango and Djuna were left alone.

Rango said: "*Your* friend the policeman was on guard at the top of the stairs. A hobo had been found murdered. So when the Guatemalans began to arrive, he asked for papers. It was dangerous." He had made his first error, in thinking the barge a good place. The head of the group had been severe. Had called him a romantic. . . . "He also knows about you. Asked if you were a member. I had to tell the truth."

"Should I sign the papers?" she asked, with a docility which was so much like a child's that Rango was moved.

"If you do it for me, that's bad. You have to do it for yourself."

"Oh, for myself. You know what I believe. The world today is rootless; it's like a forest with all the trees with their heads in the ground and their roots gesticulating wildly in the air, withering. The only remedy is to begin a world of two; in two there is hope of perfection, and that in turn may spread to all. . . . But it must begin at the base, in relationship of man and woman."

"I'm going to give you books to read, to study."

Would his new philosophy change his overindulgence and slavishness to Zora, would he see her with new eyes, see the waste, the criminality of her self-absorption? Would he say to her, too: there are more important things in the world than your little pains. One must forget one's personal life. Would his personal life be altered as she had not been able to alter it? Would his confusions and errors be clarified?

Djuna began to hope. She began to study. She noted analogies between the new philosophy and what she had been expounding uselessly to Rango.

For instance, to die romantically, recklessly, unintelligently, was not approved by the party. Waste. Confusion. Indiscipline. The party developed a kind of stoicism, an armature, a form of behavior and thinking.

Djuna gradually allied herself to the essence of the philosophy, to its results rather, and overlooked the rigid dogmas.

The essence was construction. In a large way she could adopt this because it harmonized with her obsessional battle against destruction and negativism.

She was not alone against the demoralizing, dissolving influence of Zora.

Perhaps the trap was opening a little, in an unforeseen direction.

What he could not do for her (because she was his pleasure, his self-indulgence, his sensually fulfilling mistress, and this gave him guilt), he might do for the party and for a large, anonymous mass of people.

The trap was the fixation on the impossible. A change in Zora, instead of an aggravation. A change in Rango, instead of a gradual strangulation.

Passion alone had not made him whole. But it had made him whole enough to be useful to the world.

When the barge failed to become the meeting place for Rango's fellow workers, it was suddenly transformed into its opposite: a shelter for the dreamers looking for a haven. The more bitter the atmosphere of Paris, the more intense the dissensions, the rising tide of political antagonisms, dangers, fears, the more they came to the barge as if it were Noah's Ark against a new deluge.

It was no longer the secret boat of a voyage of two. The unicellular nights had come to an end. Rango was but a visitor-lover in transit.

The divergence between them became sharply exteriorized: while Rango attended meetings, talked feverishly in cafés, sought to convert, to teach, to organize, worked among the poor he had known, among the artists, Djuna's friends brought to the barge the values they believed in danger of being lost, a passionate clinging to aesthetic and human creation.

Rango brought stories of cruelty and personal sacrifice: Ramon had been four years without seeing his wife and child. He had been working in Guatemala. Now his wife in Paris was gravely ill, and he wanted to throw off his duties there and come, at any cost. "Think of a man forgetting his loyalty to his party, just because his wife and child need him. Willing to sacrifice the good of millions, perhaps, for just two."

"Rango, that's just what you would do, and you know it. That's what you have done with Zora. You've given twenty years of your strength to one human being, when you could have done greater things, too. . . ."

Another day he came and was sick in her arms, vomited all night, and only at dawn, weak, and feverish did he confess: they had had to arrest a traitor. He had been a friend of Rango's. The group had been obliged to judge him. Rango had been forced to question him. The man was not really a traitor. He was weak. He had needed money for his family. He was tired of working for the party without pay. The party never worried about a man's family, what they needed while he was away on duty. He had given his whole life, and now, at forty, he had weakened. He had been tempted by a good position in the embassy. At first he had intended to exploit his position for the benefit of the party. But after awhile he got tired of danger. He had ceased to be of help. . . . Rango had had to force himself to turn him over to the party. It had made him sick. It was his first cruel, difficult, disciplined act. But he didn't sleep for a week, and each time he remembered the man's face as he told his story, and repeated: just tired, very tired, worn out, at forty, too many times in prison, too many hardships, couldn't take any more. Had been in the party from the age of seventeen, had been useful, courageous, but now he was tired.

Every day he brought a story like this one. When the conflict grew too great he drank. Djuna did not have this escape. When the stories burnt into her and hurt her, she turned away and into the dream again, as she had done in childhood. There was another world visible to practiced eyes, easy to enter and inhabit, another chamber to which only the initiate could follow.

(Moods flowing like the river finding its way to the sea and vastness and depth. In this world the river was the flow; tap the secret of its flow, in the lulling rhythm of its waves, in the continuity of its current. Love is a madness shared by two, love is the crystal in which people find their unity. In this world Rango was capable of giving himself to a dream of love, which is a city of only two inhabitants. In this world, when Rango buys shoes so heavy and so strong, they seem like the hooves of the centaur, hooves of iron, whose head was in the heavens but whose hooves must pound the battlefields.)

There are drugs to escape reality, a Rango vomiting from the spectacle of cruelty, Rango's harshness toward her feelings. He should, by laws of accuracy, be angry at his own emotionalism and human fallibility. But because of his blindness, he gets angry at Djuna's face turned away and attacks her swift departures from horror. He drinks but does not consider *that* a trap door opening on the infinite, an inferior drug to dispel pain. . . . But Djuna's excursions into astronomy, her sheltering of the artists in the barge . . . He is merciless toward their kind of drug to transform reality into something bearable. . . .

340

"To me, it is the world of history which appears mad, treacherous and full of contradictions," said Djuna.

"In Guatemala," said Rango, with an ironic twist of his lips which Djuna disliked, "they placed madmen by the side of the river, and that cured them. If your madmen don't get cured, we'll make a hole in the floor and sink them."

"I may sink with them, you know."

Walking along the quay, they saw a hobo sitting under a tree, a hobo with a Scotch cap, a plaid, and a crooked pipe.

Rango adopted his best imitation of a Scotch accent and said: "Weel, and where d'ya come from, ma good friend?"

But the hobo looked up bewildered and said in pure Montmartre French: "Mon Dieu, I'm no foreigner, sir. What makes you think I am?"

"The cap and the blanket," said Rango.

"Oh, that, sir, it's just that I'm always digging in the garbage can of the Opéra Comique, and I found this rig. It was the only one I could wear, you understand, the others were a little too fancy, and most of them pretty indecent, I must say."

Then he took a faded gray sporran out of his pocket: "Could you tell me what this is for?"

Rango laughed: "That's a wig. The use of the skirt has caused premature baldness of an unusual kind in Scotland. Hold on to it, it might come useful one day. . . ."

Sabina walked with her feet flat on the ground, which gave to her heavy body the poise of Biblical water carriers.

Djuna saw her and Rango as composed of the same elements, and felt that perhaps they would love each other. She imagined a parting scene with Rango, surrendering his black hair to hers heavy and straight, his burnt-sienne skin to her incandescent gold one, his rough dry hands to her strong peasant ones, his laughter to hers, his Indian slyness to her Semitic labyrinthian mind. They will recognize each other's climate of fever and chaos, and embrace each other.

Djuna was amazed to see her predictions unfulfilled. Rango fled from Sabina's intensity and violence. They met like two armed warriors, and the part of Rango which longed to be yielded to, who longed for warmth, found in Sabina an unyielding armor. She yielded only at the last moment, merely to achieve a sensual embrace, and immediately after was poised for battle again. No aperture for tenderness to lodge itself, for his secret timidity to flow into, as it flew into Djuna's breast. Not a woman one could nestle into.

They sought grounds for a duel. Rango hated her presence about Djuna, and woud have liked to drive her away from the barge.

Once sitting in a restaurant together, with Djuna and two other friends, they decided to see which one could eat the most red chilies.

They ate the red chilies with ostentatious insolence, watching each other. At first mixed with rice and vegetables, then with the salad, and finally by themselves.

Both might have died of the contest, for neither one would yield. Each little red chili like a concentrate of fire which burned them both.

Now and then they opened their mouths wide and breathed quickly in and out, as if to cool their insides.

As in the old myths, they sat like fire eaters partaking of a fire banquet. Tears came to Sabina's intense dark eyes. A sepia flush came to Rango's laughing cheeks, but neither would yield, though they might scar their entrails.

Fortunately the restaurant was closing, and the waiters

maliciously washed the floor under their feet with ammonia, piled chairs on the table, and finally put an end to the marathon by turning out the lights.

Not one but many Djunas descended the staircase of the barge, one layer formed by the parents, the childhood, another molded by her profession and her friends, still another born of history, geology, climate, race, economics, and all the backgrounds and backdrops, the sky and nature of the earth, the pure sources of birth, the influence of a tree, a word dropped carelessly, an image seen, and all the corrupted sources: books, art, dogmas, tainted friendships, and all the places where a human being is wounded, defeated, crippled, and which fester. . . .

People add up their physical mishaps, the stubbed toes, the cut finger, the burn scar, the fever, the cancer, the microbe, the infection, the wounds and broken bones. They never add up the accumulated bruises and scars of the inner lining, forming a complete universe of reactions, a reflected world through which no event could take place without being subjected to a personal and private interpretation, through this kaleidoscope of memory, through the peculiar formation of the psyche's sensitive photographic plates, to this assemblage of emotional chemicals through which every word, every event, every experience is filtered, digested, deformed, before it is projected again upon people and relationships.

The movement of the many layers of the self described by Duchamp's "Nude Descending a Staircase," the multiple selves grown in various proportions, not singly, not evenly developed, not moving in one direction, but composed of multiple juxtapositions revealing endless spirals of character as the earth revealed its strata, an infinite constellation of feelings expanding as mysteriously as space and light in the realm of the planets.

Man turned his telescope outward and far, not seeing character emerging at the opposite end of the telescope by subtle accumulations, fragments, accretions, and encrustations.

Woman turned her telescope to the near, and the warm.

Djuna felt at this moment a crisis, a mutation, a need to leap from the self born of her relationship to Rango and Zora, a need to resuscitate in another form. She was unable to follow Rango in his faith, unable either to live in the dream in peace, or to sail the barge accurately through a stormy Seine.

She found herself defending Sabina against Rango's ruthless mockery. She defended Sabina's philosophy of the many loves against the One.

(Rango, your anger should not be directed against Sabina. Sabina is only behaving as all women do in their dreams, at night. I feel responsible for her acts, because when we walk together and I listen to her telling me about her adventures, a part of me is not listening to her telling me a story but recognizing scenes familiar to a secret part of myself. I recognize scenes I have dreamed and which therefore I have committed. What is dreamed is committed. In my dreams I have been Sabina. I have escaped from your tormenting love, caressed all the interchangeable lovers of the world. Sabina cannot be made alone responsible for acting the dreams of many women, just because the others sit back and participate with a secret part of their selves. Through secret and small vibrations of the flesh they admit being silent accomplices to Sabina's acts. At night we have all tossed with fever and desire for strangers. During the day we deride Sabina, and revile her. You're angry at Sabina because she lives out all her wishes overtly as you have done. To love Sabina's fever, Sabina's impatience, Sabina's evasion of traps in the games of love, was being Sabina. To be only at night what Sabina dared to be during the day, to bear the responsibility for one's secret dream of escape from the torments of one love into many loves.)

Sabina sat astride a chair, flinging her hair back with her hands and laughing.

She always gave at this moment the illusion that she was going to confess. She excelled in this preparation for unveiling, this setting of a mood for intimate revelations. She excelled equally in evasion. When she wished it, her life was like a blackboard on which she wrote swiftly and then erased almost before anyone could read what she had written. Her words then did not seem like words but like smoke issuing from her mouth and nostrils, a heavy smoke screen against detection. But at other times, if she felt secure from judgment, then she opened a story of an incident with direct, stabbing thoroughness. . . .

"Our affair lasted . . . lasted for the duration of an elevator ride! And I don't mean that symbolically either! We took such a violent fancy to each other, the kind that will not last, but will not wait either. It was cannibalistic, and of no importance, but it had to be fulfilled once. Circumstances were against us. We had no place to go. We wandered through the streets, we were ravenous for each other. We got into an elevator, and he began to kiss me. . . . First floor, second floor, and he still kissing me, third floor, fourth floor, and when the elevator came to a standstill, it was too late . . . we could not stop, his hands were everywhere, his mouth. . . . I pressed the button wildly and went on kissing as the elevator came down. . . . When we got to the bottom it was worse . . . He pressed the button and we went up and down, up and down, madly, while people kept ringing for the elevator. . . ."

She laughed again, with her entire body, even her feet, marking the rhythm of her gaiety, stamping the ground like a delighted spectator, while her strong thighs rocked the chair like an Amazon's wooden horse.

One evening while Djuna was waiting for Rango at the barge, she heard a footstep which was not the watchman's and not Rango's.

The shadows of the candles on the tarpapered walls played a scene from a Balinese theatre as she moved toward the door and called: "Who's there?"

There was a complete silence, as if the river, the barge, and the visitor had connived to be silent at the same moment, put a tension in the air which she felt like a vibration through her body.

She did not know what to do, whether to stay in the room and lock the door, awaiting Rango, or to explore the barge. If she stayed in the room quietly and watched for his coming, she could shout a warning to him out of the window, and then together they might corner the intruder.

She waited.

The shadows on the walls were still, but the reflections of the lights on the river played on the surface like a ghost's carnival. The candles flickered more than usual, or was it her anxiety?

When the wood beams ceased to creak, she heard the footsteps again, moving toward the room, cautiously but not light enough to prevent the boards from creaking.

Djuna took her revolver from under her pillow, a small one which had been given to her and which she did not know how to use.

She called out: "Who is there? If you come any nearer, I'll shoot."

She knew there was a safety clasp to open. She wished Rango would arrive. He had no physical fear. He feared truth, he feared to confront his motives, feared to face, to understand, to examine in the realm of feelings and thought, but he did not fear to act, he did not fear physical danger. Djuna was intrepid in awareness, in painful exposures of the self, and dared more than most in matter of emotional surgery, but she had a fear of violence.

She waited another long moment, but again the silence was complete, suspended.

Rango did not come.

Out of exhaustion, she lay down with her revolver in hand. The doors and windows were locked. She waited, listening for Rango's uneven footsteps on the deck.

The candles burnt down one by one, gasping out their last flame, throwing one last long, agonized skeleton on the wall.

The river rocked the barge.

Hours passed and Djuna fell into a half sleep.

The catch of the door was gradually lifted off the hinge by some instrument or other and Zora stood at the opened door.

Djuna saw her when she was bending over her, and screamed.

Zora held a long old-fashioned hatpin in her hand and tried to stab Djuna with it. Djuna at first grasped her hands at the wrists, but Zora's anger gave her greater strength. Her face was distorted with hatred. She pulled her hands free and stabbed at Djuna several times blindly, striking her at the shoulder, and then once more, with her eyes wide open, she aimed at the breast and missed. Then Djuna pushed her off, held her.

"What harm have I done you, Zora?"

"You forced Rango to join the party. He's trying to become someone now, in politics, and it's for you. He wants you to be proud of him. With me he never cared; he wasn't ashamed of his laziness. . . . It's your fault that he is never home . . . Your fault that he's in danger every day."

Djuna looked at Zora's face and felt again as she did with Rango, the desperate hopelessness of talking, explaining, clarifying. Zora and Rango were fanatics.

She shook Zora by the shoulders, as if to force her to listen and said: "Killing me won't change anything, can't you understand that? We're the two faces of Rango's character. If you kill me, that side of him remains unmated and another woman will take my place. He's divided within himself, between destruction and construction. While he's divided there will be two women, always. I wished you would die, too, once, until I understood this. I once thought Rango could be saved if you died. And here you are, thinking that I would drive him into danger. He's driving himself into danger. He is ashamed of his futility. He can't bear the conflict of his split being enacted in us before his eyes. He is trying a third attempt at wholeness. For his peace of mind, if you and I could have been friends it would have been easier. He didn't consider us, whether or not we could sincerely like each other. We tried and failed. You were too selfish. You and I stand at opposite poles. I don't like you, and you don't like me either; even if Rango did not exist you and I could never like each other. Zora, if you harm me you'll be punished for it and sent to a place without Rango. . . . And Rango will be angry with you. And if you died, it would be the same. He would not be mine either, because I can't fulfill his love of destruction. . . ."

Words, words, words . . . all the words Djuna had turned in her mind at night when alone, she spoke them wildly, blindly, not hoping for Zora to understand, but they were said with such anxiety and vehemence that aside from their meaning Zora caught the pleading, the accents of truth, dissolving her hatred, her violence.

At the sight of each other their antagonism always dissolved. Zora, faced with the sadness of Djuna's face, her voice, her slender body, could never sustain her anger. And Djuna faced with Zora's haggard face, limp hair, uncontrolled lips, lost her rebellion.

Whatever scenes took place between them, there was a sincerity in each one's sadness which bound them too.

It was at this moment that Rango arrived, and stared at the two women with dismay.

"What happened? Djuna, you're bleeding!"

"Zora tried to kill me. The wounds aren't bad."

Djuna hoped once more that Rango would say, "Zora is mad," and that the nightmare would cease.

"You wanted us to be friends, because that would have made it easier for you. We tried. But it was impossible. I feel that Zora destroys all my efforts to create with you, and she thinks I sent you into a dangerous political life. . . . We can never understand each other."

Rango found nothing to say. He stared at the blood showing through Djuna's clothes. She showed him that the stabs were not deep and had struck fleshy places without causing harm.

"I'll take Zora home. I'll come back."

When he returned he was still silent, crushed, bowed.

"Zora has moments of madness," he said. "She's been threatening people in the street lately. I'm so afraid the police may catch her and put her in an institution."

"You don't care about the people she might kill, do you?"

"I do care, Djuna. If she had killed you I don't think I could ever have forgiven her. But you aren't angry, when you have a right to be. You're generous and good. . . ."

"No, Rango. I can't let you believe that. It isn't true. I have often wished Zora's death, but I only had the courage to wish it. . . . I had a dream one night in which I saw myself killing her with a long old-fashioned hatpin. Do you realize where she got the idea of the hatpin? From my own dream, which I told her. She was being more courageous, more honest, when she attacked me."

Rango took his head in his hands and swayed back and forth as if in pain. A dry sob came out of his chest.

"Oh, Rango, I can't bear this any more. I will go away. Then you'll have peace with Zora."

"Something else happened today, Djuna, something which reminded me of some of the things you said. Something so terrible that I did not want to see you tonight. I don't know what instinct of danger made me come, after all. But what happened tonight is worse than Zora's fit of madness. You know that once a month the workers of the party belonging to a certain group meet for what they call autocriticism. It's part of the discipline. It's done with kindness, great objectivity, and very justly. I have been at such meetings. A man's way of working, his character traits, are analyzed. Last night it was my turn. The men who sat in a circle, they were the ones I see every day, the butcher, the postman, the grocer, the shoemaker on my own street. The head of our particular section is the bus driver. At first, you know, they had been doubtful about signing me in. They knew I was an artist, a bohemian, an intellectual. But they liked me . . . and they took me in. I've worked for them two months now. Then last night. . . ."

He stopped as if he would not have the courage to relive the scene. Djuna's hand in his calmed him. But he kept his head bowed. "Last night they talked, very quietly and moderately as the French do. . . . They analyzed me, how I work. They told me some of the things you used to tell me. They made an analysis of my character. They observed everything, the good and the bad. Not only the laziness, the disorder, the lack of discipline, the placing of personal life before the needs of the party, the nights at the café, the immoderate talking, irresponsibility, but they also mentioned my capabilities, which made it worse, as they showed how I sabotage myself. . . . They analyzed my power to influence others, my eloquence, my fervor and enthusiasm, my contagious enthusiasm and energy, my gift for making an impression on a crowd, the fact that people are inclined to trust me, to elect me as their leader. Everything. They knew about my fatalism, too. They talked about character changing, as you do. They even intimated that Zora should be placed in an institution, because they knew about her behavior."

All the time he kept his head bowed.

"When you said these things gently, it didn't hurt me. It was our secret and I could get angry with you, or contradict you. But when they said them before all the other men I knew it was true, and worse still, I knew that if I had not been able to change with all that you gave me, years of love and devotion, I wouldn't change for the party either. . . . Any other man, taking what you gave, would have accomplished the greatest changes . . . any other man but me."

The barge was sailing nowhere, moored to the port of despair.

Rango stretched himself and said: "I'm tired out . . . so tired, so tired. . . ." And fell asleep almost instantly in the pose of a big child, with his fists tightly closed, his arms over his head.

Djuna walked lightly to the front cabin, looked once through the small barred portholes like the windows of a prison, leaned over the mildewed floor, and tore up one of the bottom boards, inviting the deluge to sink this Noah's Ark sailing nowhere.

The wood being old and half rotted had made it easy for Djuna to pull on the plank where it had once been patched, but the influx of the water had been partly blocked by the outer layer of barnacles and corrugated seaweeds which she could not reach.

She returned to the bed on the floor and lay beside Rango, to wait patiently for death.

She saw the river sinuating toward the sea and wondered if they would float unhampered toward the ocean.

Below the level of identity lay an ocean, an ocean of which human beings carry only a drop in their veins; but some sink below cognizance and the drop becomes a huge wave, the tide of memory, the undertows of sensation. . . .

Beneath the cities of the interior flowed many rivers carrying a multitude of images. . . .

All the women she had been spread their hair in a halo on the surface of the river, extended multiple arms like the idols of India, their essence seeping in and out of the meandering dreams of men. . . .

Djuna, lying face upward like a water lily of amniotic

352

lakes; Djuna, floating down to the organ grinder's tune of a pavana for a defunct infanta of Spain, the infanta who never acceded to the throne of maturity, the one who remained a pretender. . . .

As for Rango, the drums would burst and all the painted horses of the carnival would turn a polka. . . .

She saw their lives over and over again until she caught a truth which was not simple and divisible but fluctuating and elusive; but she saw it clearly from the places under the surface where she had been accustomed to exist: all the women she had been like many rivers running out of her and with her into the ocean. . . .

She saw, through this curtain of water, all of them as personages larger than nature, more visible to sluggish hearts being in the focus of death, a stage on which there are no blurred passages, no missed cues. . . .

She saw, now that she was out of the fog of imprecise relationships, with the more intense light of death upon these faces which had caused her despair, she saw these same faces as pertaining to gentle clowns. Zora dressed in comical trappings, in Rango's outsized socks, in dyed kimonos, in strangled rags and empty-armed brooches, a comedy to awaken guilt in others. . . .

. . . on this stage, floating down the Seine toward death, the actors drifted along and love no longer seemed a trap . . . *the trap was the static pause in growth, the arrested self caught in its own web of obstinacy and obsession.* . . .

. . . you grow, as in the water the algae grow taller and heavier and are caried by their own weight into different currents. . . .

. . . I was afraid to grow or move away, Rango, I was ashamed to desert you in your torment, but now I know your choice is your own, as mine was my own. . . .

. . . fixation is death . . . death is fixation . . .

. . . on this precarious ship, devoid of upholstery and self-deception, the voyage can continue into tomorrow. . . .

. . . what I see now is the vastness, and the places where I have not been and the duties I have not fulfilled, and the uses for this unusual cargo of past sorrows all ripe for transmutations. . . .

. . . the messenger of death, like all adventurers, will accelerate your heart toward change and mutation. . . .

. . . if one sinks deep enough and then deeper, all these women she had been flowed into one at night and lost their separate identities; she would learn from Sabina how to make love laughing, and from Stella how to die only for a little while and be born again as children die and are reborn at the slightest encouragement. . . .

. . . from the end in water to the beginning in water, she would complete the journey, from origin to birth and birth to flow. . . .

. . . she would abandon her body to flow into a vaster body than her own, as it was at the beginning, and return with many other lives to be unfolded. . . .

. . . with her would float the broken doll of her childhood, the Easter egg which had been smaller than the one she had asked for, debris of fictions. . . .

. . . she would return to the life above the waters of the unconscious and see the magnifications of sorrow which had taken place and been the true cause of the deluge. . . .

. . . there were countries she had not yet seen. . . .

. . . this image created a pause in her floating. . . .

. . . there must also be loves she had not yet encountered. . . .

. . . as the barge ran swiftly down the current of despair, she saw the people on the shore flinging their arms in desolation, those who had counted on her Noah's Ark to save themselves. . . .

. . . she was making a selfish journey. . . .

. . . she had intended the barge for other purposes than for a mortuary. . . .

. . . war was coming. . . .

. . . the greater the turmoil, the confusion, the greater had been her effort to maintain an individually perfect world, a cocoon of faith, which would be a symbol and a refuge. . . .

354

... the curtain of dawn would rise on a deserted river. ...

... on two deserters. ...

... in the imminence of death she seized this intermediary region of our being in which we rehearse our future sorrows and relive the past ones. ...

... in this heightened theatre their lives appeared in their true color because there was no witness to distort the private admissions, the most absurd pretensions. ...

... in the last role Djuna became immune from the passageway of pretense, from a suspended existence in reflection, from impostures. ...

... and she saw what had appeared immensely real to her as charades. ...

... *in the theatre of death, exaggeration is the cause of despair.* ...

... the red Easter egg I had wanted to be so enormous when I was a child, if it floats by today in its natural size, so much smaller than my invention, I will be able to laugh at its shrinking. ...

... I had chosen death because I was ashamed of this shrinking and fading, of what time would do to our fiction of magnificence, time like the river would wear away the pain of defeats and broken promises, time and the river would blur the face of Zora as a giant incubus, time and the river would mute the vibrations of Rango's voice upon my heart. ...

... the organ grinder will play all the time but it will not always seem like a tragic accompaniment to separations. ...

... the organ grinder will play all the time but the images will change, as the feelings will change, Rango's gestures will seem less violent, and sorrows will fall off like leaves to fecundate the heart for a new love. ...

... the organ grinder will accelerate his rhythm into arabesques of delight to match the vendor's cries: "Mimosa! mimosa!" to the tune of Brahm's "Lullaby." ... *"Couteaux! couteaux à aiguiser!"* to the tune from *Madame Butterfly.* ... *"Pommes de terre! pommes de terre!"* to the tune from

Ravel's *Bolero*.

. . . *"Bouteilles! bouteilles!"* to the tune from *Tristan and Isolde*.
She laughed.

. . . tomorrow the city would ferment with new disasters, the
paper vendors would raise their voices to the pitch of hysteria,
the crowds would gather to discuss the news, the trains would
carry away the cowards. . . .

. . . the cowards. . . .

. . . floating down the river. . . .

. . . with the barge that had been intended not only to house
a single love but as a refuge for faith. . . .

. . . she was sinking a faith. . . .

. . . instead of solidifying the floating kingdom with its cargo
of eternal values. . . .

("An individually perfect world," said Rango, "is destroyed
by reality, war, revolutions.")

"Rango, wake up wake up wake up, there's a leak!"

He was slow in awakening, his dreams of greatness and
magnificence were heavy on his body like royal garments, but
the face he opened to the dawn was the face of innocence, as
every man presents innocence to the new day. Djuna read on
it what she had refused to see, the other face of Rango the
child lodged in a big man's body by a merry freak.

It had been a game: "Djuna, you stand there and watch
while I am the king and savior. You will admire me when I
give the cue." She will now laugh and say: "But actually, you
know, I prefer a hobo who plays the guitar."

She will laugh when he refuses to see Zora's madness, because it was like her refusal to see his madness, his impersonations, his fictions, his illusions. . . .

In the face of death the barge was smaller, Rango did not
loom so immense, Zora had shrunk. . . .

In the face of death they were playing games, Zora absurdly
overdressed in the trappings of tragedy, muddying, aborting,
confusing, delighted with the purple colors of catastrophe as
children delight in fire engines. When their absence of wisdom

and courage tormented her, she would avenge herself by descending into their realm and adding to the difficulties. She had once told Rango that her father would have to live in the south of France for his health and that they would have to separate. Being helpless, they had believed she would let this happen, since they were accustomed to bowing to the inevitable. Rango had jumped and leaped with pain. Zora had said to him, not without mixing it with a delicate shading of poison: "This must happen sooner or later . . .Djuna will leave you."

Then she had gone to see Zora, Zora awkwardly, laboriously moving her small and flabby hands, Zora appearing helpless while Djuna knew she was the strongest of the three because she had learned to exploit her weakness. She told Djuna that Rango had not eaten that day. He was just pacing around, and he had been so cruel to Zora. He had said to her: "If Djuna goes to the south of France, I'll send you home to your relatives."

"Alone? And what about you?"

"Oh, me," he said with a shrug. Zora added: "He will kill himself."

By this time her game had given her enough pleasure. She felt mature again. But after a week of torment the stage was set for a great love scene; she knew now that if she left Rango he would not console himself with Zora. That was all she needed to know. Perhaps she was not so much wiser than they were . . . perhaps she did not have herself too great a faith in love. . . . Perhaps there was in her a Zora in need of protection and a wildly anxious Rango in need of reassurances. And perhaps that was why she loved them, and perhaps Zora was right to believe in her love as she did in her moments of lucidity. . . .

In the face of death Rango seemed less violent, Zora less tyrannical, and Djuna less wise. And when Zora looked at Djuna above the rim of her glasses which she had picked up in a scrap basket at somebody's door and which were not suited to her eyes—she looked as children do when they stare and frown over the rim of their parents' glasses, these pretenders to the throne of maturity. . . .

"Rango, wake up wake up wake up wake up wake up, there's a leak."

Rango opened his eyes and then jumped: "Oh, I forgot to pump the water yesterday."

The second face of Rango, after awakening, following the bewildered and innocent one, contained this expression of total, of absolute, distress common to children and adolescents betraying an exaggeration in the vision of reality, a sense of the menacing, disproportionate stature of this reality. Only children and adolescents know this total despair, as if every wound were fatal and irremediable, every moment the last, death and dangers looming immense as they had loomed in Djuna's mind during the night. . . .

Rango repaired the leak vigorously, and they walked out on the quay. It was a moment before dawn, and some fishermen were already installed because the river was smooth for fishing. One of them had caught something unusual and was holding it out for Djuna to see, and laughing.

It was a doll.

It was a doll who had committed suicide during the night. The water had washed off its features. Her hair aureoled her face with crystalline glow.

Noah's Ark had survived the flood.

Hugo 1942

A Spy in the
House of Love

THE LIE DETECTOR WAS ASLEEP when he heard the telephone ringing.

At first he believed it was the clock ordering him to rise, but then he awakened completely and remembered his profession.

The voice he heard was rusty, as if disguised. He could not distinguish what altered it: alcohol, drugs, anxiety or fear.

It was a woman's voice; but it could have been an adolescent imitating a woman, or a woman imitating an adolescent.

"What is it?" he asked. "Hello. Hello. Hello."

"I had to talk to someone; I can't sleep. I had to call someone."

"You have something to confess . . ."

"To confess?" echoed the voice incredulously; this time, the ascending tonalities unmistakably feminine.

"Don't you know who I am?"

"No, I just dialed blindly. I've done this before. It is good to hear a voice in the middle of the night, that's all."

"Why a stranger? You could call a friend."

"A stranger doesn't ask questions."

"But it's my profession to ask questions."

"Who are you?"

"A lie detector."

There was a long silence after his words. The lie detector expected her to hang up. But he heard her cough through the telephone.

"Are you there?"

"Yes."

"I thought you would hang up."

There was laughter through the telephone, a lax, spangled, spiralling laughter. "But you don't practice your profession over the telephone!"

"It's true. Yet you wouldn't have called me if you were innocent. Guilt is the one burden human beings can't bear alone. As soon as a crime is committed, there is a telephone call, or a confession to strangers."

"There was no crime."

"There is only one relief: to confess, to be caught, tried, punished. That's the ideal of every criminal. But it's not quite so simple. Only half of the self wants to atone, to be freed of the torments of guilt. The other half of man wants to continue to be free. So only half of the self surrenders, calling out "catch me," while the other half creates obstacles, difficulties; seeks to escape. It's a flirtation with justice. If justice is nimble, it will follow the clue with the criminal's help. If not, the criminal will take care of his own atonement."

"Is that worse?"

"I think so. I think we are more severe judges of our own acts than professional judges. We judge our thoughts, our intents, our secret curses, our secret hates, not only our acts."

ˌShe hung up.

The lie detector called up the operator, gave orders to have the call traced. It came from a bar. Half an hour later, he was sitting there.

He did not allow his eyes to roam or examine. He wanted his ears alone to be attentive, that he might recognize the voice.

When she ordered a drink, he lifted his eyes from his newspaper.

Dressed in red and silver, she evoked the sounds and imagery of fire engines as they tore through the streets of New York, alarming the heart with the violent gong of catastrophe; all dressed in red and silver, the tearing red and silver cutting a pathway through the flesh. The first time he looked at her he felt: *everything will burn!*

Out of the red and silver and the long cry of alarm to the poet who survives in all human beings, as the child survives in him; to this poet she threw an unexpected ladder in the middle of the city and ordained, "Climb!"

As she appeared, the orderly alignment of the city gave way before this ladder one was invited to climb, standing straight in space like the ladder of Baron Münchhausen which led to the sky.

Only her ladder led to fire.

He looked at her again with a professional frown.

She could not sit still. She talked profusely and continuously with a feverish breathlessness like one in fear of silence. She sat as if she could not bear to sit for long; and, when she rose to buy cigarettes, she was equally eager to return to her seat. Impatient, alert, watchful, as if in dread of being attacked, restless and keen, she drank hurriedly; she smiled so swiftly that he was not even certain it had been a smile; she listened only partially to what was being said to her; and, even when

362

someone in the bar leaned over and shouted a name in her direction, she did not respond at first, as if it were not her own.

"Sabina!" shouted the man from the bar, leaning towards her perilously but not losing his grip on the back of his chair for fear of toppling.

Someone nearer to her gallantly repeated the name for her, which she finally acknowledged as her own. At this moment, the lie detector threw off the iridescence which the night, the voice, the drug of sleep and her presence had created in him, and determined that she behaved like someone who had all the symptoms of guilt: her way of looking at the door of the bar, as if expecting the proper moment to make her escape; her unpremeditated talk, without continuity; her erratic and sudden gestures, unrelated to her talk; the chaos of her phrases; her sudden, sulky silences.

As friends drifted towards her, sat with her, and then drifted away to other tables, she was forced to raise her voice, usually low, to be heard above the cajoling blues.

She was talking about a party at which indistinct incidents had taken place, hazy scenes from which the lie detector could not distinguish the heroine or the victim; talking a broken dream, with spaces, reversals, retractions, and galloping fantasies. She was now in Morocco visiting the baths with the native women, sharing their pumice stone, and learning from the prostitutes how to paint her eyes with kohl from the market place. "It's coal dust, and you place it right inside the eyes. It smarts at first, and you want to cry; but that spreads it out on the eyelids, and that is how they get that shiny, coal black rim around the eyes."

"Didn't you get an infection?" asked someone at her right whom the lie detector could not see clearly, an indistinct personage she disregarded even as she answered, "Oh, no, the prostitutes have the kohl blessed at the mosque." And then, when everyone laughed at this which she did not consider humorous, she laughed with them; and now it was as if all she had said had been written on a huge blackboard, and she took a sponge and effaced it all by a phrase which left in suspense who had been at the baths; or, perhaps, this was a story she had read, or heard at a bar; and, as soon as it was erased in the mind of her listeners, she began another . . .

The faces and the figures of her personages appeared only half drawn; and, when the lie detector had just begun to perceive them, another face and figure were interposed as in a dream. And when he believed she had been talking about a woman, it turned out that it was not a woman, but a man; and when the image of the man began to form, it turned out the lie detector had not heard aright: it was a young man who resembled a woman who had once taken care of Sabina; and this young man was instantly metamorphosed into a group of people who had humiliated her one night.

He could not retain a sequence of the people she had loved, hated, escaped from, any more than he could keep track of the changes in her personal appearance by phrases such as "at that time my hair was blond," "at that time I was married," and who it was that had been forgotten or betrayed; and when in desperation he clung to the recurrences of certain words, they formed no design by their repetition, but rather an absolute contradiction. The word "actress" recurred most persistently; and yet the lie detector could not, after hours of detection, tell whether she was an actress, or wanted to be one, or was pretending.

She was compelled by a confessional fever which forced her into lifting a corner of the veil, and then frightened when anyone listened too attentively. She repeatedly took a giant sponge and erased all she had said by absolute denial, as if this confusion were in itself a mantle of protection.

At first she beckoned and lured one into her world; then she blurred the passageways, confused all the images, as if to elude detection.

The dawn appearing at the door silenced her. She tightened her cape around her shoulders as if it were the final threat, the greatest enemy of all. To the dawn she would not even address a feverish speech. She stared at it angrily, and left the bar.

The lie detector followed her.

Before she awakened, Sabina's dark eyes showed the hard light of precious stones through a slit in the eyelids, pure dark green beryl shining, not yet warmed by her feverishness.

Then instantly she was awake, on guard.

She did not awaken gradually, in abandon and trust to the new day. As soon as light or sound registered on her consciousness, danger was in the air and she sat up to meet its thrusts.

Her first expression was one of tension, which was not beauty. Just as anxiety dispersed the strength of the body, it also gave to the face a wavering, tremulous vagueness, which was not beauty, like that of a drawing out of focus.

Slowly what she composed with the new day was her own focus, to bring together body and mind. This was made with an effort, as if all the dissolutions and dispersions of her self the night before were difficult to reassemble. She was like an actress who must compose a face, an attitude to meet the day.

The eyebrow pencil was no mere charcoal emphasis on blond eyebrows, but a design necessary to balance a chaotic asymmetry. Make up and powder were not simply applied to heighten a porcelain texture, to efface the uneven swellings caused by sleep, but to smooth out the sharp furrows designed by nightmares, to reform the contours and blurred surfaces of the cheeks, to erase the contradictions and conflicts which strained the clarity of the face's lines, disturbing the purity of its forms.

She must redesign the face, smooth the anxious brows, separate the crushed eyelashes, wash off the traces of secret interior tears, accentuate the mouth as upon a canvas, so it will hold its luxuriant smile.

Inner chaos, like those secret volcanoes which suddenly lift the neat furrows of a peacefully ploughed field, awaited behind all disorders of face, hair and costume for a fissure through which to explode.

What she saw in the mirror now was a flushed, clear-eyed face, smiling, smooth, beautiful. The multiple acts of composure and artifice had merely dissolved her anxieties; now that she felt prepared to meet the day, her true beauty, which had been frayed and marred by anxiety, emerged.

She considered her clothes with the same weighing of possible external dangers as she had the new day which had entered through her closed windows and doors.

Believing in the danger which sprang from objects as well as people, which dress, which shoes, which coat demanded less of her panicked heart and body? For a costume was a challenge too, a discipline, a trap which once adopted could influence the actor.

She ended by choosing a dress with a hole in its sleeve. The last time she had worn it she had stood before a restaurant which was too luxurious, too ostentatious, which she was frightened to enter, but instead of saying: "I am afraid to enter here," she had been able to say: "I can't enter here with a hole in my sleeve."

She selected her cape which seemed more protective, more enveloping.

Also the cape held within its folds something of what she imagined was a quality possessed exclusively by man: some dash, some audacity, some swagger of freedom denied to woman.

The toreador's provocative flings, the medieval horsemen's floating flag of attack, a sail unfurled in full collision with the wind, the warrior's shield for his face in battle, all these she experienced when she placed a cape around her shoulder.

A spread-out cape was the bed of nomads, a cape unfurled was the flag of adventure.

Now she was dressed in a costume most appropriate to flights, battles, tournaments.

The curtain of the night's defenselessness was rising to expose a personage prepared.

Prepared, said the mirror, prepared said the shoes, prepared said the cape.

She stood contemplating herself arrayed for no peaceful or trusting encounter with life.

She was not surprised when she looked out of her window and saw the man who had been following her standing at the corner pretending to be reading a newspaper.

It was not a surprise because it was a materialization of a feeling she had known for many years: that of an Eye watching and following her throughout her life.

She walked along 18th St. towards the river. She walked slightly out of rhythm, like someone not breathing deeply, long steps and inclined forward as if racing.

It was a street completely lined with truck garages. At this hour they were sliding open the heavy iron doors and huge trucks were rolling out, obscuring the sun. Their wheels were as tall as Sabina.

They lined up so close together that she could no longer see the street or the houses across the way. On her right they made a wall of throbbing motors, and giant wheels starting to turn. On her left more doors were opening, more trucks advanced slowly as if to engulf her. They loomed threateningly, inhuman, so high she could not see the drivers.

Sabina felt a shrinking of her whole body, and as she shrank from the noise the trucks seemed to enlarge in her eyes, their scale becoming monstrous, the rolling of their wheels uncontrollable. She felt as a child in an enormous world of menacing giants. She felt her bones fragile in her sandals. She felt brittle and crushable. She felt overwhelmed by danger, by a mechanized evil.

Her feeling of fragility was so strong that she was startled by the appearance of a woman at her left, who walked in step with her. Sabina glanced at her profile and was comforted by her tallness, the assurance of her walk. She too was dressed in black, but walked without terror.

And then she vanished. The mirror had come to an end. Sabina had been confronted with herself, the life size image walking beside the shrunk inner self, proving to her once more the disproportion between her feelings and external truth.

As many other times Sabina had experienced smallness, a sense of gigantic dangers, but she faced in the mirror a tall, strong, mature woman of thirty, equal to her surroundings. In the mirror was the image of what she had become and the image she gave to the world, but her secret inner self could be overwhelmed by a large truck wheel.

It was always at this precise moment of diminished power that the image of her husband Alan appeared. It required a mood of weakness in her, some inner unbalance, some exaggeration in her fears, to summon the image of Alan. He appeared as a fixed point in space. A calm face. A calm bearing. A tallness which made him visible in crowds and which harmonized with her concept of his uniqueness. The image of Alan appeared in her vision like a snap-shot. It did not reach her through tactile memory or any of the senses but the eyes. She did not remember his touch, or his voice. He was a photograph in her mind, with the static pose which characterized him: either standing up above average tallness so that he must carry his head a little bent, and something calm which gave the impression of a kind of benediction. She could not see him playful, smiling, or reckless, or carefree. He would never speak first, assert his mood, likes or dislikes, but wait, as confessors do, to catch first of all the words or the moods of others. It gave him the passive quality of a listener, a reflector. She could not imagine him wanting anything badly (except that she should come home) or taking anything for himself. In the two snap-shots she carried he showed two facets but no contrasts: one listening and waiting, wise and detached, the other sitting in meditation as a spectator.

Whatever event (in this case the trivial one of the walk down 18th St.) caused in Sabina either a panic, a shrinking, these two images of Alan would appear, and her desire to return home.

She walked back to the room in which she had awakened that morning. She pulled her valise out from under the bed and began to pack it.

The cashier at the desk of the hotel smiled at her as she passed on her way out, a smile which appeared to Sabina as expressing a question, a doubt. The man at the desk stared at her valise. Sabina walked up to the desk and said haltingly: "Didn't . . . my husband pay the bill?"

"Your husband took care of everything," said the desk man.

Sabina flushed angrily. She was about to say: Then why did you stare at me? And why the undertone of irony in your faces? And why had she herself hesitated at the word husband?

The mockery of the hotel personnel added to her mood of weight and fatigue. Her valise seemed to grow heavier in her hand. In this mood of lostness every object became extraordinarily heavy, every room oppressive, every task overwhelming. Above all, the world seemed filled with condemning eyes. The cashier's smile had been ironic and the desk man's scrutiny not friendly.

Haven was only two blocks away, yet distance seemed enormous, difficulties insuperable. She stopped a taxi and said: "55 Fifth Avenue."

The taxi driver said rebelliously: "Why, lady, that's only two blocks away, you can walk it. You look strong enough." And he sped away.

She walked slowly. The house she reached was luxurious, but as many houses in the village, without elevators. There was no one around to carry her bag. The two floors she had to climb appeared like the endless stairways in a nightmare. They would drain the very last of her strength.

But I am safe. He will be asleep. He will be happy at my coming. He will be there. He will open his arms. He will make room for me. I will no longer have to struggle.

Just before she reached the last floor she could see a thin ray of light under his door and she felt a warm joy permeate her entire body. *He is there. He is awake.*

As if everything else she had experienced were but ordeals and this the shelter, the place of happiness.

I can't understand what impels me to leave this, this is happiness.

When his door opened it always seemed to open upon an unchanging room. The furniture was never displaced, the lights were always diffused and gentle like sanctuary lamps.

Alan stood at the door and what she saw first of all was his smile. He had strong, very even teeth in a long and narrow head. The smile almost closed his eyes which were narrow and shed a soft fawn light. He stood very erect with an almost military bearing, and being very tall his head bent down as if from its own weight to look down upon Sabina.

He always greeted her with a tenderness which seemed to assume she had always been in great trouble. He automatically rushed to comfort and to shelter. The way he opened his arms and the tone in which he greeted her implied: "First of all I will comfort and console you, first of all I will gather you together again, you're always so battered by the world outside."

The strange, continuous, almost painful tension she felt away from him always dissolved in his presence, at his very door.

He took her valise, moving with deliberate gestures, and deposited it with care in her closet. There was a rock-like center to his movements, a sense of perfect gravitation. His emotions, his thoughts revolved around a fixed center like a well-organized planetary system.

The trust she felt in his evenly modulated voice, both warm

and light, in his harmonious manners never sudden or violent, in his thoughts which he weighed before articulating, in his insights which were moderate, was so great that it resembled a total abandon of herself to him, a total giving.

In trust she flowed out to him, grateful and warm.

She placed him apart from other men, distinct and unique. He held the only fixed position in the fluctuations of her feelings.

"Tired, my little one?" he said. "Was it a hard trip? Was it a success?"

He was only five years older than she was. He was thirty-five and had gray hairs on his temples, and he talked to her as if he were her father. Had he always talked in this tone to her? She tried to remember Alan as a very young man. When she was twenty years old and he twenty-five. But she could not picture him any differently than at this moment. At twenty-five he stood the same way, he spoke the same way, and even then he said: "My little one."

For a moment, because of the caressing voice, the acceptance and the love he showed, she was tempted to say: "Alan, I am not an actress. I was not playing a part on the road. I never left New York, it was all an invention. I stayed in a hotel, with . . ."

She held her breath. That was what she was always doing, holding her breath so that the truth would never come out, at any time, not here with Alan, and not in the hotel room with a lover who had asked questions about Alan. She held her breath to choke the truth, made one more effort to be the very actress she denied being, to act the part she denied acting, to describe this trip she had not taken, to recreate the woman who had been away for eight days, so that the smile would not vanish from Alan's face, so that his trustingness and happiness would not be shattered.

During the brief suspense of her breathing she was able to make the transition. It was an actress who stood before Alan now, re-enacting the past eight days.

"The trip was tiring, but the play went well. I hated the role at first, as you know. But I began to feel for Madame Bovary, and the second night I played it well, I even understood her particular kind of voice and gestures. I changed myself completely. You know how tension makes the voice higher and thinner, and nervousness increases the number of gestures?"

"What an actress you are," said Alan. "You're still doing it! You've entered into this woman's part so thoroughly you can't get out of it! You're actually making so many more gestures than you ever did, and your voice has changed. Why do you keep covering your mouth with your hand? As if you were holding back something you were strongly tempted to say?"

"Yes, that is what *she* was doing. I must stop. I'm so tired, so tired, and I can't stop . . . can't stop being her."

"I want my own Sabina back."

Because Alan had said this was a part she had been playing, because he had said this was not Sabina, not the genuine one, the one he loved, Sabina began to feel that the woman who had been away eight days, who had stayed at a small hotel with a lover, who had been disturbed by the instability of that other relationship, the strangeness of it, into a mounting anxiety expressed in multiple movements, wasted, unnecessary, like the tumult of wind or water, was indeed another woman, a part she had played on the road. The valise, the impermanency, the evanescent quality of the eight days were thus explained. Nothing that had happened had any connection with Sabina herself, only with her profession. She had returned home intact, able to answer his loyalty with loyalty, his trust with trust, his single love with a single love.

"I want my own Sabina back, not this woman with a new strange gesture she had never made before, of covering her face, her mouth with her hand as if she were about to say something she did not want to say or should not say."

He asked more questions. And now that she was moving away from the description of the role she had played into descriptions of a town, a hotel and other people in the cast, she felt this secret, this anguishing constriction tightening her heart, an invisible flush of shame, invisible to others but burning in her like a fever.

It was this shame which dressed her suddenly, permeated her gestures, clouded her beauty, her eyes with a sudden opaqueness. She experienced it as a loss of beauty, an absence of quality.

Every improvisation, every invention to Alan was always followed not by any direct knowledge of this shame, but by a substitution: almost as soon as she had talked, she felt as if her dress had faded, her eyes dimmed, she felt unlovely, unlovable, not beautiful enough, not of a quality deserving to be loved.

Why am I loved by him? Will he continue to love me? His love is for something I am not. I am not beautiful enough, I am not good, I am not good for him, he should not love me, I do not deserve it, shame shame shame for not being beautiful enough, there are other women so much more beautiful, with radiant faces and clear eyes. Alan says my eyes are beautiful, but I cannot see them, to me they are lying eyes, my mouth lies, only a few hours ago it was kissed by another . . . He is kissing the mouth kissed by another, he is kissing eyes which adored another . . . shame . . . shame . . . shame . . . the lies, the lies . . . The clothes he is hanging up for me with such care were caressed and crushed by another, the other was so impatient he crushed and tore at my dress. I had no time to undress. It is this dress he is hanging up lovingly . . . Can I forget yesterday, forget the vertigo, this wildness, can I come home and stay home? Sometimes I cannot bear the quick changes of scene, the quick transitions, I cannot make the changes smoothly, from one relationship to another. Some parts of me tear off like a fragment, fly here and there. I lose vital parts of myself, some part of me stays in that hotel room, a part of me is walking away from this place of haven, a part of me is following another as he walks down the street alone, or perhaps not alone: someone may take my place at his side while I am here, that will be my punishment, and someone will take my place here when I leave. I feel guilty for leaving each one alone, I feel responsible for their being alone, and I feel guilty twice over, towards both men. Wherever I am, I am in many pieces, not daring to bring them all together, anymore than I would dare to bring the two men together. Now I am here where I will not be hurt, for a few days at least I will not be hurt in any way, by any word or gesture . . . but I am not all of me here, only half of me is being sheltered. Well, Sabina, you failed as an actress. You rejected the discipline, the routine, the monotony, the repetitions, any sustained effort, and now you have a role which must be changed every day, to protect one human being from sorrow. Wash your lying eyes and lying face, wear the clothes which stayed in the house, which are his, baptized by his hands, play the role of a whole woman, at least you have always wished to be that, it is not altogether a lie . . .

Alan never understood her eagerness to take a bath, her immediate need to change her clothes, to wash off the old make up.

The pain of dislocation and division abated, the shame dissolved as Sabina passed into Alan's mood of contentment.

At this moment she feels impelled by a force outside of herself to be the woman he demands, desires, and creates. Whatever he says of her, about her, she will fulfill. She no longer feels responsibility for what she has been. There is a modification of her face and body, of her attitudes and her voice. She has become the woman Alan loves.

The feelings which flow through her and which carry her along are of love, protection, devotion. These feelings create a powerful current on which she floats. Because of their strength they have engulfed all her doubts, as in the case of fanatic devotions to a country, a science, an art, when all minor crimes are absolved by the unquestioned value of the aim.

374

A light like a small diamond facet appeared in her eyes, fixed in a narrower precision on her intent. At other times her pupils were dilated, and did not seem to focus on the present, but now their diamond precision was at work on this laborious weaving of life-giving lies, and it gave them a clarity which was even more transparent than that of truth.

Sabina wants to be the woman whom Alan wants her to be.

At times Alan is not certain of what he wishes. Then the stormy, tumultuous Sabina waits in incredible stillness, alert and watchful for signs of his wishes and fantasies.

The new self she offered him, created for him, appeared intensely innocent, newer than any young girl could have been, because it was like a pure abstraction of a woman, an idealized figure, not born of what she was, but of his wish and hers. She even altered her rhythm for him, surrendered her heavy restless gestures, her liking for large objects, large rooms, for timelessness, for caprice and sudden actions. Even her hands which were sturdy, for his sake rested more gently upon objects around her.

"You always wanted to be an actress, Sabina. It makes me happy that you're fulfilling this wish. It consoles me for your absences."

For his pleasure she began to reconstruct the events of the last week of her absence: the trip to Provincetown, the behavior of the cast, the problems in the play, directing errors, the reactions of the public, the night when the fuses burnt out, the night when the sound track broke down.

At the same time she wished she could tell him what had actually happened; she wished she could rest her head upon his shoulder as upon a protective force, a protective understanding not concerned with possession of her but a complete knowledge of her which would include absolution. Wishing he might judge her acts with the same detachment and wisdom he applied to other's acts, wishing he might absolve her as he absolved strangers from a knowledge of their motivations.

Above all she wished for his *absolution* so that she might

sleep deeply. She knew what awaited her instead of sleep: an anxious watch in the night. For after she had reconstructed the events of the last week for Alan's peace of mind, after he had kissed her with gratitude, and with a hunger accumulated during her absence, he fell into a deep sleep in utter abandon and confidence in the night which had brought Sabina back, while Sabina lay awake wondering whether among her inventions there might be one which could be exposed later, wondering whether her description of the Provincetown hotel might be proved false, being based on hearsay. Wondering whether she would remember what she had said about it, and what she had said about the other members of the cast. Wondering if Alan might meet one of the actors in the cast some day and discover Sabina had never worked with them at all.

The night came merely as a dark stage upon which invented scenes took on a greater sharpness than by day. Scenes surrounded by darkness were like the scenes in a dream, heightened, delineated intensely, and all the while suggesting the abysses surrounding the circles of light.

Outside of this room, this bed, there was a black precipice. She had escaped danger for a day, that was all. Other dangers awaited her tomorrow.

At night too she puzzled the mystery of her desperate need of kindness. As other girls prayed for handsomeness in a lover, or for wealth, or for power, or for poetry, she had prayed fervently: let him be kind.

Why should she have had such a need of kindness? Was she a cripple? What if instead she had married a man of violence or a man of cruelty?

At the mere word "cruelty" her heart started to beat feverishly. The enormity of the dangers she had averted was so great she did not even dare picture them. She had desired and obtained kindness. And now that she had found it she risked its loss every day, every hour, on other quests!

Alan slept so peacefully. Even in sleep he maintained a serenity of gesture. The firm design of his nose, mouth and chin, the angular lines of the body, all sculptured from some material of rectitude that would not slacken. In moments of desire even, he did not have the wildness of the eyes, disordered hair of others. He would never grow almost delirious with pleasure or utter sounds not quite human, from the jungle of man's earlier animalism.

Was it this quietism that inspired her trust? He told no lies. What he felt and thought he could tell Sabina. At the thought of confession, of confiding in him, she was almost asleep when out of the darkness the image of Alan appeared vividly and he was sobbing, sobbing desperately as he had at his father's death. This image awakened her with horror, with compassion, and again her feeling was: I must always be on guard, to protect his happiness, always on guard to protect my guardian angel . . .

In the darkness she relived entirely the eight days spent in Provincetown.

She had walked into the dunes in quest of O'Neill's house, and had lost her way. The sand dunes were so white in the sun, so immaculate, that she felt like the first inhabitant at the top of a glacier.

The sea churned at the base as if struggling to drag back the sand into its depths, carrying a little away each time only to replace it at high tide in the form of geological designs, a static sea of crystallized sand waves.

There she stopped and took off her bathing suit to lie in the sun. Drifts of sand were lifted by the wind and deposited over her skin like muslin. She wondered whether if she stayed there long enough it would cover her, and would she disappear in a natural tomb. Immobility always brought this image to her, the image of death, and it was this which impelled her to rise and seek activity. Repose, to her, resembled death.

But here in this moment of warmth and light with her face towards the sky, the sea coiling and uncoiling violently at her feet, she did not fear the image of death. She lay still watching the wind forming sand drawings and felt a momentary suspense from anxiety and fever. Happiness had been defined once as the absence of fever. Then what was it she possessed which was the opposite of fever?

She was grateful that, hypnotized by the sun's reassuring splendor and the sea's incurable restlessness, her own nerves did not coil and spring within her to destroy this moment of repose.

It was at this moment that she heard a song. It was not a casual song anyone might sing walking along the beach. It was a powerful, developed voice with a firm core of gravity, accustomed to vast halls and a large public. Neither the sand nor wind nor sea nor space could attenuate it. It was flung out with assurance, in defiance of them all, a vital hymn of strength equal to the elements.

The man who appeared had a body which was a full match to his voice, a perfect case for this instrument. He had a strong neck, a large head with high brow, wide shoulders and long legs. A full strong box for the vocal cords, good for resonance, thought Sabina, who had not moved, hoping he would walk by without seeing her and without interrupting this song from *Tristan and Isolde*.

As the song continued she found herself in the Black Forest of the German fairytales which she had read so avidly in her childhood. Giant trees, castles, horsemen, all out of proportion in a child's eyes.

The song ascended, swelled, gathered together all the turmoil of the sea, the rutilant gold carnival of the sun, rivalled the wind and flung its highest notes into space like the bridge span of a flamboyant rainbow. And then the incantation broke.

He had seen Sabina.

He hesitated.

378

Her silence as perfectly eloquent as his song, her immobility as flowing an essence of her meaning as his voice had been.

(Later he told her: "If you had spoken then I would have walked away. You had the talent of letting everything else speak for you. It was because you were silent that I came up to you.")

She allowed him to continue his dream.

She watched him walk freely and easily up the sand dune, smiling. His eyes took their color from the sea. A moment ago she had seen the sea as a million diamond eyes and now only two, bluer, colder, approached her. If the sea and the sand and the sun had formed a man to incarnate the joyousness of the afternoon they would have spouted a man like this.

He stood before her, blocking the sun, still smiling as she covered herself. The silence continued to transmit messages between them.

"*Tristan and Isolde* sounded more beautiful here than at the Opera," she said, and donned her bathing suit and her necklace quietly, as if this were the end of a performance of his voice and her body.

He sat down beside her. "There is only one place where it sounds better: the Black Forest itself, where the song was born."

By his accent she knew that he came from there, and that his physical resemblance to the Wagnerian hero was not accidental.

"I sang it there very often. There's an echo there, and I had the feeling the song was being preserved in hidden sources and that it will spring up again long after I am dead."

Sabina seemed to be listening to the echo of his song, and of his description of a place where there was memory, where the past itself was like a vast echo retaining experience; whereas here there was this great determination to dispose of memories and to live only in the present, as if memory were but a cumbersome baggage. That was what he meant, and Sabina understood.

Then her tidal movement caught her again, and she said impatiently: "Let's walk."

"I'm thirsty," he said. "Let's walk back to where I was sitting. I left a bag of oranges."

They descended the sand dunes sliding as if it were a hill of snow and they had been on skis. They walked along the wet sand.

"I saw a beach once where each step you took made the phosphorous sparkle under the feet."

"Look at the sand-peckers," said the singer inaccurately, but Sabina liked his invention, and laughed.

"I came here to rest before my opening at the Opera."

They ate the oranges, swam, and walked again. Only at sundown did they lie on the sand.

She expected a violent gesture from him, in keeping with his large body, heavy arms, muscular neck.

He turned his eyes, now a glacial blue, fully upon her. They were impersonal and seemed to gaze beyond her at all women who had dissolved into one, but who might at any moment again become dissolved into all. This was the gaze Sabina had always encountered in Don Juan, everywhere; it was the gaze she mistrusted. It was the alchemy of desire fixing itself upon the incarnation of all women into Sabina for a moment but as easily by a second process able to alchemize Sabina into many others.

Her identity as the "unique" Sabina loved by Alan was threatened. Her mistrust of his glance made the blood flow cold within her.

She examined his face to see if he divined that she was nervous, that every moment of experience brought on this nervousness, almost paralyzing her.

But instead of a violent gesture he took hold of her finger tips with his smoothly designed hands, as if he were inviting her for an airy waltz, and said: "Your hands are cold."

He caressed the rest of her arm, kissing the nook between the elbows, the shoulders, and said: "Your body is feverishly

380

hot. Have you had too much sun?"

To reassure him she said unguardedly: "Stage fright."

At this he laughed, mockingly, unbelieving, as she had feared he would. (There was only one man who believed she was afraid and at this moment she would have liked to run back to Alan, to run away from this mocking stranger whom she had attempted to deceive by her poise, her expert silences, her inviting eyes. This was too difficult to sustain and she would fail. She was straining, and she was frightened. She did not know how to regain prestige in his eyes, having admitted a weakness which the stranger mockingly disbelieved and which was not in harmony with her provocative behavior. This mocking laughter she was to hear once more when later he invited her to meet his closest friend, his companion in adventure, his brother Don Juan, as suave, as graceful and confident as himself. They had treated her merrily as one of their own kind, the adventuress, the huntress, the invulnerable woman, and it had offended her!)

When he saw she did not share his laughter, he became serious, lying at her side, but she was still offended and her heart continued to beat loudly with stage fright.

"I have to go back," she said, rising and shaking the sand off with vehemence.

With immediate gallantry he rose, denoting a long habit of submission to women's whims. He rose and dressed himself, swung his leather bag over his shoulder and walked beside her, ironically courteous, impersonal, unaffected.

After a moment he said: "Would you like to meet me for dinner at the Dragon?"

"Not for dinner but later, yes. About ten or eleven."

He again bowed, ironically, and walked with cool eyes beside her. His nonchalance irritated her. He walked with such full assurance that he ultimately always obtained his desire, and she hated this assurance, she envied it.

When they reached the beach town everyone turned to gaze at them. The Bright Messenger, she thought, from the Black

Forest of the fairytales. Breathing deeply, expanding his wide chest, walking very straight, and then this festive smile which made her feel gay and light. She was proud of walking at his side, as if bearing a trophy. As a woman she was proud in her feminine vanity, in her love of conquest. This vainglorious walk gave her an illusion of strength and power: she had charmed, won, such a man. She felt heightened in her own eyes, while knowing this sensation was not different than drunkenness, and that it would vanish like the ecstasies of drink, leaving her the next day even more shaky, even weaker at the core, deflated, defeated, possessing nothing within herself.

The core, where she felt a constant unsureness, this structure always near collapse, which could so easily be shattered by a harsh word, a slight, a criticism, which floundered before obstacles, was haunted by the image of catastrophe, by the same obsessional forebodings which she heard in Ravel's Waltz.

The waltz leading to catastrophe: swirling in spangled airy skirts, on polished floors, into an abyss, the minor notes simulating lightness, a mock dance, the minor notes always recalling that man's destiny was ruled by ultimate darkness.

This core of Sabina's was temporarily supported by an artificial beam, the support of vanity's satisfaction when this man so obviously handsome walked by her side, and everyone who saw him envied the woman who had charmed him.

When they separated he bowed over her hand in a European manner, with mock respect, but his voice was warm when he repeated: "You will come?" When none of his handsomeness, perfection and nonchalance had touched her, this slight hesitation did. Because he was for a moment uncertain, she felt him for a moment as a human being, a little closer to her when not altogether invulnerable.

She said: "Friends are waiting for me."

Then a slow to unfold but utterly dazzling smile illumined his face as he stood to his full height and saluted: "Change of guards at Buckingham Palace!"

By his tone of irony she knew he did not expect her to be

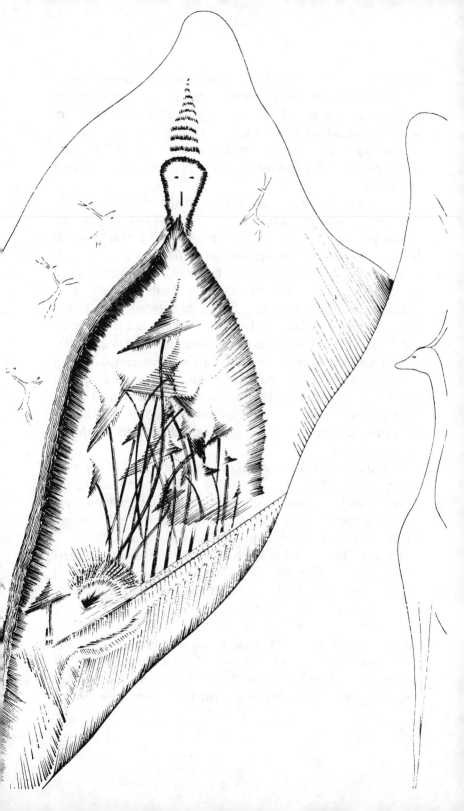

meeting friends but most probably another man, another lover.

He would not believe that she wanted to return to her room to wash the sand out of her hair, to put oil over her sunburnt skin, to paint a fresh layer of polish on her nails, to relive every step of their encounter as she lay in the bath, in her habit of wanting to taste the intoxications of experience not once but twice.

To the girl she shared the room with she owed but a slight warning that she would be out that evening, but on this particular evening there was a third person staying with them for just one night, and this woman was a friend of Alan as well as hers; so her departure would be more complicated. Once more she would have to steal ecstasy and rob the night of its intoxications. She waited until they were both asleep and went silently out, but did not go towards the main street where all her friends the artists would be walking and who might offer to join her. She leaped over the wharf's railing and slid down the wooden pole, scratching her hands and her dress against the barnacles, and leaped on to the beach. She walked along the wet sand towards the most brightly lighted of the wharves where the Dragon offered its neon-lighted body to the thirsty night explorers.

None of her friends could afford to come there, where even the piano had discarded its modest covering and added the dance of its bare inner mechanism to the other motions, extending the pianist's realm from abstract notes to a disciplined ballet of reclining chess figures on agitated wires.

To reach the nightclub she had to climb large iron ladders planted on the glistening poles, on which her dress caught and her hair. She arrived out of breath as if she had been diving from there and were returning after freeing herself from the clasp of the sea weeds. But no one noticed her except Philip, the spotlight being on the singer of cajoling blues.

A flush of pleasure showed even through the deep tan. He held a chair out for her and bent over to whisper: "I was afraid you were not coming. When I passed by your studio at ten o'clock, I didn't see any light, so I walked up and knocked at the window, not too hard, because I don't see well at night, and I was afraid I had made a mistake. There was no answer. I stumbled about in the dark . . . waited . . ."

At the terror that Philip might have awakened her friends, at the danger that had barely been averted, she felt fever mounting, the heat of the blood set off by danger. His handsomeness at night became a drug, and the image of his night-blinded self seeking her, touched her and disarmed her. Her eyes now turned dark and rimmed with coal dust like those of oriental women. The eyelids had a bluish tint, and her eyebrows which she did not pluck, threw shadows which made here eyes' dark glints seem to come from a deeper source than during the day.

Her eyes absorbed the vivid modelling of his features, and the contrast between his strong head and the long fingered hands, hairless, covered by the finest down. He not only caressed her skin along her arm, but seemed to exert a subtle musician's pressure on the concealed nerves of an instrument he knew well, saying: "The beauty of your arm is exactly like that of your body. If I didn't know your body I would want it, just from seeing the shape of your arm."

Desire made a volcanic island on which they lay in a trance, feeling the subterranean whirls lying beneath them, dance floor and table and the magnetic blues uprooted by desire, the avalanches of the body's tremors. Beneath the delicate skin, the tendrils of secret hair, the indentations and valleys of flesh, the volcanic lava flowed, desire incandescent, and where it burned the voices of the blues being sung became a harsh wilderness cry, bird and animal's untamed cry of pleasure and cry of danger and cry of fear and cry of childbirth and cry of wound pain from the same hoarse delta of nature's pits.

The trembling premonitions shaking the hand, the body, made dancing unbearable, waiting unbearable, smoking and talking unbearable. Soon would come the untamable seizure of sensual cannibalism, the joyous epilepsies.

385

They fled from the eyes of the world, the singer's prophetic, harsh, ovarian prologues. Down the rusty bars of ladders to the undergrounds of the night propitious to the first man and woman at the beginning of the world, where there were no words by which to possess each other, no music for serenades, no presents to court with, no tournaments to impress and force a yielding, no secondary instruments, no adornments, necklaces, crowns to subdue, but only one ritual, a joyous, joyous, joyous, joyous impaling of woman on man's sensual mast.

She reopened her eyes to find herself lying at the bottom of a sail boat, lying over Philip's coat gallantly protecting her from sediments, water seepage and barnacles. Philip lies beside her, only his head is above hers, and his feet extend further down than hers. He lies asleep, content, breathing very deeply. She sits up in the moonlight, angry, restless, defeated. The fever had reached its peak, and waned separately from her desire, leaving it unfulfilled, stranded. High fever and no climax—Anger, Anger—at this core which will not melt, while Sabina wills to be like man, free to possess and desire in adventure, to enjoy a stranger. Her body will not melt, will not obey her fantasy of freedom. It cheated her of the adventure she had pursued. The fever, the hope, the mirage, the suspended desire, unfulfilled, would remain with her all night and the next day, burn undimmed within her and make others who saw her say: "How sensual she is!"

Philip awakened and smiled gratefully. He had given and taken and was content.

Sabina lay thinking she would not see him again, and wishing desperately she might. He was talking about his childhood and his love of snow. He had loved to ski. Then without transition, some image came to disturb this idyllic scene and he said: "Women will never leave me alone."

386

Sabina said: "If you ever want to be with a woman who will not always expect you to make love, come to me. I will understand."

"You're wonderful to say that, Sabina. Women are so offended if you are not always ready and in the mood to play the romantic lover, when you look the part."

It was her words which brought him back the next day when he had confessed to her that he never spent more than one evening with a woman for: "After that she begins to demand too much, to lay claims . . ."

He came and they walked to the sand dunes. He was talkative but always impersonal. Secretly Sabina hoped he might tell her something that would melt the unmeltable sensual core, that she might respond, that he might break through her resistance.

Then the absurdity of her expectation amazed her: seeking another kind of fusion because she had failed to achieve the sensual one, when what she wanted was only the sensual one, to reach man's freedom in adventure, to arrive at enjoyment without dependence which might liberate her from all her anxieties connected with love.

For a moment she saw her love anxieties as resembling those of a drug addict, of alcoholics, of gamblers. The same irresistible impulse, tension, compulsion and then depression following the yielding to the impulse, revulsion, bitterness, depression, and the compulsion once more . . .

Three times the sea, the sun, and the moon witnessed and mocked her efforts at truly possessing Philip, this adventure, this man whom other women so envied her.

And now in the city, in autumn purple, she was walking towards his apartment after a telephone call from him. The bells on the Indian ring he had given her were tinkling merrily.

She remembered her fear that he would vanish with the summer. He had not asked for her address. The day before he left, a friend arrived. He had spoken of this woman with reserve. Sabina had divined that she was the essential one. She was a singer, he had taught her, music bound them. Sabina heard in his voice a tone of respect which she did not like to inspire, but which was like Alan's tone when he talked about her. For this other woman Philip had the sympathy Alan had for Sabina. He spoke tenderly of her health not being good, to Sabina who had kept so fiercely the secret of being cold when they swam, or tired when they walked too long, or feverish in too much sun.

Sabina invented a superstitious game: if this woman were beautiful, then Sabina would not see him again. If not, if she was the steadfastly loved one, then Sabina could be the whim, the caprice, the drug, the fever.

When Sabina saw her she was amazed. The woman was not beautiful. She was pale, self-effacing. But in her presence Philip walked softly, happy, subdued in his happiness, less erect, less arrogant, but gently serene. No streaks of lightning in his ice-blue eyes, but a soft early morning glow.

And Sabina knew that when he would want fever he would call her.

Whenever she felt lost in the endless deserts of insomnia she would take up the labyrinthian thread of her life again from the beginning to see if she could find at what moment the paths had become confused.

Tonight she remembered the moon-baths, as if this had marked the beginning of her life instead of the parents, school, birthplace. As if they had determined the course of her life rather than inheritance or imitation of the parents. In the moon-baths, perhaps, lay the secret motivation of her acts.

At sixteen Sabina took moon-baths, first of all because everyone else took sun-baths, and second, she admitted, because she had been told it was dangerous. The effect of moon-baths was unknown, but it was intimated that it might be the opposite of the sun's effect.

The first time she exposed herself she was frightened. What would the consequences be? There were many taboos against gazing at the moon, many old legends about the evil effects of falling asleep in moonlight. She knew that the insane found the full moon acutely disturbing, that some of them regressed to animal habits of howling at the moon. She knew that in astrology the moon ruled the night life of the unconscious, invisible to consciousness.

But then she had always preferred the night to the day.

Moonlight fell directly over her bed in the summer. She lay naked in it for hours before falling asleep, wondering what its rays would do to her skin, her hair, her eyes, and then deeper, to her feelings.

By this ritual it seemed to her that her skin acquired a different glow, a night glow, an artificial luminousness which showed its fullest effulgence only at night, in artificial light. People noticed it and asked her what was happening. Some suggested she was using drugs.

It accentuated her love of mystery. She meditated on this planet which kept half of itself in darkness. She felt related to it because it was the planet of lovers. Her attraction for it, her desire to bathe in its rays, explained her repulsion for home, husband and children. She began to imagine she knew the life which took place on the moon. Homeless, childless, free lovers, not even tied to each other.

The moon-baths crystallized many of Sabina's desires and orientations. Up to that moment she had only experienced a simple rebellion against the lives which surrounded her, but now she began to see the forms and colors of other lives, realms much deeper and stranger and remote to be discovered, and that her denial of ordinary life had a purpose: to send her off like a rocket into other forms of existence. Rebellion was merely the electric friction accumulating a charge of power that would launch her into space.

She understood why it angered her when people spoke of

life as one life. She became certain of myriad lives within herself. Her sense of time altered. She felt acutely and with grief the shortness of life's physical span. Death was terrifyingly near, and the journey towards it, vertiginous; but only when she considered the lives around her, accepting their time tables, clocks, measurements. Everything they did constricted time. They spoke of one birth, one childhood, one adolescence, one romance, one marriage, one maturity, one aging, one death, and then transmitted the monotonous cycle to their children. But Sabina, activated by the moon-rays, felt germinating in her the power to extend time in the ramifications of myriad lives and loves, to expand the journey to infinity, taking immense and luxurious detours as the courtesan depositor of multiple desires. The seeds of many lives, places, of many women in herself were fecundated by the moon-rays because they came from that limitless night life which we usually perceive only in our dreams, containing roots reaching for all the magnificences of the past, transmitting the rich sediments into the present, projecting them into the future.

In watching the moon she acquired the certainty of the expansion of time by depth of emotion, range and infinite multiplicity of experience.

It was this flame which began to burn in her, in her eyes and skin, like a secret fever, and her mother looked at her in anger and said: "You look like a consumptive." The flame of accelerated living by fever glowed in her and drew people to her as the lights of night life drew passersby out of the darkness of empty streets.

When she did finally fall asleep it was the restless sleep of the night watchman continuously aware of danger and of the treacheries of time seeking to cheat her by permitting clocks to strike the passing hours when she was not awake to grasp their contents.

She watched Alan closing the windows, watched him light the lamps and fasten the lock on the door which led to the porch. All the sweet enclosures, and yet Sabina, instead of slipping languorously into the warmth and gentleness, felt a sudden restlessness like that of a ship pulling against its moorings.

The image of the ship's cracking, restless bones arrived on the waves of Debussy's "Ile Joyeuse" which wove around her all the mists and dissolutions of remote islands. The notes arrived charged like a caravan of spices, gold mitres, ciboriums and chalices bearing messages of delight setting the honey flowing between the thighs, erecting sensual minarets on men's bodies as they lay flat on the sand. Debris of stained glass wafted up by the seas, splintered by the radium shafts of the sun and the waves and tides of sensuality covered their bodies, desires folding in every lapping wave like an accordion of aurora borealis in the blood. She saw an unreachable dance at which men and women were dressed in rutilant colors, she saw their gaiety, their relations to each other as unparalleled in splendor.

By wishing to be there where it was more marvellous she made the near, the palpable seem like an obstruction, a delay to the more luminous life awaiting her, the incandescent personages kept waiting.

The present—Alan, with his wrists hidden in silky brown hair, his long neck always bending towards her like a very tree of faithfulness—was murdered by the insistent, whispering, interfering dream, a compass pointing to mirages flowing in the music of Debussy like an endless beckoning, alluring, its voices growing fainter if she did not listen with her whole being, its steps lighter if she did not follow, its promises, its sighs of pleasure growing clearer as they penetrated deeper regions of her body directly through the senses bearing on airy canopies all the fluttering banners of gondolas and divertissements.

Debussy's "Clair de Lune" shone on other cities . . . She

wanted to be in Paris, the city propitious to lovers, where policemen smiled absolution and taxi drivers never interrupted a kiss . . .

Debussy's "Clair de Lune" shone upon many stranger's faces, upon many Iles Joyeuses, music festivals in the Black Forest, marimbas praying at the feet of smoking volcanoes, frenzied intoxicating dances in Haiti, and she was not there. She was lying in a room with closed windows under a lamplight.

The music grew weary of calling her, the black notes bowed to her inertia ironically in the form of a pavanne for a defunct infanta, and dissolved. All she could hear now were the fog horns on the Hudson from ships she would never be able to board.

Sabina emerged a week later dressed in purple and waited for one of the Fifth Avenue buses which allowed smoking. Once seated she opened an overfull handbag and brought out a Hindu ring with minuscule bells on it, and slipped it on in place of her wedding ring. The wedding ring was pushed to the bottom of the bag. Each gesture she made was now accompanied by the tinkling of bells.

At Sixty-Fourth Street she leaped out of the bus before it had entirely stopped and her walk had changed. She now walked swiftly, directly, with a power and vigor to her hips. She walked with her whole foot flat on the ground as the Latins and the Negroes do. Whereas on her way to Alan's her shoulders had been bowed, now they were vigorously thrown back and she was breathing deeply, feeling her breasts pushing against the purple dress.

The ripples of her walk started from the pelvis and hips, a strong undulation like waves of muscles flowing from the feet to the knees, to the hips and back to the waist. She walked with her entire body as if to gain momentum for an event in which her entire body would participate. On her face there was no longer any bewilderment, but a vehemence which caused people to stop and glance at her face as if they had been touched by a magnet.

The evening lights were being turned on, and at this hour Sabina felt like the city, as if all the lights were turned on at once causing a vast illumination. There were lights on her hair, in her eyes, on her nails, on the ripples of her purple dress now turning black.

When she finally reached the apartment, she realized she still did not know whether he lived alone.

He guided her into a room which looked like him and had been arranged for him alone. His skiing trophies hung on the walls: on a Viennese curtain of damask hung a whole army of tin soldiers in army formation. On the piano lay stacks of music in disorder, and in the center of the room, under an umbrella hung open from the ceiling, a partly constructed telescope.

"I want to see the stars with my own handmade telescope. I'm now polishing the glass. It takes a long, long time and a great deal of patience."

"But the umbrella!" exclaimed Sabina laughing.

"The children in the apartment above mine jump around and fine particles of plaster kept falling over my glass, scratching it. The finest grain of dust can spoil a whole day's polishing."

She understood his desire to observe the planets through an instrument made by his own hands. She was eager to see it finished and wanted to know how long it would take. Absorbed by the telescope they behaved like friends, and for a moment abandoned the tense challenges and teasings of conquest.

In this mood they undressed. Philip was playfully inventing endless grimaces, as children do. He loved to make himself grotesque as if he were tired of being always flawlessly handsome. He could turn himself into Frankenstein.

393

Sabina laughed, but uneasily, fearful that if his handsomeness truly vanished she would no longer desire him, aware of the evanescence and fragility of this desire. If the singer of *Tristan and Isolde* singing in the Black Forest of the fairytales disappeared, whom would she desire then?

Then his cool eyes became aware of the intensity of her eyes and they stirred him. His detachment was ignited by the smouldering violence in her. He did not want fires or explosions of feeling in a woman, but he wanted to know it was there. He wanted the danger of touching it off only in the dark depths of her flesh, but without rousing a heart that would bind him. He often had fantasies of taking a woman whose arms were bound behind her back.

Once he had seen a heavy storm cloud settle over a twin-nippled mountain, so closely knit, like an embrace and he had said: "Wonderful copulation, the mountain has no arms!"

Now he grew tired of making faces, and having resumed the perfectly modelled features, he bent over her to pay homage to her body.

And then it happened like a miracle, this pulsation of pleasure unequalled by the most exalted musicians, the summits of perfection in art or science or wars, unequalled by the most regal beauties of nature, this pleasure which transformed the body into a high tower of fireworks gradually exploding into fountains of delight through the senses.

She opened her eyes to contemplate the piercing joy of her liberation: she was free, free as man was, to enjoy without love.

Without any warmth of the heart, as a man could, she had enjoyed a stranger.

And then she remembered what she had heard men say: "Then I wanted to leave."

She gazed at the stranger lying naked beside her and saw him as a statute she did not want to touch again. As a statue he lay far from her, strange to her, and there welled in her something resembling anger, regret, almost a desire to take this gift of herself back, to efface all traces of it, to banish it from her body. She wanted to become swiftly and cleanly detached from him, to disentangle and unmingle what had been fused for a moment, their breaths, skins, exhalations, and body's essences.

She slid very softly out of the bed, dressed with adroit soundlessness while he slept. She tiptoed to the bathroom.

On the shelf she found face powder, comb, lipstick in shell rose wrappings. She smiled at them. Wife? Mistress? How good it was to contemplate these objects without the lightest tremor of regret, envy or jealousy. That was the meaning of freedom. Free of attachment, dependency and the capacity for pain. She breathed deeply and felt she had found this source of pleasure for good. Why had it been so difficult? So difficult that she had often simulated this pleasure?

While combing her hair and repainting her eyelashes, she enjoyed this bathroom, this neutral zone of safety. While moving between men, lovers, she always entered with pleasure a natural safety zone (in the bus, in the taxi, on the way from one to another, at this moment the bathroom) safe from grief. If she had loved Philip, how each one of these objects—face powder, hair pins, comb—each one would have hurt her!

(He is not to be trusted. I am only passing by. I am on my way to another place, another life, where he cannot even find me, claim me. How good not to love; I remember the eyes of the woman who met Philip at the beach. Her eyes were in a panic as she looked at me. She wondered if I were the one who would take him away. And how this panic disappeared at the tone of Philip's voice as he introduced her: "Meet Doña Juana." The woman had understood the tone of his voice and the fear had vanished from her eyes.)

What new reassurance Sabina felt as she laced her sandals, swirled her cape and smoothed her long, straight hair. She was not only free from danger but free for a quick get-away. That is what she called it. (Philip had observed he had never seen a woman dress so quickly, never seen a woman gather up her belongings as quickly and never forgetting a single one!)

How she had learned to flush love letters down the toilet, to leave no hairs on the borrowed comb, to gather up hair pins, to erase traces of lipstick anywhere, to brush off clouds of face powder.

Her eyes like the eyes of a spy.

Her habits like the habits of a spy. How she lay all her clothes on one chair, as if she might be called away suddenly and must not leave any traces of her presence.

She knew all the trickeries in this war of love.

And her neutral zone, the moment when she belonged to none, when she gathered her dispersed self together again. The moment of non-loving, non-desiring. The moment when she took flight, if the man had admired another woman passing by, or talked too long about an old love, the little offenses, the small stabs, a mood of indifference, a small unfaithfulness, a small treachery, all of them were warnings of possibly larger ones, to be counter-acted by an equal or larger or total unfaithfulness, her own, the most magnificent of counterpoisons, prepared in advance for the ultimate emergencies. She was accumulating a supply of treacheries, so that when the shock came, she would be prepared: "I was not taken unaware, the trap was not sprung on my naivete, on my foolish trustingness. I had already betrayed. To be always ahead, a little ahead of the expected betrayals by life. To be there first and therefore prepared . . ."

When she returned to the room Philip was still asleep. It was the end of the afternoon and the rain sent cooler winds over the bed, but she felt no desire to cover or shelter him, or to give him warmth.

She had only been away five days but because of all the emotions and experiences which had taken place, all the inner expansions and explorations, Sabina felt that she had been away for many years. Alan's image had receded far into the past, and a great fear of complete loss of him assailed her. Five days containing so many changes within her body and feelings lengthened the period of absence, added unmeasurable mileage to her separation from Alan.

Certain roads one took emotionally also appeared on the map of the heart as travelling away from the center, and ultimately leading to exile.

Driven by this mood, she appeared at his home.

"Sabina! I'm so happy. I didn't expect you for another week. What happened? Nothing went wrong?"

He was there. Five days had not altered his voice, the all-enveloping expression of his eyes. The apartment had not changed. The same book was still open by his bed, the same magazines had not yet been thrown away. He had not finished some fruit she had bought the last time she had been there. Her hands caressed the overfull ash trays, her fingers designed rivers of meditation on the coats of dust on the table. Here living was gradual, organic, without vertiginous descents or ascents.

As she stood there the rest of her life appeared like a fantasy. She sought Alan's hand and searched for the familiar freckle on his wrist. She felt a great need to take a bath before he touched her, to wash herself rigorously of other places, other hands, other odors.

Alan had obtained for her, as a surprise, some records of drumming and singing from the Ile Joyeuse. They listened to the drumming which began at first remotely as if playing in a distant village smothered in jungle vines. At first like small children's steps running through dry rushes, and then heavier steps on hollow wood, and then sharp powerful fingers on the drum skins, and suddenly a mass of crackling stumpings, animal skins slapped and knuckled, stirred and pecked so swiftly there was no time for echoes. Sabina saw the ebony and cinnamon bodies through which the structure of the bones never showed, glistening with the sea's wild baths, leaping and dancing as quick as the necklaces of drum beats, in emerald greens, indigo blue, tangerines in all the colors of fruits and flowers, flaming eucalyptus of flesh.

There were places where only the beat of the blood guided

the body, where there was no separation from the speed of wind, the tumult of waves, and the sun's orgies. The voices rich with sap sang joyously . . . cascabel . . . guyabana . . . chinchinegrites . . .

"I wish we could go there together," said Sabina.

Alan looked at her reproachfully as if it hurt him to be obliged to remind her: "I can't leave my work. Later this year perhaps. . ."

Sabina's eyes grew fixed. Alan interpreted it as disappointment and added: "Please be patient, Sabina."

But Sabina's gaze was not transfixed by disappointment. It was the fixation of the visionary. She was watching a mirage take form, birds were being born with new names: "cuchuchito," "Pito real." They perched on trees called "liquidambar," and over her head stretched a roof made of palm leaves tied with reeds. *Later was always too late; later did not exist.* There was only great distance to overcome to reach the inaccessible. The drums had come bearing the smell of cinnamon skins in a dance of heartbeats. They would soon bring an invitation which she would not refuse.

When Alan looked at her face again, her eyelashes had dropped in a simulacrum of obedience. He felt the imminence of departure had been averted by a sudden docility. He did not observe that her quiescence was already in itself a form of absence. She was already inhabiting the Ile Joyeuse.

Perhaps because of this, when she heard drumming, as she walked along McDougall Street she found it natural to stop, to climb down the steps into a cellar room of orange walls and sit on one of the fur-covered drums.

The drummers were playing in complete self-absorption intended for a ritual, seeking their own trances. A smell of spices came from the kitchen and gold earrings danced over the steaming dishes.

The voices started an incantation to Alalle, became the call of birds, the call of animals, rapids falling over rocks, reeds dipping their fingered roots into the lagoon waters. The drums

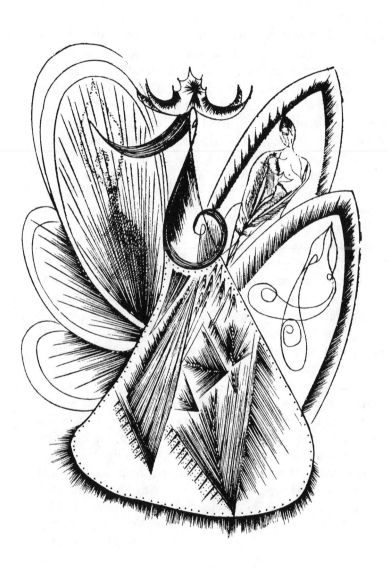

beat so fast the room turned into a forest of tap-dancing foliage, wind chimes cajoling Alalle, the dispenser of pleasure.

Among the dark faces there was one pale one. A grandfather from France or Spain, and a stream of shell-white had been added to the cauldron of ebony, leaving his hair as black but with a reflector depth like that of a black mirror. His head was round, his brow wide, his cheeks full, his eyes soft and brilliant. His fingers on the drum nimble yet fluid, playing with a vehemence which rippled from his hips and shoulders.

Sabina could see him swimming, squatting over a fire by the beach, leaping, climbing trees. No bones showing, only the smoothness of the South Sea islander, muscles strong but invisible as in cats.

The diffusion of color on his face also gave his gestures a nerveless firmness, quite different from the nervous staccato of the other drummers. He came from the island of softness, of soft wind and warm sea, where violence lay in abeyance and exploded only in cycles. The life too sweet, too lulling, too drugging for continuous anger.

When they stopped playing they sat at a table near hers, and talked in an elaborate, formal, sixteenth century colonial Spanish, in the stilted language of old ballads. They practiced an elaborate politeness which made Sabina smile. The stylization imposed by the conquerors upon African depths was like a baroque ornamentation on a thatched palm leaf hut. One of them, the darkest one, wore a stiff white collar and had a long-stemmed umbrella by his chair. He held his hat with great care on his knees, and in order not to disturb the well-ironed lines of his suit he drummed almost entirely from the wrists and moved his head from left to right of the starched collar, separate from his shoulders like that of a Balinese dancer.

She was tempted to disrupt their politeness, to break the polished surface of their placidity with her extravagance. As she shook her cigarette on her vanity case, the Hindu ring given to her by Philip tinkled, and the pale-faced drummer

400

turned his face towards her and smiled, as if this fragile sound were an inadequate response to his drumming.

When he returned to his singing an invisible web had already been spun between their eyes. She no longer watched his hands on the drumskin but his mouth. His lips were full, evenly so, rich but firmly designed, but the way he held them was like an offer of fruit. They never closed tightly or withdrew by the slightest contraction, but remained offered.

His singing was offered to her in this cup of his mouth, and she drank it intently, without spilling a drop of this incantation of desire. Each note was the brush of his mouth upon her. His singing grew exalted and the drumming deeper and sharper and it showered upon her heart and body. Drum - drum - drum - drum - drum - upon her heart, she was the drum, her skin was taut under his hands, and the drumming vibrated through the rest of her body. Wherever he rested his eyes, she felt the drumming of his fingers upon her stomach, her breasts, her hips. His eyes rested on her naked feet in sandals and they beat an answering rhythm. His eyes rested on the indented waist where the hips began to swell out, and she felt possessed by his song. When he stopped drumming he left his hands spread on the drumskin, as if he did not want to remove his hands from her body, and they continued to look at each other and then away as if fearing everyone had seen the desire flowing between them.

But when they danced he changed. The direct, the inescapable way he placed his knees between hers, as if implanting the rigidity of his desire. He held her firmly, so encompassed that every movement they made was made as one body. He held her head against his, with a physical finiteness, as if for eternity. His desire became a center of gravity, a final welding. He was not much taller than she but held himself proudly, and when she raised her eyes into his, his eyes thrust into her very being, so sensually direct that she could not bear their radiance, their claim. Fever shone in his face like moonlight. At the same time a strange wave of anger appeared which she

401

felt and could not understand.

When the dance ended, his bow was a farewell, as finite as his desire had been.

She waited in anguish and bewilderment.

He went back to his singing and drumming but no longer offered them to her.

Yet she knew he had desired her, and why was he destroying it now? Why?

Her anxiety grew so violent she wanted to stop the drumming, stop the others from dancing. But she checked this impulse, sensing it would estrange him. There was his pride. There was this strange mixture of passivity and aggressivity in him. In music he had been glowing and soft and offered; in the dance, tyrannical. She must wait. She must respect the ritual.

The music stopped, he came to her table, sat down and gave her a smile mixed with a contraction of pain.

"I know," he said. "I know . . ."

"You know?"

"I know, but it cannot be," he said very gently. And then suddenly the anger overflowed: "For me, it's everything or nothing. I've known this before . . . a woman like you. Desire. It's desire, but not for *me*. *You don't know me*. It's for my race, it's for a sensual power we have."

He reached for her wrists and spoke close to her face: "It destroys me. Everywhere desire, and in the ultimate giving, withdrawal. Because I am African. What do you know of me? I sing and drum and you desire me. But I'm not an entertainer. I'm a mathematician, a composer, a writer." He looked at her severely, the fullness of his mouth difficult to compress in anger but his eyes lashing: "You wouldn't come to Ile Joyeuse and be my wife and bear me black children and wait patiently upon my Negro grandmother!"

Sabina answered him with equal vehemence, throwing her hair away from her face, and lowering the pitch of her voice until it sounded like an insult: "I'll tell you one thing: if it were only what you say, I've had that, and it didn't hold me, it was not enough. It was magnificent, but it didn't hold me. You're destroying everything, with your bitterness. You're angry, you've been hurt . . ."

"Yes, it's true, I've been hurt, and by a woman who resembled you. When you first came in, I thought it was she . . ."

"My name is Sabina."

"I don't trust you, I don't trust you at all."

But when she rose to dance with him, he opened his arms and as she rested her head on his shoulder he looked down at her face drained of all anger and bitterness.

Mambo's studio was situated in Patchen Place, a street without issue. An iron railing half blocked its entrance, like an entrance to a prison. The houses all being identical added to this impression of an institution where all variations in the human personality would be treated like eccentricities and symptoms of disintegration.

Sabina hated this street. She always considered it a trap. She was certain that the lie detector had seen her enter and would wait at the gate to see her come out. How simple it would be for him to find out who lived there, whom she visited, which house she came out of in the morning.

She imagined him searching every house, reading all the names on the letter boxes: E. E. Cummings, Djuna Barnes, Mambo of Mambo's Nightclub, known to everyone.

At dawn, the lie detector himself would see her come out of the house, holding her cape tightly around her against the morning sharpness, her hair not smoothly combed, and her eyes not fully opened.

Any other street but this one.

Once in the early summer, she had been awakened by a painful tension of the nerves. All the windows were open. It

403

was near dawn. The little street was absolutely silent. She could hear the leaves shivering on the trees. Then a cat wailing. Why had she awakened? Was there any danger? Was Alan watching at the gate?

She heard a woman's voice call out distinctly: "Betty! Betty!" And a voice answered in the muffled tones of half-sleep: "What's the matter?"

"Betty! There's a man hiding in one of the doorways. I saw him sneak in."

"Well . . . what do you want me to do about it? He's just a drunk getting home."

"No, Betty. He was trying to hide when I leaned out of the window. Ask Tom to go and see. I'm frightened."

"Oh, don't be childish. Go to sleep. Tom worked late last night. I can't wake him. The man can't get in anyhow, unless you press the button and let him in!"

"But he'll be there when I go to work. He'll wait there. Call Tom."

"Go to sleep."

Sabina began to tremble. She was certain it was Alan. Alan was waiting down below, to see her come out. For her this was the end of the world. Alan was the core of her life. These other moments of fever were moments in a dream: insubstantial and vanishing as quickly as they came. But if Alan repudiated her, it was the death of Sabina. Her existence in Alan's eyes was her only true existence. To say to herself "Alan cast me off," was like saying: "Alan killed me."

The caresses of the night before were acutely marvellous, like all the multicolored flames from an artful fireworks, bursts of exploded suns and neons within the body, flying comets aimed at all the centers of delight, shooting stars of piercing joys, and yet if she said: "I will stay here and live with Mambo forever," it was like the children she had seen trying to stand under the showers of sparks from the fireworks lasting one instant and covering them with ashes.

She saw two scenes before her eyes: Alan sobbing as he had

sobbed at the death of his father, and this image caused her an intolerable pain. And the second image was Alan angry, as he had never shown himself to her but to others, and this was equally intolerable; both equally annihilating.

It was not dawn yet. What could she do? Her anxiety was so great she could not continue to lie there in silence. How would she explain to Mambo her leaving so early in the morning? Nevertheless she rose quietly after sliding gradually out of bed, and dressed. She was trembling and her clothes slipped awkwardly between her fingers.

She must go and see who was the man hiding in the doorway. She could not bear the suspense.

She left the apartment slowly, noiselessly. She walked barefoot down the stairs, carrying her sandals. When one step creaked, she stopped. Perspiration showed on her eyebrows. A feeling of utter weakness kept her hands trembling. She finally reached the door and saw a man's outline behind the frosted glass of the door. He stood there smoking a pipe as Alan smoked it. Sabina's heart was paralyzed. She knew why she had always hated this street without issue. She stood there fully ten minutes, paralyzed by terror and guilt, by regrets for what she was losing.

"It's the end of the world," she whispered.

As if she were about to die, she summarized her existence: the heightened moments of passion dissolved as unimportant in the face of the loss of Alan as if this love were the core of her existence.

Formulating this, the anguish increased to the point where she could no longer stand still. She pushed the door open violently.

A stranger stood there, with red, blood-shot eyes and unsteady legs. He was frightened by her sudden appearance and muttered, leaning backwards: "Can't find my name on the doorbell, lady, can you help me?"

Sabina looked at him with a wild fury and ran past him, the corner of her cape slapping his face.

Mambo reproached her constantly: "You don't love me."
He felt that she embraced in him, kissed on his lips the music,
the legends, the trees, the drums of the island he came from,
that she sought to possess ardently both his body and his
island, that she offered her body to his hands as much as to
tropical winds, and that the undulations of pleasure resembled
those of swimmers in tropical seas. She savored on his lips
his island spices, and it was from his island too that he had
learned his particular way of caressing her, a silken volup-
tuousness without harshness or violence, like the form of his
island body on which no bone showed.

Sabina did not feel guilty for drinking of the tropics through
Mambo's body: she felt a more subtle shame, that of bringing
him a fabricated Sabina, feigning a single love.

Tonight when the drug of caresses whirled them into space,
free—free for an instant of all the interferences to complete
union created by human beings themselves, she would give
him an undisguised Sabina.

When their still throbbing bodies lay side by side, there
was always silence, and in this silence each one began to
weave the separating threads, to disunite what had been
united, to return to each what had been for a moment equally
shared.

There were essences of caresses which could penetrate the
heaviest insulations, filtering through the heaviest defenses,
but these, so soon after the exchange of desires, could be
destroyed like the seeds of birth.

Mambo proceeded to this careful labor by renewing his
secret accusation against Sabina, that she sought only pleasure,
that she loved in him only the island man, the swimmer and
the drummer, that she never touched in him, or ardently desired, or took into her body, the artist that he most valued in
himself, the composer of music which was a distillation of
the barbaric themes of his origin.

He was a run-away from his own island, seeking awareness,
seeking shading and delicate balances as in the music of

Debussy, and at his side lay Sabina, feverishly dispersing all the delicacies as she demanded: "Drum! Mambo, drum! Drum for me."

Sabina too was slipping out of the burning moment which had almost welded their differences. Her secret self unveiled and naked in his arms must be costumed once more for what she felt in the silence were his withdrawal and silent accusations.

Before he could speak and harm her with words while she lay naked and exposed, while he prepared a judgment, she was preparing her metamorphosis, so that whatever Sabina he struck down she could abandon like a disguise, shedding the self he had seized upon and say: "That was not me."

Any devastating words addressed to the Sabina he had possessed, the primitive one, could not reach her then; she was already halfway out of the forest of their desire, the core already far away, invulnerable, protected by flight. What remained was a costume: it was piled on the floor of his room, and empty of her.

Once in an ancient city in South America, Sabina had seen streets which had been ravaged by an earthquake. Nothing was left but façades, as in Chirico paintings; the façades of granite had remained with doors and windows half unhinged, opening unexpectedly, not upon a household nestled around a hearth, but whole families camping under the sky, protected from strangers only by one wall and door, but otherwise completely free of walls or roofs from the other three sides.

She realized that it was this illimitable space she had expected to find in every lover's room, the sea, the mountains visible all around, the world shut off on one side. A hearth without roof or walls, growing between trees, a floor through which wild flowers pushed to show smiling faces, a column housing stray birds, temples and pyramids and baroque churches in the distance.

But when she saw four walls and a bed pushed against the corner as if it had been flying and had collided against an obstacle, she did not feel as other voyagers: "I have arrived at my destination and can now remove my travelling costume," but: "I have been captured and from here, sooner or later, I must escape."

No place, no human being could bear to be gazed at with the critical eye of the absolute, as if they were obstacles to the reaching of a place or person of greater value created by the imagination. This was the blight she inflicted upon each room when she asked herself: "Am I to live here forever?" This was the blight, the application of the irrevocable, the endless fixation upon a place or relationship. It aged it prematurely, it accelerated the process of decay by staleness. A chemical death ray, this concentrate of time, inflicting the fear of stasis like a consuming ray, deteriorating at the high speed of a hundred years per minute.

At this moment she was aware of her evil, of an invisible crime equal to murder in life. It was her secret sickness, one she believed incurable, unnameable.

Having touched the source of death, she turned back to her source of life; it was only in Stravinsky's *The Firebird* that Sabina found her unerring musical autobiography. It was only here she could find the lost Sabina, her self-revelation.

Even when the first sensual footsteps of the orange bird first appeared, phosphorescent tracks along magnolia forests, she recognized her first sensations, the adolescent stalking of emotion, of its shadow first of all, the echo of its dazzling presence, not yet daring to enter the circle of frenzy.

She recognized the first prologue waltzes, the paintings on glass which might shatter at the touch of warm hands, the moon's haloes around featureless heads, the preparations for festivities and the wild drums announcing feasts of the hearts and senses. She recognized the crimson suspenses, the elevations which heightened the pulse, the wind which thrust its hieroglyphs through the swan necks of the trombones.

The fireworks were mounted on wire bodies waving amorous arms, tiptoeing on the purple tongues of the Holy Ghost, leaping out of captivity, Mercury's wings of orange on pointed torches hurled like javelins into space sparring through the clouds, the purple vulvas of the night.

On many of the evenings Sabina spent with Mambo they did not go anywhere.

On evenings when Sabina had agreed to return to Alan at midnight, her going out with a friend would not have been fatal or too difficult to explain; but there were evenings (when she wanted to spend a few whole nights with her lover) when she had been obliged to say she was travelling, and then when Mambo suggested: "Let's go to a movie," the conflict was started. She did not like to answer: "I don't want Alan to see me." This made her feel like a child being watched, or a woman in a state of subjection, so much did her feelings about Alan seem not like those of a woman wanting to be faithful or loyal but those of an adolescent escaping home for some forbidden games. She could only see Alan as a kind father who might become angry at her lies and punish her. She would also, if she mentioned Alan's rights, be forced to confess to Mambo the division in her affections. At times her lies seemed to her like the most intricate act of protectiveness instead of the greatest treachery. Other days she felt tempted to confess, but would be blocked by the knowledge that even if she were forgiven, Alan would expect then a change of life, and this she knew she was powerless to achieve.

At mention of the movies she would assent, but as if it were a game of chance she were playing, each time that Mambo suggested one movie, or another, or still another, she weighed them not so much for their qualities as movies, but according to what quarter of the city they were shown at, whether or not it was a movie Alan might care to see, whether it was near at hand (knowing Alan was lazy about going uptown). If she were with Alan she would have to try and remember the movies Mambo had seen, or the ones he wanted to see, and knowing how fanatical he was about movies, to gauge even those he might see twice.

Ultimately, like a gambler, she had to question her instinct.

Once seated at the movies her anxiety increased. Alan might have liked this movie enough to want to see it again, or a friend might have persuaded him to make the effort to go uptown. Could Mambo be sitting in the audience while she sat with Alan, could he have seen her walking down the aisle?

Sometimes she discarded her anxiety as nervousness. At other times she was compelled to go to the ladies' room at the very beginning in order to be able to walk slowly and carefully down the aisle examining the crowd from behind before settling down beside Mambo or Alan. This would relieve her anxiety for awhile, until some fragment of the movie story itself would reawaken it, if a lie were pictured, a false situation, exposure. Above all if it were a spy story.

It was when she saw the lives of spies that she realized fully the tension with which she lived every moment, equal to theirs. The fear of committing themselves, of sleeping too soundly, of talking in their sleep, of carelessness of accent or behavior, the need for continuous pretending, quick improvisations of motivations, quick justifiications of their presence here or there.

It seemed to Sabina that she could have offered her services or been of great value in that profession.

I am an international spy in the house of love.

When the anxiety became absolutely intolerable it was transmuted into playfulness. The excitement and risks appeared as a highly flavored, highly humorous game. Then she shifted

410

her position entirely to that of a child escaping surveillance and being amused by her own ingenuity. Then she passed from secrecy to a need of boasting openly of her maneuvres and would describe them with such gaiety that it would shock her hearers. Both anxiety and humor became interchangeable. The pretenses, escapades, trickeries seemed to her in her humorous moods like gay and gallant efforts at protecting everyone from the cruelties of existence for which she was not responsible. Wits and good acting were employed for such justifiable ends: to protect human beings from unbearable truths.

But no one who listened ever shared her sudden gaiety: in their glances she read condemnations. Her laughter seemed a desecration, a mockery of what should be considered tragic. She could see in their eyes the wish that she should fall from this incandescent trapeze on which she walked with the aid of delicate Japanese paper umbrellas, for no guilty party has a right to such adroitness and to live only by its power to balance over the rigidities of life which dictated a choice, according to its taboos against multiple lives. No one would share with her this irony and playfulness against the rigidities of life itself; no one would applaud when she succeeded by her ingenuity in defeating life's limitations.

These moments when she reached a humorous peak above the morass of dangers, the smothering swamps of guilt, were the ones when everyone left her alone, unabsolved; they seemed to be awaiting her hour of punishment after living like a spy in the house of many loves, for avoiding exposure, for defeating the sentinels watching definite boundaries, for passing without passports and permits from one love to another.

Every spy's life had ended in ignominious death.

She stood waiting for the light to change at the crossroad of the beach town.

411

What startled Sabina and made her examine the cyclist waiting beside her was the extraordinary brilliance of his large eyes. They shone with a wet, silver sparkle which was almost frightening because it highlighted the tumultuous panic close to the surface. The molten silver was disquieting, like blinding reflectors on the edge of annihilation by darkness. She was caught in the contagion of this panic, the transparent film of precious stone trembling, about to be sucked in by a hidden cyclone.

It was only later that she notice the delicately chiselled face, the small nose, the mouth modelled by gentleness, unrelated to the deeper disturbance of the eyes, a very young man's mouth, a pure design on the face not yet enslaved by his feelings. These feeling not yet known to him, had not yet acid-bitten through his body. His gestures were free and nimble, the gestures of an adolescent, restless and light. The eyes alone contained all the fever.

He had driven his bicycle like a racing car on an airplane. He had come down upon her as if he did not see trees, cars, people, and almost overlooked the stop signal.

To free herself of the shock his eyes had given her she sought to diminish their power by thinking: "They are just beautiful eyes, they are just passionate eyes, young men rarely have such passionate eyes, they are just more alive than other eyes." But no sooner had she said this to herself to exorcise his spell than a deeper instinct in her added: "He has seen something other young men have not seen."

The red light changed to green; he gave a wild spurt to his pedalling, so swift that she had no time to step on the curb, then just as wildly he stopped and asked her the way to the beach in a breathless voice which seemed to miss a beat. The voice matched the eyes as his tan, healthy, smooth skin did not.

The tone in which he asked directions was as if the beach were a shelter to which he was speeding away from grave dangers.

He was no handsomer than the other young men she had

seen in the place, but his eyes left a memory and stirred in her a wild rebellion against the place. With bitter irony she remembered ruins she had seen in Guatemala, and an American visitor saying: "I hate ruins, I hate dilapidation, tombs." But this new town at the beach was infinitely more static and more disintegrated than the ancient ruins. The clouds of monotony, uniformity, which hung over the new, neat mansions, the impeccable lawns, the dustless garden furniture. The men and women at the beach, all in one dimension, without any magnetism to bring them together, zombies of civilization, in elegant dress with dead eyes.

Why was she here? Waiting for Alan to end his work, Alan who had promised to come. But the longing for other places kept her awake.

She walked and collided against a sign which read: "This is the site of the most costly church on Long Island."

She walked. At midnight the town was deserted. Everyone was at home with bottles from which they hoped to extract a gaiety bottle elsewhere.

"It's the kind of drinking one does at wakes," thought Sabina, looking into the bars, where limp figures clutched at bottles containing oblivion.

At one o'clock she looked for a drug store to buy sleeping pills. They were closed. She walked. At two o'clock she was worn out but still tormented by a place which refused to have feasts on the street, dances, fireworks, orgies of guitars, marimbas, shouts of delight, tournaments of poetry and courtships.

At three o'clock she swung towards the beach to ask the moon why she had allowed one of her night children to become so lost in a place long ago deprived of human life.

A car stopped beside her, and a very tall, white-haired Irish policeman addressed her courteously.

"Can I give you a lift home?"

"I couldn't sleep," said Sabina. "I was looking for a drug store to buy sleeping pills, or aspirin. They're all closed. I was trying to walk until I felt sleepy . . ."

"Boy trouble?" he said, his white-haired head very gallantly held with a suave rectitude which did not come from his policeman's training but from some deeper pride in rectitude itself as the image of man's erotic pride.

But the words so inadequate that they inhibited whatever she would have liked to confide in him, for fear of another adolescent stunted comment. His appearance of maturity was belied by the clumsy words. So she said vaguely: "I'm homesick for all the beach towns I have known, Capri, Mallorca, the south of France, Venice, the Italian Riviera, South America."

"I understand that," he said. "I was homesick when I first came to this country from Ireland."

"A year ago I was dancing on the beach under palm trees. The music was wild, and the waves washed our feet while we danced."

"Yes, I know. I was a bodyguard for a rich man. Everybody sat in the port cafés at night. It was like the Fourth of July every night. Come along, I'll take you to my home. The wife and kids are asleep, but I can give you some aspirin."

She sat beside him. He continued to recall his life as a bodyguard, when he had travelled all around the world. He controlled the car without a dissonance.

"I hate this town," she said vehemently.

He had driven smoothly beside a neat white house. He said: "Wait here," and went into the house.

When he returned he was carrying a glass of water and two aspirin in the palm of his hand. Sabina's nerves began to untangle. She took the water and aspirin obediently.

He turned his powerful flashlight upon a bush in his garden and said: "Look at this!"

In the night she saw flowers of velvet with black hearts and gold eyes.

"What kind of a flower is that?" she asked, to please him.

"Roses of Sharon," he said reverently and with the purest of Irish accents. "They only grow in Ireland and on Long

414

Island."

Sabina's rebellion was subsiding. She felt a tenderness for the roses of Sharon, for the policeman's protectiveness, for his effort to find a substitute for tropical flowers, a little beauty in the present night.

"I'll sleep now," she said. "You can drop me off at the Penny Cottage."

"Oh no," he said, sitting at the wheel. "We'll drive around by the sea until you're so sleepy you can't bear it anymore. You can't sleep, you know, until you find something to be grateful for, you can never sleep when you're angry."

She could not hear very distinctly his long and rambling stories about his life as a bodyguard, except when he said: "There's two of you giving me trouble with homesickness today. The other was a young fellow in the English Air Corps. Aviator all through the war, seventeen when he volunteered. He's grounded now, and he can't take it. He's restless and keeps speeding and breaking traffic laws. The red lights drive him crazy. When I saw what it was, I stopped giving him tickets. He's used to airplanes. Being grounded is tough. I know how he feels."

She felt the mists of sleep rising from the gorund, bearing the perfume of roses of Sharon; in the sky shone the eyes of the grounded aviator not yet accustomed to small scales, to shrunken spaces. There were other human beings attempting vast flights, with a kind policeman as tall as the crusaders watching over them with a glass of water and two aspirins; she could sleep now, she could sleep, she could find her bed with his flashlight shining on the keyhole, his car so smoothly so gently rolling away, his white hair saying sleep . . .

Sabina in the telephone booth. Alan had just said that he was unable to come that day. Sabina felt like sliding down on the floor and sobbing out the loneliness. She wanted to return to New York but he begged her to wait.

415

There were places which were like ancient tombs in which a day was a century of non-existence. He had said: "Surely you can wait another day. I'll be there tomorrow. Don't be unreasonable."

She could not explain that perfect lawns, costly churches, new cement and fresh paint can make a vast tomb without stone gods to admire, without jewels, or urns full of food for the dead, without hieroglyphs to decipher.

Telephone wires only carried literal messages, never the subterranean cries of distress, of desperation. Like telegrams they delivered only final and finite blows: arrivals, departures, births and deaths, but no room for fantasies such as: Long Island is a tomb, and one more day in it would bring on suffocation. Aspirin, Irish policemen, and roses of Sharon were too gentle a cure for suffocation.

Grounded. Just before she slid down to the floor, the bottom of the telephone cabin, the bottom of her loneliness, she saw the grounded aviator waiting to use the telephone. When she came out of the booth he looked distressed again as he seemed to be by everything that happened in time of peace. But he smiled when he recognized her, saying: "You told me the way to the beach."

"You found it? You liked it?"

"A little flat for my taste. I like rocks and palm trees. Got used to them in India, during the war."

War as an abstraction had not yet penetrated Sabina's consciousness. She was like the communion seekers who received religion only in the form of a wafer on the tongue. War as a wafer placed on her tongue directly by the young aviator came suddenly very close to her, and she saw that if he shared with her his contempt for the placidities of peace it was only to take her straight into the infernal core of war. That was his world. When he said: "Get your bicycle then, and I'll show you a better beach further on . . ." it was not only to escape from fashionable reclining figures on the beach, from golf players and human barnacles glued to damp bar flanks, it was

416

to bicycle into his inferno. As soon as they started to walk along the beach, he began to talk:

"I've had five years of war as a rear gunner. Been to India a couple of years, been to North Africa, slept in the desert, crashed several times, made about one hundred missions, saw all kinds of things . . . Men dying, men yelling when they're trapped in burning planes. Their arms charred, their hands like claws of animals. The first time I was sent to the field after a crash . . . the smell of burning flesh. It's sweet and sickening, and it sticks to you for days. You can't wash it off. You can't get rid of it. It haunts you. We had good laughs, though, laughs all the time. We laughed plenty. We would steal prostitutes and push them into the beds of the men who didn't like women. We had drunks that lasted several days. I liked that life. India. I'd like to go back. This life here, what people talk about, what they do, think, bores me. I liked sleeping in the desert. I saw a black woman giving birth . . . She worked on the fields carrying dirt for a new airfield. She stopped carrying dirt to give birth under the wing of the plane, just like that, and then bound the kid in some rags and went back to work. Funny to see the big plane, so modern, and this half naked black woman giving birth and then continuing to carry dirt in pails for an airfield. You know, only two of us came back alive of the bunch I started with. We played pranks, though. My buddies always warned me: 'Don't get grounded; once you're grounded you're done for.' Well, they grounded me too. Too many rear gunners in the service. I didn't want to come home. What's civilian life? Good for old maids. It's a rut. It's drab. Look at this: the young girls giggle, giggle at nothing. The boys are after me. Nothing ever happens. They don't laugh hard, and they don't yell. They don't get hurt, and they don't die, and they don't laugh either."

Always something in his eyes which she could not read, something he had seen but would not talk about.

"I like you because you hate this place, and because you don't giggle," he said taking her hand with gentleness.

They walked endlessly, tirelessly, along the beach, until there were no more houses, no more cared-for gardens, no more people, until the beach became wild and showed no footsteps, until the debris from the sea lay "like a bombed museum," he said.

"I'm glad I found a woman who walks my stride as you do," he said. "And who hates what I hate."

As they bicycled homeward he looked elated, his smooth skin flushed with sun and pleasure. The slight trembling of his gestures had vanished.

The fireflies were so numerous they flew into their faces.

"In South America," said Sabina, "the women wear fireflies in their hair, but fireflies stop shining when they go to sleep so now and then the women have to rub the fireflies to keep them awake."

John laughed.

At the door of the cottage where she stayed, he hesitated. He could see it was a rooming house in a private family's jurisdiction. She made no movement but fixed her enlarged, velvet-pupilled eyes on his and held them, as if to subdue the panic in them.

He said in a very low voice: "I wish I could stay with you." And then bent over to kiss her with a fraternal kiss, missing her mouth.

"You can if you wish."

"They will hear me."

"You know a great deal about war," said Sabina, "but I know a great deal about peace. There's a way you can come in and they will never hear you."

"Is that true?" But he was not reassured and she saw that he had merely shifted his mistrust of the critical family to mistrust of her knowledge of intrigue which made her a redoubtable opponent.

She was silent and made a gesture of abdication, starting to run towards the house. It was then he grasped her and kissed her almost desperately, digging his nervous, lithe fingers into

418

her shoulders, into her hair, grasping her hair as if he were drowning, to hold her head against his as if she might escape his grasp.

"Let me come in with you."

"Then take off your shoes," she whispered.

He followed her.

"My room is on the first floor. Keep in step with me as we go up the stairs; they creak. But it will sound like one person."

He smiled.

When they reached her room, and she closed the door, he examined his surroundings as if to assure himself he had not fallen into an enemy trap.

His caresses were so delicate that they were almost like a teasing, an evanescent challenge which she feared to respond to as it might vanish. His fingers teased her, and withdrew when they had aroused her, his mouth teased her and then eluded hers, his face and body came so near, espoused her every limb and then slid away into the darkness. He would seek every curve and nook he could exert the pressure of his warm slender body against and suddenly lie still, leaving her in suspense. When he took her mouth he moved away from her hands, when she answered the pressure of his thighs, he ceased to exert it. Nowhere would he allow a long enough fusion, but tasting every embrace, every area of her body and then deserting it, as if to ignite only and then elude the final welding. A teasing, warm, trembling, elusive short circuit of the senses as mobile and restless as he had been all day, and here at night, with the street lamp revealing their nudity but not his eyes, she was roused to an almost unbearable expectation of pleasure. He had made of her body a bush of roses of Sharon, exfoliating pollen, each prepared for delight.

So long delayed, so long teased that when possession came it avenged the waiting by a long, prolonged, deep thrusting ecstasy.

The trembling passed into her body. She had amalgamated his anxieties, she had absorbed his delicate skin, his dazzling eyes.

The moment of ecstasy had barely ended when he moved away and he murmured: Life is flying, flying.

"This is flying," said Sabina. But she saw his body lying there no longer throbbing, and knew she was alone in her feeling, that this moment contained all the speed, all the altitude, all the space she wanted.

Almost immediately he began to talk in the dark, about burning planes, about going out to find the fragments of the living ones, to check on the dead.

"Some die silent," he said. "You know by the look in their eyes that they are going to die. Some die yelling, and you have to turn your face away and not look into their eyes. When I was being trained, you know, the first thing they told me: 'Never look into a dying man's eyes'."

"But you did," said Sabina.

"No, I didn't, I didn't."

"But I know you did. I can see it in your eyes; you did look into dying men's eyes, the first time perhaps . . ."

She could see him so clearly, at seventeen, not yet a man, with the delicate skin of a girl, the finely carved features, the small straight nose, the mouth of a woman, a shy laugh, something very tender about the whole face and body, looking into the eyes of the dying.

"The man who trained me said: 'Never look into the eyes of the dying or you'll go mad.' Do you think I'm mad? Is that what you mean?"

"You're not mad. You're very hurt, and very frightened, and very desperate, and you feel you have no right to live, to enjoy, because your friends are dead or dying, or flying still. Isn't that it?"

"I wish I were there now, drinking with them, flying, seeing new countries, new faces, sleeping in the desert, feeling you may die any moment and so you must drink fast, and fight hard, and laugh hard. I wish I were there now, instead of here, being bad."

420

"Being bad?"

"This is being bad, isn't it? You can't say it isn't, can you?"

He slipped out of bed and dressed. His words had destroyed her elation. She covered herself up to her chin with the sheet and lay silent.

When he was ready, before he gathered up his shoes, he bent over her, and in the voice of a tender young man playing at being a father he said: "Would you like me to tuck you in before I leave?"

"Yes, yes," said Sabina, her distress melting. "Yes," she said, with gratitude not for the gesture of protectiveness, but because if he considered her bad in his own vision, he would not have tucked her in. *One does not tuck in a bad woman.* And surely this gesture meant that perhaps he would see her again.

He tucked her in gently and with all the neatness of a flyer's training, using the deftness of long experience with camping. She lay back accepting this, but what he tucked in so gently was not a night of pleasure, a body satiated, but a body in which he had injected the poison which was killing him, the madness of hunger, guilt and death by proxy which tormented him. He had injected into her body his own venomous guilt for living and desiring. He had mingled poison with every drop of pleasure, a drop of poison in every kiss, every thrust of sensual pleasure the thrust of a knife killing what he desired, killing with guilt.

The following day Alan arrived, his equable smile and equable temper unchanged. His vision of Sabina unchanged. Sabina had hoped he would exorcise the obsession which had enslaved her the night before, but he was too removed from her chaotic despair, and his extended hand, his extended love was uneual to the power of what was dragging her down.

421

The sharp, the intense moment of pleasure which had taken possession of her body, and the sharp intense poison amalgamated with it.

She wanted to rescue John from a distortion she knew led to madness. She wanted to prove to him that his guilt was a distortion, that his vision of her and desire as bad, and of his hunger as bad, was a sickness.

The panic, the hunger and terror of his eyes had passed into her. She wished she had never looked into his eyes. She felt a desperate need to abolish his guilt, the need of rescuing him because for a reason she could not fathom, she had sunk with him into the guilt; she had to rescue him and herself. He had poisoned her, transmitted his doom to her. She would go mad with him if she did not rescue him and alter his vision.

If he had not tucked her in she might have rebelled against him, hated him, hated his blindness. But this act of tenderness had abolished all defenses: he was blind in error, frightened and tender, cruel and lost, and she was all these with him, by him, through him.

She could not even mock at his obsession with flying. His airplanes were not different from her relationships, by which she sought other lands, strange faces, forgetfulness, the unfamiliar, the fantasy and the fairytale.

She could not mock his rebellion against being grounded. She understood it, experienced it each time that, wounded, she flew back to Alan. If only he had not tucked her in, not as a bad woman, but as the child, the child he was in a terrifying, confusing world. If only he had left brutally, projecting his shame on her as so often woman bore the brunt of man's shame, shame thrown at her in place of stones, for seducing and tempting. Then she could have hated him, and forgotten him, but because he had tucked her in, he would come back. He had not thrown his shame at her, he had not said: "You're bad." One does not tuck in a bad woman.

But when they met accidentally, and he saw her walking beside Alan, at this moment, in the glance he threw at her,

Sabina saw that he had succeeded in shifting the shame and that now what he felt was: *"You're* a bad woman," and that he would never come back to her. Only the poison remained, without hope of the counter-poison.

Alan left, and Sabina stayed with the hope of seeing John again. She sought him vainly at bars, restaurants, movie houses and at the beach. She inquired at the place where he rented his bicycle: they had not seen him but he still had his bicycle.

In desperation she inquired at the house where he rented a room. The room was paid for the next week, but he had not been there for three days and the woman was concerned because John's father had been telephoning every day.

The last time he had been seen was at the bar, with a group of strangers who had driven away with him.

Sabina felt she should return to New York and forget him, but his eager face and the distress in his eyes made this act seem one of desertion.

At other moments the pleasure he had given her ignited her body like flowing warm mercury darting through the veins. The memory of it flowed through the waves when she swam, and the waves seemed like his hands, or the form of his body in her hands.

She fled from the waves and his hands. But when she lay on the warm sand, it was his body again on which she lay; it was his dry skin and his swift elusive movements slipping through her fingers, shifting beneath her breasts. She fled from the sand of his caresses.

But when she bicycled home, she was racing him, she heard his merry challenges, faster—faster—faster in the wind, his face pursued her in flight or she pursued his face.

That night she raised her face to the moon, and the gesture awakened the pain, because to receive his kiss she had had to raise her face this way, but with the support of his two hands. Her mouth opened to receive his kiss once more but closed on emptiness. She almost shouted out with pain, shouted at the moon, the deaf, impassible goddess of desire shining down mockingly at an empty night, an empty bed.

She decided to pass once more by his house, although it was late, although she dreaded to see once more the empty dead face of his window.

His window was alight and open!

Sabina stood under it and whispered his name. She was hidden by a bush. She dreaded that anyone else in the house should hear her. She dreaded the eyes of the world upon a woman standing under a young man's window.

"John! John!"

He leaned out of the window, his hair tousled, and even in the moonlight she could see his face was burning and his eyes hazy.

"Who's there?" he said, always with the tone of a man at war, fearing ambush.

"Sabina. I just wanted to know . . . Are you all right?"

"Of course I'm all right. I was in the hospital."

"The hospital?"

"A bout of malaria, that's all."

"Malaria?"

"I get it, when I drink too much . . ."

"Will I see you tomorrow?"

He laughed softly: "My father is coming to stay with me."

"We won't be able to see each other then. I'd better return to New York."

"I'll call you when I get back."

"Will you come down and kiss me goodnight?"

He hesitated: "They will hear me. They will tell my father."

"Goodbye, goodnight . . ."

"Goodbye," he said, detached, cheerful.

But she could not leave Long Island. It was as if he had thrown a net around her by the pleasure she wanted again, by his creation of a Sabina she wanted to erase, by a poison he alone had the cure for, of a mutual guilt which only an act of love could transmute into something else than a one-night encounter with a stranger.

424

The moon mocked her as she walked back to her empty bed. The moon's wide grin which Sabina had never noticed before, never before its mockery of this quest of love which she influenced. *I understand his madness, why does he run away from me? I feel close to him, why does he not feel close to me, why doesn't he see the resemblance between us, between our madness. I want the impossible, I want to fly all the time, I destroy ordinary life, I run towards all the dangers of love as he ran towards all the dangers of war. He runs away, war is less terrifying to him than life . . .*

John and the moon left this madness unexorcised. No trace of it was revealed except when she was taunted:

"Aren't you interested in war news, don't you read the papers?"

"I *know* war, I know all about war."

"You never seem very close to it."

(*I slept with war, all night I slept with war once. I received deep war wounds into my body, as you never did, a feat of arms for which I will never be decorated!*)

In the multiple peregrinations of love, Sabina was quick to recognize the echoes of larger loves and desires. The large ones, particularly if they had not died a natural death, never died completely and left reverberations. Once interrupted, broken artificially, suffocated accidentally, they continued to exist in separate fragments and endless smaller echoes.

A vague physical resemblance, an almost similar mouth, a slightly similar voice, some particle of the character of Philip, or John, would emigrate to another, to whom she recognized immediately in a crowd, at a party, by the erotic resonance it reawakened.

The echoes struck at first through the mysterious instrumentation of the senses which retained sensations as instruments retain a sound after being touched. The body remained vulnerable to certain repetitions long after the mind believed it had made a clear, a final severance.

A similar design of a mouth was sufficient to retransmit the interrupted current of sensations, to recreate a contact by way of the past receptivity, like a channel conducting perfectly only a part of the former ecstasy through the channel of the senses arousing vibrations and sensibilities formerly awakened by a total love or total desire for the entire personality.

The senses created river beds of responses formed in part from the sediments, the waste, the overflow from the original experience. A partial resemblance could stir what remained of the imperfectly rooted-out love which had not died a natural death.

Whatever was torn out of the body, as out of the earth, cut, violently uprooted, left such deceptive, such lively roots below the surface, all ready to bloom again under an artificial association, by a grafting of sensation, given new life through this graft of memory.

Out of the loss of John, Sabina retained such musical vibration below visibility which made her insensitive to men totally different from John and prepared her for a continuation of her interrupted desire for John.

When she saw the slender body of Donald, the same small nose, the head carried on a long-stemmed neck, the echo of the old violent emotions was strong enough to appear like a new desire.

She did not observe the differences, that Donald's skin was even more transparent, his hair silkier, that he did not spring, but glided, dragging his feet a little, that his voice was passive, indolent, slightly whining.

At first Sabina thought he was gently clowning by his parodies of women's feathery gestures, by a smile so deliberately seductive imitating the corolla's involutionary attractions.

She smiled indulgently when he lay down on the couch preparing such a floral arrangement of limbs, head, hands as to suggest a carnal banquet.

She laughed when he trailed his phrases like southern vines, or practiced sudden exaggerated severities as children do when they play charades of the father's absurd arrogances, of the mother's hot-house exudations of charm.

When Sabina crossed the street, she nourished herself upon the gallant smile of the policeman who stopped the traffic for her, she culled the desire of the man who pushed the revolving door for her, she gathered the flash of adoration from the drug clerk: "Are you an actress?" She picked the bouquet of the shoe salesman trying on her shoes: "Are you a dancer?" As she sat in the bus she received the shafts of the sun as a personal, intimate visit. She felt a humorous connivance with the truck driver who had to pull the brakes violently before her impulsive passages, and who did so smiling because it was Sabina and they were glad to see her crossing their vision.

But she considered this feminine sustenance like pollen. To her amazement, Donald, walking beside her, assumed these offerings were intended for him.

He passed what she believed to be from one mimicry to another: the pompous policeman, for which he filled his lungs with air, the sinuosities of the woman walking in front of them, for which he tangoed his hips.

Sabina was still laughing, wondering when the charades would end and the true Donald appear.

At this moment, in front of her at the restaurant table he was ordering with the exaggerated tyranny of the business executive, or he became prim with the salesgirl like a statesman with little time for charm. He ridiculed women in their cycles of periodic irrationality with an exact reproduction of whims, contrariness, and commented on the foibles of fashion with a minute expertness Sabina lacked. He made her doubt her femininity by the greater miniature precision of his miniature interests. His love of small roses, of delicate jewelry seemed more feminine than her barbaric heavy necklaces and her dislike of small flowers and nursery pastel blues.

At any moment, she believed, this playfulness would cease, he would stand more erect and laugh with her at his own absurdities of dress, a shirt the color of her dress, a baroque watch, a woman's billfold, or a strand of hair dyed silver gray on his young luxuriant gold head.

But he continued to assume mock professions, to mock all of them. Above all, he possessed a most elaborate encyclopedia of women's flaws. In this gallery he had most carefully avoided Joan of Arc and other women heroines, Madame Curie and other women of science, the Florence Nightingales, the Amelia Earharts, the women surgeons, the therapists, the artists, the collaborative wives. His wax figures of women were an endless concentrate of puerilities and treacheries.

"Where did you find all these repulsive women?" she asked one day, and then suddenly she could no longer laugh: caricature was a form of hatred.

In his gentleness lay his greatest treachery. His submission and gentleness lulled one while he collected material for future satires. His glance always came from below as if he were still looking up at the monumental figures of the parents from a child's vantage point. These immense tyrants could only be undermined with the subtlest parody: the mother, his mother, with her flurry of feathers and furs, always preoccupied with people of no importance, while he wept with loneliness and fought the incubus of nightmares alone.

She danced, she flirted, she whined, she whirled without devotion to his sorrows. Her caressing voice contained all the tormenting contradictions: the voice read him fairytales, and when he believed them and proceeded to pattern his life after them, this same voice gave an acid bath to all his wishes, longings, desires, and distributed words worse than a slap, a closed door or dessertless dinner.

And so today, with Sabina walking at his side believing she could destroy the corrosive mother by enacting her opposite, by full attentiveness to his secret wishes, not dancing with others, not flirting, never whining, focussing the full search-light of her heart upon him, his eyes did not see her alone, but Sabina and a third woman forever present in a perpetual triangle, a *menage à trois*, in which the mother's figure often stood between them, intercepting the love Sabina desired, translating her messages to Donald in terms of repetitions of early disappointments, early treacheries, all the mother's sins against him.

He kneeled at her feet to relace the sandal which was un-done, an act he performed with the delicacy not of an enam-ored man, but of a child at a statue's feet, of a child intent on dressing woman, adorning her, but not for himself to claim. In performing these adulations he fulfilled a secret love for satin, for feathers, for trinkets, for adornment, and it was a caress not to Sabina's feet but to the periphery of all that he could caress without breaking the ultimate taboo: touching his mother's body.

To touch the silk which enwrapped her, the hair which stemmed from her, the flowers she wore.

Suddenly his face, which had been bent over the task, lifted to her with the expression of a blind man suddenly struck with vision. He explained: "Sabina! I felt a shock all through my body while I tied your sandals. It was like an electric shock."

And then as quickly, his face clouded with the subdued light of filtered emotions, and he returned to his neutral zone: some early, pre-man fin-knowledge of woman, indirect, en-veloping, but without any trace of a passageway for erotic penetration. Brushings, silken radiations, homage of eyes alone, possession of a little finger, of a sleeve, never a full hand on a bare shoulder but a flight from touch, wavelets and rivulets of delicate incense, that was all that flowed from him to her.

The electric shock sank beneath his consciousness.

By touching her naked foot he had felt a unity resembling the first unity of the world, unity with nature, unity with the mother, early memories of an existence within the silk, warmth and effortlessness of a vast love. By touching her foot this empty desert which lay between him and other human beings, bristling with all the plants of defenses, the cactus varieties of emotional repellents, grown impenetrable between himself and other young men, even when they lay body to body, was annihilated. There were sensual acts in which he had not felt this sudden flowing together which had happened between her naked foot and his hands, between the heart of her and the core of himself. This heart of Sabina's, which he imagined panoplied for refuge, and the core of himself, which he had never felt before except as the crystal structure of his young man's body which he knew, in her presence, he discovered to be soft and vulnerable.

He became aware of all his fragilities at once, his dependence, his need. Nearer she came, her face growing larger as she bent over him, her eyes brighter and warmer, nearer and nearer, melting his hostilities.

It was terribly sweet to be so naked in her presence. As in all the tropical climates of love, his skin softened, his hair felt silkier on his skin, his nerves untangled from their sharp wiry contortions. All the tensions of pretenses ceased. He felt himself growing smaller, back to his natural size, as in tales of magic, shrinking painlessly in order to enter this refuge of her heart, relinquishing the straining for maturity. But with this came all the corresponding moods of childhood: the agonized helplessness, the early defenselessness, the anguish at being at other's complete mercy.

It was necessary to arrest this invasion of her warmth which drugged his will, his uprightness in anger, to arrest this dissolution and flowing of one being into another which had already taken place once between his mother and then been violently shattered with the greatest shock and pain by her fickleness and frivolities. It was necessary to destroy this fluid warmth in which he felt himself absorbed, drowning as within the sea itself, her body a chalice, a ciborium, a niche of

430

shadows. Her gray cotton dress folded like an accordion around her feet, with the gold dust of secrecy between each rivulet of tissue, a journey of infinite detours in which his manhood would be trapped, captured.

He dropped her naked foot and rose stiffly. He took up where he had left off, took up the adolescent charades. His gentleness turned to limpness, the hand he extended to take the cape off her shoulders was as if severed from the rest of his body.

He took up following her, carrying her cape. He incensed her with words, he sat in the closest proximity, in her shadow, always near enough to bask in the warmth emanating from her body, always within reach of her hand, always with his shirt open at the throat in an oblique challenge to her hands, but the mouth in flight. Wearing around his waist the most unique belts so that her eyes would admire his waist, but the body in flight.

This design in space was a continuation of John's way of caressing her, the echo of his teasings. The tantalizing night spent in seeking the sources of pleasure but avoiding all possible dangers of welding their bodies into any semblance of marriage. It aroused in Sabina a similar suspense, all the erotic nerves awakened, throwing off futile, wasted sparks in space.

She saw his charades as a child's jealous imitations of a maturity he could not reach.

"You're sad, Sabina," he said. "Come with me. I have things to show you." As if rising with her in his gyroscope of fantasy he took her to visit his collection of empty cages.

Cages crowded his room, some of bamboo from the Philippines, some in gilt, wrought with intricate designs from Persia, others peaked like tents, others like miniature adobe houses, others like African huts of palm leaves. To some of the cages he himself had added turrets, towers from the Middle Ages, trapezes and baroque ladders, bathtubs made of mirrors, and a complete miniature jungle sufficient to give these prisons the illusion of freedom to any wild or mechanical bird imprisoned

431

in them.

"I prefer empty cages, Sabina, until I find a unique bird I once saw in my dreams."

Sabina placed *The Firebird* on the phonograph. The delicate footsteps of the Firebird were heard at first through infinite distance, each step rousing the phosphorescent sparks from the earth, each note a golden bugle to marshal delight. A jungle of dragon tails thrashing in erotic derisions, a brazier of flesh-smoking prayers, the multiple debris of the stained glass fountains of desire.

She lifted the needle, cut the music harshly in mid-air.

"Why? Why? Why?" cried Donald, as if wounded.

Sabina had silenced the firebirds of desire, and now she extended her arms like widely extended wings, wings no longer orange, and Donald gave himself to their protective embrace. The Sabina he embraced was the one he needed, the dispenser of food, of fulfilled promises, of mendings and knitting, comforts and solaces, of blankets and reassurances, of heaters, medicines, potions and scaffolds.

"You're the firebird, Sabina, and that was why, until you came, all my cages were empty. It was you I wanted to capture." Then with a soft, a defeated tenderness he lowered his eyelashes and added: "I know I have no way to keep you here, nothing to hold you here . . ."

Her breasts were no longer tipped with fire, they were the breasts of the mother, from which flowed nourishment. She deserted her other loves to fulfill Donald's needs. She felt: "I am a woman, I am warm, tender and nourishing. I am fecund and I am good."

Such serenity came with this state of being woman the mother! The humble, the menial task-performing mother as she had known her in her own childhood.

When she found chaotic, hasty little notes from Donald telling her where he was and when he would return he always ended them: "You are wonderful. You are wonderful and good. You are generous and kind."

And these words calmed her anxiety more than sensual fulfillment had, calmed her fevers. She was shedding other Sabinas, believing she was shedding anxiety. Each day the colors of her dresses became more subdued, her walk less animal. It was as if in captivity her brilliant plumage were losing its brilliance. She felt the metamorphosis. She knew she was moulting. But she did not know what she was losing in molding herself to Donald's needs.

Once, climbing his stairs with a full market bag, she caught a dim silhouette of herself on a damp mirror, and was startled to see a strong resemblance to her mother.

What Donald had achieved by capturing her into his net of fantasy as the firebird (while in the absence of erotic climate he had subtly dulled her plumage) was not only to reach his own need's fulfillment but to enable her to rejoin her mother's image which was her image of goodness: her mother, dispenser of food, of solace—soft warm and fecund.

On the stained mirror stood the shadow and echo of her mother, carrying food. Wearing the neutral-toned clothes of self-effacement, the faded garments of self-sacrifice, the external uniform of goodness.

In this realm, her mother's realm, she had found a moment's surcease from guilt.

Now she knew what she must say to Donald to cure his sense of smallness, and the smallness of what he had given her. She would say to him:

"Donald! Donald! You did give me something no one else could give me, you gave me my innocence! You helped me to find again the way to gain peace which I had learned as a child. When I was a child, only a little younger than you are now, after days of drugging myself with reading, with playing, with fantasies about people, with passionate friendships, with days spent hiding from my parents, with escapes, and all the activities which were termed bad, I found that by helping my mother, by cooking, mending, cleaning, scrubbing, and doing all the chores I most hated, I could appease this hungry and tyrannical conscience. It's no crime that you have remained a child, Donald. In some of the old fairytales, you know, many mature characters were shrunk back into midgets, as Alice was made small again to re-experience her childhood. It's the rest of us who are pretenders; we all pretend to be large and strong. You just are not able to pretend."

When she entered his room, she found a letter on her table.

Once she had said to him, when his moods had been too contradictory: "Adolescence is like cactus," and he had answered: "I'll write you a letter some day, with cactus milk!"

And here it was!

Letter to an actress: "From what you told me last night I see that you do not know your power. You are like a person who consumes herself in love and giving and does not know the miracles that are born of this. I felt this last night as I watched you act Cinderella, that you were whatever you acted, that you touched that point at which art and life meet and there is only BEING. I felt your hunger and your dreams, your pities and your desires at the same time as you awakened all of mine. I felt that you were not acting but dreaming; I felt that all of us who watched you could come out of the theatre and without transition could pass magically into another Ball, another snowstorm, another love, another dream. Before our very eyes you were being consumed by love and the dream of love. The burning of your eyes, of your gestures, a bonfire of faith and dissolution. You have the power. Never again use the word exhibitionism. Acting in you is a revelation. What the soul so often cannot say through the body because the body is not subtle enough, you can say. The body usually betrays the soul. You have the power of contagion, of transmitting emotion through the infinite shadings of your movements, the variations of your mouth's designs, the feathery palpitations of your eyelashes. And your voice, your voice more than any other voice, linked to your breath, the breathlessness of feeling, so that you take one's breath away with you and carry one into

434

the realm of breathlessness and silence. So much power you have Sabina! The pain you felt afterwards was not the pain of failure or of exhibitionism, as you said, it must be the pain of having revealed so much that was of the spirit, like some great mystic revelation of compassion and love and secret illusion, so that you expected this to have been communicated to others, and that they should respond as to a magic ritual. It must have been a shock when it did not happen to the audience, when they remained untransformed. But to those who respond as I did, you appear as something beyond the actor who can transmit to others the power to feel, to believe. For me the miracle took place. You seemed the only one alive among the actors. What hurt you was that it was not acting, and that when it ended there was a break in the dream. You should have been protected from the violent transition. You should have been carried off the stage, so that you would not feel the change of level, from the stage to the street, and from the street to your home, and from there to another party, another love, another snowstorm, another pair of gold slippers.

It must take great courage to give to many what one often gives but to the loved one. A voice altered by love, desire, the smile of open naked tenderness. We are permitted to witness the exposure of all feelings, tenderness, anger, weakness, abandon, childishness, fear, all that we usually reveal only to the loved one. That is why we love the actress. They give us the intimate being who is only revealed in the act of love. We receive all the treasures, a caressing glance, an intimate gesture, the secret ranges of the voice. This openness, which is closed again as soon as we face a partial relationship, the one who understands only one part of us, is the miraculous openness which takes place in whole love. And so I witnessed, on the stage, this mystery of total love which in my life is hidden from me. And now, Sabina, I cannot bear the little loves, and yet I cannot claim all of yours, and every day I see you now, immense, complete, and I but a fragment, wandering . . ."

Sabina touched the letter which rested on her breast, the sharp corners of the pages hurting her a little . . . "What can I give you?" he asked. "What have I to give you?" he cried out in anguish, thinking this was the reason why he had not seen her for three days, or heard from her. Another time he had said playfully: "I can only nibble at you." And had pressed his small, perfect teeth into her shoulder.

The ascensions of the ballet dancers into space and their return to the ground, brought before her eyes a Japanese umbrella made of colored paper which she once wore in her hair. It was lovely to see, so delicately made. When it rained and others opened their umbrellas then it was time for her to close hers.

But a high wind had torn it, and when she went into Chinatown to buy another the woman who ran the shop shouted violently: "It's made in Japan, throw it in the gutter!"

Sabina had looked at the parasol, innocent and fragile, made in a moment of peace by a workman dreaming of peace, made like a flower, lighter than war and hatred. She left the shop and looked down at the gutter and could not bring herself to throw it. She folded it quietly, folded tender gardens, the fragile structure of dream, a workman's dream of peace, innocent music, innocent workman whose hands had not made bullets. In time of war hatred confused all the values, hatred fell upon cathedrals, paintings, music, rare books, children, the innocent passersby.

She folded the letter, as she had folded the parasol, out of sight of hatred and violence. She could not keep pace with the angry pulse of the world. She was engaged in a smaller cycle, the one opposite to war. There were truths women had been given to protect while the men went to war. When everything would be blown away, a paper parasol would raise its head among the debris, and man would be reminded of peace and tenderness.

Alan always believed he was giving Sabina pleasure when he took her to the theatre, and at first her face was always illuminated with suspense and curiosity. But inevitably she would grow restive and tumultuous, chaotic and disturbed; she would even weep quietly in the dark and disappear in between acts, so as not to expose a ravaged face.

"What is it, what is it?" repeated Alan patiently, suspecting her of envy or jealousy of the roles given to others. "You could be the most marvelous actress of our period if you wanted to give your whole life to it, but you know how you feel about discipline and monotony."

"It isn't that, no, it isn't that," and Sabina would say no more.

To whom could she explain that what she envied them was the ease with which they would step out of their roles, wash themselves of it after the play and return to their true selves. She would have wanted these metamorphoses of her personality to take place on the stage so that at a given signal she would know for certain they were ended and she might return to a permanent immutable Sabina.

But when she wished to end a role, to become herself again, the other felt immensely betrayed, and not only fought the alteration but became angered at her. Once a role was established in a relationship, it was almost impossible to alter. And even if she succeeded, when the time came to return to the original Sabina, where was she? If she rebelled against her role towards Donald, if she turned on the "Firebird" record again, the drumming of the senses, the tongues of fire, and denied her mother within her, was she then returning to the true Sabina?

When she replaced the needle on the record and set off on her first assignation with desire was it not her father then walking within her, directing her steps? Her father who, having fed on her mother's artful cooking, having dressed in the shirt she had ironed, having kissed her unbeautiful forehead damp from ironing, having allowed her marred hands

437

to tie his tie, proceeded to leave her mother and Sabina for his vainglorious walk down the streets of the neighborhood who knew him for his handsomeness and his wanderings?

How many times had a perfumed, a painted, a handsome woman stopped her on the street to kiss her, caress her long hair and say: "You're Sabina! You're his daughter! I know your father *so* well." It was not the words, it was the intimate glance, the boudoir tone of the voice which alarmed her. This knowledge of her father always brought to women's eyes a sparkle not there before, an intimation of secret pleasures. Even as a child Sabina could read their messages. Sabina was the daughter of delight born of his amorous genius and they caressed her as another manifestation of a ritual she sensed and from which her mother had been estranged forever.

"I knew your father so well!" Always the handsome women bending over her, hateful with perfume one could not resist smelling, with starched petticoats and provocative ankles. For all these humiliations she would have wanted to punish her father, for all his desecrations of multiple summer evenings of wanderings which gave these women the right to admire her as another of his women. She was also angry at her mother for not being angry, for preparing and dressing him for these intruders.

Was it Sabina now rushing into her own rituals of pleasure, or was it her father within her, his blood guiding her into amorousness, dictating her intrigues, he who was inexorably woven with her by threads of inheritance she could never separate again to know which one was Sabina, which one her father whose role she had assumed by alchemy of mimetic love.

Where was Sabina?

She looked at the sky and she saw the face of John speeding in the pursued clouds, his charm fading like smoke from celestial pyres; she saw the soft night glow of Mambo's eyes saying: "You don't love me," while bearing down on her; and Philip laughing a conqueror's laugh, bearing down on her and his charm vanishing too before the thoughtful, withdrawn face of Alan. The entire sky a warm blanket of eyes and mouths shining down on her, the air full of voices now raucous from the sensual spasm, now gentle with gratitude, now doubtful, and she was afraid because there was no Sabina, not ONE, but a multitude of Sabinas lying down yielding and being dismembered, constellating in all directions and breaking. A small Sabina who felt weak at the center carried on a giant wave of dispersion. She looked at the sky arched overhead but it was not a protective sky, not a cathedral vault, not a haven; it was a limitless vastness to which she could not cling, and she was weeping: "Someone hold me—hold me, so I will not continue to race from one love to another, dispersing me, disrupting me . . . *Hold me to one . . .*"

Leaning out of the window at dawn, pressing her breasts upon the window sill, she still looked out of the window hoping to see what she had failed to possess. She looked at the ending nights and the passersby with the keen alertness of the voyager who can never reach termination as ordinary people reach peaceful terminals at the end of each day, accepting pauses, deserts, havens, as she could not accept them.

Sabina felt lost.

The wild compass whose fluctuations she had always obeyed, making for tumult and motion in place of direction, was suddenly fractured so that she no longer knew even the relief of ebbs and flows and dispersions.

She felt lost. The dispersion had become too vast, too

extended. A shaft of pain cut through the nebulous pattern. Sabina had always moved so fast that all pain had passed swiftly, as through a sieve, leaving a sorrow like children's sorrows, soon forgotten, soon replaced by another interest. She had never known a pause.

Her cape, which was more than a cape, which was a sail, which was the feelings she threw to the four winds to be swelled and swept by the wind in motion, lay becalmed.

Her dress was becalmed.

It was as if now she were nothing that the wind could catch, swell and propel.

For Sabina, to be becalmed meant to die.

Anxiety had entered her body and refused to run through it. The silvery holes of her sieve against sorrow granted her at birth, had clogged. Now the pain had lodged itself inside of her, inescapable.

She had lost herself somewhere along the frontier between her inventions, her stories, her fantasies and her true self. The boundaries had become effaced, the tracks lost; she had walked into pure chaos, and not a chaos which carried her like the galloping of romantic riders in operas and legends, but which suddenly revealed the stage props: A papier-mâché horse.

She had lost her sails, her cape, her horse, her seven-league boots, and all of them at once. She was stranded in the semi-darkness of a winter evening.

Then, as if all the energy and warmth had been drawn inward for the first time, killing the external body, blurring the eyes, dulling the ears, thickening the palate and tongue, slowing the movements of the body, she felt intensely cold and shivered with the same tremor as leaves, feeling for the first time some withered leaves of her being detaching themselves from her body.

As she entered Mambo's Night Club she noticed new paintings on the walls and for a moment imagined herself back in Paris, seven years back, when she had first met Jay

440

in Montparnasse.

She recognized his paintings instantly.

It was now as before in Paris exhibits, all the methods of scientific splitting of the atom applied to the body and to the emotions. His figures exploded and constellated into fragments, like spilled puzzles, each piece having flown far enough away to seem irretrievable and yet not far enough to be dissociated. One could, with an effort of the imagination, reconstruct a human figure completely from these fragments kept from total annihilation in space by an invisible tension. By one effort of contraction at the core they might still amalgamate to form the body of a woman.

No change in Jay's painting, but a change in Sabina who understood for the first time what they meant. She could see at this moment on the wall *an exact portrait of herself as she felt inside.*

Had he painted Sabina, or something happening to all of them as it was happening in chemistry, in science? They had found all the corrosive acids, all the disintegrations, all the alchemies of separateness.

But when the painter exposed what took place inside the body and emotions of man, they starved him, or gave him Fifth Avenue shop windows to do, where Paris La Nuit in the background allowed fashions to display hats and shoes and handbags and waists floating in mid-air, and waiting to be assembled on one complete woman.

She stood before the paintings and she now could see the very minute fragments of her acts, which she had believed unimportant, causing minute incisions, erosions of the personality. A small act, a kiss given at a party to a young man who benefitted from his resemblance to a lost John, a hand abandoned in a taxi to a man not desired but because the other woman's hand had been claimed and Sabina could not bear to have her hand lie unclaimed on her lap: it seemed an affront to her powers of seduction. A word of praise about a painting she had not liked but uttered out of fear that the painter would say: "Oh, Sabina ... Sabina doesn't understand painting."

All the small insincerities had seeped like invisible rivulets of acid and caused profound damages. The erosions had sent each fragment of Sabina rotating like separate pieces of colliding planets into other spheres, yet not powerful enough to fly into space like a bird, not organic enough to become another life, to rotate on its own core.

Jay's painting was a dance of fragments to the rhythm of debris. It was also a portrait of the present Sabina.

And all her seeking of fire to weld these fragments together, seeking in the furnace of delight a welding of fragments into one total love, one total woman, had failed!

When she turned away from the paintings she saw Jay sitting at one of the tables, his face more than ever before resembling Lao Tze. His half-bald head rimmed now with frosty white hair, his half-closed, narrow, small eyes laughing.

Someone standing between Sabina and Jay leaned over to compliment him on his Fifth Avenue windows. Jay laughed merrily and said: "I have the power to stun them, and while they are stunned by modern art the advertisers can do their poisonous jobs."

He waved at Sabina to sit down with him.

"You've been watching my atomic pile in which men and women are bombarded to find the mysterious source of power in them, a new source of strength." He talked to her as if no years had intervened between their last meeting at a café in Paris. He was always continuing the same conversation begun no one knew when, perhaps in Brooklyn where he had been born, everywhere and anywhere until he had reached the country of cafés where he found an audience, so that he could paint and talk perpetually in one long chain of dissertations.

"Have you found your power, your new strength?" asked Sabina. "I haven't."

"I haven't either," said Jay, with mock contrition. "I've

just come home, because of the war. They asked us to leave. Whoever couldn't be drafted was only one more mouth to feed for France. The consulate sent us a messenger: 'Let all the useless ones leave Paris.' In one day all the artists deserted, as if the plague had come. I never knew the artists occupied so much space! We, the international artists, were faced with either hunger or concentration camps. Do you remember Hans, Sabina? They wanted to send him back to Germany. A minor Paul Klee, that's true, but still deserving a better fate. And Suzanne was sent back to Spain; she had no papers. Her Hungarian husband with the polio was put in a camp. Remember the corner of Montparnasse and Raspail where we all stood for hours saying good night? Because of the blackouts you'd have no time to say good night, you'd be lost as soon as you were out of the café, you'd vanish in the black night. Innocense was gone from all our acts. Our habitual state of rebellion became a serious political crime. Djuna's house boat was drafted for the transportation of coal. Everything could undergo conversion except the artists. How can you convert disorganizers of past and present order, the chronic dissenters, those dispossessed of the present anyway, the atom bomb throwers of the mind, of the emotions, seeking to generate new forces and a new order of mind out of continuous upheavals?"

As he looked at Sabina his eyes seemed to say that she had not changed, that she was still, for him, the very symbol of this fever and restlessness and upheaval and anarchy in life which he had applauded in Paris seven years ago.

At this moment another personage sat down next to Jay. "Meet Cold Cuts, Sabina. Cold Cuts is our best friend here. When people get transplanted, it's exactly like plants; at first there's a wilting, a withering; some die of it. We're all at the critical stage, suffering from a change of soil. Cold Cuts works at the morgue. His constant familiarity with suicides and terrifying description of them keeps us from committing it. He speaks sixteen languages and thus he's the only one who can talk to all the artists, at least early in the evening. Later he'll be drunk in extremis and will only be able to speak the esperanto of alcoholics, which is a language full of stutterings from the geological layers of our animal ancestors."

Satisfied with this introduction, Cold Cuts left the table and busied himself with the microphone. But Jay was wrong. Although it was only nine o'clock, Cold Cuts was already in difficulties with the microphone. He was struggling to maintain an upright relationship, but the microphone would yield, bend, sway under his embrace like a flexible young reed. In his desperate embraces, it seemed as if the instrument and Cold Cuts would finally lie on the floor entangled like uncontrollable lovers.

When a momentary equilibrium was established, Cold Cuts became voluble and sang in sixteen various languages (including alcoholic esperanto), becoming in quick succession a French street singer, a German opera singer, a Viennese organ grinder singer, etc.

Then he returned to sit with Jay and Sabina.

"Tonight Mambo cut off my food supply earlier than usual. Why, do you think? I shouldn't be so loyal to him. But he doesn't want me to lose my job. At midnight I must be fit to receive the dead politely. I musn't stutter or bungle anything. The dead are sensitive. Oh, I have a perfect suicide to report to the exiles: a European singer who was spoiled and pampered in her own country. She strangled herself with all her colored scarves tied together. Do you think she wanted to imitate the death of Isadora Duncan?"

"I don't believe that," said Jay. "I can reconstruct the scene. She was a failure as a singer here. Her present life was gray, she was forgotten and not young enough to conquer a second time perhaps . . . She opened her trunk full of programs of past triumphs, full of newspaper clippings praising her voice and her beauty, full of dried flowers which had been given to her, full of love letters grown yellow, full of colored scarves which brought back the perfumes and the colors of her past successes, and by contrast her life today became unbearable."

"You're absolutely right," said Cold Cuts. "I'm sure that's the way it happened. She hung herself on the umbilical cord of the past." He sputtered as if all the alcohol he contained had begun to bubble within him, and he said to Sabina: "Do you know why I'm so loyal to Mambo? I'll tell you. In my profession people would rather forget me. No one wants to be reminded of death. Maybe they don't want to ignore *me*, but the company I keep. Now I don't mind this the rest of the year, but I do mind it at Christmas. Christmas comes and I'm the only one who never gets a Christmas card. And that's the one thing about my work at the morgue which I can't stand. So a few days before Christmas I said to Mambo: 'Be sure and send me a Christmas card. I've got to receive at least *one* Christmas card. I've got to feel one person at least thinks of me at Christmas time, as if I were a human being like any other.' But you know Mambo . . . He promised, he smiled, and then once he starts drumming it's like a jag of some kind, and you can't sober him up. I couldn't sleep for a week thinking he might forget and how I would feel on Christmas day to be forgotten *as if I were dead* . . . Well, he didn't forget."

Then with unexpected swiftness, he pulled an automobile horn out of his pocket, affixed it to his buttonhole and pressed it with the exuberance of a woman squeezing perfume from an atomizer and said: "Listen to the language of the future. The word will disappear altogether and that is how human beings will talk to each other!"

And bowing with infinite control of the raging waters of alcohol which were pressing against the dam of his politeness, Cold Cuts prepared to leave for his duties at the morgue.

Mambo began his drumming and Sabina began to look feverish and trapped as she had looked the first time Jay had seen her.

Dressed in red and silver, she evoked the sounds and imagery of fire engines as they tore through the streets of New

York, alarming the heart with the violent accelerations of catastrophes.

All dressed in red and silver, she evoked the tearing red and silver siren cutting a pathway through the flesh.

The first time he had looked at her he had felt: "Everything will burn!"

Out of the red and silver and the long cry of alarm to the poet who survives (even if secretly and invisibly) in every human being as the child survives in him (denied and disguised), to this poet she threw an unexpected challenge, a ladder in the middle of the city and ordained: "Climb!"

As she appeared, all orderly alignment of the city gave way before this ladder one was invited to climb, standing straight in space like the ladder of Baron Münchhausen which led to the sky.

Only her ladders led to fire.

Jay laughed and shook his head from side to side at the persistence of the image he had of Sabina. After seven years she *still had not learned to sit still. She talked profusely and continuously with a feverish breathlessness like one in fear of silence. She sat as if she could not bear to sit for long and when she rose to buy cigarettes she was equally eager to return to her seat. Impatient, alert, watchful, as if in dread of being attacked, restless and keen. She drank hurriedly, she smiled so swiftly that he was never certain it had been a smile, she listened only partially to what was being said to her, and even when someone in the bar leaned over and shouted out her name in her direction she did not respond at first, as if it were not her own.*

Her way of looking at the door of the bar as if expecting the proper moment to make her escape, her erratic and sudden gestures, her sudden sulky silences. She behaved like someone who had all the symptoms of guilt.

Above the iridescence of the candles, above the mists of cigarette smoke and the echoes of the cajoling blues, Sabina was aware that Jay was meditating on her. But it would be too dangerous to question him; he was a satirist, and all she would obtain from him at this moment was a caricature which she could not take lightly or dismiss, and which would, in her present mood, add heavily to the weights pulling her downward.

Whenever Jay shook his head kindly, with the slow heavy playfulness of a bear, he was about to say something devastating, which he called his brutal honesty. And Sabina would not challenge this. So she began a swift, spiralling, circuitous story about a party at which indistinct incidents had taken place, hazy scenes from which no one could distinguish the heroine or the victim. By the time Jay felt he recognized the place (Montparnasse, seven years ago, a party at which Sabina had actually been jealous of the strong bond between Jay and Lillian which she was seeking to break), Sabina was already gone from there, and talking as in a broken dream, with spaces, reversals, retractions and galloping fantasies.

She was now in Morocco, visiting the Arabian baths with the native women, sharing their pumice stone, and learning from the prostitutes how to paint her eyes with kohl from the market place.

"It's coal dust," explained Sabina, "and you place it right inside of the eyes. It smarts at first, and it makes you cry, but that spreads it out on the edge of the eyelids and that is how they get that shiny, coal black rim around the eyes."

"Didn't you get an infection?" asked Jay.

"Oh, no, the prostitutes are very careful to have the kohl blessed at the mosque."

Everyone laughed at this—Mambo who had been standing near, Jay, and two indistinct personages who had been sitting at the next table but who had been sliding their chairs to listen to Sabina. Sabina did not laugh; she was invaded by another memory of Morocco. Jay could see the images passing through her eyes like a film being censored. He knew she was busy eliminating other stories she was about to tell; she might even be regretting the story about the bath, and now

447

it was as if all she had said had been written on a huge blackboard and she took a sponge and effaced it all by adding: "Actually, this did not happen to me. It was told to me by someone who went to Morocco," and before anyone could ask: "Do you mean that you never went to Morocco at all?" she continued to confuse the threads by adding that this was a story she had read somewhere or heard at a bar, and as soon as she had erased in the minds of her listeners any facts which could be directly attributed to her own responsibility, she began another story . . .

The faces and the figures of her personages appeared only half-drawn, and when Jay had barely begun to reconstruct the missing fragment (when she told about the man who was polishing his own telescope glass she did not want to say too much for fear Jay would recognize Philip whom he had known in Vienna and whom they all called playfully in Paris: "Vienna-as-it-was-before-the-war"), when Sabina would interpose another face and figure as one does in dreams, and when Jay had laboriously decided she was talking about Philip (with whom he was sure now she had had an affair), it turned out that she was no longer talking about a man polishing a telescope glass with the umbrella hung up in the middle of the room above his work, but about a woman who continued to play the harp at a concert in Mexico City during the revolution when someone had shot at the lights of the concert hall, and she had felt that if she continued to play she would prevent a panic; and as Jay knew this story had been told of Lillian, and that it was not as a harpist but as a pianist that Lillian had continued to play, Sabina became aware that she did not want to remind Jay about Lillian as the memory would be painful to him, for Sabina's seduction of Jay in Paris had been in part responsible for Lillian's desertion of him, and so she quickly reversed her story, and it was Jay who wondered whether he was not hearing right, whether perhaps he had been drinking too much and had imagined she was talking about Lillian, because actually at this very moment she was

448

talking about a young man, an aviator, who had been told not to look into the eyes of the dead.

Jay could not retain any sequence of the people she had loved, hated, escaped from, anymore than he could keep track of her very personal appearance as she herself would say: "At that time I was a blond, and I wore my hair very short," or "This was before I was married when I was only nineteen" (and once she had told him she had been married at the age of eighteen). Impossible to know who she had betrayed, forgotten, married, deserted, or clung to. It was like her profession. The first time he had questioned her, she had answered immediately: "I am an actress." But when he pressed her, he could not find in what play she had acted, whether she had been a success or a failure, whether, perhaps, (as he decided later) she had merely *wished* to be an actress but had never worked persistently enough, seriously enough except in the way she was working now, changing personalities with such rapidity that Jay was reminded of a kaleidoscope.

He sought to capture the recurrence of certain words in her talk, thinking they might be used as keys, but if the word "actress," "miraculous," "travel," "wandering," "relationship" did occur frequently, it remained impossible to know whether or not she used them in their literal sense of symbolically, for they were the same to her. He had heard her say once: "When you are hurt, you travel as far as you can from the place of the hurt," and when he examined her meaning found she was referring to a change of quarters within fifty blocks in the city of New York.

She was compelled by a confessional fever which forced her into lifting the veil slightly, only a corner of it, and then frightened when anyone listened too attentively, especially Jay whom she did not trust, whom she knew found the truth only in the sense of exposure of the flaws, the weaknesses, the foibles.

As soon as Jay listened too attentively, she took a giant

449

sponge and erased all she had said by an absolute denial as if this confusion were in itself a mantle of protection.

At first she beckoned and lured one into her world, then she blurred the passageways, confused all the images *as if to elude detection.*

"False mysteries," said Jay savagely, baffled and irritated by her elusiveness. "But what is she hiding behind these false mysteries?"

Her behavior always aroused in him (in the kind of mind he had with an obsession for truth, for revelation, for openness, brutal exposure) a desire which resembled the desire of a man to violate a woman who resists him, to violate a virginity which creates a barrier to his possession. Sabina always incited him to a violent desire to rip all her pretenses, her veils, and to discover the core of her self which, by this perpetual change of face and mobility, escaped all detection.

How right he had been to paint Sabina always as *a mandrake with fleshly roots, bearing a solitary purple flower in a purple-bell-shaped corolla of narcotic flesh. How right he had been to paint her born with red-gold eyes always burning as from caverns, from behind trees, as one of the luxuriant women, a tropical growth, excommunicated from the bread line as too rich a substance for everyday living, placing her there merely as a denizen of the world of fire, and content with her intermittent, parabolic appearances.*

"Sabina, do you remember our elevator ride in Paris?"

"Yes, I do remember."

"We had no place to go. We wandered through the streets. I remember it was your idea to take an elevator."

(We were ravenous for each other, I remember, Sabina. We got into an elevator and I began to kiss her. First floor. Second floor. I couldn't let go of her. Third floor, and when the elevator came to a standstill it was too late . . . I couldn't stop, I couldn't let go of her if all Paris had been watching us. She pressed the button wildly, and we went on kissing as the elevator came down. When we got to the bottom it was worse, so she pressed the button again, and we went up and down, up and down, while people kept trying to stop it and get on . . .)

Jay laughed uncontrollably at the memory, at Sabina's audacity. At that moment Sabina had been stripped of all mystery and Jay had tasted what the mystery contained: the most ardent frenzy of desire.

The dawn appearing weakly at the door silenced them. The music had ceased long ago and they had not noticed. They had continued their own drumming in talk.

Sabina tightened her cape around her shoulders as if daylight were the greatest enemy of all. To the dawn she would not even address a feverish speech. She stared at it angrily, and left the bar.

There is no bleaker moment in the life of the city than that one which crosses the boundary lines between those who have not slept all night and those who are going to work. It was for Sabina as if two races of men and women lived on earth, the night people and the day people, never meeting face to face except at this moment. Whatever Sabina had worn which seemed to glitter during the night, lost its colors in the dawn. The determined expressions of those going to work appeared to her like a reproach. Her fatigue was not like theirs. Hers marked her face like a long fever, left purple shadows under her eyes. She wanted to conceal her face from them. She hung her head so that her hair would partly cover it.

The mood of lostness persisted. For the first time she felt she could not go to Alan. She carried too great a weight of untold stories, too heavy a weight of memories, she was followed by too many ghosts of personages unsolved, of experiences not yet understood, of blows and humiliations not

451

yet dissolved. She might return and plead extreme tiredness, and fall asleep, but her sleep would be restive, and she might talk in her dreams.

This time Alan would not have the power to exorcise her mood. Nor could she tell him about the event which most tormented her: the man she had first seen some months ago from the window of her hotel room, standing under her very window reading a newspaper, as if waiting for her to come out. Once more she had seen him on her way to visit Philip. She had encountered him in the subway station, and he had let several subway cars pass by in order to take the one she was taking.

It was not a flirtation. He made no effort to speak to her. He seemed engaged in an impersonal observation of her. In Mambo's Night Club he had sat a few tables away and he was writing in a notebook.

This was the way criminals were shadowed, just before being caught. Was he a detective? What did he suspect her of? Would he report to Alan? Or to her parents? Or would he take his notes downtown to all the awesome buildings in which they carried on investigations of one kind or another, and would she receive one day a notice asking her to leave the United States and return to her place of birth, Hungary, because the life of Ninon de l'Enclos, or Madame Bovary was not permitted by the law?

If she told Alan that she had been followed by a man, Alan would smile and say: "Why, of course, this isn't the first time, is it? That's the penalty you pay for being a beautiful woman. You wouldn't want it not to happen, would you?"

For the first time, on this bleak early morning walk through New York streets not yet cleaned of the night people's cigarette butts and empty liquor bottles, she understood Duchamp's painting of a "Nude Descending a Staircase." Eight or ten outlines of the same woman, like many multiple exposures of a woman's personality, neatly divided into many layers, walking down the stairs in unison.

452

If she went to Alan now it would be like detaching one of these cut-outs of a woman, and forcing it to walk separately from the rest, but once detached from the unison, it would reveal that it was a mere outline of a woman, the figure design as the eye could see it, but empty of substance, this substance having evaporated through the spaces between each layer of the personality. A divided woman indeed, a woman divided into numberless silhouettes, and she could see this apparent form of Sabina leaving a desperate and a lonely one walking the streets in quest of hot coffee, being greeted by Alan as a transparently innocent young girl he had married ten years before and sworn to cherish, as he had, only he had continued to cherish the same young girl he had married, the first exposure of Sabina, the first image delivered into his hands, the first dimension, of this elaborated, complex and extended series of Sabinas which had been born later and which she had not been able to give him. Each year, just as a tree puts forth a new ring of growth, she should have been able to say: "Alan, here is a new version of Sabina. Add it to the rest, fuse them well, hold on to them when you embrace her, hold them all at once in your arms, or else, divided, separated, each image will live a life of ts own, and it will not be one but six, or seven, or eight Sabinas who will walk sometimes in unison, by a great effort of synthesis, sometimes separately, one of them following a deep drumming into forests of black hair and luxurious mouths, another visiting Vienna-as-it-was-before-the-war, and still another lying beside an insane young man, and still another opening maternal arms to a trembling frightened Donald. Was this the crime to have sought to marry each Sabina to another mate, to match each one in turn by a different life?

Oh, she was tired, but it was not from loss of sleep, or from talking too much in a smoke-filled room, or from eluding Jay's caricatures, or Mambo's reproaches, or Philip's distrust of her, or because Donald by his behavior so much like a child had made her feel that her thirty years were a grandmother's age. She was tired of pulling these disparate fragments together. She understood Jay's paintings too. It was perhaps at such a moment of isolation that Madame Bovary had taken the poison. It was the moment when the hidden life is in danger of being exposed, and no woman could bear the condemnation.

But why should she fear exposure? At this moment Alan was deeply asleep, or quietly reading if he were not asleep.

Was it merely this figure of a lie detector dogging her steps which caused her so acute an anxiety?

Guilt is the one burden human beings cannot bear alone.

After taking a cup of coffee, she went to the hotel where they knew her already, took a sleeping pill, and took refuge in sleep.

When she awakened at ten o'clock that night she could hear from her hotel room the music from Mambo's Night Club across the street.

She needed a confessor! Would she find it there, in the world of the artists? All over the world they had their meeting places, their affiliations, their rules of membership, their kingdoms, their chiefs, their secret channels of communication. They established common beliefs in certain painters, certain musicians, certain writers. They were the misplaced persons too, unwanted at home usually, or repudiated by their families. But they established new families, their own religions, their own doctors, their own communities.

She remembered someone asking Jay: "Can I be admitted if I show proofs of excellent taste?"

"That is not enough," said Jay. "Are you also willing to become an exile? Or a scapegoat? We are the notorious scapegoats, for living as others live only in their dreams at night, for confessing openly what others only confess to doctors under guarantee of professional secret. We are also underpaid: people feel that we are in love with our work, and that one should not be paid for doing what you most love to do."

In this world they had criminals too. Gangsters in the world of art, who produced corrosive works born of hatred, who killed and poisoned with their art. You can kill with a painting or a book too.

Was Sabina one of them? What had she destroyed?

She entered Mambo's Night Club. The artificial palm trees seemed less green, the drums less violent. The floor, doors, walls were slightly askew with age.

Djuna arrived at the same moment, her black rehearsal tights showing under her raincoat, her hair bound in a ribbon like a school-girl's.

When such magical entrances and exits take place in a ballet, when the dancers vanish behind columns or dense hills of shadows, no one asks them for passports or identifications. Djuna arrived as a true dancer does, walking as naturally from her ballet bar work a few floors above the night club as she had in Paris when she studied with the Opera ballet dancers. Sabina was not surprised to see her. But what she remembered of her was not so much her skill in dancing, her smooth dancer's legs, tense, but the skill of her compassion, as if she exercised everyday on an invisible bar of pain, her understanding as well as her body.

Djuna would know who had stolen, who had betrayed, and what had been stolen, what had been betrayed. And Sabina might cease falling—falling from all her incandescent trapezes, from all her ladders to fire.

They were all brothers and sisters, moving on the revolving stages of the unconscious, never intentionally mystifying others as much as themselves, caught in a ballet of errors and impersonations, but Djuna could distinguish between illusion and living and loving. She could detect the shadow of a crime which others could not bring to trial. She would know the identity of the criminal.

Sabina had only to wait now.

The drums ceased to play as if they were muffled by several forests of intricate impenetrable vegetation. Sabina's anxiety had ceased to beat against her temples and deafen her to outer sounds. Rhythm was restored to her blood and her hands lay still on her lap.

While she waited for Djuna to be free she thought about the lie detector who had been watching her actions. He was there in the café again, sitting alone, and writing in a notebook. She prepared herself mentally for the interview.

She leaned over and called him: "How do you do? Have you come to arrest me?"

He closed his notebook, walked over to her table, sat down beside her. She said: *I knew it would happen, but not quite so soon. Sit down. I know exactly what you think of me. You are saying to yourself: here is the notorious imposter, the international spy in the house of love. (Or should I specify: in the house of many loves?) I must warn you, you must handle me delicately: I am covered with a mantle of iridescence as easily destroyed as a dust flower, and although I am quite willing to be arrested, if you handle me roughly you will lose much of the evidence. I don't want you to taint that fragile coat of astonishing colors created by my illusions, which no painter has ever been able to reproduce. Strange, isn't it, that no chemical will give a human being the iridescence that illusions give them? Give me your hat. You look so formal and uncomfortable! And so you finally tracked down my impersonations! But are you aware of the courage, the audacity which my profession requires? Very few people are gifted for it. I had the vocation. It showed very early in my capacity for deluding myself. I was one who could call a backyard a garden, a tenement apartment a house, and if I were late when I came home, to avoid a scolding I could imagine and recreate instantly such interesting obstacles, adventures, that it would take my parents several minutes before they could shake off the spell and return to reality. I could step out of my ordinary self or my ordinary life into multiple selves and lives without attracting attention. I mean that my first crime, as you may be surprised to hear, was committed against myself. I was then a corrupter of minors, and this minor was my-*

456

self. What I corrupted was what is called the truth in favor of a more marvelous world. I could always improve on the facts. I was never arrested for this: it concerned only myself. My parents were not wise enough to see that such prestigitation of facts might produce a great artist, or at least a great actress. They beat me, to shake out the dust of delusions. But strangely enough, the more my father beat me, the more abundantly did this dust gather again, and it was not gray or brown dust as you find it in its daily form, but what is known to adventurers as fool's gold. Give me your coat. As an investigator you may be more interested to know that in self defense, I accuse the writers of fairytales. Not hunger, not cruelty, not my parents, but these tales which promised that sleeping in the snow never caused pneumonia, that bread never turned stale, that trees blossomed out of season, that dragons could be killed with courage, that intense wishing would be followed immediately by fufillment of the wish. Intrepid wishing, said the fairytales, was more effective than labor. The smoke issuing from Aladdin's lamp was my first smokescreen, and the lies learned from fairytales were my first perjuries. Let us say I had perverted tendencies: I believed everything I read.

Sabina laughed at her own words. Djuna thought she was drinking too much and looked at her.

"What made you laugh, Sabina?"

"Meet the lie detector, Djuna. He may arrest me."

"Oh, Sabina. You've never done anything to be arrested for!"

Djuna gazed at Sabina's face. The intentness of it, the feverishness she had always seen on it was no longer that of burning aliveness. There was a tightness to the features, and fear in the eyes.

"I have to talk to you, Djuna . . . . I can't sleep . . ."

"I tried to find you when I came from Paris. You change your address so often, and even your name."

"You know I've always wanted to break the molds which

life forms around one if one lets them."

"Why?"

"I want to trespass boundaries, erase all identifications, anything which fixes one permanently into one mold, one place, without hope of change."

"This is the opposite of what everyone usually wants, isn't it?"

"Yes, I used to say that I had housing problems: mine was that I didn't want a house. I wanted a boat, a trailer, anything that moved freely. I feel safest of all when no one knows where I am, when for instance, I'm in a hotel room where even the number is scratched off the door."

"But safe from what?"

"I don't know what I'm saving from detection, except perhaps that I'm guilty of several loves, of many loves instead of one."

"That's no crime. Merely a case of divided loves!"

"But the lies, the lies I have to tell . . . You know, just as some criminals tell you: 'I never found a way to get what I wanted except by robbery,' I often feel like saying: 'I have never found a way to get what I wanted except by lies'."

"Are you ashamed of it?"

Sabina grew frightened again. "There comes a moment with each man, in each relationship, when I feel lonely."

"Because of the lies?"

"But if I told the truth I would be not only lonely but also alone, and I would cause each one great harm. How can I tell Alan that for me he is like a father."

"That's why you deserted him over and over again as one must desert the parent, it's a law of maturity."

"You seem to exonerate me."

"I'm only exonerating you in relationship to Alan, toward whom you acted like a child."

"He is the only one I trust, the only one whose love is infinite, tireless, all-forgiving."

"That's not a man's love you are describing, and not even a

father's love. It's a fantasy-father, an idealized father once invented by a needy child. This love you need, Alan has given you. In this form of love you are right to trust him. But you will lose him one day, for there are other Alans exactly as there are other Sabinas, and they too demand to live and to be matched. The enemy of a love is never outside, it's not a man or woman, it's what we lack in ourselves."

Sabina's head had fallen on her chest in a pose of contrition.

"You don't believe that this man is here to arrest me?"

"No, Sabina, that is what you imagine. It is your own guilt which you have endowed this man with. You probably see this guilt mirrored in every policeman, every judge, every parent, every personage with authority. You see it with other's eyes. It's a reflection of what you feel. It's your interpretation: the eyes of the world on your acts."

Sabina raised her head. Such a flood of memories submerged her and hurt her so deeply she was left without breath. She felt such pain. It was like the pain of the "bends" felt by deep sea divers when they come to the surface too quickly.

"In your fabricated world, Sabina, men were either crusaders who would fight your battles for you, or judges continuing your parent's duties, or princes who had not yet come of age, and therefore could not be husbands."

"Free me," said Sabina to the lie detector. "Set me free. I've said that to so many men: 'Are you going to set me free?'" She laughed. "I was all ready to say it to you."

"You have to set yourself free. That will come with love . . ." said the lie detector.

"Oh, I've loved enough, if that could save one. I've loved plenty. Look at your notebook. I'm sure it is full of addresses."

"You haven't loved yet," he said. "You've only been trying to love, beginning to love. Trust alone is not love, desire alone is not love, illusion is not love, dreaming is not love. All these were paths leading you out of yourself, it is true, and so you thought they led to another, but you never reached the other. You were only on the way. Could you go out now and find the other faces of Alan, which you never struggled to see, or accept? Would you find the other face of Mambo which he so delicately hid from you? Would you struggle to find the other face of Philip?"

"Is it my fault if they only turned *one* of their faces towards me?"

"You're a danger to other human beings. First of all you dress them in the costume of the myth: poor Philip, he is Siegfried, he must always sing in tune, and be everlastingly handsome. Do you know where he is now? In a hospital with a broken ankle. Due to immobility he has gained a great deal of weight. You turn your face away, Sabina? That was not the myth you made love to, is it? If Mambo stopped drumming to go home and nurse his sick mother, would you go with him and boil injection needles? Would you, if another woman loved Alan, would you relinquish your child's claims upon his protectiveness? Will you go and make of yourself a competent actress and not continue to play Cinderella for amateur theatres only, keeping the artificial snow drop which fell on your nose during the snow storm long after the play is over as if to say: 'For me there is no difference at all between stage snow and the one falling now over Fifth Avenue?' Oh Sabina, how you juggled the facts in your games of desire, so that you might always win. The one intent on winning has not loved yet!"

To the lie detector Sabina said: "And if I did all you ask of me, will you stop haunting my steps, will you stop writing in your notebook?"

"Yes, Sabina. I promise you," he said.

"But, how could you know so much about my life . . ."

"You forget that you invited me yourself to shadow you. You endowed me with the power to judge your acts. You have endowed so many people with this power: priest, policemen, doctors. Shadowed by your conscience, interchangeable, you felt safer. You felt you could keep your sanity. Half of you wanted to atone, to be freed of the torments of guilt, but the other half wanted to be free. Only half of you surrendered, calling out to strangers: 'Catch me!' while the other half sought industriously to escape final capture. It was just another one of your flirtations, a flirtation with justice. And now you are in flight, from the guilt of love divided, and from the guilt of not loving. Poor Sabina, there was not enough to go around. You sought your wholeness in music . . . Yours is a story of non-love . . . And do you know Sabina, if you had been caught and tried, you would have been meted out a less severe punishment than you mete out to yourself. We are much more severe judges of our own acts. We judge our thoughts, our secret intents, our dreams even . . . You never considered the mitigating circumstances. Some shock shattered you and made you distrustful of a single love. You divided them as a measure of safety. So many trap doors opened between the night club world of Mambo, to the Vienna-before-the-war of Philip, to the studious world of Alan, or the adolescent evanescent world of Donald. Mobility in love became a condition for your existence. There is nothing shameful in seeking safety measures. Your fear was very great."

"My trap doors failed me."

"Come with me, Sabina."

Sabina and Djuna went up to her studio, where they could still hear the drumming.

As if to silence it, Djuna placed a record in her phonograph.

"Sabina . . ." But no words came as one of Beethoven's Quartets began to tell Sabina, as Djuna could not, of what they both knew for absolute certainty: the continuity of existence and of the chain of summits, of elevations by which such continuity is reached. By elevation the consciousness reached

461

a perpetual movement, transcending death, and in the same manner attained the continuity of love by seizing upon its impersonal essence, which was a summation of all the alchemies producing life and birth, a child, a work of art, a work of science, a heroic act, an act of love. The identity of the human couple was not eternal but interchangeable, to protect this exchange of spirits, transmissions of character, all the fecundations of new selves being born, and faithfulness only to the continuity, the extensions and expansions of love achieving their crystallizations into high moments and summits equal to the high moments and summits of art or religion.

Sabina slid to the floor and sat there with her head against the phonograph, with her wide skirt floating for one instant like an expiring parachute; and then deflating completely and dying in the dust.

The tears on Sabina's face were not round and separate like ordinary tears, but seemed to have fallen like a water veil, as if she had sunk to the bottom of the sea by the weight and dissolutions of the music. There was a complete dissolution of the eyes, features, as if she were losing her essence.

The lie detector held out his hands as if to rescue her, in a light gesture, as if this were a graceful dance of sorrow rather than the sorrow itself, and said: "In homeopathy there is a remedy called pulsatile for those who weep at music."

Seduction of the Minotaur

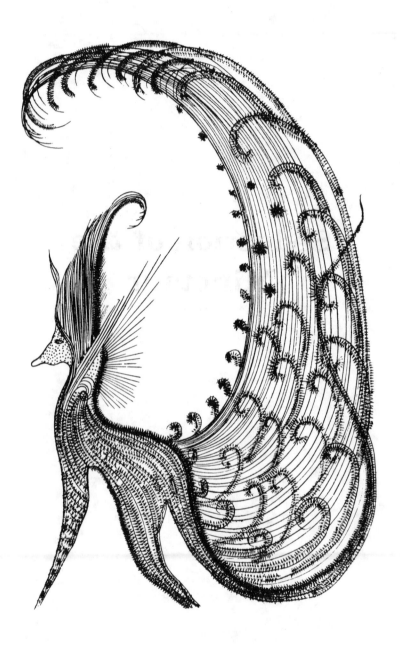

SOME VOYAGES HAVE THEIR INCEPTION in the blueprint of a dream, some in the urgency of contradicting a dream. Lillian's recurrent dream of a ship that could not reach the water, that sailed laboriously, pushed by her with great effort, through city streets, had determined her course toward the sea, as if she would give this ship, once and for all, its proper sea bed.

She had landed in the city of Golconda, where the sun painted everything with gold, the lining of her thoughts, the worn valises, the plain beetles, Golconda of the golden age, the golden aster, the golden eagle, the golden goose, the golden fleece, the golden robin, the goldenrod, the goldenseal, the golden warbler, the golden wattles, the golden wedding, and the gold fish, and the gold of pleasure, the goldstone, the gold thread, the fool's gold.

With her first swallow of air she inhaled a drug of forgetfulness well known to adventurers.

Tropic, from the Greek, signified change and turning. So she changed and turned and was metamorphosed by the light and caressing heat into a spool of silk. Every movement she made from that moment on, even the carrying of her valise, was softened and pleasurable. Her nerves, of which she had always been sharply aware, had become instead strands from a spool of silk, spiraling through the muscles.

"How long do you intend to stay?" asked the official. "How much money do you carry with you? In what currency? Do you have a return ticket?"

You had to account for every move, arrival or exit. In the world there was a conspiracy against improvisation. It was only permitted in jazz.

The guitars and the singing opened fire. Her skin blossomed and breathed. A heavy wave of perfume came down the jungle on the right, and a fine spray of waves came from the left. On the beach the natives swung in hammocks of reeds. The tender Mexican voices sang love songs which cradled and rocked the body as did the hammocks.

Where she came from only jewels were placed in satin-lined, cushioned boxes, but here it was thoughts and memories which the air, the scents, and the music conspired to hypnotize by softness.

But the airport official who asked cactus-pointed questions wore no shirt, nor did the porters, so that Lillian decided to be polite to the smoothest torso and show respect only to the strongest muscle.

The absence of uniforms restored the dignity and importance of the body. They all looked untamed and free in their bare feet, as if they had assumed the duties of receiving the travelers only temporarily and would soon return to their hammocks, to swimming and singing. Work was one of the absurdities of existence. Don't you think so, Señorita? said their laughing eyes while they appraised her from head to toe. They looked at her openly, intently, as children and animals do, with a physical vision, measuring only physical attributes, charm, aliveness, and not titles, possessions, or occupations. Their full, complete smile was not always answered by the foreigners, who blinked at such sudden warmth of smile as they did at the dazzling sun. Against the sun they wore dark glasses, but against these smiles and open naked glances they could only defend their privacy with a half-smile. Not Lillian. Her very full, rounded lips had always given such a smile. She could respond to this naked curiosity, naked interest, proximity. Thus animals and children stare, with their whole, concentrated attentiveness. The natives had not yet learned from the white man his inventions for traveling away from the present, his scientific capacity for analyzing warmth into a chemical substance, for abstracting human beings into symbols. The white man had invented glasses which made objects too near or too far, cameras, telescopes, spyglasses, objects which put glass between living and vision. It was the image he sought to possess, not the texture, the living warmth, the human closeness.

The natives saw only the present. This communion of eyes and smiles was elating. Where Lillian came from people seemed intent on not seeing each other. Only children looked at her with this unashamed curiosity. Poor white man, wandering and lost in his proud possession of a dimension in which bodies became invisible to the naked eye, as if staring were an immodest act. Already she felt incarnated, in full possession of her own body because the porter was in full possession of his, and this concentration upon the present allowed no interruption or short circuits of the physical contact. When she turned away from the porter it was to find a smiling taxi driver who seemed to be saying: "I am not keen on going anywhere. It is just as good right here, right now. . . ."

He was scratching his luxuriant black hair, and he carried his wet bathing suit around his neck.

The guitars kept up their musical fire. The beggars squatted around the airport. Blind or crippled, they smiled. The festivities of nature bathed them in gold and anesthetized their suffering.

Clothes seemed ponderous and superfluous in the city of Golconda.

Golconda was Lillian's private name for this city which she wanted to rescue from the tourist-office posters and propaganda. Each one of us possesses in himself a separate and distinct city, a unique city, as we possess different aspects of the same person. She could not bear to love a city which thousands believed they knew intimately. Golconda was hers. True, it had been at first a pearl-fishing village. True, a Japanese ship had been wrecked here, slave ships had brought Africans, other ships delivered spices, and Spanish ships had brought the art of filigree, of lace making. A shipwrecked Spanish galley had scattered on the beach baptism dresses which the women of southern Mexico had adopted as headgear.

The legend was that when the Japanese pearl divers had been driven away they had destroyed the pearl caches, and Golconda became a simple fishing village. Then the artists had come on donkeys and discovered the beauty of the place. They had been followed by the real-estate men and hotelkeepers. But none could destroy Golconda. Golconda remained a city where the wind was like velvet, where the sun was made of radium, and the sea as warm as a mother's womb.

The porters were deserting before all the baggage was distributed. They had earned enough, just enough for the day for food, beer, a swim, and enough to take a girl dancing, and they did not want any more. So the little boys of ten and twelve, who had been waiting for this opening, were seeking to carry bags bigger than themselves.

The taxi driver, who was in no hurry to go anywhere in his dilapidated car, saw his car filling up, and decided it was time to put on his clean laundry-blue shirt.

The three men who were to share the taxi with Lillian were already installed. Perhaps because they were in city clothes or perhaps because they were not smiling, they seemed to be the only subjects the sun could not illumine. The sea's aluminum reflectors had even penetrated the old taxi and found among the cracked leather some stuffing which had come out of the seat and which the sun transformed into angel hair such as grows on Christmas trees.

One of the men helped her into the car and introduced himself with Spanish colonial courtesy: "I am Doctor Hernandez."

He had the broad face she had seen in Mayan sculpture, the round high cheekbones, the aquiline nose, the full mouth slanting downward while the eyes slanted upward. His skin was a light olive which came from the mixture of Indian and Spanish blood. His smile was like the natives', open and total, but it came less often and faded quickly, leaving a shadow over his face.

She looked out the window to explore her new territory of pleasure. Everything was novel. The green of the foliage was not like any other greens: it was deeper, lacquered, and moist. The leaves were heavier, fuller, the flowers bigger. They seemed surcharged with sap, and more alive, as if they never had to close against the frost, or even a colder night. As if they had no need of sleep.

The huts made of palm leaves recalled Africa. Some were pointed on top and on stilts. Others had slanting roofs, and the palm leaves extended far enough to create shadows all around the house.

The lagoon on the left of the road showed a silver surface which sometimes turned to sepia. It was half filled with floating lagoon flowers. Trees and bushes seemed like new vegetation, also on stilts, dipping twisted roots into the water as the reeds dipped their straight and flexible roots. Herons stood on one leg. Iguanas slithered away, and parrots became hysterically gay.

Lillian's eyes returned to the Doctor. His thoughts were elsewhere, so she looked at the American who had introduced himself as Hatcher. He was an engineer who had come to Mexico years before to build roads and bridges, and had remained and married a Mexican woman. He spoke perfect Spanish, and was a leathery-skinned man who had been baked by the sun as dark as the natives. The tropics had not relaxed his forward-jutting jaw and shoulders. He looked rigid, lean, hard-fleshed. His bare feet were in Mexican sandals, the soles made of discarded rubber tires. His shirt was open at the neck. But on him the negligent attire still seemed a uniform to conquer, rather than a way of submitting to, the tropics.

"Golconda may seem beautiful to you, but it's spoiled by tourism. I found a more beautiful place farther on. I had to hack my way to it. I have a beach where the sand is so white it hurts the eyes like a snow slope. I'm building a house. I come to Golconda once a week to shop. I have a jeep. If you like you can drive out with me for a visit. Unless, like most Americans, you have come here to drink and dance. . . ."

"I'm not free to drink and dance. I have to play every night with the jazz orchestra."

"Then you must be Lillian Beye," said the passenger who had not yet spoken. He was a tall blond Austrian who spoke a harsh Spanish but with authority. "I'm the owner of the Black Pearl. I engaged you."

"Mr. Hansen?"

He shook her hand without smiling. He was fair-skinned. The tropics had not been able to warm him or to melt the icicle-blue eyes.

Lillian felt that these three men were somehow interfering with her own tasting of Golconda. They seemed intent on giving her an image of Golconda she did not want. The Doctor wanted her to notice only that the children were in need of care, the American wanted her to recoil from tourism, and the owner of the Black Pearl made the place seem like a night club.

The taxi stopped for gasoline. An enormously fat American,

unshaved for many days, rose from a hammock to wait on them.

"Hello, Sam," said Doctor Hernandez. "How is Maria? You didn't bring her to me for her injection."

Sam shouted to a woman dimly visible inside the palmleaf shack. She came to the door. Her long black shawl was fastened to her shoulders and her baby was cradled in the folds of it as if inside a hammock.

Sam repeated the Doctor's question. She shrugged her shoulders: "No time," she said and called: "Maria!"

Maria came forward from a group of children, carrying a boat made out of a coconut shell. She was small for her age, delicately molded, like a miniature child, as Mexican children often are. In the eyes of most Mexican painters, these finely chiseled beings with small hands and feet and slender necks and waists become larger than nature, with the sinews and muscles of giants. Lillian saw them tender and fragile and neat. The Doctor saw them ill.

The engineer said to Lillian: "Sam was sent here twenty years ago to build bridges and roads. He married a native. He does nothing but sleep and drink."

"It's the tropics," said Hansen.

"You've never been to the Bowery," said Lillian.

"But in the tropics all white men fall apart."

"I've heard that but I never believed it. Any more than I believe all adventurers are doomed. I think such beliefs are merely an expression of fear, fear of expatriation, fear of adventure."

"I agree with you," said the Doctor. "The white man who falls apart in the tropics is the same one who would fall apart anywhere. But in foreign lands they stand out more because they are few, and we notice them more."

"And then at home, if you want to fall apart, there are so many people to stop you. Relatives and friends foil your attempts! You get sermons, lectures, threats, and you are even rescued."

The Austrian laughed: "I can't help thinking how much

encouragement you would get here."

"You, Mr. Hatcher, didn't disintegrate in the tropics!"

Hatcher answered solemnly: "But I am a happy man. I have succeeded in living and feeling like a native."

"Is that the secret, then? It's those who don't succeed in going native, in belonging, who get desperately lonely and self-destructive?"

"Perhaps," said the Doctor pensively. "It may also be that you Americans are work-cultists, and work is the structure that holds you up, not the joy of pure living."

His words were accompanied by a guitar. As soon as one guitar moved away, the sound of another took its place, to continue this net of music that would catch and maintain you in flight from sadness, suspended in a realm of festivities.

Just as every tree carried giant brilliant flowers playing chromatic scales, runs and trills of reds and blues, so the people vied with them in wearing more intense indigoes, more flaming oranges, more platinous whites, or else colors which resembled the purple insides of mangoes, the flesh tones of pomegranates.

The houses were covered with vines bearing bell-shaped flowers playing coloraturas. The guitars inside of the houses or on the doorsteps took up the color chromatics and emitted sounds which evoked the flavor of guava, papaya, cactus figs, anise, saffron, and red pepper.

Big terra-cotta jars, heavily loaded donkeys, lean and hungry dogs, all recalled images from the Bible. The houses were all open; Lillian could see babies asleep in hammocks, holy pictures on the white stucco walls, old people on rocking chairs, and photographs of relatives pinned on the walls together with old palm leaves from the Palm Sunday feast.

The sun was setting ostentatiously, with all the pomp of embroidered silks and orange tapestries of Oriental spectacles. The palms had a naked elegance and wore their giant plumes like languid feather dusters sweeping the tropical sky of all clouds, keeping it as transparent as a sea shell.

Restaurants served dinner out in the open. On one long communal table was a bowl of fish soup and fried fish. Inside the houses people had begun to light the oil lamps which had a more vivacious flicker than candles.

The Doctor had been talking about illness. "Fifteen years ago this place was actually dangerous. We had malaria, dysentery, elephantiasis, and other illnesses you would not even know about. They had no hospital and no doctor until I came. I had to fight dysentery alone, and teach them not to sleep in the same bed with their farm animals."

"How did you happen to come here?"

"We have a system in Mexico. Before obtaining their degrees, young medical students have to have a year of practice in whatever small town needs them. When I first came here I was only eighteen. I was irresponsible and a bit sullen at having to take care of fishermen who could neither read nor write nor follow instructions of any kind. When I was not needed, I read French novels and dreamed of the life in large cities which I was missing. But gradually I came to love my fishermen, and when the year was over I chose to stay."

The eyes of the people were full of burning life. They squatted like Orientals next to their wide flat baskets filled with fruits and vegetables. The fruit was not piled negligently but arranged in a careful Persian design of decorative harmonies. Strings of chili hung from the rafters, chili to wake them from their dreams, dreams born of scents and rhythms, and the warmth that fell from the sky like the fleeciest blanket. Even the twilight came without a change of temperature or alteration in the softness of the air.

It was not only the music from the guitars but the music of the body that Lillian heard—a continuous rhythm of life. There was a rhythm in the way the women lifted the water jugs onto their heads, and walked balancing them. There was a rhythm in the way the shepherds walked after their lambs and their cows. It was not just the climate, but the people themselves who exuded a more ardent life.

Hansen was looking out the taxi window with a detached

and bored expression. He did not see the people. He did not notice the children who, because of their black hair cut in square bangs and their slanted eyes, sometimes looked like Japanese. He questioned Lillian on entertainers. What entertainers from New York or Paris or London should he bring to the Black Pearl?

The hotel was at the top of the hill, one main building and a cluster of small cottages hidden by olive trees and cactus. It faced the sea at a place where huge boiling waves were trapped by crevices in the rocks and struck at their prison with cannon reverberations. Two narrow gorges were each time assaulted, the waves sending foam high in the air and leaping up as if in a fury at being restrained.

The receptionist at the desk was dressed in rose silk, as if registering guests and handing out keys were part of the festivities. The manager came out, holding out his hand paternally, as though his immense bulk conferred on him a patriarchy, and said: "You are free to enjoy yourself tonight. You won't have to start playing until tomorrow night. Did you see the posters?"

He led her to the entrance where her photograph, enlarged, faced her like the image of a total stranger. She never recognized herself in publicity photographs. "I look pickled," she thought.

A dance was going on, on the leveled portion of the rock beside the hotel. The music was intermittent, for the wind carried some of the notes away, and the sound of the sea absorbed others, so that these fragments of mambos had an abstract distinction like the music of Erik Satie. It also made the couples seem to be dancing sometimes in obedience to it, and sometimes in obedience to the gravitations of their secret attractions.

A barefoot boy carried Lillian's bags along winding paths. Flowers brushed her face as she passed. Both music and sea sounds grew fainter as they climbed. Cottages were set capriciously on rock ledges, hidden by reeds, or camouflaged in bougainvillaea. The boy stopped before a cottage with a palm-leaf roof.

In front of it was a long tile terrace with a hemp hammock strung across it. The room inside had whitewashed walls and contained only a bed, a table, and a chair. Parasoling over the cottage was a giant tree which bore leaves shaped like fans. The encounter of the setting sun and rising moon had combined to paint everything in the changing colors of mercury.

As Lillian opened a bureau drawer, a mouse that had been making a nest of magnolia petals suddenly fled.

She showered and dressed hastily, feeling that perhaps the beauty and velvety softness of the night might not last, that if she delayed it would change to coldness and harshness. She put on the only dress she had that matched the bright flowers, an orange cotton. Then she opened the screen door. The night lay unchanged, serene, filled with tropical whisperings, as if leaves, birds, and sea breezes possessed musicalities unknown to northern countries, as if the richness of the scents kept them all intently alive.

The tiles under her bare feet were warm. The perfume she had sprayed on herself evaporated before the stronger perfumes of carnation and honeysuckle.

She walked back to the wide terrace where people sat on deck chairs waiting for each other and for dinner.

The expanse of sky was like an infinite canvas on which human beings were incapable of projecting images from their human life because they would seem out of scale and absurd.

Lillian felt that nature was so powerful it absorbed her into itself. It was a drug for forgetting. People seemed warmer and nearer, as the stars seemed nearer and the moon warmer.

The sea's orchestration carried away half the spoken words and made talking and laughing seem a mere casual accompaniment, like the sound of birds. Words had no weight. The intensity of the colors made them float in space like balloons, and the velvet texture of the climate gave them a purely decorative quality like no other flowers. They had no abstract meaning, being received by the senses which only recognized touch, smell, and vision, so that these people sitting in their chairs became a part of a vivid animated mural. A brown shoulder emerging from a white dress, the limpidity of a smile in a tanned face, the muscular tension of a brown leg, seemed more eloquent than the voices.

This is an exaggerated spectacle, thought Lillian, and it makes me comfortable. I was always an exaggerated character because I was trying to create all by myself a climate which suited me, bigger flowers, warmer words, more fervent relationships, but here nature does it for me, creates the climate I need within myself, and I can be languid and at rest. It is a drug . . . a drug . . .

Why were so many people fearful of the tropics? "All adventurers came to grief." Perhaps they had not been able to make the transition, to alchemize the life of the mind into the life of the senses. They died when their minds were overpowered by nature, yet they did not hesitate to dilute it in alcohol.

Even while Golconda lulled her, she was aware of several mysteries entering her reverie. One she called the sorrows of Doctor Hernandez. The other was why do exiles come to a bad end (if they did, of which she was not sure). From where she sat, she saw the Doctor arrive with his professional valise. But this burden he deposited at the hotel desk, and then he walked toward Lillian as if he had been seeking her.

"You haven't had dinner yet? Come and have it with me. We'll have it in the Black Pearl, so you will become familiar with the place where you are going to play every night."

The Black Pearl had been built of driftwood. It was a series of terraces overhanging the sea. Red ship lanterns illumined a jazz band playing for a few dancers.

Because the hiss of the sea carried away some of the overtones, the main drum beat seemed more emphatic, like a giant heart pulsing. The more volatile cadences, the ironic notes, the lyrical half-sobs of the trombone rose like sea spray and were lost. As if the instrumentalists knew this, they repeated their climbs up invisible antennae into vast spaces of volatile joys and shrank the sorrows by speed and flight, decanting all the

476

essences, and leaving always at the bottom the blood beat of the drums.

The Doctor was watching her face. "Did I frighten you with all my talk about sickness?"

"No, Doctor Hernandez, illness does not frighten me. Not physical illness. The one that does is unknown in Golconda. And I'm a convalescent. And in any case, it's one which does not inspire sympathy."

Her words had been spoken lightly, but they caused the Doctor's smooth face to wrinkle with anxiety. Anxiety? Fear? She could not read his face. It had the Indian sculptural immobility. Even when the skin wrinkled with some spasm of pain, the eyes revealed nothing, and the mouth was not altered.

She felt compelled to ask: "Are you unhappy? Are you in trouble?"

She knew it was dangerous to question those who were accustomed to doing the questioning, to being depended on (and well did Lillian know that those who were in the position of consolers, guides, healers, felt uncomfortable in any reversal), but she took the risk.

He answered, laughing: "No, I'm not, but if being unhappy would arouse your interest, I'm willing to be. It was tactless of me to speak of illness in this place created for pleasure. I nearly spoiled *your* pleasure. And I can see you are one who has not had too much of it, one of the underprivileged of pleasure! Those who have too much nauseate me. I don't know why. I'm glad when they get dysentery or serious sunburns. It is as if I believed in an even distribution of pleasure. Now you, for instance, have a right to some . . . not having had very much."

"I didn't realize it was so apparent."

"It is not so apparent. Permit me to say I am unusually astute. Diagnostic habit. You *appear* free and undamaged, vital and without wounds."

"Diagnostic clairvoyance, then?"

"Yes. But here comes our professional purveyor of pleasure. He may be more beneficent for you."

Hansen sat down beside them and began to draw on the tablecloth. "I'm going to add another terrace, then I will flood-light the trees and the divers. I will also have a light around the statue of the Virgin so that everyone can see the boys praying before they dive." His glance was cold, managerial. The sea, the night, the divers were all, in his eyes, properties of the night club. The ancient custom of praying before diving one hundred feet into a narrow rocky gorge was going to become a part of the entertainment.

Lillian turned her face away from him, and listened to the jazz.

Jazz was the music of the body. The breath came through aluminum and copper tubes, it was the body's breath, and the strings' wails and moans were echoes of the body's music. It was the body's vibrations which rippled from the fingers. And the mystery of the withheld theme known to the musicians alone was like the mystery of our secret life. We give to others only peripheral improvisations. The plots and themes of the music, like the plots and themes of our life, never alchemized into words, existed only in a state of music, stirring or numbing, exalting or despairing, but never named.

When she turned her face unwillingly towards Hansen, he was gone, and then she looked at the Doctor and said: "This is a drugging place. . . ."

"There are so many kinds of drugs. One for remembering and one for forgetting. Golconda is for forgetting. But it is not a permanent forgetting. We may seem to forget a person, a place, a state of being, a past life, but meanwhile what we are doing is selecting a new cast for the reproduction of the same drama, seeking the closest reproduction to the friend, the lover, or the husband we are striving to forget. And one day we open our eyes, and there we are caught in the same pattern, repeating the same story. How could it be otherwise? The design comes from within us. It is internal."

There were tears in Lillian's eyes, for having made friends immediately not with a new, a beautiful, a drugging place, but with a man intent on penetrating the mysteries of the human labyrinth from which she was a fugitive. She was almost angered by his persistence. A man should respect one's desire to have no past. But even more damaging was his conviction that we live by a series of repetitions until the experience is solved, understood, liquidated. . . .

"You will never rest until you have discovered the familiar within the unfamiliar. You will go around as these tourists do, searching for flavors which remind you of home, begging for Coca-Cola instead of tequila, cereal foods instead of papaya. Then the drug will wear off. You will discover that barring a few divergences in skin tone, or mores, or language, you are still related to the same kind of person because it all comes from within you, you are the one fabricating the web."

Other people were dancing around them, so obedient to the rhythms that they seemed like algae in the water, welded to each other, and swaying, the colored skirts billowing, the white suits like frames to support the flower arrangements made by the women's dresses, their hair, their jewels, their lacquered nails. The wind sought to carry them away from the orchestra, but they remained in its encirclement of sound like Japanese kites moved by strings from the instruments.

Lillian asked for another drink. But as she drank it, she knew that one of the drops of the Doctor's clairvoyance had fallen into her glass, that a part of what he had said was already proved true. The first friend she had made in Golconda, choosing him in preference to the engineer and the nightclub manager, resembled, at least in his role, a personage she had known who was nicknamed "The Lie Detector"; for many months this man had lived among a group of artists extracting complete confessions from them without effort and subtly changing the course of their lives.

Not to yield to the Doctor's challenge, she brusquely turned the spotlight on him: "Are you engaged in such a repetition now, with me? Have you left anyone behind?"

"My wife hates this place," said the Doctor simply. "She

comes here rarely. She stays in Mexico City most of the time, on the excuse that the children must go to good schools. She is jealous of my patients, and says they are not really ill, that they pretend to be. And in this she is right. Tourists in strange countries are easily frightened. More frightened of strangeness. They call me to reassure themselves that they will not succumb to the poison of strangeness, to unfamiliar foods, exotic flavors, or the bite of an unfamiliar insect. They do call me for trivial reasons, often out of fear. But is fear trivial? And my native patients do need me desperately . . . I built a beautiful house for my wife. But I cannot keep her here. And I love this place, the people. Everything I have created is here. The hospital is my work. And if I leave, the drug traffic will run wild. I have been able to control it."

Lillian no longer resented the Doctor's probings. He was suffering, and it was this which made him so aware of others' difficulties.

"That's a very painful conflict, and not easily solved," she said. She wanted to say more, but she was stopped by a messenger boy with bare feet, who had come to fetch the Doctor on an emergency case.

Lillian and the Doctor sat in a hand-carved canoe. The pressure of the human hand on the knife had made uneven indentations in the scooped-out tree trunk which caught the light like the scallops of the sea shell. The sun on the high rims of these declivities and the shadows within their valleys gave the canoe a stippled surface like that of an impressionist painting, made it seem a multitude of spots moving forward on the water in ripples of changeable colors and textures.

The fisherman was paddling it quietly through the varied colors of the lagoon water, colors that ranged from the dark sepia of the red earth bottom to silver gray when the colors of the bushes triumphed over the earth, to gold when the sun conquered them both, to purple in the shadows.

He paddled with one arm. His other had been blown off when he was a young fisherman of seventeen first learning the use of dynamite sticks for fishing.

The canoe had once been painted in laundry blue. This blue had faded and become like the smoky blue of old Mayan murals. a blue which man could not create, only time.

The lagoon trees showed their naked roots, as though on stilts, an intricate maze of silver roots as fluent below as they were interlaced above, and overhung, casting shadows before the bow of the canoe so dense that Lillian could scarcely believe they would open and divide to let them through.

Emerald sprays and fronds projected from a mass of wasp nests, of pendant vines and lianas. Above her head the branches formed metallic green parabolas and enameled pennants, while the canoe and her body accomplished the magical feat of cutting smoothly through the roots and dense tangles.

The boat undulated the aquatic plants and the grasses that bore long plumes, and traveled through reflections of the clouds. The absence of visible earth made Lillian feel as if the forest were afloat, an archipelago of green vapors.

The snowy herons, the shell-pink flamingos meditated upon one leg like yogis of the animal world.

Now and then she saw a single habitation by the waterside, an ephemeral hut of palm leaves wading on frail stilts and a canoe tied to a toy-sized jetty. Before each hut, watching Lillian and the Doctor float by would be a smiling woman and several naked children. They stood against a backdrop of impenetrable foliage, as if the jungle allowed them, along with the butterflies, dragonflies, praying mantises, beetles, and parrots, to occupy only its fringe. The exposed giant roots of the trees made the children seem to be standing between the toes of Gulliver's feet.

Once when the earth showed itself on the right bank, Lillian saw on the mud the tracks of a crocodile that had come to quench his thirst. The scaly carapaces of the iguanas were colored so exactly like the ashen roots and tree trunks that she could not spot them until they moved. When they did not move they lay as still as stones in the sun, as if petrified.

The canoe pushed languid water lettuce out of the way, and water orchids, magnolias, and giant clover leaves.

A flowing journey, a contradiction to the persistent dream from which Lillian sought to liberate herself. The dream of a boat, sometimes large and sometimes small, but invariably caught in a waterless place, in a street, in the jungle, in the desert. When it was large it was in city streets, and the deck reached to the upper windows of the houses. She was in this boat and aware that it could not float unless it were pushed, so she would get down from it and seek to push it along so that it might move and finally reach water. The effort of pushing the boat along the street was immense, and she never accomplished her aim. Whether she pushed it along cobblestones or over asphalt, it moved very little, and no matter how much she strained she always felt she would never reach the sea. When the boat was small the pushing was less difficult; nevertheless she never reached the lake or river or the sea in which it could sail. Once the boat was stuck between rocks, another time on a mud bank.

Today she was fully aware that the dream of pushing the boat through waterless streets was ended. In Golconda she had attained a flowing life, a flowing journey. It was not only the presence of water, but the natives' flowing rhythm: they never became caught in the past, or stagnated while awaiting the future. Like children, they lived completely in the present.

She had read that certain Egyptian rulers had believed that after death they would join a celestial caravan in an eternal journey toward the sun. Scientists had found two solar barques, which they recognized from ancient texts and mortuary paintings, in a subterranean chamber of limestone. The chamber was so well sealed that no air, dust, or cobwebs had been found in it. There were always two such barques—one for the night's journey toward the moon, one for the day's journey toward the sun.

In dreams one perpetuated these journeys in solar barques. And in dreams, too, there were always two: one buried in limestone and unable to float on the waterless routes of anxiety, the other flowing continuously with life. The static one made the voyage of memories, and the floating one proceeded into endless discoveries.

This canoe, thought Lillian, as she dipped her hand into the lagoon water, was to be her solar barque, magnetized by sun and water, gyrating and flowing, without strain or effort.

The Doctor's thoughts had also been wandering through other places. Mexico City, where his wife was? His three small children? His past? His medical studies in Paris and in New York? His first book of poems, published when he was twenty years old?

Lillian smiled at him as if saying, you too have taken a secret journey into the past.

Simultaneously they returned to the present.

Lillian said: "There is a quality in this place which does not come altogether from its beauty. What is it? Is it the softness which annihilates all thought and lulls the body for enjoyment? Is it the continuity of music which prevents thoughts from arresting the flow of life? I have seen other trees, other rivers; they did not have the power to intoxicate the senses. Do you feel this? Does everyone feel this? Is this what kept South Seas travelers from ever returning home?"

"It does not affect everyone in the same way," said the Doctor with bitterness in his voice, and Lillian realized he was thinking of his wife.

Was this the mystery in Doctor Hernandez's life? A wife he could not win over to the city he liked, the life he loved?

She waited for him to say more. But he was silent, and his face had become placid again.

Her hand, which she had left in the waters of the lagoon to

feel the gliding, the uninterrupted gentleness of the flowing, to assure herself of this union with a living current, she now felt she must lift, to prove to the Doctor that she shared his anxiety, and that his sadness affected her. She must surrender the pleasure of touching the flow of water, as if she were touching the flow of life within her, out of sympathy for his anguish.

As she lifted her hand and waited for the drops of water to finish dripping from it, a shot was heard, and water spattered over her. They all three sat still, stunned.

"Hunters?" she asked. She wanted to stand up and shout and wave so the hunters would know they were there.

The Doctor answered quietly: "They were not hunters. It was not a mistake. They intended to shoot me, but they missed."

"But why? Why? You're the most needed, the most loved man here!"

"I refuse to give them drugs. Don't you understand? As a doctor I have access to drugs. They want to force me to give them some. Drugs for forgetting. And I have no right to do this, no right except in cases of great physical pain. That's why when you compared Golconda to a drug I felt bitter. For some people, Golconda is not enough."

The fisherman did not understand their talk in English. He said in Spanish, with a resigned air: "Bad hunters. They missed the crocodile. I could catch him with my bare hands and a knife. I often have. Without guns. What bad hunters!"

The swimming pool was at the lowest level of the hotel and only about ten feet above the sea, so that it was dominated by the roar of the waves hurling themselves against the rocks. The quietness of its surface did not seem like the quietness of a pool but more like that of a miniature bay formed within rocks which miraculously escaped the boiling sea for a few moments.

484

It did not seem an artificial pool dug into cement and fed by water pipes, but rather one of the sea's own moods, one of the sea's moments of response, an intermittent haven.

It was surrounded by heavy, lacquered foliage, and flowers so tenuously held that they fell of their own weight into the pool and floated among the swimmers like children's boats.

It was an island of warm, undangerous water in which one man at least had sought eternal repose by throwing himself out of one of the overhanging hotel windows. Ever since that night the pool had been locked at midnight. Those who knew that the watchman preferred to watch the dancers on the square and that the gate could easily be leaped over, came to sit there in the evenings before going to sleep. The place was barred to any loud frivolity but open for secret assignations after dancing.

It was also Lillian's favorite place before going to sleep. The gentleness of the water, its warmth, was the lulling atmosphere she had missed when she had passed from childhood to womanhood.

She felt an unconfessed need of receiving from some gentle source the reassurance that the world was gentle and warm, and not, as it may have seemed during the day, cold and cruel. This reassurance was never granted to the mature, so that Lillian told no one of the role the pool played in her life today. It was the same role played by another watchman whom she had heard when she was ten years old and living in Mexico while her father built bridges and roads. The town watchman, a figure out of the Middle Ages, walked the streets at night chanting: "All is well, all is calm and peaceful. All is well."

Lillian had always waited for this watchman to pass before going to sleep. No matter how tense she had been during the day, no matter what catastrophes had taken place in school, or in the street, or at home, she knew that this moment would come when the watchman would walk all alone in the darkened streets swinging his lantern and his keys, crying monotonously, "All is well, all is well and calm and peaceful." No sooner had he said this and no sooner had she heard the jangling keys and seen the flash of his lantern on the wall of her room, than she would fall instantly asleep.

Others who came to the pool were of the fraternity who liked to break laws, who liked to steal their pleasures, who liked the feeling that at any time the hotel watchman might appear at the top of the long stairs; they knew his voice would not carry above the hissing sea, and that as he was too lazy to walk downstairs he would merely turn off the lights as if this were enough to disperse the transgressors. To be forced to swim in the darkness and slip away from the pool in darkness was not, as the watchman believed, a punishment, but an additional pleasure.

In the darkness one became even more aware of the softness of the night, of pulsating life in the muscles, of the pleasure of motion. The silence that ensued was the silence of conspiracy and at this hour everyone dropped his disguises and spoke from some realm of innocence preserved from the corrosion of convention.

The Doctor would come to the pool, leaving his valise at the hotel desk. He talked as if he wanted to forget that everyone needed him, and that he had little time for pleasure or leisure. But Lillian felt that he never rested from diagnosis. It was as if he did not believe anyone free of pain, and could not rest until he had placed his finger on the core of it.

Lillian now sat in one of the white string chairs that looked like flattened harps, and played abstractedly with the white cords as if she were composing a song.

The Doctor watched her and said: "I can't decide which of the two drugs you need: the one for forgetting or the one for remembering."

Lillian abandoned the harp chair and slipped into the pool, floating on her back and seeking immobility.

"Golconda is for forgetting, and that's what I need," she said, laughing.

"Some memories are imbedded in the flesh like splinters," said the Doctor, "and you have to operate to get them out."

486

She swam underwater, not wanting to hear him, and then came up nearer to where he sat on the steps and said: "Do I really seem to you like someone with a splinter in her flesh?"

"You act like a fugitive."

She did not want to be touched by the word. She plunged into the deep water again as if to wash her body of all memories, to wash herself of the past. She returned gleaming, smooth, but not free. The word had penetrated and caused an uneasiness in her breast like that caused by diminished oxygen. The search for truth was like an explorer's deep-sea diving, or his climb into impossible altitudes. In either case it was a problem of oxygen, whether you went too high or too low. Any world but the familiar neutral one caused such difficulty in breathing. It may have been for this reason that the mystics believed in a different kind of training in breathing for each different realm of experience.

The pressure in her chest compelled her to leave the pool and sit beside the Doctor, who was looking out to sea.

In the lightest voice she could find, and with the hope of discouraging the Doctor's seriousness, she said: "I was a woman who was so ashamed of a run in my stocking that it would prevent me from dancing all evening. . . ."

"It wasn't the run in your stocking. . . ."

"You mean . . . other things . . . ashamed . . . just vaguely ashamed. . . ."

"If you had not been ashamed of other things you would not have cared about the run in your stocking. . . ."

"I've never been able to describe or understand what I felt. I've lived so long in an impulsive world, desiring without knowing why, destroying without knowing why, losing without knowing why, being defeated, hurting myself and others. . . . All this was painful, like a jungle in which I was constantly lost. A chaos."

"Chaos is a convenient hiding place for fugitives. You are a fugitive from truth."

"Why do you want to force me to remember? The beauty of

Golconda is that one does not remember. . . ."

"In Eastern religions there was a belief that human beings gathered the sum total of their experiences on earth, to be examined at the border. And according to the findings of the celestial customs officer one would be directed either to a new realm of experience, or back to re-experience the same drama over and over again. The condemnation to repetition would only cease when one had understood and transcended the old experience."

"So you think I am condemned to repetition? You think that I have not liquidated the past?"

"Yes, unless you know what it is you ran away from. . . ."

"I don't believe this, Doctor. I know I can begin anew here."

"So you will plunge back into chaos, and this chaos is like the jungle we saw from the boat. It is also your smoke screen."

"But I do feel new. . . ."

The Doctor's expression at the moment was perplexed, as if he were no longer certain of his diagnosis; or was it that what he had discovered about Lillian was so grave he did not want to alarm her? He very unexpectedly withdrew at the word "new," smiled with indulgence, raised his shoulders as if he had been persuaded by her eloquence, and finally said: "Maybe only the backdrop has changed."

Lillian examined the pool, the sea, the plants, but could not see them as backdrops. They were too charged with essences, with penetrating essences like the newest drugs which altered the chemistry of the body. The softness entered the nerves, the beauty surrounded and enveloped the thoughts. It was impossible that in this place the design of her past life should repeat itself, and the same characters reappear, as the Doctor had implied. Did the self which lived below visibility really choose its characters repetitiously and with only superficial variations, intent on reproducing the same basic drama, like a well-trained actor with a limited repertory?

And exactly at the moment when she felt convinced of the

deep power of the tropics to alter a character, certain personages appeared who seemed to bear no resemblance to the ones she had left in the other country, personages whom she received with delight because they were gifts from Golconda itself, intended to heal her of other friendships, other loves, and other places.

The hitchhiker Fred was a student from the University of Chicago who had been given a job in the hotel translating letters from prospective guests. Lillian called him "Christmas," because at everything he saw which delighted him—a coppery sunrise or a flamingo bird, a Mexican girl in her white starched dress or a bougainvillaea bush in full bloom—he would exclaim: "It's like Christmas!"

He was tall and blond but undecided in his movements, as if he were not sure yet that his arms and legs belonged to him. He was at that adolescent age when his body hampered him, as though it were a shell he was seeking to outgrow. He was still concerned with the mechanics of living, unable as yet to enjoy it. For him it was still an initiation, an ordeal. He still belonged to the Nordic midnight sun; the tropical sun could not tan him, only freckle him. Sometimes he had the look of a blond angel who had just come from a Black Mass. He smiled innocently although one felt sure that in his dreams he had undressed the angels and the choir boys and made love to them. He had the small smile of Pan. His eyes conveyed only the wide expanse of desert that lay between human beings, and his mouth expressed the tremors he felt when other human beings approached him. The eyes said: do not come too near. But his body glowed with warmth. It was his mouth, compressed and controlled, which revealed his timidity.

At everything new he marveled, but with persistent reference to the days of his childhood which had given him a permanent joy. Every day was Christmas day; the turtle eggs served at lunch were a gift from the Mexicans, the opened coconut spiked with rum was a new brand of candy.

His only anxiety centered around the problem of returning

home. He did not have time enough to hitchhike back; it had taken him a full month to get here. He had no money, so he had decided to work his way back on a cargo ship.

Everyone offered to contribute, to perpetuate his Christmas day. But a week after his arrival he was already inquiring about cargo ships which would take him back home in time to finish college, and back to Shelley, the girl he was engaged to.

But about Shelley there was no hurrry, he explained. It was because of Shelley that he had decided to spend the summer hitchhiking. He was engaged and he was afraid. Afraid of the girl. He needed time, time to adventure, time to become a man. Yes, to become a man. (He always showed Shelley's photograph, and there was nothing in the tilted-up nose, the smile, and her soft hair to frighten anyone.)

Lillian asked him: "Couldn't Shelley have helped you to become a man?"

He had shrugged his shoulders. "A girl can't help a boy to become a man. I have to feel I am one *before I marry*. And I don't know anything about myself . . . or about women . . . or about love. . . . I thought this trip would help me. But I find I am afraid of all girls. It was not only Shelley."

"What is the difference between a girl and a woman?"

"Girls laugh. They laugh at you. That's the one thing I can't bear, to be laughed at."

"They're not laughing at you, Christmas. They're laughing because they wish to hide their own fears, to appear free and light, or they laugh so you won't think they take you too seriously. They may be laughing from pleasure, to encourage you. Think how frightened you would be if they did not laugh, if they looked at you gravely and made you feel that their destiny was in your hands, a matter of life and death. That would frighten you even more, wouldn't it?"

"Yes, much more."

"Do you want me to tell you the truth?"

"Yes, you have a way of saying things which makes me feel you are not laughing at me."

490

"If . . . you experimented with becoming a man before you married your girl, you might also find that it was *because* you were a boy that she loved you . . . that she loves you for what you are, not for what you will be later. She might love you less if you changed. . . ."

"What makes you think this?"

"Because if you truly wanted to change, you would not be so impatient to leave. Your mind is fixed on the departure times of cargo ships!"

When he arrived at the pool Lillian could almost see him carrying his two separate and contradictory wishes, one in each hand. But at least while he was intent on juggling them without losing his balance, he no longer felt the pain of not living, of a paralysis before living.

His smile at Lillian was charged with gratitude. Lillian was thinking that the primitives were wiser in having definitely established rituals: at a certain moment, determined by the calendar, a boy becomes a man.

Meanwhile Fred was using all his energy in rituals of his own: he had to master water skiing, he had to be the champion swimmer and diver, he must initiate the Mexicans into his knowledge of jazz, he had to outdo everyone in going without sleep, in dancing.

Lillian had said: "Fears cannot bear to be laughed at. If you take all your fears, one by one, make a list of them, face them, decide to challenge them, most of them will vanish. Strange women, strange countries, strange foods, strange illnesses."

While Fred dived many times into the pool conscientiously, Diana arrived.

Diana had first come to Mexico at the age of seventeen when she had won a painting fellowship. But she had stayed, married, and built a house in Golconda. Most of the time she was alone; her husband worked and traveled.

She no longer painted, but collected textiles, paintings, and jewelry. She spent her entire morning getting dressed. She no longer sat before an easel, but before a dressing table, and made an art of dressing in native textiles and jewels.

When she finally descended the staircase into the hotel, she became an animated painting. Everyone's eyes were drawn to her. All the colors of Diego Rivera and Orozco were draped on her body. Sometimes her dress seemed painted with large brushstrokes, sometimes roughly dyed like the costumes of the poor. Other times she wore what looked like fragments of ancient Mayan murals, bold symmetrical designs in charcoal outlines with the colors dissolved by age. Heavy earrings of Aztec warriors, necklaces and bracelets of shell, gold and silver medallions and carved heads and amulets, animals and bones, all these caught the light as she moved.

It was her extreme liveliness that may have prevented her from working upon a painting, and turned a passion for color and textures upon her own body.

Lillian saw her once, later, at a costume party carrying an empty frame around her neck. It was Diana's head substituted for a canvas, her head with its slender neck, its tousled hair, tanned skin and earth-colored eyes. Her appearance within an empty frame was an exact representation of her history.

With the same care she took in dressing herself, in creating tensions of colors and metals, once she had arrived at the top of the staircase, she set out to attract all the glances, exposing the delicately chiseled face belonging to a volatile person and incongruously set upon a luxurious body which one associated with all the voluptuous reclining figures of realistic paintings. When she was satisfied that every eye was on her, she was content, and could devote herself to the second phase of her activity.

First of all she thrust her breasts forward, as if to assert that hers was a breathing, generous body, and not just a painting. But they were in curious antiphony, the quick-turning sharp-featured head with its untamed hair, and the body with its separate language, the language of the strip teaser; for, after raising her breasts upward and outward as a swimmer might before diving, she continued to undulate, and although one could not trace the passage of her hand over various places on her body, Lillian had the feeling that, like the strip teaser, she had mysteriously called attention to the roundness of her shoulder, to the indent of her waist. And what added to the illusion of provocation was that, having dressed herself with the lavishness of ancient civilizations, she proceeded gradually to strip herself. It was her artistic interpretation of going native.

She would first of all lay her earrings on the table and rub her ear lobes. The rings hurt her ears, which wanted to be free. No eyes could detach themselves from this spectacle. She would remove her light jacket, and appear in a backless sundress. After breakfast, on a chaise longue on the terrace, she would lie making plans for the beach, but on this chaise longue she turned in every ripple or motion which could escape immobility. She took off her bracelets and rubbed the wrist which they had confined. She was too warm for her beach robe. By the time she reached the beach even the bathing suit had ceased to be visible to one's eyes. By an act of prestidigitation, even though she was now dressed as was every other woman on the beach, one could see her as the naked, full, brown women of Gauguin's Tahitian scenes.

Whoever had voted that she deserved a year to dedicate herself to the art of painting had been wise and clairvoyant.

Illogically, with Diana Fred lost his fear of women who laughed. Perhaps because Diana's laughter was continuous, so that it seemed, like the music of the guitars, an accompaniment to their days in Golconda.

Every day Fred wanted Diana and Lillian to accompany him in his visits to the cargo ships which were to sail him home. The one that had accepted him was not ready yet. It was being loaded very slowly with coconuts, dried fish, crocodile skins, bananas, and baskets.

They would walk the length of the wharf, watching the fishermen catching tropical fish, or watching the giant turtle that had been turned on its back so that it would not escape until it was time to make turtle soup.

Watching the small ships preparing to sail, questioning the

captain who wore a brigand's mustache, the mate who wore no shirt, and obtaining no definite sailing date, the anxiety of Christmas reached its culmination.

He had something to prove to himself which he had not yet proved. He was simultaneously enjoying his adventure and constantly planning to put an end to it.

When the captain allowed him to visit the ship he would stand alone on its deck and watch Diana and Lillian standing on the wharf. They waved goodbye in mockery and he waved back. And it was only at this moment that he noticed how alive Lillian's hair was, as if each curl were weaving itself around his fingers, how slender Diana's neck and inviting to the hand, how full of light both their faces were, how their fluttering dresses enveloped and caressed them.

Behind them rose the soft violet mountains of Golconda. He had known intimately neither woman nor city and was already losing them. Then he felt pain and a wild desire not to sail away. He would run down the gangplank, pushing the porters to one side, run back once more to all the trepidations they caused him by their nearness.

Neither Diana nor Lillian was helping him. They both smiled so gaily, without a shadow of regret, and did not force him to stay, or cling to him. And in the deepest part of himself he knew they were helping him to become a man by allowing him to make his own decisions. That was part of the initiation. They would not steal his boyhood; he must abdicate it.

He loved them both: Diana for incarnating the spice, the color, and the fragrance of Golconda, and Lillian because her knowledge of him seemed to incarnate him, and because she was like a powerful current that transmitted life to him.

Just as he climbed the gangplank as a rehearsal for his departure, he felt then that he was not ready to leave, so when he returned to them he felt unready to live, painfully poised between crystallizations. He could not follow Diana's invitations into the unknown, unfamiliar life of the senses, and he could not sail either.

494

An invisible race was taking place between Diana's offer of a reclining nude by a Gauguin and the ship's departure. And as if the ship, the captain, the mate, and the men who loaded it had known he was not ready to leave, one day when he went to the pier at four o'clock as he did every day, the ship was gone!

He could still see it on the horizon line, a small black speck throwing off not qute enough smoke to conceal its departure.

Lillian was walking through the market. It was like walking through an Oriental bazaar. Gold filigree from Spain, silk scarves from India, embroidered skirts from Japan, glazed potteries from Africa, engraved copper from Morocco, sculptures from Egypt, herbs and incense from Arabia. At the time Golconda was an important seaport, every country had deposited some of its riches there. When it was no longer visited, the Mexicans themselves had created variations upon these themes, adding inventions of their own.

Cages containing tropical birds were panoplied with striped awnings like the tents of ancient maharajahs. From them the Mexicans had inherited the art of training birds to pick out of their hands tiny folded papers containing predictions for the future.

Lillian gave her pennies to the man and asked for one of the messages. The bird very delicately selected, from a handful, a message that read: "You will find what you are seeking." Lillian smiled. She wondered whether among those tiny folded papers the bird might pick up a message telling her *what* it was she was seeking. She decided to squander a few more pennies. But the Mexican bird trainer refused to let her try again. "It's bad luck to question destiny twice. If it gives you two answers you will be confused."

495

Beside her stood a man who was well known in Golconda as a guide. She had always disliked him. Not because she condemned his trade of selling Golconda to the spectators who could not discover it for themselves, not because she lacked sympathy for the strangers who wanted to witness others' weddings, others' fiestas, as paying guests, but because wherever he stood, at the hotel entrance, at the ticket agencies, at the bullfight entrance, he had the air of a pimp, a pimp who was ashamed of what he was selling, as if Golconda were not a radiant city but a package of obscene post cards. It was the suggestive way he had approached her the first time, whispering: "Would you like to attend a genuine Mexican wedding?" as though he were saying: "Would you like me to procure for you a fine young man?"

It may be that Lillian identified his yellow face, his averted eyes, and his constantly nibbling lips with prying, with the spectator, with all peripheral living. And yet, she thought, blushing, I am quite willing to seek guidance for my inward journeys. To ask of a trained bird that he should pick out of a pile of folded papers guidance for my inward journeys!

This thought caused her to look at the guide with more tolerance, and he sensed her weakening defenses. This made him take a step forward and whisper to her shoulder, which was on the level of his eyes: "I have something to show you that will really interest you. It isn't just an ordinary tourist sight, believe me. It is a fellow American in trouble. You're an American woman, aren't you? I was told about you. You came to Mexico as a child with your American father who was an engineer. You speak Spanish fluently, and you understand our ways. I saw you at church with a handkerchief on your head to show respect for our customs. But you are American, I know. Would you feel sorry for an American in real trouble? Would you like to help?"

Lillian struggled with her distrust of the guide, whose lizard-colored eyes remained fixed on the freckles on her shoulders.

"What kind of trouble?"

"Well, he was caught without papers, traveling in the bus to Yucatan. So they put him in jail, here, where he started from. He's been in jail one year now."

"A year? And nothing was done for him?"

The guide's mouth, which seemed to nibble and chew at words rather than utter them, nibbled in the void, uttering no word while he was thinking.

"An American trapped in a foreign country, who cannot speak Spanish. You might at least talk with him?"

"And nothing has been done? Nobody has done anything? Hasn't he appealed to the American consulate?"

The guide mimicked a gesture of indifference, not content with shrugging the imaginary weight off his shoulders, but also washing his hands of it, and when turning away and taking several steps indicating detachment from the problem. It was almost as if he were anticipating any gesture of indifference Lillian might make.

"Where is this jail?"

He walked furtively ahead of her. Whether or not he felt ashamed of taking strangers through the scenes of his native village, ashamed to be paid for invading burials and weddings, he walked as if he were leading them all to places of ill fame, as perhaps he had.

The other tourists treated him with unusual cordiality. They felt isolated and mistook him for a bridge of friendship between themselves and the natives. They fraternized with him as if he were a mediator as well as an interpreter. They drank with him and slapped his back.

But Lillian saw him as the deforming mirror which corrupted every relationship between tourist and native. Only the plight of the American prisoner drove her to follow him through streets she had never crossed before, beyond the market and behind the bullring.

They were in the tenement section, a concentration of shacks built of odds and ends, newspapers on tin slabs, palm trees, driftwood, cartons, gasoline tins. The floors were dirt and hammocks served as beds. The cooking was done out of doors on braziers. No matter how poor the houses, they were camouflaged in flowers, and at each window hung a singing bird. And no matter how poor, the laundry on the line was like a palette from which all the Mexican painters could have drawn their warmest, most burning colors.

Why did the plight of the American prisoner affect her so keenly? The knowledge of his being a stranger in a country whose language he did not speak? She visualized him in jail, drinking the polluted water which made all foreigners sick with dysentery, perhaps being bitten by mosquitoes injecting him with malaria.

All her protectiveness was aroused, so that even the guide no longer seemed like a pimp selling the intimate life of Golconda, but a man of kindness, capable of understanding that tourists could be in genuine trouble and not always absurdly rich and powerful figures.

The jail had been built inside a discarded and ruined church. The ogival windows were heavily barred. The original ochre and coral still remained on the walls and gave the prison a joyous air. The church bells were used to call the prisoners to meals, bedtime, or to announce an escaped convict.

The guide was familiar with the place. The guards did not stop playing cards when he entered. They needed shaves so badly that if they had not worn uniforms one might have taken them for prisoners. The place retained a smell of incense which mixed with the smell of tobacco. Some of the stands which had supported statues now served as coat racks, and gun racks. Belts filled with cartridges were thrown over the holy water stoup. A single statue of the Virgin, the dark-faced one from Guadalupe, had been deemed sufficient to guard the jail.

"*Buenos dias.*"

"*Muy buenos dias.*"

"The lady is here to visit the American prisoner."

One of the guards who had been asleep now pulled out his keys with vague hesitancies. He considered giving the keys to the guide and returning to his siesta, but suddenly his pride awakened and he decided to play his allotted role with exaggerated arrogance.

Inside, the walls of the prison were painted in sky blue. The ceilings retained their murals of nude angels, clouds, and vaporous young women playing harps. The cots were all occupied by sleeping prisoners. The American stood by the iron door of his cell watching the arrival of the visitor.

His thin, long-fingered hands held onto the bars of the cell door as if he would tear them down. But in his lean, unshaved face there was a glint of irony which Lillian interpreted as a show of courage. He was smiling.

"It was good of you to come," he said.

"What can I do for you? Should I telephone the American consulate?"

"Other people have tried that but he will not bother. There are too many of us."

"Too many of you?"

"Well, yes, Americans without papers, runaways from home, runaways from the draft, escaped criminals, displaced persons who claim to be Americans, ex-politicos, ex-gangsters, runaways from wives and alimony. . ."

"What happened to your papers?"

"I went for a swim one day. I left all my clothes on the beach. When I came back, all my clothes were gone, and with them my papers. So here I am."

He kept his eyes on her face. They were red, probably from not sleeping. The amusement in them might have been a form a courage.

"But what can I do for you? How can I get you out? I'm not rich. I get a small salary for playing the piano at the Black Pearl."

His eyes pleaded softly in contradiction to the clipped words. "The best way to help me is to give the guide fifty dollars. Can you spare that? He will fix things up and get me out. He knows the ropes. Can you manage that?"

"I can do that. But once you're out, how will you get back home, and won't you get caught again without papers?"

"Once I'm out I can hitchhike to Mexico City, and there go to the consulate. I can manage the rest, if you can get me out."

Later on, having delivered the money, she felt immensely light, as if she had freed a part of herself. The prisoner would have haunted her. She knew by the exaggeration of her feelings that there must be some relationship between the condition of the prisoner and herself. What she had felt was more than sympathy for a fellow American. It may have been sympathy for a fellow prisoner.

To all appearances she was free. But free of what? Had she not lost her identity papers? Was not her voyage like that of the South American bird that walked over the sands rubbing out his tracks with a special feather that grew longer than the others, like a feather duster?

The past had been dissolved by the intensity of Golconda, by its light which dazzled the thoughts, closed the eyes of memory. Freedom from the past came with unfamiliar objects; none of them possessed any evocative power. From the moment she opened her eyes she was in a new world. The colors were all hot and brilliant, not the pearly grays and attenuated pastels of her homeland. Breakfast was a tray of fruit of a humid, fleshy quality never tasted before, and even the bread did not have the same flavor. There was an herb which they burned in the oven before inserting the bread which gave it a slight flavor of anise.

All day long there was not a single familiar object to carry her back into her past life. The first human being she saw in the morning was the gardener. She could see him through the half-shut bamboo blinds, raking the pebbles and the sand, not as if he was eager to terminate the task but as if raking pebbles and sand was the most pleasurable occupation and he wanted to prolong his enjoyment. Now and then he would stop to talk with a lonely little girl in a white dress who skipped rope all around him asking questions which he answered gently.

"What makes some butterflies have such beautiful colors on their wings, and others not?"

"The plain ones were born of parents who didn't know how to paint."

And even when familiar objects turned up, they did not turn up in their accustomed places. Like the giant Coca-Cola bottle made of wood placed in the middle of the bull ring before the bullfight began—a grotesque surrealist dream. Lillian had expected the bulls to charge it, but just before the bull was let out the attendants (who usually took care of carrying away the dead bull and sweeping over the bloody tracks) had come and toppled the bottle, and the six of them had carried it away on their shoulders—publicity's defeated trophy.

So all was freedom: her hours, her time, and even the music she improvised at night, the jazz which allowed her to embroider on all her moods.

But there was one moment that was different, and it was the knowledge of this moment that perhaps created her feeling of kinship with the prisoner. That was the hour just before dinner, when she was freshly bathed and dressed, the hour when a genuine adventurer would reach the high point of his gambling with the beauty of the night and feel: Now the evening is beginning and I will discover a human being to court or to be courted by, an adventure with caprice and desire, and while gambling I might find love.

At this hour, when she took one last glance at the mirror, the screen door of her room seemed the locked door of a prison, the room an enclosure, only because she was a prisoner of anxiety: the moment before the unknown gamble with a relationship to other human beings paralyzed her with fear. Who would take her dancing? Would no one come, no one remember her existence? Would all the groups that formed in the evening forget to include her in their plans? Would she arrive at the terrace to find only the head of the Chicago stockyards for a dancing partner? Would she come downstairs and watch

Christmas a bemused spectator of Diana's provocations, and couples climbing into cars going to fiestas, and couples climbing the hill to attend the Sunday night dance on the rocks, and Doctor Hernandez appropriated by a movie star who was sure she had malaria?

This was the moment which proved she was a prisoner of timidities and not a genuine adventurer, not a gambler who could smile when he lost, who could be invulnerable before an empty evening, or untouched by an evening spent with a drunken man who insisted on describing to her how the stock-yards functioned, how the animals were killed.

This fantasy of disaster never actually took place. Several people always gathered around the piano when she played and waited for her to stop to offer her a drink and join them. But actual happenings never freed her of her inner imprisonment by fear, in anticipation of aloneness.

She would like to have seen the prisoner again but imagined he was already on his way to Mexico City. She had time to walk down to the Spanish restaurant on the square, which she preferred to the hotel. In the hotel she ate her own dinner in privacy. On the square she felt she had dinner with the entire city of Golconda, and shared a multitude of lives.

The square was the heart of the town. The church opened its doors to it on one side. The other sides were lined with cafés, restaurants with their tables on the sidewalk, a movie house; in the center was a bandstand surrounded by a small park with benches.

On the benches sat enraptured young lovers, tired hobos, men reading their newspapers while little boys shined their shoes. There was also a circle of vendors sitting on the sidewalk with their baskets full of candied fruit, colored fruit drinks, red and yellow cigarettes, and magazines. Old ladies with black shawls walked quietly in and out of the church, children begged, marimba players settled in front of each café and played as long as the pennies flowed. Singers stopped to sing. Little girls sold sea-shell necklaces and earrings. The prostitutes paraded in taffeta dresses with flowers in their black hair.

The flow of beggars was endlessly varied. They changed their handicaps. When they tired of portraying blindness they suddenly appeared with wooden legs. The genuine ones were terrifying, like nightmare figures: a child, shriveled and shrunken, lying on a little table with wheels which he pushed with withered hands; an old woman so twisted she resembled the roots of a very ancient tree; many of them sightless, with festering sores in place of eyes. But they resisted all professional help, as Doctor Hernandez had told her. They refused to be taken out of the streets, from the spectacles of religious processions, Indian fireworks, band concerts, or the flow of visitors in their eccentric costumes.

And among them now, sitting at a nearby table, was the American prisoner with the guide.

From the heightened tones of their voices, the numerous empty bottles of tequila on the table Lillian knew to what cause her donation for freedom had been diverted. They were beyond recognizing her. Unfocused eyes, vague gestures, revealed a Coney Island of the mind, with the whirlings, the crack-the-whips, the dark chambers of surprises, the deforming mirrors, the jet-plane trips, the death-defying motorcycles of drunkenness. Tongues rubberized, their words came out on oiled rollers, their laughter like sudden geysers.

Just as Lillian sat down there came to her table a short Irishman with an ageless face and round, absolutely fixed round eyes. Their roundness and fixity gave his face an expression of extreme innocence. He greeted her and asked her permission to sit down.

He wore white pants as the Mexicans did, a blue shirt open at the neck, and Spanish rope shoes, and talked briefly in such a monotone that it was difficult to hear what he said.

But his pockets were filled with small fragments from excavations: heads, arms, legs, snakes, flutes, pottery of various Indian origins. He would pull one of these objects out of his pocket and hold it for inspection in the palm of his hand. And

503

quietly he would tell the history of the piece.

He never asked anyone to buy them, but if a tourist asked: "Will you sell it?" he assented sadly, as if it belonged to a private collection and he was only a courteous host.

Every time he saw Lillian he showed her one of the pieces and taught her how to distinguish between the periods, by whether the piece was clay or stone, by the slant of the eye, the headgear, the design of the jewels, so that she began to know the history of Mexico.

O'Connor never talked of anything but the new excavations he had attended, the history of the little fragments. And after that he would fall into a tropical trance.

The theatrical scenes on the square sufficed for his happiness—two sailors quarreling, lovers meeting, a Mexican family celebrating their daughter's winning of the Carnival beauty-queen contest, men alone playing chess after dinner. He lived the life of others. Lillian could see him watching these people until he *became* them. He sat in his chair like a body empty of its spirit, and Lillian could sense him living the life of the lovers, the life of the sailors.

She felt he would understand the story of the prisoner and laugh with her at her gullibility. But he did not laugh. His eyes for the first time lost their glassy fixity. They moistened with emotion.

"I wish I had been able to warn you. . . . I never imagined . . . To think you rescued the one prisoner who did not deserve it! I never told you . . . When I'm not working with excavators and anthropologists I spend all my time rescuing foreigners in trouble—a sailor who gets into a brawl with a Mexican; a tourist whose car kills a donkey on the road. If they are poor, or if they strike a native, the Mexicans are apt to forget them in jail. This place is filled with people who don't care what happens to others. They have come here for pleasure. They are running away from burdens. There's something in the climate too. And now you . . . You went and rescued the one prisoner who makes a profession of this, who shares with the guide what

504

the tourists give him, who lives on that, and then quickly returns to jail, to wait for more."

Lillian laughed again, irrepressibly.

"I'm glad you're laughing. I guess I have taken all this too seriously. It has seemed to me almost a matter of life and death, to get all the prisoners out. I never quite understood it. Sometimes I forget them for a few days, go on my expeditions, swim, travel. But always I return to the jail, to the jailed."

"When you're so intent on freeing others, you must be trying to free some part of yourself too."

"I never gave it much thought . . . but the desperation with which I work, the amount of time I spent on this, as if it were a vice I had no control over . . . Opening jail doors, and searching for fragments of vanished civilizations. Never thought what it might mean . . . You see, I came here to forget myself. I had the illusion that if I engaged in impersonal activities, I would get rid of myself somewhere. I felt that an interest in the history of Mexico and salvaging prisoners meant I had abdicated my personal life."

"Does it disturb you so much to think that perhaps your apparently impersonal activities actually represent a personal drama in which you yourself are involved? That you are merely re-enacting your intimate drama through others, expressing it through others?"

"Yes, it does disturb me. It makes me feel I have failed to escape from myself. Yet I have known all along that I failed in some way. Because I should have been content, alive, as people are when they give of themselves. Instead I have often felt like a depersonalized ghost, a man without a self, a zombie. It is not a good feeling. It's like the old stories about the man who lost his shadow."

"You never abdicate the self, you merely find new ways of manifesting its activities."

"If you know what they mean, my two obsessions, then tell me, I would rather know. I know I have been deceiving myself. Before we began to talk tonight, when I first sat down with you,

I thought to myself, "Now I will act like a dead man again, talk like a guide about my new pieces. . . ."

"We never cast off the self. It persists in living through our impersonal activities. When it is in distress it seeks to give messages through our activities."

"Are you trying to say that I was one of the prisoners myself?"

"Yes, I would say that at some time or other you were in bondage, figuratively speaking, at least kept from doing what you wanted to do; your freedom was tampered with."

"Yes, it's true."

"And every time you can get one of those jail doors open, you feel you are settling an account with some past jailer . . . or at least trying to, as I tried today. . . ."

"Very true. At fifteen I had such a passion for archaeology that I ran away from home. I tried to get to Yucatan. The family sent police after me, who caught me and brought me back. From then on they kept me under watch."

Then his look turned once more toward the square, and he relinquished this expedition into his personal life. His eyes became round again and fixed. He had no more to say.

Watching him, Lillian was reminded of the way animals took on the immobility and the color of a tree's bark or a bush so as not to be detected. She smiled at him, but already he was far removed from the present, the personal, as if he had never talked to her, or known her.

She felt that imprisonment had deprived him of communication with his family, that it was his tongue he had lost then, a vital fragment of himself, and that no matter how many statues he unearthed and reconstructed, no matter how many fragments of history he reassembled, one part of him was missing and might never be found.

The marimba players interrupted their playing as if their instruments were a juke box that could not function without the proper amount of nickels, and began to ask for contributions.

506

In the morning it was the intense radium shafts of the sun on the seas that awakened her, penetrating the native hut. The dawns were like court scenes of Arabian magnificence. The tent of the sky took fire, a laminated coral, dispelling all the sea-shell delicacies which had preceded the birth of the sun, and it was a duel between fire and platinum. The whole sea would seem to have caught fire, until the incendiary dawn stopped burning. After the fire came a rearrangement of more subtle brocades, the turquoise and the coral separated, and transparencies appeared like curtains of the sheerest sari textiles. The rest of the day might have seemed shabby after such an opening, but not in Golconda. The dawn was merely the rain of colors from the sky which the earth and the sea would orchestrate all day, with fruits, flowers, and the dress of the natives. These were not merely spots of color, but always vividly shining and humid, as shining as human eyes, colors as alive as flesh tones.

Just as music was an unbroken chain in Golconda, so were the synchronizations of color. Where the flowers ended their jeweled displays, their pagan illuminated manuscripts, fruits took up the gradations. Once or twice, her mouth full of fruit, she stopped. She had the feeling that she was eating the dawn.

Lying in her hammock she could see both sea and the sunlight, and the rocks below between the stellated, swaying palms. From there too she could see the gardener at work with the tenderness which was the highest quality of the Mexican, a quality which made him work not just for a living, with indifference, but with a tenderness for the plants, a caressingness toward the buds, a swinging rhythm with the rake which made work seem like an act of devotion.

Her day was free until it was time to play with the orchestra for the evening cocktails and dancing.

Before, she had had the feeling that festivities began only with the evening, with the jazz musicians, but now she saw that they began with the sun's extravagance, and ended with a night which never closed up the flowers, or put the gardens to sleep, or made the birds hide their heads in their wings. The night came with such a softness that a new kind of life blossomed. If one touched the sea at night, sparks of phosphorous illuminated it, and sparkled under one's step on the wet sand.

Sometimes, at the beach, the sea seemed not like water but a pool of mercury, so iridescent, so clinging. Swimming on her back, she could see the native musicians arrive, and she would swim ashore.

A guitarist, a violinist, a cellist, and a singer would cluster around an umbrella. The singer sang with such sweetness and tenderness that the hammocks stopped swaying. He enchanted not only the bathers, but the other musicians as well, and the cellist would close his heavy-lidded eyes and play with such a relaxed hand that his brown arm seemed to be held up not by the weight of the hand on the bow, but by some miraculous yogi means of suspension. The South Sea Island shirt seemed to contain no nerves or muscles. The violinist played with one string missing, but as the sea occasionally carried away a few of the notes anyway no one detected the missing ones.

The waves, attracted by the music, would unroll like a bolt of silk, each time a little closer to the musicians, and aim at surrounding the peg of the cello dug deep into the sand. The cellist did not seem to be looking at the waves, yet each time they moved to encircle his cello, he had already lifted it up in midair and continued to play uninterruptedly while the waves washed his feet, then retreated.

After the musicians came children carrying baskets on their heads, selling fruit and fried fish. Then came the old photographer with his old-fashioned accordion box camera, and a big black box cover for his head. He was so neatly dressed, his mustache so smoothly combed that he himself looked like an old photograph. Someone had touched up the old photographer until he had become a black and white abstraction of old age.

Lillian did not enjoy being photographed, and she sought to escape him by going for a swim. But he was a figure of endless patience, and waited silently, compact, brittle, and straight. The wrinkles of his face all ran upward, controlled by an almost perpetual smile. He was like the old gardener, so ritualistic in his work, so stylized in his dignity, that Lillian felt she owed him an apology: "I'm sorry I kept you waiting."

"No harm done, no harm done," he said gently, as he proceeded to balance his camera on the sand, and just before disappearing under the black cloth he said: "We all have much more time than we have life!"

Watching Lillian being photographed was Edward, the ex-violinist with red hair and freckles who lived in a trailer on the beach. His calendar of events was determined by his multiple marriages. "Oh, the explosion of the yacht? That happened at the time of my second wife." Or if someone tried to recall when the American swimming champion had dived into the rocks: "Oh that was four wives back!" The wives disappeared, but the children remained. They were so deeply tanned it was difficult to distinguish them from the native children. Edward worked at odd jobs: designing fabrics, tending silver shops, or building a house for someone. At the time Lillian met him he was distributing Coca-Cola calendars all over Mexico. To his own amazement, the people loved them and hung them up on their walls. The last one, which he now unrolled to create a stir among the bathers, was an interpretation of a Mayan human sacrifice. The Yucatan pyramid was smaller than the woman, and the woman who was about to be sacrificed looked like Gypsy Rose Lee. The shaved and lean priest looked unequal to the task of annihilating such splendor of the body. The active volcano on the right-hand side was the size of the sacrificial virgin's breast.

Tequila always brought out in Edward a total repudiation of art. He was emphatic about the fact that he had deserted the musical world of his own volition. "In this place music is not necessary. Golconda is full of natural music, dance music, singing music, music for living. The street vendors' tunes are better than any modern composition. Life itself is full of rhythm, people sing while they work. I don't miss concerts or my own violin at all!"

The second glass of tequila unleashed reminiscences of concert halls, and the Museum of Modern Art, as if they had been his residence prior to Golconda. With the third glass came a lecture on the superfluity of art. "For example, here, with the lagoon, the jungle, you do not need the collages of Max Ernst, his artificial lagoons and swamps. With the deserts and sand dunes, the bleaching bones of cows and donkeys, there is no need of Tanguy's desert scenes and bleaching bones. And with the ruins of San Miguel what need do we have of Chirico's columns? I lack nothing here. Only a wife willing to live on bananas and coconut milk."

"When I felt cold," said Lillian, "I used to go to the Tropical Birds and Plants Department at Sears Roebuck. It was warm, humid, and pungent. Or I would go to look at the tropical plants in the Botanical Gardens. I was looking for Golconda then. I remember a palm tree there which grew so tall, too tall for the glass dome, and I would watch it pushing against the glass, wishing to grow beyond it and be free. I think of this caged palm tree often while I watch the ones of Golconda sweeping the skies."

But at the third glass of tequila, Edward's talk grew less metallic, and his glance would fall on his left hand where a finger was missing. Everyone knew, but he never mentioned it, that this was the cause of his broken career as a violinist.

Everyone knew too that his children were loved, nourished, and protected by all in Golconda. They had mysteriously accepted an interchangeable mother, one with many faces and speaking many languages, but for the moment it was Lillian they had adopted, as if they had sensed that in her there was a groove for children, already formed, once used, familiar, and which they found comfortable. And Lillian wondered at their insight, wondered how they knew that she had once possessed, and lost, children of the same age.

How did they know she had already kissed such freckles on the nose, such thin elbows, braided such tangled hair, and known where to find missing shoes? It was not only that they allowed her to play the missing mother, but that they seemed

510

intent on filling an empty niche in her, on playing the missing children.

She and the children embraced each other with a knowledge of substitution which added to their friendship, a familiarity the children did not feel with their other temporary mothers.

To her alone they confessed their concern with their father's next choice of a wife. They examined each newcomer gravely, weighing her qualifications. They had observed one infallible sign: "If she loves us first," they explained, "Father doesn't like it. If she loves him first, then she doesn't want us around."

An airline's beauty queen arrived at the beach. She walked and carried herself as if she knew she were on display and should hold herself as still as possible, arranged for other's eyes as if to allow them to photograph her. The way she held herself and did not look at others made her seem an image cut out of a poster which incited young men to go to war. A surface unblurred, unruffled, no frown of thought to mar the brow, she exposed herself to other's eyes with no sign of recognition. She neither transmitted nor received messages to and from the nerves and senses. She walked toward others without emitting any vibrations of warmth or cold. She was a plastic perfection of hair, skin, teeth, body, and form which could not rust, or wrinkle, or cry. It was as if only synthetic elements had been used to create her.

Edward's children were uneasy with this girl because they imagined their father would be spellbound by the perfect image she presented, the clear blue eyes, the graceful hair, the flawless profile. But soon she made her own choice of companion and it was the ex-Marine who had been pensioned off for exposing himself voluntarily to an experiment with the atom bomb, and had been damaged inside. No one dared to ask, or even to imagine the nature of the injury. He himself was laconic: "I got damaged inside." No injury was apparent. He was tall, strong, and blond, with so rich a coloring he could not take the sun. His blue eyes matched those of the American airline's beauty queen; both were untroubled and designed to be admired. He was reluctant to tell his story, but when he drank he would admit: "I offered myself as a volunteer to be stationed as close as possible . . . and I got damaged, that's all."

Neither one had seemed to make any movement toward the other, but as if they had both been moving in the same sphere, at the same altitude, with the same spectator's detachment, they encountered each other and continued to walk together. They did not keep their eyes fastened on each other as the Mexican lovers did.

They both carried cameras, and they methodically photographed everything. But as for themselves, it was as if they agreed to reveal nothing of themselves by word or gesture.

Edward treated them casually, like walking posters, like one-dimensional cut-outs. But Lillian believed their façade to be a disguise like any other. "They're just not acquainted with their own selves," she said.

"Will you introduce them?" asked Edward ironically.

"But you know that's a dangerous thing to do. They wouldn't recognize each other; they would treat me like a trespasser, and their unrecognized selves like house breakers."

"It is dangerous to confront people with an image of themselves they do not wish to acknowledge."

These words reawakened in her the sense of danger and mystery she felt each time she saw Doctor Hernandez. She remembered his saying: "I get bored with physical illness, which I have fought for fifteen years. As an amateur detective of secret lives, I entertain myself."

Another time he had said: "I'm fully aware, of course, that you've thrown me off the scent by involving me in the secret lives of all your friends in place of your own. But I will tell you one shocking truth. It's not the sun you're basking in, it's my people's passivity and fatalism. They believe the character of man cannot be altered or tampered with, that man is nature, unpredictable, uncontrollable. They believe whatever he is should be accepted along with poverty, illness, death. The concept of effort and change is unknown. You are born poor, good

512

or bad, or a genius, and you live with that just as you live with your relatives."

"Do people ever run amok in Golconda? As they do in Bali, or Africa, or the South Sea Islands?"

"Yes, they do. Because having based all their lives on resignation, acceptance, humility, passivity, when they find themselves in a trap, they do not know how to defeat it; they only know how to grab a revolver or a knife and kill."

"No one searches for reasons, no one prods?"

"Except me. And I will be punished for it. Whoever tampers with this empathy with animals, this osmosis with light, this absence of thought, is always made the victim of people's hatred of awareness."

"You have anesthetics for physical pain. Why not for anxiety, then?"

"Because they do not cure."

There was a masquerade dance on the Mexican general's yacht.

From its decks fireworks exploded into the bay, and the rowboats which took the guests up to the ladder had to sail courageously through a shower of comet tails.

The Mexican general was the only one who was not disguised. He awaited his guests at the top of the ladder, greeted them with an embrace; his circumference was so wide that all Lillian was able to kiss in response to his embrace was one of the medals on his chest.

From behind masks, feathers, paint, spangles, all Lillian could could see at first were eyes, sea-eyes, animal-eyes, earth-eyes, eyes of precious stones. Fixed, mobile, fluid, some were easily caught by a stare, others escaped all but a fleeting spark.

Lillian recognized the Doctor only when he spoke. He was

513

costumed as an Aztec warrior, face and body painted, and he was carrying a sharp-pointed lance, with sharp arrows slung across his neck. It was his turn to inflict deep wounds, like those he was weary of healing. That night his appearance forbade all women to rest their heads upon his shoulder and confess their difficulties. Before they crumpled into wailing children, he would challenge the potential mistress.

When Diana arrived with Christmas walking in her shadow, the Doctor said: "When patients suffer from malnutrition of the senses, I send them to Diana."

Diana, her head emerging from the empty picture frame, wearing a violet face mask and her hair covered with sea weed, was dancing with Christmas.

Christmas was dressed quite fittingly, as a man from another planet, but such affirmation of distance did not discourage Diana. She kissed him, and the frame fell around both their shoulders like a life belt to keep them afloat on the unfamiliar sea of the senses, its swell heightened by the jazz and the fireworks.

A couple was leaning over the railing, and Lillian could hear the woman say: "Even if you don't mean it, just for tonight, say you love me. I won't ever remind you of it; I will not see you again, but just for tonight say you love me, say you love me."

Would such a guarantee of freedom from responsibility make of any man a lover and a poet? Bring about a lyrical confession? In the green flare of a fireworks fountain, Lillian saw that the man hesitated to create illusion even for one night, and she thought, "He should have been disguised as the greatest of all misers!"

The woman in quest of illusion disappeared among the dancers.

Everyone was already dancing the intricate patterns of the mambo, which not only set bodies in motion but generated words which would not have been said without such propulsions.

The Doctor was transformed by his disguise; Lillian was

astonished to watch him in the role of ruthless lover who would deal only in wounds in the war of love, none of the consolations. He had separated Diana from Christmas with some ironic remarks, and caused another woman to sit alone among the cordage piled in circles on the deck like sleeping anacondas.

It was not only the champagne Lillian drank, it was the softness of the night so palpable that when she opened her mouth she felt as if she had swallowed some of it: it descended into her arteries like a new drug not yet discovered by the alchemists. She swallowed the softness, and then swallowed the showers of light from the fireworks too, and felt illumined by them. It was not only the champagne, but the merry cries of the native boys diving for silver pieces around the yacht, and then climbing on the anchor chain to watch the festivities.

There were many Golcondas—one above the horizon, dark hills wearing necklaces of shivering lights, one reflected on the satin-surfaced bay, one of oil lamps from the native huts, one of candlelights, one of cold neon lights, the neon cross on the church, the neon eyes of the future, without warmth at all— but all of them looked equally beautiful when their reflections fell into the water.

Doctor Hernandez was dancing with a woman who reminded Lillian of Man Ray's painting of a mouth: a giant mouth that took up all of the canvas. The young man the woman had discarded in order to dance with the Doctor seemed disoriented. Lillian noticed his pallor. Drunkenness? Sorrow? Jealousy? Loneliness?

She said to him: "Do you remember in all the Coney Islands of the world a slippery turntable on which we all tried to sit? As it turned more swiftly people could no longer hold onto the highly waxed surface and they slid off."

"The secret is to spit on your hands."

"Then let's both spit on our hands right now," she said, and the manner in which he compressed his mouth made her fear he would be angry. "We both slipped off at the same moment."

His smile was so forced that it came as a grimace. The cries

515

of the diving boys, the narcotic lights, the carnival of fireworks and dancing feet, no longer reached them, and they recognized the similarity of their mood.

"Every now and then, at a party, in the middle of living, I get this feeling that I have slipped off," she said, "that I am becalmed, that I have struck a snag . . . I don't know how to put it."

"I have that feeling all the time, not now and then. How would you like to escape altogether? I have a beautiful house in an ancient city, only four hours from here. My name is Michael Lomax. I know your name, I have heard you play."

In the jeep she fell asleep. She dreamed of a native guide with a brown naked torso, who stood at the entrance to an Aztec tomb. Holding a machete, he said: "Would you like to visit the tomb?"

She was about to refuse his invitation when she awakened because the jeep was acting like a camel on the rough road. She heard the hissing of the sea.

"How old are you, Michael?"

He laughed at this: "I'm twenty-nine and you're about thirty, so you need not use such a protective tone."

"Adolescence is like cactus," she said, and fell asleep again.

And she began dreaming of a Chirico painting: endless vistas of ruined columns and ghostly figures either too large, like ancient Greek statues, or too small as they sometimes appeared in dreams.

But she was not dreaming. She was awake and driving at dawn through the cobblestones of an ancient city.

Not a single house complete. The ruins of a once sumptuous baroque architecture, still buried in the silence it had been in since the volcano had erupted and half buried it in ashes and lava.

The immobility of the people, the absence of wind, gave it a static quality.

The Indians lived behind the scarred walls quietly, like mourners of an ancient splendor. The life of each family took place in an inner patio, and, as they kept the shutters closed on the street side, the city had the deserted aspect of a ghost town.

Rows of columns no longer supporting roofs, churches open to a vaulted sky, a coliseum's empty seats watching in the arena the spectacle of mutilated statues toppled by the victorious lava. A convent without doors, the nun's cells, prisons, secret stairways exposed.

"Here is my house," said Michael. "It was once a convent attached to the church. The church, by the way, is an historic monument, what's left of it."

They crossed the inner patio with its music of fountains and entered a high-ceilinged white stucco room. Dark wood beams, blood-red curtains, and wrought-iron grilles on the windows gave the dramatic contrasts which are the essence of Spanish life, a conflict between austerity and passion, poetry and discipline. The high walls gave purity and elevation, the rich, voluptuous, red primitive ardor; dark wood gave the somber nobilities; the iron grilles symbolized the separation from the world which made individuality grow intensely as it did not grow when all barriers of quality and evaluations were removed.

The church bells tolled persistently although there was not ritual to be attended, as if calling day and night to the natives buried by the volcano's eruption years before.

Walking through the muted streets of the place with Michael, Lillian wondered how the Spaniards and the Mayans now lived quietly welded, with no sign of their past warring visible to the outsider. Whatever opposition remained was so subtle and indirect that neither Spaniards nor visitors were aware of it. Michael repeated many times: "The Indians are the most stubborn people."

In the dark, slumbering eyes, white people could never find a flicker of approbation. The Indians expressed no open hostility, merely silence whenever white people approached them, and their glazed obsidian eyes had the power of reflecting without revelation of feelings, as if they had themselves become

517

their black lacquered pottery. White people would explain how they wanted a meal cooked, a house built, a dress made. In the Indian eyes there was a complete lack of adhesion, in their smiles a subtle mockery of the freakish ways of all visitors, ancient or modern. The Indians would work for these visitors, but disregard their eccentricity and disobey them with what appeared to be ignorance or lack of understanding, but which was in reality an enormous passive resistance to change, which enabled them to preserve their way of life against all outside influences.

The Catholic church bells continued to toll, but in the eyes of the Indians this was merely another external form to be adopted and mysteriously, indefinably mocked. On feast days they mixed totem poles and saint's statues, Catholic incense and Indian perfumes, the Catholic wafer and Mayan magic foods. They enjoyed the chanting, the organ and candlelight, the lace and brocades; they played with pictures of the saints and at the same time with Indian bone necklaces.

The silence of the ancient city was so noticeable and palpable that it disturbed Lillian. She did not know at first what caused it. It hung over her head like suspense itself, as menacing as the unfamiliar noises in the jungle she had crossed on the way.

She wondered what attracted Michael to living here among ruins. It was a city rendered into poetry by its recession into the past, as cities are rendered into poetry by the painters because of the elements left out, allowing each spectator to fill in the spaces for himself. The missing elements on the half-empty canvas were important because they were the only spaces in which human imagination could draw its own inferences, its own architecture from its private myths, its streets and personages from a private world.

A city in ruins, as this ancient city was, was more powerful and evocative because it had to be constructed anew by each person, therefore enhanced into illimitable beauty, never destroyed or obscured by the realism of the present, never rendered familiar and forced to expose its flaws.

To gain such altitude it was necessary to learn from the artist how to overlook, leave out, the details which weighed down the imagination and caused crash landings.

Even the prisons, where one knew that scenes of horror had taken place, acquired in the sun, under streams of ivy gently bleached by time, a serenity, a passivity, a transmutation into resignation which included forgiveness of man's crimes against man. In time man will forgive even the utmost cruelty merely because the sacred personal value of each man is lost when the father, the mother, son or daughter, brother or sister, wife of this man have ceased to exist—the ones who gave his life its importance, its irreplaceable quality. Time, powerless to love one man, promptly effaces him. His sorrows, torments, and death recede into impersonal history, or evaporate into these poetic moments which the tourists come to seek, sitting on broken columns, or focusing their cameras on empty ransacked tombs, none of them knowing they are learning among ruins and echoes to devaluate the importance of one man, and to prepare themselves for their own disappearance.

The ancient city gave Lillian a constriction of the heart. She was not given to such journeys into the past. To her it seemed like a city mourning its dead, even though it could not remember those it mourned. She saw it as the ruins of Chirico's paintings and asked Michael: "But why the heavy silence?"

"There's no wind here," said Michael.

It was true. The windlessness gave it the static beauty of a painting.

But there was another reason for the silence, which she discovered only in the afternoon. She was taking a sunbath on the terrace, alone.

The sun was so penetrating that it drugged her. She fell asleep and had a dream. A large vulture was flying above the terrace, circling over her, and then it swooped downward and she felt its beak on her shoulder. She awakened screaming, sat up, and saw that she had not been dreaming, for a vulture had

519

marked her shoulder and was flying away slowly, heavily.

Wherever vultures settled they killed the singing birds. The absence of singing birds, as well as of the wind, was the cause of that petrified silence.

She began to dislike the ancient city. The volcano began its menacing upward sweep at the edge of the city, and rose so steeply and so high that its tip was hidden in the clouds. "I have been up there," said Michael. "I looked down into its gaping top and saw the earth's inside smoldering."

Michael said on Sunday: "I wish you would spend all your free days here, every week."

That evening he and Lillian, and other guests, were sitting in the patio when suddenly there appeared in the sky what seemed at first like a flying comet, which then burst high in the air into a shower of sparks and detonations.

Lillian thought: "It's the volcano!"

They ran to the outside windows. A crowd of young men, carefully dressed in dark suits and gleaming white shirts, stood talking and laughing. Fireworks illuminated their dark, smooth faces. The marimbas played like a concert of children's pianos, small light notes so gay that they seemed the laughter of the instrument.

The fireworks were built in the shape of tall trees, and designed to go off in tiers, branch by branch. From the tips of the gold and red branches hung planets, flowers, wheels gyrating and then igniting, all propelled into space bursting, splintering, falling as if the sun and the moon and the stars themselves had been pierced open and had spilled their jewels of lights, particles of delight.

Some of the flowers spilled their pollen of gold, the planets flew into space, discarding ashes, the skeletons of their bodies. But some of the chariot wheels, gyrating wildly, spurred by each explosion of their gold spokes, wheeled themselves into space and never returned in any form, whether gold showers or ashes.

When the sparkles fell like a rain of gold, the children rushed to place themselves under them, as if the bath of gold would transform their ragged clothes and lives into light.

Beside Lillian, Michael took no pleasure in the spectacle. She saw him watching the students with an expression which had the cold glitter of hunger, not emotion. Almost the cold glitter of the hunter taking aim before killing.

"This is a fiesta for men only, Lillian. The men here love each other openly. See, there, they are holding hands."

Lillian translated this into: He wants it to be thus, this is the way he wants it to be.

"They like to be alone, among men. They enjoy being without women." He looked at her this time with malice, as if to observe the effect of his words on her.

"I lived in Mexico as a child, Michael. The women are kept away from the street, from cafés, they are kept at home. But it does not mean what you believe. . . ."

They watched the young men so neatly dressed, standing in the street with their faces turned toward the fireworks. Then they noticed that across the street from Michael's house one of the windows was brightly lit and a very young girl dressed in white stood behind the iron railing. Behind her the room was full of people, and the marimbas were playing.

Then there was a silence. One of the young students moved forward, stood under the young girl's window with his guitar and sang a ballad praising her eyes, smile, and voice.

She answered him in a clear, light voice, accepting the compliment. The young student praised her again and begged admittance to her home.

She answered him in a clear, light voice, accepting this compliment too, smiled at him, but did not invite him in. This meant that his ballad was not considered artful enough.

This was their yearly poetry tournament, at which only excellence in verse counted. It was the bad poets who were left outside to dance among themselves!

One of the student's ballads finally pleased the girl, and she invited him inside. Her family met him at the door. The other students cheered.

Lillian said: "I'm going out to dance with the bad poets!"

"No," said Michael, "you can't do that!"

"Why not?"

"It isn't done here."

"But I'm American. I don't have to conform to their traditions."

Lillian went out. When she first appeared at the door the students all stared at her in awe. Then they murmured with pleasure: "The American is allowed to dance in the streets."

A bolder one asked her to dance. She glided off with him. The marimbas played with a tinkle of music boxes, the resonances of Tibetan bells, and sometimes like Balinese cymbals. The fireworks lighted up the sky and faces.

Other students pressed around her, waiting for a dance. They offered her a flower to wear in her hair. Tactfully, they made a wall against the students who were drunk, shielding her. She passed from the arms of one student to another. As she passed she could see Michael's face at the window, cold and angry.

The dances grew faster and the change of partners swifter. They sang ballads in her ears.

As the evening wore on she began to tire because of the cobblestones, and she became a little frightened too, because the students were growing more ardent and more intoxicated. So she began to dance toward the house where Michael stood waiting. They realized she was seeking to escape, and the ones she had not yet danced with pressed forward, pleading with her. But she was out of breath and had lost one heel, so she moved eagerly toward the door. Michael opened it and closed it quickly after her. The students knocked on the door and for a moment she feared they would knock it down.

Then she noticed that Michael was trembling. He looked so pale, drawn, unhappy that Lillian asked him tenderly: "What is it, Michael? What is it, Michael? Did you mind my going out to dance? Did you mind that your fantasy about a world without women was proved not true? Why don't you come with me?

We're invited to the Queen's house."

"No, I won't go."

"I don't understand you, Michael. You make it so clear that you want a world without women."

"I don't look upon you as a woman."

"Then why should you mind if I go to a party?"

"I do mind."

She remembered that she had come because he seemed in distress; she had come to help him and not to hurt him.

"I'll stay with you, then."

They sat in the courtyard, alone.

If the city we choose, thought Lillian, represents our inner landscape, then Michael has selected a magnificent tomb, to live among the ruins of his past loves. The beauty of his house, his clothes, his paintings, his books, seem like precious jewels, urns, perfumes, gold ornaments such as were placed in the tombs of Egyptian kings.

"A long time ago," said Michael, "I decided never to fall in love again. I have made of desire an anonymous activity"

"But not to feel . . . not to love . . . is like dying within life, Michael."

The burial of emotion caused a kind of death, and it was this cadaver of his feelings he carried within him that gave him, in spite of his elegance, and the fairness of his coloring, a static quality, like that of the ancient city itself.

"Soon the rains will come," he said. "The house will grow cold and damp. The roads will become impassable. I had hoped your engagement at the hotel would last until then."

"Why don't you come back to Golconda then?"

"This place suits my present mood," said Michael. "The gaiety and liveliness of Golconda hurts me, like too much light in my eyes."

"What a strange conversation, Michael, in this patio that reminds me of the illustrations for the Thousand and One Nights—the fountain, the palm tree, the flowers, the mosaic floor, the unbelievable moon, the smell of roses. And here we sit talking like a brother and sister stricken by some mysterious malady. All the dancing and pleasure are taking place next door, nearby, and we are exiled from it . . . and by our own hand."

At night her room looked like a nun's cell, with its whitewashed walls, dark furniture, and the barred windows. She knew she would not stay, that what Michael wanted to share with her was a withdrawal from the world.

In the darkness she heard whisperings. Michael was talking vehemently, and someone was saying: "No, no." Then she heard a chair being pushed. Was it Michael courting one of the young students? Michael who had said lightly: "All I ask, since I can't keep you here, is that in your next incarnation you be born a boy, and then I will love you."

One day in Golconda she saw a bus passing by that bore the name of San Luis, the town near Hatcher's place and she climbed on it.

It was brimming full, not only with people, but with sacks of corn, chickens tied together, turkeys in baskets, church chairs in red velvet, a mail sack, babies in arms.

On the front seat sat the young bullfighter she had seen at the arena the Sunday before. He was very young and very slim. His dark hair was now wild and free, not sleek and severely tied as it was worn by bullfighters. In the arena he had seemed taut, all nerves and electric resilience. In his white pants and slack shirt he looked vulnerable and tender. Lillian had seen him wildly angry at the bull, had seen him challenge the bull recklessly because, during one of the passes, it had torn his pants with its horns, had undressed him in public. This small patch of flesh showing through the turquoise brocaded pants, this human, warm flesh glowing, exposed, had made the scene

524

with the bull more like a sensual scene, a duel between aggressor and victim, and the tension had seemed less that of a symbolic ritual between animal strength and male strength than that of a sexual encounter.

This vulnerable exposure had stirred the women, but injured the bullfighters' dignity, made him a thousand times angrier, wilder, more reckless. . . .

The bus driver was teasing him. He said he was going to visit his parents in San Luis. The bus driver thought he was going to visit Maria. The bullfighter did not want to talk. Next to him sat a very old woman, all in black, asleep with a basket of eggs on her knees. When the bus stopped someone got on carrying candelabras.

"Are they moving the whole church?" asked the man carrying turkeys. But though he was standing, he did not dare sit on one of the red velvet praying chairs. He was bartering with the man who carried chickens. The bag filled with corn undulated with each bump on the road. Finally a very small hole was made in the hemp by so much friction, and a few grains of corn began to fall out. At this the chickens, who were all tied together, began to crane their necks, and to mutiny. The owner of the bag became angry and, not finding a way to repair it, sat next to it on the floor with his hand on the hole.

In another seat sat an English woman with a young Mexican girl. The woman was a school teacher. Her English clothes were wearing out; they were mended, patched, but she would not change to Mexican clothes. She wore a colonial hat on her sparse yellow hair. The books she carried were completely yellow and brittle, the corners all chewed, the covers disintegrating.

At each station the bus stopped for the bus driver to deliver letters and messages. In exchange for this he was given a glass of beer. "Tell Josefa her daughter had a son yesterday. She'll writer later. She wants you to come to the baptism."

A man climbed in. His pants were held up with a string. His straw hat looked as if the cows had chewed on the edges until they had reached the unappetizing stains of sweat. His shirt had never been washed. He was selling cactus figs.

At the next stop a priest arrived on his bicycle. He had tied his robe with strings so it would not get caught in the wheels. When he jumped off he forgot to liberate himself, and as he began to run toward the bus he fell on the white dusty road. But nobody laughed. They helped him get his chairs and candelabras out of the bus and placed them on the side of the road. The women then picked them up and balancing them on their heads, followed the priest on his bicycle, in the wave of the dust he raised.

The bus seats were of plain hardwood. The bus jumped like a bronco on the rocky, uneven, half-gutted road. Lillian had difficulty staying in her seat. The bullfighter was gently sleeping, and did not seem like the same young man who had suffered a symbolic rape before thousands of people.

Talking to the conductor in a stream of tinkly words like a marimba was a little girl of seven who resembled Lietta, Edward's oldest daughter. Lillian felt all through her body a dissolution of tenderness for Lietta, who, even though she was so deeply tanned, as dark as a Mexican child, had a transparency and openness Lillian loved. As if children were made of phosphorous, and one saw the light shining in them. The transparent child. Her own little girl at home had had this. And then one day they lose it. How? Why? One day for no perceptible reason, they close their thoughts, veil their feelings, and one can no longer read their faces openly as before. The transparent child. Such a delight to look into open naked feelings and thoughts.

The little girl who talked to the bus driver did not mind that he was not listening. Her eyes were so large that it seemed she must see more than anyone, and reveal more of herself than any child. But her eyes were heavily fringed with eyelashes, and she was watching the road.

Lillian herself must have been transparent once, and how did this heavy wall build up, these prison walls, these silences? Unaware of this great loss, the loss of the transparent child, one

526

becomes an actor whose profession it is to manipulate his face so that others may have the illusion they are reading his soul. Illusion. How she had loved the bullfighter's fury at the bull, this gentle and tender young man sleeping now, so angry he had almost hurled himself upon its horns.

When did opaqueness set in? Mistrust, fear of judgment. The bus was passing through a tunnel.

Lietta. Lillian could not tell if she was trying to understand Lietta, or her own children, or the Lietta she had once been. She remembered watching Lietta's diminutive nose twitching almost imperceptibly when she was afraid, when one of the dazzling women approached her father, for instance. Dream of the transparent child.

The bus was like a bronco. Would they be able to stay on it? In the darkness of the tunnel she lost the image of Lietta in her blue bathing suit and found herself at the same age, herself and other children she had played with, in Mexico, at the time her father was building bridges and roads. The beginning was the whistling by which her mother called her in from playing. She had a powerful whistle. The children could hear it, no matter how far they went. Their playground was a city beneath the city, which had been partly excavated to build a subway like the American subway, and then abandoned. Cities in other centuries, once buried in lava, which ran underneath the houses, gardens, streets. Where it ran under streets there were grilles to catch the rainwater, but most of the time these grilles only served to bring in a diffuse light. People walked over them without knowing they were walking over another city. The neighborhood children had brought mats, candles, toys, shawls, and lived there a life which because of its secrecy seemed more intense than any above the ground. They had all been forbidden to go there, had been warned of wells, sewers, underground rivers.

The children all stayed together and never ventured farther than the lighted passageways. They were fearful of getting lost.

From all the corners of the underground city Lillian could

hear her mother calling when it was time to come home. She had never imagined she might disregard her mother's whistle. But one day she was learning from a Mexican playmate how to cut animals and flowers out of paper for a fiesta, and was so surprised by the shapes that appeared that when the whistle came, she decided not to hear it. Her brothers and sisters left. She went on cutting out ships, stars, lanterns, suns, and moons. Then suddenly her candle gave out.

Trailing all her streams of paper with her, she walked toward the opening that gave onto their garden wall, trusting in her memory. But the place was dark. Under her feet the clay was dry and soft. She walked confidently, until she felt the clay growing wet. She did not remember any wet clay in the places where they played. She became frightened. She remembered the stories about wells, rivers, sewers. The knowledge that people were walking about free right above her head, without knowing that she was there, augmented her fear. She had never known the exact meaning of death. But at this moment, she felt that this was death. Right above her her family was sitting down to dinner. She could faintly hear voices. But they could not hear her. Her brothers and sisters were sworn to secrecy and would not tell where she was.

She shouted through one of the grilled openings, but the street was deserted at that moment and no one answered. She took a few more steps into the wet clay and felt that her feet were sinking deeper. She stumbled on a piece of wood. With it she struck at the roof, and continued to call. Some of the dirt was loosened and fell on her. And at this she sat down and wept.

And just as she had begun to feel that she was dying, her mother arrived carrying a candle and followed by her brothers and sisters.

(*When you do not answer the whistle of duty and obedience, you risk death all alone in the forgotten cities of the past. When you engage in the delights of creating pink, blue, white animals and towers, ships and starry stems, you court solitude*

528

and catastrophe.

When you choose to play in a realm far away from the eyes of parents, you court death.)

For some, Golconda was the city of pleasure which one should be punished for visiting or for loving. Was this the beginning of the adventurers' superstitions, the secret of their doomed exiles from home?

Her father never smiled. He had so much dark hair, even along his fingers. He drank and was easily angered, particularly at the natives. The tropics and the love of pleasure were his personal enemies. They interfered with the building of roads and bridges. Roads and bridges were the most important personages in his life.

Lillian's mother did not smile either. Hers was the house of no-smile, from her father because the building of bridges and roads was such a grave matter which the natives would not take seriously, and from her mother because the children were growing up as "savages." All they were learning was to sing, dance, paint their faces, make their own toys as the Mexican children did, adopt stray donkeys and goats, and to smile. The Mexican children smiled in such a way that Lillian felt they were giving all they had, all of themselves, in that one smile. So much was said about "economy" in her house that there was perhaps also an economy of smiles! Did one have to be sparing of them, give half-smiles, small sidelong smiles, crumbs of smiles? Were the Mexican children living in the present recklessly, without thought of the future, and would these dazzling smiles wear out?

A cyclone carried away one of Lillian's father's bridges. He felt personally offended, as if nature had flaunted his dedication to his work. A flood undermined a road. Another personal affront from the realm of nature. Was it because of this that they returned home? Or because there was shooting in the streets, minor revolutions every now and then?

Once during a school concert at which Lillian was playing the piano, there was a shot in the audience. It was intended for the President but merely put out the lights. While people screamed to get out, Lillian had calmly finished her piece. If she had stayed in Mexico, would she have been so different?

Did everyone live thus in two cities at once, one above the ground, in the sun of Golconda, and one underground? And was everyone now and then metamorphosed into a child again?

There must be someone with whom one can hold a dialogue absolutely faithful to the thoughts that go on in one's head?

At a certain point human beings began to veil themselves. The key word was "transparent." Lietta was transparent. The child talking to the bus driver was transparent. The driver was not listening, but the child was willing to be transparent, exposed.

The bus stopped by a wide river, beyond the village of San Luis. It was waiting for the ferry. The ferry was a flat raft made of logs tied together. Two men pushed it along with long bamboo poles. The ferry was halfway back.

An old woman in black had set up a stand of fruit juices and Coca-Cola. The bullfighter was the first one to leap out.

"Are you going to visit your folks, Miguelito?"

"Yes," he answered sullenly. He did not want to talk.

"What's the matter, Miguelito? Usually you're as quick with your tongue as you are with your sword!"

He too, was traveling through two cities at once. Was he still in the arena, still angry at the bull? Was he concerned about the cost of a new suit?

The raft was approaching. And on the raft was Hatcher's jeep.

When he saw Lillian he smiled. "Were you coming to visit me? I would have come to get you."

"I wanted a ride in the bus."

"I'm going to pick up some bottles of water here and going right back. Where is your bag?"

"I don't have any. I'm only free for the week end. I followed an impulse."

"My wife will be glad to see you. She gets lonely up there."

The bottles of water were loaded on the jeep. Then both jeep and bus rolled onto the raft.

Hatcher had hair on his fingers, like her father. Like her father he was always commanding. The raft became his raft, the men his men, the journey his responsibility. He even wanted to change its course, a course settled hundreds of years ago. His smile too was a quarter-tone smile, as if he had no time to to radiate, to expand.

Already she regretted having come. This was not a journey in her solar barque. It was a night journey into the past, and the thread that had pulled her was one of accidental resemblances, familiarity, the past. She had been unable to live for three months a new life, in a new city, without being caught by an umbilical cord and brought back to the figure of her father. Hatcher was an echo from the past.

They were leaving the raft, starting their journey through the jungle. A dust road, with just enough room for the car. The cactus and the banana leaves touched their faces. When they were deep in the forest and seemingly far from all villages, they found a young man waiting for them on the road. He carried a heavy small bag, like a doctor's bag. He wore dark glasses.

"I'm Doctor Palas," he said. "Will you give me a ride?"

When he had settled himself beside Lillian he explained: "I just delivered a child. I'm stationed at Kulacan."

He was carrying a French novel like the one Doctor Hernandez must have carried at his age. Was he bored and indifferent, or was he already devoted to his poor patients? She wanted to ask. He seemed to divine her question, for he said: "Last night I didn't sleep a wink. A workman came in the middle of the night. He had a wood splinter in his eye. I tried to send him away, I hoped he would get tired of waiting, I just couldn't wake up. But he stayed on my porch, stayed until I had to get up. Even in my sleep I heard the way he called me. They call me the way children call their mother. And I have a year of this to endure!"

Between the trees, now and then there appeared the figure of a workman with a machete. White pants, naked torso, sandals, and a straw hat, bending over their cutting. When they heard the car they straightened up and watched them with somber eyes.

Once one of them signaled Hatcher to stop. Lillian saw him grow tense. Then they pushed before them a frightened child.

"Will you take him? He's too small to walk all the way."

"Climb over the bottles," said Hatcher.

But the child was too frightened. He clung to the extra tire in the back, and when the jeep slowed down before a deep ravine, he leaped off and disappeared into the forest.

"Here is my place," said Hatcher, and turned left up a hill until he reached a plateau. On this open space he had built a roof on posts, with only one wall in the back. The cooking was done out of doors. A Mexican woman was bending over her washing. She only came when Hatcher called her. She was small and heavy, and sad-faced, but she gave Hatcher a caressing look and a brilliant warm smile. Toward the visitors she showed only a conscious effort at politeness.

"You must excuse us, the place is not finished yet. My husband works alone, and has a lot to do."

"Bring the coffee, Maria," said Hatcher. She left them sitting around a table on the terrace, staring at an unbelievable stretch of white sand, dazzling white foam spraying a gigantic, sprawling vegetation which grew to the very edge of the sand. Birds sand deliriously, and monkeys gave humorous clown cries in the trees. The colors all seemed purer, and the whole place as if uninhabited by man.

Maria came with coffee in a thermos. Hatcher patted her shoulder and looked gratefully at her.

"She is the most marvelous wife," he said.

"And he is a wonderful husband," said Maria. "Mexican husbands never go around telling everyone they are married. Whenever Harry goes to Golconda, he keeps telling everyone about his wife."

And then, turning to Lillian, she added in a lower tone, while Hatcher talked with the young doctor: "I don't know why he loves me. I am so short and squatty. He was once married to someone like you. She was tall, and she had long, pointed, painted nails. He never talks about her. I worked for him, at first. I was his secretary. We are going to build a beautiful place here. This is only the beginning."

Against the wall at the back they had their bedroom. Lillian could imagine them together. She was sure that he lay with his head on his wife's breast. She was compliant, passive, devoted.

Lillian wondered if he were truly happy. He seemed so intent on affirming his happiness. He was not tranquil, nor capable of contemplation. He named all the beauties of his place, summoned them. When he mentioned America, his mouth grew bitter. He missed nothing. American women . . . He stopped himself, as if aware for the first time that Lillian was one of them. His eyes alighted on Lillian's nails. "I hate painted nails," he said. Until now he had been friendly. Something, a shadow of a resemblance, a recall, had sent him for a moment into the city beneath the city, the subterranean chambers of memory. But he leaped back into the present to describe all the work that had yet to be done.

"As you can see, it is still very primitive."

On the terrace, several camp beds were set side by side, as in an army barracks, with screens between them.

"I hope you won't mind sleeping out of doors."

The Mexican doctor was leaving. "Tomorrow I will be driving back with friends who are spending a few days in Golconda. If you want us to, we will pick you up."

Lillian wanted to walk to the beach. She left the Hatchers discussing dinner, and followed a trail down the hill. The flowers which opened their violet red velvety faces toward her

533

were so eloquent, they seemed about to speak. The sand did not seem like sand, but like vaporized glass, which reflected lights. The spray and the foam from the waves was of a whiteness impossible to match. The sea folded its layers around her, touched her legs, her hips, her breasts—a liquid sculptor, the warm hands of the sea all over her body.

She closed her eyes.

When she came out and put on her clothes she felt reborn, born anew. She had closed the eyes of memory. She felt as though she were one of the red flowers, that she would speak only with the texture of her skin, the tendrils of hair at the core, remain open, feel no contractions ever again.

She thought of the simplified life. Of cooking over a wood fire, of swimming every day, of sleeping out of doors in a cot without sheets with only a Mexican wool blanket. Of sandals, and freedom of the body in light dresses, hair washed by the sea and curled by the air. Unpainted nails.

When she arrived Maria had set the table. The lights were weak bulbs hanging from a string. The generator was working and could be heard. But the trees were full of fireflies, crickets, and pungent odors.

"If you want to wash the salt off, there is a creek just down toward the left, and a natural pool. Take a candle."

"No, I like the salt on my skin."

On the table were dishes of black beans, rice, and tamales. And again coffee in the thermos bottle.

After dinner Hatcher wanted to show Lillian all of the half-built house. She saw their bedroom, with its white-washed walls and flowered curtains. And behind the wall a vast storage room.

"He is very proud of his storage room," said Maria.

It was enormous, as large as the entire front of the house. As large as a supermarket. With shelves reaching to the ceiling. Organized, alphabetized, catalogued.

Every brand of canned food, every brand of medicine, every brand of clothing, glasses, work gloves, tools, magazines, books, hunting guns, fishing equipment.

"Will you have cling peaches? Asparagus? Quinine?"

He was swollen with pride. "Magazines? Newspapers?"

Lillian saw a pair of crutches on a hook at the side of the shelf. His eyes followed her glance, and he said without embarrassment: "That's in case I should break a leg."

Lillian did not know why the place depressed her. She suddenly felt deeply tired. Maria seemed grateful to be left alone with her husband. They went into their bedroom in the back, and Lillian sat on her cot at the front of the open terrace, and undressed behind a screen.

She had imagined Hatcher free. That was what had depressed her. She had been admiring him for several weeks as a figure who had attained independence, who could live like a native, a simplified existence with few needs. He was not even free of his past, of his other wife. The goodness of this one, her warmth, her servitude, only served to underline the contrast between her and the *other*. Lillian had felt him making comparisons between her and his Mexican wife. The *other* still existed in his thoughts. It may even have been why he invited Lillian the very first day in the taxi.

She couldn't sleep, having witnessed Hatcher's umbilical ties with his native land's protectiveness. (America alone could supply crutches if one broke one's leg, America alone could cure him of malaria, America-the-mother, America-the-father had been transported into the supplies shed, canned and bottled.) He had been unable to live here naked, without possessions, without provisions, with his Mexican mother and the fresh fruits and vegetables in abundance, the goat's milk, and hunting.

Close the eyes of memory . . . but was she free? Hatcher's umbilical cord had stirred her own roots. His fears had lighted up these intersections of memory which were like double exposures. Like the failed photograph of the Mayan temple, in which by an accident, a failure to turn a small key, Lillian had been photographed both standing up and lying down, and her head had seemed to lie inside the jaws of a giant king snake of stone, and the stairs of the pyramid to have been built across her body as if she had been her own ghostly figure transcending the stone.

The farther she traveled into unknown places, unfamiliar places, the more precisely she could find within herself a map showing only the cities of the interior.

This place resembled none other, with its colonnade of palm-tree trunks, its walled back set against the rocks, its corrugated roof on which monkeys clowned. The cactus at night took shapes of arthritic old men, bearded scarecrows of the tropics, and the palms were always swaying with a rhythm of fans in the heat, of hammocks in the shade.

Was there no open road, simple, clear, unique? Would all her roads traverse several worlds simultaneously, bordered by the fleeting shadows of other roads, other mountains? She could not pass by a little village in the present without passing as well by some other little village in some other country, even the village of a country she had wished to visit once and had not reached!

Lillian could see the double exposure created by memory. A lake once seen in Italy flowed into the lagoon which encircled Golconda, a hotel on a snowy mountain in Switzerland was tied to Hatcher's unfinished mountain home by a long continuous cable, and this folding cot behind a Mexican screen lay alongside a hundred other beds in a hundred other rooms, New York, Paris, Florence, San Francisco, New Orleans, Bombay, Tangiers, San Luis.

The map of Mexico lay open on her knees, but she could not find the thick jungle line which indicated her journeys. They divided into two, four, six, eight skeins.

She was speeding at the same rhythm along several dusty roads, as a child with parents, as a wife driving her husband, as a mother taking her children to school, as a pianist touring the world, and all these roads intersected noiselessly and without damage.

536

Swinging between the drug of forgetfulness and the drug of awareness, she closed her eyes, she closed the eyes of memory.

When she awakened she saw first of all a casuarina tree with orange flowers that seemed like tongues of flames. Between its branches rose a thin wisp of smoke from Maria's *brasero*. Maria was patting tortillas between her hands with an even rhythm and at the same time watching over genuine American pancakes saying: "Señorita, I have tortillas *a la Americana* for you."

The table was set in the sun, with Woolworth dishes and oilcloth and paper napkins.

The young doctor had arrived with his friends. They would take her back to Golconda.

Maria was gazing at Lillian pensively. She was trying to imagine that a woman just like this one had hurt Hatcher so deeply that he never talked about it. She was trying to imagine the nature of the hurt. She knew that Hatcher no longer loved that woman. But she knew also that he still hated her, and that she was still present in his thoughts.

Lillian wanted to talk to her, help her exorcise the American woman with the painted nails. But Hatcher would be lonely without his memories, lonely without his canned asparagus, and his American-made crutches. Did he truly love Maria, with her oily black hair, her maternal body, her compassionate eyes, or did he love her for not being his first wife?

He looked at Lillian with hardness. Because she did not want to stay? Could she explain that she had spent the night in the subterranean cities of memory, instead of outside in the spicy, lulling tropical night?

Doctor Palas had been called during the night, and was in

a bad humor. His friends had found the new beach hotel lacking in comfort. "The cot had a large stain, as if a crime had been committed there. The mosquito netting had a hole, and we were bitten by mosquitoes. And in the morning we had to wash our faces from a pail of water. We gave some pennies to the children. They were so eager that they scratched our hands. And only fish and black beans to eat, even for breakfast."

"Some day," said Hatcher, "when my place is built, it will attract everyone. I am sure the movie colony will come."

"But I thought you came here to be isolated, to enjoy a primitive life, a simple life."

"It isn't the first time a human being has had two wishes, diametrically opposed," said Doctor Palas.

In the car, driving back in the violent sun, no one talked. The light filled the eyes, the mind, the nerves, the bones, and it was only when they drove through shade that they came out of this anesthesia of sunlight. In the shade they would find women washing clothes in the river, children swimming naked, old men sitting on fences, and the younger men behind the plough, or driving huge wheeled carts pulled by white Brahma bulls. In the eyes of the Mexicans there were no questions, no probings; only resignation, passivity, endurance, patience. Except when one of them ran amok.

Lillian could feel as they did at times. There were states of being which resembled the time before the beginning of the world, unformed, undesigned, unseparated. Chaos. Mountains, sea and earth undifferentiated, nebulous, intertwined. States of mind and feeling which would never appear under any spiritual X-ray. Dense, invisible, inaccessible to articulate people. She would live here, would be lost. At every moment of anxiety, of probing, she would slip into the sea for rebirth. Her body would be restored to her. She would feel her face as a face, fleshy, sunburned, warm, and not as a mask concealing a flow of thoughts. She would be given back her neck as a firm, living, palpitating, warm neck, not as a support for a head heavy with fever and questions. Her whole body would be restored to her, breasts relaxed, no longer compressed by the emotions of the chest, legs restored, smooth and gleaming. All of it cool, smooth, washed of thought.

She would plunge back with these people into silence, into meditation and contemplation. When she washed her clothes in the river she would feel only the flow of the water, the sun on her back. The light of the sun would fill every corner of her mind and create refractions of light and color and send messages to her senses which would dissolve into humid shining fields, purple mountains, and the rhythms of the sea and the Mexican songs.

No thoughts like the fingers of a surgeon, feeling here and there, where is the pain, where did destruction spring from, what cell has broken, where is the broken mirror that distorts the images of human life?

Chaos was rich, destructive, and protective, like the dense jungle they had traveled through. Could she return to the twilight marshes of a purely natural, inarticulate, impulsive world, feel safe there from inquiry and exposure?

But in this jungle, a pair of eyes, not her own, had followed and found her. Her mother's eyes. She had first seen the world through her mother's eyes, and seen herself through her mother's eyes. Children were like kittens, at first they did not have vision, they did not see themselves except reflected in the eyes of the parents. Lillian seen through her mother's eyes.

Her mother was a great lady. She wore immaculate dresses, was always pulling on her gloves. She had tidy hair which the wind could not disarrange, she wore veils, perfume. Lillian's outbursts of affection were always curtailed because they threatened this organization. "Don't wrinkle my dress. You will tear my veil. Don't muss my hair." And once when Lillian had buried her face in the folds of her dress and cried: "Oh, Mother, you smell so good," she had even said: "Don't behave like a savage." If this is a woman, thought Lillian, I do not want to be one. Lillian was impetuous, but this barrier had driven her into an excess, into exaggerations of her tumultuousness.

She threw her clothes about, she soiled and crumpled up her dresses. Her hair was never tidy. At the same time, she felt that this was the cause of her mother's coolness. She did not want this coldness. She thought she would rather be chaotic, and stutter and be rough but warm. When she disobeyed, when she ran amok, she felt she was rescuing her warmth and naturalness from her mother's formal hands. And at the same time she felt despair, that because she was as she was, and unable to be like HER, she would never be loved. She took to music passionately, and there too her wildness, her lack of discipline, hampered her playing. In music too there was a higher organization of experience. Yes, she knew that, she was undisciplined and wayward. Only today, traveling through Mexico, a country of warmth, of naturalness, and looking into eyes that did not criticize, did she realize she had never yet used her own eyes to look at herself.

Her mother, a very tall woman with critical eyes. She had eyes like Lillian's, a vivid electric blue. Lillian looked into them for everything. They were her mirror. She thought she could read them clearly, and what she saw made her uneasy. There were never any words. Only her eyes. Was this dissatisfaction due to other causes? She used her eyes to stop Lillian when Lillian wanted to draw physically close to her. It was a kind of signal. Her mother had told her only much later that she did think her an awkward and ardent child, chaotic, impulsive, did think how emotional she was, how she could not civilize her. Those were her mother's words.

Lillian had never seen herself with her own eyes. Children do not possess eyes of their own. You retained as upon a delicate retina, your mother's image of you, as the first and the only authentic one, her judgment of your acts.

They had reached a place of shade by the river. They had to wait for the barge to take them across. They got out of the car and sat on the grass. A woman was hanging her laundry on the branches of a low tree, and the blues, oranges, pinks looked like giant flowers wilted by tropical rains.

Another woman approached them with a basket on her head. She took it down with calm, deliberate gestures and put before them a neatly arranged pile of small fried fish.

"Do you have any beer?" asked Doctor Palas.

The houses by the river did not have any walls. They were palm leaves on four palm trunks. A woman was pushing a small hammock monotonously to keep a baby asleep. Children were playing naked in the dust and by the edge of the river.

It was Doctor Palas' friends who noticed that the radiator was leaking profusely. They would never reach Golconda. They would be lucky if they reached San Luis, on the other side of the river.

Lillian was thinking that at this time Diana, Christmas, and her other friends were starting on a colorful safari to the beach.

The barge drifted in slowly, languidly. The men who had pushed it wiped the perspiration from their shoulders. In their dark red-brown eyes, fawn eyes, there were always specks of gold. From the sun, or from some deep Indian irony. Catastrophe always made them laugh. Was it a religion unknown to Lillian? A dog half drowned once, at the beach, made them laugh. The leaking radiator, the stranded tourists. And this was New Year's Eve. They would not reach Golconda for the fireworks and street dances.

San Luis was a village of dirt streets, shacks, in which bands of pigs were left to find their nourishment in the garbage, and bands of children followed the foreigners asking for pennies. There was only a square, with a church of gold and blue mosaics, a cafe, a grocery, a garage. They took the car there and Doctor Palas translated for them. Lillian understood the palaver. It consisted, on the Indian side, in avoiding a direct answer to a simple question: "When will the car be ready?" As if a direct answer would bring down on them some fatal wrath, some superstitious punishment. It was impossible to say. Would they care to sit at the café while they waited? It was four o'clock. They sat there until six. Doctor Palas went back to the garage several times. In between he sought to continue with Lillian an intimate conversation in Spanish which his American friends would not understand. Without knowing the trend of meditation that Lillian had embarked on, on the theme of eyes, the eyes of her mother with which she had looked at herself, it was her eyes he praised, and her hair. Her eyes which were not her own when she looked at herself. But when she looked at others, she saw them with love, with compassion. She truly saw them. She saw the American couple, uncomfortable, not understanding this mixture of dirt and gaiety. The children took delight in chasing away the pigs and imitating their cries.

She saw young Doctor Palas not yet humanly connected with the poor as Doctor Hernandez was.

"Will you go dancing with me tonight?"

"If we get to Golconda," said Lillian, laughing. "I hope the Hungarian violinist will sweep them off their feet, so they will not notice my absence."

At seven o'clock the streets were silent and it began to grow dark. The owner of the café was a fair-faced Spaniard with the manners of a courtier. He was helping them to pass the time. He had sent for a guitar player and a singer. He had fixed them a dinner.

When all of them realized they would not be leaving that night, that the car seemed to be losing vigor rather than regaining it, he came and talked to them with vehemence.

"San Luis looks quiet now, but it is only because they are dressing for New Year's Eve. Pretty soon they will all be out in the streets. There will be dancing. But the men will drink heavily. I advise you not to mix with them. The women know when to leave. Gradually they disappear with the children. The men continue drinking, and soon they begin to shoot at mirrors, at glasses, at bottles, at anything. Sometimes they shoot at each other. I entreat you, *Señores y Señoras* to stay right here. I have clean rooms I can let you have for the night. Stay in our rooms. I strongly advise you . . ."

The rooms he showed them gave on a peaceful patio full of flowers and fountains. Lillian was tempted to go out with the Doctor, at least to dance a while. But traditional protectiveness toward women made him obstinately refuse to take the risk. At ten o'clock the fireworks, the music, and the shouts and quarrels began. They went to their rooms. Lillian's room was like a white nun's cell. Whitewashed walls, a cot buried in white mosquito netting, no sheets or blankets. The walls did not reach to the ceiling, to let the air through, and her shutter door let in all the sounds of the village. After the fireworks, the shooting began. The café owner had been wise.

It was in such rooms that Lillian always made the devastating discovery that she was not free. Out in the sun, with others, swimming or dancing, she was free. But alone, she was still in that underground city of her childhood. Even though she knew the magic formula: life is dreamed, life is a nightmare, you can awaken, and when you awaken you know the monsters were self-created.

If she could have danced with Doctor Palas, maintained the speed of elation, sat at a table and let him rest his hand lightly on her bare arm, participated in a carnival of affection.

All of them with navigation troubles. The American couple fearful of unfamiliarity. Doctor Palas lonely.

I can see, I can see that it is in this distorted vision of the world's proper proportions that lies the secret of our fears. We make the animals bigger with our fears. We make our creations and our loves smaller, we shrink by our vision, and enlarge and shrink according to the whims of our interchangeable vision, not according to an immutable law of growth. The size of each world we live in is individual and relative, and the objects and people vary in each EYE.

Lillian remembered when she had believed that her mother was the tallest woman on earth, and her father the heaviest man. She remembered that her mother never had a wrinkle on her dress, or a lock of hair out of place, and was always putting on her gloves as if she were a noted surgeon about to operate.

Her presence was antiseptic, particularly in Mexico, where she was unsuited to the humanity of the life, the acceptance of flaws, spots, stains, wrinkles. Children changed the size of all they saw, but so did the parents, and they continued to see one *small.*

She was too cold to fall asleep. The wind from the mountain had descended upon San Luis as soon as the sun had set.

I see my parents smaller, they have assumed a natural size. My father must have been like Hatcher, terribly afraid of a strange country on which he was dependent for a living. But how could my mother's whistle have penetrated through all those underground passages? There must have been an echo!

If she still could hear this whistle, there must be echos in the soul. But she was regaining her own eyes, and with these eyes, with her own vision, she would return home.

The patio was full of birds in cages. The noises of the fiesta kept them awake too. Why should it be among these shadows, these furtive illuminations, these descending passageways that her true self would hide? Driven so far below the surface! She was now like those French speleologists who had descended thousands of feet into the earth and found ancient caves covered with paintings and carvings. But Lillian carried no searchlight and no nourishment. Nothing but the wafer granted to those who believe in symbolism, a wafer in place of bread. And all she had to follow were the inscriptions of her dreams, half-effaced hieroglyphs on half-broken statues. And no guide in the darkness but a scream through the eyes of a statue.

In the morning she returned to life above the ground. Outside in the patio there was a washstand, and the water in the pitcher was cool spring water. The mirror was broken, and the towel had been used by many people. But after the loneliness of the night's journey Lillian was happy to use a collective towel and to see her face in two pieces which could be made to fit together again. She had made a long journey, the journey of the smile and the eyes. There were no decorations for such discoveries. The journey had in reality taken only three months. According to the calendar her trip had taken only the time of an engagement in a night club. The voyage underground had taken longer, and had taken her farther. She would return to Golconda to drink her last cup of flowing gold, iridescent water, sun and air, to pack her treasures, her geological discoveries, the statues which, once unearthed, had become so eloquent.

When they arrived at Golconda it was the end of the New Year celebrations. The streets were still littered with confetti. The street vendor's baskets were empty, and they were sleeping beside them rolled in their ponchos. The scent of malabar was in the air, and that of burnt fireworks.

Lillian walked down the hill to the center of town, past the old woman in black who sold colored fruit juices and white coconut candy, past the church with its wide doors open so that she could see the bouquets of candlelights and the women praying while they fanned their faces. Cats and dogs were allowed to stray in and out, the workmen continued to work on their scaffolds while Mass was being said, the children were allowed to cry, or were fed right there while lying in the black shawls slung from their mother's necks like hammocks.

She walked in a glittering sunlight that annihilated all thought, that left only the eyes awake, and a procession of images marching through the retina, no thoughts around them, no thoughts interpreting them.

She walked more heavily on her heels, on flat sandals, as the natives walked, and although she weighed exactly the same as when she had first arrived, a medium weight, she felt heavier, and more aware of her body. The swimming, the sun, the air, all contributed to sculpture a firm, elastic, balanced body, free in its movements.

She was preparing herself to talk to the Doctor, as he had wanted her to talk. She had awakened with a clear image of the Doctor's character.

Doctor Hernandez in the taxi, the first day, concerned over his village's state of health, aware of others' moods and needs, unable to forget the secret sorrow of his own life. Doctor Hernandez probing into her life with a doctor's conviction of his right to probe, and evading her questions.

She had seen him in his home, in a Spanish setting, and met his wife, who had come for one of her brief visits. Under a semblance of Latin submission, under her thoughtfulness in serving him his drink, saving him from telephone calls, there was a mockery in his wife's attitude toward his patients. This had been instilled in the children who played the game of "being a doctor" differently from other children; they expressed distaste for his profession. The sick were not really sick, and the sick who came from the poor, with the desperate illnesses that attacked the undernourished natives, both children and wife totally ignored.

Lillian had seen in the Doctor's eyes a sadness which seemed out of proportion to the children's irony. He watched them perform their doctor act. The patient was a beautiful movie star. She was covered with bandages. Doctor Hernandez' daughter took this role. As soon as the "doctor" came near to her, she herself unwound all the bandages, threw herself upon him, embraced him and said: "Now that you have come I am not sick any more."

This morning as she walked, all these fragments had coalesced into the figure of a man in trouble, and Lillian understood that his persistence in making her confess was a defense against all that he himself wanted to confess.

At first she had not understood the game, nor his need. But she did now. And even if it meant that first of all (to play it as he wished it) she must confide in him, she was now willing, because it would liberate him of his secret. It was a habitual role for him to take: that of confessor. In any other role he would be uncomfortable.

The street climbed halfway up the hill, and there was the Doctor's office. The waiting room was a patio, with wicker chairs placed between potted palms and rubber plants. Pink and purple bougainvillaea trailed down the walls. A servant in

546

bedroom slippers was mopping the mosaic floor. The nurse was not dressed like a nurse but, like all the native girls who worked in Golconda, she wore a party dress, a rose pastel taffeta which made her seem much more like a nurse to pleasure than to illness. There were ribbons in her hair, and sea-shell earrings on her ears.

"The Doctor has not yet arrived," she said.

This was no unusual occurrence in the Doctor's life. Added to the demands of his profession and their uncertain timing, was the natives' own religion of timelessness. They absolutely refused to live in obedience to clocks, and it was always their mood that dictated their movements.

But Lillian felt an uneasiness which compelled her to walk instead of waiting patiently in the office.

She walked along the docks, watching the fishermen returning from their day's work. Each boat that had made a large catch had a pennanet waving on its mast. The wind caught the banners and imprinted on them the same ripples and billows as it did on the skirts of the women, and the ribbons on their hair.

She sat down at a little café and had a dark coffee, watching the boats heaving up and down, and the families taking a walk with all their children. How they installed themselves in the present! They looked at everything that was happening as if nothing else existed, as if there were no work to be done, no home to return to. They abandoned themselves to the rhythm, let the wind animate scarves and hair, as if every undulation and ripple of color and motion hypnotized them into contentment.

By the time she returned to the Doctor's office it was growing dark.

None of the patients showed uneasiness. But the nurse said: "I don't understand. I called the Doctor's home. He left there an hour ago saying he was coming straight to his office."

Just as she turned on the electric lights, they went out again. This often happened in Golconda. The power was weak. But it increased Lillian's anxiety, and to relieve it she decided to walk toward the Doctor's home, hoping to meet him on the way.

The long walk uphill oppressed her. The electric lights were on again, but the houses grew farther apart from each other, the gardens darker and denser as she walked.

Then in an isolated field she noticed a car which had run into an electric pole. A group of people were gathered around it.

In the dark she could not see the color of the car. But she heard the screams of the Doctor's wife.

Lillian began to tremble. *He had tried to prepare her for this.*

She continued to walk. She was not aware that she was weeping. The Doctor's wife broke away from the group and ran toward Lillian, blindly. Lillian took her in her arms and held her, but the woman fought against her. Her mouth was contorted but no sounds came from it, as if her cries had been strangled. The wife fell on her knees and hid her face in Lillian's dress.

Lillian could not believe in the Doctor's death. She consoled the wife as if she were a child with an exaggerated sorrow. She heard the ambulance come, the one he had raised the funds to buy. She saw the doctors and the people around the car. She realized that it was his car's hitting the pole that had cut off the electric current for a moment. The wife now talked incoherently: "They shot him, they finally shot him . . . They shot him and the car went against the pole. I wanted to get him away from here. Who would be capable of killing such a man? Who? Tell me. Tell me."

Who would be capable of killing such a man? Who, thinking of the sick people who would need him and not find him, thinking how gently he took his short moments of pleasure without rebelling when they were interrupted. Thinking how deep his pleasure was in curing illness. Thinking how he had tried to control the drug traffic and refused to dispense dangerous forgetfulness. Thinking of his nights spent in studying drugs for remembrance, which were known to the Indians. As a port doctor, what underworld had he known which neither Lillian nor his wife could ever have known, but which his wife had sensed as dangerous.

Lillian was helping the wife up the hill, helping the woman who had hated the city he loved, and whose hatred was now justified by events.

"I have to prepare the children, but they are so young. What can I say to such young children about death?"

Lillian did not want to know whether he had bled, been cut by glass. It seemed to her that he alone knew how to bandage, how to stop bleeding, how to heal.

The siren of the ambulance grew fainter. People walked behind them in silence.

If it were true that what we practice on others is secretly what we wish practiced upon ourselves, then he had wanted, needed all the care he gave.

To the wife with her too-high heels, her coiled black hair, her dark and jealous eyes, her small hands and feet, what could he have confided when from the beginning she turned against the city and the sick people he loved?

Lillian did not believe in the death of Doctor Hernandez, and yet she heard the shot, she felt in her body the sound of the car hitting the pole, she knew the moment of death, as if all of them had happened to her.

He had something to say, which he had not said, and he had gone, taking with him his secrets.

If only Doctor Hernandez had not postponed that deeper, wilder talk which ran underground through the myths of dreams, shouted through architectural crevices, screamed eloquently through the eyes of statues, from the depths of all the ancient cities within ourselves, if he had not merely signaled distress like a deaf-mute . . . . if only awareness had not appeared through the interstices of memory, between bars of lights and bars of shadows . . . if only human beings did not draw the blinds, don disguises, and live in isolation cells marked: not yet time for revelations . . . . . . if only they had gone down together, down the caverns of the soul with picks, lanterns, cords, oxygen, X-rays, food, following the blueprints of all the messages from the geological depths where lay hidden the imprisoned self. . . .

According to the definition, tropic meant a turning and changing, and with the tropics Lillian turned and changed, and she swung between the drug of forgetfulness and the drug of awareness, as the natives swung in their hammocks, as the jazz players swung into their rhythms, as the sea swung in its bed

turned

changed

Lillian was journeying homeward.

The other travelers were burdened with Mexican baskets, serapes, shawls, silver jewelry, painted clay figurines and Mexican hats.

Lillian carried no objects, because none of them would have incarnated what she was bringing back, the softness of the atmosphere, the tenderness of the voices, the caressing colors and the whispering presence of an underworld of memory which had serpentined under her every footstep and which was the past she had not been able to forget. Her husband and her children had traveled with her. Had she not loved Larry in the prisoner she had liberated? Her first image of Larry had been of him standing behind a garden iron grille, watching her dance. He was the only one of her fellow students she had forgotten to invite to her eighteenth birthday party. He had stood with his hands on the railing as the prisoner had stood in the Mexican jail, and she had seen him as a prisoner of his own silence and self-effacement. It was Larry and not the fraudulent prisoner she had wanted to liberate. Had she not loved her own children in Edwards' children, kissed Lietta's freckles because they were Adele's freckles, sat up with them evenings because their loneliness was her children's loneliness?

She was bringing back new images of her husband Larry, as if while she were away, some photographer with a new chemical had made new prints of the old films in which new aspects appeared she had never noticed before. As if a softer Lillian who had absorbed some of the softness of the climate, some of the relaxed grace of the Mexicans, some of their genius for happiness had felt her senses sharpened, her vision more focused, her hearing more sensitive. As the inner turmoil quieted, she saw others more clearly. A less rebellious Lillian had become aware that when Larry was not there she had either become him or had looked for him in others.

If she had not talked to Doctor Hernandez it was because he had been seeking to bring to the surface what he knew to be her incompletely drowned marriage.

Doctor Hernandez. As she sat in the airplane, she saw him bending over his doctor's bag unrolling bandages. She could not reconstruct his face. He turned away from her because she had not given him the confidence he asked for. This fleeting glimpse of him appeared as if on glass, and vanished, dissolved in the sun.

Diana had told Lillian just before she left: I believe I know the real cause of his death. He felt alone, divided from his wife, dealing only in the casual, intermittent friendships with people who changed every day. It was not a bullet which killed him. He was too deeply trained to combat death, to consider death as a private enemy, to accept suicide. But he brought it about in such a roundabout way, in so subtle a way that he could delude himself that he had no hand in his own death. HE COULD HAVE AVOIDED THE CONFLICT WITH THE DRUG SMUGGLERS. It was not his responsibility. He could have left this task to the police, better equipped to handle them. Something impelled him to seek danger, to challenge these violent men. ALMOST TO INVITE THEM TO KILL HIM. I often warned him, and he would smile. I knew what was truly killing him: an accumulation of defeats, the knowledge that even his wife loved in him the doctor and not the man. Did you know that she had been near death when they met, that he had cured her, and that even after their marriage it was his care of others that she was jealous of? To you he may have seemed beloved, but in his own eyes all the love went to the Doctor with the miraculous valise. Golconda was a place for fluctuating friendships, so many strangers passing through for a few days. Once he reproached me bitterly for my mobility and flexibility.

"You never hang on," he said. "This constant flow suits your fickle temperament. But I would like something deeper and more permanent. The more gaiety there is around me, the more alone I feel."

And Lillian must have added to his feeling. She had failed to give him that revelation of herself which he had wanted, a gift which might have enabled him to confide too. He was suffering from denials she had not divined. And how tired he must have been of people's disappearances. They came to Golconda, they sat at the beach with him, they had dinner with him, they talked with him for the length of a consultation, and then left for other countries. What a relief it may have been to have become at last the one who left!

Diana was certain that he had subtly sought out his death. And now to this image Lillian could add others which until now had not fitted in. The image of his distress magnetized a series of impressions caught at various times but abandoned like impressionistic fragments which did not coagulate. The shutters of the eyes opening to reveal anxiety, discouragement, solitude, all the more somber by contrast with the landscape of orange, turquoise, and gold. He seemed to flow with all the life currents of Golconda. She had accepted only the surface evidence. But the selves of Doctor Hernandez which had lived in the periphery, backstage, now emerged unexpectedly. And with them all the invisible areas of life, his and hers, and others', which the eyes of the psyche sees but which the total

552

self refuses to acknowledge, when at times these "ghosts" contain the living self and it is the personage on the stage who is empty and somnambulistic. It was as if having begun to see the true Doctor Hernandez, solitary, estranged from his wife and his children by her jealousy and hatred of Golconda immersed only in the troubled, tragic life of a pleasure city, she could also see for the first time, around the one-dimensional profile of her husband, a husband leaving for work, a father bending over his children, an immense new personality. It was Larry, the prisoner of his own silences which she had liberated the day she visited the fraudulent one in jail. It was Larry's silent messages she had been able to read through the bars of the Mexican jail. Once the vision becomes dual, or triple, like those lenses which fracture the designs one turns them on but also repeats them to infinity in varied arrangements, she could see at least two Larrys, one bearing an expression of hunger and longing which had penetrated her the day of her birthday party more deeply than the gaiety of her dancing partners, the other as the kind father and husband who dispensed care and gifts and tenderness perhaps as Doctor Hernandez had done, while desiring some unattainable pleasure.

Another image of Larry which appeared through the thick glass window of the plane, was of him standing behind the glass partition of a television studio. Lillian had been playing with an orchestra for a recording and Larry had sat in the recording room. He had forgotten that she could not hear him, and when the music had ended had stood up and talked, smiling and gesturing, in an effort to convey his enthusiasm for the music. The perplexed expression of her face urged him to magnify his gestures, to exaggerate the expression of his face, to dramatize beyond his usual manner, hoping that by a mime of his entire body and face he could transmit a message without the help of words.

At the time the scene had been baffling to Lillian, but only today did she understand it. She had failed to hear Larry, because he did not employ the most obvious means of communication. These two images seemed like a condensation of the drama of their marriage. First her response to his mute needs, his mute calling to her, and then her failure to discern his message. He had been a prisoner of his own silences, and these silences she had interpreted as absences.

He had answered her needs! What she had required of love was something that should never be expected of a human being, a love so strong that it might neutralize her self-disparagement, a love that would be occupied day and night with the reconstruction of a lovable Lillian, an image she would tear down as quickly as he created it. A love of such mathematical precision, occupied in keeping an inward balance between her self-caricature and a Lillian she might accept. A love tirelessly repeating: Lillian you are beautiful, Lillian you are wonderful, Lillian you are generous, and kind, and inspiring, while she, on the other side of the ledger made her own entries: Lillian, you were unjustly angry, you were thoughtless, you hurt someone's feelings, you were not patient with your child.

Endless accounting, endless revising of accounts.

But what had Larry wanted? It was true that Larry had accepted this abdication from life and seemed fulfilled when she lived for him in the musicians' world (because he had first wanted to be a musician, and had not fulfilled this wish). It was true that he seemed content in his silences, content to let her and her jazz musicians play and talk. This peripheral life seemed natural to him. But this division of labor had become a charade. When they grew tired of it (Lillian tired of Larry's indirect spectatorships, and Larry tired of Lillian's predominant role) they had not known how to exchange roles! Larry began to crystallize, not having any direct flow into life, not having his own aqualungs, his own oxygen. They were like twins with one set of lungs. And all Lillian knew was to sustain the flow by escaping into other lives, a movement which gave her the illusion of a completed circle. No other relationship could complete her, for it was Larry she had wanted to share life with, and ultimately she was seeking Larry in the other personages.

This last voyage without him had confronted her with her own incompleteness. She had deluded herself that the lungs, the capacity to live, were hers alone. How much of Larry she had carried within herself and enacted as soon as he was not there to act it for her. It was she who did not talk then, who let the Mexicans talk nimbly and flowingly, as she let Doctor Hernandez monologue. It was she who had remained at a distance from the life of Golconda except for the moment of abandon to the lulling drugs of nature. She had behaved as Larry would have behaved. Her courage, her flow in life had only existed in relation to Larry, by comparison with his withdrawals. What had he done while deprived of her presence? Probably had lived out the Lillian he carried within himself, her traits. Toward what Larry was she voyaging now?

Was it not an act of love to impersonate the loved one? Was it not like the strange "possessions" which take place at the loss of a parent by death? When her mother died, Lillian *became* her mother for at least a long year of mourning. It had been an imperceptible possession, for Lillian did not belong to the race who had rituals at which these truths were dramatized, rituals at which the spirit of the "departed" entered the body of the living, at which the spirit of the dead parent was acknowledged to be capable of entering the body of the son or daughter and inhabit until driven, or prayed, or chased away. To all appearances these primitive beliefs and what happened to Lillian were not related. Yet the spirit of her mother had passed into her. When she died, leaving Lillian a thimble and a sewing machine (when Lillian could not sew), Lillian did not know that she took on some of her moods, characteristics, attitudes. She once thought it was that as one grew older one had less resistance to the influences of the family and one surrendered to family resemblances.

Lillian laughed at the primitive rituals of "possession" she had seen in Haiti. But there was a primitive Lillian who had combated the total loss of her mother by a willingness to take into herself some of her mannerisms and traits (the very ones she had rebelled against while her mother was alive, the very ones which had injured her own growth). It was not only that she began to sew, to use the thimble and the sewing machine, but that she began to whistle when her children strayed from the house, she scolded her children for the very traits her mother had censured in her: neglect in dress, impulsive, chaotic behavior. A strange way to erect a monument to the memory of her mother, a monument to her continuity.

Thus she had also been "possessed" by Larry, and it was his selectivity in people which spoke against Diana's lack of discrimination. For the first time, in Golconda, she had practiced Larry's choice of withdrawing if the people were not of quality. Of preferring solitude to the effort of pretending he was interested in them.

Nearing home, she wondered if both of them had not accepted roles handed to them by others' needs as conditions of the marriage. It was the need which had dictated the role. And roles dictated by a need and not the whole self caused a withering in time. They had been married to parts of themselves only. Just as Dr. Hernandez had married a woman who loved only the Doctor, and who never knew the man who had tried to shed the role by entering the violent world of the smugglers, to feel himself in the heart of life, even at the cost of death.

Lillian had felt responsible for the Doctor's death, but now she knew it was not a personal responsibility; it was because she too had lived with only a part of Larry, and when you live with only a part of a person, you symbolically condemn the rest of it to indifference, to oblivion.

She knew it was not a bullet which had killed Dr. Hernandez. He had placed himself in the bullet's path. Certainly at times his intelligence and knowledge of human nature must have warned him that he was courting sudden death when he refused to surrender his supply of drugs or to underwrite fake permits to obtain more.

She knew that by similar detours of the labyrinth, it was not the absence of love or the death of it which had estranged her from Larry, but the absence of communication between all the parts of themselves, the sides of their character which each one feared to uncover in the other. The channels of emotions were just like the passageways running through our physical body which some illness congests, and renders narrower and narrower until the supply of oxygen and blood is diminished and brings on death. The passageways of their communication with each other had shrunk. They had singled out their first image of each other as if they had selected the first photograph of each other to live with forever, regardless of change or growth. They had set it upon their desks, and within their hearts, a photograph of Larry as he had first appeared behind the garden gate, mute and hungry, and a photograph of Lillian in distress because her faith in herself had been killed by her parents.

If they had been flowing together in life, they would not have created these areas of vacuum into which other relationships had penetrated, just as if Doctor Hernandez had been loved and happy in Golconda, he would have found a way to escape his enemies. (Diana had proofs that he had been warned, offered help, and recklessly disregarded both.)

The manner in which Lillian had finally immured herself against the life in Golconda betrayed how she, as well as Larry, often closed doors against experience, and lived by patterns.

Diana had said: "People only called him when they were in distress. When they gave parties they never thought of him. I knew that what he gave to others was what he deeply wanted for himself. This sympathy . . . for those in trouble. I do believe he was in greater trouble than any of us."

His death set in motion a chain of disappearances, an awareness of the dangers of disappearances. And this fear fecundated Lillian, stirred all life and feeling into bloom again. Sudden death had exposed the preciousness of human love and human life. All the negations, withdrawals, indifferences seemed like the precursors of absolute death, and were to be condemned.

She had a vision of a world without Larry and without her children, and then she knew that her love of Golconda had only been possible because of the knowledge that her absence was temporary.

And now the words spoken by Doctor Hernandez were clear to her, their meaning reached her. "We may seem to forget a person, a place, a state of being, a past life, but meanwhile what we are doing is selecting new actors, seeking the closest reproduction to the friend, the lover, the husband we are trying to forget, in order to re-enact the drama with understudies. And one day we open our eyes and there we are, repeating the same story. How could it be otherwise? The design comes from within us. It is internal. It is what the old mystics described as karma, repeated until the spiritual or emotional experience was understood, liquidated, achieved."

All the personages had been there, not to be described in words but by a series of images. The prisoner had touched her only because he vaguely echoed the first image of Larry as he appeared behind the iron gate. Even if this prisoner had been fraudulent, his acting had been good enough to reawaken in Lillian her feelings towards the first Larry she had known, a Larry in trouble, a trouble which she deeply shared, was married to, not only by empathy but by affinity. She had disguised it by throwing herself into life and relationships, by appearing fearless and passionate, and it had taken the true freedom of Golconda, its fluid, soft, flowing life, to expose her own imprisonment, her own awkwardness. She had been more mated to Larry than she had known. She had been as much afraid, only fear had made her active, leaping and courting and loving and giving and seeking, but driven by the same fear which made Larry recoil into his home and solitude. In losing this first intuitive knowledge she had of the bond between them, she had also lost a truth about herself. She had been taken in by the myth of her courage, the myth of her warmth and flow. And it was the belief in this myth which had caused her to pass judgment on the static quality of Larry, concealing the static elements in herself.

One night Doctor Hernandez, Fred, Diana, and Edward had decided to visit the native dance halls of Golconda which opened on small, unpaved streets behind the market. They leaped across an open trench of sewer water, onto a dirt floor, and sat at a table covered with a red oilcloth. Tropical plants growing out of gasoline cans partly veiled them from the street. Red bulbs strung on wires cast charcoal shadows and painted the skins in the changing tones of leaping flames. A piano out of tune gave out a sound of broken glass. The drums always dominated the melodies, whether songs or juke boxes, insistent like the drums of Africa. The houses being like gardens with roofs, the various musics mingled: guitars, a Cuban dance orchestra, a woman's voice. But the dancers obeyed the drums.

The skins matched all the tones of chocolate, coffee, and wood. There were many white suits and dresses, and many of those flowered dresses which in the realm of printed dresses stand in the same relation as the old paintings of flowers and fruit done by maiden aunts to a Matisse, or a Braque. They had been unwilling to separate themselves from their daily fare in food, the daily appearance of a dining table.

All the people she had seen in Golconda were there: taxi drivers, policemen, shopkeepers, truck drivers, life savers, beach photographers, lemon vendors, and the owner of the glass bottom boat. The men danced with the prostitutes of Golconda, and these were the girls Lillian had seen sewing quietly at windows, selling fruit at the market, and they brought to their evening profession the same lowered eyes, gentle voices, and passive quietude. They were dressed more enticingly, showed more shoulders and arms, but not provocatively. It was the men who drank and raised their voices. The policemen had tied their gun halters to their chairs.

The natives danced in bare feet, and Lillian kicked off her sandals. The dirt floor was warm and dry, and just as the night she had danced on the beach with the sea licking her toes, she felt no interruption between the earth and her body as if the

559

same sap and rhythm ran through both simultaneously: gold, green, watery, or fiery when you touched the core.

Everyone spoke to Doctor Hernandez. Even tottering drunk, they bowed with respect.

A singer was chanting the Mexican plainsong, a lamentation on the woes of passion. Tequila ran freely, sharpened by lemon and salt on the tongue. The voices grew husky and the figures blurred. The naked feet trampled the dirt, and the bodies lost their identities and flowed into a single dance, moved by one beat. The heat from the bowels of the earth warmed their feet.

Doctor Hernandez frowned and said: "Lillian, put your sandals on!" His tone was protective; she knew he could justify this as a grave medical counsel. But she felt fiercely rebellious at anyone who might put an end to this magnetic connection with others, with the earth, and with the dance, and with the messages of sensuality passing between them.

With Fred, too, whom she had once baptized "Christmas," she was unaccountably angry. Because he looked pale and withdrawn, and because he was watching, not entering. He kept his shoes on, and not even the monodic jubilance of the singer could dissolve this peregrine, this foreign visitor. And then it was no longer Fred who sat there, spectator and fire extinguisher, but all those who had been an obstacle to her efforts to touch the fiery core.

The plants which overflowed into the dance hall and brushed the shoulders, uninvited guests from the jungle, the sharp stinging scent of tequila, the milk of cactus, the cries of the street like the cries of animals in the forest, bird, monkey, the burning eyes of the urchins watching through the leaves almost as phosphorescent as the eyes of wildcats; the water of the sewers running through the trench hissing like a fountain, the taxis throwing their headlights upon the dancers, beacons of a tumultuous sea of the senses, the perspiration on the shirt backs, the touch of toes more intimate than the touch of hands, the round tables seeming to turn like ouija boards of censurable messages, every

560

message a caress, all this orchestration of the effulgence of the tropics served to measure by contrast these moments of existence which did not bloom completely, moments lived dimly, conjunctions and fusions which did not take place.

Larry and she had touched at one point, caught a glimpse of their undisguised self, but had not fused completely. Poor receptivity, poor connections, and at times no contact at all. Lillian knew now that it was an illusion that one lived in full possession of one's body. It could slip away from one. She could see Fred achieving this by impermeability to the sensuality of the place and people.

"Put your sandals on!" repeated Doctor Hernandez, and Lillian translated it: he wanted to protect her from promiscuity. That had been his role. She must defy him from causing more short circuits, more disconnections. And she must defy Fred, who, as in those dreams in which the identity is not clear, became all the ones who had not answered her love and particularly the first one, Gerard. When Fred danced with her, clumsily, soberly, she looked down at his boots as a sign of deliberate insulation, and she pushed him away and said: "Your shoes hurt me."

The time was past when her body could be ravished from her by visitations from the world of guilt. Such pleasurable sensations as a kiss on the inside of her arm, in the nook within the elbow, given by a stranger at a dance had been enough at one time to cause sudden departures. But no one could break now her feeling of oneness with Golconda. She had betrayed Larry with all the voluptuous textures, pungent smells, and with pleasure.

The girls had noticed that Lillian would not dance with Fred, and they came to sit at his side. One of them wore a black satin dress with an edge of white lace which seemed like a petticoat making an indiscreet appearance. The other a shawl which was slipped off her shoulders constantly as by an invisible hand. One had the expression of a schoolgirl intent upon her work. Her hair was still damp from the beach, and hung straight down like a Tahitian's. The other smiled and rested a fine-boned, delicate, small hand upon Fred's knees. Then she leaned over and, still smiling, whispered in his ear a request which made the blood rush to Fred's face, and his body stiffen with panic. The girl on his left, her small earrings trembling, and her medal of the Virgin engraved in blue lacquer which she held between her fingers like a cigarette, added: "The two of us? More exciting?"

Fred threw a distressed glance at Lillian, who was laughing. One girl was kissing the lobe of his ear, and the other slipping her hand inside his shirt.

"Lillian, help me."

He could not extricate himself. He had seen them at the beach selling shells, fish, lace. He had seen them entering the church, with black veils over their hair.

Seeing the depth of his distress, Lillian said: "Let's go swimming. It's too hot to dance anymore." It was true: their clothes were glued to their bodies, and their hair looked as if they had been swimming.

The girls clung to Fred: "You stay," they said.

Lillian leaned over to them and said in Spanish: "Some other night. Tonight he feels he must stay with me."

Their hands fell off his shoulders.

Now they were in a taxi, joggling over dirt roads.

Fred did not know that during the evening he had lost his identity in Lillian's eyes and become Gerard, her first defeat at the hands of passivity. A Gerard whose paralysis she now recognized and no longer desired. One could not lust for a wall, an obstacle, an inert mass, yet she had once been seduced by just such gentleness and passivity. It had calmed her fears. She did not know then what she knew now: it had been an encounter with a fear greater than her own. She could desire him violently (Gerard) because she had an instinctive knowledge that he would not respond. She could desire him without restraint (and even admire her own spontaneity) because the restraint was safely prearranged within him. She was free to desire, knowing that she would not be swept away into any fusion. It seemed absurd to say that one would refuse a glass of water when one was thirsty, *but if this glass of water also represented all the dangers of love?* When Lillian was sixteen or seventeen, fulfillment itself was the danger, love itself was the danger, a shared passion was slavery. She would be at the mercy of another human being. (Just as Fred now feared to be at the mercy of a woman.) Whereas by desiring someone who would not desire her, she could allow this fire to burn and feel: how alive I am! I am capable of desire. Poor Gerard, what a coward he is. He is afraid of life. It was not, as she thought, the pain of being alive she felt, but the pain of frustration.

How elated she was now not to have been seduced by Fred's mute pleadings and his retractions. How grateful to have discovered not a failed love affair, but the secret of that failure to lie in the choice of partner, a choice which came out of fear. So it was fear which had designed her life, and not desire or love.

If they did not arrive too soon at the secret cove known only to Doctor Hernandez, she would have time to make inevitable deductions. She and Larry had selected each other and each had played the role which kept their fears from overwhelming them. How could they pass judgment on each other for playing the role they had assigned to each other? You, Larry, must not change, or move, must represent fixed, unalterable love. You, Lillian, must change and move for both to sustain the myth of freedom.

Fred was afraid of the night, afraid of Diana who was cooling her body by pulling her dress out away from her breasts, waving it before her like a fan. He was afraid of Lillian who was fanning her face with the edge of her cotton dress, exposing the lacy petticoat.

The taxi left them at the top of the hill, and Doctor Hernandez guided them through brambles and rocks, downhill, to his secret cove.

Fred was afraid of the night, afraid his body would slip away from him, dissolve in that purple velvet with diamond eyes, the tropical night. The tropical night did not lie inert like a painted movie backdrop, but was filled with whisperings, and seemed to have arms like the foliage.

Beauty was a drug. The small beach shone like mercury at their feet. They undressed in the rocks which formed a cavern. The waves absorbed the words; one only heard the laughter, or a name. Diana, painted by the moonlight, walked like a phosphorescent Venus into the waves. The oil lamps on the fishermen's small boats trembled like candlelight. The neon lights softened by the haze threw beams on the bay like miniature searchlights.

Fred was as troubled as if he had encountered the singing mermaids. He did not undress. Doctor Hernandez swam far out; he was familiar with every rock. Lillian and Edward stayed near the shore. The fatigue and the heat of the dance were washed away. The sea swung like a hammock. One could grow a new skin over the body. The undulations of the sea were like their breathing, as if the sea and the swimmers had but one lung.

Out of the full beauty of the tropical night, the full moon, the full bloom of the stars, the full velvet of the night, a full woman might be born. No more scattered fragments of herself living separate cellular lives, living at times in the temporary homes of others' lives.

Fred stood further away, clinging to his locks and his clocks, to peripheries, islands, bridges. The taxi driver smoked a cigarette and was singing the *melopée* of love.

Fred's immobility, sitting by the rock, not sharing in the baptismal immersion, gave birth to an image of Larry's absence of mobility. But as the psyche changes, it recreates semantics, and the word "fixity" had once been considered a virtue. It was this fixity she had summoned, needed, loved, because in her chaos and confusions, fixity was the symbol of immutability, eternity. An unchanging love. How unjust to change its meaning when this unchanging love had been the hot house in which she had been born as a woman. Was it possible to begin one's life anew with a knowledge of what lay behind the charades one had created? Would she circumvent the masks they had donned, those she had pinned upon the face of Larry? She now knew her responsibility in the symbolic drama of their marriage.

Lillian was journeying homeward. The detours of the labyrinth did not expose disillusion, but unexplored dimensions. Archeologists of the soul never returned empty-handed. Lillian had felt the existence of the labyrinth beneath her feet like the excavated passageways under Mexico City, but she had feared entering it and meeting the Minotaur who would devour her.

Yet now that she had come face to face with it, the Minotaur resembled someone she knew. It was not a monster. It was a reflection upon a mirror, a masked woman, Lillian herself, the hidden masked part of herself unknown to her, who had ruled her acts. She extended her hand toward this tyrant who could no longer harm her. It lay upon the mirror of the plane's round portholes, traveling through the clouds, a fleeting face, her own, clear and definable only when darkness came.

Even though the airplane was taking her back to White Plains after an engagement of three months in Golconda, a little girl of six running up and down the aisle of the plane carried her by a detour into the past, to a certain day in her childhood in Mexico, where her father, frustrated by enigmatic natives and elemental cataclysms, would come home to the one kingdom, at least, where his will was unquestioned. He would receive from the mother a report on the day. And no matter how mild she made this, how much she attenuated the children's infractions, the father always found the cause enough to march them up to the top floor, an attic filled with dusty objects. And there, one by one, he spanked them.

As the rest of the time he did not talk to them, nor play with them nor cuddle them, nor sing to them, nor read to them, as he acted in fact as if they were not there, this moment in the attic produced in Lillian two distinct emotions: one of humiliation, the other the pleasure of intimacy. As there were no other moments of intimacy with her father, Lillian began to regard the attic as a place which was both the scene of spankings but also of the only rite shared with her father. For years, in telling of it, she only stressed the injustice, the ignominy of it. She stressed how there came a day when she openly rebelled and frightened her father into giving up this punishment.

But once in Paris, she strayed into an arcade and saw people watching penny movies with such delight and interest that she waited her turn and slipped a penny in a slot. A little movie scene appeared, awkward and jerky like the movies of the 1920s. A family sat at dinner, father (with a mustache), mother in a ruffled dress, and three children. The young and pretty maid was serving the soup. She was dressed in black. Her dress was very short. It revealed a white lace-edged petticoat, and she wore a butterfly of white lace on her hair. She spilled the soup on the father's lap. The father rose in a fury and left the table to go and change his clothes. The maid had not only to help him change his clothes, but to atone for the accident.

Lillian was about to leave, unmoved, amused, when the machine clicked and a new film began. The scene this time took place in a classroom. The students were little girls of six or seven (Lillian's age when she was receiving the spankings). They were dressed in old-fashioned frilly and bouffant dresses. The teacher was angered by their mockeries and laughter, and asked them to come up, one by one, to be spanked (just as Lillian and her sisters and brothers were lined up and made to march up the stairs). At this scene Lillian's heart began to beat wildly. She thought she was about to relive the pain and humiliation caused by ther father.

But when the teacher lifted up the little girl, stretched her across his knees, turned up her skirt, pulled down her panties, and began to spank her, what Lillian experienced after twenty years was not pain, but a flooding joy of sensual excitement. As if the spankings, while hurting her, had been at the same time the only caress she had known from her father. Pain had become

inextricably mixed with joy at his presence, the distorted closeness had alchemized into pleasure. The rite, intended as a punishment, had become the only intimacy she had known, the
only contact, a substitution of anger and tears in place of
tenderness.

She wanted to be in the little girl's place!

She hurried away from the arcade, trembling with joy, as
if she were returning from an erotic adventure.

Thus the real dictator, the organizer and director of her
life, had been this quest for a chemical compound—so many
ounces of pain mixed with so many ounces of pleasure in a
formula known only to the unconscious. The failure lay in the
enormous difference between the relationship she had needed,
and the one she had, on a deeper level, more deeply wanted.
The need was created out of an aggregate of negativities and
deformations. When Lillian thought that in her relationship to
Jay she was only in bondage to a passion, she was also in bondage to a need. When she thought her stays in Paris were directed entirely by a desire for Jay, they were in fact prede-
termined on those days in Mexico when she was six or seven
years old.

Not enough of that measure of pain had existed in her marriage to Larry.

In the laboratories the scientists were trying to isolate the
virus which might be the cause of cancer. Djuna believed one
could isolate the virus which destroys love. But then there were
outcries: that this would be the end of illusion, when it was
only the beginning! Lillian had learned from Djuna that each
cell, once separated from the diseased one, was capable of
new life.

Erasing the grooves. It was not that Lillian had remained
attached to the father, and incapable of other attachments. It
was that the form of the relationship, the mold, had become
a groove, the groove itself was familiar, her footsteps followed
it habitually, unquestioningly, the familiar groove of pain and
pleasure, of closeness at the cost of pain.

Lillian remembered Djuna's words: Man is not falling apart. He *is* undergoing a kind of fission, but I believe in those who are trying quietly to isolate the destructive cells, so that after fission each part is illumined and alive, waiting for a new fusion.

Was this why Lillian had always wept at weddings? Had she known obscurely that each human being might lie wrapped in his self-created myth, in the first plaster cast made by his emotions. Static and unchangeable, each could move only in the grooves etched by the past.

Jay had appeared at first as the bearer of joy. She had loved his complete union with the earth, his acceptance of the hungry, the greedy animal within himself. He lived with blinders on, seeking only pleasure, avoiding responsibilities and duties, swimming skillfully on the surface, enjoying, suspicious of depths, out in the world, preferring the many to the few, intoxication with life only, wherever it carried him, not faithful to individuals, or to ideas. Seeking the flow, the living moment only. Never looking back or looking into the future.

His talk of violence suited her tumultuous nature. But then he had made love without violence, and then asked her: "Did you expect more brutality?" She did not know this man. The first room he had taken her to was shabby. He had said: "Look how worn the carpet is." But all she could see was the golden glow, the sun behind the curtain. All she could hear were his words: "Lillian, your eyes are full of wonder. You expect a miracle every day." His brown shirt hung behind the door, there was only one glass to drink from and a mountain of sketches and notebooks she was to sort out later, silk screen, and arrange into the famous Portfolio. He had no time to stop. There was too much to see in the streets. He had just discovered the Algerian street, with its smell of saffron, and the Algerian *melopée* issuing from dark medieval doorways.

Lillian felt they would live out something new. They had first known each other in New York when Lillian was disconnected from Larry. Jay had left for Paris because he wanted to live near the painters he admired. Lillian's engagement took her there for several months each year. New for her, this total acceptance of all life, ugliness, poverty, sensuality, Jay's total acceptance, lack of selectivity or discrimination or withdrawals. Lillian thought him a gentle savage, a passionate cannibal. Motherhood prepared Lillian for this abdication of herself. Lillian adopted all his infatuations and enthusiasms: she sat with him contemplating from a café table the orange face of a clock, the prostitute with the wooden leg; played chess at the Café de La Regence at the very table where Napoleon and Robespierre had played chess. She helped him gather and note fifty ways of saying drunk.

She abandoned classical music and became a jazz pianist. Classical music could not contain her improvisations, her tempo, her vehemences.

She watched over Jay's work, searched Paris shops for the best paint, even learned to make some from ancient crafts. She watched over his needs. She had his sketch book silk screened and carried the Portfolios to New York and sold them. People were asking questions about Jay. They laughed at his casual gifts to them, loved the freedom, the unbound pages, the surprises, which gave them the feeling they were sharing an intimate, private document, like a personal sketch book.

His rooms remained the same everywhere: the plain iron bed, the hard pillows, the one glass. They were illumined by orgies: let us see how long we can make love, how long, how many hours, days, nights.

When she went to New York to visit her children, he wrote to her: "Terribly alive but pained, and feeling absolutely that I need you. But I must see you soon. I see you bright and wonderful. I want to get more familiar with you. I love you. I loved you when you came and sat on the edge of the bed. All that afternoon like warm mist. Get closer to me, I promise you it will be beautiful. I like so much your frankness, your humility almost. I could never hurt that. It was to a woman like you I should have been married."

569

Small room, so shabby, like a deep-set alcove. Immediately there was the richness of Jay's voice, the feeling of sinking into warm flesh, every twist of the body awakening new centers of pleasure. "Everything is good, good," murmured Jay. "Have I been less brutal than you expected? Did the violence of my painting lead you to expect more?" Lillian was baffled by these questions. What was he measuring himself against? A myth in his own mind of what women expected?

In his own work everything was larger than nature. Was he trying to match his own extravagances? If in his eyes he carried magnifying glasses, did he see himself in life as a smaller figure?

In the same letter he wrote: "I don't know what I expect of you, Lillian, but it is something in the way of a miracle. I am going to demand everything of you, even the impossible, because you are strong."

Lillian's secret weakness then became the cause of pain. She had a need of a mirror in which she could see her image loved by Jay. Or perhaps a shrine, with herself in the place of honor. Unique and irreplaceable Lillian (as she had been for Larry). But with Jay this was impossible. The whole world flowed through his being in one day. Lillian was apt to find sitting in her place (or lying in her bed) the most unlovely of all women, undernourished, unkempt, anonymous, ordinary, he had picked up in a café, with nothing to explain her presence except that she was perhaps the opposite of Lillian. To her he gave the coat Lillian had left in his room. The visitor had even brought with her a little grey wilted dog and Jay who hated animals was even kind to this dusty mongrel that was moulting.

For Jay's kindness was his greatest expression of anarchy. It was always an act of defiance to those one loved, to those one lived with. His was a mockery of the laws of devotion. He could not give to Lillian. He was always generous to outsiders, to those he owed nothing to, giving paints to those who did not paint, a drink to the man who was over-saturated with drink, his time to one who did not value it, the painting Lillian favored to anyone who came to the studio.

His giving was a defiance of evaluation and selection. He wanted to assert the value of what others discarded or neglected. His favorite friend was not a great painter but the most mediocre of all painters, who reflected Jay like a caricature, a diminished echo, who hummed his words as Jay did, nodded his head as Jay did, laughed when Jay laughed. They practiced dadaism together: everything was absurd, everything was a joke. Jay would launch into frenzied praise of his paintings. (Lillian called him Sancho Panza.)

Lillian would ask with candor: "Do you really admire him so much, as much as all that? Is he truly greater than Gauguin? Greater than Picasso?"

Jay would laugh at her gravity. "Oh no, I was carried away by my own words, just got going. I think I was talking about my own painting, really. I enjoy mystifying, confusing, contradicting. Deep down, you know, I don't believe in anything."

"But people will believe you."

"They admire the wrong painters anyway."

"But you're adding to the absurdities."

Lillian had the feeling that Sancho did not exist. True, he presented a Chinese face, but when she sought to know Sancho she found an evasive smile which was a reflection of Jay's smile, a sympathy which was an act of politeness, an opinion which, at the slightest opposition, vanished, a head waiter at a banquet, a valet for your coat, a shadow at the top of the stairs. His eyes carried no messages. If her fingers touched him she felt his body was fluid, evasive, anonymous. What Jay asserted he did not deny. He imitated Jay's adventures, but Lillian felt he had neither possessed life, nor lost it, neither devoured it nor spat it out. He was the wool in the bedroom slipper, the storm strip on the window, the felt stop on the piano key, the shock absorber on the car spring. He was the invisible man, and Lillian could not understand their fraternal bond. She suffered to see a reduced replica of Jay, his shrunken double.

"Right after being with me," Lillian said once, "did you have to take up with such an unlovely woman?"

"Oh that," said Jay. "Reichel believes me to be callous, amoral, ungrateful. He thinks because I have you I'm the luckiest man in the world, and it irritated me, his lecturing, so I launched into a role, to shock him. I talked to him about the whores, and had him gasping to think I might be callous about you. Can you understand that? I realize that it's all childish, but don't take it seriously."

"Eh? Sancho?" Sancho would laugh hysterically. It was what Lillian called the Village Idiot Act. Lillian laughed with them, but not with all of herself.

"I'm finding my own world," said Jay. "A certain condition of existence, a universe of mere BEING, where one lives like a plant, instinctively. No will. The great indifference, like that of the Hindu who lets himself be passive in order to let the seeds in him flower. Something between the will of the European and the karma of the Oriental. I want just the joy of illumination, the joy of what I see in the world. Just to receive vibrations. Susceptibility to all life. Acceptance. Taking it all in. Just BE. That was always the role of the artist: to reveal the joy, the ecstasy. My life has been one long opposition to will. I have practiced letting things happen. I have dodged jobs, responsibilities, and I want to express in painting the relaxing of will and straining for the sake of enjoyment."

This was the climate he created and to which Lillian responded, the yieldingness of the body, relaxed gestures, yielding to flow, seeking pleasure and being nourished with it, giving it to others. When something threatened his pleasure, how skillful he was at evasion. He had created something which on the surface seemed untainted by the anxiety of his time, yet Lillian felt there was a flaw in it. She did not know what it was.

The flaw she was to discover was that his world was like a child's world, depending on others' care, others' devotions, others' taking on the burdens.

He received a letter from his first wife, telling him about his daughter now fourteen years old, and showing exceptional gifts for painting. At first Jay wept: "I cannot help her." He remem-

572

bered saying to her when she was five years old: "Now remember, I am your brother, not your father." The idea of fatherhood repulsed him. It threatened his desire for everlasting freedom and youthfulness.

"Let her come and share our life," said Lillian.

"No," said Jay. "I want to be free. I have too much work to do. I have to take the frames off my paintings. I want them to become a part of the wall, a continuous frieze. My colors are about to fly off the edge, and I don't want restraint. Let them fly!"

While Lillian cooked dinner in the small kitchen off the studio, he fell asleep. When he awakened he had forgotten his daughter and his guilt. "Is dinner ready? Is the wine good?"

How I wish his indifference were contagious, thought Lillian. He can forget his daughter, and I cannot forget my children. Every night I leave Jay's side to go and say goodnight to my children across the ocean. I have to give Jay the same kind of love I gave my children. As if I knew no other expression of love outside of care and devotion.

She spent all her time consoling the friends he had misused, paying his debts, preventing him from paying too high a price for his rebellions.

When they first met he was proofreading in a newspaper office. His paintings were not selling yet. The work irritated his eyes. He would come to his room and the first thing he would do was to wash his inflamed eyelids. Lillian watched him, watched the red-rimmed eyes, usually laughing, and now withered by fatigue, and watering. These eyes which he needed for his work, wasted on proofreading under weak lights on greyish paper. These eyes he needed to drink in the world and all its profusion of images.

"Jay," said Lillian, extending a glass of red wine. "Drink to the end of your job at the paper. You will never have to do it again. I earn enough for both of us when I play every night."

He had at times the air of a gnome, a satyr, or at other times the air of a serious scholar. His body appeared fragile in proportion to his exuberance. His appetite for life was enormous. His parents had given him money to go to college. He had put it in his pocket and gone to wander all over America, taking any job that came along, and sometimes none, travelling with hoboes, as a hitchhiker, a fruit picker, a dishwasher, seeking adventure, enriching his experience. He did not see his parents again for many years. In one blow, he had severed himself from his childhood, his adolescence, from all his past.

What richness, Lillian felt, what a torrent. In a world chilled by the mind, his work poured out like a volcano and raised the surrounding temperature.

"Lillian, let's drink to my Pissoir Period. I have been painting the joys of urinating. It's wonderful to urinate while looking up at the Sacre Coeur and thinking of Robinson Crusoe. Even better still in the urinoir of the Jardin des Plantes, while listening to the roar of the lions, and while the monkeys, high up in the trees, watch the performance and sometimes imitate me. Everything in nature is good."

He loved the boiling streets. While he walked the streets he was happy. He learned their names amorously as if they were the names of women. He knew them intimately, noted those which disappeared and those which were born. He took Lillian to the Rue d'Ulm which sounded like a poem by Edgar Allan Poe, to the Rue Feuillantine which sounded like a soufflé of leaves, to the Quai de Valmy where the barges waited patiently in the locks for a change of level while the wives hung their laundry on the decks, watered their flower pots and ironed their lace curtains to make the barges seem more like cottages in the country. Rue de la Fourche, like the trident of Neptune or of the devil, Rue Dolent with its mournful wall encircling the prison. Impasse du Mont Tonnerre! How he loved the Impasse du Mont Tonnerre. It was guarded at the entrance by a small café, three round tables on the sidewalk. A rusted iron gate which once opened to the entrance of carriages, now left open. A hotel filled with Algerians who worked in a factory nearby. Rusty Algerian voices, monotone songs, shouts, spice smells,

574

fatal quarrels, knife wounds.

Once having walked past the iron gate, over the uneven cobblestones, they entered the Middle Ages. Dogs were eating garbage, women were going to market in their bedroom slippers. An old concierge stared through half-closed shutters, her skin the color of a mummy, a shrivelled mouth munching words he could not hear. "Who do you want to see?" The classical words of concierges. Jay answered: "Marat, Voltaire, Mallarme, Rimbaud."

"Every time I see one of those concierges," said Jay, "I am reminded of how in the Middle Ages they believed that a cat must be buried in the walls of a newly built house; it would bring luck. I feel that these are the cats come back to avenge themselves by losing your mail and misleading visitors."

Through an entrance as black and as narrow as the entrance to Mayan tombs, they entered gentle courtyards, with humble flower pots in bloom, a cracked window one expected to be opened by Ninon de L'Enclos. The smallness of the window, the askewness of the frame, the hood of the grey pointed slate roof overhanging it had been painted so many times on canvas that it receded into the past, fixed, eternal, like the sea-shell colored clouds suspended in time which could not be blown away by a change of wind.

Jay was sitting at the small coffee-stained table like a hunter on the watch for adventure. Lillian said: "The painters and the writers heightened these places and those people so well that they seem more alive than today's houses, today's people. I can remember the words spoken by Leon Paul Fargue more than the words I hear today. I can hear the very sound of his restless cane on the pavement better than I can hear my own footsteps. Was their life as rich, as intense? Was it the artist who touched it up?"

Time and art had done for Suzanne Valadon, the mother of Utrillo, what Jay would never do for Sabina. Flavor by accretion, poetry by decantation. The artists of that time had placed their subject in a light which would forever entrance us, their love re-infected us. By the opposite process which he did not understand, but which he shared with many other artists of his time, he was conveying *his* inability to love. It was *his* hatred he was painting.

Jay once said: "I arrived by the same boat that takes the prisoners to Devil's Island. And I was thinking how strange it would be if I sailed back with them as a murderer. It was in Marseilles. I had picked up two girls in a café, and we were returning by taxi after a night of night clubs. One of the girls kept after me not to let myself get cheated. When we arrived at the hotel the taxi driver asked me for a ridiculously high sum. I argued with him. I was very angry, and yet during that moment I was conscious that I was looking at his face with terrific intensity, as if I were going to kill him, but it was not that; my hatred was like a magnifying glass, taking in all the details, his porous meaty face, his moles with hair growing out of them, his soggy hair falling over his forehead, his cloudy eyes the color of Pernod. Finally we came to an agreement. That night I dreamed that I strangled him. The next day I painted him as I saw him in my dream. It was as if I had done it in reality. People will hate this painting."

"No, they will probably love it," said Lillian. "Djuna says that the criminal relieves others of their wish to commit murder. He acts out the crimes of the world. In your painting you depict the desire of thousands. In your erotic drawings you do the same. They will love your freedom."

At dawn they stood on the Place du Tertre, among houses which seemed about to crumble, to slide away, having been for so long the façades of Utrillo's houses.

Three policemen were strolling, watching. A street telephone rang hysterically in the vaporous dawn. The policemen began to run towards it.

"Someone committed your murder," said Lillian.

Two waiters and a woman began to run after the policemen. The loud ringing continued. One of the policemen picked up the telephone and to a question put to him he answered: "No, not at all, not at all. Don't worry. Everything is absolutely calm. A very calm night."

Lillian and Jay had sat on the curb and laughed.

But whatever Jay's secret of freedom was, it could not be imparted to Lillian. She could not gain it by contagion. All she could feel were Jay's secret needs: "Lillian, I need you. Lillian, be my guardian angel. Lillian, I need peace in which to work." Love, faithfulness, attentiveness, devotion, always created the same barriers around Lillian, the same limitations, the same taboos.

Jay avoided the moments of beauty in human beings. He stressed their analogies with animals. He added inert flesh, warts, oil to the hair, claws to the nails. He was suspicious of beauty. It was like a puritan's suspicion of make up, a crowd's suspicion of prestidigitators. He had divorced nature from beauty. Nature was neglect, unbuttoned clothes, uncombed hair, homeliness.

Lillian was bewildered by the enormous discrepancy which existed between Jay's models and what he painted. Together they would walk along the same Seine river, she would see it silky grey, sinuous and glittering, he would draw it opaque with fermented mud, and a shoal of wine bottle corks and weeds caught in the stagnant edges.

He had discovered a woman hobo who slept every night in exactly the same place, in the middle of the sidewalk, in front of the Pantheon. She had found a subway ventilator from which a little heat arose and sometimes a pale grey smoke, so that she seemed to be burning. She lay in a tidy way, her head resting on her market bag packed with her few belongings, her brown dress pulled over her ankles, her shawl neatly tied under her chin. She slept calm and dignified as if she were in her own bed. Jay had painted her soiled and scratched feet, the corns on her toes, the black nails. But he overlooked the story Lillian loved and remembered of her, that when they tried to remove her to an old woman's home she had refused saying: "I prefer to stay here where all the great men of France are buried. They keep me company. They watch over me."

Lillian was reminded of the Talmudic words: "We do not see things as they are, we see them as we are."

Lillian would become so confused by Jay's chaotic living, his dadaism, his contradictions, that she submitted to Djuna's clarifications. Jay's "realism," his need to expose, debunk, as he said, his need for reality, did not seem as real as Djuna's intuitive interpretations of their acts.

Lillian had no confidence in herself as a woman. She thought that it was because her father had wanted her to be a boy. She did not see herself as beautiful, and as a girl loved to put on her brother's clothes at first to please her father, and later because it gave her a feeling of strength to take flights from the problems of being a woman. In her brother's jeans, with short hair, with a heavy sweater and tennis shoes, she took on some of her brother's assurance, and reached the conviction that men determined their own destiny and women did not. She chose a man's costume as the primitives chose masks to frighten away the enemy. But the mystery play she had acted was too mysterious. Pretend to be a boy, when what she most wanted was to be loved by one. Act the active lover so the lover will understand she wished him to be active with her. She acted the active lover not because she was the aggressor but because she wanted to demonstrate. . . .

Because her father had wanted her to be a boy she felt she had acquired some masculine traits: courage, activity. When she shifted her ground she felt greater confidence. She thought a woman might love her some day for other qualities as they loved men for their strength, or genius, or wit.

Sabina's appearance, first as a model for Jay's paintings, then more and more into their intimate life, her chaotic and irresistible flow swept Lillian along into what seemed like a passion. But Lillian, with Djuna's help, had discovered the real nature of the relationship. It was a desire for an impossible union: she wanted to lose herself in Sabina and BECOME Sabina. This wanting to BE Sabina she had mistaken for love of Sabina's night beauty. She wanted to lie beside her and become her and be one with her and both arise as ONE woman; she wanted to add herself to Sabina, re-enforce the woman in herself, the submerged woman, intensify this woman Lillian she could not liberate fully. She wanted to merge with Sabina's freedom, her capacity for impulsive action, her indifference to consequences. She wanted to smooth her rebellious hair with Sabina's clinging hair, smooth her own denser skin by the touch of Sabina's silkier one, set her own blue eyes on fire with Sabina's fawn eyes, drink Sabina's voice in place of her own, and, disguised as Sabina, out of her own body for good, to become one of the women so loved by her father.

She had loved in Sabina an unborn Lillian. By adding herself to Sabina she would become a more potent woman. In the presence of Sabina she existed more vividly. She chose a body she could love (being critical of her own), a freedom she could obey (which she could never possess), a face she could worship (not being pleased with her own). She believed love quite capable of such metamorphosis.

These feelings had been obscure, unformulated until the night the three of them had gone out together and Sabina had drunk a whole bottle of Pernod. She had become violently ill. Jay and Lillian had nursed her. Sabina was almost delirious. She was easily prone to fever and Lillian was alarmed by the way her face seemed to be consumed from within. She stretched out beside her to watch over her. Jay had gone to sleep in the studio.

In the first version of that night, gathered from Sabina's smoky talk and Lillian's evasions. Jay had believed that jealousy of him had sprung between them and separated them. But this was only on the surface. Later Lillian saw another drama.

Both Sabina and Lillian, faced with a woman, realized they felt closeness but not desire. They had kissed, and that was all. Sabina wanted something of Lillian: her inexperience, her newness, as if she wanted to begin her own life anew. They both wanted intangible things. Impossible to explain to Jay who made everything so simple, and reduced to acts. He could not understand atmosphere, moods, mysteries.

The true bridge of fascination was the recognition that in Sabina lay a dormant Lillian. A Lillian Jay had not been able to awaken, a liberated Lillian. For he had needed the devoted Lillian.

Sabina was a drought of freedom. Every gesture she made, every word she uttered. She was free of faithfulness, loyalty, gratitude, devotion, duties, responsibilities, guilts. Even the roles she played were chosen by herself.

Faced with the culmination of their fantasies of a possible closeness to woman, neither one wanted to go further. They both realized the comedy of their pretences. Something so absurd in their bravado towards all experience, in their arrogance about playing Jay's role. They could not escape their femininity, their woman's role, no matter how difficult or complex.

The story which had filtered out had become wrapped in poetry, myth, and drama. It became more and more difficult to reveal the truth, for it was so much more simple, so much more human. Lillian kept the secret because she felt it would make Jay love Sabina more. Jay thought Sabina loved women and that this would explain her water-tight compartments.

What would Jay have thought of their hesitations, awkwardnesses, their own bewilderment. He might have laughed at them. They had both played roles: Sabina in a theatrical way, with capes, make up, late arrivals, dramatic effects, disappearances, mysteries; Lillian the one dictated by her outward appearance of naturalness and honesty. "From you I expect honesty," said Jay. Everyone knew Sabina was an actress. Everyone believed Lillian sincere.

Lillian loved Sabina's fluidity, because she wanted it for herself. When she thought she was courting a woman, she was courting Sabina's gift for escape from whatever interrupted the course of passion, whatever interfered with life as an adventure.

They kissed once. It was soft and lovely, but like touching your own flesh. All this was on the edge of their bodies, not at the core. Sabina was touched to see Lillian's bedazzlement. She smiled a triumphant smile.

Lillian had imagined that by loving Sabina a miraculous alchemy would take place. What took place that night was not love of woman. It was a hope of an exchange of selves.

It was Sabina's feelings Jay was curious about.

But there were so many things Lillian could not tell Jay. So many things he did not want to hear. Jay thought he could arrive at a dissolution of Sabina's potency by an acid bath of truth. He was seeking to exorcise her power.

He would never believe that they had contemplated allying themselves because they felt incomplete and exposed and less strong than he imagined them. Jay was tone deaf to such secret weaknesses, needs, moments of helplessness.

He would not believe that they both wanted to be consoled as by a sister, or a mother, for his erratic behavior, his multitude of treacheries.

Antiphonal music of desires at cross currents repeated to infinity. Jay the gate-crasher seeking a truth too black and white. And the key lay in prefabricated myths which appeared in dreams with veiled faces, mute, undecipherable.

Until Djuna took up each strand, delicately separating each one from pain and blindness, the pain of blindness. Strange how in this light, high above the earth, flying through the regions of awareness which Djuna had taken her into by a method of ascension she had finally learned from her. Djuna's words, Djuna the aviator of language, air force for grounded lives.

For awhile Lillian had been devoted to both Jay and Sabina. And what had Jay wanted? To own them both? She remembered his letter to her: "You are really strong. I warn you. I am no angel. I am insatiable. I will ask the impossible of you. What it is I don't know."

And a few years later he demanded of her that she understand the presence of Sabina at first only in his paintings, and then later in their lives. He even wanted Lillian to help him know Sabina.

Just before she left Paris for the last time, abdicating, Lillian said to Jay: "Now the time has come for me to tell you of the Sabina I know, because it will make you love her more. You see, what I was given to see was a glimpse of Sabina's innocence. That night . . . we had both dreamed of escaping from our bodies, our molds. At a certain stage of exaltation all the boundaries are lost, identity too. Sabina was awkward too; she did not know how to behave before a woman. She kept repeating: "I'd like to be at the beginning of everything, when I could believe, I'd like to be at the beginning of all experience, as you are, able to give yourself, trusting.' She wanted my innocence, and what we want is what we are. And I . . . all my life I could hardly live or breathe for fear of hurting anyone, I had seen Sabina take what she wanted and being loved for it. And I wanted to catch from her by contagion that irresponsibility. Now you will love her more."

"No," said Jay, "much less. Because she would never tell me what you have told me. What you describe—I could not hate that. There's some beauty to it. I have just realized that what I gave you was something coarse and plain compared with that."

"No, Jay, you made me a woman. Sabina would have thrust me back into being a half woman, as I was before I met you."

"Beyond the love," said Jay, "we were friends. Sabina and I will never be friends. I hate her unnecessary complications."

"But they interest you. They are your drugs. I could not give you that. It is I who gave you something plain. I am not a drug."

She looked at the grey blond hair on the nape of his neck, and felt almost capable of staying at his side while he experienced his passion for Sabina. But she was too certain that the body of Sabina would triumph. They were better matched in violence. But what would become of the tender Jay she had known?

So she said: "I must go and see my children. Adele is ill."

"Whatever you do is right. For the first time I see some beauty in it."

582

The plane was flying into the night now. At times it shivered as from too great an effort to gain altitude.

Jay had been concerned with being the lover of the world, naming all it contained, caressing it with his short and stocky hands, appropriating it, exploring it. And Djuna concerned only with the longitude and latitude and altitude of human beings in relation to each other.

For a while it seemed as if Lillian were flying into a storm. Luminous signs informed her she must strap herself to her chair. Other passengers slept, confident that strapped to their chairs they would safely reach earth again. Lillian slid the curtain open and through the porthole watched the immensity of space in which sorrows seemed to lose their weight. She looked at the moon, as if to communicate with it, as if it would assure her that the storms of earth could not reach her. Looking at the moon intently it seemed to her that the plane flew more steadily.

It was the year when everyone's attention was focused on the moon. "The first terrestrial body to be explored will undoubtedly be the moon." Yet how little we know about human beings, thought Lillian. All the telescopes are focused on the distant. No one is willing to turn his vision inward.

What she had seen of Larry during their marriage was only what he allowed her to see, giant albatross wings, the wings of his goodness. She had been unable to see above or beyond the rim of them. Larry had collaborated in this. He only offered his goodness. He never said: "I want, I like, I take," but "What do you want? What do you like?" He deliberately obscured any vision into his being.

"The moon is the earth's nearest neighbor."

They had slept side by side. In the night, or at dawn, his body had been there. She had felt its radiations. In his voice there were caresses. In his sympathy, a tropical balm. In his goodness, a universe. His attentiveness blinded her. If he had another life, other selves, he turned like a planet, only one face towards Lillian.

"A rocket that woud take months to reach one of the planets

can travel to the moon in a day or two."

"An instrument station on the moon could communicate with the earth with greater ease than one on Mars or Venus." It was not necessary to circle around Larry or go to Paris, to Mexico. At last she was a receptor for Larry's messages!

"To investigators preoccupied with the remarkable developments in contemporary astronomy and physics the moon had seemed a dead and changeless world."

But only because she had not looked beyond the mask. The rim of density around Larry had been his goodness. It was selfless, almost anonymous. He was present only when summoned, and summoned only by distress. Lillian had fixed the distorted image, but Larry had contributed the mask.

"The moon is an astronomical stone. Because its surface has preserved the record of ancient events, it holds the key to the solar system."

The key to the marriage? Larry had achieved changelessness. Whereas Lillian was created "out of the air and water that support life on earth which continuously wear away the surface of our planets. Processes in the interior of the earth heave up chains of mountains for demolition by the forces of erosion, and the cycles of building and erosion from one epoch to the next erase the records of the past." That was a portrait of Lillian's turbulences in planetary terms! And of Larry's conservation of the past, of their life together.

"The moon, on the other hand, has neither atmosphere nor oceans, and has never been eroded by wind and water. Furthermore, the circular formations that dominate the moon's topography indicate that its crust has never undergone the violent changes which are involved in mountain-building processes on earth."

Larry had sought to present such an undisturbed surface to Lillian's investigations. But this evenness had been as much a mask as Sabina's more theatrical disguises. What do you feel? Where are you? Will you share my enthusiasms? My friendships?

What had sent Larry so far away from human life into the position of a spectator, so far away from earth? What had made him wrap himself in an unbreathable atmosphere of self-lessness and then be absent from his own body? There were in-cidents she knew. But she had never coordinated them. She was landing for the first time on this new planet, Larry. "In any case, a planet would be cool at birth." His mother had not wanted him to be born. This was the first denial. He had arrived unsummoned by love and jealously resented by his father.

"A cool birth does not exclude the later heating and melting of planetary bodies by radioactive elements they contain."

The child, inhibited by such "a cool birth," sought warmth by running away from home to the huts of the Negroes living and working nearby for his father. His father was drilling oil wells in Brazil for an American firm.

His pale mother had faded blue eyes, and wore white dresses which covered her neck and arms, and on which the sewing machine, as if in fear the material would undulate, swell, or fly off like a parachute, had criss-crossed a thousand stitches, tight and overlapping, controlling every inch in a stifling design called "shirring."

The father believed in unremitting work, and no idleness or dreaming. He clocked the universe, constantly pulling out his watch like a judge at a running match. His mother was beset with fear. Every pleasure was dangerous. Swimming led to drowning, fireworks could blow your finger off, hunting fireflies could anger a rattlesnake, associating with native children would turn you into a "savage."

Larry ran to the Negro huts for warmth of voices, warmth of gestures, and warmth of food. He liked the half-nakedness, the soft laughter. Home here seemed like a nest, with joyous flesh proximity. Caressess were lavish. There was a hum of content, a hiss of doves. Violence came and went like tropical storms, leaving no traces. (At home a quarrel led to weeks of silence and resentment.) It was Larry's first closeness to human beings. He threw off his too tight clothes. The Negro mother was his nurse. She smiled upon his fairness. Her flowered cotton dress smelled of spices, and she moved as easily as cotton tree seeds. When she was happy her body undulated with laughter. Their laundry, swollen like sail boats, was more vivid than a rainbow.

Yet she betrayed him.

He had played with the naked dark children. After swimming in all the forbidden lagoons and rivers, they had openly admired each other, half mocking, half tender. In his own home Larry had wanted to repeat these games with his younger brother. But it was not a swimming adventure as it was out in the country, among plants and grass and reeds. It was in the bathroom. Larry thought all discoveries of bodies could be made as merrily as by the riverside. His younger brother was so delicate, his hair so fragile, his skin like a girl's. With delight they contrasted skin tones, breadth of chest, length of legs, strength of legs. But this scientific erotic exploration was watched by the nurse through the transom window, and the same thing she laughed at in nature, she now reported like a policeman on the frontier of some forbidden land.

A shocking treachery from the world he loved with a trusting passion, a treachery which came not from where he might have expected it, the shaggy-browed father with his eyes too deeply set in tired flesh, or from the cool eyes of the pale mother, but from the spice-scented, barefooted, tenderhanded black mother he loved. Such treacheries throw human beings into outer space, at a safe distance from human beings. They are propelled into space by attacks from the human species. Could not the nurse have laughed at the children exploring the wonders of the body? Could she not have laughed at their games as she laughed at their games while swimming? Did she not herself keep her warm dry hand on his coltish shoulder blades and comb his hair with her fingers "To feel the silk of it"? He had almost reached the earth with her, with her he had almost been born fully to his molten life.

The child has set his planet's course, has chosen his place in outer space, according to the waves of hostility or fear he has encountered. Pain was the instrument which set him afloat and determined his course. The sun, whether gold, white, or black, having failed him, he will exist henceforward in a more temperate zone, twilit ones, less exposed to danger.

Lillian had a first misinterperted his silences. He communicated only with children, and with animals. His absences (if only I knew where he was when he was gone) distressed her. Never knowing until later that, as a measure of safety he had sought the periphery, the region of no-pain, where human beings could not reach him.

The first betrayal had thrust him into space to rotate at a certain distance from the source and origin of the first collision.

Lillian calculated the effect of his not having been wanted. The effect of adopting a family and then being betrayed. The atmosphere of gaiety and freedom was altered. When the negro shack was accidentally destroyed by fire he had no regrets. When he was made to sail away from the Brazilian planet to England, he was sullen. The parents had decided he could not grow up into a native "savage." He needed discipline. Larry already preferred drumming to sixteenth-century English songs. He liked the stamping of bare feet more than the waltzing of high heels and patent leather shoes. He liked vivid pinks, not his mother's colorless dresses. He liked time for dreaming, not his father's tightly filled days.

He entered a cold atmosphere of discipline and puritanism. His mother's sister held the watch now, and also a whip. Every infraction was severely punished. The long walk to school was timed. The purchase of a water pistol was a crime. Pulling a little girl's hair or pushing her down on the grass was a crime. And as for the mystery of where her legs started and asking if inside the bouffant dress there was a corolla as in the heart of a poppy. . . . Whatever food she served had no taste, because she imposed it. She measured and enforced time and appetite, just as she commanded the flowers to bloom at a certain date.

Larry disappeared behind a façade of obedience. There was a Sea of Tranquillity on the moon. Larry lived there. There were no ruffles on the surface. Outwardly he conformed until his marriage to Lillian. Lillian having spent her childhood in Mexico, seemed to be a messenger from the happier days of Brazil.

"The relative smoothness of the lunar surface poses a question."

Much of men's energies were being spent on such questions, Lillian's on the formation of Larry's character. Their minds were fixed on space; hers on the convolutions of Larry's feelings.

Her vehement presence became the magnet. She summoned him back from solitude. She was curious about his feelings, about his silences, about his retractions. His mother's first wish that he should not exist at all was pitted against Lillian's wish that he exist in a more vivid and heightened way. She made a game of his retreats, pretended to discover his "caves." He was truly born in her warmth and her conviction of his existence.

How slender was the form he offered to the world's vision, how slender a slice of his self, a thin sliver of an eighth of the moon on certain nights. She was not deceived as to the dangers of another eclipse. She could hear, as you hear in *musique concrète*, the echo in vast space which corresponds to new dimensions in science, the echo which was never heard in classical music.

Lillian felt that in the husband playing the role of husband, in the scientist playing his role of scientist, in the father playing his role of father, there was always the danger of detachment. He had to be maintained on the ground, given a body. She breathed, laughed, stirred, and was tumultuous for him. Together they moved as one living body and Larry was passionately willed into being born, this time permanently. Larry, Larry, what can I bring you? Intimacy with the world? She was on intimate terms with the world. While he maintained a world in which Lillian was the only inhabitant, or at least the reigning one.

Such obsession with reaching the moon, because they had failed to reach each other, each a solitary planet! In silence, in mystery, a human being was formed, was exploded, was struck by other passing bodies, was burned, was deserted. And then it was born in the molten love of the one who cared.

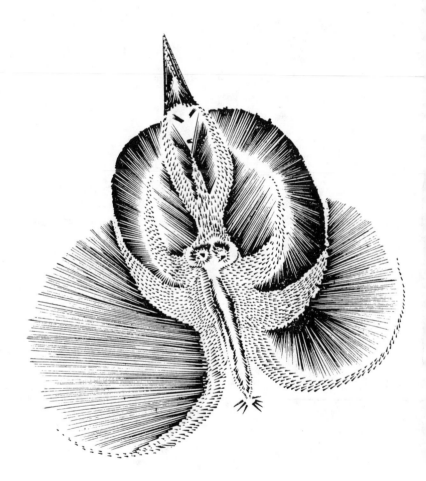